THE NONESUCH STORYTELLERS

W. Somerset Maugham

The
Nonesuch Storytellers

W. Somerset Maugham

Short Stories

INTRODUCED BY

Anthony Curtis

THE NONESUCH PRESS

LONDON

THE NONESUCH PRESS

Published by
REINHARDT BOOKS

Distributed by the Penguin Group
Penguin Books Ltd, 27 Wrights Lane, London w8 5 tz, England
Viking Penguin, a division of Penguin Books USA Inc.
375 Hudson Street, New York, New York 10014, USA
Penguin Books Australia Ltd, Ringwood, Victoria, Australia
Penguin Books Canada Ltd, 2801 John Street, Markham, Ontario, Canada l3r 1b4
Penguin Books (NZ) Ltd, 182–190 Wairau Road, Auckland 10, New Zealand

Penguin Books Ltd, Registered Offices: Harmondsworth, Middlesex, England

This selection first published by Reinhardt Books Ltd 1990

1 3 5 7 9 10 8 6 4 2

Typeset in 10½/12pt Linotype Janson 55
Printed in Great Britain by Butler & Tanner Ltd.

A CIP catalogue record for this book is available from the British Library

isbn 1–871–06125–3

'The Pacific', 'Mackintosh', 'The Fall of Edward Barnard', 'Rain', 'Envoi', from *The
Trembling of a Leaf*, Copyright 1921 by Royal Literary Fund; 'The Casuarina Tree', 'Before
the Party', 'P & O', 'The Letter', from *The Casuarina Tree*, Copyright 1926 by Royal Literary
Fund; 'Mr Harrington's Washing', from *Ashenden*, Copyright 1928 by Royal Literary Fund;
'Sanatorium', 'The Colonel's Lady', 'The Kite', from *Creatures of Circumstance*, Copyright
1947 by Royal Literary Fund; 'The Princess and the Nightingale', from *The Gentleman in the
Parlour*, Copyright 1930 by Royal Literary Fund; 'The Round Dozen', 'Jane', 'The Alien
Corn', from *Six Stories Written in the First Person Singular*, Copyright 1931 by Royal Literary
Fund; 'The Door of Opportunity', 'The Vessel of Wrath', 'The Book-Bag', from *Ah King*,
Copyright 1933 by Royal Literary Fund; 'Salvatore', 'The Judgement Seat', from
Cosmopolitans, Copyright 1936 by Royal Literary Fund; 'Gigolo and Gigolette', from *The
Mixture as Before*, Copyright 1940 by Royal Literary Fund; 'Daisy', from *Orientations*,
Copyright 1899 by Royal Literary Fund.

CONTENTS

Introduction, vii

From *The Trembling of a Leaf* (1921)
The Pacific, 3
Mackintosh, 5
The Fall of Edward Barnard, 52
Rain, 96
Envoi, 151

From *The Casuarina Tree* (1926)
The Casuarina Tree, 155
Before the Party, 157
P & O, 192
The Letter, 235

From *Ashenden* (1928)
Mr Harrington's Washing, 283

From *Creatures of Circumstance* (1947)
Sanatorium, 339

From *The Gentleman in the Parlour* (1930)
The Princess and the Nightingale, 375

From *Six Stories Written
in the First Person Singular* (1931)
The Round Dozen, 389
Jane, 426
The Alien Corn, 461

From *Ah King* (1933)
The Door of Opportunity, 517
The Vessel of Wrath, 563
The Book-Bag, 615

From *Cosmopolitans* (1936)
Salvatore, 667
The Judgement Seat, 673

From *The Mixture as Before* (1940)
Gigolo and Gigolette, 683

From *Creatures of Circumstance* (1947)
The Colonel's Lady, 709
The Kite, 734

From *Orientations* (1899)
Daisy, 769

Introduction

Somerset Maugham's gift for storytelling first became apparent when he was a small child. His father was a solicitor for the British Embassy in Paris after the Franco-Prussian war. Maugham, born in 1874, grew up in the Embassy circle to which his parents belonged. He would entertain the other British children with puppet-shows, manipulating the characters and playing all the roles himself, holding his infant audience spellbound. Mrs Violet Hammersley, the daughter of another official, had vivid memories of these performances she attended as a girl.

Maugham's parents died within a few years of each other by the time he was ten. Still emotionally shattered, he went to live with a clerical uncle and his German wife in Whitstable on the coast of Kent. He was sent to the King's School in nearby Canterbury, where once again he attracted a faithful audience. Maugham was one of those boys who are listened to by their contemporaries, despite, in his case, a bad stammer. He was known and feared for making memorable, sometimes cutting, remarks. It was after he had left school and university to study medicine at St Thomas's Hospital in Lambeth that he decided to make storytelling, in the form of story-writing, his profession.

The 1890s were good years for an aspiring author to be writing stories for newspapers and magazines.

There was, of course, no cinema, no television, no radio, and many people relied on reading periodicals to escape for a while from the stress of the workaday world. In 1891 George Newnes started the *Strand Magazine* at 6d. a copy, offering new urban middle-class readers gripping self-contained stories by Conan Doyle and others, and it rapidly caught on. Maugham's 'A Point of Law' was published there in 1904. Other outlets for the short-story writer were the *Fortnightly Review*, *Pall Mall*, the *Illustrated London News*, the *Sketch*, *Punch* and the *Daily Mail*, all of which printed stories by Maugham in the first decade of the twentieth century.

Maugham's early novel, *Liza of Lambeth* (1897), was hardly more than an extended short story, modelled on Arthur Morrison's verbal portraits of the London poor that had appeared in *Macmillan's Magazine* and the *National Observer* and were published as *Tales of Mean Streets*. When considering Maugham's outstanding contribution to the story as literature, we should remember this late-Victorian flowering of the magazine story. That was where he served his apprenticeship, and it conditioned his future outlook. The magazine story had to capture the reader's attention in the first paragraph and hold it through a developing situation in which the writer was always one or two jumps ahead. At length, after as many twists and turns as the plot would stand, a climax was reached and the initial situation was resolved with nothing left unexplained. These requirements suited Maugham's cast of mind perfectly. They became his articles of literary faith and were encapsulated in his famous saying that a story should have a beginning, a middle and an end.

Liza was a success, with reviews everywhere. Although by now he had qualified, Maugham gave up all thoughts of practising medicine to become a full-time writer. His next book but one, *Orientations* (1899), was a gathering together of his early magazine stories. Some thirty years later, when the moment came for a collected edition of his works, Maugham did not consider this book, or any of his early stories, worth reprinting. Since his death, however, they have been reissued in two volumes: *Seventeen Lost Stories*, compiled by Craig V. Showalter (New York, 1969), and *A Traveller in Romance*, edited by John Whitehead (London, 1984).

The aim of this collection is to present Maugham as a consummate master of the short story, so we need merely nod in passing to the majority of these early works. I have, though, rescued a single story, 'Daisy', from *Orientations* and included it at the end. (With one other exception – 'Sanatorium' – the stories are arranged in chronological order of publication of the books in which they originally appeared.) The work of a man who was barely twenty, 'Daisy' earns its place not just because it remains a good story but because it shows all the qualities characteristic of the mature stories. Here are the assurance, irony, clarity, the observation of a self-contained world and triumph of the wicked over the virtuous that readers familiar with his work will recognize. Here too is his first attempt to give an impression of the Whitstable of his boyhood which in the story he calls Blackstable. (He was to use the name again when the town came under closer scrutiny in *Of Human Bondage* and *Cakes and*

Ale.) Maugham identifies with the plight of the heroine, who leaves Blackstable as a girl, to flout its stuffy, late-Victorian values, and returns later in life, a rich, influential individual who had won renown in the theatre.

Such was Maugham's own plan of campaign when he turned his back on medicine as a career. He shared a flat in the Victoria area of London with a male friend who had a regular nine-to-five job, leaving Maugham in sole occupation of the sitting-room in which to pursue his rigorous routine of four hours' writing every day. With a good record of one successful novel already published, Maugham was not content merely to write stories. He wrote another novel, and then another and another. He was a furious worker. He felt he was fighting for his life – he had to prove himself in his chosen profession and to secure his financial independence. Freelance writers are inevitably pre-occupied with money. Maugham was obsessed by it and remained obsessed by it even after he had become a rich man through the efforts of his pen. He studied the market and aimed to turn out the kind of work that would sell.

Another genre he considered was drama. Ever since his puppet-show days he had loved the theatre and had nursed dreams of becoming an acclaimed playwright. Moreover, the technique of writing the kind of play fashionable on the London stage at this time was not dissimilar to that of the magazine short story. Look at 'Daisy' and you will see how naturally it would adapt to the stage.

The tale of Maugham's triumph in the theatre, which began with *Lady Frederick* in 1907, has been told many times. Here it is necessary to note only that his work as a playwright diverted him for some time from story-writing, for he was far too busy with his plays. But Maugham did not completely give up writing fiction even then. He took a long break from play writing in 1913, at the height of his pre-war popularity, to write the autobiographical novel *Of Human Bondage*.

By the time it was published in 1915 the First World War was raging and Maugham's life had altered a great deal. He was rich. He was widely known. He was fashionable on both sides of the Atlantic. The flat in Victoria had been replaced by a house in Mayfair. Maugham was not, however, to remain a civilian throughout the war. He joined an ambulance unit as an interpreter and was sent to serve near the French front at Doullens, Montdidier and Amiens. At Doullens he worked in a school that had been turned into a temporary hospital for three hundred severely wounded men. Maugham moved freely among them, trying to interpret their needs. One of his colleagues was a charming homosexual American called Gerald Haxton. Maugham's instant attraction to Gerald proved to be lifelong. He invited Gerald to join him now on a South Seas tour he was planning; this came about, after they had left the unit, in 1916.

Maugham's main idea was to find out as much as he could about Gauguin, of whom he had heard from Bohemian friends in Paris and whose rejection of family responsibility he saw as a promising subject for a novel. He soon found that in addition he was acquiring excellent material for fiction from the Britons and Americans they met on board ship and on the different islands they visited. Haxton was good at getting people to talk about their experiences over a drink or two, and Maugham, who was no mean conversationalist himself, listened.

Maugham did not turn these reminiscences into stories straight away, but saved them, noting an outline of a plot or a fragment of talk to jog his memory when he came back home. Some of his jottings were later published in *A Writer's Notebook* (1949), giving an interesting insight into his working method. After his return to London from this trip he was still busy with plays, and his life was undergoing two momentous changes.

The first was marriage to Syrie Barnardo, the former wife of the pharmaceuticals magnate Henry Wellcome. Syrie was an elegant, talented woman with a flair for interior decoration and a knowledge of antique furniture, which she later developed professionally. Quite why Maugham, a confirmed homosexual, should at this precise moment have married this passionate, demanding woman, none of his biographers has satisfactorily explained. Perhaps he was not quite as confirmed then as he later became. Whatever the reason, from that time there was a split in his private life between Syrie on the one hand and Gerald on the other, which would ultimately prove fatal to the marriage.

It was through Syrie that Maugham met the British spymaster William Wiseman, who recruited him for the intelligence service. This second great change brought considerable benefits to Maugham's work. If the role of husband in a conventional marriage was one to which Maugham was congenitally unsuited, that of secret agent in wartime fitted him to perfection. After completing a number of assignments, including information gathering and controlling a string of what Le Carré calls Joes, based in Geneva, he was given the more delicate task of going to Russia to try to prop up the Kerensky government to prevent it from making a separate peace.

Maugham wrote several stories about this period in his life. Some of them he later burnt because, according to his secretary Alan Searle, he felt publication would contravene the Official Secrets Act. But the most considerable of them were published, linked to each other through the movements of the British agent whose name (borrowed from a contemporary at the King's School) gave the volume its title. In my short selection from *Ashenden* I have followed Maugham's practice for anthology purposes of running together connected episodes under a single title. I have added the last Ashenden story, 'Sanatorium' (first published in a later collection), in which Ashenden has been invalided out of active service to be treated for tuberculosis in a sanatorium in the north of Scotland. Maugham and Ashenden may have failed to stop the Russian Revolution; they opened up a genre of spy fiction whose remarkable development in our own time would, surely, have surprised them.

Ashenden was not published until 1928, though some of its contents had appeared in magazines a year earlier. This gives a good idea of the amount of time – ten years or more – that often passed between Maugham's experiencing something that suggested a story to him and the appearance of the completed story in print. Thus in the early years after the armistice Maugham brooded on the material he had acquired in the Pacific Islands while he resumed his distinguished career as a dramatist, setting his comedies firmly in the metropolitan and country-house world of post-war England. These were the years of the premières of such perennial Maugham favourites as *Home and Beauty* (*Too Many Husbands* in the USA) and *The Circle*.

The short-story market he had known as a young man had by now disappeared. Maugham was not at all sure the one that had replaced it, where the big rewards lay in being accepted by the glossy American magazines, was going to suit him. He decided to proceed cautiously by writing up one or two episodes from the South Sea voyage as stories of around 15,000 words and giving them to his American literary agent, Charles Hanson Towne, to try out on editors. There was, for instance, the episode when the ship had been delayed in Pago-Pago because one member of the crew had caught measles, and the passengers, including an American missionary and his wife from New England and a blowzy English prostitute on her way to Apia, were all herded together in a cheap, run-down hotel. The rain had battered maddeningly all night on the corrugated-iron roof.

'Miss Thompson', as the story was called until its inclusion in a volume as 'Rain', was rejected by every major American magazine, but was eventually picked up by H. L. Mencken, editor of *Smart Set*, and printed there in April 1921. (It reappeared as 'Sadie Thompson' in a cheap edition of Maugham's Pacific tales in 1928; the first book ever sold in Woolworths, it continued to be reissued until 1940.) By the early 1920s editors were becoming less reluctant to accept Maugham's work. He had written five more stories of a similar length, and his publishers, George H. Doran and Company in the USA and Heinemann in London, brought them out between hard covers under the title *The Trembling of a Leaf* in America in September of 1921 and in London in October. A first printing of 3,000 copies in both countries rapidly sold out.

Although each story in *The Trembling of a Leaf* is quite separate, they gain from being read in sequence, as do those in the other volumes depicting the Far East, *The Casuarina Tree* (1926) and *Ah King* (1933). 'Mackintosh', in which colonial paternalism is seen at its most odious, echoes in the mind as the reader turns to 'The Fall of Edward Barnard', which sets the materialistic outlook of early-twentieth-century Chicago against the idealism of a young man exiling himself on a South Sea island. Maugham was to return to this theme when he came to write the novel *The Razor's Edge*.

Because of the immense surfeit of riches, in making my selection I have had to leave out several fine stories. I have preserved the order of their first publication in book form, and I have also kept the lyrical mood-setting passages that opened and closed the earliest collections.

From the 1920s, then, Maugham acquired a renewed reputation as a story-writer alongside his existing one as a playwright. For another dozen years he was happy to work hard in both fields, alternating new stage productions with volumes of fiction. But he had begun to be wearied by the constrictions imposed upon a writer for the mainstream theatre in such areas as the development of character. He chafed at the limitations of the form that had attracted him so much when he was young and yearned to be free to concentrate his energies wholly on fiction. In 1933, in a blaze of publicity and to the consternation of his admirers, he announced he would, after *Sheppey*, write no more plays.

Maugham had always been clear in his mind about whether an idea would work best as a play or a story. The Miss Thompson anecdote, for example, was a story idea. He never thought it would do as a play, and he was most agreeably surprised when, having given permission for John Colton and Clemence Randolph to dramatize it, the play *Rain* became one of the most commercially successful of all his works. Other stories were adapted for the stage by Guy Bolton, S. N. Behrman and Rodney Ackland. The only time Maugham himself dramatized a story was when he made a play out of 'The Letter', and that also proved extremely lucrative.

The writer whom Maugham adopted as a model in his youth and with whose stories Maugham's are most frequently compared – usually to their detriment – is Guy de Maupassant (1850–93), the great French exponent of the form. In *The Summing Up* Maugham presents a picture of himself (one to be taken with a pinch of salt) as a penniless young man in Paris, standing for hours at bookstalls absorbing the works of the master, sometimes even cutting the pages to do so. Certainly it was within the tradition of French naturalist fiction, with its insistence upon a precisely realized setting, a firm, unblurred delineation of character and a linear narrative, that Maugham operated. He aimed to emulate Maupassant's succinct and dispassionate pursuit of his quarry, the truth. But in turning the lives of ordinary people into stories these two virtuosos of short fiction were working on quite dissimilar material. Britain after the First World War, the last period of the British Empire, was a very different place from France during and after the Franco-Prussian war.

The main area in which Maugham moved away from his French model lies in his treatment of the Englishman as a colonial administrator. The leading members of French society were not nearly as involved in the running and commercial exploitation of colonial territory as were the British during Maugham's years as a writer of short stories. After their voyage to the South Seas, Maugham and Haxton went to Malaya, an expedition that resulted in *The Casuarina Tree*. Set in and around the Federated Malay States (FMS), the stories give startling insights into how the British behaved when they were in charge of that region. Here Maugham had lighted upon one of his richest veins of fictional material as well as one of his greatest sources of enjoyment as a traveller. From then on he and Haxton made it their business to go on regular, almost annual, tours of the Far East, starting from the Villa Mauresque in the south of France where Maugham had become a permanent expatriate after the collapse of his marriage at the end of the 1920s.

A comparison of Maugham with Kipling is more valid in this respect than one with Maupassant. In the selection he made in 1952, *A Choice of Kipling's Prose*, Maugham wrote of Kipling: 'He is our greatest short-story writer. I can't believe he will ever be equalled. I am sure he can never be excelled.' This verdict rests on a body of work ranging from the very short stories Kipling, then a precociously gifted youth, published in *The Civil and Military Gazette* in Lahore to the last collection, *Limits and Renewals* (1932), where in much longer stories he describes various states of acute mental breakdown. It is when Kipling looks at the code of behaviour of his own countrymen in India – which Maugham visited once and wrote about in *The Razor's Edge* but never in a short story – that they are on a more or less equal footing.

The basic difference is that, although they are dealing with similar themes – the odd white man out, the obduracy of the natives, sexual relations between the races – Kipling (in *Plain Tales from the Hills*) writes as a member of the ruling British community, revealing with approval its rigid code of conduct and the retribution that immediately followed any violation. Kipling is an insider writing for fellow members of the club. Maugham is a guest, an inquisitive outsider writing for other outsiders. He observes the code in operation; he leaves the reader in no doubt as to the awkward moral questions the working of it sometimes raises, and then he stops. It is not for him, a mere storyteller, to question the whole system of British administration overseas, as it was for E. M. Forster, Orwell and later Paul Scott.

As his reputation grew around the world, Maugham became supremely confident of his powers as a short-story writer, and he adopted an increasingly relaxed stance towards his readers. He began to address them directly, uttering asides of a general kind and challenging them to guess what on earth the story was going to be about. Compare these two openings from stories that first appeared in *Ah King*:

They got a first-class carriage to themselves. It was lucky, because they were taking a good deal in with them, Alban's suit-case and a hold-all, Anne's dressing-case and her hat-box.

There are few books in the world that contain more meat than the *Sailing Directions* published by the Hydrographic Department by order of the Lords Commissioners of the Admiralty. They are handsome volumes, bound (very flimsily) in cloth of different colours, and the most expensive of them is cheap.

The first, from 'The Door of Opportunity', is the classic, brisk, into-the-middle-of-things beginning. Alert readers might prick up their ears on hearing that, in a crowded train, the characters got a first-class carriage to themselves. It later transpires that Alban has been sent home in disgrace from his posting as District Officer and Anne is about to leave him for good. The theme is cowardice, depicted here as an attribute of a music-loving aesthete who is arrogant about his intellectual superiority to his colleagues.

The second opening is a tease. What could be more tiresome to the non-sailor than that manual? But Maugham dwells on it for a couple of pages in 'The Vessel of Wrath', without a hint of any story. Gradually he creates out of the Admiralty's impersonal tones a picture of an utterly remote group of islands where an intrepid explorer might find complete release from worldly pressures. This is to be the venue for his comic tale of *The Taming of the Shrew* the other way round. In it the white scapegrace and bully is cowed into marital docility by the missionary's prudish sister.

'The Book-Bag' has an even more extended, digressive opening, a mini-essay on the question of making sure one has adequate reading-matter during a long spell of travel. It allows Maugham to let his people discuss a biography of Byron that tells of the incestuous relations between the poet and his half-sister, Augusta. After several leisurely rubbers of bridge in the club, Maugham broaches the tale proper, which turns on the love between a planter and his sister and ends, when he marries, in her suicide. It represents the most extreme case of exclusive love of all Maugham's stories – so much so that it was rejected by *Cosmopolitan* (the American magazine where the stories were appearing in the early 1930s) because the editor thought that, in spite of Maugham's tactful approach to this taboo subject, it might offend some readers.

Maugham came to favour the voice of the first person for telling a story. It appealed to his sense of irony. The 'I' character or narrator is able to drop pregnant hints, leaving it to the reader to take them or not. In 1931 he published *Six Stories Written in the First Person Singular*, whose literal title is another sign of his confidence in his power over his vast readership. Even more unabashed was the collection in 1940 entitled simply *The Mixture as Before*. Maugham carefully explains that the 'I' in his stories is not to be identified with the author. We tend to ignore this caveat as we read, however, and to regard the wise, courteous, completely unshockable novelist, our amusingly affable host, as Maugham, albeit in his professional mask.

Maugham leaps about in time and place in these later works, and they reflect his mature, cosmopolitan way of life. He is just as at home in a fashionable London drawing-room, a smart restaurant on the Riviera, an embassy banquet or a weekend country-house party as he was in the depths of Borneo when the river burst its banks. His characters are mainly British, but occasionally he deals with Americans, Spaniards and the French. 'The Alien Corn', which tells of wealthy, anglicized Jews, reveals his fascination for the way in which people conform to inherited patterns of behaviour in moments of crisis. He casts a quizzical eye at the vagaries of the marriage market in 'Jane' and in 'Gigolo and Gigolette' extends his sympathy to those who risk their necks to entertain the public.

The stories set in England tend to hark back to the Edwardian England Maugham knew when he lived there as a struggling young author. His entertaining tale 'The Round Dozen', for example, takes place in a quiet resort on the south coast, where Mortimer Ellis, a confidence trickster, preys upon gullible women and persuades them to marry him. For all his duplicity his victims experience romance. Other characters find it outside marriage and sexual passion, as Maugham often did. They discover it in travel and in their experience of different forms of art. The difficulty of a life dedicated to the practice of art is another favourite topic.

At one time Maugham was asked for stories that could be printed in full on two facing pages of a magazine, testing his skill as a miniaturist. I have included two of these: the justly famous account of a good man, 'Salvatore', and 'The Judgement Seat'. The latter puts forward in the form of a celestial parable Maugham's often stated view that far too much fuss is made about marital infidelity (a view not apparent in his private life when he considered himself the injured party). 'The Princess and the Nightingale' comes from his early travel book *The Gentleman in the Parlour* (1930). It was originally a children's story he told to his young daughter Liza. When Maugham was requested to contribute something to a volume to be placed in the library of the doll's house belonging to Queen Mary, the wife of George V, he submitted this fable in tiny hand-writing.

Maugham went on publishing stories into the Second World War; his last collection, *Creatures of Circumstance*, was issued in 1947. Soon after that some were made into films in which he appeared – the 'Old Party', as he now styled himself – on the terrace of the Villa Mauresque to introduce and link them, and since then there have been many television and radio versions. By the end of the 1940s, however, his interest in the form had been well-nigh exhausted. In old age he found an alternative to it in setting down reflections on literary and artistic topics. As he had from play-writing, Maugham again retired with his public still thirsting for more, this time to become an essayist. But his short stories live on, to be rediscovered by each succeeding generation.

Anthony Curtis
London, 1990

FROM

The Trembling of a Leaf

(1 9 2 1)

The Pacific

The Pacific is inconstant and uncertain, like the soul of man. Sometimes it is grey like the English Channel off Beachy Head, with a heavy swell, and sometimes it is rough, capped with white crests, and boisterous. It is not so often that it is calm and blue. Then, indeed, the blue is arrogant. The sun shines fiercely from an unclouded sky. The trade wind gets into your blood and you are filled with an impatience for the unknown. The billows, magnificently rolling, stretch widely on all sides of you, and you forget your vanished youth, with its memories, cruel and sweet, in a restless, intolerable desire for life. On such a sea as this Ulysses sailed when he sought the Happy Isles. But there are days also when the Pacific is like a lake. The sea is flat and shining. The flying fish, a gleam of shadow on the brightness of a mirror, make little fountains of sparkling drops when they dip. There are fleecy clouds on the horizon, and at sunset they take strange shapes so that it is impossible not to believe that you see a range of lofty mountains. They are the mountains of the country of your dreams. You sail through an unimaginable silence upon a magic sea. Now and then a few gulls suggest that land is not far off, a forgotten island hidden in a wilderness of waters; but the gulls, the melancholy gulls, are the only sign you have of it. You see never a tramp, with its friendly smoke, no stately bark or trim schooner, not a fishing boat even: it is an empty desert; and presently the emptiness fills you with a vague foreboding.

Mackintosh

He splashed about for a few minutes in the sea; it was too shallow to swim in and for fear of sharks he could not go out of his depth; then he got out and went into the bath-house for a shower. The coldness of the fresh water was grateful after the heavy stickiness of the salt Pacific, so warm, though it was only just after seven, that to bathe in it did not brace you but rather increased your languor; and when he had dried himself, slipping into a bath-gown, he called out to the Chinese cook that he would be ready for breakfast in five minutes. He walked barefoot across the patch of coarse grass which Walker, the administrator, proudly thought was a lawn, to his own quarters and dressed. This did not take long, for he put on nothing but a shirt and a pair of duck trousers and then went over to his chief's house on the other side of the compound. The two men had their meals together, but the Chinese cook told him that Walker had set out on horseback at five and would not be back for another hour.

Mackintosh had slept badly and he looked with distaste at the paw-paw and eggs and bacon which were set before him. The mosquitoes had been maddening that night; they flew about the net under which he slept in such numbers that their humming, pitiless and menacing, had the effect of a note, infinitely drawn out, played on a distant organ, and whenever he dozed off he awoke with a start in the belief that one had found its way inside his curtains. It was so hot that he lay naked. He turned from side to side. And gradually the dull roar of the breakers on the reef, so unceasing and so regular that generally you did not hear it, grew distinct on his consciousness, its rhythm hammered on his tired nerves and he held himself with clenched hands in the effort to bear it. The thought that nothing could stop that sound, for it would continue to all eternity, was almost impossible to bear, and, as though his strength were a match for the ruthless forces of nature, he had an insane impulse to do some violent thing. He felt he must cling to his self-control or he would go mad. And now, looking out of the window at the lagoon and the strip of foam which marked the reef, he shuddered with hatred of the brilliant scene. The cloudless sky was like an inverted bowl that hemmed it in. He lit his pipe and turned over the pile of Auckland papers that had come over from Apia a few days before. The newest of them was three weeks old. They gave an impression of incredible dullness.

Then he went into the office. It was a large, bare room with two desks in it and a bench along one side. A number of natives were seated on this, and a couple of women. They gossiped while they waited for the administrator, and when Mackintosh came in they greeted him.

'*Talofa li.*'

He returned their greeting and sat down at his desk. He began to write, working on a report which the governor of Samoa had been clamouring for and which Walker, with his usual dilatoriness, had neglected to prepare. Mackintosh as he made his notes reflected vindictively that Walker was late with his report because he was so illiterate that he had an invincible distaste for anything to do with pens and paper; and now when it was at last ready, concise and neatly official, he would accept his subordinate's work without a word of appreciation, with a sneer rather or a gibe, and send it on to his own superior as though it were his own composition. He could not have written a word of it. Mackintosh thought with rage that if his chief pencilled in some insertion it would be childish in expression and faulty in language. If he remonstrated or sought to put his meaning into an intelligible phrase, Walker would fly into a passion and cry:

'What the hell do I care about grammar? That's what I want to say and that's how I want to say it.'

At last Walker came in. The natives surrounded him as he entered, trying to get his immediate attention, but he turned on them roughly and told them to sit down and hold their tongues. He threatened that if they were not quiet he would have them all turned out and see none of them that day. He nodded to Mackintosh.

'Hulloa, Mac; up at last? I don't know how you can waste the best part of the day in bed. You ought to have been up before dawn like me. Lazy beggar.'

He threw himself heavily into his chair and wiped his face with a large bandana.

'By heaven, I've got a thirst.'

He turned to the policeman who stood at the door, a picturesque figure in his white jacket and *lava-lava*, the loincloth of the Samoan, and told him

(7)

to bring *kava*. The *kava* bowl stood on the floor in the corner of the room, and the policeman filled a half coconut shell and brought it to Walker. He poured a few drops on the ground, murmured the customary words to the company, and drank with relish. Then he told the policeman to serve the waiting natives, and the shell was handed to each one in order of birth or importance and emptied with the same ceremonies.

Then he set about the day's work. He was a little man, considerably less than of middle height, and enormously stout; he had a large, fleshy face, clean-shaven, with the cheeks hanging on each side in great dew-laps, and three vast chins; his small features were all dissolved in fat; and, but for a crescent of white hair at the back of his head, he was completely bald. He reminded you of Mr Pickwick. He was grotesque, a figure of fun, and yet, strangely enough, not without dignity. His blue eyes, behind large gold-rimmed spectacles, were shrewd and vivacious, and there was a great deal of determination in his face. He was sixty, but his native vitality triumphed over advancing years. Notwithstanding his corpulence his movements were quick, and he walked with a heavy, resolute tread as though he sought to impress his weight upon the earth. He spoke in a loud, gruff voice.

It was two years now since Mackintosh had been appointed Walker's assistant. Walker who had been for a quarter of a century administrator of Talua, one of the larger islands in the Samoan group, was a man known in person or by report through the length and breadth of the South Seas; and it was with lively curiosity that Mackintosh looked forward to his first meeting with him. For one reason or another he stayed a couple of weeks at Apia before he took up his post and both at Chaplin's hotel and at the English club he heard innumerable stories about the administrator. He thought now with irony of his interest in them. Since then he had heard them a hundred times from Walker himself. Walker knew that he was a character, and, proud of his reputation, deliberately acted up to it. He was jealous of his 'legend' and anxious that you should know the exact details of any of the celebrated stories that were told of him. He was ludicrously angry with anyone who had told them to the stranger incorrectly.

There was a rough cordiality about Walker which Mackintosh at first found not unattractive, and Walker, glad to have a listener to whom all he said was fresh, gave of his best. He was good-humoured, hearty, and considerate. To Mackintosh, who had lived the sheltered life of a government official in London till at the age of thirty-four an attack of pneumonia, leaving him with the threat of tuberculosis, had forced him to seek a post in the Pacific. Walker's existence seemed extraordinarily romantic. The adventure with which he started on his conquest of circumstance was typical of the man. He ran away to sea when he was fifteen and for over a year was employed in shovelling coal on a collier. He was an undersized boy and both men and mates were kind to him, but the captain for some reason conceived a savage dislike of him. He used the lad cruelly so that, beaten and kicked, he often could not sleep for the pain that racked his limbs. He loathed the captain with all his soul. Then he was given a tip for some race and managed to borrow twenty-five pounds from a friend he had picked up in Belfast. He put it on the horse, an outsider, at long odds. He had no means of repaying the money if he lost, but it never occurred to him that he could lose. He felt himself in luck. The horse won and he found himself with something over a thousand pounds in hard cash. Now his chance had come. He found out who was the best solicitor in the town – the collier lay then somewhere on the Irish coast – went to him, and, telling him that he heard the ship was for sale, asked him to arrange the purchase for him. The solicitor was amused at his small client, he was only sixteen and did not look so old, and, moved perhaps by sympathy, promised not only to arrange the matter for him but to see that he made a good bargain. After a little while Walker found himself the owner of the ship. He went back to her and had what he described as the most glorious moment of his life when he gave the skipper notice and told him that he must get off *his* ship in half an hour. He made the mate captain and sailed on the collier for another nine months, at the end of which he sold her at a profit.

He came out to the islands at the age of twenty-six as a planter. He was one of the few white men settled in Talua at the time of the German occupation and had then already some influence with the natives. The Germans made him administrator, a position, which he occupied for twenty years, and when the island was seized by the British he was confirmed in his post. He ruled the island despotically, but with complete success. The prestige of this success was another reason for the interest that Mackintosh took in him.

But the two men were not made to get on. Mackintosh was an ugly man, with ungainly gestures, a tall thin fellow, with a narrow chest and bowed shoulders. He had sallow, sunken cheeks, and his eyes were large and sombre. He was a great reader, and when his books arrived and were unpacked Walker came over to his quarters and looked at them. Then he turned to Mackintosh with a coarse laugh.

'What in hell have you brought all this muck for?' he asked.

Mackintosh flushed darkly.

'I'm sorry you think it muck. I brought my books because I want to read them.'

'When you said you'd got a lot of books coming I thought there'd be something for me to read. Haven't you got any detective stories?'

'Detective stories don't interest me.'

'You're a damned fool then.'

'I'm content that you should think so.'

Every mail brought Walker a mass of periodical literature, papers from New Zealand and magazines from America, and it exasperated him that Mackintosh showed his contempt for these ephemeral publications. He had no patience with the books that absorbed Mackintosh's leisure and thought it only a pose that he read Gibbon's *Decline and Fall* or Burton's *Anatomy of Melancholy*. And since he had never learned to put any restraint on his tongue, he expressed his opinion of his assistant freely. Mackintosh began to see the real man, and under the boisterous good-humour he discerned a vulgar cunning which was hateful; he was vain and domineering, and it was strange that he had notwithstanding a shyness which made him dislike people who were not quite of his kidney. He judged others, naïvely, by their language, and if it was free from the oaths and the obscenity which made up the greater part of his own conversation, he looked upon them with suspicion. In the evening the two men played piquet. He played badly but vaingloriously, crowing over his opponent when he won and losing his temper when he lost. On rare occasions a couple of planters or traders would drive over to play bridge, and then Walker showed himself in what Mackintosh considered a characteristic light. He played regardless of his partner, calling up in his desire to play the hand, and argued interminably, beating down opposition by the loudness of his voice. He constantly revoked, and when he did so said with an ingratiating whine: 'Oh, you wouldn't count it against an old man who can hardly see.' Did he know that his opponents thought it as well to keep on the right side of him and hesitated to insist on the rigour of the game? Mackintosh watched him with an icy contempt. When the game was over, while they smoked their pipes and drank whisky, they would begin telling stories. Walker told with gusto the story of his marriage. He had got so drunk at the wedding feast that the bride had fled and he had never seen her since. He had had numberless adventures, commonplace and sordid, with the women of the island and he described them with a pride in his own prowess which was an offence to Mackintosh's fastidious ears. He was a gross, sensual old man. He thought Mackintosh a poor fellow because he would not share his promiscuous amours and remained sober when the company was drunk.

He despised him also for the orderliness with

which he did his official work. Mackintosh liked to do everything just so. His desk was always tidy, his papers were always neatly docketed, he could put his hand on any document that was needed, and he had at his fingers' ends all the regulations that were required for the business of their administration.

'Fudge, fudge,' said Walker. 'I've run this island for twenty years without red tape, and I don't want it now.'

'Does it make it any easier for you that when you want a letter you have to hunt half an hour for it?' answered Mackintosh.

'You're nothing but a damned official. But you're not a bad fellow; when you've been out here a year or two you'll be all right. What's wrong about you is that you won't drink. You wouldn't be a bad sort if you got soused once a week.'

The curious thing was that Walker remained perfectly unconscious of the dislike for him which every month increased in the breast of his subordinate. Although he laughed at him, as he grew accustomed to him, he began almost to like him. He had a certain tolerance for the peculiarities of others, and he accepted Mackintosh as a queer fish. Perhaps he liked him, unconsciously, because he could chaff him. His humour consisted of coarse banter and he wanted a butt. Mackintosh's exactness, his morality, his sobriety, were all fruitful subjects; his Scot's name gave an opportunity for the usual jokes about Scotland; he enjoyed himself thoroughly when two or three men were there and he could make them all laugh at the expense of Mackintosh. He would say ridiculous things about him to the natives, and Mackintosh, his knowledge of Samoan still imperfect, would see their unrestrained mirth when Walker had made an obscene reference to him. He smiled good-humouredly.

'I'll say this for you, Mac,' Walker would say in his gruff loud voice, 'you can take a joke.'

'Was it a joke?' smiled Mackintosh. 'I didn't know.'

'Scots wha hae!' shouted Walker, with a bellow of laughter. 'There's only one way to make a Scotchman see a joke and that's by a surgical operation.'

Walker little knew that there was nothing Mackintosh could stand less than chaff. He would wake in the night, the breathless night of the rainy season, and brood sullenly over the gibe that Walker had uttered carelessly days before. It rankled. His heart swelled with rage, and he pictured to himself ways in which he might get even with the bully. He had tried answering him, but Walker had a gift of repartee, coarse and obvious, which gave him an advantage. The dullness of his intellect made him impervious to a delicate shaft. His self-satisfaction made it impossible to wound him. His loud voice, his bellow of laughter, were weapons against which Mackintosh had nothing to counter, and he learned that the wisest thing was never to betray his irritation. He learned to control himself. But his hatred grew till it was a monomania. He watched Walker with an insane vigilance. He fed his own self-esteem by every instance of meanness on Walker's part, by every exhibition of childish vanity, of cunning and of vulgarity. Walker ate greedily, noisily, filthily, and Mackintosh watched him with satisfaction. He took note of the foolish things he said and of his mistakes in grammar. He knew that Walker held him in small esteem, and he found a bitter satisfaction in his chief's opinion of him; it increased his own contempt for the narrow, complacent old man. And it gave him a singular pleasure to know that Walker was entirely unconscious of the hatred he felt for him. He was a fool who liked popularity, and he blandly fancied that everyone admired him. Once Mackintosh had overheard Walker speaking of him.

'He'll be all right when I've licked him into shape,' he said. 'He's a good dog and he loves his master.'

Mackintosh silently, without a movement of his long, sallow face, laughed long and heartily.

But his hatred was not blind; on the contrary, it was peculiarly clear-sighted, and he judged Walker's capabilities with precision. He ruled his small kingdom with efficiency. He was just and honest. With opportunities to make money he was a poorer man than when he was first appointed to his post, and his only support for his old age was the pension which he expected when at last he retired from official life. His pride was that with an assistant and a half-caste clerk he was able to administer the island more competently than Upolu, the island of which Apia is the chief town, was administered with its army of functionaries. He had a few native policemen to sustain his authority, but he made no use of them. He governed by bluff and his Irish humour.

'They insisted on building a gaol for me,' he said. 'What the devil do I want a gaol for? I'm not going to put the natives in prison. If they do wrong I know how to deal with them.'

One of his quarrels with the higher authorities at

Apia was that he claimed entire jurisdiction over the natives of his island. Whatever their crimes he would not give them up to courts competent to deal with them, and several times an angry correspondence had passed between him and the Governor at Upolu. For he looked upon the natives as his children. And that was the amazing thing about this coarse, vulgar, selfish man; he loved the island on which he had lived so long with passion, and he had for the natives a strange rough tenderness which was quite wonderful.

He loved to ride about the island on his old grey mare and he was never tired of its beauty. Sauntering along the grassy roads among the coconut trees he would stop every now and then to admire the loveliness of the scene. Now and then he would come upon a native village and stop while the head man brought him a bowl of *kava*. He would look at the little group of bell-shaped huts with their high thatched roofs, like beehives, and a smile would spread over his fat face. His eyes rested happily on the spreading green of the bread-fruit trees.

'By George, it's like the garden of Eden.'

Sometimes his rides took him along the coast and through the trees he had a glimpse of the wide sea, empty, with never a sail to disturb the loneliness; sometimes he climbed a hill so that a great stretch of country, with little villages nestling among the tall trees, was spread out before him like the kingdom of the world, and he would sit there for an hour in an ecstasy of delight. But he had no words to express his feelings and to relieve them would utter an obscene jest; it was as though his emotion was so violent that he needed vulgarity to break the tension.

Mackintosh observed this sentiment with an icy disdain. Walker had always been a heavy drinker, he was proud of his capacity to see men half his age under the table when he spent a night in Apia, and he had the sentimentality of the toper. He could cry over the stories he read in his magazines and yet would refuse a loan to some trader in difficulties whom he had known for twenty years. He was close with his money. Once Mackintosh said to him:

'No one could accuse you of giving money away.'

He took it as a compliment. His enthusiasm for nature was but the drivelling sensibility of the drunkard. Nor had Mackintosh any sympathy for his chief's feelings towards the natives. He loved them because they were in his power, as a selfish man loves his dog, and his mentality was on a level with theirs. Their humour was obscene and he was never at a loss for the lewd remark. He understood them and they understood him. He was proud of his influence over them. He looked upon them as his children and he mixed himself in all their affairs. But he was very jealous of his authority; if he ruled them with a rod of iron, brooking no contradiction, he would not suffer any of the white men on the island to take advantage of them. He watched the missionaries suspiciously and, if they did anything of which he disapproved, was able to make life so unendurable to them that if he could not get them removed they were glad to go of their own accord. His power over the natives was so great that on his word they would refuse labour and food to their pastor. On the other hand he showed the traders no favour. He took care that they should not cheat the natives; he saw that they got a fair reward for their work and their copra and that the traders made no extravagant profit on the wares they sold them. He was merciless to a bargain that he thought unfair. Sometimes the traders would complain at Apia that they did not get fair opportunities. They suffered for it. Walker then hesitated at no calumny, at no outrageous lie, to get even with them, and they found that if they wanted not only to live at peace, but to exist at all, they had to accept the situation on his own terms. More than once the store of a trader obnoxious to him had been burned down, and there was only the appositeness of the event to show that the administrator had instigated it. Once a Swedish half-caste, ruined by the burning, had gone to him and roundly accused him of arson. Walker laughed in his face.

'You dirty dog. Your mother was a native and you try to cheat the natives. If your rotten old store is burned down it's a judgement of Providence; that's what it is, a judgement of Providence. Get out.'

And as the man was hustled out by two native policemen the administrator laughed fatly.

'A judgement of Providence.'

And now Mackintosh watched him enter upon the day's work. He began with the sick, for Walker added doctoring to his other activities, and he had a small room behind the office full of drugs. An elderly man came forward, a man with a crop of curly grey hair, in a blue *lava-lava*, elaborately tattooed, with the skin of his body wrinkled like a wine-skin.

'What have you come for?' Walker asked him abruptly.

In a whining voice the man said that he could not eat without vomiting and that he had pains here and pains there.

'Go to the missionaries,' said Walker. 'You know that I only cure children.'

'I have been to the missionaries and they do me no good.'

'Then go home and prepare yourself to die. Have you lived so long and still want to go on living? You're a fool.'

The man broke into querulous expostulation, but Walker, pointing to a woman with a sick child in her arms, told her to bring it to his desk. He asked her questions and looked at the child.

'I will give you medicine,' he said. He turned to the half-caste clerk. 'Go into the dispensary and bring me some calomel pills.'

He made the child swallow one there and then and gave another to the mother.

'Take the child away and keep it warm. Tomorrow it will be dead or better.'

He leaned back in his chair and lit his pipe.

'Wonderful stuff, calomel. I've saved more lives with it than all the hospital doctors at Apia put together.'

Walker was very proud of his skill, and with the dogmatism of ignorance had no patience with the members of the medical profession.

'The sort of case I like,' he said, 'is the one that all the doctors have given up as hopeless. When the doctors have said they can't cure you, I say to them, "come to me." Did I ever tell you about the fellow who had a cancer?'

'Frequently,' said Mackintosh.

'I got him right in three months.'

'You've never told me about the people you haven't cured.'

He finished this part of the work and went on to the rest. It was a queer medley. There was a woman who could not get on with her husband and a man who complained that his wife had run away from him.

'Lucky dog,' said Walker. 'Most men wish their wives would too.'

There was a long complicated quarrel about the ownership of a few yards of land. There was a dispute about the sharing out of a catch of fish. There was a complaint against a white trader because he had given short measure. Walker listened attentively to every case, made up his mind quickly, and gave his decision. Then he would listen to nothing more; if the complainant went on he was hustled out of the office by a policeman. Mackintosh listened to it all with sullen irritation. On the whole, perhaps, it might be admitted that rough justice was done, but it exasperated the assistant that his chief trusted his instinct rather than the evidence. He would not listen to reason. He browbeat the witnesses and when they did not see what he wished them to called them thieves and liars.

He left to the last a group of men who were sitting in the corner of the room. He had deliberately ignored them. The party consisted of an old chief, a tall, dignified man with short, white hair, in a new *lava-lava*, bearing a huge fly wisp as a badge of office, his son, and half a dozen of the important men of the village. Walker had had a feud with them and had beaten them. As was characteristic of him he meant now to rub in his victory, and because he had them down to profit by their helplessness. The facts were peculiar. Walker had a passion for building roads. When he had come to Talua there were but a few tracks here and there, but in course of time he had cut roads through the country, joining the villages together, and it was to this that a great part of the island's prosperity was due. Whereas in the old days it had been impossible to get the produce of the land, copra chiefly, down to the coast where it could be put on schooners or motor launches and so taken to Apia, now transport was easy and simple. His ambition was to make a road right round the island and a great part of it was already built.

'In two years I shall have done it, and then I can die or they can fire me. I don't care.'

His roads were the joy of his heart and he made excursions constantly to see that they were kept in order. They were simple enough, wide tracks, grass covered, cut through the scrub or through the plantations; but trees had to be rooted out, rocks dug up or blasted, and here and there levelling had been necessary. He was proud that he had surmounted by his own skill such difficulties as they presented. He rejoiced in his disposition of them so that they were not only convenient, but showed off the beauties of the island which his soul loved. When he spoke of his roads he was almost a poet. They meandered through those lovely scenes, and Walker had taken care that here and there they should run in a straight line, giving you a green vista through the tall trees, and here and there should turn and curve so that the heart was rested by the diversity. It was amazing that this coarse and sensual man should exercise so subtle an ingenuity to get the effects which his fancy suggested to him. He had used in making his roads all the fantastic skill of a Japanese gardener. He received a grant from headquarters for the work but took a curious pride in using but a small part of it, and the year before had spent only a hundred pounds of the thousand assigned to him.

'What do they want money for?' he boomed. 'They'll only spend it on all kinds of muck they don't want; what the missionaries leave them, that is to say.'

For no particular reason, except perhaps pride in the economy of his administration and the desire to contrast his efficiency with the wasteful methods of the authorities at Apia, he got the natives to do the work he wanted for wages that were almost nominal. It was owing to this that he had lately had difficulty with the village whose chief men now were come to see him. The chief's son had been in Upolu for a year and on coming back had told his people of the large sums that were paid at Apia for the public works. In long, idle talks he had inflamed their hearts with the desire for gain. He held out to them visions of vast wealth and they thought of the whisky they could buy – it was dear, since there was a law that it must not be sold to natives, and so it cost them double what the white man had to pay for it – they thought of the great sandal-wood boxes in which they kept their treasures, and the scented soap and potted salmon, the luxuries for which the Kanaka will sell his soul; so that when the administrator sent for them and told them he wanted a road made from their village to a certain point along the coast and offered them twenty pounds, they asked him a hundred. The chief's son was called Manuma. He was a tall, handsome fellow, copper-coloured, with his fuzzy hair dyed red with lime, a wreath of red berries round his neck, and behind his ear a flower like a scarlet flame against his brown face. The upper part of his body was naked, but to show that he was no longer a savage, since he had lived in Apia he wore a pair of dungarees instead of a *lava-lava*. He told them that if they held together the administrator would be obliged to accept their terms. His heart was set on building the road and when he found they would not work for less he would give them what they asked. But they must not move; whatever he said they must not abate their claim; they had asked a hundred and that they must keep to. When they mentioned the figure, Walker burst into a shout of his long, deep-voiced laughter. He told them not to make fools of themselves, but to set about the work at once. Because he was in a good humour that day he promised to give them a feast when the road was finished. But when he found that no attempt was made to start work, he went to the village and asked the men what silly game they were playing. Manuma had coached them well. They were quite calm, they did not attempt to argue – and argument is a passion with the Kanaka – they merely shrugged their shoulders: they would do it for a hundred pounds, and if he would not give them that they would do no work. He could please himself. They did not care. Then Walker flew into a passion. He was ugly then. His short fat neck swelled ominously, his red face grew purple, he foamed at the mouth. He set upon the natives with invective. He knew well how to wound and how to humiliate. He was terrifying.

The older men grew pale and uneasy. They hesitated. If it had not been for Manuma, with his knowledge of the great world, and their dread of his ridicule, they would have yielded. It was Manuma who answered Walker.

'Pay us a hundred pounds and we will work.'

Walker, shaking his fist at him, called him every name he could think of. He riddled him with scorn. Manuma sat still and smiled. There may have been more bravado than confidence in his smile, but he had to make a good show before the others. He repeated his words.

'Pay us a hundred pounds and we will work.'

They thought that Walker would spring on him. It would not have been the first time that he had thrashed a native with his own hands; they knew his strength, and though Walker was three times the age of the young man and six inches shorter they did not doubt that he was more than a match for Manuma. No one had ever thought of resisting the savage onslaught of the administrator. But Walker said nothing. He chuckled.

'I am not going to waste my time with a pack of fools,' he said. 'Talk it over again. You know what I have offered. If you do not start in a week, take care.'

He turned round and walked out of the chief's hut. He untied his old mare and it was typical of the relations between him and the natives that one of the elder men hung on to the off stirrup while Walker from a convenient boulder hoisted himself heavily into the saddle.

That same night when Walker according to his habit was strolling along the road that ran past his house, he heard something whizz past him and with a thud strike a tree. Something had been thrown at him. He ducked instinctively. With a shout, 'Who's that?' he ran towards the place from which the missile had come and he heard the sound of a man escaping through the bush. He knew it was hopeless to pursue in the darkness, and besides he was soon out of breath, so he stopped and made his way back to the road. He looked about for what had been thrown, but could find nothing. It was quite dark. He went quickly back to the house and called Mackintosh and the Chinese boy.

'One of those devils has thrown something at me. Come along and let's find out what it was.'

He told the boy to bring a lantern and the three of them made their way back to the place. They hunted about the ground, but could not find what they sought. Suddenly the boy gave a guttural cry. They turned to look. He held up the lantern, and there, sinister in the light that cut the surrounding darkness, was a long knife sticking into the trunk of a coconut tree. It had been thrown with such force that it required quite an effort to pull it out.

'By George, if he hadn't missed me I'd have been in a nice state.'

Walker handled the knife. It was one of those knives, made in imitation of the sailor knives brought to the islands a hundred years before by the first white men, used to divide the coconuts in two so that the copra may be dried. It was a murderous weapon, and the blade, twelve inches long, was very sharp. Walker chuckled softly.

'The devil, the impudent devil.'

He had no doubt it was Manuma who had flung the knife. He had escaped death by three inches. He was not angry. On the contrary, he was in high spirits; the adventure exhilarated him, and when they got back to the house, calling for drinks, he rubbed his hands gleefully.

'I'll make them pay for this!'

His little eyes twinkled. He blew himself out like a turkey-cock, and for the second time within half an hour insisted on telling Mackintosh every detail of the affair. Then he asked him to play piquet, and while they played he boasted of his intentions. Mackintosh listened with tightened lips.

'But why should you grind them down like this?' he asked. 'Twenty pounds is precious little for the work you want them to do.'

'They ought to be precious thankful I give them anything.'

'Hang it all, it's not your own money. The government allots you a reasonable sum. They won't complain if you spend it.'

'They're a bunch of fools at Apia.'

Mackintosh saw that Walker's motive was merely vanity. He shrugged his shoulders.

'It won't do you much good to score off the fellows at Apia at the cost of your life.'

'Bless you, they wouldn't hurt me, these people. They couldn't do without me. They worship me. Manuma is a fool. He only threw that knife to frighten me.'

The next day Walker rode over again to the village. It was called Matautu. He did not get off his horse. When he reached the chief's house he saw that the men were sitting round the floor in a circle, talking, and he guessed they were discussing again the question of the road. The Samoan huts are formed in this way: Trunks of slender trees are placed in a circle at intervals of perhaps five or six feet; a tall tree is set in the middle and from this downwards slopes the thatched roof. Venetian blinds of coconut leaves can be pulled down at night or when it is raining. Ordinarily the hut is open all round so that the breeze can blow through freely. Walker rode to the edge of the hut and called out to the chief.

'Oh, there, Tangatu, your son left his knife in a tree last night. I have brought it back to you.'

He flung it down on the ground in the midst of the circle, and with a low burst of laughter ambled off.

On Monday he went out to see if they had started work. There was no sign of it. He rode through the village. The inhabitants were about their ordinary avocations. Some were weaving mats of the pandanus leaf, one old man was busy with a *kava* bowl, the children were playing, the women went about their household chores. Walker, a smile on his lips, came to the chief's house.

'*Talofa li,*' said the chief.

'*Talofa,*' answered Walker.

Manuma was making a net. He sat with a cigarette between his lips and looked up at Walker with a smile of triumph.

'You have decided that you will not make the road?'

The chief answered.

'Not unless you pay us one hundred pounds.'

'You will regret it.' He turned to Manuma. 'And you, my lad, I shouldn't wonder if your back was very sore before you're much older.'

He rode away chuckling. He left the natives vaguely uneasy. They feared the fat sinful old man, and neither the missionaries' abuse of him nor the scorn which Manuma had learnt in Apia made them forget that he had a devilish cunning and that no man had ever braved him without in the long run suffering for it. They found out within twenty-four hours what scheme he had devised. It was characteristic. For next morning a great band of men, women, and children came into the village and the chief men said that they had made a bargain with Walker to build the road. He had offered them twenty pounds and they had accepted. Now the cunning lay in this, that the Polynesians have rules of hospitality which have all the force of laws; an etiquette of absolute rigidity made it necessary for the people of the village not only to give lodging to the strangers, but to provide them with food and drink as long as they wished to stay. The inhabitants of Matautu were outwitted. Every morning the workers went out in a joyous band, cut down trees, blasted rocks, levelled here and there and then in the evening tramped back again, and ate and drank, ate heartily, danced, sang hymns, and enjoyed life. For them it was a picnic. But soon their hosts began to wear long faces; the strangers had enormous appetites, and the plantains and the bread-fruit vanished before their rapacity; the alligator-pear trees, whose fruit sent to Apia might sell for good money, were stripped bare. Ruin stared them in the face. And then they found that the strangers were working very slowly. Had they received a hint from Walker that they might take their time? At this rate by the time the road was finished there would not be a scrap of food in the village. And worse than this, they were a laughing-stock; when one or other of them went to some distant hamlet on an errand he found that the story had got there before him, and he was met with derisive laughter. There is nothing the Kanaka can endure less than ridicule. It was not long before much angry talk passed among the sufferers. Manuma was no longer a hero; he had to put up with a good deal of plain speaking, and one day what Walker had suggested came to pass: a heated argument turned into a quarrel and half a dozen of the young men set upon the chief's son and gave him such a beating that for a week he lay bruised and sore on the pandanus mats. He turned from side to side and could find no ease. Every day or two the administrator rode over on his old mare and watched the progress of the road. He was not a man to resist the temptation of taunting the fallen foe, and he missed no opportunity to rub into the shamed inhabitants of Matautu the bitterness of their humiliation. He broke their spirit. And one morning, putting their pride in their pockets, a figure of speech, since pockets they had not, they all set out with the strangers and started working on the road. It was urgent to get it done quickly if they wanted to save any food at all, and the whole village joined in. But they worked silently, with rage and mortification in their hearts, and even the children toiled in silence. The women wept as they carried away bundles of brushwood. When Walker saw them he laughed so much that he almost rolled out of his saddle. The news spread quickly and tickled the people of the island to death. This was the greatest joke of all, the crowning triumph of that cunning old white man whom no Kanaka had ever been able to circumvent; and they came from distant villages, with their wives and children, to look at the foolish folk who had refused twenty pounds to make the road and now were forced to work for nothing. But the harder they worked the more easily went the guests. Why should they hurry, when they were getting good food for nothing and the longer they took about the job the better the joke became? At last the wretched villagers could stand it no longer, and they were come this morning to beg the administrator to send the strangers back to their own homes. If he would do this they promised to finish the road themselves for nothing. For him it was a victory complete and unqualified. They were humbled. A look of arrogant complacence spread over his large, naked face, and he seemed to swell in his chair like a great bullfrog. There was something sinister in his appearance, so that Mackintosh shivered with disgust. Then in his booming tones he began to speak.

'Is it for my good that I make the road? What benefit do you think I get out of it? It is for you, so that you can walk in comfort and carry your copra in comfort. I offered to pay you for your work, though it was for your own sake the work was done. I offered to pay you generously. Now *you* must pay. I will send the people of Manua back to their homes if you will finish the road and pay the twenty pounds that I have to pay them.'

There was an outcry. They sought to reason with him. They told him they had not the money. But to everything they said he replied with brutal gibes. Then the clock struck.

'Dinner time,' he said. 'Turn them all out.'

He raised himself heavily from his chair and walked out of the room. When Mackintosh followed him he found him already seated at table, a napkin tied round his neck, holding his knife and fork in readiness for the meal the Chinese cook was about to bring. He was in high spirits.

'I did 'em down fine,' he said, as Mackintosh sat down. 'I shan't have much trouble with the roads after this.'

'I suppose you were joking,' said Mackintosh icily.

'What do you mean by that?'

'You're not really going to make them pay twenty pounds?'

'You bet your life I am.'

'I'm not sure you've got any right to.'

'Ain't you? I guess I've got the right to do any damned thing I like on this island.'

'I think you've bullied them quite enough.'

Walker laughed fatly. He did not care what Mackintosh thought.

'When I want your opinion I'll ask for it.'

Mackintosh grew very white. He knew by bitter experience that he could do nothing but keep silence, and the violent effort at self-control made him sick and faint. He could not eat the food that was before him and with disgust he watched Walker shovel meat into his vast mouth. He was a dirty feeder, and to sit at table with him needed a strong stomach. Mackintosh shuddered. A tremendous desire seized him to humiliate that gross and cruel man; he would give anything in the world to see him in the dust, suffering as much as he had made others suffer. He had never loathed the bully with such loathing as now.

The day wore on. Mackintosh tried to sleep after dinner, but the passion in his heart prevented him; he tried to read, but the letters swam before his eyes. The sun beat down pitilessly, and he longed for rain; but he knew that rain would bring no coolness; it would only make it hotter and more steamy. He was a native of Aberdeen and his heart yearned suddenly for the icy winds that whistled through the granite streets of that city. Here he was a prisoner, imprisoned not only by that placid sea, but by his hatred for that horrible old man. He pressed his hands to his aching head. He would like to kill him. But he pulled himself together. He must do something to distract his mind, and since he could not read he thought he would set his private papers in order. It was a job which he had long meant to do and which he had constantly put off. He unlocked the drawer of his desk and took out a handful of letters. He caught sight of his revolver. An impulse, no sooner realized than set aside, to put a bullet through his head and so escape from the intolerable bondage of life flashed through his mind. He noticed that in the damp air the revolver was slightly rusted, and he got an oil rag and began to clean it. It was while he was thus occupied that he grew aware of someone slinking round the door. He looked up and called:

'Who is there?'

There was a moment's pause, then Manuma showed himself.

'What do you want?'

The chief's son stood for a moment, sullen and silent, and when he spoke it was with a strangled voice.

'We can't pay twenty pounds. We haven't the money.'

'What am I to do?' said Mackintosh. 'You heard what Mr Walker said.'

Manuma began to plead, half in Samoan and half

in English. It was a sing-song whine, with the quavering intonations of a beggar, and it filled Mackintosh with disgust. It outraged him that the man should let himself be so crushed. He was a pitiful object.

'I can do nothing,' said Mackintosh irritably. 'You know that Mr Walker is master here.'

Manuma was silent again. He still stood in the doorway.

'I am sick,' he said at last. 'Give me some medicine.'

'What is the matter with you?'

'I do not know. I am sick. I have pains in my body.'

'Don't stand there,' said Mackintosh sharply. 'Come in and let me look at you.'

Manuma entered the little room and stood before the desk.

'I have pains here and here.'

He put his hands to his loins and his face assumed an expression of pain. Suddenly Mackintosh grew conscious that the boy's eyes were resting on the revolver which he had laid on the desk when Manuma appeared in the doorway. There was a silence between the two which to Mackintosh was endless. He seemed to read the thoughts which were in the Kanaka's mind. His heart beat violently. And then he felt as though something possessed him so that he acted under the compulsion of a foreign will. Himself did not make the movements of his body, but a power that was strange to him. His throat was suddenly dry, and he put his hand to it mechanically in order to help his speech. He was impelled to avoid Manuma's eyes.

'Just wait here,' he said, his voice sounded as

though someone had seized him by the windpipe, 'and I'll fetch you something from the dispensary.'

He got up. Was it his fancy that he staggered a little? Manuma stood silently, and though he kept his eyes averted, Mackintosh knew that he was looking dully out of the door. It was this other person that possessed him that drove him out of the room, but it was himself that took a handful of muddled papers and threw them on the revolver in order to hide it from view. He went to the dispensary. He got a pill and poured out some blue draught into a small bottle, and then came out into the compound. He did not want to go back into his own bungalow, so he called to Manuma.

'Come here.'

He gave him the drugs and instructions how to take them. He did not know what it was that made it impossible for him to look at the Kanaka. While he was speaking to him he kept his eyes on his shoulder. Manuma took the medicine and slunk out of the gate.

Mackintosh went into the dining-room and turned over once more the old newspapers. But he could not read them. The house was very still. Walker was upstairs in his room asleep, the Chinese cook was busy in the kitchen, the two policemen were out fishing. The silence that seemed to brood over the house was unearthly, and there hammered in Mackintosh's head the question whether the revolver still lay where he had placed it. He could not bring himself to look. The uncertainty was horrible, but the certainty would be more horrible still. He sweated. At last he could stand the silence no longer, and he made up his mind to go down the road to the trader's, a man named Jervis, who had a store about a mile away. He was a half-caste, but even that amount of white blood made him possible to talk to. He wanted to get away from his bungalow, with the desk littered with untidy papers, and underneath them something, or nothing. He walked along the road. As he passed the fine hut of a chief a greeting was called out to him. Then he came to the store. Behind the counter sat the trader's daughter, a swarthy broad-featured girl in a pink blouse and a white drill skirt. Jervis hoped he would marry her. He had money, and he had told Mackintosh that his daughter's husband would be well-to-do. She flushed a little when she saw Mackintosh.

'Father's just unpacking some cases that have come in this morning. I'll tell him you're here.'

He sat down and the girl went out behind the shop. In a moment her mother waddled in, a huge old woman, a chiefess, who owned much land in her own right; and gave him her hand. Her monstrous obesity was an offence, but she managed to convey an impression of dignity. She was cordial without obsequiousness; affable, but conscious of her station.

'You're quite a stranger, Mr Mackintosh. Teresa was saying only this morning: "Why, we never see Mr Mackintosh now."'

He shuddered a little as he thought of himself as that old native's son-in-law. It was notorious that she ruled her husband, notwithstanding his white blood, with a firm hand. Hers was the authority and hers the business head. She might be no more than Mrs Jervis to the white people, but her father had been a chief of the blood royal, and his father and his father's father had ruled as kings. The trader came in, small beside his imposing wife, a dark man with a black beard going grey, in ducks, with handsome eyes and flashing teeth. He was very British, and his conversation was slangy, but you felt he spoke English as a foreign tongue; with his family he used the language of his native mother. He was a servile man, cringing and obsequious.

'Ah, Mr Mackintosh, this is a joyful surprise. Get the whisky, Teresa; Mr Mackintosh will have a gargle with us.'

He gave all the latest news of Apia, watching his guest's eyes the while, so that he might know the welcome thing to say.

'And how is Walker? We've not seen him just lately. Mrs Jervis is going to send him a sucking-pig one day this week.'

'I saw him riding home this morning,' said Teresa.

'Here's how,' said Jervis, holding up his whisky.

Mackintosh drank. The two women sat and looked at him, Mrs Jervis in her black Mother Hubbard, placid and haughty, and Teresa, anxious to smile whenever she caught his eye, while the trader gossiped insufferably.

'They were saying in Apia it was about time Walker retired. He ain't so young as he was. Things have changed since he first come to the islands and he ain't changed with them.'

'He'll go too far,' said the old chiefess. 'The natives aren't satisfied.'

'That was a good joke about the road,' laughed the trader. 'When I told them about it in Apia they fair split their sides with laughing. Good old Walker.'

Mackintosh looked at him savagely. What did he mean by talking of him in that fashion? To a half-caste trader he was Mr Walker. It was on his tongue to utter a harsh rebuke for the impertinence. He did not know what held him back.

'When he goes I hope you'll take his place, Mr Mackintosh,' said Jervis. 'We all like you on the island. You understand the natives. They're educated now, they must be treated differently to the old days. It wants an educated man to be administrator now. Walker was only a trader same as I am.'

Teresa's eyes glistened.

'When the time comes if there's anything anyone can do here, you bet your bottom dollar we'll do it. I'd get all the chiefs to go over to Apia and make a petition.'

Mackintosh felt horribly sick. It had not struck him that if anything happened to Walker it might be he would would succeed him. It was true that no one in his official position knew the island so well. He got up suddenly and scarcely taking his leave walked back to the compound. And now he went straight to his room. He took a quick look at his desk. He rummaged among the papers.

The revolver was not there.

His heart thumped violently against his ribs. He looked for the revolver everywhere. He hunted in the chairs and in the drawers. He looked desperately, and all the time he knew he would not find it. Suddenly he heard Walker's gruff, hearty voice.

'What the devil are you up to, Mac?'

He started. Walker was standing in the doorway and instinctively he turned round to hide what lay upon his desk.

'Tidying up?' quizzed Walker. 'I've told 'em to put the grey in the trap. I'm going down to Tafoni to bathe. You'd better come along.'

'All right,' said Mackintosh.

So long as he was with Walker nothing could happen. The place they were bound for was about three miles away, and there was a fresh-water pool, separated by a thin barrier of rock from the sea, which the administrator had blasted out for the natives to bathe in. He had done this at spots round the island, wherever there was a spring; and the fresh water, compared with the sticky warmth of the sea, was cool and invigorating. They drove along the silent grassy road, splashing now and then through fords, where the sea had forced its way in, past a couple of native villages, the bell-shaped huts spaced out roomily and the white chapel in the middle, and at the third village they got out of the trap, tied up the horse, and walked down to the pool. They were accompanied by four or five girls and a dozen children. Soon they were all splashing about, shouting and laughing, while Walker, in a *lava-lava*, swam to and fro like an unwieldy porpoise. He made lewd jokes with the girls, and they amused themselves by diving under him and wriggling away when he tried to catch them. When he was tired he lay down on a rock, while the girls and children surrounded him; it was a happy family; and the old man, huge, with his crescent of white hair and his shining bald crown, looked like some old sea god. Once Mackintosh caught a queer soft look in his eyes.

'They're dear children,' he said. 'They look upon me as their father.'

And then without a pause he turned to one of the

girls and made an obscene remark which sent them all into fits of laughter. Mackintosh started to dress. With his thin legs and thin arms he made a grotesque figure, a sinister Don Quixote, and Walker began to make coarse jokes about him. They were acknowledged with little smothered laughs. Mackintosh struggled with his shirt. He knew he looked absurd, but he hated being laughed at. He stood silent and glowering.

'If you want to get back in time for dinner you ought to come soon.'

'You're not a bad fellow, Mac. Only you're a fool. When you're doing one thing you always want to do another. That's not the way to live.'

But all the same he raised himself slowly to his feet and began to put on his clothes. They sauntered back to the village, drank a bowl of *kava* with the chief, and then, after a joyful farewell from all the lazy villagers, drove home.

After dinner, according to his habit, Walker, lighting his cigar, prepared to go for a stroll. Mackintosh was suddenly seized with fear.

'Don't you think it's rather unwise to go out at night by yourself just now?'

Walker stared at him with his round blue eyes.

'What the devil do you mean?'

'Remember the knife the other night. You've got those fellows' backs up.'

'Pooh! They wouldn't dare.'

'Someone dared before.'

'That was only a bluff. They wouldn't hurt me. They look upon me as a father. They know that whatever I do is for their own good.'

Mackintosh watched him with contempt in his heart. The man's self-complacency outraged him, and yet something, he knew not what, made him insist.

'Remember what happened this morning. It wouldn't hurt you to stay at home just tonight. I'll play piquet with you.'

'I'll play piquet with you when I come back. The Kanaka isn't born yet who can make me alter my plans.'

'You'd better let me come with you.'

'You stay where you are.'

Mackintosh shrugged his shoulders. He had given the man full warning. If he did not heed it that was his own lookout. Walker put on his hat and went out. Mackintosh began to read; but then he thought of something; perhaps it would be as well to have his own whereabouts quite clear. He crossed over to the kitchen and, inventing some pretext, talked for a few minutes with the cook. Then he got out the gramophone and put a record on it, but while it ground out its melancholy tune, some comic song of a London music-hall, his ear was strained for a sound away there in the night. At his elbow the record reeled out its loudness, the words were raucous, but notwithstanding he seemed to be surrounded by an unearthly silence. He heard the dull roar of the breakers against the reef. He heard the breeze sigh, far up, in the leaves of the coconut trees. How long would it be? It was awful.

He heard a hoarse laugh.

'Wonders will never cease. It's not often you play yourself a tune, Mac.'

Walker stood at the window, red-faced, bluff and jovial.

'Well, you see I'm alive and kicking. What were you playing for?'

Walker came in.

'Nerves a bit dicky, eh? Playing a tune to keep your pecker up?'

'I was playing your requiem.'

'What the devil's that?'

''Alf o' bitter an' a pint of stout.'

'A rattling good song too. I don't mind how often I hear it. Now I'm ready to take your money off you at piquet.'

They played and Walker bullied his way to victory, bluffing his opponent, chaffing him, jeering at his mistakes, up to every dodge, browbeating him, exulting. Presently Mackintosh recovered his coolness, and standing outside himself, as it were, he was able to take a detached pleasure in watching the overbearing old man and in his own cold reserve. Somewhere Manuma sat quietly and awaited his opportunity.

Walker won game after game and pocketed his winnings at the end of the evening in high good humour.

'You'll have to grow a little bit older before you stand much chance against me, Mac. The fact is I have a natural gift for cards.'

'I don't know that there's much gift about it when I happen to deal you fourteen aces.'

'Good cards come to good players,' retorted Walker. 'I'd have won if I'd had your hands.'

He went on to tell long stories of the various occasions on which he had played cards with notorious sharpers and to their consternation had taken all their money from them. He boasted. He praised himself. And Mackintosh listened with absorption. He wanted now to feed his hatred; and everything Walker said, every gesture, made him more detestable. At last Walker got up.

'Well, I'm going to turn in,' he said with a loud yawn. 'I've got a long day tomorrow.'

'What are you going to do?'

'I'm driving over to the other side of the island. I'll start at five, but I don't expect I shall get back to dinner till late.'

They generally dined at seven.

'We'd better make it half-past seven then.'

'I guess it would be as well.'

Mackintosh watched him knock the ashes out of his pipe. His vitality was rude and exuberant. It was strange to think that death hung over him. A faint smile flickered in Mackintosh's cold, gloomy eyes.

'Would you like me to come with you?'

'What in God's name should I want that for? I'm using the mare and she'll have enough to do to carry me; she don't want to drag you over thirty miles of road.'

'Perhaps you don't quite realize what the feeling is at Matautu. I think it would be safer if I came with you.'

Walker burst into contemptuous laughter.

'You'd be a fine lot of use in a scrap. I'm not a great hand at getting the wind up.'

Now the smile passed from Mackintosh's eyes to his lips. It distorted them painfully.

'*Quem deus vult perdere prius dementat.*'

'What the hell is that?' said Walker.

'Latin,' answered Mackintosh as he went out.

And now he chuckled. His mood had changed. He had done all he could and the matter was in the hands of fate. He slept more soundly than he had done for weeks. When he awoke next morning he went out. After a good night he found a pleasant exhilaration in the freshness of the early air. The sea was a more vivid blue, the sky more brilliant, than on most days, the trade wind was fresh, and there was a ripple on the lagoon as the breeze brushed over it like velvet brushed the wrong way. He felt himself stronger and younger. He entered upon the day's work with zest. After luncheon he slept again, and as evening drew on he had the bay saddled and sauntered through the bush. He seemed to see it all with new eyes. He felt more normal. The extraordinary thing was that he was able to put Walker out of his mind altogether. So far as he was concerned he might never have existed.

He returned late, hot after his ride, and bathed again. Then he sat on the veranda, smoking his pipe, and looked at the day declining over the lagoon. In the sunset the lagoon, rosy and purple and green, was very beautiful. He felt at peace with the world and with himself. When the cook came out to say that dinner was ready and to ask whether he should wait, Mackintosh smiled at him with friendly eyes. He looked at his watch.

'It's half-past seven. Better not wait. One can't tell when the boss'll be back.'

The boy nodded, and in a moment Mackintosh saw him carry across the yard a bowl of steaming soup. He got up lazily, went into the dining-room, and ate his dinner. Had it happened? The uncertainty was amusing and Mackintosh chuckled in the silence. The food did not seem so monotonous as usual, and even though there was Hamburger steak, the cook's invariable dish when his poor invention failed him, it tasted by some miracle succulent and spiced. After dinner he strolled over lazily to his bungalow to get a book. He liked the intense stillness, and now that the night had fallen the stars were blazing in the sky. He shouted for a lamp and in a moment the Chink pattered over on his bare feet, piercing the darkness with a ray of light. He put the lamp on the desk and noiselessly slipped out of the room. Mackintosh stood rooted to the floor, for there, half hidden by untidy papers, was his revolver. His heart throbbed painfully, and he broke into a sweat. It was done then.

He took up the revolver with a shaking hand. Four of the chambers were empty. He paused a moment and looked suspiciously out into the night, but there was no one there. He quickly slipped four cartridges into the empty chambers and locked the revolver in his drawer.

He sat down to wait.

An hour passed, a second hour passed. There was nothing. He sat at his desk as though he were writing, but he neither wrote nor read. He merely listened. He strained his ears for a sound travelling from a far distance. At last he heard hesitating footsteps and knew it was the Chinese cook.

'Ah-Sung,' he called.

The boy came to the door.

'Boss velly late,' he said. 'Dinner no good.'

Mackintosh stared at him, wondering whether he knew what had happened, and whether, when he knew, he would realize on what terms he and Walker had been. He went about his work, sleek, silent, and smiling, and who could tell his thoughts?

'I expect he's had dinner on the way, but you must keep the soup hot at all events.'

The words were hardly out of his mouth when the silence was suddenly broken into by a confusion, cries, and a rapid patter of naked feet. A number of natives ran into the compound, men and women and children; they crowded round Mackintosh and they all talked at once. They were unintelligible. They were excited and frightened and some of them were crying. Mackintosh pushed his way through them and went to the gateway. Though he had scarcely understood what they said he knew quite well what had happened. And as he reached the gate the dog-cart arrived. The old mare was being led by a tall Kanaka, and in the dog-cart crouched two men, trying to hold Walker up. A little crowd of natives surrounded it.

The mare was led into the yard and the natives surged in after it. Mackintosh shouted to them to stand back and the two policemen, sprang suddenly from God knows where, pushed them violently aside. By now he had managed to understand that some lads who had been fishing, on their way back to their village had come across the cart on the home side of the ford. The mare was nuzzling about the herbage and in the darkness they could just see the great white bulk of the old man sunk between the seat and the dashboard. At first they thought he was drunk and they peered in, grinning, but then they heard him groan, and guessed that something was amiss. They ran to the village and called for help. It was when they returned, accompanied by half a hundred people, that they discovered Walker had been shot.

With a sudden thrill of horror Mackintosh asked himself whether he was already dead. The first thing at all events was to get him out of the cart, and that, owing to Walker's corpulence, was a difficult job. It took four strong men to lift him. They jolted him and he uttered a dull groan. He was still alive. At last they carried him into the house, up the stairs, and placed him on his bed. Then Mackintosh was able to see him, for in the yard, lit only by half a dozen hurricane lamps, everything had been obscured. Walker's white ducks were stained with blood, and the men who had carried him wiped their hands, red and sticky, on their *lava-lavas*. Mackintosh held up the lamp. He had not expected the old man to be so pale. His eyes were closed. He was breathing still, his pulse could be just felt, but it was obvious that he was dying. Mackintosh had not bargained for the shock of horror that convulsed him. He saw that the native clerk was there, and in a voice hoarse with fear told him to go into the dispensary and get what was necessary for a hypodermic injection. One of the policemen had brought up the whisky, and Mackintosh forced a little into the old man's mouth. The room was crowded with natives. They sat about the floor, speechless now and terrified, and every now and then one wailed aloud. It was very hot, but Mackintosh felt cold, his hands and his feet were like ice, and he had to make a violent effort not to tremble in all his limbs. He did not know what to do. He did not know if Walker was bleeding still, and if he was, how he could stop the bleeding.

The clerk brought the hypodermic needle.

'You give it to him,' said Mackintosh. 'You're more used to that sort of thing than I am.'

His head ached horribly. It felt as though all sorts of little savage things were beating inside it, trying to get out. They watched for the effect of the injection. Presently Walker opened his eyes slowly. He did not seem to know where he was.

'Keep quiet,' said Mackintosh. 'You're at home. You're quite safe.'

Walker's lips outlined a shadowy smile.

'They've got me,' he whispered.

'I'll get Jervis to send his motor-boat to Apia at once. We'll get a doctor out by tomorrow afternoon.'

There was a long pause before the old man answered:

'I shall be dead by then.'

A ghastly expression passed over Mackintosh's pale face. He forced himself to laugh.

'What rot! You keep quiet and you'll be as right as rain.'

'Give me a drink,' said Walker. 'A stiff one.'

With shaking hand Mackintosh poured out whisky and water, half and half, and held the glass while Walker drank greedily. It seemed to restore him. He gave a long sigh and a little colour came into his great fleshy face. Mackintosh felt extraordinarily helpless. He stood and stared at the old man.

'If you tell me what to do I'll do it,' he said.

'There's nothing to do. Just leave me alone. I'm done for.'

He looked dreadfully pitiful as he lay on the great bed, a huge, bloated, old man; but so wan, so weak, it was heart-rending. As he rested, his mind seemed to grow clearer.

'You were right, Mac,' he said presently. 'You warned me.'

'I wish to God I'd come with you.'

'You're a good chap, Mac, only you don't drink.'

There was another long silence, and it was clear that Walker was sinking. There was an internal haemorrhage and even Mackintosh in his ignorance could not fail to see that his chief had but an hour or two to live. He stood by the side of the bed stock still. For half an hour perhaps Walker lay with his eyes closed, then he opened them.

'They'll give you my job,' he said, slowly. 'Last time I was in Apia I told them you were all right. Finish my road. I want to think that'll be done. All round the island.'

'I don't want your job. You'll get all right.'

Walker shook his head wearily.

'I've had my day. Treat them fairly, that's the great thing. They're children. You must always remember that. You must be firm with them, but you must be kind. And you must be just. I've never made a bob out of them. I haven't saved a hundred pounds in twenty years. The road's the great thing. Get the road finished.'

Something very like a sob was wrung from Mackintosh.

'You're a good fellow, Mac. I always liked you.'

He closed his eyes, and Mackintosh thought that he would never open them again. His mouth was so dry that he had to get himself something to drink. The Chinese cook silently put a chair for him. He sat down by the side of the bed and waited. He did not know how long a time passed. The night was endless. Suddenly one of the men sitting there broke into uncontrollable sobbing, loudly, like a child, and Mackintosh grew aware that the room was crowded by this time with natives. They sat all over the floor on their haunches, men and women, staring at the bed.

'What are all these people doing here?' said Mackintosh. 'They've got no right. Turn them out, turn them out, all of them.'

His words seemed to rouse Walker, for he opened his eyes once more, and now they were all misty. He wanted to speak, but he was so weak that Mackintosh had to strain his ears to catch what he said.

'Let them stay. They're my children. They ought to be here.'

Mackintosh turned to the natives.

'Stay where you are. He wants you. But be silent.'

A faint smile came over the old man's white face.

'Come nearer,' he said.

Mackintosh bent over him. His eyes were closed and the words he said were like a wind sighing through the fronds of the coconut trees.

'Give me another drink. I've got something to say.'

This time Mackintosh gave him his whisky neat. Walker collected his strength in a final effort of will.

'Don't make a fuss about this. In ninety-five when there were troubles white men were killed, and the fleet came and shelled the villages. A lot of people were killed who'd had nothing to do with it. They're damned fools at Apia. If they make a fuss they'll only punish the wrong people. I don't want anyone punished.'

He paused for a while to rest.

'You must say it was an accident. No one's to blame. Promise me that.'

'I'll do anything you like,' whispered Mackintosh.

'Good chap. One of the best. They're children. I'm their father. A father don't let his children get into trouble if he can help it.'

A ghost of a chuckle came out of his throat. It was astonishingly weird and ghastly.

'You're a religious chap, Mac. What's that about forgiving them? You know.'

For a while Mackintosh did not answer. His lips trembled.

'Forgive them, for they know not what they do?'

'That's right. Forgive them. I've loved them, you know, always loved them.'

He sighed. His lips faintly moved, and now Mackintosh had to put his ears quite close to them in order to hear.

'Hold my hand,' he said.

Mackintosh gave a gasp. His heart seemed wrenched. He took the old man's hand, so cold and weak, a coarse, rough hand, and held it in his own. And thus he sat until he nearly started out of his seat, for the silence was suddenly broken by a long rattle. It was terrible and unearthly. Walker was dead. Then the natives broke out with loud cries. The tears ran down their faces, and they beat their breasts.

Mackintosh disengaged his hand from the dead man's, and staggering like one drunk with sleep he went out of the room. He went to the locked drawer in his writing-desk and took out the revolver. He walked down to the sea and walked into the lagoon; he waded out cautiously, so that he should not trip against a coral rock, till the water came to his arm-pits. Then he put a bullet through his head.

An hour later half a dozen slim brown sharks were splashing and struggling at the spot where he fell.

The Fall of Edward Barnard

Bateman Hunter slept badly. For a fortnight on the boat that brought him from Tahiti to San Francisco he had been thinking of the story he had to tell, and for three days on the train he had repeated to himself the words in which he meant to tell it. But in a few hours now he would be in Chicago, and doubts assailed him. His conscience, always very sensitive, was not at ease. He was uncertain that he had done all that was possible, it was on his honour to do much more than the possible, and the thought was disturbing that, in a matter which so nearly touched his own interest, he had allowed his interest to prevail over his quixotry. Self-sacrifice appealed so keenly to his imagination that the inability to exercise it gave him a sense of disillusion. He was like the philanthropist who with altruistic motives builds model dwellings for the poor and finds that he has made a lucrative investment. He cannot prevent the satisfaction he feels in the ten per cent which rewards the bread he had cast upon the waters, but he has an awkward feeling that it detracts somewhat from the savour of his virtue. Bateman Hunter knew that his heart was pure, but he was not quite sure how steadfastly, when he told her his story, he would endure the scrutiny of Isabel Longstaffe's cool grey eyes. They were far-seeing and wise. She measured the standards of others by her own meticulous uprightness and there could be no greater censure than the cold silence with which she expressed her disapproval of a conduct that did not satisfy her exacting code. There was no appeal from her judgement, for, having made up her mind, she never changed it. But Bateman would not have had her different. He loved not only the beauty of her person, slim and straight, with the proud carriage of her head, but still more the beauty of her soul. With her truthfulness, her rigid sense of honour, her fearless outlook, she seemed to him to collect in herself all that was most admirable in his countrywomen. But he saw in her something more than the perfect type of the American girl, he felt that her exquisiteness was peculiar in a way to her environment, and he was assured that no city in the world could have produced her but Chicago. A pang seized him when he remembered that he must deal so bitter a blow to her pride, and anger flamed up in his heart when he thought of Edward Barnard.

But at last the train steamed in to Chicago and he exulted when he saw the long streets of grey houses. He could hardly bear his impatience at the thought of State and Wabash with their crowded pavements, their hustling traffic, and their noise. He was at home. And he was glad that he had been born in the most important city in the United States. San Francisco was provincial, New York was effete; the future of America lay in the development of its economic possibilities, and Chicago, by its position and by the energy of its citizens, was destined to become the real capital of the country.

'I guess I shall live long enough to see it the

biggest city in the world,' Bateman said to himself as he stepped down to the platform.

His father had come to meet him, and after a hearty handshake, the pair of them, tall, slender, and well-made, with the same fine, ascetic features and thin lips, walked out of the station. Mr Hunter's automobile was waiting for them and they got in. Mr Hunter caught his son's proud and happy glance as he looked at the street.

'Glad to be back, son?' he asked.

'I should just think I was,' said Bateman.

His eyes devoured the restless scene.

'I guess there's a bit more traffic here than in your South Sea island,' laughed Mr Hunter. 'Did you like it there?'

'Give me Chicago, dad,' answered Bateman.

'You haven't brought Edward Barnard back with you.'

'No.'

'How was he?'

Bateman was silent for a moment, and his handsome, sensitive face darkened.

'I'd sooner not speak about him, dad,' he said at last.

'That's all right, my son. I guess your mother will be a happy woman today.'

They passed out of the crowded streets in the Loop and drove along the lake till they came to the imposing house, an exact copy of a château on the Loire, which Mr Hunter had built himself some years before. As soon as Bateman was alone in his room he asked for a number on the telephone. His heart leaped when he heard the voice that answered him.

'Good-morning, Isabel,' he said gaily.

'Good-morning, Bateman.'

'How did you recognize my voice?'

'It is not so long since I heard it last. Besides, I was expecting you.'

'When may I see you?'

'Unless you have anything better to do perhaps you'll dine with us tonight.'

'You know very well that I couldn't possibly have anything better to do.'

'I suppose that you're full of news?'

He thought he detected in her voice a note of apprehension.

'Yes,' he answered.

'Well, you must tell me tonight. Good-bye.'

She rang off. It was characteristic of her that she should be able to wait so many unnecessary hours to know what so immensely concerned her. To Bateman there was an admirable fortitude in her restraint.

At dinner, at which beside himself and Isabel no one was present but her father and mother, he watched her guide the conversation into the channels of an urbane small-talk, and it occurred to him that in just such a manner would a marquise under the shadow of the guillotine toy with the affairs of a day that would know no morrow. Her delicate features, the aristocratic shortness of her upper lip, and her wealth of fair hair suggested the marquise again, and it must have been obvious, even if it were not notorious, that in her veins flowed the best blood in Chicago. The dining-room was a fitting frame in her fragile beauty, for Isabel had caused the house, a replica of a palace on the Grand Canal at Venice, to be furnished by an English expert in the style of Louis XV; and the graceful decoration linked with the name of that amorous monarch enhanced her loveliness and at the same time acquired from it a more profound significance. For Isabel's mind was richly stored, and her conversation, however light, was never flippant. She spoke now of the *Musicale* to which she and her mother had been in the afternoon, of the lectures which an English poet was giving at the Auditorium, of the political situation, and of the Old Master which her father had recently bought for fifty thousand dollars in New York. It comforted Bateman to hear her. He felt that he was once more in the civilized world, at the centre of culture and distinction; and certain voices, troubling and yet against his will refusing to still their clamour, were at last silent in his heart.

'Gee, but it's good to be back in Chicago,' he said.

At last dinner was over, and when they went out of the dining-room Isabel said to her mother:

'I'm going to take Bateman along to my den. We have various things to talk about.'

'Very well, my dear,' said Mrs Longstaffe. 'You'll find your father and me in the Madame du Barry room when you're through.'

Isabel led the young man upstairs and showed him into the room of which he had so many charming memories. Though he knew it so well he could not repress the exclamation of delight which it always wrung from him. She looked round with a smile.

'I think it's a success,' she said. 'The main thing is that it's right. There's not even an ash-tray that isn't of the period.'

'I suppose that's what makes it so wonderful.

Like all you do it's so superlatively right.'

They sat down in front of a log fire and Isabel looked at him with calm grave eyes.

'Now what have you to say to me?' she asked.

'I hardly know how to begin.'

'Is Edward Barnard coming back?'

'No.'

There was a long silence before Bateman spoke again, and with each of them it was filled with many thoughts. It was a difficult story he had to tell, for there were things in it which were so offensive to her sensitive ears that he could not bear to tell them, and yet in justice to her, no less than in justice to himself, he must tell her the whole truth.

It had all begun long ago when he and Edward Barnard, still at college, had met Isabel Longstaffe at the tea-party given to introduce her to society. They had both known her when she was a child and they long-legged boys, but for two years she had been in Europe to finish her education and it was with a surprised delight that they renewed acquaintance with the lovely girl who returned. Both of them fell desperately in love with her, but Bateman saw quickly that she had eyes only for Edward, and, devoted to his friend, he resigned himself to the role of confidant. He passed bitter moments, but he could not deny that Edward was worthy of his good fortune, and, anxious that nothing should impair the friendship he so greatly valued, he took care never by a hint to disclose his own feelings. In six months the young couple were engaged. But they were very young and Isabel's father decided that they should not marry at least till Edward graduated. They had to wait a year. Bateman remembered the winter at the end of which Isabel and Edward were to be married, a winter of dances and theatre-parties and of informal gaieties at which he, the constant third, was always present. He loved her no less because she would shortly be his friend's wife; her smile, a gay word she flung him, the confidence of her affection, never ceased to delight him; and he congratulated himself, somewhat complacently, because he did not envy them their happiness. Then an accident happened. A great bank failed, there was a panic on the exchange, and Edward Barnard's father found himself a ruined man. He came home one night, told his wife that he was penniless, and after dinner, going into his study, shot himself.

A week later, Edward Barnard, with a tired, white face, went to Isabel and asked her to release him. Her only answer was to throw her arms round his neck and burst into tears.

'Don't make it harder for me, sweet,' he said.

'Do you think I can let you go now? I love you.'

'How can I ask you to marry me? The whole thing's hopeless. Your father would never let you. I haven't a cent.'

'What do I care? I love you.'

He told her his plans. He had to earn money at once, and George Braunschmidt, an old friend of his family, had offered to take him into his own business. He was a South Sea merchant, and he had agencies in many of the islands of the Pacific. He had suggested that Edward should go to Tahiti for a year or two, where under the best of his managers he could learn the details of that varied trade, and at the end of that time he promised the young man a position in Chicago. It was a wonderful opportunity, and when he had finished his explanations Isabel was once more all smiles.

'You foolish boy, why have you been trying to make me miserable?'

His face lit up at her words and his eyes flashed.

'Isabel, you don't mean to say you'll wait for me?'

'Don't you think you're worth it?' she smiled.

'Ah, don't laugh at me now. I beseech you to be serious. It may be for two years.'

'Have no fear. I love you, Edward. When you come back I will marry you.'

Edward's employer was a man who did not like delay and he had told him that if he took the post he offered he must sail that day week from San Francisco. Edward spent his last evening with Isabel. It was after dinner that Mr Longstaffe, saying he wanted a word with Edward, took him into the smoking-room. Mr Longstaffe had accepted good-naturedly the arrangement which his daughter had told him of and Edward could not imagine what mysterious communication he had now to make. He was not a little perplexed to see that his host was embarrassed. He faltered. He talked of trivial things. At last he blurted it out.

'I guess you've heard of Arnold Jackson,' he said, looking at Edward with a frown.

Edward hesitated. His natural truthfulness obliged him to admit a knowledge he would gladly have been able to deny.

'Yes, I have. But it's a long time ago. I guess I didn't pay very much attention.'

'There are not many people in Chicago who haven't heard of Arnold Jackson,' said Mr Longstaffe bitterly, 'and if there are they'll have no difficulty in finding someone who'll be glad to tell them. Did you know he was Mrs Longstaffe's brother?'

'Yes, I knew that.'

'Of course we've had no communication with him for many years. He left the country as soon as he was able to, and I guess the country wasn't sorry to see the last of him. We understand he lives in Tahiti. My advice to you is to give him a wide berth, but if you do hear anything about him Mrs Longstaffe and I would be very glad if you'd let us know.'

'Sure.'

'That was all I wanted to say to you. Now I daresay you'd like to join the ladies.'

There are few families that have not among their members one whom, if their neighbours permitted, they would willingly forget, and they are fortunate when the lapse of a generation or two has invested his vagaries with a romantic glamour. But when he is actually alive, if his peculiarities are not of the kind that can be condoned by the phrase, 'he is nobody's enemy but his own', a safe one when the culprit has no worse to answer for than alcoholism or wandering affections, the only possible course is silence. And it was this which the Longstaffes had adopted towards Arnold Jackson. They never talked of him. They would not even pass through the street in which he had lived. Too kind to make his wife and children suffer for his misdeeds, they had supported them for years, but on the understanding that they should live in Europe. They did everything they could to blot out all recollection of Arnold Jackson and yet were conscious that the story was as fresh in the public mind as when first the scandal burst upon a gaping world. Arnold

Jackson was as black a sheep as any family could suffer from. A wealthy banker, prominent in his church, a philanthropist, a man respected by all, not only for his connections (in his veins ran the blue blood of Chicago), but also for his upright character, he was arrested one day on a charge of fraud; and the dishonesty which the trial brought to light was not of the sort which could be explained by a sudden temptation; it was deliberate and systematic. Arnold Jackson was a rogue. When he was sent to the penitentiary for seven years there were few who did not think he had escaped lightly.

When at the end of this last evening the lovers separated it was with many protestations of devotion. Isabel, all tears, was consoled a little by her certainty of Edward's passionate love. It was a strange feeling that she had. It made her wretched to part from him and yet she was happy because he adored her.

This was more than two years ago.

He had written to her by every mail since then, twenty-four letters in all, for the mail went but once a month, and his letters had been all that a lover's letters should be. They were intimate and charming, humorous sometimes, especially of late, and tender. At first they suggested that he was homesick, they were full of his desire to get back to Chicago and Isabel; and, a little anxiously, she wrote begging him to persevere. She was afraid that he might throw up his opportunity and come racing back. She did not want her lover to lack endurance and she quoted to him the lines:

> *I could not love thee, dear, so much,*
> *Loved I not honour more.*

But presently he seemed to settle down and it made Isabel very happy to observe his growing enthusiasm to introduce American methods into that forgotten corner of the world. But she knew him, and at the end of the year, which was the shortest time he could possibly stay in Tahiti, she expected to have to use all her influence to dissuade him from coming home. It was much better that he should learn the business thoroughly, and if they had been able to wait a year there seemed no reason why they should not wait another. She talked it over with Bateman Hunter, always the most generous of friends (during those first few days after Edward went she did not know what she would have done without him), and they decided that Edward's future must stand before everything. It was with relief that she found as the time passed that he made no suggestion of returning.

'He's splendid, isn't he?' she exclaimed to Bateman.

'He's white, through and through.'

'Reading between the lines of his letter I know he hates it over there, but he's sticking it out because ...'

She blushed a little and Bateman, with the grave smile which was so attractive in him, finished the sentence for her.

'Because he loves you.'

'It makes me feel so humble,' she said.

'You're wonderful, Isabel, you're perfectly wonderful.'

But the second year passed and every month Isabel continued to receive a letter from Edward, and presently it began to seem a little strange that he did not speak of coming back. He wrote as though he were settled definitely in Tahiti, and what was more, comfortably settled. She was surprised. Then she read his letters again, all of them, several times; and now, reading between the lines indeed, she was puzzled to notice a change which had escaped her. The later letters were as tender and as delightful as the first, but the tone was different. She was vaguely suspicious of their humour, she had the instinctive mistrust of her sex for that unaccountable quality, and she discerned in them now a flippancy which perplexed her. She was not quite certain that the Edward who wrote to her now was the same Edward that she had known. One afternoon, the day after a mail had arrived from Tahiti, when she was driving with Bateman he said to her:

'Did Edward tell you when he was sailing?'

'No, he didn't mention it. I thought he might have said something to you about it.'

'Not a word.'

'You know what Edward is,' she laughed in reply, 'he has no sense of time. If it occurs to you next time you wrote you might ask him when he's thinking of coming.'

Her manner was so unconcerned that only Bateman's acute sensitiveness could have discerned in her request a very urgent desire. He laughed lightly.

'Yes. I'll ask him. I can't imagine what he's thinking about.'

A few days later, meeting him again, she noticed that something troubled him. They had been much together since Edward left Chicago; they were both devoted to him and each in his desire to talk of the absent one found a willing listener; the consequence was that Isabel knew every expression of Bateman's face, and his denials now were useless against her keen instinct. Something told her that his harassed look had to do with Edward and she did not rest till she had made him confess.

'The fact is,' he said at last, 'I heard in a roundabout way that Edward was no longer working for Braunschmidt & Co., and yesterday I took the opportunity to ask Mr Braunschmidt himself.'

'Well?'

'Edward left his employment with them nearly a year ago.'

'How strange he should have said nothing about it!'

Bateman hesitated, but he had gone so far now that he was obliged to tell the rest. It made him feel dreadfully embarrassed.

'He was fired.'

'In heaven's name what for?'

'It appears they warned him once or twice, and at last they told him to get out. They say he was lazy and incompetent.'

'Edward?'

They were silent for a while, and then he saw that Isabel was crying. Instinctively he seized her hand.

'Oh, my dear, don't, don't,' he said. 'I can't bear to see it.'

She was so unstrung that she let her hand rest in his. He tried to console her.

'It's incomprehensible, isn't it? It's so unlike Edward. I can't help feeling there must be some mistake.'

She did not say anything for a while, and when she spoke it was hesitatingly.

'Has it struck you that there was anything queer in his letters lately?' she asked, looking away, her eyes all bright with tears.

He did not quite know how to answer.

'I have noticed a change in them,' he admitted. 'He seems to have lost that high seriousness which I admired so much in him. One would almost think that the things that matter – well, don't matter.'

Isabel did not reply. She was vaguely uneasy.

'Perhaps in his answer to your letter he'll say when he's coming home. All we can do is to wait for that.'

Another letter came from Edward for each of them, and still he made no mention of his return; but when he wrote he could not have received Bateman's inquiry. The next mail would bring them an answer to that. The next mail came, and Bateman brought Isabel the letter he had just received; but the first glance of his face was enough to tell her that he was disconcerted. She read it through carefully and then, with slightly tightened lips, read it again.

'It's a very strange letter,' she said. 'I don't quite understand it.'

'One might almost think that he was joshing me,' said Bateman, flushing.

'It reads like that, but it must be unintentional. That's so unlike Edward.'

'He says nothing about coming back.'

'If I weren't so confident of his love I should think . . . I hardly know what I should think.'

It was then that Bateman had broached the scheme which during the afternoon had formed itself in his brain. The firm, founded by his father, in which he was now a partner, a firm which manufactured all manner of motor vehicles, was about to establish agencies in Honolulu, Sydney, and Wellington; and Bateman proposed that himself should go instead of the manager who had been suggested. He could return by Tahiti; in fact, travelling from Wellington, it was inevitable to do so; and he could see Edward.

'There's some mystery and I'm going to clear it up. That's the only way to do it.'

Oh, Bateman, how can you be so good and kind?' she exclaimed.

'You know there's nothing in the world I want more than your happiness, Isabel.'

She looked at him and she gave him her hands.

'You're wonderful, Bateman. I didn't know there was anyone in the world like you. How can I ever thank you?'

'I don't want your thanks. I only want to be allowed to help you.'

She dropped her eyes and flushed a little. She was so used to him that she had forgotten how handsome he was. He was as tall as Edward and as well made, but he was dark and pale of face, while Edward was ruddy. Of course she knew he loved her. It touched her. She felt very tenderly towards him.

It was from this journey that Bateman Hunter was now returned.

The business part of it took him somewhat longer than he expected and he had much time to think of his two friends. He had come to the conclusion that it could be nothing serious that prevented Edward from coming home, a pride, perhaps, which made him determined to make good before he claimed the bride he adored; but it was a pride that must be reasoned with. Isabel was unhappy. Edward must come back to Chicago with him and marry her at once. A position could be found for him in the works of the Hunter Motor Traction and Automobile Company. Bateman, with a bleeding heart, exulted at the prospect of giving happiness to the two persons he loved best in the world at the cost of his own. He would never marry. He would be godfather to the children of Edward and Isabel, and many years later when they were both dead he would tell Isabel's daughter how long, long ago he had loved her mother. Bateman's eyes were veiled with tears when he pictured this scene to himself.

Meaning to take Edward by surprise he had not cabled to announce his arrival, and when at last he landed at Tahiti he allowed a youth, who said he was the son of the house, to lead him to the Hotel de la Fleur. He chuckled when he thought of his friend's amazement on seeing him, the most unexpected of visitors, walk into his office.

'By the way,' he asked, as they went along, 'can you tell me where I shall find Mr Edward Barnard?'

'Barnard?' said the youth. 'I seem to know the name.'

'He's an American. A tall fellow with light brown hair and blue eyes. He's been here over two years.'

'Of course. Now I know who you mean. You mean Mr Jackson's nephew.'

'Whose nephew?'

'Mr Arnold Jackson.'

'I don't think we're speaking of the same person,' answered Bateman, frigidly.

He was startled. It was queer that Arnold Jackson, known apparently to all and sundry, should live here under the disgraceful name in which he had been convicted. But Bateman could not imagine whom it was that he passed off as his nephew. Mrs Longstaffe was his only sister and he had never had a brother. The young man by his side talked volubly in an English that had something in it of the intonation of a foreign tongue, and Bateman, with a sidelong glance, saw, what he had not noticed before, that there was in him a good deal of native blood. A touch of hauteur involuntarily entered into his manner. They reached the hotel. When he had arranged about his room Bateman asked to be directed to the premises of Braunschmidt & Co. They were on the front, facing the lagoon and, glad to feel the solid earth under his feet after eight days at sea, he sauntered down the sunny road to the water's edge. Having found the place he sought, Bateman sent in his card to the manager and was led through a lofty barn-like room, half store and half warehouse, to an office in which sat a stout, spectacled, bald-headed man.

'Can you tell me where I shall find Mr Edward Barnard? I understand he was in this office for some time.'

'That is so. I don't know just where he is.'

'But I thought he came here with a particular recommendation from Mr Braunschmidt. I know Mr Braunschmidt very well.'

The fat man looked at Bateman with shrewd, suspicious eyes. He called to one of the boys in the warehouse.

'Say, Henry, where's Barnard now, d'you know?'

'He's working at Cameron's, I think,' came the answer from someone who did not trouble to move.

The fat man nodded.

'If you turn to your left when you get out of here you'll come to Cameron's in about three minutes.'

Bateman hesitated.

'I think I should tell you that Edward Barnard is my greatest friend. I was very much surprised when I heard he'd left Braunschmidt & Co.'

The fat man's eyes contracted till they seemed like pin-points, and their scrutiny made Bateman so uncomfortable that he felt himself blushing.

'I guess Braunschmidt & Co. and Edward Barnard didn't see eye to eye on certain matters,' he replied.

Bateman did not quite like the fellow's manner, so he got up, not without dignity, and with an apology for troubling him bade him good-day. He left the place with a singular feeling that the man he had just interviewed had much to tell him, but no intention of telling it. He walked in the direction indicated and soon found himself at Cameron's. It was a trader's store, such as he had passed half a dozen of on his way, and when he entered the first person he saw, in his shirt sleeves, measuring out a length of trade cotton, was Edward. It gave him a start to see him engaged in so humble an occupation. But he had scarcely appeared when Edward, looking up, caught sight of him, and gave a joyful cry of surprise.

'Bateman! Who ever thought of seeing you here?'

He stretched his arm across the counter and wrung Bateman's hand. There was no self-consciousness in his manner and the embarrassment was all on Bateman's side.

'Just wait till I've wrapped this package.'

With perfect assurance he ran his scissors across

the stuff, folded it, made it into a parcel, and handed it to the dark-skinned customer.

'Pay at the desk, please.'

Then, smiling with bright eyes, he turned to Bateman.

'How did you show up here? Gee, I am delighted to see you. Sit down, old man. Make yourself at home.'

'We can't talk here. Come along to my hotel. I suppose you can get away?'

This he added with some apprehension.

'Of course I can get away. We're not so business-like as all that in Tahiti.' He called out to a Chinese who was standing behind the opposite counter. 'Ah-Ling, when the boss comes tell him a friend of mine's just arrived from America and I've gone out to have a drain with him.'

'All-light,' said the Chinese, with a grin.

Edward slipped on a coat and, putting on his hat, accompanied Bateman out of the store. Bateman attempted to put the matter facetiously.

'I didn't expect to find you selling three and a half yards of rotten cotton to a greasy nigger,' he laughed.

'Braunschmidt fired me, you know, and I thought that would do as well as anything else.'

Edward's candour seemed to Bateman very sur-prising, but he thought it indiscreet to pursue the subject.

'I guess you won't make a fortune where you are,' he answered, somewhat dryly.

'I guess not. But I earn enough to keep body and soul together, and I'm quite satisfied with that.'

'You wouldn't have been two years ago.'

'We grow wiser as we grow older,' retorted Edward, gaily.

Bateman took a glance at him. Edward was dressed in a suit of shabby white ducks, none too clean, and a large straw hat of native make. He was thinner than he had been, deeply burned by the sun, and he was certainly better looking than ever. But there was something in his appearance that disconcerted Bateman. He walked with a new jauntiness; there was a carelessness in his demeanour, a gaiety about nothing in particular, which Bateman could not precisely blame, but which exceedingly puzzled him.

'I'm blest if I can see what he's got to be so darned cheerful about,' he said to himself.

They arrived at the hotel and sat on the terrace. A Chinese boy brought them cocktails. Edward was most anxious to hear all the news of Chicago and bombarded his friend with eager questions. His interest was natural and sincere. But the odd thing was that it seemed equally divided among a multitude of subjects. He was as eager to know how Bateman's father was as what Isabel was doing. He talked of her without a shade of embarrassment, but she might just as well have been his sister as his promised wife; and before Bateman had done analysing the exact meaning of Edward's remarks he found that the conversation had drifted to his own work and the buildings his father had lately erected. He was determined to bring the conversation back to Isabel and was looking for the occasion when he saw Edward wave his hand cordially. A man was advancing towards them on the terrace, but Bateman's back was turned to him and he could not see him.

'Come and sit down,' said Edward gaily.

The new-comer approached. He was a very tall, thin man, in white ducks, with a fine head of curly white hair. His face was thin too, long, with a large, hooked nose and a beautiful expressive mouth.

'This is my old friend Bateman Hunter. I've told you about him,' said Edward, his constant smile breaking on his lips.

'I'm pleased to meet you, Mr Hunter. I used to know your father.'

The stranger held out his hand and took the young man's in a strong, friendly grasp. It was not till then that Edward mentioned the other's name.

'Mr Arnold Jackson.'

Bateman turned white and he felt his hands grow cold. This was the forger, the convict, this was Isabel's uncle. He did not know what to say. He tried to conceal his confusion. Arnold Jackson looked at him with twinkling eyes.

'I daresay my name is familiar to you.'

Bateman did not know whether to say yes or no, and what made it more awkward was that both Jackson and Edward seemed to be amused. It was bad enough to have forced on him the acquaintance of the one man on the island he would rather have avoided, but worse to discern that he was being made a fool of. Perhaps, however, he had reached this conclusion too quickly, for Jackson, without a pause, added:

'I understand you're very friendly with the Longstaffes. Mary Longstaffe is my sister.'

Now Bateman asked himself if Arnold Jackson could think him ignorant of the most terrible scandal that Chicago had ever known. But Jackson put his hand on Edward's shoulder.

'I can't sit down, Teddie,' he said. 'I'm busy. But you two boys had better come up and dine tonight.'

'That'll be fine,' said Edward.

'It's very kind of you, Mr Jackson,' said Bateman, frigidly, 'but I'm here for so short a time; my boat sails tomorrow, you know; I think if you'll forgive me, I won't come.'

'Oh nonsense. I'll give you a native dinner. My wife's a wonderful cook. Teddie will show you the way. Come early so as to see the sunset. I can give you both a shake-down if you like.'

'Of course we'll come,' said Edward. 'There's always the devil of a row in the hotel on the night a boat arrives and we can have a good yarn up at the bungalow.'

'I can't let you off, Mr Hunter,' Jackson continued with the utmost cordiality. 'I want to hear all about Chicago and Mary.'

He nodded and walked away before Bateman could say another word.

'We don't take refusals in Tahiti,' laughed Edward. 'Besides, you'll get the best dinner on the island.'

'What did he mean by saying his wife was a good cook? I happen to know his wife's in Geneva.'

'That's a long way off for a wife, isn't it?' said Edward. 'And it's a long time since he saw her. I guess it's another wife he's talking about.'

For some time Bateman was silent. His face was set in grave lines. But looking up he caught the amused look in Edward's eyes, and he flushed darkly.

'Arnold Jackson is a despicable rogue,' he said.

'I greatly fear he is,' answered Edward, smiling.

'I don't see how any decent man can have anything to do with him.'

'Perhaps I'm not a decent man.'

'Do you see much of him, Edward?'

'Yes, quite a lot. He's adopted me as his nephew.'

Bateman leaned forward and fixed Edward with his searching eyes.

'Do you like him?'

'Very much.'

'But don't you know, doesn't everyone here know, that he's a forger and that he's been a convict? He ought to be hounded out of civilized society.'

Edward watched a ring of smoke that floated from his cigar into the still, scented air.

'I suppose he is a pretty unmitigated rascal,' he said at last. 'And I can't flatter myself that any repentance for his misdeeds offers one an excuse for condoning them. He was a swindler and a hypocrite. You can't get away from it. I never met a more agreeable companion. He's taught me everything I know.'

'What has he taught you?' cried Bateman in amazement.

'How to live.'

Bateman broke into ironical laughter.

'A fine master. Is it owing to his lessons that you lost the chance of making a fortune and earn your living now by serving behind a counter in a ten cent store?'

'He has a wonderful personality,' said Edward, smiling good-naturedly. 'Perhaps you'll see what I mean tonight.'

'I'm not going to dine with him if that's what you mean. Nothing would induce me to set foot within that man's house.'

'Come to oblige me, Bateman. We've been

friends for so many years, you won't refuse me a favour when I ask it.'

Edward's tone had in it a quality new to Bateman. Its gentleness was singularly persuasive.

'If you put it like that, Edward, I'm bound to come,' he smiled.

Bateman reflected, moreover, that it would be as well to learn what he could about Arnold Jackson. It was plain that he had a great ascendency over Edward, and if it was to be combated it was necessary to discover in what exactly it consisted. The more he talked with Edward the more conscious he became that a change had taken place in him. He had an instinct that it behooved him to walk warily and he made up his mind not to broach the real purport of his visit till he saw his way more clearly. He began to talk of one thing and another, of his journey and what he had achieved by it, of politics in Chicago, of this common friend and that, of their days together at college.

At last Edward said he must get back to his work and proposed that he should fetch Bateman at five so that they could drive out together to Arnold Jackson's house.

'By the way, I rather thought you'd be living at this hotel,' said Bateman, as he strolled out of the garden with Edward. 'I understand it's the only decent one here.'

'Not I,' laughed Edward. 'It's a deal too grand for me. I rent a room just outside the town. It's cheap and clean.'

'If I remember right those weren't the points that seemed most important to you when you lived in Chicago.'

'Chicago!'

'I don't know what you mean by that, Edward. It's the greatest city in the world.'

'I know,' said Edward.

Bateman glanced at him quickly, but his face was inscrutable.

When are you coming back to it?'

'I often wonder,' smiled Edward.

This answer, and the manner of it, staggered Bateman, but before he could ask for an explanation Edward waved to a half-caste who was driving a passing motor.

'Give us a ride down, Charlie,' he said.

He nodded to Bateman, and ran after the machine that had pulled up a few yards in front. Bateman was left to piece together a mass of perplexing impressions.

Edward called for him in a rickety trap drawn by an old mare, and they drove along a road that ran by the sea. On each side of it were plantations, coconut and vanilla; and now and then they saw a great mango, its fruit yellow and red and purple among the massy green of the leaves; now and then they had a glimpse of the lagoon, smooth and blue, with here and there a tiny islet graceful with tall palms. Arnold Jackson's house stood on a little hill and only a path led to it, so they unharnessed the mare and tied her to a tree, leaving the trap by the side of the road. To Bateman it seemed a happy-go-lucky way of doing things. But when they went up to the house they were met by a tall, handsome native woman, no longer young, with whom Edward cordially shook hands. He introduced Bateman to her.

'This is my friend Mr Hunter. We're going to dine with you, Lavina.'

'All right,' she said, with a quick smile. 'Arnold ain't back yet.'

'We'll go down and bathe. Let us have a couple of *pareos*.'

The woman nodded and went into the house.

'Who is that?' asked Bateman.

'Oh, that's Lavina. She's Arnold's wife.'

Bateman tightened his lips, but said nothing. In a moment the woman returned with a bundle, which she gave to Edward; and the two men, scrambling down a steep path, made their way to a grove of coconut trees on the beach. They undressed and Edward showed his friend how to make the strip of red trade cotton which is called a *pareo* into a very neat pair of bathing-drawers. Soon they were splashing in the warm, shallow water. Edward was in great spirits. He laughed and shouted and sang. He might have been fifteen. Bateman had never seen him so gay, and afterwards when they lay on the beach, smoking cigarettes, in the limpid air, there was such an irresistible light-heartedness in him that Bateman was taken aback.

'You seem to find life mighty pleasant,' said he.

'I do.'

They heard a soft movement and looking round saw that Arnold Jackson was coming towards them.

'I thought I'd come down and fetch you two boys back,' he said. 'Did you enjoy your bath, Mr Hunter?'

'Very much,' said Bateman.

Arnold Jackson, no longer in spruce ducks, wore nothing but a *pareo* round his loins and walked barefoot. His body was deeply browned by the sun. With his long, curling white hair and his ascetic face he made a fantastic figure in the native dress, but he bore himself without a trace of self-consciousness.

'If you're ready we'll go right up,' said Jackson.

'I'll just put on my clothes,' said Bateman.

'Why, Teddie, didn't you bring a *pareo* for your friend?'

'I guess he'd rather wear clothes,' smiled Edward.

'I certainly would,' answered Bateman, grimly, as he saw Edward gird himself in the loincloth and stand ready to start before he himself had got his shirt on.

'Won't you find it rough walking without your shoes?' he asked Edward. 'It struck me the path was a trifle rocky.'

'Oh, I'm used to it.'

'It's a comfort to get into a *pareo* when one gets back from town,' said Jackson. 'If you were going to stay here I should strongly recommend you to adopt it. It's one of the most sensible costumes I have ever come across. It's cool, convenient, and inexpensive.'

They walked up to the house, and Jackson took them into a large room with white-washed walls and an open ceiling in which a table was laid for dinner. Bateman noticed that it was set for five.

'Eva, come and show yourself to Teddie's friend, and then shake us a cocktail,' called Jackson.

Then he led Bateman to a long low window.

'Look at that,' he said, with a dramatic gesture. 'Look well.'

Below them coconut trees tumbled down steeply to the lagoon, and the lagoon in the evening light had the colour, tender and varied, of a dove's breast. On a creek, at a little distance, were the clustered huts of a native village, and towards the reef was a canoe, sharply silhouetted, in which were a couple of natives fishing. Then, beyond, you saw the vast calmness of the Pacific and twenty miles away, airy and unsubstantial like the fabric of a poet's fancy, the unimaginable beauty of the island which is called Murea. It was all so lovely that Bateman stood abashed.

'I've never seen anything like it,' he said at last.

Arnold Jackson stood staring in front of him, and in his eyes was a dreamy softness. His thin, thoughtful face was very grave. Bateman, glancing at it, was once more conscious of its intense spirituality.

'Beauty,' murmured Arnold Jackson. 'You seldom see beauty face to face. Look at it well, Mr Hunter, for what you see now you will never see again, since the moment is transitory, but it will be an imperishable memory in your heart. You touch eternity.'

His voice was deep and resonant. He seemed to breathe forth the purest idealism, and Bateman had to urge himself to remember that the man who spoke was a criminal and a cruel cheat. But Edward, as though he heard a sound, turned round quickly.

'Here is my daughter, Mr Hunter.'

Bateman shook hands with her. She had dark, splendid eyes and a red mouth tremulous with laughter; but her skin was brown, and her curling hair, rippling down her shoulders, was coal black. She wore but one garment, a Mother Hubbard of pink cotton, her feet were bare, and she was crowned with a wreath of white scented flowers. She was a lovely creature. She was like a goddess of the Polynesian spring.

She was a little shy, but not more shy than Bateman, to whom the whole situation was highly embarrassing, and it did not put him at his ease to see this sylph-like thing take a shaker and with a practised hand mix three cocktails.

'Let us have a kick in them, child,' said Jackson.

She poured them out and smiling delightfully handed one to each of the men. Bateman flattered himself on his skill in the subtle art of shaking cocktails and he was not a little astonished, on tasting this one, to find that it was excellent. Jackson laughed proudly when he saw his guest's involuntary look of appreciation.

'Not bad, is it? I taught the child myself, and in the old days in Chicago I considered that there wasn't a bar-tender in the city that could hold a candle to me. When I had nothing better to do in the penitentiary I used to amuse myself by thinking out new cocktails, but when you come down to brass tacks there's nothing to beat a dry Martini.'

Bateman felt as though someone had given him a violent blow on the funny-bone and he was conscious that he turned red and then white. But before he could think of anything to say a native boy brought in a great bowl of soup and the whole party sat down to dinner. Arnold Jackson's remark seemed to have aroused in him a train of recollections, for he began to talk of his prison days. He talked quite naturally, without malice, as though he were relating his experiences at a foreign university. He addressed himself to Bateman and Bateman was confused and then confounded. He saw Edward's eyes fixed on him and there was in them a flicker of amusement. He blushed scarlet, for it struck him that Jackson was making a fool of him, and then because he felt absurd – and knew there was no reason why he should – he grew angry. Arnold Jackson was impudent – there was no other word for it – and his callousness, whether assumed or not, was outrageous. The dinner proceeded. Bateman was asked to eat sundry messes, raw fish and he knew not what, which only his civility induced him to swallow, but which he was amazed to find very good eating. Then an incident happened which to Bateman was the most mortifying experience of the evening. There was a little circlet of flowers in front of him, and for the sake of conversation he hazarded a remark about it.

'It's a wreath that Eva made for you,' said Jackson, 'but I guess she was too shy to give it you.'

Bateman took it up in his hand and made a polite little speech of thanks to the girl.

'You must put it on,' she said, with a smile and a blush.

'I? I don't think I'll do that.'

'It's the charming custom of the country,' said Arnold Jackson.

There was one in front of him and he placed it on his hair. Edward did the same.

'I guess I'm not dressed for the part,' said Bateman, uneasily.

'Would you like a *pareo*?' said Eva quickly. 'I'll get you one in a minute.'

'No, thank you. I'm quite comfortable as I am.'

'Show him how to put it on, Eva,' said Edward.

At that moment Bateman hated his greatest friend. Eva got up from the table and with much laughter placed the wreath on his black hair.

'It suits you very well,' said Mrs Jackson. 'Don't it suit him, Arnold?'

'Of course it does.'

Bateman sweated at every pore.

'Isn't it a pity it's dark?' said Eva. 'We could photograph you all three together.'

Bateman thanked his stars it was. He felt that he must look prodigiously foolish in his blue serge suit and high collar – very neat and gentlemanly – with this ridiculous wreath of flowers on his head. He was seething with indignation, and he had never in his life exercised more self-control than now when he presented an affable exterior. He was furious with that old man, sitting at the head of the table, half-naked, with his saintly face and the flowers on his handsome white locks. The whole position was monstrous.

Then dinner came to an end, and Eva and her mother remained to clear away while the three men sat on the veranda. It was very warm and the air was scented with the white flowers of the night. The full moon, sailing across an unclouded sky, made a pathway on the broad sea that led to the boundless realms of Forever. Arnold Jackson began to talk. His voice was rich and musical. He talked now of the natives and of the old legends of the country. He told strange stories of the past, stories of hazardous expeditions into the unknown, of love and death, of hatred and revenge. He told of the adventurers who had discovered those distant islands, of the sailors who, settling in them, had married the daughters of great chieftains, and of the beach-combers who had led their varied lives on those silvery shores. Bateman, mortified and exasperated, at first listened sullenly, but presently some magic in the words possessed him and he sat entranced. The mirage of romance obscured the light of common day. Had he forgotten that Arnold Jackson had a tongue of silver, a tongue by which he had charmed vast sums out of the credulous public, a tongue which very nearly enabled him to escape the penalty of his crimes? No one had a sweeter eloquence, and no one had a more acute sense of climax. Suddenly he rose.

'Well, you two boys haven't seen one another for a long time. I shall leave you to have a yarn. Teddie will show you your quarters when you want to go to bed.'

'Oh, but I wasn't thinking of spending the night, Mr Jackson,' said Bateman.

'You'll find it more comfortable. We'll see that you're called in good time.'

Then with a curteous shake of the hand, stately as though he were a bishop in canonicals, Arnold Jackson took leave of his guest.

'Of course I'll drive you back to Papeete if you like,' said Edward, 'but I advise you to stay. It's bully driving in the early morning.'

For a few minutes neither of them spoke. Bateman wondered how he should begin on the conversation which all the events of the day made him think more urgent.

'When are you coming back to Chicago?' he asked, suddenly.

For a moment Edward did not answer. Then he turned rather lazily to look at his friend and smiled.

'I don't know. Perhaps never.'

'What in heaven's name do you mean?' cried Bateman.

'I'm very happy here. Wouldn't it be folly to make a change?'

'Man alive, you can't live here all your life. This is no life for a man. It's a living death. Oh, Edward, come away at once, before it's too late. I've felt that something was wrong. You're infatuated with the place, you've succumbed to evil influences, but it only requires a wrench, and when you're free from these surroundings you'll thank all the gods there be. You'll be like a dope-fiend when he's broken from his drug. You'll see then that for two years you've been breathing poisoned air. You can't imagine what a relief it will be when you fill your lungs once more with the fresh, pure air of your native country.'

He spoke quickly, the words tumbling over one another in his excitement, and there was in his voice sincere and affectionate emotion. Edward was touched.

'It is good of you to care so much, old friend.'

'Come with me tomorrow, Edward. It was a mistake that you ever came to this place. This is no life for you.'

'You talk of this sort of life and that. How do you think a man gets the best out of life?'

'Why, I should have thought there could be no two answers to that. By doing his duty, by hard work, by meeting all the obligations of his state and station.'

'And what is his reward?'

'His reward is the consciousness of having achieved what he set out to do.'

'It all sounds a little portentous to me,' said Edward, and in the lightness of the night Bateman could see that he was smiling. 'I'm afraid you'll think I've degenerated sadly. There are several things I think now which I daresay would have seemed outrageous to me three years ago.'

'Have you learnt them from Arnold Jackson?' asked Bateman, scornfully.

'You don't like him? Perhaps you couldn't be expected to. I didn't when I first came. I had just the same prejudice as you. He's a very extraordinary man. You saw for yourself that he makes no secret of the fact that he was in a penitentiary. I do not know that he regrets it or the crimes that led him there. The only complaint he ever made in my hearing was that when he came out his health was impaired. I think he does not know what remorse is. He is completely unmoral. He accepts everything and he accepts himself as well. He's generous and kind.'

'He always was,' interrupted Bateman, 'on other people's money.'

'I've found him a very good friend. Is it unnatural that I should take a man as I find him?'

'The result is that you lose the distinction between right and wrong.'

'No, they remain just as clearly divided in my mind as before, but what has become a little confused in me is the distinction between the bad man and the good one. Is Arnold Jackson a bad man who does good things or a good man who does bad things? It's a difficult question to answer. Perhaps we make too much of the difference between one man and another. Perhaps even the best of us are sinners and the worst of us are saints. Who knows?'

'You will never persuade me that white is black and that black is white,' said Bateman.

'I'm sure I shan't, Bateman.'

Bateman could not understand why the flicker of a smile crossed Edward's lips when he thus agreed with him. Edward was silent for a minute.

'When I saw you this morning, Bateman,' he said then, 'I seemed to see myself as I was two years ago. The same collar, and the same shoes, the same blue suit, the same energy. The same determination. By God, I was energetic. The sleepy methods of this place made my blood tingle. I went about and everywhere I saw possibilities for development and enterprise. There were fortunes to be made here. It seemed to me absurd that the copra should be taken away from here in sacks and the oil extracted in America. It would be far more economical to do all that on the spot, with cheap labour, and save freight, and I saw already the vast factories springing up on the island. Then the way they extracted it from the coconut seemed to me hopelessly inadequate, and I invented a machine which divided the nut and scooped out the meat at the rate of two hundred and forty an hour. The harbour was not large enough. I made plans to enlarge it, then to form a syndicate to buy land, put up two or three large hotels, and bungalows for occasional residents; I had a scheme for improving the steamer service in order to attract visitors from California. In twenty years, instead of this half French, lazy little town of Papeete I saw a great American city with ten storey buildings and street-cars, a theatre and an opera house, a stock exchange and a mayor.'

'But go ahead, Edward,' cried Bateman, springing up from the chair in excitement. 'You've got the ideas and the capacity. Why, you'll become the richest man between Australia and the States.'

Edward chuckled softly.

'But I don't want to,' he said.

'Do you mean to say you don't want money, big money, money running into millions? Do you know what you can do with it? Do you know the power it brings? And if you don't care about it for yourself think what you can do, opening new channels for human enterprise, giving occupation to thousands. My brain reels at the visions your words have conjured up.'

'Sit down, then, my dear Bateman,' laughed Edward. 'My machine for cutting the coconuts will always remain unused, and so far as I'm concerned street-cars shall never run in the idle streets of Papeete.'

Bateman sank heavily into his chair.

'I don't understand you,' he said.

'It came upon me little by little. I came to like the life here, with its ease and its leisure, and the people, with their good-nature and their happy smiling faces. I began to think. I'd never had time to do that before. I began to read.'

'You always read.'

'I read for examinations. I read in order to be able to hold my own in conversation. I read for instruction. Here I learned to read for pleasure. I learned to talk. Do you know that conversation is one of the greatest pleasures in life? But it wants leisure. I'd always been too busy before. And gradually all the life that had seemed so important to me began to seem rather trivial and vulgar. What is the use of all this hustle and this constant striving? I think of

Chicago now and I see a dark, grey city, all stone –
it is like a prison – and a ceaseless turmoil. And
what does all that activity amount to? Does one get
there the best out of life? Is that what we come into
the world for, to hurry to an office, and work hour
after hour till night, then hurry home and dine and
go to a theatre? Is that how I must spend my
youth? Youth lasts so short a time, Bateman. And
when I am old, what have I to look forward to? To
hurry from my home in the morning to my office
and work hour after hour till night, and then hurry
home again, and dine and go to a theatre? That may
be worth while if you make a fortune; I don't know,
it depends on your nature; but if you don't, is it
worth while then? I want to make more out of my
life than that, Bateman.'

'What do you value in life then?'

'I'm afraid you'll laugh at me. Beauty, truth, and
goodness.'

'Don't you think you can have those in Chicago?'

'Some men can, perhaps, but not I.' Edward
sprang up now. 'I tell you when I think of the life I
led in the old days I am filled with horror,' he cried
violently. 'I tremble with fear when I think of the
danger I have escaped. I never knew I had a soul till
I found it here. If I had remained a rich man I
might have lost it for good and all.'

'I don't know how you can say that,' cried Bateman indignantly. 'We often used to have discussions about it.'

'Yes, I know. They were about as effectual as the
discussions of deaf mutes about harmony. I shall
never come back to Chicago, Bateman.'

'And what about Isabel?'

Edward walked to the edge of the veranda and
leaning over looked intently at the blue magic of the

night. There was a slight smile on his face when he turned back to Bateman.

'Isabel is infinitely too good for me. I admire her more than any woman I have ever known. She has a wonderful brain and she's as good as she's beautiful. I respect her energy and her ambition. She was born to make a success of life. I am entirely unworthy of her.'

'She doesn't think so.'

'But you must tell her so, Bateman.'

'I?' cried Bateman. 'I'm the last person who could ever do that.'

Edward had his back to the vivid light of the moon and his face could not be seen. Is it possible that he smiled again?

'It's no good your trying to conceal anything from her, Bateman. With her quick intelligence she'll turn you inside out in five minutes. You'd better make a clean breast of it right away.'

'I don't know what you mean. Of course I shall tell her I've seen you.' Bateman spoke in some agitation. 'Honestly I don't know what to say to her.'

'Tell her that I haven't made good. Tell her that I'm not only poor, but that I'm content to be poor. Tell her I was fired from my job because I was idle and inattentive. Tell her all you've seen tonight and all I've told you.'

The idea which on a sudden flashed through Bateman's brain brought him to his feet and in uncontrollable perturbation he faced Edward.

'Man alive, don't you want to marry her?'

Edward looked at him gravely.

'I can never ask her to release me. If she wishes to hold me to my word I will do my best to make her a good and loving husband.'

'Do you wish me to give her that message,

Edward? Oh, I can't. It's terrible. It's never dawned on her for a moment that you don't want to marry her. She loves you. How can I inflict such a mortification on her?'

Edward smiled again.

'Why don't you marry her yourself, Bateman? You've been in love with her for ages. You're perfectly suited to one another. You'll make her very happy.'

'Don't talk to me like that. I can't bear it.'

'I resign in your favour, Bateman. You are the better man.'

There was something in Edward's tone that made Bateman look up quickly, but Edward's eyes were grave and unsmiling. Bateman did not know what to say. He was disconcerted. He wondered whether Edward could possibly suspect that he had come to Tahiti on a special errand. And though he knew it was horrible he could not prevent the exultation in his heart.

'What will you do if Isabel writes and puts an end to her engagement with you?' he said, slowly.

'Survive,' said Edward.

Bateman was so agitated that he did not hear the answer.

'I wish you had ordinary clothes on,' he said, somewhat irritably. 'It's such a tremendously serious decision you're taking. That fantastic costume of yours makes it seem terribly casual.'

'I assure you, I can be just as solemn in a *pareo* and a wreath of roses, as in a high hat and a cutaway coat.'

Then another thought struck Bateman.

'Edward, it's not for my sake you're doing this? I don't know, but perhaps this is going to make a tremendous difference to my future. You're not sacrificing yourself for me? I couldn't stand for that, you know.'

'No, Bateman, I have learnt not to be silly and sentimental here. I should like you and Isabel to be happy, but I have not the least wish to be unhappy myself.'

The answer somewhat chilled Bateman. It seemed to him a little cynical. He would not have been sorry to act a noble part.

'Do you mean to say you're content to waste your life here? It's nothing less than suicide. When I think of the great hopes you had when we left college it seems terrible that you should be content to be no more than a salesman in a cheap-John store.'

'Oh, I'm only doing that for the present, and I'm gaining a great deal of valuable experience. I have another plan in my head. Arnold Jackson has a small island in the Paumotas, about a thousand miles from here, a ring of land round a lagoon. He's planted coconut there. He's offered to give it me.'

'Why should he do that?' asked Bateman.

'Because if Isabel releases me I shall marry his daughter.'

'You?' Bateman was thunderstruck. 'You can't marry a half-caste. You wouldn't be so crazy as that.'

'She's a good girl, and she has a sweet and gentle nature. I think she would make me very happy.'

'Are you in love with her?'

'I don't know,' answered Edward reflectively. 'I'm not in love with her as I was in love with Isabel. I worshipped Isabel. I thought she was the most wonderful creature I had ever seen. I was not half good enough for her. I don't feel like that with Eva. She's like a beautiful exotic flower that must be sheltered from bitter winds. I want to protect her. No one ever thought of protecting Isabel. I think she loves me for myself and not for what I may become. Whatever happens to me I shall never disappoint her. She suits me.'

Bateman was silent.

'We must turn out early in the morning,' said Edward at last. 'It's really about time we went to bed.'

Then Bateman spoke and his voice had in it a genuine distress.

'I'm so bewildered, I don't know what to say. I came here because I thought something was wrong. I thought you hadn't succeeded in what you set out to do and were ashamed to come back when you'd failed. I never guessed I should be faced with this. I'm so desperately sorry, Edward. I'm so disappointed. I hoped you would do great things. It's almost more than I can bear to think of you wasting your talents and your youth and your chance in this lamentable way.'

'Don't be grieved, old friend,' said Edward. 'I haven't failed. I've succeeded. You can't think with what zest I look forward to life, how full it seems to me and how significant. Sometimes, when you are married to Isabel, you will think of me. I shall build myself a house on my coral island and I shall live there, looking after my trees – getting the fruit out of the nuts in the same old way that they have done for unnumbered years – I shall grow all sorts of things in my garden, and I shall fish. There will be enough work to keep me busy and not enough to make me dull. I shall have my books and Eva, children, I hope, and above all, the infinite variety of the sea and the sky, the freshness of the dawn and the beauty of the sunset, and the rich magnificence of the night. I shall make a garden out of what so short a while ago was a wilderness. I shall have created something. The years will pass insensibly, and when I am an old man I hope that I shall be able to look back on a happy, simple, peaceful life. In my small way I too shall have lived in beauty. Do you think it is so little to have enjoyed contentment? We know that it will profit a man little if he gain the whole world and lose his soul. I think I have won mine.'

Edward led him to a room in which there were two beds and he threw himself on one of them. In ten minutes Bateman knew by his regular breathing, peaceful as a child's, that Edward was asleep. But for his part he had no rest, he was disturbed in mind, and it was not till the dawn crept into the room, ghostlike and silent, that he fell asleep.

Bateman finished telling Isabel his long story. He had hidden nothing from her except what he thought would wound her or what made himself ridiculous. He did not tell her that he had been forced to sit at dinner with a wreath of flowers round his head and he did not tell her that Edward was prepared to marry her uncle's half-caste daughter the moment she set him free. But perhaps Isabel had keener intuitions than he knew, for as he went on with his tale her eyes grew colder and her lips closed upon one another more tightly. Now and then she looked at him closely, and if he had been less intent on his narrative he might have wondered at her expression.

'What was this girl like?' she asked when he

finished. 'Uncle Arnold's daughter. Would you say there was any resemblance between her and me?'

Bateman was surprised at the question.

'It never struck me. You know I've never had eyes for anyone but you and I could never think that anyone was like you. Who could resemble you?'

'Was she pretty?' said Isabel, smiling slightly at his words.

'I suppose so. I daresay some men would say she was very beautiful.'

'Well, it's of no consequence. I don't think we need give her any more of our attention.'

'What are you going to do, Isabel? he asked then.

Isabel looked down at the hand which still bore the ring Edward had given her on their betrothal.

'I wouldn't let Edward break our engagement because I thought it would be an incentive to him. I wanted to be an inspiration to him. I thought if anything could enable him to achieve success it was the thought that I loved him. I have done all I could. It's hopeless. It would only be weakness on my part not to recognize the facts. Poor Edward, he's nobody's enemy but his own. He was a dear, nice fellow, but there was something lacking in him, I suppose it was backbone. I hope he'll be happy.'

She slipped the ring off her finger and placed it on the table. Bateman watched her with a heart beating so rapidly that he could hardly breathe.

'You're wonderful, Isabel, you're simply wonderful.'

She smiled, and, standing up, held out her hand to him.

'How can I ever thank you for what you've done

for me?' she said. 'You've done me a great service. I knew I could trust you.'

He took her hand and held it. She had never looked more beautiful.

'Oh, Isabel, I would do so much more for you than that. You know that I only ask to be allowed to love and serve you.'

'You're so strong, Bateman,' she sighed. 'It gives me such a delicious feeling of confidence.'

'Isabel, I adore you.'

He hardly knew how the inspiration had come to him, but suddenly he clasped her in his arms, and she, all unresisting, smiled into his eyes.

'Isabel, you know I wanted to marry you the very first day I saw you,' he cried passionately.

'Then why on earth didn't you ask me?' she replied.

She loved him. He could hardly believe it was true. She gave him her lovely lips to kiss. And as he held her in his arms he had a vision of the works of the Hunter Motor Traction and Automobile Company growing in size and importance till they covered a hundred acres, and of the millions of motors they would turn out, and of the great collection of pictures he would form which should beat anything they had in New York. He would wear horn spectacles. And she, with the delicious pressure of his arms about her, sighed with happiness, for she thought of the exquisite house she would have, full of antique furniture, and of the concerts she would give, and of the *thés dansants*, and the dinners to which only the most cultured people would come. Bateman should wear horn spectacles.

'Poor Edward,' she sighed.

Rain

It was nearly bed-time and when they awoke next morning land would be in sight. Dr Macphail lit his pipe and, leaning over the rail, searched the heavens for the Southern Cross. After two years at the front and a wound that had taken longer to heal than it should, he was glad to settle down quietly at Apia for twelve months at least, and he felt already better for the journey. Since some of the passengers were leaving the ship next day at Pago-Pago they had had a little dance that evening and in his ears hammered still the harsh notes of the mechanical piano. But the deck was quiet at last. A little way off he saw his wife in a long chair talking with the Davidsons, and he strolled over to her. When he sat down under the light and took off his hat you saw that he had very red hair, with a bald patch on the crown, and the red, freckled skin which accompanies red hair; he was a man of forty, thin, with a pinched face, precise and rather pedantic; and he spoke with a Scots accent in a very low, quiet voice.

Between the Macphails and the Davidsons, who were missionaries, there had arisen the intimacy of shipboard, which is due to propinquity rather than to any community of taste. Their chief tie was the disapproval they shared of the men who spent their days and nights in the smoking-room playing poker or bridge and drinking. Mrs Macphail was not a little flattered to think that she and her husband were the only people on board with whom the Davidsons were willing to associate, and even the doctor, shy but no fool, half unconsciously acknowledged the compliment. It was only because he was of an argumentative mind that in their cabin at night he permitted himself to carp.

'Mrs Davidson was saying she didn't know how they'd have got through the journey if it hadn't been for us,' said Mrs Macphail, as she neatly brushed out her transformation. 'She said we were really the only people on the ship they cared to know.'

'I shouldn't have thought a missionary was such a big bug that he could afford to put on frills.'

'It's not frills. I quite understand what she means. It wouldn't have been very nice for the Davidsons to have to mix with all that rough lot in the smoking-room.'

'The founder of their religion wasn't so exclusive,' said Dr Macphail with a chuckle.

'I've asked you over and over again not to joke about religion,' answered his wife. 'I shouldn't like to have a nature like yours, Alec. You never look for the best in people.'

He gave her a sidelong glance with his pale, blue eyes, but did not reply. After many years of married life he had learned that it was more conducive to peace to leave his wife with the last word. He was undressed before she was, and climbing into the upper bunk he settled down to read himself to sleep.

When he came on deck next morning they were

close to land. He looked at it with greedy eyes. There was a thin strip of silver beach rising quickly to hills covered to the top with luxuriant vegetation. The coconut trees, thick and green, came nearly to the water's edge, and among them you saw the grass houses of the Samoans; and here and there, gleaming white, a little church. Mrs Davidson came and stood beside him. She was dressed in black and wore round her neck a gold chain, from which dangled a small cross. She was a little woman, with brown, dull hair very elaborately arranged, and she had prominent blue eyes behind invisible pince-nez. Her face was long, like a sheep's, but she gave no impression of foolishness, rather of extreme alertness; she had the quick movements of a bird. The most remarkable thing about her was her voice, high, metallic, and without inflection; it fell on the ear with a hard monotony, irritating to the nerves like the pitiless clamour of the pneumatic drill.

'This must seem like home to you,' said Dr Macphail, with his thin, difficult smile.

'Ours are low islands, you know, not like these. Coral. These are volcanic. We've got another ten days' journey to reach them.'

'In these parts that's almost like being in the next street at home,' said Dr Macphail facetiously.

'Well, that's rather an exaggerated way of putting it, but one does look at distances differently in the South Seas. So far you're right.'

Dr Macphail sighed faintly.

'I'm glad we're not stationed here,' she went on. 'They say this is a terribly difficult place to work in. The steamers' touching makes the people unsettled; and then there's the naval station; that's bad for the natives. In our district we don't have difficulties like that to contend with. There are one or two traders, of course, but we take care to make them behave, and if they don't we make the place so hot for them they're glad to go.'

Fixing the glasses on her nose she looked at the green island with a ruthless stare.

'It's almost a hopeless task for the missionaries here. I can never be sufficiently thankful to God that we are at least spared that.'

Davidson's district consisted of a group of islands to the North of Samoa; they were widely separated and he had frequently to go long distances by canoe. At these times his wife remained at their headquarters and managed the mission. Dr Macphail felt his heart sink when he considered the efficiency with which she certainly managed it. She spoke of the depravity of the natives in a voice which nothing could hush, but with a vehemently unctuous horror. Her sense of delicacy was singular. Early in their acquaintance she had said to him:

'You know, their marriage customs when we first settled in the islands were so shocking that I couldn't possibly describe them to you. But I'll tell Mrs Macphail and she'll tell you.'

Then he had seen his wife and Mrs Davidson, their deck-chairs close together, in earnest conversation for about two hours. As he walked past them backwards and forwards for the sake of exercise, he had heard Mrs Davidson's agitated whisper, like the distant flow of a mountain torrent, and he saw by his wife's open mouth and pale face that she was enjoying an alarming experience. At night in their cabin she repeated to him with bated breath all she had heard.

'Well, what did I say to you?' cried Mrs Davidson, exultant, next morning. 'Did you ever hear anything more dreadful? You don't wonder that I couldn't tell you myself, do you? Even though you are a doctor.'

Mrs Davidson scanned his face. She had a dramatic eagerness to see that she had achieved the desired effect.

'Can you wonder that when we first went there our hearts sank? You'll hardly believe me when I tell you it was impossible to find a single good girl in any of the villages.'

She used the word *good* in a severely technical manner.

'Mr Davidson and I talked it over, and we made up our minds the first thing to do was to put down the dancing. The natives were crazy about dancing.'

'I was not averse to it myself when I was a young man,' said Dr Macphail.

'I guessed as much when I heard you ask Mrs Macphail to have a turn with you last night. I don't think there's any real harm if a man dances with his wife, but I was relieved that she wouldn't. Under the circumstances I thought it better that we should keep ourselves to ourselves.'

'Under what circumstances?'

Mrs Davidson gave him a quick look through her pince-nez, but did not answer his question.

'But among white people it's not quite the same,' she went on, 'though I must say I agree with Mr Davidson, who says he can't understand how a husband can stand by and see his wife in another man's arms, and as far as I'm concerned I've never danced a step since I married. But the native dancing is quite another matter. It's not only immoral in itself, but it distinctly leads to immorality. However, I'm thankful to God that we stamped it out, and I don't think I'm wrong in saying that no one has danced in our district for eight years.'

But now they came to the mouth of the harbour and Mrs Macphail joined them. The ship turned sharply and steamed slowly in. It was a great land-locked harbour big enough to hold a fleet of battle-ships; and all around it rose, high and steep, the green hills. Near the entrance, getting such breeze as blew from the sea, stood the governor's house in a garden. The Stars and Stripes dangled languidly from a flagstaff. They passed two or three trim bungalows, and a tennis court, and then they came to the quay with its warehouses. Mrs Davidson pointed out the schooner, moored two or three hundred yards from the side, which was to take them to Apia. There was a crowd of eager, noisy, and good-humoured natives come from all parts of the island, some from curiosity, others to barter with the travellers on their way to Sydney; and they brought pineapples and huge bunches of bananas, *tapa* cloths, necklaces of shells or sharks' teeth, *kava*-bowls, and models of war canoes. American sailors, neat and trim, clean-shaven and frank of face, sauntered among them, and there was a little group of officials. While their luggage was being landed the Macphails and Mrs Davidson watched the crowd. Dr Macphail looked at the yaws from which most of the children and the young boys seemed to suffer, disfiguring sores like torpid ulcers, and his professional eyes glistened when he saw for the first time in his experience cases of elephantiasis, men going about with a huge, heavy arm or dragging along a grossly disfigured leg. Men and women wore the *lava-lava*.

'It's a very indecent costume,' said Mrs Davidson. 'Mr Davidson thinks it should be prohibited by law. How can you expect people to be moral when they wear nothing but a strip of red cotton round their loins?'

'It's suitable enough to the climate,' said the doctor, wiping the sweat off his head.

Now that they were on land the heat, though it was so early in the morning, was already oppressive. Closed in by its hills, not a breath of air came in to Pago-Pago.

'In our islands,' Mrs Davidson went on in her high-pitched tones, 'we've practically eradicated the *lava-lava*. A few old men still continue to wear it, but that's all. The women have all taken to the Mother Hubbard, and the men wear trousers and singlets. At the very beginning of our stay Mr Davidson said in one of his reports: the inhabitants of these islands will never be thoroughly Christianized till every boy of more than ten years is made to wear a pair of trousers.'

But Mrs Davidson had given two or three of her birdlike glances at heavy grey clouds that came floating over the mouth of the harbour. A few drops began to fall.

'We'd better take shelter,' she said.

They made their way with all the crowd to a great shed of corrugated iron, and the rain began to fall in torrents. They stood there for some time and then were joined by Mr Davidson. He had been polite enough to the Macphails during the journey, but he had not his wife's sociability, and had spent much of his time reading. He was a silent, rather sullen man, and you felt that his affability was a duty that he imposed upon himself Christianly; he was by nature reserved and even morose. His appearance was singular. He was very tall and thin, with long limbs loosely jointed; hollow cheeks and curiously high cheek-bones; he had so cadaverous an air that it surprised you to notice how full and sensual were his lips. He wore his hair very long. His dark eyes, set deep in their sockets, were large and tragic; and his hands with their big, long fingers, were finely shaped; they gave him a look of great strength. But the most striking thing about him was the feeling he gave you of suppressed fire. It was impressive and vaguely troubling. He was not a man with whom any intimacy was possible.

He brought now unwelcome news. There was an epidemic of measles, a serious and often fatal disease among the Kanakas, on the island, and a case had developed among the crew of the schooner which was to take them on their journey. The sick man had been brought ashore and put in hospital on the quarantine station, but telegraphic instructions had been sent from Apia to say that the schooner would not be allowed to enter the harbour till it was certain no other member of the crew was affected.

'It means we shall have to stay here for ten days at least.'

'But I'm urgently needed at Apia,' said Dr Macphail.

'That can't be helped. If no more cases develop on board, the schooner will be allowed to sail with white passengers, but all native traffic is prohibited for three months.'

'Is there a hotel here?' asked Mrs Macphail.

Davidson gave a low chuckle.

'There's not.'

'What shall we do then?'

'I've been talking to the governor. There's a trader along the front who has rooms that he rents, and my proposition is that as soon as the rain lets up we should go along there and see what we can do. Don't expect comfort. You've just got to be thankful if we get a bed to sleep on and a roof over our heads.'

But the rain showed no sign of stopping, and at length with umbrellas and waterproofs they set out. There was no town, but merely a group of official buildings, a store or two, and at the back, among the coconut trees and plantains, a few native dwellings. The house they sought was about five minutes' walk from the wharf. It was a frame house of two storeys, with broad verandas on both floors and a roof of corrugated iron. The owner was a half-caste named Horn, with a native wife surrounded by little brown children, and on the ground-floor he had a store where he sold canned goods and cottons. The rooms he showed them were almost bare of furniture. In the Macphails' there was nothing but a poor, worn bed with a ragged mosquito net, a rickety chair, and a washstand. They looked round with dismay. The rain poured down without ceasing.

'I'm not going to unpack more than we actually need,' said Mrs Macphail.

Mrs Davidson came into the room as she was unlocking a portmanteau. She was very brisk and alert. The cheerless surroundings had no effect on her.

'If you'll take my advice you'll get a needle and cotton and start right in to mend the mosquito net,' she said, 'or you'll not be able to get a wink of sleep tonight.'

'Will they be very bad?' asked Dr Macphail.

'This is the season for them. When you're asked to a party at Government House at Apia you'll notice that all the ladies are given a pillow-slip to put their – their lower extremities in.'

'I wish the rain would stop for a moment,' said Mrs Macphail. 'I could try to make the place comfortable with more heart if the sun were shining.'

'Oh, if you wait for that, you'll wait a long time. Pago-Pago is about the rainiest place in the Pacific. You see, the hills, and that bay, they attract the water, and one expects rain at this time of year anyway.'

She looked from Macphail to his wife, standing helplessly in different parts of the room, like lost souls, and she pursed her lips. She saw that she must take them in hand. Feckless people like that made her impatient, but her hands itched to put everything in the order which came so naturally to her.

'Here, you give me a needle and cotton and I'll mend that net of yours, while you go on with your unpacking. Dinner's at one. Dr Macphail, you'd better go down to the wharf and see that your heavy luggage has been put in a dry place. You know what these natives are, they're quite capable of storing it where the rain will beat in on it all the time.'

The doctor put on his waterproof again and went downstairs. At the door Mr Horn was standing in conversation with the quartermaster of the ship they had just arrived in and a second-class passenger whom Dr Macphail had seen several times on board. The quartermaster, a little, shrivelled man, extremely dirty, nodded to him as he passed.

'This is a bad job about the measles, doc,' he said. 'I see you've fixed yourself up already.'

Dr Macphail thought he was rather familiar, but he was a timid man and he did not take offence easily.

'Yes, we've got a room upstairs.'

'Miss Thompson was sailing with you to Apia, so I've brought her along here.'

The quartermaster pointed with his thumb to the woman standing by his side. She was twenty-seven perhaps, plump, and in a coarse fashion pretty. She wore a white dress and a large white hat. Her fat calves in white cotton stockings bulged over the tops of long white boots in glacé kid. She gave Macphail an ingratiating smile.

'The feller's tryin' to soak me a dollar and a half a day for the meanest sized room,' she said in a hoarse voice.

'I tell you she's a friend of mine, Jo,' said the quartermaster. 'She can't pay more than a dollar, and you've sure got to take her for that.'

The trader was fat and smooth and quietly smiling.

'Well, if you put it like that, Mr Swan, I'll see what I can do about it. I'll talk to Mrs Horn and if we think we can make a reduction we will.'

'Don't try to pull that stuff with me,' said Miss Thompson. 'We'll settle this right now. You get a dollar a day for the room and not one bean more.'

Dr Macphail smiled. He admired the effrontery

with which she bargained. He was the sort of man who always paid what he was asked. He preferred to be over-charged than to haggle. The trader sighed.

'Well, to oblige Mr Swan I'll take it.'

'That's the goods,' said Miss Thompson. 'Come right in and have a shot of hooch. I've got some real good rye in that grip if you'll bring it along, Mr Swan. You come along too, doctor.'

'Oh, I don't think I will, thank you,' he answered. 'I'm just going down to see that our luggage is all right.'

He stepped out into the rain. It swept in from the opening of the harbour in sheets and the opposite shore was all blurred. He passed two or three natives clad in nothing but the *lava-lava*, with huge umbrellas over them. They walked finely, with leisurely movements, very upright; and they smiled and greeted him in a strange tongue as they went by.

It was nearly dinner-time when he got back, and their meal was laid in the trader's parlour. It was a room designed not to live in but for purposes of prestige, and it had a musty, melancholy air. A suite of stamped plush was arranged neatly round the walls, and from the middle of the ceiling, protected from the flies by yellow tissue paper, hung a gilt chandelier. Davidson did not come.

'I know he went to call on the governor,' said Mrs Davidson, 'and I guess he's kept him to dinner.'

A little native girl brought them a dish of Hamburger steak, and after a while the trader came up to see that they had everything they wanted.

'I see we have a fellow lodger, Mr Horn,' said Dr Macphail.

'She's taken a room, that's all,' answered the trader. 'She's getting her own board.'

He looked at the two ladies with an obsequious air.

'I put her downstairs so she shouldn't be in the way. She won't be any trouble to you.'

'Is it someone who was on the boat?' asked Mrs Macphail.

'Yes, ma'am, she was in the second cabin. She was going to Apia. She has a position as cashier waiting for her.'

'Oh!'

When the trader was gone Macphail said:

'I shouldn't think she'd find it exactly cheerful having her meals in her room.'

'If she was in the second cabin I guess she'd rather,' answered Mrs Davidson. 'I don't exactly know who it can be.'

'I happened to be there when the quartermaster brought her along. Her name's Thompson.'

'It's not the woman who was dancing with the quartermaster last night?' asked Mrs Davidson.

'That's who it must be,' said Mrs Macphail. 'I wondered at the time what she was. She looked rather fast to me.'

'Not good style at all,' said Mrs Davidson.

They began to talk of other things, and after dinner, tired with their early rise, they separated and slept. When they awoke, though the sky was still grey and the clouds hung low, it was not raining and they went for a walk on the high road which the Americans had built along the bay.

On their return they found that Davidson had just come in.

'We may be here for a fortnight,' he said irritably. 'I've argued it out with the governor, but he says there is nothing to be done.'

'Mr Davidson's just longing to get back to his work,' said his wife, with an anxious glance at him.

'We've been away for a year,' he said, walking up and down the veranda. 'The mission has been in charge of native missionaries and I'm terribly nervous that they've let things slide. They're good men, I'm not saying a word against them, God-fearing, devout, and truly Christian men – their Christianity would put many so-called Christians at home to the blush – but they're pitifully lacking in energy. They can make a stand once, they can make a stand twice, but they can't make a stand all the time. If you leave a mission in charge of a native missionary, no matter how trustworthy he seems, in course of time you'll find he's let abuses creep in.'

Mr Davidson stood still. With his tall, spare form, and his great eyes flashing out of his pale face, he was an impressive figure. His sincerity was obvious in the fire of his gestures and in his deep, ringing voice.

'I expect to have my work cut out for me. I shall act and I shall act promptly. If the tree is rotten it shall be cut down and cast into the flames.'

And in the evening after the high tea which was their last meal, while they sat in the stiff parlour, the ladies working and Dr Macphail smoking his pipe, the missionary told them of his work in the islands.

'When we went there they had no sense of sin at all,' he said. 'They broke the commandments one after the other and never knew they were doing wrong. And I think that was the most difficult part of my work, to instil into the natives the sense of sin.'

The Macphails knew already that Davidson had worked in the Solomons for five years before he met his wife. She had been a missionary in China, and they had become acquainted in Boston, where they were both spending part of their leave to attend a missionary congress. On their marriage they had been appointed to the islands in which they had laboured ever since.

In the course of all the conversations they had had with Mr Davidson one thing had shone out clearly and that was the man's unflinching courage. He was a medical missionary, and he was liable to be called at any time to one or other of the islands in the group. Even the whaleboat is not so very safe a conveyance in the stormy Pacific of the wet season, but often he would be sent for in a canoe, and then the danger was great. In cases of illness or accident he never hesitated. A dozen times he had spent the whole night baling for his life, and more than once Mrs Davidson had given him up for lost.

'I'd beg him not to go sometimes,' she said, 'or at least to wait till the weather was more settled, but he'd never listen. He's obstinate, and when he's once made up his mind, nothing can move him.'

'How can I ask the natives to put their trust in the Lord if I am afraid to do so myself?' cried Davidson. 'And I'm not, I'm not. They know that if they send for me in their trouble I'll come if it's humanly possible. And do you think the Lord is going to abandon me when I am on his business? The wind blows at his bidding and the waves toss and rage at his word.'

Dr Macphail was a timid man. He had never

been able to get used to the hurtling of the shells over the trenches, and when he was operating in an advanced dressing-station the sweat poured from his brow and dimmed his spectacles in the effort he made to control his unsteady hand. He shuddered a little as he looked at the missionary.

'I wish I could say that I've never been afraid,' he said.

'I wish you could say that you believed in God,' retorted the other.

But for some reason, that evening the missionary's thoughts travelled back to the early days he and his wife had spent on the islands.

'Sometimes Mrs Davidson and I would look at one another and the tears would stream down our cheeks. We worked without ceasing, day and night, and we seemed to make no progress. I don't know what I should have done without her then. When I felt my heart sink, when I was very near despair, she gave me courage and hope.'

Mrs Davidson looked down at her work, and a slight colour rose to her thin cheeks. Her hands trembled a little. She did not trust herself to speak.

'We had no one to help us. We were alone, thousands of miles from any of our own people, surrounded by darkness. When I was broken and weary she would put her work aside and take the Bible and read to me till peace came and settled upon me like sleep upon the eyelids of a child, and when at last she closed the book she'd say: "We'll save them in spite of themselves." And I felt strong again in the Lord, and I answered: "Yes, with God's help I'll save them. I must save them."'

He came over to the table and stood in front of it as though it were a lectern.

'You see, they were so naturally depraved that

they couldn't be brought to see their wickedness. We had to make sins out of what they thought were natural actions. We had to make it a sin, not only to commit adultery and to lie and thieve, but to expose their bodies, and to dance and not to come to church. I made it a sin for a girl to show her bosom and a sin for a man not to wear trousers.'

'How?' asked Dr Macphail, not without surprise.

'I instituted fines. Obviously the only way to make people realize that an action is sinful is to punish them if they commit it. I fined them if they didn't come to church, and I fined them if they danced. I fined them if they were improperly dressed. I had a tariff, and every sin had to be paid for either in money or work. And at last I made them understand.'

'But did they never refuse to pay?'

'How could they?' asked the missionary.

'It would be a brave man who tried to stand up against Mr Davidson,' said his wife, tightening her lips.

Dr Macphail looked at Davidson with troubled eyes. What he heard shocked him, but he hesitated to express his disapproval.

'You must remember that in the last resort I could expel them from their church membership.'

'Did they mind that?'

Davidson smiled a little and gently rubbed his hands.

'They couldn't sell their copra. When the men fished they got no share of the catch. It meant something very like starvation. Yes, they minded quite a lot.'

'Tell him about Fred Ohlson,' said Mrs Davidson.

The missionary fixed his fiery eyes on Dr Macphail.

'Fred Ohlson was a Danish trader who had been in the islands a good many years. He was a pretty rich man as traders go and he wasn't very pleased when we came. You see, he'd had things very much his own way. He paid the natives what he liked for their copra, and he paid in goods and whisky. He had a native wife, but he was flagrantly unfaithful to her. He was a drunkard. I gave him a chance to mend his ways, but he wouldn't take it. He laughed at me.'

Davidson's voice fell to a deep bass as he said the last words, and he was silent for a minute or two. The silence was heavy with menace.

'In two years he was a ruined man. He'd lost everything he'd saved in a quarter of a century. I broke him, and at last he was forced to come to me like a beggar and beseech me to give him a passage back to Sydney.'

'I wish you could have seen him when he came to see Mr Davidson,' said the missionary's wife. 'He had been a fine, powerful man, with a lot of fat on him, and he had a great big voice, but now he was half the size, and he was shaking all over. He'd suddenly become an old man.'

With abstracted gaze Davidson looked out into the night. The rain was falling again.

Suddenly from below came a sound, and Davidson turned and looked questioningly at his wife. It was the sound of a gramophone, harsh and loud, wheezing out a syncopated tune.

'What's that?' he asked.

Mrs Davidson fixed her pince-nez more firmly on her nose.

'One of the second-class passengers has a room in the house. I guess it comes from there.'

They listened in silence and presently they heard the sound of dancing. Then the music stopped, and they heard the popping of corks and voices raised in animated conversation.

'I daresay she's giving a farewell party to her friends on board,' said Dr Macphail. 'The ship sails at twelve, doesn't it?'

Davidson made no remark, but he looked at his watch.

'Are you ready?' he asked his wife.

She got up and folded her work.

'Yes, I guess I am,' she answered.

'It's early to go to bed yet, isn't it?' said the doctor.

'We have a good deal of reading to do,' explained Mrs Davidson. 'Wherever we are, we read a chapter of the Bible before retiring for the night and we study it with the commentaries, you know, and discuss it thoroughly. It's a wonderful training for the mind.'

The two couples bade one another good-night. Dr and Mrs Macphail were left alone. For two or three minutes they did not speak.

'I think I'll go and fetch the cards,' the doctor said at last.

Mrs Macphail looked at him doubtfully. Her conversation with the Davidsons had left her a little uneasy, but she did not like to say that she thought they had better not play cards when the Davidsons might come in at any moment. Dr Macphail brought them and she watched him, though with a vague sense of guilt, while he laid out his patience. Below the sound of revelry continued.

It was fine enough next day, and the Macphails, condemned to spend a fortnight of idleness at Pago-Pago, set about making the best of things. They went down to the quay and got out of their boxes a number of books. The doctor called on the chief surgeon of the naval hospital and went round the beds with him. They left cards on the governor. They passed Miss Thompson on the road. The doctor took off his hat, and she gave him a 'Good-morning, doc,' in a loud cheerful voice. She was dressed as on the day before, in a white frock, and her shiny white boots with their high heels, her fat legs bulging over the tops of them, were strange things on that exotic scene.

'I don't think she's very suitably dressed, I must say,' said Mrs Macphail. 'She looks extremely common to me.'

When they got back to their house, she was on the veranda playing with one of the trader's dark children.

'Say a word to her,' Dr Macphail whispered to his wife. 'She's all alone here, and it seems rather unkind to ignore her.'

Mrs Macphail was shy, but she was in the habit of doing what her husband bade her.

'I think we're fellow lodgers here,' she said, rather foolishly.

'Terrible, ain't it, bein' cooped up in a one-horse burg like this?' answered Miss Thompson. 'And they tell me I'm lucky to have gotten a room. I don't see myself livin' in a native house, and that's what some have to do. I don't know why they don't have a hotel.'

They exchanged a few more words. Miss Thompson, loud-voiced and garrulous, was evidently quite willing to gossip, but Mrs Macphail had a poor stock of small talk and presently she said:

'Well, I think we must go upstairs.'

In the evening when they sat down to their high tea Davidson on coming in said:

'I see that woman downstairs has a couple of sailors sitting there. I wonder how she's gotten acquainted with them.'

'She can't be very particular,' said Mrs Davidson.

They were all rather tired after the idle, aimless day.

'If there's going to be a fortnight of this, I don't know what we shall feel like at the end of it,' said Dr Macphail.

'The only thing to do is to portion out the day to different activities,' answered the missionary. 'I shall set aside a certain number of hours to study and a certain number to exercise, rain or fine – in the wet season you can't afford to pay any attention to the rain – and a certain number to recreation.'

Dr Macphail looked at his companion with misgiving. Davidson's programme oppressed him. They were eating Hamburger steak again. It seemed the only dish the cook knew how to make. Then below the gramophone began. Davidson started nervously when he heard it, but said nothing. Men's voices floated up. Miss Thompson's guests were joining in a well-known song and presently they heard her voice too, hoarse and loud. There was a good deal of shouting and laughing. The four people upstairs, trying to make conversation, listened despite themselves to the clink of glasses and the scrape of chairs. More people had evidently come. Miss Thompson was giving a party.

'I wonder how she gets them all in,' said Mrs Macphail, suddenly breaking into a medical conversation between the missionary and her husband.

It showed whither her thoughts were wandering. The twitch of Davidson's face proved that, though he spoke of scientific things, his mind was busy in the same direction. Suddenly, while the doctor was giving some experience of practice on the Flanders front, rather prosily, he sprang to his feet with a cry.

'What's the matter, Alfred?' asked Mrs Davidson.

'Of course! It never occurred to me. She's out of Iwelei.'

'She can't be.'

'She came on board at Honolulu. It's obvious. And she's carrying on her trade here. Here.'

He uttered the last word with a passion of indignation.

'What's Iwelei?' asked Mrs Macphail.

He turned his gloomy eyes on her and his voice trembled with horror.

'The plague spot of Honolulu. The Red Light district. It was a blot on our civilization.'

Iwelei was on the edge of the city. You went down side streets by the harbour, in the darkness, across a rickety bridge, till you came to a deserted road, all ruts and holes, and then suddenly you came out into the light. There was parking room for motors on each side of the road, and there were saloons, tawdry and bright, each one noisy with its mechanical piano, and there were barbers' shops and tobacconists. There was a stir in the air and a sense of expectant gaiety. You turned down a narrow alley, either to the right or to the left, for the road divided Iwelei into two parts, and you found yourself in the district. There were rows of little bungalows, trim and neatly painted in green, and the pathway between them was broad and straight. It was laid out like a garden-city. In its respectable regularity, its order and spruceness, it gave an impression of sardonic horror; for never can the search for love have been so systematized and ordered. The pathways were lit by a rare lamp, but they would have been dark except for the lights that came from the open windows of the bungalows. Men wandered about, looking at the women who sat at their windows, reading or sewing, for the most part taking no notice of the passers-by; and like the women they were of all nationalities. There were Americans, sailors from the ships in port, enlisted men off the gunboats, sombrely drunk, and soldiers from the regiments, white and black, quartered on the island; there were Japanese, walking in twos and threes; Hawaiians, Chinese in long robes, and Filipinos in preposterous hats. They were silent and as it were oppressed. Desire is sad.

'It was the most crying scandal of the Pacific,' exclaimed Davidson vehemently. 'The missionaries had been agitating against it for years, and at last the local press took it up. The police refused to stir. You know their argument. They say that vice is inevitable and consequently the best thing is to localize and control it. The truth is, they were paid. Paid. They were paid by the saloon-keepers, paid by the bullies, paid by the women themselves. At last they were forced to move.'

'I read about it in the papers that came on board in Honolulu,' said Dr Macphail.

'Iwelei, with its sin and shame, ceased to exist on the very day we arrived. The whole population was brought before the justices. I don't know why I didn't understand at once what that woman was.'

'Now you come to speak of it,' said Mrs Macphail, 'I remember seeing her come on board only a few minutes before the boat sailed. I remember thinking at the time she was cutting it rather fine.'

'How dare she come here!' cried Davidson indignantly. 'I'm not going to allow it.'

He strode towards the door.

'What are you doing to do?' asked Macphail.

'What do you expect me to do? I'm going to stop it. I'm not going to have this house turned into – into . . .'

He sought for a word that should not offend the ladies' ears. His eyes were flashing and his pale face was paler still in his emotion.

'It sounds as though there were three or four men down there,' said the doctor. 'Don't you think it's rather rash to go in just now?'

The missionary gave him a contemptuous look and without a word flung out of the room.

'You know Mr Davidson very little if you think the fear of personal danger can stop him in the performance of his duty,' said his wife.

She sat with her hands nervously clasped, a spot of colour on her high cheek-bones, listening to what was about to happen below. They all listened. They heard him clatter down the wooden stairs and throw open the door. The singing stopped suddenly, but the gramophone continued to bray out its vulgar tune. They heard Davidson's voice and then the noise of something heavy falling. The music stopped. He had hurled the gramophone on the floor. Then again they heard Davidson's voice, they could not make out the words, then Miss Thompson's, loud and shrill, then a confused clamour as though several people were shouting together at the top of their lungs. Mrs Davidson gave a little gasp, and she clenched her hands more tightly. Dr Macphail looked uncertainly from her to his wife. He did not want to go down, but he wondered if they expected him to. Then there was something that sounded like a scuffle. The noise now was more distinct. It might be that Davidson was being thrown out of the room. The door was slammed. There was a moment's silence and they heard Davidson come up the stairs again. He went to his room.

'I think I'll go to him,' said Mrs Davidson.

She got up and went out.

'If you want me, just call,' said Mrs Macphail, and then when the other was gone: 'I hope he isn't hurt.'

'Why couldn't he mind his own business?' said Dr Macphail.

They sat in silence for a minute or two and then they both started, for the gramophone began to play once more, defiantly, and mocking voices shouted hoarsely the words of an obscene song.

Next day Mrs Davidson was pale and tired. She complained of headache, and she looked old and wizened. She told Mrs Macphail that the missionary had not slept at all; he had passed the night in a state of frightful agitation and at five had got up and gone out. A glass of beer had been thrown over him and his clothes were stained and stinking. But a sombre fire glowed in Mrs Davidson's eyes when she spoke of Miss Thompson.

'She'll bitterly rue the day when she flouted Mr Davidson,' she said. 'Mr Davidson has a wonderful heart and no one who is in trouble has ever gone to him without being comforted, but he has no mercy for sin, and when his righteous wrath is excited he's terrible.'

'Why, what will he do?' asked Mrs Macphail.

'I don't know, but I wouldn't stand in that creature's shoes for anything in the world.'

Mrs Macphail shuddered. There was something positively alarming in the triumphant assurance of the little woman's manner. They were going out together that morning, and they went down the stairs side by side. Miss Thompson's door was open, and they saw her in a bedraggled dressing-gown, cooking something in a chafing-dish.

'Good-morning,' she called. 'Is Mr Davidson better this morning?'

They passed her in silence, with their noses in the air, as if she did not exist. They flushed, however, when she burst into a shout of derisive laughter. Mrs Davidson turned on her suddenly.

'Don't you dare to speak to me,' she screamed. 'If you insult me I shall have you turned out of here.'

'Say, did I ask Mr Davidson to visit with me?'

'Don't answer her,' whispered Mrs Macphail hurriedly.

They walked on till they were out of earshot.

'She's brazen, brazen,' burst from Mrs Davidson.

Her anger almost suffocated her.

And on their way home they met her strolling towards the quay. She had all her finery on. Her great white hat with its vulgar, showy flowers was an affront. She called out cheerily to them as she went by, and a couple of American sailors who were standing there grinned as the ladies set their faces to an icy stare. They got in just before the rain began to fall again.

'I guess she'll get her fine clothes spoilt,' said Mrs Davidson with a bitter sneer.

Davidson did not come in till they were half way through dinner. He was wet through but he would not change. He sat, morose and silent, refusing to eat more than a mouthful, and he stared at the slanting rain. When Mrs Davidson told him of their two encounters with Miss Thompson he did not answer. His deepening frown alone showed that he had heard.

'Don't you think we ought to make Mr Horn turn her out of here?' asked Mrs Davidson. 'We can't allow her to insult us.'

'There doesn't seem to be any other place for her to go,' said Macphail.

'She can live with one of the natives.'

'In weather like this a native hut must be a rather uncomfortable place to live in.'

'I lived in one for years,' said the missionary.

When the little native girl brought in the fried bananas which formed the sweet they had every day, Davidson turned to her.

'Ask Miss Thompson when it would be convenient for me to see her,' he said.

The girl nodded shyly and went out.

'What do you want to see her for, Alfred?' asked his wife.

'It's my duty to see her. I won't act till I've given her every chance.'

'You don't know what she is. She'll insult you.'

'Let her insult me. Let her spit on me. She has an immortal soul, and I must do all that is in my power to save it.'

Mrs Davidson's ears rang still with the harlot's mocking laughter.

'She's gone too far.'

'Too far for the mercy of God?' His eyes lit up suddenly and his voice grew mellow and soft. 'Never. The sinner may be deeper in sin than the depth of hell itself, but the love of the Lord Jesus can reach him still.'

The girl came back with the message.

'Miss Thompson's compliments and as long as Rev. Davidson don't come in business hours she'll be glad to see him any time.'

The party received it in stony silence, and Dr Macphail quickly effaced from his lips the smile which had come upon them. He knew his wife would be vexed with him if he found Miss Thompson's effrontery amusing.

They finished the meal in silence. When it was over the two ladies got up and took their work, Mrs Macphail was making another of the innumerable comforters which she had turned out since the beginning of the war, and the doctor lit his pipe. But Davidson remained in his chair and with abstracted eyes stared at the table. At last he got up and without a word went out of the room. They heard him go down and they heard Miss Thompson's defiant 'Come in' when he knocked at the door. He remained with her for an hour. And Dr Macphail watched the rain. It was beginning to get on his nerves. It was not like our soft English rain that drops gently on the earth; it was unmerciful and somehow terrible: you felt in it the malignancy of the primitive powers of nature. It did not pour, it flowed. It was like a deluge from heaven, and it rattled on the roof of corrugated iron with a steady persistence that was maddening. It seemed to have a fury of its own. And sometimes you felt that you must scream if it did not stop, and then suddenly you felt powerless, as though your bones had suddenly become soft; and you were miserable and hopeless.

Macphail turned his head when the missionary came back. The two women looked up.

'I've given her every chance. I have exhorted her to repent. She is an evil woman.'

He paused, and Dr Macphail saw his eyes darken and his pale face grow hard and stern.

'Now I shall take the whips with which the Lord Jesus drove the usurers and the money changers out of the Temple of the Most High.'

He walked up and down the room. His mouth was close set, and his black brows were frowning.

'If she fled to the uttermost parts of the earth I should pursue her.'

With a sudden movement he turned round and strode out of the room. They heard him go downstairs again.

'What is he going to do?' asked Mrs Macphail.

'I don't know.' Mrs Davidson took off her pincenez and wiped them. 'When he is on the Lord's work I never ask him questions.'

She sighed a little.

'What is the matter?'

'He'll wear himself out. He doesn't know what it is to spare himself.'

Dr Macphail learnt the first results of the missionary's activity from the half-caste trader in whose house they lodged. He stopped the doctor when he passed the store and came out to speak to him on the stoop. His fat face was worried.

'The Rev. Davidson has been at me for letting Miss Thompson have a room here,' he said, 'but I didn't know what she was when I rented it to her. When people come and ask if I can rent them a room all I want to know is if they've the money to pay for it. And she paid me for hers a week in advance.'

Dr Macphail did not want to commit himself.

'When all's said and done it's your house. We're very much obliged to you for taking us in at all.'

Horn looked at him doubtfully. He was not certain yet how definitely Macphail stood on the missionary's side.

'The missionaries are in with one another,' he said, hesitatingly. 'If they get it in for a trader he may just as well shut up his store and quit.'

'Did he want you to turn her out?'

'No, he said so long as she behaved herself he couldn't ask me to do that. He said he wanted to be just to me. I promised she shouldn't have no more visitors. I've just been and told her.'

'How did she take it?'

'She gave me Hell.'

The trader squirmed in his old ducks. He had found Miss Thompson a rough customer.

'Oh, well, I daresay she'll get out. I don't suppose she wants to stay here if she can't have anyone in.'

'There's nowhere she can go, only a native house, and no native'll take her now, not now that the missionaries have got their knife in her.'

Dr Macphail looked at the falling rain.

'Well, I don't suppose it's any good waiting for it to clear up.'

In the evening when they sat in the parlour Davidson talked to them of his early days at college. He had had no means and had worked his way through by doing odd jobs during the vacations. There was silence downstairs. Miss Thompson was sitting in her little room alone. But suddenly the gramophone began to play. She had set it on in defiance, to cheat her loneliness, but there was no one to sing, and it had a melancholy note. It was like a cry for help. Davidson took no notice. He was in the middle of a long anecdote and without change of expression went on. The gramophone continued. Miss Thompson put on one reel after another. It looked as though the silence of the night were getting on her nerves. It was breathless and sultry. When the Macphails went to bed they could not sleep. They lay side by side with their eyes wide open, listening to the cruel singing of the mosquitoes outside their curtain.

'What's that?' whispered Mrs Macphail at last.

They heard a voice, Davidson's voice, through the wooden partition. It went on with a monotonous, earnest insistence. He was praying aloud. He was praying for the soul of Miss Thompson.

Two or three days went by. Now when they passed Miss Thompson on the road she did not greet them with ironic cordiality or smile; she passed with her nose in the air, a sulky look on her painted face, frowning, as though she did not see them. The trader told Macphail that she had tried to get lodging elsewhere, but had failed. In the evening she played through the various reels of her gramophone, but the pretence of mirth was obvious now. The ragtime had a cracked, heart-broken rhythm as though it were a one-step of despair. When she began to play on Sunday Davidson sent Horn to beg her to stop at once since it was the Lord's day. The reel was taken off and the house was silent except for the steady pattering of the rain on the iron roof.

'I think she's getting a bit worked up,' said the trader next day to Macphail. 'She don't know what Mr Davidson's up to and it makes her scared.'

Macphail had caught a glimpse of her that morning and it struck him that her arrogant expression had changed. There was in her face a hunted look. The half-caste gave him a sidelong glance.

'I suppose you don't know what Mr Davidson is doing about it?' he hazarded.

'No, I don't.'

It was singular that Horn should ask him that question, for he also had the idea that the missionary was mysteriously at work. He had an impression that he was weaving a net around the woman, carefully, systematically, and suddenly, when everything was ready would pull the strings tight.

'He told me to tell her,' said the trader, 'that if at any time she wanted him she only had to send and he'd come.'

'What did she say when you told her that?'

'She didn't say nothing. I didn't stop. I just said what he said I was to and then I beat it. I thought she might be going to start weepin'.'

'I have no doubt the loneliness is getting on her nerves,' said the doctor. 'And the rain – that's enough to make anyone jumpy,' he continued irritably. 'Doesn't it ever stop in this confounded place?'

'It goes on pretty steady in the rainy season. We have three hundred inches in the year. You see, it's the shape of the bay. It seems to attract the rain from all over the Pacific.'

'Damn the shape of the bay,' said the doctor.

He scratched his mosquito bites. He felt very short-tempered. When the rain stopped and the sun shone, it was like a hothouse, seething, humid, sultry, breathless, and you had a strange feeling that everything was growing with a savage violence. The natives, blithe and childlike by reputation, seemed then, with their tattooing and their dyed hair, to have something sinister in their appearance; and when they pattered along at your heels with their naked feet you looked back instinctively. You felt they might at any moment come behind you swiftly and thrust a long knife between your shoulder blades. You could not tell what dark thoughts lurked behind their wide-set eyes. They had a little the look of ancient Egyptians painted on a temple wall, and there was about them the terror of what is immeasurably old.

The missionary came and went. He was busy, but the Macphails did not know what he was doing. Horn told the doctor that he saw the governor every day, and once Davidson mentioned him.

'He looks as if he had plenty of determination,' he said, 'but when you come down to brass tacks he has no backbone.'

'I suppose that means he won't do exactly what you want,' suggested the doctor facetiously.

The missionary did not smile.

'I want him to do what's right. It shouldn't

be necessary to persuade a man to do that.'

'But there may be differences of opinion about what is right.'

'If a man had a gangrenous foot would you have patience with anyone who hesitated to amputate it?'

'Gangrene is a matter of fact.'

'And Evil?'

What Davidson had done soon appeared. The four of them had just finished their midday meal, and they had not yet separated for the siesta which the heat imposed on the ladies and on the doctor. Davidson had little patience with the slothful habit. The door was suddenly flung open and Miss Thompson came in. She looked round the room and then went up to Davidson.

'You low-down skunk, what have you been saying about me to the governor?'

She was spluttering with rage. There was a moment's pause. Then the missionary drew forward a chair.

'Won't you be seated, Miss Thompson? I've been hoping to have another talk with you.'

'You poor low-life bastard.'

She burst into a torrent of insult, foul and insolent. Davidson kept his grave eyes on her.

'I'm indifferent to the abuse you think fit to heap on me, Miss Thompson,' he said, 'but I must beg you to remember that ladies are present.'

Tears by now were struggling with her anger. Her face was red and swollen as though she were choking.

'What has happened?' asked Dr Macphail.

'A feller's just been in here and he says I gotter beat it on the next boat.'

Was there a gleam in the missionary's eyes? His face remained impassive.

'You could hardly expect the governor to let you stay here under the circumstances.'

'You done it,' she shrieked. 'You can't kid me. You done it.'

'I don't want to deceive you. I urged the governor to take the only possible step consistent with his obligations.'

'Why couldn't you leave me be? I wasn't doin' you no harm.'

'You may be sure that if you had I should be the last man to resent it.'

'Do you think I want to stay on in this poor imitation of a burg? I don't look no busher, do I?'

'In that case I don't see what cause of complaint you have,' he answered.

She gave an inarticulate cry of rage and flung out of the room. There was a short silence.

'It's a relief to know that the governor has acted at last,' said Davidson finally. 'He's a weak man and he shilly-shallied. He said she was only here for a fortnight anyway, and if she went on to Apia that was under British jurisdiction and had nothing to do with him.'

The missionary sprang to his feet and strode across the room.

'It's terrible the way the men who are in authority seek to evade their responsibility. They speak as though evil that was out of sight ceased to be evil. The very existence of that woman is a scandal and it does not help matters to shift it to another of the islands. In the end I had to speak straight from the shoulder.'

Davidson's brow lowered, and he protruded his

firm chin. He looked fierce and determined.

'What do you mean by that?'

'Our mission is not entirely without influence at Washington. I pointed out to the governor that it wouldn't do him any good if there was a complaint about the way he managed things here.'

'When has she got to go?' asked the doctor, after a pause.

'The San Francisco boat is due here from Sydney next Tuesday. She's to sail on that.'

That was in five days' time. It was next day, when he was coming back from the hospital where for want of something better to do Macphail spent most of his mornings, that the half-caste stopped him as he was going upstairs.

'Excuse me, Dr Macphail, Miss Thompson's sick. Will you have a look at her.'

'Certainly.'

Horn led him to her room. She was sitting in a chair idly, neither reading nor sewing, staring in front of her. She wore her white dress and the large hat with the flowers on it. Macphail noticed that her skin was yellow and muddy under her powder, and her eyes were heavy.

'I'm sorry to hear you're not well,' he said.

'Oh, I ain't sick really. I just said that, because I just had to see you. I've got to clear on a boat that's going to 'Frisco.'

She looked at him and he saw that her eyes were suddenly startled. She opened and clenched her hands spasmodically. The trader stood at the door, listening.

'So I understand,' said the doctor.

She gave a little gulp.

'I guess it ain't very convenient for me to go to

'Frisco just now. I went to see the governor yesterday afternoon, but I couldn't get to him. I saw the secretary, and he told me I'd got to take that boat and that was all there was to it. I just had to see the governor, so I waited outside his house this morning, and when he come out I spoke to him. He didn't want to speak to me, I'll say, but I wouldn't let him shake me off, and at last he said he hadn't no objection to my staying here till the next boat to Sydney if the Rev. Davidson will stand for it.'

She stopped and looked at Dr Macphail anxiously.

'I don't know exactly what I can do,' he said.

'Well, I thought maybe you wouldn't mind asking him. I swear to God I won't start anything here if he'll just only let me stay. I won't go out of the house if that'll suit him. It's no more'n a fortnight.'

'I'll ask him.'

'He won't stand for it,' said Horn. 'He'll have you out on Tuesday, so you may as well make up your mind to it.'

'Tell him I can get work in Sydney, straight stuff, I mean. 'Tain't asking very much.'

'I'll do what I can.'

'And come and tell me right away, will you? I can't set down to a thing till I get the dope one way or the other.'

It was not an errand that much pleased the doctor, and, characteristically perhaps, he went about it indirectly. He told his wife what Miss Thompson had said to him and asked her to speak to Mrs Davidson. The missionary's attitude seemed rather arbitrary and it could do no harm if the girl were allowed to stay in Pago-Pago another fortnight. But he was not prepared for the result of his diplomacy. The missionary came to him straightway.

'Mrs Davidson tells me that Thompson has been speaking to you.'

Dr Macphail, thus directly tackled, had the shy man's resentment at being forced out into the open. He felt his temper rising, and he flushed.

'I don't see that it can make any difference if she goes to Sydney rather than to San Francisco, and so long as she promises to behave while she's here it's dashed hard to persecute her.'

The missionary fixed him with his stern eyes.

'Why is she unwilling to go back to San Francisco?'

'I didn't inquire,' answered the doctor with some asperity. 'And I think one does better to mind one's own business.'

Perhaps it was not a very tactful answer.

'The governor has ordered her to be deported by the first boat that leaves the island. He's only done his duty and I will not interfere. Her presence is a peril here.'

'I think you're very harsh and tyrannical.'

The two ladies looked up at the doctor with some alarm, but they need not have feared a quarrel, for the missionary smiled gently.

'I'm terribly sorry you should think that of me, Dr Macphail. Believe me, my heart bleeds for that unfortunate woman, but I'm only trying to do my duty.'

The doctor made no answer. He looked out of the window sullenly. For once it was not raining and across the bay you saw nestling among the trees the huts of a native village.

'I think I'll take advantage of the rain stopping to go out,' he said.

'Please don't bear me malice because I can't accede to your wish,' said Davidson, with a melancholy smile. 'I respect you very much, doctor, and I should be sorry if you thought ill of me.'

'I have no doubt you have a sufficiently good opinion of yourself to bear mine with equanimity,' he retorted.

'That's one on me,' chuckled Davidson.

When Dr Macphail, vexed with himself because he had been uncivil to no purpose, went downstairs, Miss Thompson was waiting for him with her door ajar.

'Well,' she said, 'have you spoken to him?'

'Yes, I'm sorry, he won't do anything,' he answered, not looking at her in his embarrassment.

But then he gave her a quick glance, for a sob broke from her. He saw that her face was white with fear. It gave him a shock of dismay. And suddenly he had an idea.

'But don't give up hope yet. I think it's a shame the way they're treating you and I'm going to see the governor myself.'

'Now?'

He nodded. Her face brightened.

'Say, that's real good of you. I'm sure he'll let me stay if you speak for me. I just won't do a thing I didn't ought all the time I'm here.'

Dr Macphail hardly knew why he had made up his mind to appeal to the governor. He was perfectly indifferent to Miss Thompson's affairs, but the missionary had irritated him, and with him temper was a smouldering thing. He found the governor at home. He was a large, handsome man, a

sailor, with a grey toothbrush moustache; and he
wore a spotless uniform of white drill.

'I've come to see you about a woman who's lodging in the same house as we are,' he said. 'Her
name's Thompson.'

'I guess I've heard nearly enough about her, Dr
Macphail,' said the governor, smiling. 'I've given
her the order to get out next Tuesday and that's all
I can do.'

'I wanted to ask you if you couldn't stretch a
point and let her stay here till the boat comes in
from San Francisco so that she can go to Sydney. I
will guarantee her good behaviour.'

The governor continued to smile, but his eyes
grew small and serious.

'I'd be very glad to oblige you, Dr Macphail, but
I've given the order and it must stand.'

The doctor put the case as reasonably as he
could, but now the governor ceased to smile at all.
He listened sullenly, with averted gaze. Macphail
saw that he was making no impression.

'I'm sorry to cause any lady inconvenience, but
she'll have to sail on Tuesday and that's all there is
to it.'

'But what difference can it make?'

'Pardon me, doctor, but I don't feel called upon
to explain my official actions except to the proper
authorities.'

Macphail looked at him shrewdly. He remembered Davidson's hint that he had used threats, and
in the governor's attitude he read a singular
embarrassment.

'Davidson's a damned busybody,' he said hotly.

'Between ourselves, Dr Macphail, I don't say
that I have formed a very favourable opinion of Mr

Davidson, but I am bound to confess that he was within his rights in pointing out to me the danger that the presence of a woman of Miss Thompson's character was to a place like this where a number of enlisted men are stationed among a native population.'

He got up and Dr Macphail was obliged to do so too.

'I must ask you to excuse me. I have an engagement. Please give my respects to Mrs Macphail.'

The doctor left him crest-fallen. He knew that Miss Thompson would be waiting for him, and unwilling to tell her himself that he had failed, he went into the house by the back door and sneaked up the stairs as though he had something to hide.

At supper he was silent and ill-at-ease, but the missionary was jovial and animated. Dr Macphail thought his eyes rested on him now and then with triumphant good-humour. It struck him suddenly that Davidson knew of his visit to the governor and of its ill success. But how on earth could he have heard of it? There was something sinister about the power of that man. After supper he saw Horn on the veranda and, as though to have a casual word with him, went out.

'She wants to know if you've seen the governor,' the trader whispered.

'Yes. He wouldn't do anything. I'm awfully sorry, I can't do anything more.'

'I knew he wouldn't. They daren't go against the missionaries.'

'What are you talking about?' said Davidson affably, coming out to join them.

'I was just saying there was no chance of your getting over to Apia for at least another week,' said the trader glibly.

He left them, and the two men returned into the parlour. Mr Davidson devoted one hour after each meal to recreation. Presently a timid knock was heard at the door.

'Come in,' said Mrs Davidson, in her sharp voice.

The door was not opened. She got up and opened it. They saw Miss Thompson standing at the threshold. But the change in her appearance was extraordinary. This was no longer the flaunting hussy who had jeered at them in the road, but a broken, frightened woman. Her hair, as a rule so elaborately arranged, was tumbling untidily over her neck. She wore bedroom slippers and a skirt and blouse. They were unfresh and bedraggled. She stood at the door with the tears streaming down her face and did not dare to enter.

'What do you want?' said Mrs Davidson harshly.

'May I speak to Mr Davidson?' she said in a choking voice.

The missionary rose and went towards her.

'Come right in, Miss Thompson,' he said in cordial tones. 'What can I do for you?'

She entered the room.

'Say, I'm sorry for what I said to you the other day an' for – for everythin' else. I guess I was a bit lit up. I beg pardon.'

'Oh, it was nothing. I guess my back's broad enough to bear a few hard words.'

She stepped towards him with a movement that was horribly cringing.

'You've got me beat. I'm all in. You won't make me go back to 'Frisco?'

His genial manner vanished and his voice grew on a sudden hard and stern.

'Why don't you want to go back there?'

She cowered before him.

'I guess my people live there. I don't want them to see me like this. I'll go anywhere else you say.'

'Why don't you want to go back to San Francisco?'

'I've told you.'

He leaned forward, staring at her, and his great shining eyes seemed to try to bore into her soul. He gave a sudden gasp.

'The penitentiary.'

She screamed, and then she fell at his feet, clasping his legs.

'Don't send me back there. I swear to you before God I'll be a good woman. I'll give all this up.'

She burst into a torrent of confused supplication and the tears coursed down her painted cheeks. He leaned over her and, lifting her face, forced her to look at him.

'Is that it, the penitentiary?'

'I beat it before they could get me,' she gasped. 'If the bulls grab me it's three years for mine.'

He let go his hold of her and she fell in a heap on the floor, sobbing bitterly. Dr Macphail stood up.

'This alters the whole thing,' he said. 'You can't make her go back when you know this. Give her another chance. She wants to turn over a new leaf.'

'I'm going to give her the finest chance she's ever had. If she repents let her accept her punishment.'

She misunderstood the words and looked up. There was a gleam of hope in her heavy eyes.

'You'll let me go?'

'No. You shall sail for San Francisco on Tuesday.'

She gave a groan of horror and then burst into

low, hoarse shrieks which sounded hardly human, and she beat her head passionately on the ground. Dr Macphail sprang to her and lifted her up.

'Come on, you mustn't do that. You'd better go to your room and lie down. I'll get you something.'

He raised her to her feet and partly dragging her, partly carrying her, got her downstairs. He was furious with Mrs Davidson and with his wife because they made no effort to help. The half-caste was standing on the landing and with his assistance he managed to get her on the bed. She was moaning and crying. She was almost insensible. He gave her a hypodermic injection. He was hot and exhausted when he went upstairs again.

'I've got her to lie down.'

The two women and Davidson were in the same positions as when he had left them. They could not have moved or spoken since he went.

'I was waiting for you,' said Davidson, in a strange, distant voice. 'I want you all to pray with me for the soul of our erring sister.'

He took the Bible off a shelf, and sat down at the table at which they had supped. It had not been cleared, and he pushed the tea-pot out of the way. In a powerful voice, resonant and deep, he read to them the chapter in which is narrated the meeting of Jesus Christ with the woman taken in adultery.

'Now kneel with me and let us pray for the soul of our dear sister, Sadie Thompson.'

He burst into a long, passionate prayer in which he implored God to have mercy on the sinful woman. Mrs Macphail and Mrs Davidson knelt with covered eyes. The doctor, taken by surprise, awkward and sheepish, knelt too. The missionary's prayer had a savage eloquence. He was extraordinarily moved, and as he spoke the tears ran down his cheeks. Outside, the pitiless rain fell, fell steadily, with a fierce malignity that was all too human.

At last he stopped. He paused for a moment and said:

'We will now repeat the Lord's prayer.'

They said it and then, following him, they rose from their knees. Mrs Davidson's face was pale and restful. She was comforted and at peace, but the Macphails felt suddenly bashful. They did not know which way to look.

'I'll just go down and see how she is now,' said Dr Macphail.

When he knocked at her door it was opened for him by Horn. Miss Thompson was in a rocking-chair, sobbing quietly.

'What are you doing there?' exclaimed Macphail. 'I told you to lie down.'

'I can't lie down. I want to see Mr Davidson.'

'My poor child, what do you think is the good of it? You'll never move him.'

'He said he'd come if I sent for him.'

Macphail motioned to the trader.

'Go and fetch him.'

He waited with her in silence while the trader went upstairs. Davidson came in.

'Excuse me for asking you to come here,' she said, looking at him sombrely.

'I was expecting you to send for me. I knew the Lord would answer my prayer.'

They stared at one another for a moment and then she looked away. She kept her eyes averted when she spoke.

'I've been a bad woman. I want to repent.'

'Thank God! thank God! He has heard our prayers.'

He turned to the two men.

'Leave me alone with her. Tell Mrs Davidson that our prayers have been answered.'

They went out and closed the door behind them.

'Gee whizz,' said the trader.

That night Dr Macphail could not get to sleep till late, and when he heard the missionary come upstairs he looked at his watch. It was two o'clock. But even then he did not go to bed at once, for through the wooden partition that separated their rooms he heard him praying aloud, till he himself, exhausted, fell asleep.

When he saw him next morning he was surprised at his appearance. He was paler than ever, tired, but his eyes shone with an inhuman fire. It looked as though he were filled with an overwhelming joy.

'I want you to go down presently and see Sadie,' he said. 'I can't hope that her body is better, but her soul – her soul is transformed.'

The doctor was feeling wan and nervous.

'You were with her very late last night,' he said.

'Yes, she couldn't bear to have me leave her.'

'You look as pleased as Punch,' the doctor said irritably.

Davidson's eyes shone with ecstasy.

'A great mercy has been vouchsafed me. Last night I was privileged to bring a lost soul to the loving arms of Jesus.'

Miss Thompson was again in the rocking-chair. The bed had not been made. The room was in disorder. She had not troubled to dress herself, but wore a dirty dressing-gown, and her hair was tied in a sluttish knot. She had given her face a dab with a wet towel, but it was all swollen and creased with crying. She looked a drab.

She raised her eyes dully when the doctor came in. She was cowed and broken.

'Where's Mr Davidson?' she asked.

'He'll come presently if you want him,' answered Macphail acidly. 'I came here to see how you were.'

'Oh, I guess I'm OK. You needn't worry about that.'

'Have you had anything to eat?'

'Horn brought me some coffee.'

She looked anxiously at the door.

'D'you think he'll come down soon? I feel as if it wasn't so terrible when he's with me.'

'Are you still going on Tuesday?'

'Yes, he says I've got to go. Please tell him to come right along. You can't do me any good. He's the only one as can help me now.'

'Very well,' said Dr Macphail.

During the next three days the missionary spent almost all his time with Sadie Thompson. He joined the others only to have his meals. Dr Macphail noticed that he hardly ate.

'He's wearing himself out,' said Mrs Davidson pitifully. 'He'll have a breakdown if he doesn't take care, but he won't spare himself.'

She herself was white and pale. She told Mrs Macphail that she had no sleep. When the missionary came upstairs from Miss Thompson he prayed till he was exhausted, but even then he did not sleep for long. After an hour or two he got up and dressed himself, and went for a tramp along the bay. He had strange dreams.

'This morning he told me that he'd been dreaming about the mountains of Nebraska,' said Mrs Davidson.

'That's curious,' said Dr Macphail.

He remembered seeing them from the windows of the train when he crossed America. They were like huge mole-hills, rounded and smooth, and they rose from the plain abruptly. Dr Macphail remembered how it struck him that they were like a woman's breasts.

Davidson's restlessness was intolerable even to himself. But he was buoyed up by a wonderful exhilaration. He was tearing out by the roots the last vestiges of sin that lurked in the hidden corners of that poor woman's heart. He read with her and prayed with her.

'It's wonderful,' he said to them one day at supper. 'It's a true rebirth. Her soul, which was black as night, is now pure and white like the new-fallen snow. I am humble and afraid. Her remorse for all her sins is beautiful. I am not worthy to touch the hem of her garment.'

'Have you the heart to send her back to San Francisco?' said the doctor. 'Three years in an American prison. I should have thought you might have saved her from that.'

'Ah, but don't you see? It's necessary. Do you think my heart doesn't bleed for her? I love her as I love my wife and my sister. All the time that she is in prison I shall suffer all the pain that she suffers.'

'Bunkum,' cried the doctor impatiently.

'You don't understand because you're blind. She's sinned, and she must suffer. I know what she'll endure. She'll be starved and tortured and humiliated. I want her to accept the punishment of man as a sacrifice to God. I want her to accept it joyfully. She has an opportunity which is offered to very few of us. God is very good and very merciful.'

Davidson's voice trembled with excitement. He could hardly articulate the words that tumbled passionately from his lips.

'All day I pray with her and when I leave her I pray again, I pray with all my might and main, so that Jesus may grant her this great mercy. I want to put in her heart the passionate desire to be punished so that at the end, even if I offered to let her go, she would refuse. I want her to feel that the bitter punishment of prison is the thank-offering that she places at the feet of our Blessed Lord, who gave his life for her.'

The days passed slowly. The whole household, intent on the wretched, tortured woman downstairs, lived in a state of unnatural excitement. She was like a victim that was being prepared for the savage rites of a bloody idolatry. Her terror numbed her. She could not bear to let Davidson out of her sight; it was only when he was with her that she had courage, and she hung upon him with a slavish dependence. She cried a great deal, and she read the Bible, and prayed. Sometimes she was exhausted and apathetic. Then she did indeed look forward to her ordeal, for it seemed to offer an escape, direct and concrete, from the anguish she was enduring. She could not bear much longer the vague terrors which now assailed her. With her sins she had put aside all personal vanity, and she slopped about her room, unkempt and dishevelled, in her tawdry dressing-gown. She had not taken off her night-dress for four days, nor put on stockings. Her room was littered and untidy. Meanwhile the rain fell with a cruel persistence. You felt that the heavens must at last be empty of water, but still it poured down, straight and heavy, with a maddening iteration, on the iron roof. Everything was damp and clammy. There was mildew on the walls and on the boots that stood on the floor. Through the sleepless nights the mosquitoes droned their angry chant.

'If it would only stop raining for a single day it wouldn't be so bad,' said Dr Macphail.

They all looked forward to the Tuesday when the boat for San Francisco was to arrive from Sydney. The strain was intolerable. So far as Dr Macphail was concerned, his pity and his resentment were alike extinguished by his desire to be rid of the unfortunate woman. The inevitable must be accepted. He felt he would breathe more freely when the ship had sailed. Sadie Thompson was to be escorted on board by a clerk in the governor's office. This person called on the Monday evening and told Miss Thompson to be prepared at eleven in the morning. Davidson was with her.

'I'll see that everything is ready. I mean to come on board with her myself.'

Miss Thompson did not speak.

When Dr Macphail blew out his candle and crawled cautiously under his mosquito curtains, he gave a sigh of relief.

'Well, thank God that's over. By this time tomorrow she'll be gone.'

'Mrs Davidson will be glad too. She says he's wearing himself to a shadow,' said Mrs Macphail. 'She's a different woman.'

'Who?'

'Sadie. I should never have thought it possible. It makes one humble.'

Dr Macphail did not answer, and presently he fell asleep. He was tired out, and he slept more soundly than usual.

He was awakened in the morning by a hand placed on his arm, and, starting up, saw Horn by the side of his bed. The trader put his finger on his mouth to prevent any exclamation from Dr Macphail and beckoned to him to come. As a rule he wore shabby ducks, but now he was barefoot and wore only the *lava-lava* of the natives. He looked suddenly savage, and Dr Macphail, getting out of bed, saw that he was heavily tattooed. Horn made him a sign to come on to the veranda. Dr Macphail got out of bed and followed the trader out.

'Don't make a noise,' he whispered. 'You're wanted. Put on a coat and some shoes. Quick.'

Dr Macphail's first thought was that something had happened to Miss Thompson.

'What is it? Shall I bring my instruments?'

'Hurry, please, hurry.'

Dr Macphail crept back into the bedroom, put on a waterproof over his pyjamas, and a pair of rubber-soled shoes. He rejoined the trader, and together they tiptoed down the stairs. The door leading out to the road was open and at it were standing half a dozen natives.

'What is it?' repeated the doctor.

'Come along with me,' said Horn.

He walked out and the doctor followed him. The natives came after them in a little bunch. They crossed the road and came on to the beach. The doctor saw a group of natives standing round some object at the water's edge. They hurried along, a couple of dozen yards perhaps, and the natives opened out as the doctor came up. The trader pushed him forwards. Then he saw, lying half in the water and half out, a dreadful object, the body of Davidson. Dr Macphail bent down – he was not a man to lose his head in an emergency – and turned the body over. The throat was cut from ear to ear, and in the right hand was still the razor with which the deed was done.

'He's quite cold,' said the doctor. 'He must have been dead some time.'

'One of the boys saw him lying there on his way to work just now and came and told me. Do you think he did it himself?'

'Yes. Someone ought to go for the police.'

Horn said something in the native tongue, and two youths started off.

'We must leave him here till they come,' said the doctor.

'They mustn't take him into my house. I won't have him in my house.'

'You'll do what the authorities say,' replied the doctor sharply. 'In point of fact I expect they'll take him to the mortuary.'

They stood waiting where they were. The trader took a cigarette from a fold in his *lava-lava* and gave one to Dr Macphail. They smoked while they stared at the corpse. Dr Macphail could not understand.

'Why do you think he did it?' asked Horn.

The doctor shrugged his shoulders. In a little while native police came along, under the charge of a marine, with a stretcher, and immediately afterwards a couple of naval officers and a naval doctor.

They managed everything in a businesslike manner.

'What about the wife?' said one of the officers.

'Now that you've come I'll go back to the house and get some things on. I'll see that it's broken to her. She'd better not see him till he's been fixed up a little.'

'I guess that's right,' said the naval doctor.

When Dr Macphail went back he found his wife nearly dressed.

'Mrs Davidson's in a dreadful state about her husband,' she said to him as soon as he appeared. 'He hasn't been to bed all night. She heard him leave Miss Thompson's room at two, but he went out. If he's been walking about since then he'll be absolutely dead.'

Dr Macphail told her what had happened and asked her to break the news to Mrs Davidson.

'But why did he do it?' she asked, horror-stricken.

'I don't know.'

'But I can't. I can't.'

'You must.'

She gave him a frightened look and went out. He heard her go into Mrs Davidson's room. He waited a minute to gather himself together and then began to shave and wash. When he was dressed he sat down on the bed and waited for his wife. At last she came.

'She wants to see him,' she said.

'They've taken him to the mortuary. We'd better go down with her. How did she take it?'

'I think she's stunned. She didn't cry. But she's trembling like a leaf.'

'We'd better go at once.'

When they knocked at her door Mrs Davidson came out. She was very pale, but dry-eyed. To the doctor she seemed unnaturally composed. No word was exchanged, and they set out in silence down the road. When they arrived at the mortuary Mrs Davidson spoke.

'Let me go in and see him alone.'

They stood aside. A native opened a door for her and closed it behind her. They sat down and waited. One or two white men came and talked to them in undertones. Dr Macphail told them again what he knew of the tragedy. At last the door was quietly opened and Mrs Davidson came out. Silence fell upon them.

'I'm ready to go back now,' she said.

Her voice was hard and steady. Dr Macphail could not understand the look in her eyes. Her pale face was very stern. They walked back slowly, never saying a word, and at last they came round the bend on the other side of which stood their house. Mrs Davidson gave a gasp, and for a moment they stopped still. An incredible sound assaulted their ears. The gramophone which had been silent for so long was playing, playing ragtime loud and harsh.

'What's that?' cried Mrs Macphail with horror.

'Let's go on,' said Mrs Davidson.

They walked up the steps and entered the hall. Miss Thompson was standing at her door, chatting with a sailor. A sudden change had taken place in her. She was no longer the cowed drudge of the last days. She was dressed in all her finery, in her white dress, with the high shiny boots over which her fat legs bulged in their cotton stockings; her hair was elaborately arranged; and she wore that enormous hat covered with gaudy flowers. Her face was painted, her eyebrows were boldly black, and her lips were scarlet. She held herself erect. She was the flaunting quean that they had known at first. As they came in she broke into a loud, jeering laugh; and then, when Mrs Davidson involuntarily stopped, she collected the spittle in her mouth and spat. Mrs Davidson cowered back, and two red spots rose suddenly to her cheeks. Then, covering her face with her hands, she broke away and ran quickly up the stairs. Dr Macphail was outraged. He pushed past the woman into her room.

'What the devil are you doing?' he cried. 'Stop that damned machine.'

He went up to it and tore the record off. She turned on him.

'Say, doc, you can that stuff with me. What the hell are you doin' in my room?'

'What do you mean?' he cried. 'What d'you mean?'

She gathered herself together. No one could describe the scorn of her expression or the contemptuous hatred she put into her answer.

'You men! You filthy, dirty pigs! You're all the same, all of you. Pigs! Pigs!'

Dr Macphail gasped. He understood.

Envoi

When your ship leaves Honolulu they hang *leis* round your neck, garlands of sweet smelling flowers. The wharf is crowded and the band plays a melting Hawaiian tune. The people on board throw coloured streamers to those standing below, and the side of the ship is gay with the thin lines of paper, red and green and yellow and blue. When the ship moves slowly away the streamers break softly, and it is like the breaking of human ties. Men and women are joined together for a moment by a gaily coloured strip of paper, red and blue and green and yellow, and then life separates them and the paper is sundered, so easily, with a little sharp snap. For an hour the fragments trail down the hull and then they blow away. The flowers of your garlands fade and their scent is oppressive. You throw them overboard.

FROM

The Casuarina Tree

(1926)

The Casuarina Tree

Of the Casuarina tree they say that if you take in a boat with you a piece of it, be it ever so small, contrary winds will arise to impede your journey or storms to imperil your life. They say also that if you stand in its shadow by the light of the full moon you will hear, whispered mysteriously in its dark ramage, the secrets of the future. These facts have never been disputed; but they say also that when in the wide estuaries the mangrove has in due time reclaimed the swampy land from the water the Casuarina tree plants itself and in its turn settles, solidifies and fertilizes the soil till it is ripe for a more varied and luxuriant growth; and then, having done its work, dies down before the ruthless encroachment of the myriad denizens of the jungle. It occurred to me that *The Casuarina Tree* would not make so bad a title for a collection of stories about the English people who live in the Malay Peninsula and in Borneo; for I fancied that they, coming after the pioneers who had opened these lands to Western civilization, were destined in just such a manner, now that their work was accomplished and the country was peaceable, orderly and sophisticated, to give way to a more varied, but less adventurous, generation; and I was excessively disconcerted on inquiry to learn that there was not a word of truth in what I had been told. It is very hard to find a title for a volume of short stories; to give it the name of the first is to evade the difficulty and deceives the purchaser into thinking that he is about to read a novel; a good title should, however vaguely, have a reference to all the stories gathered together; the best titles have already been used. I was in a quandary. But I reflected that a symbol (as Master Francis Rabelais pointed out in a diverting chapter) can symbolize anything; and I remembered that the Casuarina tree stood along the sea shore, gaunt and rough-hewn, protecting the land from the fury of the winds, and so might aptly suggest these planters and administrators who, with all their shortcomings, have after all brought to the peoples among whom they dwell tranquillity, justice and welfare, and I fancied that they too, as they looked at the Casuarina tree, grey, rugged and sad, a little out of place in the wanton tropics, might very well be reminded of their native land; and, thinking for a moment of the heather on a Yorkshire moor or the broom on a Sussex common, see in that hardy tree, doing its best in difficult circumstances, a symbol of their own exiled lives. In short I could find a dozen reasons for keeping my title, but, of course, the best of them all was that I could think of no better.

Before the Party

Mrs Skinner liked to be in good time. She was already dressed, in black silk as befitted her age and the mourning she wore for her son-in-law, and now she put on her toque. She was a little uncertain about it, since the egrets' feathers which adorned it might very well arouse in some of the friends she would certainly meet at the party acid expostulations; and of course it was shocking to kill those beautiful white birds, in the mating season too, for the sake of their feathers; but there they were, so pretty and stylish, and it would have been silly to refuse them, and it would have hurt her son-in-law's feelings. He had brought them all the way from Borneo and he expected her to be so pleased with them. Kathleen had made herself rather unpleasant about them, she must wish she hadn't now, after what had happened, but Kathleen had never really liked Harold. Mrs Skinner, standing at her dressing-table, placed the toque on her head, it was after all the only nice hat she had, and put in a pin with a large jet knob. If anybody spoke to her about the ospreys she had her answer.

'I know it's dreadful,' she would say, 'and I wouldn't dream of buying them, but my poor son-in-law brought them back the last time he was home on leave.'

That would explain her possession of them and

excuse their use. Everyone had been very kind. Mrs Skinner took a clean handkerchief from a drawer and sprinkled a little eau-de-Cologne on it. She never used scent, and she had always thought it rather fast, but eau-de-Cologne was so refreshing. She was very nearly ready now, and her eyes wandered out of the window behind her looking-glass. Canon Heywood had a beautiful day for his garden-party. It was warm and the sky was blue; the trees had not yet lost the fresh green of the spring. She smiled as she saw her little granddaughter in the strip of garden behind the house busily raking her very own flower-bed. Mrs Skinner wished Joan were not quite so pale, it was a mistake to have kept her so long in the tropics; and she was so grave for her age, you never saw her run about; she played quiet games of her own invention and watered her garden. Mrs Skinner gave the front of her dress a little pat, took up her gloves, and went downstairs.

Kathleen was at the writing-table in the window busy with lists she was making, for she was Honorary Secretary of the Ladies' Golf Club, and when there were competitions had a good deal to do. But she too was ready for the party.

'I see you've put on your jumper after all,' said Mrs Skinner.

They had discussed at luncheon whether Kathleen should wear her jumper or her black chiffon. The jumper was black and white, and Kathleen thought it rather smart, but it was hardly mourning. Millicent, however, was in favour of it.

'There's no reason why we should all look as if we'd just come from a funeral,' she said. 'Harold's been dead eight months.'

To Mrs Skinner it seemed rather unfeeling to talk like that. Millicent was strange since her return from Borneo.

'You're not going to leave off your weeds yet, darling?' she asked.

Millicent did not give a direct answer.

'People don't wear mourning in the way they used,' she said. She paused a little and when she went on there was a tone in her voice which Mrs Skinner thought quite peculiar. It was plain that Kathleen noticed it too, for she gave her sister a curious look. 'I'm sure Harold wouldn't wish me to wear mourning for him indefinitely.'

'I dressed early because I wanted to say something to Millicent,' said Kathleen in reply to her mother's observation.

'Oh?'

Katheen did not explain. But she put her lists aside and with knitted brows read for the second time a letter from a lady who complained that the committee had most unfairly marked down her handicap from twenty-four to eighteen. It requires a good deal of tact to be Honorary Secretary to a ladies' golf club. Mrs Skinner began to put on her new gloves. The sun-blinds kept the room cool and dark. She looked at the great wooden hornbill, gaily painted, which Harold had left in her safekeeping; and it seemed a little odd and barbaric to her, but he had set much store on it. It had some religious significance and Canon Heywood had been greatly struck by it. On the wall, over the sofa, were Malay weapons, she forgot what they were called, and here and there on occasional tables pieces of silver and brass which Harold at various times had sent to them. She had liked Harold and involuntarily her eyes sought his photograph which stood on the piano with photographs of her two daughters, her grandchild, her sister and her sister's son.

'Why, Kathleen, where's Harold's photograph?' she asked.

Kathleen looked round. It no longer stood in its place.

'Someone's taken it away,' said Kathleen.

Surprised and puzzled, she got up and went over to the piano. The photographs had been rearranged so that no gap should show.

'Perhaps Millicent wanted to have it in her bedroom,' said Mrs Skinner.

'I should have noticed it. Besides, Millicent has several photographs of Harold. She keeps them locked up.'

Mrs Skinner had thought it very peculiar that her daughter should have no photographs of Harold in her room. Indeed she had spoken of it once, but Millicent had made no reply. Millicent had been strangely silent since she came back from Borneo, and had not encouraged the sympathy Mrs Skinner would have been so willing to show her. She seemed unwilling to speak of her great loss. Sorrow took people in different ways. Her husband had said the best thing was to leave her alone. The thought of him turned her ideas to the party they were going to.

'Father asked if I thought he ought to wear a top-hat,' she said. 'I said I thought it was just as well to be on the safe side.'

It was going to be quite a grand affair. They were having ices, strawberry and vanilla, from Boddy, the confectioner, but the Heywoods were making the iced coffee at home. Everyone would be there. They had been asked to meet the Bishop of Hong-Kong, who was staying with the Canon, an old college friend of his, and he was going to speak on the Chinese missions. Mrs Skinner, whose daughter had lived in the East for eight years and whose son-in-law had been Resident of a district in Borneo, was in a flutter of interest. Naturally it meant more to her than to people who had never had anything to do with the Colonies and that sort of thing.

'What can they know of England who only England know?' as Mr Skinner said.

He came into the room at that moment. He was a lawyer, as his father had been before him, and he had offices in Lincoln's Inn Fields. He went up to London every morning and came down every evening. He was only able to accompany his wife and daughters to the Canon's garden-party, because the Canon had very wisely chosen a Saturday to have it on. Mr Skinner looked very well in his tail-coat and pepper-and-salt trousers. He was not exactly dressy, but he was neat. He looked like a respectable family solicitor, which indeed he was; his firm never touched work that was not perfectly above board, and if a client went to him with some trouble that was not quite nice, Mr Skinner would look grave.

'I don't think this is the sort of case that we very much care to undertake,' he said. 'I think you'd do better to go elsewhere.'

He drew towards him his writing-block and scribbled a name and address on it. He tore off a sheet of paper and handed it to his client.

'If I were you I think I would go and see these

people. If you mention my name I believe they'll do anything they can for you.'

Mr Skinner was clean-shaven and very bald. His pale lips were tight and thin, but his blue eyes were shy. He had no colour in his cheeks and his face was much lined.

'I see you've put on your new trousers,' said Mrs Skinner.

'I thought it would be a good opportunity,' he answered. 'I was wondering if I should wear a buttonhole.'

'I wouldn't, father,' said Kathleen. 'I don't think it's awfully good form.'

'A lot of people will be wearing them,' said Mrs Skinner.

'Only clerks and people like that,' said Kathleen. 'The Heywoods have had to ask everybody, you know. And besides, we are in mourning.'

'I wonder if there'll be a collection after the Bishop's address,' said Mr Skinner.

'I should hardly think so,' said Mrs Skinner.

'I think it would be rather bad form,' agreed Kathleen.

'It's as well to be on the safe side,' said Mr Skinner. 'I'll give for all of us. I was wondering if ten shillings would be enough or if I must give a pound.'

'If you give anything I think you ought to give a pound, father,' said Kathleen.

'I'll see when the time comes. I don't want to give less than anyone else, but on the other hand I see no reason to give more than I need.'

Kathleen put away her papers in the drawer of the writing-table and stood up. She looked at her wrist-watch.

'Is Millicent ready?' asked Mrs Skinner.

'There's plenty of time. We're only asked at four, and I don't think we ought to arrive much before half-past. I told Davis to bring the car round at four-fifteen.'

Generally Kathleen drove the car, but on grand occasions like this Davis, who was the gardener, put on his uniform and acted as chauffeur. It looked better when you drove up, and naturally Kathleen didn't much want to drive herself when she was wearing her new jumper. The sight of her mother forcing her fingers one by one into her new gloves reminded her that she must put on her own. She smelt them to see if any odour of the cleaning still clung to them. It was very slight, she didn't believe anyone would notice.

At last the door opened and Millicent came in. She wore her widow's weeds. Mrs Skinner never could get used to them, but of course she knew that Millicent must wear them for a year. It was a pity they didn't suit her; they suited some people. She had tried on Millicent's bonnet once, with its white band and long veil, and thought she looked very well in it. Of course she hoped dear Alfred would survive her, but if he didn't she would never go out of weeds. Queen Victoria never had. It was different for Millicent; Millicent was a much younger woman; she was only thirty-six: it was very sad to be a widow at thirty-six. And there wasn't much chance of her marrying again. Kathleen wasn't very likely to marry now, she was thirty-five; last time Millicent and Harold had come home she had suggested that they should have Kathleen to stay with them; Harold had seemed willing enough, but Millicent said it wouldn't do. Mrs Skinner didn't know why not. It would give her a chance. Of course they didn't want to get rid of her, but a girl ought to marry, and somehow all the men they knew at home were married already. Millicent said the climate was trying. It was true she was a bad colour. No one would think now that Millicent had been the prettier of the two. Kathleen had fined down as she grew older, of course some people said she was too thin, but now that she had cut her hair, with her cheeks red from playing golf in all weathers, Mrs Skinner thought her quite pretty. No one could say that of poor Millicent; she had lost her figure completely; she had never been tall, and now that she had filled out she looked stocky. She was a good deal too fat; Mrs Skinner supposed it was due to the tropical heat that prevented her from taking exercise. Her skin was sallow and muddy; and her blue eyes, which had been her best feature, had gone quite pale.

'She ought to do something about her neck,' Mrs Skinner reflected. 'She's becoming dreadfully jowly.'

She had spoken of it once or twice to her husband. He remarked that Millicent wasn't as young as she was; that might be, but she needn't let herself go altogether. Mrs Skinner made up her mind to talk to her daughter seriously, but of course she must respect her grief, and she would wait till the year was up. She was just as glad to have this reason to put off a conversation the thought of which made her slightly nervous. For Millicent was certainly changed. There was something sullen in her face which made her mother not quite at home with her. Mrs Skinner liked to say aloud all the thoughts that passed through her head, but Millicent when you made a remark (just to say something, you know) had an awkward habit of not answering, so that you wondered whether she had heard. Sometimes Mrs Skinner found it so irritating, that not to be quite sharp with Millicent she had to remind herself that poor Harold had only been dead eight months.

The light from the window fell on the widow's heavy face as she advanced silently, but Kathleen stood with her back to it. She watched her sister for a moment.

'Millicent, there's something I want to say to you,' she said. 'I was playing golf with Gladys Heywood this morning.'

'Did you beat her?' asked Millicent.

Gladys Heywood was the Canon's only unmarried daughter.

'She told me something about you which I think you ought to know.'

Millicent's eyes passed beyond her sister to the little girl watering flowers in the garden.

'Have you told Annie to give Joan her tea in the kitchen, mother?' she said.

'Yes, she'll have it when the servants have theirs.'

Kathleen looked at her sister coolly.

'The Bishop spent two or three days at Singapore on his way home,' she went on. 'He's very fond of travelling. He's been to Borneo, and he knows a good many of the people that you know.'

'He'll be interested to see you, dear,' said Mrs Skinner. 'Did he know poor Harold?'

'Yes, he met him at Kuala Solor. He remembers him very well. He says he was shocked to hear of his death.'

Millicent sat down and began to put on her black gloves. It seemed strange to Mrs Skinner that she received these remarks with complete silence.

'Oh, Millicent,' she said, 'Harold's photo has disappeared. Have you taken it?'

'Yes, I put it away.'

'I should have thought you'd like to have it out.'

Once more Millicent said nothing. It really was an exasperating habit.

Kathleen turned slightly in order to face her sister.

'Millicent, why did you tell us that Harold died of fever?'

The widow made no gesture, she looked at Kathleen with steady eyes, but her sallow skin darkened with a flush. She did not reply.

'What *do* you mean, Kathleen?' asked Mr Skinner, with surprise.

'The Bishop says that Harold committed suicide.'

Mrs Skinner gave a startled cry, but her husband put out a deprecating hand.

'Is it true, Millicent?'

'It is.'

'But why didn't you tell us?'

Millicent paused for an instant. She fingered idly a piece of Brunei brass which stood on the table by her side. That too had been a present from Harold.

'I thought it better for Joan that her father should be thought to have died of fever. I didn't want her to know anything about it.'

'You've put us in an awfully awkward position,' said Kathleen, frowning a little. 'Gladys Heywood said she thought it rather nasty of me not to have told her the truth. I had the greatest difficulty in getting her to believe that I knew absolutely nothing about it. She said her father was rather put out. He says, after all the years we've known one another, and considering that he married you, and the terms we've been on, and all that, he does think we might have had confidence in him. And at all events, if we didn't want to tell him the truth we needn't have told him a lie.'

'I must say I sympathize with him there,' said Mr Skinner, acidly.

'Of course I told Gladys that we weren't to blame. We only told them what you told us.'

'I hope it didn't put you off your game,' said Millicent.

'Really, my dear, I think that is a most improper observation,' exclaimed her father.

He rose from his chair, walked over to the empty fireplace, and from force of habit stood in front of it with parted coat-tails.

'It was my business,' said Millicent, 'and if I chose to keep it to myself I didn't see why I shouldn't.'

'It doesn't look as if you had any affection for your mother if you didn't even tell her,' said Mrs Skinner.

Millicent shrugged her shoulders.

'You might have known it was bound to come out,' said Kathleen.

'Why? I didn't expect that two gossiping old parsons would have nothing else to talk about than me.'

'When the Bishop said he'd been to Borneo it's only natural that the Heywoods should ask him if he knew you and Harold.'

'All that's neither here nor there,' said Mr Skinner. 'I think you should certainly have told us the truth, and we could have decided what was the best thing to do. As a solicitor I can tell you that in the long run it only makes things worse if you attempt to hide them.'

'Poor Harold,' said Mrs Skinner, and the tears began to trickle down her raddled cheeks. 'It seems dreadful. He was always a good son-in-law to me. Whatever induced him to do such a dreadful thing?

'The climate.'

'I think you'd better give us all the facts, Millicent,' said her father.

'Kathleen will tell you.'

Kathleen hesitated. What she had to say really was rather dreadful. It seemed terrible that such things should happen to a family like theirs.

'The Bishop says he cut his throat.'

Mrs Skinner gasped and she went impulsively up to her bereaved daughter. She wanted to fold her in her arms.

'My poor child,' she sobbed.

But Millicent withdrew herself.

'Please don't fuss me, mother. I really can't stand being mauled about.'

'Really, Millicent,' said Mr Skinner, with a frown.

He did not think she was behaving very nicely.

Mrs Skinner dabbed her eyes carefully with her handkerchief and with a sigh and a little shake of the head returned to her chair. Kathleen fidgeted with the long chain she wore round her neck.

'It does seem rather absurd that I should have to be told the details of my brother-in-law's death by a friend. It makes us all look such fools. The Bishop wants very much to see you, Millicent; he wants to tell you how much he feels for you.' She paused, but Millicent did not speak. 'He says that Millicent had been away with Joan and when she came back she found poor Harold lying dead on his bed.'

'It must have been a great shock,' said Mr Skinner.

Mrs Skinner began to cry again, but Kathleen put her hand gently on her shoulder.

'Don't cry, mother,' she said. 'It'll make your eyes red and people will think it so funny.'

They were all silent while Mrs Skinner, drying her eyes, made a successful effort to control herself. It seemed very strange to her that at this very moment she should be wearing in her toque the ospreys that poor Harold had given her.

'There's something else I ought to tell you,' said Kathleen.

Millicent looked at her sister again, without haste, and her eyes were steady, but watchful. She had the look of a person who is waiting for a sound which he is afraid of missing.

'I don't want to say anything to wound you, dear,' Kathleen went on, 'but there's something else and I think you ought to know it. The Bishop says that Harold drank.'

'Oh, my dear, how dreadful!' cried Mrs Skinner. 'What a shocking thing to say. Did Gladys Heywood tell you? What did you say?'

'I said it was entirely untrue.'

'This is what comes of making secrets of things,' said Mr Skinner, irritably. 'It's always the same. If you try and hush a thing up all sorts of rumours get about which are ten times worse than the truth.'

'They told the Bishop in Singapore that Harold had killed himself while he was suffering from *delirium tremens*. I think for all our sakes you ought to deny that, Millicent.'

'It's such a dreadful thing to have said about

anyone who's dead,' said Mrs Skinner. 'And it'll be so bad for Joan when she grows up.'

'But what is the foundation of this story, Millicent?' asked her father. 'Harold was always very abstemious.'

'Here,' said the widow.

'Did he drink?'

'Like a fish.'

The answer was so unexpected, and the tone so sardonic, that all three of them were startled.

'Millicent, how can you talk like that of your husband when he's dead?' cried her mother, clasping her neatly gloved hands. 'I can't understand you. You've been so strange since you came back. I could never have believed that a girl of mine could take her husband's death like that.'

'Never mind about that, mother,' said Mr Skinner. 'We can go into all that later.'

He walked to the window and looked out at the sunny little garden, and then walked back into the room. He took his pince-nez out of his pocket and, though he had no intention of putting them on, wiped them with his handkerchief. Millient looked at him and in her eyes, unmistakably, was a look of irony which was quite cynical. Mr Skinner was vexed. He had finished his week's work and he was a free man till Monday morning. Though he had told his wife that this garden-party was a great nusiance and he would much sooner have tea quietly in his own garden, he had been looking forward to it. He did not care very much about Chinese missions, but it would be interesting to meet the Bishop. And now this? It was not the kind of thing he cared to be mixed up in; it was most unpleasant to be told on a sudden that his son-in-law was a drunkard and a suicide. Millicent was thoughtfully smoothing her white cuffs. Her coolness irritated him; but instead of addressing her he spoke to his younger daughter.

'Why don't you sit down, Kathleen? Surely there are plenty of chairs in the room.'

Kathleen drew forward a chair and without a word seated herself. Mr Skinner stopped in front of Millicent and faced her.

'Of course I see why you told us Harold had died of fever. I think it was a mistake, because that sort of thing is bound to come out sooner or later. I don't know how far what the Bishop has told the Heywoods coincides with the facts, but if you will take my advice you will tell us everything as circumstantially as you can, then we can see. We can't hope that it will go no further now that Canon Heywood and Gladys know. In a place like this people are bound to talk. It will make it easier for all of us if we at all events know the exact truth.'

Mrs Skinner and Kathleen thought he put the matter very well. They waited for Millicent's reply. She had listened with an impassive face; that sudden flush had disappeared and it was once more, as usual, pasty and sallow.

'I don't think you'll much like the truth if I tell it you,' she said.

'You must know that you can count on our sympathy and understanding,' said Kathleen gravely.

Millicent gave her a glance and the shadow of a smile flickered across her set mouth. She looked slowly at the three of them. Mrs Skinner had an uneasy impression that she looked at them as though they were mannequins at a dressmaker's.

She seemed to live in a different world from theirs and to have no connection with them.

'You know, I wasn't in love with Harold when I married him,' she said reflectively.

Mrs Skinner was on the point of making an exclamation when a rapid gesture of her husband, barely indicated, but after so many years of married life perfectly significant, stopped her. Millicent went on. She spoke with a level voice, slowly, and there was little change of expression in her tone.

'I was twenty-seven, and no one else seemed to want to marry me. It's true he was forty-four, and it seemed rather old, but he had a very good position, hadn't he? I wasn't likely to get a better chance.'

Mrs Skinner felt inclined to cry again, but she remembered the party.

'Of course I see now why you took his photograph away,' she said dolefully.

'Don't, mother,' exclaimed Kathleen.

It had been taken when he was engaged to Millicent and was a very good photograph of Harold. Mrs Skinner had always thought him quite a fine man. He was heavily built, tall and perhaps a little too fat, but he held himself well, and his presence was imposing. He was inclined to be bald, even then, but men did go bald very early nowadays, and he said that topis, sun-helmets, you know, were very bad for the hair. He had a small dark moustache, and his face was deeply burned by the sun. Of course his best feature was his eyes; they were brown and large, like Joan's. His conversation was interesting. Kathleen said he was pompous, but Mrs Skinner didn't think him so, she didn't mind it if a man laid down the law; and when she saw, as she very soon did, that he was attracted by Millicent she began to like him very much. He was always very attentive to Mrs Skinner, and she listened as though she were really interested when he spoke of his district, and told her of the big game he had killed. Kathleen said he had a pretty good opinion of himself, but Mrs Skinner came of a generation which accepted without question the good opinion that men had of themselves. Millicent saw very soon which way the wind blew, and though she said nothing to her mother, her mother knew that if Harold asked her she was going to accept him.

Harold was staying with some people who had been thirty years in Borneo and they spoke well of the country. There was no reason why a woman shouldn't live there comfortably; of course the children had to come home when they were seven; but Mrs Skinner thought it unnecessary to trouble about that yet. She asked Harold to dine, and she told him they were always in to tea. He seemed to be at a loose end, and when his visit to his old friends was drawing to a close, she told him they would be very much pleased if he would come and spend a fortnight with them. It was towards the end of this that Harold and Millicent became engaged. They had a very pretty wedding, they went to Venice for their honeymoon, and then they started for the East. Millicent wrote from various ports at which the ship touched. She seemed happy.

'People were very nice to me at Kuala Solor,' she said. Kuala Solor was the chief town of the state of Sembulu. 'We stayed with the Resident and everyone asked us to dinner. Once or twice I heard men ask Harold to have a drink, but he refused; he said he had turned over a new leaf now he was a married man. I didn't know why they laughed. Mrs Gray, the Resident's wife, told me they were all so glad Harold was married. She said it was dreadfully lonely for a bachelor on one of the outstations. When we left Kuala Solor Mrs Gray said good-bye to me so funnily that I was quite surprised. It was as if she was solemnly putting Harold in my charge.'

They listened to her in silence. Kathleen never took her eyes off her sister's impassive face; but Mr Skinner stared straight in front of him at the Malay arms, krises and parangs, which hung on the wall above the sofa on which his wife sat.

'It wasn't till I went back to Kuala Solor a year and a half later, that I found out why their manner had seemed so odd.' Millicent gave a queer little sound like the echo of a scornful laugh. 'I knew then a good deal that I hadn't known before. Harold came to England that time in order to marry. He didn't much mind who it was. Do you remember how we spread ourselves out to catch him, mother? We needn't have taken so much trouble.'

'I don't know what you mean, Millicent,' said Mrs Skinner, not without acerbity, for the insinuation of scheming did not please her. 'I saw he was attracted by you.'

Millicent shrugged her heavy shoulders.

'He was a confirmed drunkard. He used to go to bed every night with a bottle of whisky and empty it before morning. The Chief Secretary told him he'd have to resign unless he stopped drinking. He said he'd give him one more chance. He could take his leave then and go to England. He advised him to marry so that when he got back he'd have someone to look after him. Harold married me because he wanted a keeper. They took bets in Kuala Solor on how long I'd make him stay sober.'

'But he was in love with you,' Mrs Skinner interrupted. 'You don't know how he used to speak to me about you, and at that time you're speaking of, when you went to Kuala Solor to have Joan, he wrote me such a charming letter about you.'

Millicent looked at her mother again and a deep colour dyed her sallow skin. Her hands, lying on her lap, began to tremble a little. She thought of those first months of her married life. The Government launch took them to the mouth of the river, and they spent the night at the bungalow which Harold said jokingly was their seaside residence. Next day they went up stream in a prahu. From the novels she had read she expected the rivers of Borneo to be dark and strangely sinister, but the sky was blue, dappled with little white clouds, and the green of the mangroves and the nipahs, washed by the flowing water, glistened in the sun. On each side stretched the pathless jungle, and in the distance, silhouetted against the sky, was the rugged outline of a mountain. The air in the early morning was fresh and buoyant. She seemed to enter upon a friendly, fertile land, and she had a sense of spacious freedom. They watched the banks for monkeys sitting on the branches of the tangled trees, and once Harold pointed out something that looked like a log and said it was a crocodile. The Assistant Resident, in ducks and a topi, was at the landing-stage to meet them, and a dozen trim little soldiers were lined up to do them honour. The Assistant Resident was introduced to her. His name was Simpson.

'By Jove, sir,' he said to Harold, 'I'm glad to see

you back. It's been deuced lonely without you.'

The Resident's bungalow, surrounded by a garden in which grew wildly all manner of gay flowers, stood on the top of a low hill. It was a trifle shabby and the furniture was sparse, but the rooms were cool and of generous size.

'The kampong is down there,' said Harold, pointing.

Her eyes followed his gesture, and from among the coconut trees rose the beating of a gong. It gave her a queer little sensation in the heart.

Though she had nothing much to do the days passed easily enough. At dawn a boy brought them their tea and they lounged about the veranda, enjoying the fragrance of the morning (Harold in a singlet and a sarong, she in a dressing-gown) till it was time to dress for breakfast. Then Harold went to his office and she spent an hour or two learning Malay. After tiffin he went back to his office while she slept. A cup of tea revived them both, and they went for a walk or played golf on the nine hole links which Harold had made on a level piece of cleared jungle below the bungalow. Night fell at six and Mr Simpson came along to have a drink. They chatted till their late dinner hour, and sometimes Harold and Mr Simpson played chess. The balmy evenings were enchanting. The fireflies turned the bushes just below the veranda into coldly spark-ling, tremulous beacons, and flowering trees scen-ted the air with sweet odours. After dinner they read the papers which had left London six weeks before and presently went to bed. Millicent enjoyed being a married woman, with a house of her own, and she was pleased with the native servants, in their gay sarongs, who went about the bungalow, with bare feet, silent but friendly. It gave her a pleasant sense of importance to be the wife of the Resident. Harold impressed her by the fluency with which he spoke the language, by his air of command, and by his dignity. She went into the court-house now and then to hear him try cases. The multifariousness of his duties and the competent way in which he performed them aroused her respect. Mr Simpson told her that Harold understood the natives as well as any man in the country. He had the combination of firmness, tact and good humour, which was essential in dealing with that timid, revengeful and suspicious race. Millicent began to feel a certain admiration for her husband.

They had been married nearly a year when two English naturalists came to stay with them for a few days on their way to the interior. They brought a pressing recommendation from the Governor, and Harold said he wanted to do them proud. Their arrival was an agreeable change. Millicent asked Mr Simpson to dinner (he lived at the Fort and only dined with them on Sunday nights) and after dinner the men sat down to play bridge. Millicent left them presently and went to bed, but they were so noisy that for some time she could not get to sleep. She did not know at what hour she was awakened by Harold staggering into the room. She kept silent. He made up his mind to have a bath before getting into bed; the bath-house was just below their room, and he went down the steps that led to it. Apparently he slipped, for there was a great clatter, and he began to swear. Then he was violently sick. She heard him sluice the buckets of water over himself and in a little while, walking very cautiously this time, he crawled up the stairs and slipped into bed. Millicent pretended to be asleep. She was disgusted. Harold was drunk. She made up her mind to speak about it in the morning. What would the naturalists think of him? But in the morning Harold was so dignified that she hadn't quite the determination to refer to the matter. At eight Harold and she, with their two guests, sat down to breakfast. Harold looked round the table.

'Porridge,' he said. 'Millicent, your guests might manage a little Worcester Sauce for breakfast, but I don't think they'll much fancy anything else. Personally I shall content myself with a whisky and soda.'

The naturalists laughed, but shamefacedly.

'Your husband's a terror,' said one of them.

'I should not think I had properly performed the duties of hospitality if I sent you sober to bed on the first night of your visit,' said Harold, with his round, stately way of putting things.

Millicent, smiling acidly, was relieved to think that her guests had been as drunk as her husband. The next evening she sat up with them and the party broke up at a reasonable hour. But she was glad when the strangers went on with their journey. Their life resumed its placid course. Some months later Harold went on a tour of inspection of his district and came back with a bad attack of malaria. This was the first time she had seen the disease of which she had heard so much, and when he recovered it did not seem strange to her that Harold was very shaky. She found his manner peculiar. He would come back from the office and stare at her with glazed eyes; he would stand on the veranda, swaying slightly, but still dignified, and make long harangues about the political situation in England; losing the thread of his discourse, he would look at her with an archness which his natural stateliness made somewhat disconcerting and say:

'Pulls you down dreadfully, this confounded malaria. Ah, little woman, you little know the strain it puts upon a man to be an empire builder.'

She thought that Mr Simpson began to look worried, and once or twice, when they were alone, he seemed on the point of saying something to her which his shyness at the last moment prevented. The feeling grew so strong that it made her nervous, and one evening when Harold, she knew not why, had remained later than usual at the office she tackled him.

'What have you got to say to me, Mr Simpson?' she broke out suddenly.

He blushed and hesitated.

'Nothing. What makes you think I have anything in particular to say to you?'

Mr Simpson was a thin, weedy youth of four-and-twenty, with a fine head of waving hair which he took great pains to plaster down very flat. His wrists were swollen and scarred with mosquito bites. Millicent looked at him steadily.

'If it's something to do with Harold don't you think it would be kinder to tell me frankly?'

He grew scarlet now. He shuffled uneasily on his rattan chair. She insisted.

'I'm afraid you'll think it awful cheek,' he said at last. 'It's rotten of me to say anything about my chief behind his back. Malaria's a rotten thing, and after one's had a bout of it one feels awfully down and out.'

He hesitated again. The corners of his mouth sagged as if he were going to cry. To Millicent he seemed like a little boy.

'I'll be as silent as the grave,' she said with a smile, trying to conceal her apprehension. 'Do tell me.'

'I think it's a pity your husband keeps a bottle of whisky at the office. He's apt to take a nip more often then he otherwise would.'

Mr Simpson's voice was hoarse with agitation. Millicent felt a sudden coldness shiver through her. She controlled herself, for she knew that she must not frighten the boy if she were to get out of him all there was to tell. He was unwilling to speak. She pressed him, wheedling, appealing to his sense of duty, and at last she began to cry. Then he told her that Harold had been drunk more or less for the last fortnight, the natives were talking about it, and they said that soon he would be as bad as he had been before his marriage. He had been in the habit of drinking a good deal too much then, but details of that time, notwithstanding all her attempts, Mr Simpson resolutely declined to give her.

'Do you think he's drinking now?' she asked.

'I don't know.'

Millicent felt herself on a sudden hot with shame and anger. The Fort, as it was called because the rifles and the ammunition were kept there, was also the court-house. It stood opposite the Resident's bungalow in a garden of its own. The sun was just about to set and she did not need a hat. She got up and walked across. She found Harold sitting in the office behind the large hall in which he administered justice. There was a bottle of whisky in front of him. He was smoking cigarettes and talking to three or four Malays who stood in front of him listening with obsequious and at the same time scornful smiles. His face was red.

The natives vanished.

'I came to see what you were doing,' she said.

He rose, for he always treated her with elaborate politeness, and lurched. Feeling himself unsteady he assumed an elaborate stateliness of demeanour.

'Take a seat, my dear, take a seat. I was detained by press of work.'

She looked at him with angry eyes.

'You're drunk,' she said.

He stared at her, his eyes bulging a little, and a haughty look gradually traversed his large and fleshy face.

'I haven't the remotest idea what you mean,' he said.

She had been ready with a flow of wrathful expostulation, but suddenly she burst into tears. She sank into a chair and hid her face. Harold looked at her for an instant, then the tears began to trickle down his own cheeks; he came towards her with outstretched arms and fell heavily on his knees. Sobbing, he clasped her to him.

'Forgive me, forgive me,' he said. 'I promise you it shall not happen again. It was that damned malaria.'

'It's so humiliating,' she moaned.

He wept like a child. There was something very touching in the self-abasement of that big dignified man. Presently Millicent looked up. His eyes, appealing and contrite, sought hers.

'Will you give me your word of honour that you'll never touch liquor again?'

'Yes, yes. I hate it.'

It was then she told him that she was with child. He was overjoyed.

'That is the one thing I wanted. That'll keep me straight.'

They went back to the bungalow. Harold bathed himself and had a nap. After dinner they talked long and quietly. He admitted that before he married her he had occasionally drunk more than was good for him; in outstations it was easy to fall into bad habits. He agreed to everything that Millicent asked. And during the months before it was necessary for her to go to Kuala Solor for her confinement, Harold was an excellent husband, tender, thoughtful, proud and affectionate; he was irreproachable. A launch came to fetch her, she was to leave him for six weeks, and he promised faithfully to drink nothing during her absence. He put his hands on her shoulders.

'I never break a promise,' he said in his dignified way. 'But even without it, can you imagine that while you are going through so much, I should do anything to increase your troubles?'

Joan was born. Millicent stayed at the Resident's and Mrs Gray, his wife, a kindly creature of middle age, was very good to her. The two women had little to do during the long hours they were alone but to talk, and in course of time Millicent learnt everything there was to know of her husband's alcoholic past. The fact which she found most difficult to reconcile herself to, was that Harold had been told that the only condition upon which he would be allowed to keep his post was that he should bring back a wife. It caused in her a dull feeling of resentment. And when she discovered what a persistent drunkard he had been, she felt vaguely uneasy. She had a horrid fear that during her absence he would not have been able to resist the craving. She went home with her baby and a nurse. She spent a night at the mouth of the river and sent a messenger in a canoe to announce her arrival. She scanned the landing-stage anxiously as the launch approached it. Harold and Mr Simpson were standing there. The trim little soldiers were lined up. Her heart sank, for Harold was swaying slightly, like a man who seeks to keep his balance on a rolling ship, and she knew he was drunk.

It wasn't a very pleasant home-coming. She had almost forgotten her mother and father and her sister who sat there silently listening to her. Now she roused herself and became once more aware of their presence. All that she spoke of seemed very far away.

'I knew that I hated him then,' she said. 'I could have killed him.'

'Oh, Millicent, don't say that,' cried her mother. 'Don't forget that he's dead, poor man.'

Millicent looked at her mother, and for a moment a scowl darkened her impassive face. Mr Skinner moved uneasily.

'Go on,' said Kathleen.

'When he found out that I knew all about him he didn't bother very much more. In three months he had another attack of DTs.'

'Why didn't you leave him?' said Kathleen.

'What would have been the good of that? He would have been dismissed from the service in a fortnight. Who was to keep me and Joan? I had to stay. And when he was sober I had nothing to complain of. He wasn't in the least in love with me, but he was fond of me; I hadn't married him because I was in love with him, but because I wanted to be married. I did everything I could to keep liquor from him; I managed to get Mr Gray to prevent whisky being sent from Kuala Solor, but he got it from the Chinese. I watched him as a cat watches a mouse. He was too cunning for me. In a little while he had another outbreak. He neglected his duties. I was afraid complaints would be made. We were two days from Kuala Solor and that was our safeguard, but I suppose something was said, for Mr Gray wrote a private letter of warning to me. I showed it to Harold. He stormed and blustered, but I saw he was frightened, and for two or three months he was quite sober. Then he began again. And so it went on till our leave became due.

'Before we came to stay here I begged and prayed him to be careful. I didn't want any of you to know what sort of a man I had married. All the time he was in England he was all right and before we sailed I warned him. He'd grown to be very fond of Joan, and very proud of her, and she was devoted to him. She always liked him better than she liked me. I asked him if he wanted to have his child grow up, knowing that he was a drunkard, and I found out that at last I'd got a hold on him. The thought terrified him. I told him that *I* wouldn't allow it, and if he ever let Joan see him drunk I'd take her away from him at once. Do you know, he grew quite pale when I said it. I fell on my knees that night and thanked God, because I'd found a way of saving my husband.

'He told me that if I would stand by him he would have another try. We made up our minds to fight the thing together. And he tried so hard. When he felt as though he *must* drink he came to me. You know he was inclined to be rather pompous; with me he was so humble, he was like a child; he depended on me. Perhaps he didn't love me when he married me, but he loved me then, me and Joan. I'd hated him, because of the humiliation, because when he was drunk and tried to be dignified and impressive he was loathsome; but now I got a strange feeling in my heart. It wasn't love, but it was a queer, shy tenderness. He was something more than my husband, he was like a child that I'd carried under my heart for long and weary months. He was so proud of me and you know, I was proud too. His long speeches didn't irritate me any more, and I only thought his stately ways rather funny and charming. At last we won. For two years he never touched a drop. He lost his craving entirely. He was even able to joke about it.

'Mr Simpson had left us then and we had another young man called Francis.

'"I'm a reformed drunkard you know, Francis," Harold said to him once. "If it hadn't been for my wife I'd have been sacked long ago. I've got the best wife in the world, Francis."

'You don't know what it meant to me to hear him say that. I felt that all I'd gone through was worth while. I was so happy.'

She was silent. She thought of the broad, yellow and turbid river on whose banks she had lived so long. The egrets, white and gleaming in the tremulous sunset, flew down the stream in a flock, flew low and swift, and scattered. They were like a ripple of snowy notes, sweet and pure and spring-like, which an unseen hand drew forth, a divine arpeggio, from an unseen harp. They fluttered along between the green banks, wrapped in the shadows of evening, like the happy thoughts of a contented mind.

'Then Joan fell ill. For three weeks we were very anxious. There was no doctor nearer than Kuala Solor and we had to put up with the treatment of a native dispenser. When she grew well again I took her down to the mouth of the river in order to give her a breath of sea air. We stayed there a week. It was the first time I had been separated from Harold since I went away to have Joan. There was a fishing village, on piles, not far from us, but really we were quite alone. I thought a great deal about Harold, so tenderly, and all at once I knew that I loved him. I was so glad when the prahu came to fetch us back, because I wanted to tell him. I thought it would mean a good deal to him. I can't tell you how happy I was. As we rowed up stream the headman told me that Mr Francis had had to go up country to arrest a woman who had murdered her husband. He had been gone a couple of days.

'I was surprised that Harold was not on the landing-stage to meet me; he was always very punctilious about that sort of thing; he used to say that husband and wife should treat one another as politely as they treated acquaintances; and I could not imagine what business had prevented him. I walked up the little hill on which the bungalow stood. The ayah brought Joan behind me. The bungalow was strangely silent. There seemed to be no servants about, and I could not make it out; I wondered if Harold hadn't expected me so soon and was out. I went up the steps. Joan was thirsty and the ayah took her to the servants' quarters to give her something to drink. Harold was not in the sitting-room. I called him, but there was no answer. I was disappointed because I should have liked him to be there. I went into our bedroom. Harold wasn't out after all; he was lying on the bed asleep. I was really very much amused, because he always pretended he never slept in the afternoon. He said it was an unnecessary habit that we white people got into. I went up to the bed softly. I thought I would have a joke with him. I opened the mosquito curtains. He was lying on his back, with nothing on but a sarong, and there was an empty whisky bottle by his side. He was drunk.

'It had begun again. All my struggles for so many years were wasted. My dream was shattered. It was all hopeless. I was seized with rage.'

Millicent's face grew once again darkly red and she clenched the arms of the chair she sat in.

'I took him by the shoulders and shook him with all my might. "You beast," I cried, "you beast." I was so angry I don't know what I did, I don't know what I said. I kept on shaking him. You don't know how loathsome he looked, that large fat man, half naked; he hadn't shaved for days, and his face was bloated and purple. He was breathing heavily. I shouted at him, but he took no notice. I tried to drag him out of bed, but he was too heavy. He lay there like a log. "Open your eyes," I screamed. I shook him again. I hated him. I hated him all the more because for a week I'd loved him with all my heart. He'd let me down. He'd let me down. I wanted to tell him what a filthy beast he was. I could make no impression on him. "You shall open your eyes," I cried. I was determined to make him look at me.'

The widow licked her dry lips. Her breath seemed hurried. She was silent.

'If he was in that state I should have thought it best to have let him go on sleeping,' said Kathleen.

'There was a parang on the wall by the side of the bed. You know how fond Harold was of curios.'

'What's a parang?' said Mrs Skinner.

'Don't be silly, mother,' her husband replied irritably. 'There's one on the wall immediately behind you.'

He pointed to the Malay sword on which for some reason his eyes had been unconsciously resting. Mrs Skinner drew quickly into the corner of the sofa, with a little frightened gesture, as though she had been told that a snake lay curled up beside her.

'Suddenly the blood spurted out from Harold's throat. There was a great red gash right across it.'

'Millicent,' cried Kathleen, springing up and almost leaping towards her, 'what in God's name do you mean?'

Mrs Skinner stood staring at her with wide startled eyes, her mouth open.

'The parang wasn't on the wall any more. It was on the bed. Then Harold opened his eyes. They were just like Joan's.'

'I don't understand,' said Mr Skinner. 'How could he have committed suicide if he was in the state you describe?'

Kathleen took her sister's arm and shook her angrily.

'Millicent, for God's sake explain.'

Millicent released herself.

'The parang was on the wall, I told you. I don't know what happened. There was all the blood, and Harold opened his eyes. He died almost at once. He never spoke, but he gave a sort of gasp.'

At last Mr Skinner found his voice.

'But, you wretched woman, it was murder.'

Millicent, her face mottled with red, gave him such a look of scornful hatred that he shrank back. Mrs Skinner cried out.

'Millicent, you didn't do it, did you?'

Then Millicent did something that made them all feel as though their blood were turned to ice in their veins. She chuckled.

'I don't know who else did,' she said.

'My God,' muttered Mr Skinner.

Kathleen had been standing bolt upright, with her hands to her heart, as though its beating were intolerable.

'And what happened then?' she said.

'I screamed. I went to the window and flung it open. I called for the ayah. She came across the compound with Joan. "Not Joan," I cried. "Don't let her come." She called the cook and told him to take the child. I cried to her to hurry. And when she came I showed her Harold. "The Tuan's killed himself!" I cried. She gave a scream and ran out of the house.

'No one would come near. They were all frightened out of their wits. I wrote a letter to Mr Francis, telling him what had happened and asking him to come at once.'

'How do you mean you told him what had happened?'

'I said, on my return from the mouth of the river, I'd found Harold with his throat cut. You know, in the tropics you have to bury people quickly. I got a Chinese coffin, and the soldiers dug a grave behind the Fort. When Mr Francis came, Harold had been buried for nearly two days. He was only a boy. I could do anything I wanted with him. I told him I'd found the parang in Harold's hand and there was no doubt he'd killed himself in an attack of *delirium tremens*. I showed him the empty bottle. The servants said he'd been drinking hard ever since I left to go to the sea. I told the same story at Kuala Solor. Everyone was very kind to me, and the Government granted me a pension.'

For a little while nobody spoke. At last Mr Skinner gathered himself together.

'I am a member of the legal profession. I'm a solicitor. I have certain duties. We've always had a most respectable practice. You've put me in a monstrous position.'

He fumbled, searching for the phrases that played at hide and seek in his scattered wits. Millicent looked at him with scorn.

'What are you going to do about it?'

'It was murder, that's what it was; do you think I can possible connive at it?'

'Don't talk nonsense, father,' said Kathleen sharply. 'You can't give up your own daughter.'

'You've put me in a monstrous position,' he repeated.

Millicent shrugged her shoulders again.

'You made me tell you. And I've borne it long enough by myself. It was time that all of you bore it too.'

At that moment the door was opened by the maid.

'Davis has brought the car round, sir,' she said.

Kathleen had the presence of mind to say something, and the maid withdrew.

'We'd better be starting,' said Millicent.

'I can't go to the party now,' cried Mrs Skinner,

with horror. 'I'm far too upset. How can we face the Heywoods? And the Bishop will want to be introduced to you.'

Millicent made a gesture of indifference. Her eyes held their ironical expression.

'We must go, mother,' said Kathleen. 'It would look so funny if we stayed away.' She turned on Millicent furiously. 'Oh, I think the whole thing is such frightfully bad form.'

Mrs Skinner looked helplessly at her husband. He went to her and gave her his hand to help her up from the sofa.

'I'm afraid we must go, mother,' he said.

'And me with the ospreys in my toque that Harold gave me with his own hands,' she moaned.

He led her out of the room, Kathleen followed close on their heels, and a step or two behind came Millicent.

'You'll get used to it, you know,' she said quietly. 'At first I thought of it all the time, but now I forget it for two or three days together. It's not as if there was any danger.'

They did not answer. They walked through the hall and out of the front door. The three ladies got into the back of the car and Mr Skinner seated himself beside the driver. They had no self-starter; it was an old car, and Davis went to the bonnet to crank it up. Mr Skinner turned round and looked petulantly at Millicent.

'I ought never to have been told,' he said. 'I think it was most selfish of you.'

Davis took his seat and they drove off to the Canon's garden-party.

P & O

Mrs Hamlyn lay on her long chair and lazily watched the passengers come along the gangway. The ship had reached Singapore in the night, and since dawn had been taking on cargo; the winches had been grinding away all day, but by now her ears were accustomed to their insistent clamour. She had lunched at the Europe, and for lack of anything better to do had driven in a rickshaw through the gay, multitudinous streets of the city. Singapore is the meeting place of many races. The Malays, though natives of the soil, dwell uneasily in towns, and are few; and it is the Chinese, supple, alert and industrious, who throng the streets; the dark-skinned Tamils walk on their silent, naked feet, as though they were but brief sojourners in a strange land, but the Bengalis, sleek and prosperous, are easy in their surroundings, and self-assured; the sly and obsequious Japanese seem busy with pressing and secret affairs; and the English in their topis and white ducks, speeding past in motor-cars or at leisure in their rickshaws, wear a nonchalant and careless air. The rulers of these teeming peoples take their authority with a smiling unconcern. And now, tired and hot, Mrs Hamlyn waited for the ship to set out again on her long journey across the Indian Ocean.

She waved a rather large hand, for she was a big

woman, to the doctor and Mrs Linsell as they came on board. She had been on the ship since she left Yokohama, and had watched with acid amusement the intimacy which had sprung up between the two. Linsell was a naval officer who had been attached to the British Embassy at Tokio, and she had wondered at the indifference with which he took the attentions that the doctor paid his wife. Two men came along the gangway, new passengers, and she amused herself by trying to discover from their demeanour whether they were single or married. Close by, a group of men were sitting together on rattan chairs, planters she judged by their khaki suits and wide-brimmed double felt hats, and they kept the deck-steward busy with their orders. They were talking loudly and laughing, for they had all drunk enough to make them somewhat foolishly hilarious, and they were evidently giving one of their number a send-off; but Mrs Hamlyn could not tell which it was that was to be a fellow-passenger. The time was growing short. More passengers arrived, and then Mr Jephson with dignity strolled up the gangway. He was a consul and was going home on leave. He had joined the ship at Shanghai and had immediately set about making himself agreeable to Mrs Hamlyn. But just then she was disinclined for anything in the nature of a flirtation. She frowned as she thought of the reason which was taking her back to England. She would be spending Christmas at sea, far from anyone who cared two straws about her, and for a moment she felt a little twist at her heartstrings; it vexed her that a subject which she was so resolute to put away from her should so constantly intrude on her unwilling mind.

But a warning bell clanged loudly, and there was a general movement among the men who sat beside her.

'Well, if we don't want to be taken on we'd better be toddling,' said one of them.

They rose and walked towards the gangway. Now that they were all shaking hands she saw who it was that they had come to see the last of. There was nothing very interesting about the man on whom Mrs Hamlyn's eyes rested, but because she had nothing better to do she gave him more than a casual glance. He was a big fellow, well over six feet high, broad and stout; he was dressed in a bedraggled suit of khaki drill and his hat was battered and shabby. His friends left him, but they bandied chaff from the quay, and Mrs Hamlyn noticed that he had a strong Irish brogue; his voice was full, loud and hearty.

Mrs Linsell had gone below and the doctor came and sat down beside Mrs Hamlyn. They told one another their small adventures of the day. The bell sounded again and presently the ship slid away from the wharf. The Irishman waved a last farewell to his friends, and then sauntered towards the chair on which he had left papers and magazines. He nodded to the doctor.

'Is that someone you know?' asked Mrs Hamlyn.

'I was introduced to him at the club before tiffin. His name is Gallagher. He's a planter.'

After the hubbub of the port and the noisy bustle of departure, the silence of the ship was marked and grateful. They steamed slowly past green-clad, rocky cliffs (the P & O anchorage was in a charming and secluded cove), and came out into the main harbour. Ships of all nations lay at anchor, a great multitude, passenger boats, tugs, lighters, tramps; and beyond, behind the break-water, you saw the crowded masts, a bare straight forest, of the native junks. In the soft light of the evening the busy scene was strangely touched with mystery, and you felt that all those vessels, their activity for the moment suspended, waited for some event of a peculiar significance.

Mrs Hamlyn was a bad sleeper and when the dawn broke she was in the habit of going on deck. It rested her troubled heart to watch the last faint stars fade before the encroaching day, and at that early hour the glassy sea had often an immobility which seemed to make all earthly sorrows of little consequence. The light was wan, and there was a pleasant shiver in the air. But next morning, when she went to the end of the promenade deck, she found that someone was up before her. It was Mr Gallagher. He was watching the low coast of Sumatra which the sunrise like a magician seemed to call forth from the dark sea. She was startled and a little vexed, but before she could turn away he had seen her and nodded.

'Up early,' he said. 'Have a cigarette?'

He was in pyjamas and slippers. He took his case from his coat pocket and handed it to her. She hesitated. She had on nothing but a dressing-gown and a little lace cap which she had put over her tousled hair, and she knew that she must look a sight; but she had her reasons for scourging her soul.

'I suppose a woman of forty has no right to mind how she looks,' she smiled, as though he must know what vain thoughts occupied her. She took the cigarette. 'But you're up early too.'

'I'm a planter. I've had to get up at five in the morning for so many years that I don't know how I'm going to get out of the habit.'

'You'll not find it will make you very popular at home.'

She saw his face better now that it was not shadowed by a hat. It was agreeable without being handsome. He was of course much too fat, and his features which must have been good enough when he was a young man were thickened. His skin was red and bloated. But his dark eyes were merry; and though he could not have been less than five-and-forty his hair was black and thick. He gave you an impression of great strength. He was a heavy, ungraceful, commonplace man, and Mrs Hamlyn, except for the promiscuity of ship-board, would never have thought it worth while to talk to him.

'Are you going home on leave?' she hazarded.

'No, I'm going home for good.'

His black eyes twinkled. He was of a communicative turn, and before it was time for Mrs Hamlyn to go below in order to have her bath he had told her a good deal about himself. He had been in the Federated Malay States for twenty-five years, and for the last ten had managed an estate in Selantan. It was a hundred miles from anything that could be described as civilization and the life had been lonely; but he had made money; during the rubber boom he had done very well, and with an astuteness which was unexpected in a man who looked so happy-go-lucky he had invested his savings in Government stock. Now that the slump had come he was prepared to retire.

'What part of Ireland do you come from?' asked Mrs Hamlyn.

'Galway.'

Mrs Hamlyn had once motored through Ireland and she had a vague recollection of a sad and moody town with great stone warehouses, deserted and crumbling, which faced the melancholy sea. She had a sensation of greenness and of soft rain, of silence and of resignation. Was it here that Mr Gallagher meant to spend the rest of his life? He spoke of it with boyish eagerness. The thought of his vitality in that grey world of shadows was so incongruous that Mrs Hamlyn was intrigued.

'Does your family live there?' she asked.

'I've got no family. My mother and father are dead. So far as I know I haven't a relation in the world.'

He had made all his plans, he had been making them for twenty-five years, and he was pleased to have someone to talk to of all these things that he had been obliged for so long only to talk to himself about. He meant to buy a house and he would keep a motor-car. He was going to breed horses. He didn't much care about shooting; he had shot a lot of big game during his first years in the FMS; but now he had lost his zest. He didn't see why the beasts of the jungle should be killed; he had lived in the jungle so long. But he could hunt.

'Do you think I'm too heavy?' he asked.

Mrs Hamlyn, smiling, looked him up and down with appraising eyes.

'You must weigh a ton,' she said.

He laughed. The Irish horses were the best in the world, and he'd always kept pretty fit. You had a devil of a lot of walking exercise on a rubber estate and he'd played a good deal of tennis. He'd soon get thin in Ireland. Then he'd marry. Mrs Hamlyn looked silently at the sea coloured now with the tenderness of the sunrise. She sighed.

'Was it easy to drag up all your roots? Is there no one you regret leaving behind? I should have thought after so many years, however much you'd looked forward to going home, when the time came at last to go it must have given you a pang.'

'I was glad to get out. I was fed up. I never want to see the country again or anyone in it.'

One or two early passengers now began to walk round the deck and Mrs Hamlyn, remembering that she was scantily clad, went below.

During the next day or two she saw little of Mr Gallagher who passed his time in the smoking-room. Owing to a strike the ship was not touching at Colombo and the passengers settled down to a pleasant voyage across the Indian Ocean. They played deck-games, they gossiped about one another, they flirted. The approach of Christmas gave them an occupation, for someone had suggested that there should be a fancy-dress dance on Christmas day, and the ladies set about making their dresses. A meeting was held of the first-class passengers to decide whether the second-class passengers should be invited, and notwithstanding the heat the discussion was animated. The ladies said that the second-class passengers would only feel ill-at-ease. On Christmas day it was to be expected that they would drink more than was good for them and unpleasantness might ensue. Everyone who spoke insisted that there was in his (or her) mind no idea of class distinction, no one would be so snobbish as to think there was any difference between first- and second-class passengers as far as that went, but it would really be kinder to the second-class passengers not to put them in a false position. They would enjoy themselves much more if they had a party of their own in the second-class cabin. On the other hand, no one wanted to hurt their feelings, and of course one had to be more democratic nowadays (this was in reply to the wife of a missionary in China who said she had travelled on the P & O for thirty-five years and she had never heard of the second-class passengers being invited to a dance in the first-class saloon) and even though they wouldn't enjoy it, they might like to come. Mr Gallagher, dragged unwillingly from the card-table, because it had been foreseen that the voting would be close, was asked his opinion by the consul. He was taking home in the second-class a man who had been employed on his estate. He raised his massive bulk from the couch on which he sat.

'As far as I'm concerned I've only got this to say: I've got the man who was looking after our engines with me. He's a rattling good fellow, and he's just as fit to come to your party as I am. But he won't come because I'm going to make him so drunk on Christmas day that by six o'clock he'll be fit for nothing but to be put to bed.'

Mr Jephson, the consul, gave a distorted smile. On account of his official position, he had been chosen to preside at the meeting and he wished the matter to be taken seriously. He was a man who often said that if a thing was worth doing it was worth doing well.

'I gather from your observations,' he said, not without acidity, 'that the question before the meeting does not seem to you of great importance.'

'I don't think it matters a tinker's curse,' said Gallagher, with twinkling eyes.

Mrs Hamlyn laughed. The scheme was at last devised to invite the second-class passengers, but to go to the captain privily and point out to him the advisability of withholding his consent to their coming into the first-class saloon. It was on the evening of the day on which this happened that Mrs Hamlyn, having dressed for dinner, came on deck at the same time as Mr Gallagher.

'Just in time for a cocktail, Mrs Hamlyn,' he said jovially.

'I'd like one. To tell you the truth I need cheering up.'

'Why?' he smiled.

Mrs Hamlyn thought his smile attractive, but she did not want to answer his question.

'I told you the other morning,' she answered cheerfully. 'I'm forty.'

'I never met a women who insisted on the fact so much.'

They went into the lounge and the Irishman ordered a dry Martini for her and a gin pahit for himself. He had lived too long in the East to drink anything else.

'You've got hiccups,' said Mrs Hamlyn.

'Yes, I've had them all the afternoon,' he answered carelessly. 'It's rather funny, they came on just as we got out of sight of land.'

'I daresay they'll pass off after dinner.'

They drank, the second bell rang, and they went into the dining-saloon.

'You don't play bridge?' he said, as they parted. 'No.'

Mrs Hamlyn did not notice that she saw nothing of Gallagher for two or three days. She was occupied with her own thoughts. They crowded upon her when she was sewing; they came between her and the novel with which she sought to cheat their insistence. She had hoped that as the ship took her further away from the scene of her unhappiness, the torment of her mind would be eased; but contrariwise, each day that brought her nearer England increased her distress. She looked forward with dismay to the bleak emptiness of the life that awaited her; and then, turning her exhausted wits from a prospect that made her flinch, she considered, as she had done she knew not how many times before, the situation from which she had fled.

She had been married for twenty years. It was a long time and of course she could not expect her husband to be still madly in love with her; she was not madly in love with him; but they were good friends and they understood one another. Their marriage, as marriages go, might very well have been looked upon as a success. Suddenly she discovered that he had fallen in love. She would not have objected to a flirtation, he had had those before, and she had chaffed him about them; he had not minded that, it somewhat flattered him, and they had laughed together at an inclination which was neither deep nor serious. But this was different. He was in love as passionately as a boy of eighteen. He was fifty-two. It was ridiculous. It was indecent. And he loved without sense or prudence: by the time the hideous fact was forced upon her all the foreigners in Yokohama knew it. After the first shock of astonished anger, for he was the last man from whom such a folly might have been expected, she tried to persuade herself that she could have understood, and so have forgiven, if he had fallen in love with a girl. Middle-aged men often make fools of themselves with flappers, and after twenty years in the Far East she knew that the fifties were the dangerous age for men. But he had no excuse. He was in love with a woman eight years older than herself. It was grotesque, and it made her, his wife, perfectly absurd. Dorothy Lacom was hard on fifty. He had known her for eighteen years, for Lacom, like her own husband, was a silk merchant in Yokohama. Year in, year out, they had seen one another three or four times a week, and once, when they happened to be in England together, had shared a house at the sea-side. But nothing! Not till a year ago had there been anything between them but a chaffing friendship. It was incredible. Of course Dorothy was a handsome woman; she had a good figure, overdeveloped, perhaps, but still comely; with bold black eyes and a red mouth and lovely hair; but all that she had had years before. She was forty-eight. Forty-eight!

Mrs Hamlyn tackled her husband at once. At first he swore that there was not one word of truth in what she accused him of, but she had her proofs; he grew sulky; and at last he admitted what he could no longer deny. Then he said an astonishing thing.

'Why should you care?' he asked.

It maddened her. She answered him with angry scorn. She was voluble, finding in the bitterness of her heart wounding things to say. He listened to her quietly.

'I've not been such a bad husband to you for the twenty years we've been married. For a long time now we've only been friends. I have a great affection for you, and this hasn't altered it in the very smallest degree. I'm giving Dorothy nothing that I take away from you.'

'But what have you to complain of in me?'

'Nothing. No man could want a better wife.'

'How can you say that when you have the heart to treat me so cruelly?'

'I don't want to be cruel to you. I can't help myself.'

'But what on earth made you fall in love with her?'

'How can I tell? You didn't think I wanted to, do you?'

'Couldn't you have resisted?'

'I tried. I think we both tried.'

'You talk as though you were twenty. Why, you're both middle-aged people. She's eight years older than I am. It makes me look such a perfect fool.'

He did not answer. She did not know what emotions seethed in her heart. Was it jealousy that seemed to clutch at her throat, anger, or was it merely wounded pride?

'I'm not going to let it go on. If only you and she were concerned I would divorce you, but there's her husband, and then there are the children. Good heavens, does it occur to you that if they were girls instead of boys she might be a grandmother by now?'

'Easily.'

'What a mercy that we have no children!'

He put out an affectionate hand as though to caress her, but she drew back with horror.

'You've made me the laughing stock of all my friends. For all our sakes I'm willing to hold my tongue, but only on the condition that everything stops now, at once, and for ever.'

He looked down and played reflectively with a Japanese knick-knack that was on the table.

'I'll tell Dorothy what you say,' he replied at last.

She gave him a little bow, silently, and walked past him out of the room. She was too angry to observe that she was somewhat melodramatic.

She waited for him to tell her the result of his interview with Dorothy Lacom, but he made no further reference to the scene. He was quiet, polite and silent; and at last she was obliged to ask him.

'Have you forgotten what I said to you the other day?' she inquired, frigidly.

'No. I talked to Dorothy. She wishes me to tell you that she is desperately sorry that she has caused you so much pain. She would like to come and see you, but she is afraid you wouldn't like it.'

'What decision have you come to?'

He hesitated. He was very grave, but his voice trembled a little.

'I'm afraid there's no use in our making a promise we shouldn't be able to keep.'

'That settles it then,' she answered.

'I think I should tell you that if you brought an action for divorce we should have to contest it. You would find it impossible to get the necessary evidence and you would lose your case.'

'I wasn't thinking of doing that. I shall go back to England and consult a lawyer. Nowadays these things can be managed fairly easily, and I shall throw myself on your generosity. I daresay you will enable me to get my freedom without bringing Dorothy Lacom into the matter.'

He sighed.

'It's an awful muddle, isn't it? I don't want you to divorce me, but of course I'll do anything I can to meet your wishes.'

'What on earth do you expect me to do?' she cried, her anger rising again. 'Do you expect me to sit still and be made a damned fool of?'

'I'm awfully sorry to put you in a humiliating position.' He looked at her with harassed eyes. 'I'm quite sure we didn't want to fall in love with one another. We're both of us very conscious of our age. Dorothy, as you say, is old enough to be a grandmother and I'm a baldish, stoutish gentleman of fifty-two. When you fall in love at twenty you think your love will last for ever, but at fifty you know so much, about life and about love, and you know that it will last so short a time.' His voice was low and rueful. It was as though before his mind's eye he saw the sadness of autumn and the leaves falling from the trees. He looked at her gravely. 'And at that age you can't afford to throw away the chance of happiness which a freakish destiny has given you. In five years it will certainly be over, and perhaps in six months. Life is rather drab and grey, and happiness is so rare. We shall be dead so long.'

It gave Mrs Hamlyn a bitter sensation of pain to hear her husband, a matter-of-fact and practical man, speak in a strain which was quite new to her. He had gained on a sudden a wistful and tragic personality of which she knew nothing. The twenty years during which they had lived together had no power over him and she was helpless in face of his determination. She could do nothing but go, and now, resentfully determined to get the divorce with which she had threatened him, she was on her way to England.

The smooth sea, upon which the sun beat down so that it shone like a sheet of glass, was as empty and hostile as life in which there was no place for her. For three days no other craft had broken in upon the solitariness of that expanse. Now and again its even surface was scattered for the twinkling of an eye by the scurry of flying fish. The heat was so great that even the most energetic of passengers had given up deck-games, and now (it was after luncheon) such as were not resting in their cabins lay about on chairs. Linsell strolled towards her and sat down.

'Where's Mrs Linsell?' asked Mrs Hamlyn.

'Oh, I don't know. She's about somewhere.'

His indifference exasperated her. Was it possible that he did not see that his wife and the surgeon were falling in love with one another? Yet, not so very long ago, he must have cared. Their marriage had been romantic. They had become engaged when Mrs Linsell was still at school and he little more than a boy. They must have been a charming, handsome pair, and their youth and their mutual love must have been touching. And now, after so short a time, they were tired of one another. It was heart-breaking. What had her husband said?

'I suppose you're going to live in London when you get home?' asked Linsell lazily, for something to say.

'I suppose so,' said Mrs Hamlyn.

It was hard to reconcile herself to the fact that she had nowhere to go, and where she lived mattered not in the least to anyone alive. Some association of ideas made her think of Gallagher. She envied the eagerness with which he was returning to his native land, and she was touched, and at the same time amused, when she remembered the exuberant imagination he showed in describing the house he meant to live in and the wife he meant to marry. Her friends in Yokohama, apprised in confidence of her determination to divorce her husband, had assured her that she would marry again. She did not much want to enter a second time upon a state which had once so disappointed her, and besides, most men would think twice before they suggested marriage to a woman of forty. Mr Gallagher wanted a buxom young person.

'Where is Mr Gallagher?' she asked the submissive Linsell. 'I haven't seen him for the last day or two.'

'Didn't you know? He's ill.'

'Poor thing. What's the matter with him?'

'He's got hiccups.'

Mrs Hamlyn laughed.

'Hiccups don't make one ill, do they?'

'The surgeon is rather worried. He's tried all sorts of things, but he can't stop them.'

'How very odd.'

She thought no more about it, but next morning, chancing upon the surgeon, she asked him how Mr Gallagher was. She was surprised to see his boyish, cheerful face darken and grow perplexed.

'I'm afraid he's very bad, poor chap.'

'With hiccups?' she cried in amazement.

It was a disorder that really it was impossible to take seriously.

'You see, he can't keep any food down. He can't sleep. He's fearfully exhausted. I've tried everything I can think of.' He hesitated. 'Unless I can stop them soon – I don't quite know what'll happen.'

Mrs Hamlyn was startled.

'But he's so strong. He seemed so full of vitality.'

'I wish you could see him now.'

'Would he like me to go and see him?'

'Come along.'

Gallagher had been moved from his cabin into the ship's hospital, and as they approached it they heard a loud hiccup. The sound, perhaps owing to its connection with insobriety, had in it something ludicrous. But Gallagher's appearance gave Mrs Hamlyn a shock. He had lost flesh and the skin hung about his neck in loose folds; under the sunburn his face was pale. His eyes, before, full of fun and laughter, were haggard and tormented. His great body was shaken incessantly by the hiccups and now there was nothing ludicrous in the sound; to Mrs Hamlyn, for no reason that she knew, it seemed strangely terrifying. He smiled when she came in.

'I'm sorry to see you like this,' she said.

'I shan't die of it, you know,' he gasped. 'I shall reach the green shores of Erin all right.'

There was a man sitting beside him and he rose as they entered.

'This is Mr Pryce,' said the surgeon. 'He was in charge of the machinery on Mr Gallagher's estate.'

Mrs Hamlyn nodded. This was the second-class passenger to whom Gallagher had referred when they had discussed the part which was to be given on Christmas day. He was a very small man, but sturdy, with a pleasantly impudent countenance and an air of self-assurance.

'Are you glad to be going home?' asked Mrs Hamlyn.

'You bet I am, lady,' he answered.

The intonation of the few words told Mrs Hamlyn that he was a cockney and, recognizing the cheerful, sensible, good-humoured and careless type, her heart warmed to him.

'You're not Irish?' she smiled.

'Not me, miss. London's my 'ome and I shan't be sorry to see it again, I can tell you.'

Mrs Hamlyn never thought it offensive to be called miss.

'Well, sir, I'll be getting along,' he said to Gallagher, with the beginning of a gesture as though he were going to touch a cap which he hadn't got on.

Mrs Hamlyn asked the sick man whether she could do anything for him and in a minute or two left him with the doctor. The little cockney was waiting outside the door.

'Can I speak to you a minute or two, miss?' he asked.

'Of course.'

The hospital cabin was aft and they stood, leaning against the rail, and looked down on the well-deck where lascars and stewards off duty were lounging about on the covered hatches.

'I don't know exactly 'ow to begin,' said Pryce, uncertainly, a serious look strangely changing his lively, puckered face. 'I've been with Mr Gallagher for four years now and a better gentleman you wouldn't find in a week of Sundays.'

He hesitated again.

'I don't like it and that's the truth.'

'What don't you like?'

'Well, if you ask me 'e's for it, and the doctor

don't know it. I told 'im, but 'e won't listen to a word I say.'

'You mustn't be too depressed, Mr Pryce. Of course the doctor's young, but I think he's quite clever, and people don't die of hiccups, you know. I'm sure Mr Gallagher will be all right in a day or two.'

'You know when it come on? Just as we was out of sight of land. She said 'e'd never see 'is 'ome.'

Mrs Hamlyn turned and faced him. She stood a good three inches taller than he.

'What do you mean?'

'My belief is, it's a spell been put on 'im, if you understand what I mean. Medicine's going to do 'im no good. You don't know them Malay women like what I do.'

For a moment Mrs Hamlyn was startled, and because she was startled she shrugged her shoulders and laughed.

'Oh, Mr Pryce, that's nonsense.'

'That's what the doctor said when I told 'im. But you mark my words, 'e'll die before we see land again.'

The man was so serious that Mrs Hamlyn, vaguely uneasy, was against her will impressed.

'Why should anyone cast a spell on Mr Gallagher?' she asked.

'Well, it's a bit awkward speakin' of it to a lady.'

'Please tell me.'

Pryce was so embarrassed that at another time Mrs Hamlyn would have had difficulty in concealing her amusement.

'Mr Gallagher's lived a long time up-country, if you understand what I mean, and of course it's lonely, and you know what men are, miss.'

'I've been married for twenty years,' she replied, smiling.

'I beg your pardon, ma'am. The fact is he had a Malay girl living with him. I don't know 'ow long, ten or twelve years, I think. Well, when 'e made up 'is mind to come 'ome for good she didn't say nothing. She just sat there. He thought she'd carry on no end, but she didn't. Of course 'e provided for 'er all right, 'e gave 'er a little 'ouse for herself, an' 'e fixed it up so as so much should be paid 'er every month. 'E wasn't mean, I will say that for 'im, an' she knew all along as 'e'd be going some time. She didn't cry or anything. When 'e packed up all 'is things and sent them off, she just sat there an' watched 'em go. And when 'e sold 'is furniture to the Chinks she never said a word. He'd give 'er all she wanted. And when it was time for 'im to go so as to catch the boat she just kep' on sitting, on the steps of the bungalow, you know, and she just looked an' said nothing. He wanted to say good-bye to 'er, same as anyone would, an', would you believe it? she never even moved. "Aren't you going to say good-bye to me," he says. A rare funny look come over 'er face. And do you know what she says? "You go," she says; they 'ave a funny way of talking, them natives, not like we 'ave, "you go," she says, "but I tell you that you will never come to your own country. When the land sinks into the sea, death will come upon you, an' before them as goes with you sees the land again, death will have took you." It gave me quite a turn.'

'What did Mr Gallagher say?' asked Mrs Hamlyn.

'Oh, well, you know what 'e is. He just laughed. "Always merry and bright," 'e says and 'e jumps into the motor, an' off we go.'

Mrs Hamlyn saw the bright and sunny road that ran through the rubber estates, with their trim green trees, carefully spaced, and their silence, and then wound its way up hill and down through the tangled jungle. The car raced on, driven by a reckless Malay, with its white passengers, past Malay houses that stood away from the road among the coconut trees, sequestered and taciturn, and through busy villages where the market-place was crowded with dark-skinned little people in gay sarongs. Then towards evening it reached the trim, modern town, with its clubs and its golf links, its well-ordered resthouse, its white people, and its railway station, from which the two men could take the train to Singapore. And the woman sat on the steps of the bungalow, empty till the new manager moved in, and watched the road down which the car had panted, watched the car as it sped on, and watched till at last it was lost in the shadow of the night.

'What was she like?' Mrs Hamlyn asked.

'Oh, well, to my way of thinking them Malay women are all very much alike, you know,' Pryce answered. 'Of course she wasn't so young any more, and you know what they are, them natives, they run to fat something terrible.'

'Fat?'

The thought, absurdly enough, filled Mrs Hamlyn with dismay.

'Mr Gallagher was always one to do himself well, if you understand what I mean.'

The idea of corpulence at once brought Mrs Hamlyn back to common sense. She was impatient with herself because for an instant she had seemed to accept the little cockney's suggestion.

'It's perfectly absurd, Mr Pryce. Fat women can't throw spells on people at a distance of a thousand miles. In fact life is very difficult for a fat woman any way.'

'You can laugh, miss, but unless something's done, you mark my words, the governor's for it. And medicine ain't goin' to save him, not white man's medicine.'

'Pull yourself together, Mr Pryce. This fat lady had no particular grievance against Mr Gallagher. As these things are done in the East he seems to have treated her very well. Why should she wish him any harm?'

'We don't know 'ow they look at things. Why a man can live there for twenty years with one of them natives, and d'you think 'e knows what's goin' on in that black heart of hers? Not 'im!'

She could not smile at his melodramatic language, for his intensity was impressive. And she knew, if anyone did, that the hearts of men, whether their skins are yellow or white or brown, are incalculable.

'But even if she felt angry with him, even if she hated him and wanted to kill him, what could she do?' It was strange that Mrs Hamlyn with her questions was trying now, unconciously, to reassure herself. 'There's no poison that could start working after six or seven days.'

'I never said it was poison.'

'I'm sorry, Mr Pryce,' she smiled, 'but I'm not going to believe in a magic spell, you know.'

'You've lived in the East.'

'Off and on for twenty years.'

'Well, if you can say what they can do and what they can't, it's more than I can.' He clenched his

fist and beat it on the rail with sudden, angry violence. 'I'm fed up with the bloody country. It's got
on my nerves, that's what it is. We're no match for
them, us white men, and that's a fact. If you'll
excuse me I think I'll go an' 'ave a tiddley. I've got
the jumps.'

He nodded abruptly and left her. Mrs Hamlyn
watched him, a sturdy, shuffling little man in
shabby khaki, slither down the companion into the
waist of the ship, walk across it with bent head, and
disappear into the second-class saloon. She did not
know why he left with her a vague uneasiness. She
could not get out of her mind that picture of a stout
woman, no longer young, in a sarong, a coloured
jacket and gold ornaments, who sat on the steps of a
bungalow looking at an empty road. Her heavy face
was painted, but in her large, tearless eyes there
was no expression. The men who drove in the car
were like schoolboys going home for the holidays.
Gallagher gave a sigh of relief. In the early morning, under the bright sky, his spirits bubbled. The
future was like a sunny road that wandered through
a wide-flung, wooded plain.

Later in the day Mrs Hamlyn asked the doctor
how his patient did. The doctor shook his head.

'I'm done. I'm at the end of my tether.' He
frowned unhappily. 'It's rotten luck, striking a case
like this. It would be bad enough at home, but on
board ship . . .'

He was an Edinburghman, but recently qualified, and he was taking this voyage as a holiday
before settling down to practice. He felt himself
aggrieved. He wanted to have a good time and,
faced with this mysterious illness, he was worried
to death. Of course he was inexperienced, but he

was doing everything that could be done and it exasperated him to suspect that the passengers thought him an ignorant fool.

'Have you heard what Mr Pryce thinks?' asked Mrs Hamlyn.

'I never heard such rot. I told the captain and he's right up in the air. He doesn't want it talked about. He thinks it'll upset the passengers.'

'I'll be as silent as the grave.'

The surgeon looked at her sharply.

'Of course you don't believe that there can be any truth in nonsense of that sort?' he asked.

'Of course not.' She looked out at the sea which shone, blue and oily and still, all around them. 'I've lived in the East a long time,' she added. 'Strange things happen there.'

'This is getting on my nerves,' said the doctor.

Near them two little Japanese gentlemen were playing deck quoits. They were trim and neat in their tennis shirts, white trousers and buckram shoes. They looked very European, they even called the score to one another in English, and yet somehow to look at them filled Mrs Hamlyn at that moment with a vague disquiet. Because they seemed to wear so easily a disguise there was about them something sinister. Her nerves too were on edge.

And presently, no one quite knew how, the notion spread through the ship that Gallagher was bewitched. While the ladies sat about on their deck-chairs, stitching away at the costumes they were making for the fancy-dress party on Christmas day, they gossiped about it in undertones, and the men in the smoking-room talked of it over their cock-tails. A good many of the passengers had lived long in the East and from the recesses of their memory they produced strange and inexplicable stories. Of course it was absurd to think seriously that Gallagher was suffering from a malignant spell, such things were impossible, and yet this and that was a fact and no one had been able to explain it. The doctor had to confess that he could suggest no cause for Gallagher's condition, he was able to give a physiological explanation, but why these terrible spasms should have suddenly assailed him he did not say. Feeling vaguely to blame, he tried to defend himself.

'Why, it's the sort of case you might never come across in the whole of your practice,' he said. 'It's rotten luck.'

He was in wireless communication with passing ships, and suggestions for treatment came from here and there.

'I've tried everything they tell me,' he said irritably. 'The doctor of the Japanese boat advised adrenalin. How the devil does he expect me to have adrenalin in the middle of the Indian Ocean?'

There was something impressive in the thought of this ship speeding through a deserted sea, while to her from all parts came unseen messages. She seemed at that moment strangely alone and yet the centre of the world. In the lazaret the sick man, shaken by the cruel spasms, gasped for life. Then the passengers became conscious that the ship's course was altered, and they heard that the captain had made up his mind to put in at Aden. Gallagher was to be landed there and taken to the hospital, where he could have attention which on board was impossible. The chief engineer received orders to force his engines. The ship was an old one and she throbbed with the greater effort. The passengers had grown used to the sound and feel of her engines, and now the greater vibration shook their nerves with a new sensation. It would not pass into each one's unconsciousness, but beat on their sensibilities so that each felt a personal concern. And still the wide sea was empty of traffic, so that they seemed to traverse an empty world. And now the uneasiness which had descended upon the ship, but which no one had been willing to acknowledge, became a definite malaise. The passengers grew irritable, and people quarrelled over trifles which at another time would have seemed insignificant. Mr Jephson made his hackneyed jokes, but no one any longer repaid him with a smile. The Linsells had an altercation, and Mrs Linsell was heard late at night walking round the deck with her husband, and uttering in a low, tense voice a stream of vehement reproaches. There was a violent scene in the smoking-room one night over a game of bridge, and the reconciliation which followed it was attended with general intoxication. People talked little of Gallagher, but he was seldom absent from their thoughts. They examined the route map. The doctor said now that Gallagher could not live more than three or four days, and they discussed acrimoniously what was the shortest time in which Aden could be reached. What happened to him after he was landed was no affair of theirs; they did not want him to die on board.

Mrs Hamlyn saw Gallagher every day. With the suddenness with which after tropical rain in the spring you seem to see the herbage grow before your very eyes, she saw him go to pieces. Already his skin hung loosely on his bones, and his double chin was like the wrinkled wattle of a turkey-cock. His cheeks were sunken. You saw now how large his frame was, and through the sheet under which he lay his bony structure was like the skeleton of a prehistoric giant. For the most part he lay with his eyes closed, torpid with morphia, but shaken still with terrible spasms, and when now and again he opened his eyes they were preternaturally large; they looked at you vaguely, perplexed and troubled, from the depths of their bony sockets. But when, emerging from his stupor, he recognized Mrs Hamlyn, he forced a gallant smile to his lips.

'How are you, Mr Gallagher?' she said.

'Getting along, getting along. I shall be all right when we get out of his confounded heat. Lord, how I look forward to a dip in the Atlantic. I'd give anything for a good long swim. I want to feel the cold grey sea of Galway beating against my chest.'

Then the hiccup shook him from the crown of his head to the sole of his foot. Mr Pryce and the stewardess shared the care of him. The little cockney's face wore no longer its look of impudent gaiety, but instead was sullen.

'The captain sent for me yesterday,' he told Mrs Hamlyn when they were alone. 'He gave me a rare talking to.'

'What about?'

'He said 'e wouldn't 'ave all this hoodoo stuff. He said it was frightening the passengers and I'd better keep a watch on me tongue or I'd 'ave 'im to reckon with. It's not my doing. I never said a word except to you and the doctor.'

'It's all over the ship.'

'I know it is. D'you think it's only me that's saying it? All them Lascars and the Chinese, they all know what's the matter with him. You don't think you can teach them much, do you? They know it ain't a natural illness.'

Mrs Hamlyn was silent. She knew through the amahs of some of the passengers that there was no one on the ship, except the whites, who doubted that the woman whom Gallagher had left in distant Selantan was killing him with her magic. All were convinced that as they sighted the barren rocks of Arabia his soul would be parted from his body.

'The captain says if he hears of me trying any hanky-panky he'll confine me to my cabin for the rest of the voyage,' said Pryce, suddenly, a surly frown on his puckered face.

'What do you mean by hanky-panky?'

He looked at her for a moment fiercely as though she too were an object of the anger he felt against the captain.

'The doctor's tried every damned thing he knows, and he's wirelessed all over the place, and what good 'as 'e done? Tell me that. Can't 'e see the man's dying? There's only one way to save him now.'

'What do you mean?'

'It's magic what's killing 'im, and it's only magic what'll save him. Oh, don't you say it can't be done. I've seen it with me own eyes.' His voice rose, irritable and shrill. 'I've seen a man dragged from the jaws of death, as you might say, when they got in a *pawang*, what we call a witch-doctor, an' 'e did 'is little tricks. I seen it with me own eyes, I tell you.'

Mrs Hamlyn did not speak. Pryce gave her a searching look.

'One of them Lascars on board, he's a witch-doctor, same as the *pawang* that we 'ave in the FMS. An' 'e says he'll do it. Only he must 'ave a live animal. A cock would do.'

'What do you want a live animal for?' Mrs Hamlyn asked, frowning a little.

The cockney looked at her with quick suspicion.

'If you take my advice you won't know anything about it. But I tell you what, I'm going to leave no stone unturned to save my governor. An' if the captain 'ears of it and shuts me up in me cabin well, let 'im.'

At that moment Mrs Linsell came up and Pryce with his quaint gesture of salute left them. Mrs Linsell wanted Mrs Hamlyn to fit the dress she had been making herself for the fancy-dress ball, and on the way down to the cabin she spoke to her anxiously of the possibility that Mr Gallagher might die on Christmas day. They could not possibly have the dance if he did. She had told the doctor that she would never speak to him again if this happened, and the doctor had promised her faithfully that he would keep the man alive over Christmas day somehow.

'It would be nice for him, too,' said Mrs Linsell.

'For whom?' asked Mrs Hamlyn.

'For poor Mr Gallagher. Naturally no one likes to die on Christmas day. Do they?'

'I don't really know,' said Mrs Hamlyn.

That night, after she had been asleep a little while, she awoke weeping. It dismayed her that she should cry in her sleep. It was as though then the weakness of the flesh mastered her, and, her will broken, she were defenceless against a natural sorrow. She turned over in her mind, as so often

before, the details of the disaster which had so pro-
foundly affected her; she repeated the conversations with her husband, wishing she had said this
and blaming herself because she had said the other.
She wished with all her heart that she had remained
in comfortable ignorance of her husband's infatuation, and asked herself whether she would not have
been wiser to pocket her pride and shut her eyes to
the unwelcome truth. She was a woman of the
world, and she knew too well how much more she
lost in separating herself from her husband than his
love; she lost the settled establishment and the
assured position, the ample means and the support
of a recognized background. She had known of
many separated wives, living equivocally on small-
ish incomes, and knew how quickly their friends
found them tiresome. And she was lonely. She was
as lonely as the ship that throbbed her hasting way
through an unpeopled sea, and lonely as the friendless man who lay dying in the ship's lazaret. Mrs
Hamlyn knew that her thoughts had got the better
of her now and that she would not easily sleep
again. It was very hot in her cabin. She looked at
the time; it was between four and half-past; she
must pass two mortal hours before broke the
reassuring day.

She slipped into a kimono and went on deck.
The night was sombre and although the sky was
unclouded no stars were visible. Panting and shaking, the old ship under full steam lumbered
through the darkness. The silence was uncanny.
Mrs Hamlyn with bare feet groped her way slowly
along the deserted deck. It was so black that she
could see nothing. She came to the end of the
promenade deck and leaned against the rail. Sud-

denly she started and her attention was fixed, for on
the lower deck she caught a fitful glow. She leaned
forward cautiously. It was a little fire, and she saw
only the glow because the naked backs of men,
crouched round, hid the flame. At the edge of the
circle she divined, rather than saw, a stocky figure
in pyjamas. The rest were natives, but this was a
European. It must be Pryce and she guessed
immediately that some dark ceremony of exorcism
was in progress. Straining her ears she heard a low
voice muttering a string of secret words. She began
to tremble. She was aware that they were too intent
upon their business to think anyone was
watching them, but she dared not move. Suddenly,
rending the sultry silence of the night like a piece of
silk violently torn in two, came the crowing of a
cock. Mrs Hamlyn almost shrieked. Mrs Pryce was
trying to save the life of his friend and master by a
sacrifice to the strange gods of the East. The voice
went on, low and insistent. Then in the dark circle
there was a movement, something was happening,
she knew not what; there was a cluck-cluck from the
cock, angry and frightened, and then a strange,
indescribable sound; the magician was cutting the
cock's throat; then silence; there were vague doings
that she could not follow, and in a little while it
looked as though someone were stamping out the
fire. The figures she had dimly seen were dissolved
in the night and all once more was still. She heard
again the regular throbbing of the engines.

Mrs Hamlyn stood still for a little while,
strangely shaken, and then walked slowly along the
deck. She found a chair and lay down in it. She was
trembling still. She could only guess what had happened. She did not know how long she lay there,

but at last she felt that the dawn was approaching. It was not yet day, and it was no longer night. Against the darkness of the sky she could now see the ship's rail. Then she saw a figure come towards her. It was a man in pyjamas.

'Who's that?' she cried nervously.

'Only the doctor,' came a friendly voice.

'Oh! What are you doing here at this time of night?'

'I've been with Gallagher.' He sat down beside her and lit a cigarette. 'I've given him a good strong hypodermic and he's quiet now.'

'Has he been very ill?'

'I thought he was going to pass out. I was watching him, and suddenly he started up on his bed and began to talk Malay. Of course I couldn't understand a thing. He kept on saying one word over and over again.'

'Perhaps it was a name, a woman's name.'

'He wanted to get out of bed. He's a damned powerful man even now. By George, I had a struggle with him. I was afraid he'd throw himself overboard. He seemed to think someone was calling him.'

'When was that?' asked Mrs Hamlyn, slowly.

'Between four and half-past. Why?'

'Nothing.'

She shuddered.

Later in the morning when the ship's life was set upon its daily round, Mrs Hamlyn passed Pryce on the deck, but he gave her a brief greeting and walked on with quickly averted gaze. He looked tired and overwrought. Mrs Hamlyn thought again of that fat woman, with golden ornaments in her thick, black hair, who sat on the steps of the deserted bungalow and looked at the road which ran through the trim lines of the rubber trees.

It was fearfully hot. She knew now why the night had been so dark. The sky was no longer blue, but a dead, level white; its surface was too even to give the effect of cloud; it was as though in the upper air the heat hung like a pall. There was no breeze and the sea, as colourless as the sky, was smooth and shining like the dye in a dyer's vat. The passengers were listless; when they walked round the deck they panted, and beads of sweat broke out on their foreheads. They spoke in undertones. Something uncanny and disquieting brooded over the ship, and they could not bring themselves to laugh. A feeling of resentment arose in their hearts; they were alive and well, and it exasperated them that, so near, a man should be dying and by the fact (which was after all no concern of theirs) so mysteriously affect them. A planter in the smoking-room over a gin sling said brutally what most of them felt, though none had confessed.

'Well, if he's going to peg out,' he said, 'I wish he'd hurry up and get it over. It gives me the creeps.'

The day was interminable. Mrs Hamlyn was thankful when the dinner hour arrived. So much time, at all events, was passed. She sat at the doctor's table.

'When do we reach Aden?' she asked.

'Some time tomorrow. The captain says we shall sight land between five and six in the morning.'

She gave him a sharp look. He stared at her for a moment, then dropped his eyes and reddened. He remembered that the woman, the fat woman sitting on the bungalow steps, had said that Gallagher would never see the land. Mrs Hamlyn wondered whether he, the sceptical, matter-of-fact young doctor, was wavering at last. He frowned a little and then, as though he sought to pull himself together, looked at her once more.

'I shan't be sorry to hand over my patient to the hospital people at Aden, I can tell you,' he said.

Next day was Christmas eve. When Mrs Hamlyn awoke from a troubled sleep the dawn was breaking. She looked out of her porthole and saw that the sky was clear and silvery; during the night the haze had melted, and the morning was brilliant. With a lighter heart she went on deck. She walked as far forward as she could go. A late star twinkled palely close to the horizon. There was a shimmer on the sea as though a loitering breeze passed playful fingers over its surface. The light was exquisitely soft, tenuous like a budding wood in spring, and crystalline so that it reminded you of the bubbling of water in a mountain brook. She turned to look at the sun rising rosy in the east, and saw coming towards her the doctor. He wore his uniform; he had not been to bed all night; he was dishevelled and he walked, with bowed shoulders, as though he were dog-tired. She knew at once that Gallagher was dead. When he came up to her she saw that he was crying. He looked so young then that her heart went out to him. She took his hand.

'You poor dear,' she said. 'You're tired out.'

'I did all I could,' he said. 'I wanted so awfully to save him.'

His voice shook and she saw that he was almost hysterical.

'When did he die?' she asked.

He closed his eyes, trying to control himself, and his lips trembled.

'A few minutes ago.'

Mrs Hamlyn sighed. She found nothing to say. Her gaze wandered across the calm, dispassionate and ageless sea. It stretched on all sides of them as infinite as human sorrow. But on a sudden her eyes were held, for there, ahead of them, on the horizon was something which looked like a precipitous and massy cloud. But its outline was too sharp to be a cloud's. She touched the doctor on the arm.

'What's that?'

He looked at it for a moment and under his sunburn she saw him grow white.

'Land.'

Once more Mrs Hamlyn thought of the fat Malay woman who sat silent on the steps of Gallagher's bungalow. Did she know?

They buried him when the sun was high in the heavens. They stood on the lower deck and on the hatches, the first- and second-class passengers, the white stewards and the European officers. The missionary read the burial service.

'Man that is born of a woman hath but a short time to live, and is full of misery. He cometh up, and is cut down, like a flower; he fleeth as it were a shadow, and never continueth in one stay.'

Pryce looked down at the deck with knit brows. His teeth were tight clenched. He did not grieve, for his heart was hot with anger. The doctor and the consul stood side by side. The consul bore to a nicety the expression of an official regret, but the doctor, clean-shaven now, in his neat fresh uniform and his gold braid, was pale and harassed. From him Mrs Hamlyn's eyes wandered to Mrs Linsell.

She was pressed against her husband, weeping, and he was holding her hand tenderly. Mrs Hamlyn did not know why this sight singularly affected her. At that moment of grief, her nerves distraught, the little woman went by instinct to the protection and support of her husband. But then Mrs Hamlyn felt a little shudder pass through her and she fixed her eyes on the seams in the deck, for she did not want to see what was toward. There was a pause in the reading. There were various movements. One of the officers gave an order. The missionary's voice continued.

'Forasmuch as it has pleased Almighty God of his great mercy to take unto himself the soul of our dear brother here departed: we therefore commend his body to the deep, to be turned into corruption, looking for the resurrection of the body when the sea shall give up its dead.'

Mrs Hamlyn felt the hot tears flow down her cheeks. There was a dull splash. The missionary's voice went on.

When the service was finished the passengers scattered; the second-class passengers returned to their quarters and a bell rang to summon them to luncheon. But the first-class passengers sauntered aimlessly about the promenade deck. Most of the men made for the smoking-room and sought to cheer themselves with whiskies and sodas and with gin slings. But the consul put up a notice on the board outside the dining-saloon summoning the passengers to a meeting. Most of them had an idea for what purpose it was called, and at the appointed hour they assembled. They were more cheerful than they had been for a week and they chattered with a gaiety which was only subdued by a mannerly reserve. The consul, an eye-glass in his eye, said that he had gathered them together to discuss the question of the fancy-dress dance on the following day. He knew they all had the deepest sympathy for Mr Gallagher and he would have proposed that they should combine to send an appropriate message to the deceased's relatives; but his papers had been examined by the purser and no trace could be found of any relative or friend with whom it was possible to communicate. The late Mr Gallagher appeared to be quite alone in the world. Meanwhile he (the consul) ventured to offer his sincere sympathy to the doctor who, he was quite sure, had done everything that was possible in the circumstances.

'Hear, hear,' said the passengers.

They had all passed through a very trying time, proceeded the consul, and to some it might seem that it would be more respectful to the deceased's memory if the fancy-dress ball were postponed till New Year's eve. This, however, he told them frankly was not his view, and he was convinced that Mr Gallagher himself would not have wished it. Of course it was a question for the majority to decide. The doctor got up and thanked the consul and the passengers for the kind things that had been said of him, it had of course been a very trying time, but he was authorized by the captain to say that the captain expressly wished all the festivities to be carried out on Christmas day as though nothing had happened. He (the doctor) told them in confidence that the captain felt the passengers had got into a rather morbid state, and thought it would do them all good if they had a jolly good time on Christmas day. Then the missionary's wife rose and said they mustn't think only of themselves; it

had been arranged by the Entertainment Committee that there should be a Christmas Tree for the
children, immediately after the first-class passengers' dinner, and the children had been looking
forward to seeing everyone in fancy-dress; it would
be too bad to disappoint them; she yielded to
no one in her respect for the dead, and she
sympathized with anyone who felt too sad to think
of dancing just then, her own heart was very heavy,
but she did feel it would be merely selfish to give
way to a feeling which could do no good to anyone.
Let them think of the little ones. This very much
impressed the passengers. They wanted to forget
the brooding terror which had hung over the boat
for so many days, they were alive and they wanted
to enjoy themselves; but they had an uneasy notion
that it would be decent to exhibit a certain grief. It
was quite another matter if they could do as they
wished from altruistic motives. When the consul
called for a show of hands everyone, but Mrs
Hamlyn and one old lady who was rheumatic, held
up an eager arm.

'The ayes have it,' said the consul. 'And I venture to congratulate the meeting on a very sensible
decision.'

It was just going to break up when one of the
planters got on his feet and said he wished to offer a
suggestion. Under the circumstances didn't they all
think it would be as well to invite the second-class
passengers? They had all come to the funeral that
morning. The missionary jumped up and seconded
the motion. The events of the last few days had
drawn them all together, he said, and in the
presence of death all men were equal. The consul
again addressed them. This matter had been dis-

cussed at a previous meeting, and the conclusion had been reached that it would be pleasanter for the second-class passengers to have their own party, but circumstances alter cases, and he was distinctly of opinion that their previous decision should be reversed.

'Hear, hear,' said the passengers.

A wave of democratic feeling swept over them and the motion was carried by acclamation. They separated light-heartedly, they felt charitable and kindly. Everyone stood everyone else drinks in the smoking-room.

And so, on the following evening, Mrs Hamlyn put on her fancy-dress. She had no heart for the gaiety before her, and for a moment had thought of feigning illness, but she knew no one would believe her, and was afraid to be thought affected. She was dressed as Carmen and she could not resist the vanity of making herself as attractive as possible. She darkened her eyelashes and rouged her cheeks. The costume suited her. When the bugle sounded and she went into the saloon she was received with flattering surprise. The consul (always a humorist) was dressed as a ballet-girl and was greeted with shouts of delighted laughter. The missionary and his wife, self-conscious but pleased with themselves, were very grand as Manchus. Mrs Linsell, as Columbine, showed all that was possible of her very pretty legs. Her husband was an Arab sheik and the doctor was a Malay sultan.

A subscription had been collected to provide champagne at dinner and the meal was hilarious. The company had provided crackers in which were paper hats of various shapes and these the passengers put on. There were paper streamers too which they threw at one another and little balloons which they beat from one to the other across the room. They laughed and shouted. They were very gay. No one could say that they were not having a good time. As soon as dinner was finished they went into the saloon where the Christmas Tree, with candles lit, was ready, and the children were brought in, shrieking with delight, and given presents. Then the dance began. The second-class passengers stood about shyly round the part of the deck reserved for dancing and occasionally danced with one another.

'I'm glad we had them,' said the consul, dancing with Mrs Hamlyn. 'I'm all for democracy, and I think they're very sensible to keep themselves to themselves.'

But she noticed that Pryce was not to be seen, and when an opportunity presented asked one of the second-class passengers where he was.

'Blind to the world,' was the answer. 'We put him to bed in the afternoon and locked him up in his cabin.'

The consul claimed her for another dance. He was very facetious. Suddenly Mrs Hamlyn felt that she could not bear it any more, the noise of the amateur band, the consul's jokes, the gaiety of the dancers. She knew not why, but the merriment of those people passing on their ship through the night and the solitary sea affected her on a sudden with horror. When the consul released her she slipped away and, with a look to see that no one had noticed her, ascended the companion to the boat deck. Here everything was in darkness. She walked softly to a spot where she knew she would be safe from all intrusion. But she heard a faint laugh and she caught sight in a hidden corner of a Columbine and a Malay sultan. Mrs Linsell and the doctor had resumed already the flirtation which the death of Gallagher had interrupted.

Already all those people had put out of their minds with a kind of ferocity the thought of that poor lonely man who had so strangely died in their midst. They felt no compassion for him, but resentment rather, because on his account they had been ill-at-ease. They seized upon life avidly. They made their jokes, they flirted, they gossiped. Mrs Hamlyn remembered what the consul had said, that among Mr Gallagher's papers no letters could be found, not the name of a single friend to whom the news of his death might be sent, and she knew not why this seemed to her unbearably tragic. There was something mysterious in a man who could pass through the world in such solitariness. When she remembered how he had come on deck in Singapore, so short a while since, in such rude health, full of vitality, and his arrogant plans for the future, she was seized with dismay. Those words of the burial service filled her with a solemn awe: *Man that is born of a woman hath but a short time to live, and is full of misery. He cometh up, and is cut down, like a flower* ... Year in, year out, he had made his plans for the future, he wanted to live so much and he had so much to live for, and then just when he stretched out his hand – oh, it was pitiful; it made all the other distresses of the world of small account. Death with its mystery was the only thing that really mattered. Mrs Hamlyn leaned over the rail and looked at the starry sky. Why did people make themselves unhappy? Let them weep for the death of those they loved, death was terrible always, but for the rest, was it worth while to be wretched, to harbour malice, to be vain and uncharitable? She thought again of herself and her husband and the woman he so strangely loved. He too had said that we live to be happy so short a time and we are so long dead. She pondered long and intently, and suddenly, as summer lightning flashes across the darkness of the night, she made a discovery which filled her with tremulous surprise; for she found that in her heart was no longer anger with her husband nor jealousy of her rival. A notion dawned on some remote horizon of her consciousness and like the morning sun suffused her soul with a tender, blissful glow. Out of the tragedy of that unknown Irishman's death, she gathered elatedly the courage for a desperate resolution. Her heart beat quickly, she was impatient to carry it into effect. A passion for self-sacrifice seized her.

The music had stopped, the ball was over; most of the passengers would have gone to bed and the rest would be in the smoking-room. She went down to her cabin and met no one on the way. She took her writing pad and wrote a letter to her husband.

'My dear. It is Christmas day and I want to tell you that my heart is filled with kindly thoughts towards both of you. I have been foolish and unreasonable. I think we should allow those we care for to be happy in their own way, and we should care for them enough not to let it make us unhappy. I want you to know that I grudge you none of the joy that has so strangely come into your life. I am no longer jealous, nor hurt, nor vindictive. Do not think I shall be unhappy or lonely. If ever you feel that you need me, come to me, and I will welcome you with a cheerful spirit and without reproach or ill-will. I am most grateful for all the years of happiness and of tenderness that you gave me, and in return I wish to offer you an affection which makes no claim on you and is, I hope, utterly disinterested. Think kindly of me and be happy, happy, happy.'

She signed her name and put the letter into an envelope. Though it would not go till they reached Port Said she wanted to place it at once in the letter-box. When she had done this, beginning to undress, she looked at herself in the glass. Her eyes were shining and under her rouge her colour was bright. The future was no longer desolate, but bright with a fair hope. She slipped into bed and fell at once into a sound and dreamless sleep.

The Letter

Outside on the quay the sun beat fiercely. A stream of motors, lorries and buses, private cars and hirelings, sped up and down the crowded thoroughfare, and every chauffeur blew his horn; rickshaws threaded their nimble path amid the throng, and the panting coolies found breath to yell at one another; coolies, carrying heavy bales, sidled along with their quick jog-trot and shouted to the passer-by to make way; itinerant vendors proclaimed their wares. Singapore is the meeting-place of a hundred peoples; and men of all colours, black Tamils, yellow Chinks, brown Malays, Armenians, Jews and Bengalis, called to one another in raucous tones. But inside the office of Messrs Ripley, Joyce and Naylor it was pleasantly cool; it was dark after the dusty glitter of the street and agreeably quiet after its unceasing din. Mr Joyce sat in his private room, at the table, with an electric fan turned full on him. He was leaning back, his elbows on the arms of the chair, with the tips of the outstretched fingers of one hand resting neatly against the tips of the outstretched fingers of the other. His gaze rested on the battered volumes of the Law Reports which stood on a long shelf in front of him. On the top of a cupboard were square boxes of japanned tin, on which were painted the names of various clients.

There was a knock at the door.

'Come in.'

A Chinese clerk, very neat in his white ducks, opened it.

'Mr Crosbie is here, sir.'

He spoke beautiful English, accenting each word with precision, and Mr Joyce had often wondered at the extent of his vocabulary. Ong Chi Seng was a Cantonese, and he had studied law at Gray's Inn. He was spending a year or two with Messrs Ripley, Joyce and Naylor in order to prepare himself for practice on his own account. He was industrious, obliging, and of exemplary character.

'Show him in,' said Mr Joyce.

He rose to shake hands with his visitor and asked him to sit down. The light fell on him as he did so. The face of Mr Joyce remained in shadow. He was by nature a silent man, and now he looked at Robert Crosbie for quite a minute without speaking. Crosbie was a big fellow, well over six feet high, with broad shoulders, and muscular. He was a rubber-planter, hard with the constant exercise of walking over the estate, and with the tennis which was his relaxation when the day's work was over. He was deeply sunburned. His hairy hands, his feet in clumsy boots, were enormous, and Mr Joyce found himself thinking that a blow of that great fist would easily kill the fragile Tamil. But there was no fierceness in his blue eyes; they were confiding and gentle; and his face, with its big, undistinguished features, was open, frank and honest. But at this moment it bore a look of deep distress. It was drawn and haggard.

'You look as though you hadn't had much sleep the last night or two,' said Mr Joyce.

'I haven't.'

Mr Joyce noticed now the old felt hat, with its broad double brim, which Crosbie had placed on the table; and then his eyes travelled to the khaki shorts he wore, showing his red hairy thighs, the tennis shirt open at the neck, without a tie, and the dirty khaki jacket with the ends of the sleeves turned up. He looked as though he had just come in from a long tramp among the rubber trees. Mr Joyce gave a slight frown.

'You must pull yourself together, you know. You must keep your head.'

'Oh, I'm all right.'

'Have you seen your wife today?'

'No, I'm to see her this afternoon. You know, it is a damned shame that they should have arrested her.'

'I think they had to do that,' Mr Joyce answered in his level, soft tone.

'I should have thought they'd have let her out on bail.'

'It's a very serious charge.'

'It is damnable. She did what any decent woman would do in her place. Only, nine women out of ten wouldn't have the pluck. Leslie's the best woman in the world. She wouldn't hurt a fly. Why, hang it all, man, I've been married to her for twelve years, do you think I don't know her? God, if I'd got hold of the man I'd have wrung his neck, I'd have killed him without a moment's hesitation. So would you.'

'My dear fellow, everybody's on your side. No one had a good word to say for Hammond. We're going to get her off. I don't suppose either the assessors or the judge will go into court without having already made up their minds to bring in a verdict of not guilty.'

'The whole thing's a farce,' said Crosbie violently. 'She ought never to have been arrested in the first place, and then it's terrible, after all the poor girl's gone through, to subject her to the ordeal of a trial. There's not a soul I've met since I've been in Singapore, man or woman, who hasn't told me that Leslie was absolutely justified. I think it's awful to keep her in prison all these weeks.'

'The law is the law. After all, she confesses that she killed the man. It is terrible, and I'm dreadfully sorry for both you and for her.'

'I don't matter a hang,' interrupted Crosbie.

'But the fact remains that murder has been committed, and in a civilized community a trial is inevitable.'

'Is it murder to exterminate noxious vermin? She shot him as she would have shot a mad dog.'

Mr Joyce leaned back again in his chair and once more placed the tips of his ten fingers together. The little construction he formed looked like the skeleton of a roof. He was silent for a moment.

'I should be wanting in my duty as your legal adviser,' he said at last, in an even voice, looking at his client with his cool, brown eyes, 'if I did not tell you that there is one point which causes me just a little anxiety. If your wife had only shot Hammond once, the whole thing would be absolutely plain sailing. Unfortunately she fired six times.'

'Her explanation is perfectly simple. In the circumstances anyone would have done the same.'

'I daresay,' said Mr Joyce, 'and of course I think the explanation is very reasonable. But it's no good closing our eyes to the facts. It's always a good plan to put yourself in another man's place, and I can't deny that if I were prosecuting for the Crown that is the point on which I should centre my inquiry.'

'My dear fellow, that's perfectly idiotic.'

Mr Joyce shot a sharp glance at Robert Crosbie. The shadow of a smile hovered over his shapely lips. Crosbie was a good fellow, but he could hardly be described as intelligent.

'I daresay it's of no importance,' answered the lawyer, 'I just thought it was a point worth mentioning. You haven't got very long to wait now, and when it's all over I recommend you to go off somewhere with your wife on a trip, and forget all about it. Even though we are almost dead certain to get an acquittal, a trial of that sort is anxious work, and you'll both want a rest.'

For the first time Crosbie smiled, and his smile strangely changed his face. You forgot the uncouthness and saw only the goodness of his soul.

'I think I shall want it more than Leslie. She's borne up wonderfully. By God, there's a plucky little woman for you.'

'Yes, I've been very much struck by her self-control,' said the lawyer. 'I should never have guessed that she was capable of such determination.'

His duties as her counsel had made it necessary for him to have a good many interviews with Mrs Crosbie since her arrest. Though things had been made as easy as could be for her, the fact remained that she was in gaol, awaiting her trial for murder, and it would not have been surprising if her nerves had failed her. She appeared to bear her ordeal with composure. She read a great deal, took such exercise as was possible, and by favour of the authorities worked at the pillow lace which had always formed the entertainment of her long hours of leisure. When Mr Joyce saw her, she was neatly dressed in cool, fresh, simple frocks, her hair was carefully arranged, and her nails were manicured. Her manner was collected. She was able even to jest upon the little inconveniences of her position. There was something casual about the way in which she spoke of the tragedy, which suggested to Mr Joyce that only her good breeding prevented her from finding something a trifle ludicrous in a situation which was eminently serious. It surprised him, for he had never thought that she had a sense of humour.

He had known her off and on for a good many years. When she paid visits to Singapore she generally came to dine with his wife and himself, and once or twice she had passed a week-end with them at their bungalow by the sea. His wife had spent a fortnight with her on the estate, and had met Geoffrey Hammond several times. The two couples had been on friendly, if not on intimate, terms, and it was on this account that Robert Crosbie had rushed over to Singapore immediately after the catastrophe and begged Mr Joyce to take charge personally of his unhappy wife's defence.

The story she told him the first time he saw her, she had never varied in the smallest detail. She told it as coolly then, a few hours after the tragedy, as she told it now. She told it connectedly, in a level, even voice, and her only sign of confusion was when a slight colour came into her cheeks as she described one or two of its incidents. She was the last woman to whom one would have expected such a thing to happen. She was in the early thirties, a fragile creature, neither short nor tall, and graceful rather than pretty. Her wrists and ankles were very delicate, but she was extremely thin, and you could see the bones of her hands through the white skin, and the veins were large and blue. Her face was colourless, slightly sallow, and her lips were pale. You did not notice the colour of her eyes. She had a great deal of light brown hair, and it had a slight natural wave; it was the sort of hair that with a little touching-up would have been very pretty, but you could not imagine that Mrs Crosbie would think of resorting to any such device. She was a quiet, pleasant, unassuming woman. Her manner was engaging, and if she was not very popular it was because she suffered from a certain shyness. This was comprehensible enough, for the planter's life is lonely, and in her own house, with people she knew, she was in her quiet way charming. Mrs Joyce, after her fortnight's stay, had told her husband that Leslie was a very agreeable hostess. There was more in her, she said, than people thought; and when you came to know her you were surprised how much she had read and how entertaining she could be.

She was the last woman in the world to commit murder.

Mr Joyce dismissed Robert Crosbie with such reassuring words as he could find and, once more alone in his office, turned over the pages of the brief. But it was a mechanical action, for all its details were familiar to him. The case was the sensation of the day, and it was discussed in all the clubs, at all the dinner tables, up and down the Peninsula, from Singapore to Penang. The facts that Mrs Crosbie gave were simple. Her husband had gone to Singapore on business, and she was alone for the night. She dined by herself, late, at a quarter to nine, and after dinner sat in the sitting-room working at her lace. It opened on the veranda. There was no one in the bungalow, for the servants had retired to their own quarters at the back of the compound. She was surprised to hear a step on the gravel path in the garden, a booted step, which suggested a white man rather than a native, for she had not heard a motor drive up, and she could not imagine who could be coming to see her at that time of night. Someone ascended the few stairs that led up to the bungalow, walked across the veranda, and appeared at the door of the room in which she sat. At the first moment she did not recognize the visitor. She sat with a shaded lamp, and he stood with his back to the darkness.

'May I come in?' he said.

She did not even recognize the voice.

'Who is it?' she asked.

She worked with spectacles, and she took them off as she spoke.

'Geoff Hammond.'

'Of course. Come in and have a drink.'

She rose and shook hands with him cordially. She was a little surprised to see him, for though he was a neighbour neither she nor Robert had been lately on very intimate terms with him, and she had not seen him for some weeks. He was the manager of a rubber estate nearly eight miles from theirs, and she wondered why he had chosen this late hour to come and see them.

'Robert's away,' she said. 'He had to go to Singapore for the night.'

Perhaps he thought his visit called for some explanation, for he said:

'I'm sorry. I felt rather lonely tonight, so I thought I'd just come along and see how you were getting on.'

'How on earth did you come? I never heard a car.'

'I left it down the road. I thought you might both be in bed and asleep.'

This was natural enough. The planter gets up at dawn in order to take the roll-call of the workers, and soon after dinner he is glad to go to bed. Hammond's car was in point of fact found next day a quarter of a mile from the bungalow.

Since Robert was away there was no whisky and soda in the room. Leslie did not call the boy, who was probably asleep, but fetched it herself. Her guest mixed himself a drink and filled his pipe.

Geoff Hammond had a host of friends in the colony. He was at this time in the late thirties, but he had come out as a lad. He had been one of the first to volunteer on the outbreak of war, and had done very well. A wound in the knee caused him to be invalided out of the army after two years, but he returned to the Federated Malay States with a DSO and an MC. He was one of the best billiard-players in the colony. He had been a beautiful dancer and a fine tennis-player, but though able no longer to dance, and his tennis, with a stiff knee, was not so good as it had been, he had the gift of popularity and was universally liked. He was a tall, good-looking fellow, with attractive blue eyes and a fine head of black, curling hair. Old stagers said his only fault was that he was too fond of the girls, and after the catastrophe they shook their heads and vowed that they had always known this would get him into trouble.

He began now to talk to Leslie about the local affairs, the forthcoming races in Singapore, the price of rubber, and his chances of killing a tiger which had been lately seen in the neighbourhood. She was anxious to finish by a certain date the piece of lace on which she was working, for she wanted to send it home for her mother's birthday, and so put on her spectacles again, and drew towards her chair the little table on which stood the pillow.

'I wish you wouldn't wear those great horn-spectacles,' he said. 'I don't know why a pretty woman should do her best to look plain.'

She was a trifle taken aback at this remark. He had never used that tone with her before. She thought the best thing was to make light of it.

'I have no pretensions to being a raving beauty, you know, and if you ask me point blank, I'm bound to tell you that I don't care two pins if you think me plain or not.'

'I don't think you're plain. I think you're awfully pretty.'

'Sweet of you,' she answered, ironically. 'But in that case I can only think you half-witted.'

He chuckled. But he rose from his chair and sat down in another by her side.

'You're not going to have the face to deny that you have the prettiest hands in the world,' he said.

He made a gesture as though to take one of them. She gave him a little tap.

'Don't be an idiot. Sit down where you were before and talk sensibly, or else I shall send you home.'

He did not move.

'Don't you know that I'm awfully in love with you?' he said.

She remained quite cool.

'I don't. I don't believe it for a minute, and even if it were true I don't want you to say it.'

She was the more surprised at what he was saying, since during the seven years she had known him he had never paid her any particular attention. When he came back from the war they had seen a good deal of one another, and once when he was ill Robert had gone over and brought him back to their bungalow in his car. He had stayed with them then for a fortnight. But their interests were dissimilar, and the acquaintance had never ripened into friendship. For the last two or three years they had seen little of him. Now and then he came over to play tennis, now and then they met him at some planter's who was giving a party, but it often happened that they did not set eyes on him for a month at a time.

Now he took another whisky and soda. Leslie wondered if he had been drinking before. There was something odd about him, and it made her a trifle uneasy. She watched him help himself with disapproval.

'I wouldn't drink any more if I were you,' she said, good-humouredly still.

He emptied his glass and put it down.

'Do you think I'm talking to you like this because I'm drunk?' he asked abruptly.

'That is the most obvious explanation, isn't it?'

'Well, it's a lie. I've loved you ever since I first knew you. I've held my tongue as long as I could, and now it's got to come out. I love you, I love you, I love you.'

She rose and carefully put aside the pillow.

'Good-night,' she said.

'I'm not going now.'

At last she began to lose her temper.

'But, you poor fool, don't you know that I've never loved anyone but Robert, and even if I didn't love Robert you're the last man I should care for.'

'What do I care? Robert's away.'

'If you don't go away this minute I shall call the boys, and have you thrown out.'

'They're out of earshot.'

She was very angry now. She made a movement as though to go on to the veranda from which the house-boy would certainly hear her, but he seized her arm.

'Let me go,' she cried furiously.

'Not much. I've got you now.'

She opened her mouth and called 'Boy, boy', but with a quick gesture he put his hand over it. Then before she knew what he was about he had taken her in his arms and was kissing her passionately. She struggled, turning her lips away from his burning mouth.

'No, no, no,' she cried. 'Leave me alone. I won't.'

She grew confused about what happened then. All that had been said before she remembered accurately, but now his words assailed her ears through a mist of horror and fear. He seemed to plead for her love. He broke into violent protestations of passion. And all the time he held her in his tempestuous embrace. She was helpless, for he was a strong, powerful man, and her arms were pinioned to her sides; her struggles were unavailing, and she felt herself grow weaker; she was afraid she would faint, and his hot breath on her face made her feel desperately sick. He kissed her mouth, her eyes, her cheeks, her hair. The pressure of his arms was killing her. He lifted her off her feet. She tried to kick him, but he only held her more closely. He was carrying her now. He wasn't speaking any more, but she knew that his face was pale and his eyes hot with desire. He was taking her into the bedroom. He was no longer a civilized man, but a savage. And as he ran he stumbled against a table which was in the way. His stiff knee made him a little awkward on his feet, and with the burden of the woman in his arms he fell. In a moment she had snatched herself away from him. She ran round the sofa. He was up in a flash, and flung himself towards her. There was a revolver on the desk. She was not a nervous woman, but Robert was to be away for the night, and she had meant to take it into her room when she went to bed. That was why it happened to be there. She was frantic with terror now. She did not know what she was doing. She heard a report. She saw Hammond stagger. He gave a cry. He said something, she didn't know what. He lurched out of the room on to the veranda. She was in a frenzy now, she was beside herself, she followed him out, yes, that was it, she must have followed him out, though she remembered nothing of it, she followed firing automatically, shot after shot, till the six chambers were empty. Hammond fell down on the floor of the veranda. He crumpled up into a bloody heap.

When the boys, startled by the reports, rushed up, they found her standing over Hammond with the revolver still in her hand, and Hammond lifeless. She looked at them for a moment without speaking. They stood in a frightened, huddled bunch. She let the revolver fall from her hand, and without a word turned and went into the sitting-room. They watched her go into her bedroom and turn the key in the lock. They dared not touch the dead body, but looked at it with terrified eyes, talking excitedly to one another in undertones. Then the head-boy collected himself; he had been with them for many years, he was Chinese and a level-headed fellow. Robert had gone into Singapore on his motor-cycle, and the car stood in the garage. He told the seis to get it out; they must go at once to the Assistant District Officer and tell him what had happened. He picked up the revolver and put it in his pocket. The ADO, a man called Withers, lived on the outskirts of the nearest town, which was about thirty-five miles away. It took them an hour and a half to reach him. Everyone was asleep, and they had to rouse the boys. Presently Withers came out and they told him their errand. The head-boy showed him the revolver in proof of what he said. The ADO went into his room to dress, sent for his car, and in a little while was following them back along the deserted road. The dawn was just breaking as he reached the Crosbies' bungalow. He ran up the steps of the veranda, and stopped short as he saw Hammond's body lying where he fell. He touched the face. It was quite cold.

'Where's mem?' he asked the house-boy.

The Chinese pointed to the bedroom. Withers went to the door and knocked. There was no answer. He knocked again.

'Mrs Crosbie,' he called.

'Who is it?'

'Withers.'

There was another pause. Then the door was unlocked and slowly opened. Leslie stood before him. She had not been to bed, and wore the tea-gown in which she had dined. She stood and looked silently at the ADO.

'Your house-boy fetched me,' he said. 'Hammond. What have you done?'

'He tried to rape me, and I shot him.'

'My God. I say, you'd better come out here. You must tell me exactly what happened.'

'Not now. I can't. You must give me time. Send for my husband.'

Withers was a young man, and he did not know exactly what to do in an emergency which was so out of the run of his duties. Leslie refused to say anything till at last Robert arrived. Then she told the two men the story, from which since then, though she had repeated it over and over again, she had never in the slightest degree diverged.

The point to which Mr Joyce recurred was the shooting. As a lawyer he was bothered that Leslie had fired not once, but six times, and the examination of the dead man showed that four of the shots had been fired close to the body. One might almost have thought that when the man fell she stood over him and emptied the contents of the revolver into him. She confessed that her memory, so accurate for all that had preceded, failed her here. Her mind was blank. It pointed to an uncontrollable fury; but uncontrollable fury was the last thing you would have expected from this quiet and demure woman. Mr Joyce had known her a good many years, and had always thought her an unemotional person; during the weeks that had passed since the tragedy her composure had been amazing.

Mr Joyce shrugged his shoulders.

'The fact is, I suppose,' he reflected, 'that you can never tell what hidden possibilities of savagery there are in the most respectable of women.'

There was a knock at the door.

'Come in.'

The Chinese clerk entered and closed the door behind him. He closed it gently, with deliberation, but decidedly, and advanced to the table at which Mr Joyce was sitting.

'May I trouble you, sir, for a few words' private conversation?' he said.

The elaborate accuracy with which the clerk expressed himself always faintly amused Mr Joyce, and now he smiled.

'It's no trouble, Chi Seng,' he replied.

'The matter on which I desire to speak to you, sir, is delicate and confidential.'

'Fire away.'

Mr Joyce met his clerk's shrewd eyes. As usual Ong Chi Seng was dressed in the height of local fashion. He wore very shiny patent leather shoes and gay silk socks. In his black tie was a pearl and ruby pin, and on the fourth finger of his left hand a diamond ring. From the pocket of his neat white coat protruded a gold fountain pen and a gold pencil. He wore a gold wrist-watch, and on the bridge of his nose invisible pince-nez. He gave a little cough.

'The matter has to do with the case R. *v.* Crosbie, sir.'

'Yes?'

'A circumstance has come to my knowledge, sir, which seems to me to put a different complexion on it.'

'What circumstance?'

'It has come to my knowledge, sir, that there is a letter in existence from the defendant to the unfortunate victim of the tragedy.'

'I shouldn't be at all surprised. In the course of the last seven years I have no doubt that Mrs Crosbie often had occasion to write to Mr Hammond.'

Mr Joyce had a high opinion of his clerk's intelligence and his words were designed to conceal his thoughts.

'That is very probable, sir. Mrs Crosbie must have communicated with the deceased frequently, to invite him to dine with her for example, or to propose a tennis game. That was my first thought when the matter was brought to my notice. This letter, however, was written on the day of the late Mr Hammond's death.'

Mr Joyce did not flicker an eyelash. He continued to look at Ong Chi Seng with the smile of faint amusement with which he generally talked to him.

'Who has told you this?'

'The circumstances were brought to my knowledge, sir, by a friend of mine.'

Mr Joyce knew better than to insist.

'You will no doubt recall, sir, that Mrs Crosbie has stated that until the fatal night she had had no communication with the deceased for several weeks.'

'Have you got the letter?'

'No, sir.'

'What are its contents?'

'My friend gave me a copy. Would you like to peruse it, sir?'

'I should.'

Ong Chi Seng took from an inside pocket a bulky wallet. It was filled with papers, Singapore dollar notes and cigarette cards. From the confusion he presently extracted a half sheet of thin notepaper and placed it before Mr Joyce. The letter read as follows:

'R. will be away for the night. I absolutely must see you. I shall expect you at eleven. I am desperate, and if you don't come I won't answer for the consequences. Don't drive up. – L.'

It was written in the flowing hand which the Chinese were taught at the foreign schools. The writing, so lacking in character, was oddly incongruous with the ominous words.

'What makes you think that this note was written by Mrs Crosbie?'

'I have every confidence in the veracity of my informant, sir,' replied Ong Chi Seng. 'And the matter can very easily be put to the proof. Mrs Crosbie will, no doubt, but able to tell you at once whether she wrote such a letter or not.'

Since the beginning of the conversation Mr Joyce had not taken his eyes off the respectable countenance of his clerk. He wondered now if he discerned in it a faint expression of mockery.

'It is inconceivable that Mrs Crosbie should have written such a letter,' said Mr Joyce.

'If that is your opinion, sir, the matter is of course ended. My friend spoke to me on the subject only because he thought, as I was in your office, you might like to know of the existence of this letter before a communication was made to the Deputy Public Prosecutor.'

'Who has the original?' asked Mr Joyce sharply.

Ong Chi Seng made no sign that he perceived in this question and its manner a change of attitude.

'You will remember, sir, no doubt, that after the death of Mr Hammond it was discovered that he had had relations with a Chinese woman. The letter is at present in her possession.'

That was one of the things which had turned public opinion most vehemently against Hammond. It came to be known that for several months he had had a Chinese woman living in his house.

For a moment neither of them spoke. Indeed everything had been said and each understood the other perfectly.

'I'm obliged to you, Chi Seng. I will give the matter my consideration.'

'Very good, sir. Do you wish me to make a communication to that effect to my friend?'

'I daresay it would be as well if you kept in touch with him,' Mr Joyce answered with gravity.

'Yes, sir.'

The clerk noiselessly left the room, shutting the door again with deliberation, and left Mr Joyce to his reflections. He stared at the copy, in its neat, impersonal writing, of Leslie's letter. Vague suspicions troubled him. They were so disconcerting that he made an effort to put them out of his mind. There must be a simple explanation of the letter, and Leslie without doubt could give it at once, but, by heaven, an explanation was needed. He rose from his chair, put the letter in his pocket, and took his topi. When he went out Ong Chi Seng was busily writing at his desk.

'I'm going out for a few minutes, Chi Seng,' he said.

'Mr George Reed is coming by appointment at twelve o'clock, sir. Where shall I say you've gone?'

Mr Joyce gave him a thin smile.

'You can say that you haven't the least idea.'

But he knew perfectly well that Ong Chi Seng was aware that he was going to the gaol. Though the crime had been committed in Belanda and the trial was to take place at Belanda Bharu, since there was in the gaol no convenience for the detention of a white woman Mrs Crosbie had been brought to Singapore.

When she was led into the room in which he waited she held out her thin, distinguished hand, and gave him a pleasant smile. She was as ever neatly and simply dressed, and her abundant, pale hair was arranged with care.

'I wasn't expecting to see you this morning,' she said, graciously.

She might have been in her own house, and Mr Joyce almost expected to hear her call the boy and tell him to bring the visitor a gin pahit.

'How are you?' he asked.

'I'm in the best of health, thank you.' A flicker of amusement flashed across her eyes. 'This is a wonderful place for a rest cure.'

The attendant withdrew and they were left alone.

'Do sit down,' said Leslie.

He took a chair. He did not quite know how to begin. She was so cool that it seemed almost impossible to say to her the thing he had come to say. Though she was not pretty there was some-thing agreeable in her appearance. She had ele-gance, but it was the elegance of good breeding in which there was nothing of the artifice of society. You had only to look at her to know what sort of people she had and what kind of surroundings she had lived in. Her fragility gave her a singular refinement. It was impossible to associate her with the vaguest idea of grossness.

'I'm looking forward to seeing Robert this afternoon,' she said, in her good-humoured, easy voice. (It was a pleasure to hear her speak, her voice and her accent were so distinctive of her class.) 'Poor dear, it's been a great trial to his nerves. I'm thankful it'll all be over in a few days.'

'It's only five days now.'

'I know. Each morning when I awake I say to myself, "one less".' She smiled then. 'Just as I used to do at school and the holidays were coming.'

'By the way, am I right in thinking that you had no communication whatever with Hammond for several weeks before the catastrophe?'

'I'm quite positive of that. The last time we met was at a tennis-party at the MacFarrens. I don't think I said more than two words to him. They have two courts, you know, and we didn't happen to be in the same sets.'

'And you haven't written to him?'

'Oh, no.'

'Are you quite sure of that?'

'Oh, quite,' she answered, with a little smile. 'There was nothing I should write to him for except to ask him to dine or to play tennis, and I hadn't done either for months.'

'At one time you'd been on fairly intimate terms with him. How did it happen that you had stopped asking him to anything?'

Mrs Crosbie shrugged her thin shoulders.

'One gets tired of people. We hadn't anything very much in common. Of course, when he was ill Robert and I did everything we could for him, but the last year or two he'd been quite well, and he was very popular. He had a good many calls on his time, and there didn't seem to be any need to shower invitations upon him.'

'Are you quite certain that was all?'

Mrs Crosbie hesitated for a moment.

'Well, I may just as well tell you. It had come to our ears that he was living with a Chinese woman, and Robert said he wouldn't have him in the house. I had seen her myself.'

Mr Joyce was sitting in a straight-backed arm-chair, resting his chin on his hand, and his eyes were fixed on Leslie. Was it his fancy that, as she made this remark, her black pupils were filled on a sudden, for the fraction of a second, with a dull red light? The effect was startling. Mr Joyce shifted in his chair. He placed the tips of his ten fingers together. He spoke very slowly, choosing his words.

'I think I should tell you that there is in existence a letter in your handwriting to Geoff Hammond.'

He watched her closely. She made no move-ment, nor did her face change colour, but she took a noticeable time to reply.

'In the past I've often sent him little notes to ask him to something or other, or to get me something when I knew he was going to Singapore.'

'This letter asks him to come and see you because Robert was going to Singapore.'

'That's impossible. I never did anything of the kind.'

'You'd better read it for youself.'

He took it out of his pocket and handed it to her. She gave it a glance and with a smile of scorn handed it back to him.

'That's not my handwriting.'

'I know, it's said to be an exact copy of the original.'

She read the words now, and as she read a horrible change came over her. Her colourless face grew dreadful to look at. It turned green. The flesh seemed on a sudden to fall away and her skin was tightly stretched over the bones. Her lips receded, showing her teeth, so that she had the appearance of making a grimace. She stared at Mr Joyce with eyes that started from their sockets. He was looking now at a gibbering death's head.

'What does it mean?' she whispered.

Her mouth was so dry that she could utter no more than a hoarse sound. It was no longer a human voice.

'That is for you to say,' he answered.

'I didn't write it. I swear I didn't write it.'

'Be very careful what you say. If the original is in your handwriting it would be useless to deny it.'

'It would be a forgery.'

'It would be difficult to prove that. It would be easy to prove that it was genuine.'

A shiver passed through her lean body. But great beads of sweat stood on her forehead. She took a handkerchief from her bag and wiped the palms of her hands. She glanced at the letter again and gave Mr Joyce a sidelong look.

'It's not dated. If I had written it and forgotten all about it, it might have been written years ago. If you'll give me time, I'll try and remember the circumstances.'

'I noticed there was no date. If this letter were in the hands of the prosecution they would cross-examine the boys. They would soon find out whether someone took a letter to Hammond on the day of his death.'

Mrs Crosbie clasped her hands violently and swayed in her chair so that he thought she would faint.

'I swear to you that I didn't write that letter.'

Mr Joyce was silent for a little while. He took his eyes from her distraught face, and looked down on the floor. He was reflecting.

'In these circumstances we need not go into the matter further,' he said slowly, at last breaking the silence. 'If the possesser of this letter sees fit to place it in the hands of the prosecution you will be prepared.'

His words suggested that he had nothing more to say to her, but he made no movement of departure. He waited. To himself he seemed to wait a very long time. He did not look at Leslie, but he was conscious that she sat very still. She made no sound. At last it was he who spoke.

'If you have nothing more to say to me I think I'll be getting back to my office.'

'What would anyone who read the letter be inclined to think that it meant?' she asked then.

'He'd know that you had told a deliberate lie,' answered Mr Joyce sharply.

'When?'

'You have stated definitely that you had had no communication with Hammond for at least three months.'

'The whole thing has been a terrible shock to me. The events of that dreadful night have been a nightmare. It's not very strange if one detail has escaped my memory.'

'It would be unfortunate when your memory has reproduced so exactly every particular of your interview with Hammond, that you should have forgotten so important a point as that he came to see you in the bungalow on the night of his death at your express desire.'

'I hadn't forgotten. After what happened I was afraid to mention it. I thought you'd none of you believe my story if I admitted that he'd come at my invitation. I daresay it was stupid of me; but I lost my head, and after I'd said once that I'd had no communication with Hammond I was obliged to stick to it.'

By now Leslie had recovered her admirable composure, and she met Mr Joyce's appraising glance with candour. Her gentleness was very disarming.

'You will be required to explain, then, *why* you asked Hammond to come and see you when Robert was away for the night.'

She turned her eyes full on the lawyer. He had been mistaken in thinking them insignificant, they were rather fine eyes, and unless he was mistaken they were bright now with tears. Her voice had a little break in it.

'It was a surprise I was preparing for Robert. His birthday is next month. I knew he wanted a new gun and you know I'm dreadfully stupid about sporting things. I wanted to talk to Geoff about it. I thought I'd get him to order it for me.'

'Perhaps the terms of the letter are not very clear to your recollection. Will you have another look at it.'

'No, I don't want to,' she said quickly.

'Does it seem to you the sort of letter a woman would write to a somewhat distant acquaintance because she wanted to consult him about buying a gun?'

'I daresay it's rather extravagant and emotional. I do express myself like that, you know. I'm quite prepared to admit it's very silly.' She smiled. 'And after all, Geoff Hammond wasn't quite a distant acquaintance. When he was ill I'd nursed him like a mother. I asked him to come when Robert was away, because Robert wouldn't have him in the house.'

Mr Joyce was tired of sitting so long in the same position. He rose and walked once or twice up and down the room, choosing the words he proposed to say; then he leaned over the back of the chair in which he had been sitting. He spoke slowly in a tone of deep gravity.

'Mrs Crosbie, I want to talk to you very, very seriously. This case was comparatively plain sailing. There was only one point which seemed to me to require explanation: as far as I could judge, you had fired no less than four shots into Hammond when he was lying on the ground. It was hard to accept the possibility that a delicate, frightened, and habitually self-controlled woman, of gentle nature and refined instincts, should have surrendered to an absolutely uncontrolled frenzy. But of course it was admissible. Although Geoffrey Hammond was much liked and on the whole thought highly of, I was prepared to prove that he was the sort of man who might be guilty of the crime which in justification of your act you accused him of. The fact, which was discovered after his death, that he had been living with a Chinese woman gave us something very definite to go upon. That robbed him of any sympathy which might have been felt for him. We made up our minds to make use of the odium which such a connection cast upon him in the minds of all respectable people. I told your husband this morning that I was certain of an acquittal, and I wasn't just telling him that to give him heart. I do not believe the assessors would have left the court.'

They looked into one another's eyes. Mrs Crosbie was strangely still. She was like a little bird paralysed by the fascination of a snake. He went on in the same quiet tones.

'But this letter has thrown an entirely different complexion on the case. I am your legal adviser, I shall represent you in court. I take your story as you tell it me, and I shall conduct your defence according to its terms. It may be that I believe your statements, and it may be that I doubt them. The duty of counsel is to persuade the court that the evidence placed before it is not such as to justify it in bringing in a verdict of guilty, and any private opinion he may have of the guilt or innocence of his client is entirely beside the point.'

He was astonished to see in Leslie's eyes the flicker of a smile. Piqued, he went on somewhat dryly.

'You're not going to deny that Hammond came to your house at your urgent, and I may even say, hysterical invitation?'

Mrs Crosbie, hesitating for an instant, seemed to consider.

'They can prove that the letter was taken to his bungalow by one of the house-boys. He rode over on his bicycle.'

'You mustn't expect other people to be stupider than you. The letter will put them on the track of suspicions which have entered nobody's head. I will not tell you what I personally thought when I saw the copy. I do not wish you to tell me anything but what is needed to save your neck.'

Mrs Crosbie gave a shrill cry. She sprang to her feet, white with terror.

'You don't think they'd hang me?'

'If they came to the conclusion that you hadn't killed Hammond in self-defence, it would be the duty of the assessors to bring in a verdict of guilty. The charge is murder. It would be the duty of the judge to sentence you to death.'

'But what can they prove?' she gasped.

'I don't know what they can prove. You know. I don't want to know. But if their suspicions are aroused, if they begin to make inquiries, if the natives are questioned – what is it that can be discovered?'

She crumpled up suddenly. She fell on the floor before he could catch her. She had fainted. He looked round the room for water, but there was none there, and he did not want to be disturbed. He stretched her out on the floor, and kneeling beside her waited for her to recover. When she opened her eyes he was disconcerted by the ghastly fear that he saw in them.

'Keep quite still,' he said. 'You'll be better in a moment.'

'You won't let them hang me,' she whispered.

She began to cry, hysterically, while in undertones he sought to quieten her.

'For goodness sake pull yourself together,' he said.

'Give me a minute.'

Her courage was amazing. He could see the

effort she made to regain her self-control, and soon she was once more calm.

'Let me get up now.'

He gave her his hand and helped her to her feet. Taking her arm, he led her to the chair. She sat down wearily.

'Don't talk to me for a minute or two,' she said.

'Very well.'

When at last she spoke it was to say something which he did not expect. She gave a little sigh.

'I'm afraid I've made rather a mess of things,' she said.

He did not answer, and once more there was a silence.

'Isn't it possible to get hold of the letter?' she said at last.

'I do not think anything would have been said to me about it, if the person in whose possession it is was not prepared to sell it.'

'Who's got it?'

'The Chinese woman who was living in Hammond's house.'

A spot of colour flickered for an instant on Leslie's cheek-bones.

'Does she want an awful lot for it?'

'I imagine that she has a very shrewd idea of its value. I doubt if it would be possible to get hold of it except for a very large sum.'

'Are you going to let me be hanged?'

'Do you think it's so simple as all that to secure possession of an unwelcome piece of evidence? It's no different from suborning a witness. You have no right to make any such suggestion to me.'

'Then what is going to happen to me?'

'Justice must take its course.'

She grew very pale. A little shudder passed through her body.

'I put myself in your hands. Of course I have no right to ask you to do anything that isn't proper.'

Mr Joyce had not bargained for the little break in her voice which her habitual self-restraint made quite intolerably moving. She looked at him with humble eyes, and he thought that if he rejected their appeal they would haunt him for the rest of his life. After all, nothing could bring poor Hammond back to life again. He wondered what really was the explanation of that letter. It was not fair to conclude from it that she had killed Hammond without provocation. He had lived in the East a long time and his sense of professional honour was not perhaps so acute as it had been twenty years before. He stared at the floor. He made up his mind to do something which he knew was unjustifiable, but it stuck in his throat and he felt dully resentful towards Leslie. It embarrassed him a little to speak.

'I don't know exactly what your husband's circumstances are?'

Flushing a rosy red, she shot a swift glance at him.

'He has a good many tin shares and a small share in two or three rubber estates. I suppose he could raise money.'

'He would have to be told what it was for.'

She was silent for a moment. She seemed to think.

'He's in love with me still. He would make any sacrifice to save me. Is there any need for him to see the letter?'

Mr Joyce frowned a little, and, quick to notice, she went on.

'Robert is an old friend of yours. I'm not asking you to do anything for me, I'm asking you to save a rather simple, kind man who never did you any harm from all the pain that's possible.'

Mr Joyce did not reply. He rose to go and Mrs Crosbie, with the grace that was natural to her, held out her hand. She was shaken by the scene, and her look was haggard, but she made a brave attempt to speed him with courtesy.

'It's so good of you to take all this trouble for me. I can't begin to tell you how grateful I am.'

Mr Joyce returned to his office. He sat in his own room, quite still, attempting to do no work, and pondered. His imagination brought him many strange ideas. He shuddered a little. At last there was the discreet knock on the door which he was expecting. Ong Chi Seng came in.

'I was just going out to have my tiffin, sir,' he said.

'All right.'

'I didn't know if there was anything you wanted before I went, sir.'

'I don't think so. Did you make another appointment for Mr Reed?'

'Yes, sir. He will come at three o'clock.'

'Good.'

Ong Chi Seng turned away, walked to the door, and put his long slim fingers on the handle. Then, as though on an afterthought, he turned back.

'Is there anything you wish me to say to my friend, sir?'

Although Ong Chi Seng spoke English so admirably he had still a difficulty with the letter R, and he pronounced it 'fliend'.

'What friend?'

'About the letter Mrs Crosbie wrote to Hammond deceased, sir.'

'Oh! I'd forgotten about that. I mentioned it to Mrs Crosbie and she denies having written anything of the sort. It's evidently a forgery.'

Mr Joyce took the copy from his pocket and handed it to Ong Chi Seng. Ong Chi Seng ignored the gesture.

'In that case, sir, I suppose there would be no objection if my fliend delivered the letter to the Deputy Public Prosecutor.'

'None. But I don't quite see what good that would do your friend.'

'My fliend, sir thought it was his duty in the interests of justice.'

'I am the last man in the world to interfere with anyone who wishes to do his duty, Chi Seng.'

The eyes of the lawyer and of the Chinese clerk met. Not the shadow of a smile hovered on the lips of either, but they understood each other perfectly.

'I quite understand, sir,' said Ong Chi Seng, 'but from my study of the case R. *v.* Crosbie I am of opinion that the production of such a letter would be damaging to our client.'

'I have always had a very high opinion of your legal acumen, Chi Seng.'

'It has occurred to me, sir, that if I could persuade my fliend to induce the Chinese woman who has the letter to deliver it into our hands it would save a great deal of trouble.'

Mr Joyce idly drew faces on his blotting-paper.

'I suppose your friend is a business man. In what circumstances do you think he would be induced to part with the letter?'

'He has not got the letter. The Chinese woman

has the letter. He is only a relation of the Chinese woman. She is an ignorant woman; she did not know the value of that letter till my fliend told her.'

'What value did he put on it?'

'Ten thousand dollars, sir.'

'Good God! Where on earth do you suppose Mrs Crosbie can get ten thousand dollars! I tell you the letter's a forgery.'

He looked up at Ong Chi Seng as he spoke. The clerk was unmoved by the outburst. He stood at the side of the desk, civil, cool, and observant.

'Mr Crosbie owns an eighth share of the Betong Rubber Estate and a sixth share of the Selantan River Rubber Estate. I have a fliend who will lend him the money on the security of his property.'

'You have a large circle of acquaintances, Chi Seng.'

'Yes sir.'

'Well, you can tell them all to go to hell. I would never advise Mr Crosbie to give a penny more than five thousand for a letter that can be very easily explained.'

'The Chinese woman does not want to sell the letter, sir. My fliend took a long time to persuade her. It is useless to offer her less than the sum mentioned.'

Mr Joyce looked at Ong Chi Seng for at least three minutes. The clerk bore the searching scrutiny without embarrassment. He stood in a respectful attitude with downcast eyes. Mr Joyce knew his man. Clever fellow, Chi Seng, he thought, I wonder how much he's going to get out of it.

'Ten thousand dollars is a very large sum.'

'Mr Crosbie will certainly pay it rather than see his wife hanged, sir.'

Again Mr Joyce paused. What more did Chi Seng know than he had said? He must be pretty sure of his ground if he was obviously so unwilling to bargain. That sum had been fixed because whoever it was that was managing the affair knew it was the largest amount that Robert Crosbie could raise.

'Where is the Chinese woman now?' asked Mr Joyce.

'She is staying at the house of my fliend, sir.'

'Will she come here?'

'I think it more better if you go to her, sir. I can take you to the house tonight and she will give you the letter. She is a very ignorant woman, sir, and she does not understand cheques.'

'I wasn't thinking of giving her a cheque. I will bring banknotes with me.'

'It would only be waste of valuable time to bring less than ten thousand dollars, sir.'

'I quite understand.'

'I will go and tell my fliend after I have had my tiffin, sir.'

'Very good. You'd better meet me outside the club at ten o'clock tonight.'

'With pleasure, sir,' said Ong Chi Seng.

He gave Mr Joyce a little bow and left the room. Mr Joyce went out to have luncheon, too. He went to the club and here, as he had expected, he saw Robert Crosbie. He was sitting at a crowded table, and as he passed him, looking for a place, Mr Joyce touched him on the shoulder.

'I'd like a word or two with you before you go,' he said.

'Right you are. Let me know when you're ready.'

Mr Joyce had made up his mind how to tackle him. He played a rubber of bridge after luncheon in order to allow time for the club to empty itself. He did not want on this particular matter to see Crosbie in his office. Presently Crosbie came into the card-room and looked on till the game was finished. The other players went on their various affairs, and the two were left alone.

'A rather unfortunate thing has happened, old man,' said Mr Joyce, in a tone which he sought to render as casual as possible. 'It appears that your wife sent a letter to Hammond asking him to come to the bungalow on the night he was killed.'

'But that's impossible,' cried Crosbie. 'She's always stated that she had had no communication with Hammond. I know from my own knowledge that she hadn't set eyes on him for a couple of months.'

'The fact remains that the letter exists. It's in the possession of the Chinese woman Hammond was living with. Your wife meant to give you a present on your birthday, and she wanted Hammond to help her get it. In the emotional excitement that she suffered from after the tragedy, she forgot all about it, and having once denied having any communication with Hammond she was afraid to say that she had made a mistake. It was, of course, very unfortunate, but I daresay it was not unnatural.'

Crosbie did not speak. His large, red face bore an expression of complete bewilderment, and Mr Joyce was at once relieved and exasperated by his lack of comprehension. He was a stupid man, and Mr Joyce had no patience with stupidity. But his distress since the catastrophe had touched a soft spot in the lawyer's heart; and Mrs Crosbie had struck the right note when she asked him to help her, not for her sake, but for her husband's.

'I need not tell you that it would be very awkward if this letter found its way into the hands of the prosecution. Your wife has lied, and she would be asked to explain the lie. It alters things a little if Hammond did not intrude, an unwanted guest, but came to your house by invitation. It would be easy to arouse in the assessors a certain indecision of mind.'

Mr Joyce hesitated. He was face to face now with his decision. If it had been a time for humour, he could have smiled at the reflection that he was taking so grave a step, and that the man for whom he was taking it had not the smallest conception of its gravity. If he gave the matter a thought, he probably imagined that what Mr Joyce was doing was what any lawyer did in the ordinary run of business.

'My dear Robert, you are not only my client, but my friend. I think we must get hold of that letter. It'll cost a good deal of money. Except for that I should have preferred to say nothing to you about it.'

'How much?'

'Ten thousand dollars.'

'That's a devil of a lot. With the slump and one thing and another it'll take just about all I've got.'

'Can you get it at once?'

'I suppose so. Old Charlie Meadows will let me have it on my tin shares and on those two estates I'm interested in.'

'Then will you?'

'Is it absolutely necessary?'

'If you want your wife to be acquitted.'

Crosbie grew very red. His mouth sagged strangely.

'But . . .' he could not find words, his face now was purple. 'But I don't understand. She can explain. You don't mean to say they'd find her guilty? They couldn't hang her for putting a noxious vermin out of the way.'

'Of course they wouldn't hang her. They might only find her guilty of manslaughter. She'd probably get off with two or three years.'

Crosbie started to his feet and his red face was distraught with horror.

'Three years.'

Then something seemed to dawn in that slow intelligence of his. His mind was darkness across which shot suddenly a flash of lightning, and though the succeeding darkness was as profound, there remained the memory of something not seen but perhaps just descried. Mr Joyce saw that Crosbie's big red hands, coarse and hard with all the odd jobs he had set them to, trembled.

'What was the present she wanted to make me?'

'She says she wanted to give you a new gun.'

Once more that great red face flushed a deeper red.

'When have you got to have the money ready?'

There was something odd in his voice now. It sounded as though he spoke with invisible hands clutching at his throat.

'At ten o'clock tonight. I thought you could bring it to my office at about six.'

'Is the woman coming to you?'

'No, I'm going to her.'

'I'll bring the money. I'll come with you.'

Mr Joyce looked at him sharply.

'Do you think there's any need for you to do that? I think it would be better if you left me to deal with this matter by myself.'

'It's my money, isn't it? I'm going to come.'

Mr Joyce shrugged his shoulders. They rose and shook hands. Mr Joyce looked at him curiously.

At ten o'clock they met in the empty club.

'Everything all right?' asked Mr Joyce.

'Yes. I've got the money in my pocket.'

'Let's go then.'

They walked down the steps. Mr Joyce's car was waiting for them in the square, silent at that hour, and as they came to it Ong Chi Seng stepped out of the shadow of a house. He took his seat beside the driver and gave him a direction. They drove past the Hotel de l'Europe and turned up by the Sailors' Home to get into Victoria Street. Here the Chinese shops were still open, idlers lounged about, and in the roadway rickshaws and motor-cars and gharries gave a busy air to the scene. Suddenly their car stopped and Chi Seng turned round.

'I think it more better if we walk here, sir,' he said.

They got out and he went on. They followed a step or two behind. Then he asked them to stop.

'You wait here, sir. I go in and speak to my fliend.'

He went into a shop, open to the street, where three or four Chinese were standing behind the counter. It was one of those strange shops where nothing was on view, and you wondered what it was they sold there. They saw him address a stout man in a duck suit with a large gold chain across his breast, and the man shot a quick glance out into the night. He gave Chi Seng a key and Chi Seng came out. He beckoned to the two men waiting and slid into a doorway at the side of the shop. They followed him and found themselves at the foot of a flight of stairs.

'If you wait a minute I will light a match,' he said, always resourceful. 'You come upstairs, please.'

He held a Japanese match in front of them, but it scarcely dispelled the darkness and they groped their way up behind him. On the first floor he unlocked a door and going in lit a gas-jet.

'Come in, please,' he said.

It was a small square room, with one window, and the only furniture consisted of two low Chinese beds covered with matting. In one corner was a large chest, with an elaborate lock, and on this stood a shabby tray with an opium pipe on it and a lamp. There was in the room the faint, acrid scent of the drug. They sat down and Ong Chi Seng offered them cigarettes. In a moment the door was opened by the fat Chinaman whom they had seen behind the counter. He bade them good-evening in very good English, and sat down by the side of his fellow-countryman.

'The Chinese woman is just coming,' said Chi Seng.

A boy from the shop brought in a tray with a teapot and cups and the Chinaman offered them a cup of tea. Crosbie refused. The Chinese talked to one another in undertones, but Crosbie and Mr Joyce were silent. At last there was the sound of a voice outside; someone was calling in a low tone; and the Chinaman went to the door. He opened it, spoke a few words, and ushered a woman in. Mr Joyce looked at her. He had heard much about her since Hammond's death, but he had never seen her. She was a stoutish person, not very young, with a broad, phlegmatic face, she was powdered and rouged and her eyebrows were a thin black line, but she gave you the impression of a woman of character. She wore a pale blue jacket and a white skirt, her costume was not quite European nor quite Chinese, but on her feet were little Chinese silk slippers. She wore heavy gold chains round her neck, gold bangles on her wrists, gold ear-rings and elaborate gold pins in her black hair. She walked in slowly, with the air of a woman sure of herself, but with a certain heaviness of tread, and sat down on the bed beside Ong Chi Seng. He said something to her and nodding she gave an incurious glance at the two white men.

'Has she got the letter?' asked Mr Joyce.

'Yes, sir.'

Crosbie said nothing, but produced a roll of five-hundred-dollar notes. He counted out twenty and handed them to Chi Seng.

'Will you see if that is correct?'

The clerk counted them and gave them to the fat Chinaman.

'Quite correct, sir.'

The Chinaman counted them once more and put them in his pocket. He spoke again to the woman and she drew from her bosom a letter. She gave it to Chi Seng who cast his eyes over it.

'This is the right document, sir,' he said, and was about to give it to Mr Joyce when Crosbie took it from him.

'Let me look at it,' he said.

Mr Joyce watched him read and then held out his hand for it.

'You'd better let me have it.'

Crosbie folded it up deliberately and put it in his pocket.

'No, I'm going to keep it myself. It's cost me enough money.'

Mr Joyce made no rejoinder. The three Chinese watched the little passage, but what they thought about it, or whether they thought, it was impossible to tell from their impassive countenances. Mr Joyce rose to his feet.

'Do you want me any more tonight, sir?' said Ong Chi Seng.

'No.' He knew that the clerk wished to stay behind in order to get his agreed share of the money, and he turned to Crosbie. 'Are you ready?'

Crosbie did not answer, but stood up. The Chinaman went to the door and opened it for them. Chi Seng found a bit of candle and lit it in order to light them down, and the two Chinese accompanied them to the street. They left the woman sitting quietly on the bed smoking a cigarette. When they reached the street the Chinese left them and went once more upstairs.

'What are you going to do with that letter?' asked Mr Joyce.

'Keep it.'

They walked to where the car was waiting for them and here Mr Joyce offered his friend a lift. Crosbie shook his head.

'I'm going to walk.' He hesitated a little and shuffled his feet. 'I went to Singapore on the night of Hammond's death partly to buy a new gun that a man I knew wanted to dispose of. Good-night.'

He disappeared quickly into the darkness.

Mr Joyce was quite right about the trial. The assessors went into court fully determined to acquit Mrs Crosbie. She gave evidence on her own behalf. She told her story simply and with straight-forwardness. The DPP was a kindly man and it was plain that he took no great pleasure in his task. He asked the necessary questions in a deprecating manner. His speech for the prosecution might really have been a speech for the defence, and the assessors took less than five minutes to consider their popular verdict. It was impossible to prevent the great outburst of applause with which it was received by the crowd that packed the court house. The judge congratulated Mrs Crosbie and she was a free woman.

No one had expressed a more violent disapproba-tion of Hammond's behaviour than Mrs Joyce; she was a woman loyal to her friends and she had insisted on the Crosbies' staying with her after the trial, for she in common with everyone else had no doubt of the result, till they could make arrange-ments to go away. It was out of the question for poor, dear, brave Leslie to return to the bungalow at which the horrible catastrophe had taken place. The trial was over by half-past twelve and when they reached the Joyces' house a grand luncheon was awaiting them. Cocktails were ready, Mrs Joyce's million-dollar cocktail was celebrated through all the Malay States, and Mrs Joyce drank Leslie's health. She was a talkative, vivacious woman, and now she was in the highest spirits. It was fortunate, for the rest of them were silent. She did not wonder, her husband never had much to say, and the other two were naturally exhausted from the long strain to which they had been subjected. During luncheon she carried on a bright and spirited monologue. Then coffee was served.

'Now, children,' she said in her gay, bustling fashion, 'you must have a rest and after tea I shall take you both for a drive to the sea.'

Mr Joyce, who lunched at home only by exception, had of course to go back to his office.

'I'm afraid I can't do that, Mrs Joyce,' said Crosbie. 'I've got to get back to the estate at once.'

'Not today?' she cried.

'Yes, now. I've neglected it for too long and I have urgent business. But I shall be very grateful if you will keep Leslie until we have decided what to do.'

Mrs Joyce was about to expostulate, but her husband prevented her.

'If he must go, he must, and there's an end of it.'

There was something in the lawyer's tone which made her look at him quickly. She held her tongue and there was a moment's silence. Then Crosbie spoke again.

'If you'll forgive me, I'll start at once so that I can get there before dark.' He rose from the table. 'Will you come and see me off, Leslie?'

'Of course.'

They went out of the dining-room together.

'I think that's rather inconsiderate of him,' said Mrs Joyce. 'He must know that Leslie wants to be with him just now.'

'I'm sure he wouldn't go if it wasn't absolutely necessary.'

'Well, I'll just see that Leslie's room is ready for her. She wants a complete rest, of course, and then amusement.'

Mrs Joyce left the room and Joyce sat down again. In a short time he heard Crosbie start the engine of his motor-cycle and then noisily scrunch over the gravel of the garden path. He got up and went into the drawing-room. Mrs Crosbie was standing in the middle of it, looking into space, and in her hand was an open letter. He recognized it. She gave him a glance as he came in and saw that she was deathly pale.

'He knows,' she whispered.

Mr Joyce went up to her and took the letter from her hand. He lit a match and set the paper afire. She watched it burn. When he could hold it no longer he dropped it on the tiled floor and they both looked at the paper curl and blacken. Then he trod it into ashes with his foot.

'What does he know?'

She gave him a long, long stare and into her eyes came a strange look. Was it contempt or despair? Mr Joyce could not tell.

'He knows that Geoff was my lover.'

Mr Joyce made no movement and uttered no sound.

'He'd been my lover for years. He became my lover almost immediately after he came back from the war. We knew how careful we must be. When we became lovers I pretended I was tired of him, and he seldom came to the house when Robert was there. I used to drive out to a place we knew and he met me, two or three times a week, and when Robert went to Singapore he used to come to the bungalow late, when the boys had gone for the night. We saw one another constantly, all the time, and not a soul had the smallest suspicion of it. And then lately, a year ago, he began to change. I didn't know what was the matter. I couldn't believe that he didn't care for me any more. He always denied it. I was frantic. I made him scenes. Sometimes I thought he hated me. Oh, if you knew what agonies I endured. I passed through hell. I knew he didn't want me any more and I wouldn't let him go. Misery! Misery! I loved him. I'd given him everything. He was all my life. And then I heard he was living with a Chinese woman. I couldn't believe it. I wouldn't believe it. At last I saw her, I saw her with my own eyes, walking in the village, with her gold bracelets and her necklaces, an old, fat, Chinese woman. She was older than I was. Horrible! They all knew in the kampong that she was his mistress. And when I passed her, she looked at me and I knew that she knew I was his mistress too. I sent for him. I told him I must see him. You've read the letter. I was mad to write it. I didn't know what I was doing. I didn't care. I hadn't seen him for ten days. It was a lifetime. And when last we'd parted he took me in his arms and kissed me, and told me not to worry. And he went straight from my arms to hers.'

She had been speaking in a low voice, vehemently, and now she stopped and wrung her hands.

'That damned letter. We'd always been so careful. He always tore up any word I wrote to him the moment he'd read it. How was I to know he'd leave that one? He came, and I told him I knew about the Chinawoman. He denied it. He said it was only scandal. I was beside myself. I don't know what I said to him. Oh, I hated him then. I tore him limb from limb. I said everything I could to wound him. I insulted him. I could have spat in his face. And at last he turned on me. He told me he was sick and tired of me and never wanted to see me again. He said I bored him to death. And then he acknowledged that it was true about the Chinawoman. He said he'd known her for years, before the war, and she was the only woman who really meant anything to him, and the rest was just pastime. And he said he was glad I knew, and now at least I'd leave him alone. And then I don't know what happened, I was beside myself, I saw red. I seized the revolver and I fired. He gave a cry and I saw I'd hit him. He staggered and rushed for the veranda. I ran after him and fired again. He fell, and I stood over him and I fired and fired till the revolver went click, click, and I knew there were no more cartridges.'

At last she stopped, panting. Her face was no longer human, it was distorted with cruelty, and rage and pain. You would never have thought that this quiet, refined woman was capable of such fiendish passion. Mr Joyce took a step backwards. He was absolutely aghast at the sight of her. It was not a face, it was a gibbering, hideous mask. Then they heard a voice calling from another room, a loud, friendly, cheerful voice. It was Mrs Joyce.

'Come along, Leslie darling, your room's ready. You must be dropping with sleep.'

Mrs Crosbie's features gradually composed themselves. Those passions, so clearly delineated, were smoothed away as with your hand you would smooth a crumpled paper, and in a minute the face was cool and calm and unlined. She was a trifle pale, but her lips broke into a pleasant, affable smile. She was once more the well-bred and even distinguished woman.

'I'm coming, Dorothy dear. I'm sorry to give you so much trouble.'

Ashenden

(1928)

Mr Harrington's Washing

When Ashenden went on deck and saw before him a low-lying coast and a white town he felt a pleasant flutter of excitement. It was early and the sun had not long risen, but the sea was glassy and the sky was blue; it was warm already and one knew that the day would be sweltering. Vladivostok. It really gave one the sensation of being at the end of the world. It was a long journey that Ashenden had made from New York to San Francisco, across the Pacific in a Japanese boat to Yokohama, then from Tsuruki in a Russian boat, he the only Englishman on board, up the Sea of Japan. From Vladivostok he was to take the Trans-Siberian to Petrograd. It was the most important mission that he had ever had and he was pleased with the sense of responsibility that it gave him. He had no one to give him orders, unlimited funds (he carried in a belt next to his skin bills of exchange for a sum so enormous that he was staggered when he thought of them), and though he had been set to do something that was beyond human possibility he did not know this and was prepared to set about his task with confidence. He believed in his own astuteness. Though he had both esteem and admiration for the sensibility of the human race he had little respect for their intelligence: man has always found it easier to sacrifice his life than to learn the multiplication table.

Ashenden did not much look forward to ten days on a Russian train and in Yokohama he had heard rumours that in one or two places bridges had been blown up and the line cut. He was told that the soldiers, completely out of hand, would rob him of everything he possessed and turn him out on the steppe to shift for himself. It was a cheerful prospect. But the train was certainly starting and whatever happened later (and Ashenden had always a feeling that things never turned out as badly as you expected) he was determined to get a place on it. His intention on landing was to go at once to the British Consulate and find out what arrangements had been made for him; but as they neared the shore and he was able to discern the untidy and bedraggled town he felt not a little forlorn. He knew but a few words of Russian. The only man on the ship who spoke English was the purser and though he promised Ashenden to do anything he could to help him Ashenden had the impression that he must not too greatly count upon him. It was a relief then, when they docked, to have a young man, small and with a mop of untidy hair, obviously a Jew, come up to him and ask if his name was Ashenden.

'Mine is Benedict. I'm the interpreter at the British Consulate. I've been told to look after you. We've got you a place on the train tonight.'

Ashenden's spirits went up. They landed. The little Jew looked after his luggage and had his passport examined and then, getting into a car that waited for them, they drove off to the Consulate.

'I've had instructions to offer you every facility,'

said the Consul, 'and you've only got to tell me what you want. I've fixed you up all right on the train, but God knows if you'll ever get to Petrograd. Oh, by the way, I've got a travelling companion for you. He's a man called Harrington, an American, and he's going to Petrograd for a firm in Philadelphia. He's trying to fix up some deal with the Provisional Government.'

'What's he like?' asked Ashenden.

'Oh, he's all right. I wanted him to come with the American Consul to luncheon, but they've gone for an excursion in the country. You must get to the station a couple of hours before the train starts. There's always an awful scrimmage and if you're not there in good time someone will pinch your seat.'

The train started at midnight and Ashenden dined with Benedict at the station restaurant which was, it appeared, the only place in that slatternly town where you could get a decent meal. It was crowded. The service was intolerably slow. Then they went on to the platform, where, though they had still two hours to spare, there was already a seething mob. Whole families, sitting on piles of luggage, seemed to be camped there. People rushed to and fro, or stood in little groups violently arguing. Women screamed. Others were silently weeping. Here two men were engaged in a fierce quarrel. It was a scene of indescribable confusion. The light in the station was wan and cold and the white faces of all those people were like the white faces of the dead waiting, patient or anxious, distraught or penitent, for the judgement of the last day. The train was made up and most of the carriages were already filled to overflowing. When at last Benedict found that in which Ashenden had his place a man sprang out of it excitedly.

'Come in and sit down,' he said. 'I've had the greatest difficulty in keeping your seat. A fellow wanted to come in here with a wife and two children. My Consul has just gone off with him to see the station-master.'

'This is Mr Harrington,' said Benedict.

Ashenden stepped into the carriage. It had two berths in it. The porter stowed his luggage away. He shook hands with his travelling companion.

Mr John Quincy Harrington was a very thin man of somewhat less than middle height, he had a yellow, bony face, with large, pale-blue eyes and when he took off his hat to wipe his brow wet from the perturbation he had endured he showed a large, bald skull; it was very bony and the ridges and protuberances stood out disconcertingly. He wore a bowler hat, a black coat and waistcoat, and a pair of striped trousers; a very high white collar and a neat, unobtrusive tie. Ashenden did not know precisely how you should dress in order to take a ten days' journey across Siberia, but he could not but think that Mr Harrington's costume was eccentric. He spoke with precision in a high-pitched voice and in an accent that Ashenden recognized as that of New England.

In a minute the station-master came accompanied by a bearded Russian, suffering evidently from profound emotion, and followed by a lady holding two children by the hand. The Russian, tears running down his face, was talking with quivering lips to the station-master and his wife between her sobs was apparently telling him the story of her life. When they arrived at the carriage the altercation became more violent and Benedict joined in with his fluent Russian. Mr Harrington did not know a word of the language, but being obviously of an excitable turn broke in and explained in voluble English that these seats had been booked by the Consuls of Great Britain and the United States respectively, and though he didn't know about the King of England, he could tell them straight and they could take it from him that the President of the United States would never permit an American citizen to be done out of a seat on the train that he had duly paid for. He would yield to force, but to nothing else, and if they touched him he would register a complaint with the Consul at once. He said all this and a great deal more to the station-master, who of course had no notion what he was talking about, but with much emphasis and a good deal of gesticulation made him in reply a passionate speech. This roused Mr Harrington to the utmost pitch of indignation, for shaking his fist in the station-master's face, his own pale with fury, he cried out:

'Tell him I don't understand a word he says and I don't want to understand. If the Russians want us to look upon them as a civilized people why don't they talk a civilized language? Tell him that I am Mr John Quincy Harrington and I'm travelling on behalf of Messrs Crewe and Adams of Philadelphia with a special letter of introduction to Mr Kerensky and if I'm not left in peaceful possession of this carriage Mr Crewe will take the matter up with the Administration in Washington.'

Mr Harrington's manner was so truculent and his gestures so menacing that the station-master, throwing up the sponge, turned on his heel without another word and walked moodily away. He was followed by the bearded Russian and his wife arguing heatedly with him and the two apathetic children. Mr Harrington jumped back into the carriage.

'I'm terribly sorry to have to refuse to give up my seat to a lady with two children,' he said. 'No one knows better than I the respect due to a woman and a mother, but I've got to get to Petrograd by this train if I don't want to lose a very important order and I'm not going to spend ten days in a corridor for all the mothers in Russia.'

'I don't blame you,' said Ashenden.

'I am a married man and I have two children myself. I know that travelling with your family is a difficult matter, but there's nothing that I know to prevent you from staying at home.'

When you are shut up with a man for ten days in a railway carriage you can hardly fail to learn most of what there is to know about him, and for ten days (for eleven to be exact) Ashenden spent twenty-four hours a day with Mr Harrington. It is true that they went into the dining-room three times a day for their meals, but they sat opposite to one another; it is true that the train stopped for an hour morning and afternoon so that they were able to have a tramp up and down the platform, but they walked side by side. Ashenden made acquaintance with some of his fellow-travellers and sometimes they came into the compartment to have a chat, but if they only spoke French or German Mr Harrington would watch them with aciduous disapproval and if they spoke English he would never let them get a word in. For Mr Harrington was a talker. He talked as though it were a natural function of the human being, automatically, as men breathe or digest their food; he talked not because he had something to say, but because he could not help himself, in a high-pitched, nasal voice, without inflection, at one dead level of tone. He talked with precision, using a copious vocabulary and forming his sentences with deliberation; he never used a short word when a longer one would do; he never paused. He went on and on. It was not a torrent, for there was nothing impetuous about it, it was like a stream of lava pouring irresistibly down the side of a volcano. It flowed with a quiet and steady force that overwhelmed everything that was in its path.

Ashenden thought he had never known as much about anyone as he knew about Mr Harrington, and not only about him, with all his opinions, habits and circumstances, but about his wife and his wife's family, his children and their school-fellows, his employers and the alliances they had made for three or four generations with the best families of Philadelphia. His own family had come from Devonshire early in the eighteenth century and Mr Harrington had been to the village where the graves of his forebears were still to be seen in the churchyard. He was proud of his English ancestry, but proud too of his American birth, though to him America was a little strip of land along the Atlantic coast and Americans were a small number of persons of English or Dutch origin whose blood had never been sullied by foreign admixture. He looked upon the Germans, Swedes, Irish and the inhabitants of Central and Eastern Europe who for the last hundred years have descended upon the United States as interlopers.

He turned his attention away from them as a maiden lady who lived in a secluded manor might avert her eyes from the factory chimneys that had trespassed upon her retirement.

When Ashenden mentioned a man of vast wealth who owned some of the finest pictures in America Mr Harrington said:

'I've never met him. My great-aunt Maria Penn Warmington always said his grandmother was a very good cook. My great-aunt Maria was terribly sorry when she left her to get married. She said she never knew anyone who could make an apple pancake as she could.'

Mr Harrington was devoted to his wife and he told Ashenden at unbelievable length how cultivated and what a perfect mother she was. She had delicate health and had undergone a great number of operations all of which he described in detail. He had had two operations himself, one on his tonsils and one to remove his appendix and he took Ashenden day by day through his experiences. All his friends had had operations and his knowledge of surgery was encyclopedic. He had two sons, both at school, and he was seriously considering whether he would not be well-advised to have them operated on. It was curious that one of them should have enlarged tonsils, and he was not at all happy about the appendix of the other. They were more devoted to one another than he had ever seen two brothers be and a very good friend of his, the brightest surgeon in Philadelphia, had offered to operate on them both together so that they should not be separated. He showed Ashenden photographs of the boys and their mother. This journey of his to Russia was the first time in their lives that

he had been separated from them and every morning he wrote a long letter to his wife telling her
everything that had happened and a good deal of
what he had said during the day. Ashenden
watched him cover sheet after sheet of paper with
his neat, legible and precise handwriting.

Mr Harrington had read all the books on conversation and knew its technique to the last detail. He
had a little book in which he noted down the stories
he heard and he told Ashenden that when he was
going out to dinner he always looked up half a
dozen so that he should not be at a loss. They were
marked with a G if they could be told in general
society and with an M (for men) if they were more
fit for rough masculine ears. He was a specialist in
that peculiar form of anecdote that consists in nar-
rating a long serious incident, piling detail upon
detail, till a comic end is reached. He spared you
nothing and Ashenden foreseeing the point long
before he arrived would clench his hands and knit
his brows in the strenuous effort not to betray his
impatience and at last force from his unwilling
mouth a grim and hallow laugh. If someone came
into the compartment in the middle Mr Harrington
would greet him with cordiality.

'Come right in and sit down. I was just telling
my friend a story. You must listen to it, it's one of
the funniest things you ever heard.'

Then he would begin again from the very beginning and repeat it word for word, without altering a
single apt epithet, till he reached the humorous
end. Ashenden suggested once that they should see
whether they could find two people on the train
who played cards so that they might while away
the time with a game of bridge, but Mr Harrington

said he never touched cards and when Ashenden in desperation began to play patience he pulled a wry face.

'It beats me how an intelligent man can waste his time card playing, and of all the unintellectual pursuits I have ever seen it seems to me that solitaire is the worst. It kills conversation. Man is a social animal and he exercises the highest part of his nature when he takes part in social intercourse.'

'There is a certain elegance in wasting time,' said Ashenden. 'Any fool can waste money, but when you waste time you waste what is priceless. Besides,' he added with bitterness, 'you can still talk.'

'How can I talk when your attention is taken up by whether you are going to get a black seven to put on a red eight? Conversation calls forth the highest powers of the intellect and if you have made a study of it you have the right to expect that the person you're talking to will give you the fullest attention he is capable of.'

He did not say this acrimoniously, but with the good-humoured patience of a man who has been much tried. He was just stating a plain fact and Ashenden could take it or leave it. It was the claim of the artist to have his work taken seriously.

Mr Harrington was a diligent reader. He read pencil in hand, underlining passages that attracted his attention and on the margin making in his neat writing comments on what he read. This he was fond of discussing and when Ashenden himself was reading and felt on a sudden that Mr Harrington, book in one hand and pencil in the other, was looking at him with his large pale eyes he began to have violent palpitations of the heart. He dared not look up, he dared not even turn the page, for he knew that Mr Harrington would regard this as ample excuse to break into a discourse, but remained with his eyes fixed desperately on a single word, like a chicken with its beak to a chalk line, and only ventured to breathe when he realized that Mr Harrington, having given up the attempt, had resumed his reading. He was then engaged on a History of the American Constitution in two volumes and for recreation was perusing a stout volume that purported to contain all the great speeches of the world. For Mr Harrington was an after-dinner speaker and had read all the best books on speaking in public. He knew exactly how to get on good terms with his audience, just where to put in the serious words that touched their hearts, how to catch their attention by a few apt stories and finally with what degree of eloquence, suiting the occasion, to deliver his peroration.

Mr Harrington was very fond of reading aloud. Ashenden had had frequent occasion to observe the distressing propensity of Americans for this pastime. In hotel drawing-rooms at night after dinner he had often seen the father of a family seated in a retired corner and surrounded by his wife, his two sons and his daughter, reading to them. On ships crossing the Atlantic he had sometimes watched with awe the tall, spare gentleman of commanding aspect who sat in the centre of fifteeen ladies no longer in their first youth and in a resonant voice read to them the history of Art. Walking up and down the promenade deck he had passed honeymooning couples lying on deck-chairs and caught the unhurried tones of the bride as she read to her young husband the pages of a popular novel. It had always seemed to him a curious way of showing affection. He had had friends who had offered to read to him and he had known women who had said they loved being read to, but he had always politely refused the invitation and firmly ignored the hint. He liked neither reading aloud nor being read aloud to. In his heart he thought the national predilection for this form of entertainment the only flaw in the perfection of the American character. But the immortal gods love a good laugh at the expense of human beings and now delivered him, bound and helpless, to the knife of the high priest. Mr Harrington flattered himself that he was a very good reader and he explained to Ashenden the theory and practice of the art. Ashenden learned that there were two schools, the dramatic and the natural: in the first you imitated the voices of those who spoke (if you were reading a novel) and when the heroine wailed you wailed and when emotion choked her you choked too; but in the other you read as impassively as though you were reading the price-list of a mail-order house in Chicago. This was the school Mr Harrington belonged to. In the seventeen years of his married life he had read aloud to his wife, and to his sons as soon as they were old enough to appreciate them, the novels of Sir Walter Scott, Jane Austen, Dickens, the Brontë Sisters, Thackeray, George Eliot, Nathaniel Hawthorne and W. J. Howells. Ashenden came to the conclusion that it was second nature with Mr Harrington to read aloud and to prevent him from doing so made him as uneasy as cutting off his tobacco made the confirmed smoker. He would take you unawares.

'Listen to this,' he would say, 'you must listen to

this,' as though he were suddenly struck by the excellence of a maxim or the neatness of a phrase. 'Now just tell me if you don't think this is remarkably well put. It's only three lines.'

He read them and Ashenden was willing to give him a moment's attention, but having finished them, without pausing for a moment to take breath, he went on. He went right on. On and on. In his measured high-pitched voice, without emphasis or expression, he read page after page. Ashenden fidgeted, crossed and uncrossed his legs, lit cigarettes and smoked them, sat first in one position, then in another. Mr Harrington went on and on. The train went leisurely through the interminable steppes of Siberia. They passed villages and crossed rivers. Mr Harrington went on and on. When he finished a great speech by Edmund Burke he put down the book in triumph.

'Now that in my opinion is one of the finest orations in the English language. It is certainly a part of our common heritage that we can look upon with genuine pride.'

'Doesn't it seem to you a little ominous that the people to whom Edmund Burke made that speech are all dead?' asked Ashenden gloomily.

Mr Harrington was about to reply that this was hardly to be wondered at since the speech was made in the eighteenth century when it dawned upon him that Ashenden (bearing up wonderfully under affliction as any unprejudiced person could not fail to admit) was making a joke. He slapped his knee and laughed heartily.

'Gee, that's a good one,' he said. 'I'll write that down in my little book. I see exactly how I can bring it in one time when I have to speak at our luncheon club.'

Mr Harrington was a highbrow; but that appellation, invented by the vulgar as a term of abuse, he had accepted like the instrument of a saint's martyrdom, the gridiron of Saint Laurence for instance or the wheel of Saint Catherine, as an honorific title. He gloried in it.

'Emerson was a highbrow,' he said. 'Longfellow was a highbrow. Oliver Wendell Holmes was a highbrow. James Russell Lowell was a highbrow.'

Mr Harrington's study of American literature had taken him no further down the years than the period during which those eminent, but not precisely thrilling authors, flourished.

Mr Harrington was a bore. He exasperated Ashenden, and enraged him; he got on his nerves, and drove him to frenzy. But Ashenden did not dislike him. His self-satisfaction was enormous but so ingenuous that you could not resent it; his conceit was so childlike that you could only smile at it. He was so well-meaning, so thoughtful, so deferential, so polite that though Ashenden would willingly have killed him he could not but own that in that short while he had conceived for Mr Harrington something very like affection. His manners were exquisite, formal, a trifle elaborate perhaps (there is no harm in that, for good manners are the product of an artificial state of society and so can bear a touch of the powdered wig and the lace ruffle) but though natural to his good breeding they gained a pleasant significance from his good heart. He was ready to do anyone a kindness and seemed to find nothing too much trouble if he could thereby oblige his fellow man. He was eminently *serviable*. And it may be that this is a word for which there is no exact translation because the charming quality it denotes is not very common among our practical people. When Ashenden was ill for a couple of days Mr Harrington nursed him with devotion. Ashenden was embarrassed by the care he took of him and though racked with pain could not help laughing at the fussy attention with which Mr Harrington took his temperature, from his neatly packed valise extracted a whole regiment of tabloids and firmly doctored him; and he was touched by the trouble he gave himself to get from the dining-car the things that he thought Ashenden could eat. He did everything in the world for him but stop talking.

It was only when he was dressing that Mr Harrington was silent, for then his maidenly mind was singly occupied with the problem of changing his clothes before Ashenden without indelicacy. He was extremely modest. He changed his linen every day, neatly taking it out of his suit-case and neatly putting back what was soiled; but he performed miracles of dexterity in order during the process not to show an inch of bare skin. After a day or two Ashenden gave up the struggle to keep neat and clean in that dirty train, with one lavatory for the whole carriage, and soon was as grubby as the rest of the passengers; but Mr Harrington refused to yield to the difficulties. He performed his toilet with deliberation, notwithstanding the impatient persons who rattled the door-handle, and returned from the lavatory every morning washed, shining and smelling of soap. Once dressed, in his black coat, striped trousers and well-polished shoes, he looked as spruce as though he had just stepped out of his tidy little red-brick house in Philadelphia and was about to board the street-car that would take him down town to his office. At one point of the journey it was announced that an attempt had been made to blow up a bridge and that there were disturbances at the next station over the river; it might be that the train would be stopped and the passengers turned adrift or taken prisoners. Ashenden, thinking he might be separated from his luggage, took the precaution to change into his thickest clothes so that if he had to pass the winter in Siberia he need suffer as little as necessary from the cold; but Mr Harrington would not listen to reason; he made no preparations for the possible experience and Ashenden had the conviction that if he spent three months in a Russian prison he would still preserve that smart and natty appearance. A troop of Cossacks boarded the train and stood on the platform of each carriage with their guns loaded, and the train rattled gingerly over the damaged bridge; then they came to the station at which they had been warned of danger, put on steam and dashed straight through it. Mr Harrington was mildly satirical when Ashenden changed back into a light summer suit.

Mr Harrington was a keen business man. It was obvious that it would need someone very astute to over-reach him and Ashenden was sure that his employers had been well-advised to send him on this errand. He would safeguard their interests with all his might and if he succeeded in driving a bargain with the Russians it would be a hard one. His loyalty to his firm demanded that. He spoke of the partners with affectionate reverence. He loved them and was proud of them; but he did not envy them because their wealth was great. He was quite content to work on a salary and thought himself adequately paid; so long as he could educate his boys and leave his widow enough to live on what was money to him? He thought it a trifle vulgar to be rich. He looked upon culture as more important than money. He was careful of it and after every meal put down in his note-book exactly what it had cost him. His firm might be certain that he would not charge a penny more for his expenses than he had spent. But having discovered that poor people came to the station at the stopping places of the train to beg and seeing that the war had really brought them to destitution he took care before each halt to supply himself with ample small change and in a shame-faced way, mocking himself for being taken in by such imposters, distributed everything in his pocket.

'Of course I know they don't deserve it,' he said, 'and I don't do it for them. I do it entirely for my own peace of mind. I should feel so terribly badly if I thought some man really was hungry and I'd refused to give him the price of a meal.'

Mr Harrington was absurd, but lovable. It was inconceivable that anyone should be rude to him, it would have seemed as dreadful as hitting a child; and Ashenden, chafing inwardly but with a pretence of amiability, suffered meekly and with a truly Christian spirit the affliction of the gentle, ruthless creature's society. It took eleven days at that time to get from Vladivostok to Petrograd and Ashenden felt that he could not have borne another day. If it had been twelve he would have killed Mr Harrington.

When at last (Ashenden tired and dirty, Mr Harrington neat, sprightly and sententious) they reached the outskirts of Petrograd and stood at the window looking at the crowded houses of the city, Mr Harrington turned to Ashenden and said:

'Well, I never would have thought that eleven days in the train would pass so quickly. We've had a wonderful time. I've enjoyed your company and I know you've enjoyed mine. I'm not going to pretend I don't know that I'm a pretty good conversationalist. But now we've come together like this we must take care to stay together. We must see as much of one another as we can while I'm in Petrograd.'

'I shall have a great deal to do,' said Ashenden. 'I'm afraid my time won't be altogether my own.'

'I know,' answered Mr Harrington cordially. 'I expect to be pretty busy myself, but we can have breakfast together anyway and we'll meet in the evening and compare notes. It would be too bad if we drifted apart now.'

'Too bad,' sighed Ashenden.

When Ashenden found himself in his bedroom at the hotel and, for the first time for it seemed an age, alone he sat down and looked about him. He had not the energy to start immediately to unpack. How many of these hotel bedrooms had he known since the beginning of the war, grand or shabby, in one place and one land after another! It seemed to him that he had been living in his luggage for as long as he could remember. He was weary. He asked himself how he was going to set about the work that he had been sent to do. He felt lost in the immensity of Russia and very solitary. He had protested when he was chosen for this mission, it looked too large an order, but his protests were ignored. He was chosen not because those in authority thought him particularly suited for the job, but because there was no one to be found who was more suited. There was a knock at the door and Ashenden, pleased to make use of the few words of the language he knew, called out in Russian. The door was opened. He sprang to his feet.

'Come in, come in,' he cried. 'I'm awfully glad to see you.'

Three men entered. He knew them by sight, since they had travelled on the same boat with him from San Francisco to Yokohama, but following their instructions no communications had passed between them and Ashenden. They were Czechs, exiled from their country for their revolutionary activity and long settled in America, who had been sent over to Russia to help Ashenden in his mission and put him in touch with Professor Z whose authority over the Czechs in Russia was absolute. Their chief was a certain Dr Egon Orth, a tall thin man, with a little grey head; he was minister to some church in the Middle West and a doctor of divinity; but had abandoned his cure to work for the liberation of his country, and Ashenden had the impression that he was an intelligent fellow who would not put too fine a point on matters of conscience. A parson with a fixed idea has this advantage over common men that he can persuade himself of the Almighty's approval for almost any goings on. Dr Orth had a merry twinkle in his eye and a dry humour.

Ashenden had had two secret interviews with him in Yokohama and had learnt that Professor Z, though eager to free his country from the Austrian rule and since he knew that this could only come about by the downfall of the Central Powers with the allies body and soul, yet had scruples; he would not do things that outraged his conscience, all must be straightforward and above board, and so some things that it was necessary to do had to be done without his knowledge. His influence was so great that his wishes could not be disregarded, but on occasion it was felt better not to let him know too much of what was going on.

Dr Orth had arrived in Petrograd a week before Ashenden and now put before him what he had learned of the situation. It seemed to Ashenden that it was critical and if anything was to be done it must be done quickly. The army was dissatisfied and mutinous, the Government under the weak Kerensky was tottering and held power only because no one else had the courage to seize it, famine was staring the country in the face and already the possibility had to be considered that the Germans would march on Petrograd. The ambassadors of Great Britain and the United States had been apprised of Ashenden's coming, but his mission was secret even from them, and there were particular reasons why he could demand no assistance from them. He arranged with Dr Orth to make an appointment with Professor Z so that he could learn his views and explain to him that he had the financial means to support any scheme that seemed likely to prevent the catastrophe that the Allied governments foresaw of Russia's making a separate peace. But he had to get in touch with influential persons in all classes. Mr Harrington with his business proposition and his letters to Ministers of State would be thrown in contact with members of the Government and Mr Harrington wanted an interpreter. Dr Orth spoke Russian almost as well as his own language and it struck Ashenden that he would be admirably suited to the post. He explained the circumstances to him and it was arranged that while Ashenden and Mr Harrington were at luncheon Dr Orth should come in, greeting Ashenden as though he had not seen him before, and be introduced to Mr Harrington; then Ashenden, guiding the conversation, would suggest to Mr Harrington that the heavens had sent in Dr Orth the ideal man for his purpose.

But there was another person on whom Ashenden had fixed as possibly useful to him and now he said:

'Have you ever heard of a woman called Anastasia Alexandrovna Leonidov? She's the daughter of Alexander Denisiev.'

'I know all about him of course.'

'I have reason to believe she's in Petrograd. Will you find out where she lives and what she's doing?'

'Certainly.'

Dr Orth spoke in Czech to one of the two men who accompanied him. They were sharp-looking fellows both of them, one was tall and fair and the other was short and dark, but they were younger than Dr Orth and Ashenden understood that they were there to do as he bade them. The man nodded, got up, shook hands with Ashenden and went out.

'You shall have all the information possible this afternoon.'

'Well, I think there's nothing more we can do for the present,' said Ashenden. 'To tell you the truth I haven't had a bath for eleven days and I badly want one.'

Ashenden had never quite made up his mind whether the pleasure of reflection was better pursued in a railway carriage or in a bath. So far as the act of invention was concerned he was inclined to prefer a train that went smoothly and not too fast, and many of his best ideas had come to him when he was thus traversing the plains of France; but for the delight of reminiscence or the entertainment of embroidery upon a theme already in his head he had no doubt that nothing could compare with a hot bath. He considered now, wallowing in soapy water like a water-buffalo in a muddy pond, the grim pleasantry of his relations with Anastasia Alexandrovna Leonidov.

In these stories no more than the barest suggestion has been made that Ashenden was capable on occasions of the passion ironically called tender. The specialists in this matter, those charming creatures who make a business of what philosophers know is but a diversion, assert that writers, painters and musicians, all in short who are connected with the arts, in the relation of love cut no very conspicuous figure. There is much cry but little wool. They rave or sigh, make phrases and strike many a romantic attitude, but in the end, loving art or themselves (which with them is one and the same thing) better than the object of their emotion offer a shadow when the said object, with the practical common sense of the sex, demands a substance. It may be so and this may be the reason (never before suggested) why women in their souls look upon art with such a virulent hatred. Be this as it may Ashenden in the last twenty years had felt his heart go pit-a-pat because of one charming person after another. He had had a good deal of fun and had paid for it with a great deal of misery, but even when suffering most acutely from the pangs of unrequited love he had been able to say to himself, albeit with a wry face, after all, it's grist to the mill.

Anastasia Alexandrovna Leonidov was the daughter of a revolutionary who had escaped from Siberia after being sentenced to penal servitude for life and had settled in England. He was an able man and had supported himself for thirty years by the activity of a restless pen and had even made himself a distinguished position in English letters. When Anastasia Alexandrovna reached a suitable age she married Vladimir Semenovich Leonidov, also an exile from his native country, and it was after she had been married to him for some years that Ashenden made her acquaintance. It was at the time when Europe discovered Russia. Everyone was reading the Russian novelists, the Russian dancers captivated the civilized world, and the Russian composers set shivering the sensibility of persons who were beginning to want a change from Wagner. Russian art seized upon Europe with the virulence of an epidemic of influenza. New phrases became the fashion, new colours, new emotions, and the highbrows described themselves without a moment's hesitation as members of the intelligentsia. It was a difficult word to spell but an easy one to say. Ashenden fell like the rest, changed the cushions of his sitting-room, hung an eikon on the wall, read Chekoff and went to the ballet.

Anastasia Alexandrovna was by birth, circumstances and education very much a member of the intelligentsia. She lived with her husband in a tiny house near Regent's Park and here all the literary folk in London might gaze with humble reverence at pale-faced bearded giants who leaned against the wall like caryatids taking a day off; they were revolutionaries to a man and it was a miracle that they were not in the mines of Siberia. Women of letters tremulously put their lips to a glass of vodka. If you were lucky and greatly favoured you might shake hands there with Diaghileff and now and again, like a peach-blossom wafted by the breeze, Pavlova herself hovered in and out. At this time Ashenden's success had not been so great as to affront the highbrows, he had very distinctly been one of them in his youth, and though some already looked askance, others (optimistic creatures with a faith in human nature) still had hopes of him. Anastasia Alexandrovna told him to his face that he was a member of the intelligentsia. Ashenden was quite ready to believe it. He was in a state when he was ready to believe anything. He was thrilled and excited. It seemed to him that at last he was about to capture that illusive spirit of romance that he had so long been chasing. Anastasia Alexandrovna had fine eyes and a good, though for these days, too voluptuous figure, high cheek-bones and a snub nose (this was very Tartar), a wide mouth full of large square teeth and a pale skin. She dressed somewhat flamboyantly. In her dark melancholy eyes Ashenden saw the boundless steppes of Russia, and the Kremlin with its pealing bells, and the solemn ceremonies of Easter at St Isaac's, and forests of silver beeches and the Nevsky Prospekt; it was astonishing how much he saw in her eyes. They were round and shining and slightly protuberant like those of a Pekinese. They talked together of Alyosha in the *Brothers Karamazov*, of Natasha in *War and Peace*, of Anna Karenina and of *Fathers and Sons*.

Ashenden soon discovered that her husband was quite unworthy of her and presently learned that she shared his opinion. Vladimir Semenovich was a little man with a large, long head that looked as though it had been pulled like a piece of liquorice, and he had a great shock of unruly Russian hair. He was a gentle, unobtrusive creature and it was hard to believe that the Czarist government had really feared his revolutionary activities. He taught Russian and wrote for papers in Moscow. He was amiable and obliging. He needed these qualities for Anastasia Alexandrovna was a woman of character: when she had a toothache Vladimir Semenovich suffered the agonies of the damned and when her heart was wrung by the suffering of her unhappy country Vladimir Semenovich might well have wished he had never been born. Ashenden could not help admitting that he was a poor thing, but he was so harmless that he conceived quite a liking for him, and when in due course he had disclosed his passion to Anastasia Alexandrovna and to his joy found it was returned he was puzzled to know what to do about Vladimir Semenovich. Neither Anastasia Alexandrovna nor he felt that they could live another minute out of one another's pockets, and Ashenden feared that with her revolutionary views and all that she would never consent to marry him; but somewhat to his surprise, and very much to his relief, she accepted the suggestion with alacrity.

'Would Vladimir Semenovich let himself be divorced, do you think?' he asked, as he sat on the sofa, leaning against the cushions the colour of which reminded him of raw meat just gone bad, and held her hand.

'Vladimir adores me,' she answered. 'It'll break his heart.'

'He's a nice fellow, I shouldn't like him to be very unhappy. I hope he'll get over it.'

'He'll never get over it. That is the Russian spirit. I know that when I leave him he'll feel that he has lost everything that made life worth living for him. I've never known anyone so wrapped up in a woman as he is in me. But of course he wouldn't want to stand in the way of my happiness. He's far too great for that. He'll see that when it's a question of my own self-development I haven't the right to hesitate. Vladimir will give me my freedom without question.'

At that time the divorce law in England was even more complicated and absurd than it is now and in case she was not acquainted with its peculiarities Ashenden explained to Anastasia Alexandrovna the difficulties of the case. She put her hand gently on his.

'Vladimir would never expose me to the vulgar notoriety of the divorce court. When I tell him that I have decided to marry you he will commit suicide.'

'That would be terrible,' said Ashenden.

He was startled, but thrilled. It was really very much like a Russian novel and he saw the moving and terrible pages, pages and pages, in which Dostoievsky would have described the situation. He knew the lacerations his characters would have suffered, the broken bottles of champagne, the visits to the gipsies, the vodka, the swoonings, the catalepsy and the long, long speeches everyone would have made. It was all very dreadful and wonderful and shattering.

'It would make us horribly unhappy,' said Anastasia Alexandrovna, 'but I don't know what else he could do. I couldn't ask him to live without me. He would be like a ship without a rudder or a car without a carburettor. I know Vladimir so well. He will commit suicide.'

'How?' asked Ashenden, who had the realist's passion for the exact detail.

'He will blow his brains out.'

Ashenden remembered *Rosmerholm*. In his day he had been an ardent Ibsenite and had even flirted with the notion of learning Norwegian so that he might, by reading the master in the original, get at the secret essence of his thought. He had once seen Ibsen in the flesh drink a glass of Munich beer.

'But do you think we could ever pass another easy hour if we had the death of that man on our conscience?' he asked. 'I have a feeling that he would always be between us.'

'I know we shall suffer, we shall suffer dreadfully,' said Anastasia Alexandrovna, 'but how can we help it? Life is like that. We must think of Vladimir. There is his happiness to be considered too. He will prefer to commit suicide.'

She turned her face away and Ashenden saw that the heavy tears were coursing down her cheeks. He was much moved. For he had a soft heart and it was dreadful to think of poor Vladimir lying there with a bullet in his brain.

These Russians, what fun they have!

But when Anastasia Alexandrovna had mastered her emotion she turned to him gravely. She looked at him with her humid, round and slightly protuberant eyes.

'We must be quite sure that we're doing the right thing,' she said. 'I should never forgive myself if I'd allowed Vladimir to commit suicide and then found I'd made a mistake. I think we ought to make sure that we really love one another.'

'But don't you know?' exclaimed Ashenden in a low, tense voice. 'I know.'

'Let's go over to Paris for a week and see how we get on. Then we shall know.'

Ashenden was a trifle conventional and the suggestion took him by surprise. But only for a moment. Anastasia was wonderful. She was very quick and she saw the hesitation that for an instant troubled him.

'Surely you have no bourgeois prejudices?' she said.

'Of course not,' he assured her hurriedly, for he would much sooner have been thought knavish than bourgeois, 'I think it's a splendid idea.'

'Why should a woman hazard her whole life on a throw? It's impossible to know what a man is really like till you've lived with him. It's only fair to give her the opportunity to change her mind before it's too late.'

'Quite so,' said Ashenden.

Anastasia Alexandrovna was not a woman to let the grass grow under her feet and so having made their arrangements forthwith on the following Saturday they started for Paris.

'I shall not tell Vladimir that I am going with you,' she said. 'It would only distress him.'

'It would be a pity to do that,' said Ashenden.

'And if at the end of the week I come to the conclusion that we've made a mistake he need never know anything about it.'

'Quite so,' said Ashenden.

They met at Victoria station.

'What class have you got?' she asked him.

'First.'

'I'm glad of that. Father and Vladimir travel third on account of their principles, but I always feel sick on a train and I like to be able to lean my head on somebody's shoulder. It's easier in a first-class carriage.'

When the train started Anastasia Alexandrovna said she felt dizzy, so she took off her hat and leaned her head on Ashenden's shoulder. He put his arm round her waist.

'Keep quite still, won't you?' she said.

When they got on to the boat she went down to the ladies' cabin and at Calais was able to eat a very hearty meal, but when they got into the train she took off her hat again and rested her head on Ashenden's shoulder. He thought he would like to read and took up a book.

'Do you mind not reading?' she said. 'I have to be held and when you turn the pages it makes me feel all funny.'

Finally they reached Paris and went to a little hotel on the Left Bank that Anastasia Alexandrovna knew of. She said it had atmosphere. She could not bear those great big grand hotels on the other side; they were hopelessly vulgar and bourgeois.

'I'll go anywhere you like,' said Ashenden, 'as long as there's a bathroom.'

She smiled and pinched his cheek.

'How adorably English you are. Can't you do without a bathroom for a week? My dear, my dear, you have so much to learn.'

They talked far into the night about Maxim

Gorki and Karl Marx, human destiny, love and brotherhood of man; and drank innumerable cups of Russian tea, so that in the morning Ashenden would willingly have breakfasted in bed and got up for luncheon; but Anastasia Alexandrovna was an early riser. When life was so short and there was so much to do it was a sinful thing to have breakfast a minute after half-past eight. They sat down in a dingy little dining-room the windows of which showed no signs of having been opened for a month. It was full of atmosphere. Ashenden asked Anastasia Alexandrovna what she would have for breakfast.

'Scrambled eggs,' she said.

She ate heartily. Ashenden had already noticed that she had a healthy appetite. He supposed it was a Russian trait: you could not picture Anna Karenina making her midday meal off a bath-bun and a cup of coffee, could you?

After breakfast they went to the Louvre and in the afternoon they went to the Luxembourg. They dined early in order to go to the Comédie Française; then they went to a Russian cabaret where they danced. When next morning at eight-thirty they took their places in the dining-room and Ashenden asked Anastasia Alexandrovna what she fancied, her reply was:

'Scrambled eggs.'

'But we had scrambled eggs yesterday,' he expostulated.

'Let's have them again today,' she smiled.

'All right.'

They spent the day in the same manner except that they went to the Carnavalet instead of the Louvre and the Musée Guimet instead of the Luxembourg. But when the morning after in answer to Ashenden's inquiry Anastasia Alexandrovna again asked for scrambled eggs, his heart sank.

'But we had scrambled eggs yesterday and the day before,' he said.

'Don't you think that's a very good reason to have them again today?'

'No, I don't.'

'Is it possible that your sense of humour is a little deficient this morning?' she asked. 'I eat scrambled eggs every day. It's the only way I like them.'

'Oh, very well. In that case of course we'll have scrambled eggs.'

But the following morning he could not face them.

'Will you have scrambled eggs as usual?' he asked her.

'Of course,' she smiled affectionately, showing him two rows of large square teeth.

'All right, I'll order them for you, I shall have mine fried.'

The smile vanished from her lips.

'Oh?' She paused a moment. 'Don't you think that's rather inconsiderate? Do you think it's fair to give the cook unnecessary work? You English, you're all the same, you look upon servants as machines. Does it occur to you that they have hearts like yours, the same feelings and the same emotions? How can you be surprised that the proletariat are seething with discontent when the bourgeoisie like you are so monstrously selfish?'

'Do you really think that there'll be a revolution in England if I have my eggs in Paris fried rather than scrambled?'

She tossed her pretty head in indignation.

'You don't understand. It's the principle of the thing. You think it's a jest, of course I know you're being funny, I can laugh at a joke as well as anyone, Chekoff was well-known in Russia as a humorist; but don't you see what is involved? Your whole attitude is wrong. It's a lack of feeling. You wouldn't talk like that if you had been through the events of 1905 in Petersburg. When I think of the crowds in front of the Winter Palace kneeling in the snow while the Cossacks charged them, women and children! No, no, no.'

Her eyes filled with tears and her face was all twisted with pain. She took Ashenden's hand.

'I know you have a good heart. It was just thoughtless on your part and we won't say anything more about it. You have imagination. You're very sensitive. I know. You'll have your eggs done in the same way as mine, won't you?'

'Of course,' said Ashenden.

He ate scrambled eggs for breakfast every morning after that. The waiter said: '*Monsieur aime les œufs brouillés.*' At the end of the week they returned to London. He held Anastasia Alexandrovna in his arms, her head resting on his shoulder, from Paris to Calais and again from Dover to London. He reflected that the journey from New York to San Francisco took five days. When they arrived at Victoria and stood on the platform waiting for a cab she looked at him and her round, shining and slightly protuberant eyes.

'We've had a wonderful time, haven't we?' she said.

'Wonderful.'

'I've quite made up my mind. The experiment

has justified itself. I'm willing to marry you whenever you like.'

But Ashenden saw himself eating scrambled eggs every morning for the rest of his life. When he had put her in a cab, he called another for himself, went to the Cunard office and took a berth on the first ship that was going to America. No immigrant, eager for freedom and a new life, ever looked upon the Statue of Liberty with more heartfelt thankfulness than did Ashenden, when on that bright and sunny morning his ship steamed into the harbour of New York.

Some years had passed time since then and Ashenden had not seen Anastasia Alexandrovna again. He knew that on the outbreak of the revolution in March she and Vladimir Semenovich had gone to Russia. It might be that they would be able to help him, in a way Vladimir Semenovich owed him his life, and he made up his mind to write to Anastasia Alexandrovna to ask if he might come to see her.

When Ashenden went down to lunch he felt somewhat rested. Mr Harrington was waiting for him and they sat down. They ate what was put before them.

'Ask the waiter to bring us some bread,' said Mr Harrington.

'Bread?' replied Ashenden. 'There's no bread.'

'I can't eat without bread,' said Mr Harrington.

'I'm afraid you'll have to. There's no bread, no butter, no sugar, no eggs, no potatoes. There's fish and meat and green vegetables, and that's all.'

Mr Harrington's jaw dropped.

'But this is war,' he said.

'It looks very much like it.'

Mr Harrington was for a moment speechless; then he said: 'I'll tell you what I'm going to do, I'm going to get through with my business as quick as I can and then I'm going to get out of this country. I'm sure Mrs Harrington wouldn't like me to go without sugar or butter. I've got a very delicate stomach. The firm would never have sent me here if they'd thought I wasn't going to have the best of everything.'

In a little while Dr Egon Orth came in and gave Ashenden an envelope. On it was written Anastasia Alexandrovna's address. He introduced him to Mr Harrington. It was soon clear that he was pleased with Dr Egon Orth and so without further to do he suggested that here was the perfect interpreter for him.

'He talks Russian like a Russian. But he's an American citizen so that he won't do you down. I've known him a considerable time and I can assure you that he's absolutely trustworthy.'

Mr Harrington was pleased with the notion and after luncheon Ashenden left them to settle the matter by themselves. He wrote a note to Anastasia Alexandrovna and presently received an answer to say that she was going to a meeting, but would look in at his hotel about seven. He awaited her with apprehension. Of course he knew now that he had not loved her, but Tolstoi and Dostoievsky, Rimsky-Korsakoff, Stravinsky and Bakst; but he was not quite sure if the point had occurred to her. When between eight and half-past she arrived he suggested that she should join Mr Harrington and him at dinner. The presence of a third party, he thought, would prevent any awkwardness their meeting might have; but he need not have had any anxiety, for five minutes after they had sat down to a plate of soup it was borne in upon him that the feelings of Anastasia Alexandrovna towards him were as cool as were his towards her. It gave him a momentary shock. It is very hard for a man, however modest, to grasp the possibility that a woman who has once loved him may love him no longer, and though of course he did not imagine that Anastasia Alexandrovna had languished for five years with a hopeless passion for him, he did think that by a heightening of colour, a flutter of the eyelashes, or a quiver of the lips she would betray the fact that she had still a soft place in her heart for him. Not at all. She talked to him as though he were a friend she was very glad to see again after an absence of a few days, but whose intimacy with her was purely social. He asked after Vladimir Semenovich.

'He has been a disappointment to me,' she said. 'I never thought he was a clever man, but I thought he was an honest one. He's going to have a baby.'

Mr Harrington who was about to put a piece of fish into his mouth, stopped, his fork in the air, and stared at Anastasia Alexandrovna with astonishment. In extenuation it must be explained that he had never read a Russian novel in his life. Ashenden, slightly perplexed too, gave her a questioning look.

'I'm not the mother,' she said with a laugh. 'I am not interested in that sort of thing. The mother is a friend of mine and a well-known writer on Political Economy. I do not think her views are sound, but I should be the last to deny that they deserve consideration. She has a good brain, quite a good brain.' She turned to Mr Harrington. 'Are you interested in Political Economy?'

For once in his life Mr Harrington was speechless. Anastasia Alexandrovna gave them her views on the subject and they began to speak on the situation in Russia. She seemed to be on intimate terms with the leaders of the various political parties and Ashenden made up his mind to sound her on the possibility of her working with him. His infatuation had not blinded him to the fact that she was an extremely intelligent woman. After dinner he told Mr Harrington that he wished to talk business with Anastasia Alexandrovna and took her to a retired corner of the lounge. He told her all he thought necessary and found her interested and anxious to help. She had a passion for intrigue and a desire for power. When he hinted that he had command of large sums of money she saw at once that through him she might acquire an influence in the affairs of Russia. It tickled her vanity. She was immensely patriotic, but like many patriots she had an impression that her own aggrandisement tended to the good of her country. When they parted they had come to a working agreement.

'That was a very remarkable woman,' said Mr Harrington next morning when they met at breakfast.

'Don't fall in love with her,' smiled Ashenden.

This, however, was not a matter on which Mr Harrington was prepared to jest.

'I have never looked at a woman since I married Mrs Harrington,' he said. 'That husband of hers must be a bad man.'

'I could do with a plate of scrambled eggs,' said Ashenden, irrelevantly, for their breakfast consisted of a cup of tea without milk and a little jam instead of sugar.

With Anastasia Alexandrovna to help him and Dr Orth in the background, Ashenden set to work. Things in Russia were going from bad to worse. Kerensky, the head of the Provisional Government, was devoured by vanity and dismissed any minister who gave evidence of a capacity that might endanger his own position. He made speeches. He made endless speeches. At one moment there was a possibility that the Germans would make a dash for Petrograd. Kerensky made speeches. The food shortage grew more serious, the winter was approaching and there was no fuel. Kerensky made speeches. In the background the Bolsheviks were active, Lenin was hiding in Petrograd, it was said that Kerensky knew where he was, but dared not arrest him. He made speeches.

It amused Ashenden to see the unconcern with which Mr Harrington wandered through this turmoil. History was in the making and Mr Harrington minded his own business. It was uphill work. He was made to pay bribes to secretaries and underlings under the pretence that the ear of great men would be granted to him. He was kept waiting for hours in antechambers and then sent away without ceremony. When at last he saw the great men he found they had nothing to give him but idle words. They made him promises and in a day or two he discovered that the promises meant nothing. Ashenden advised him to throw in his hand and return to America; but Mr Harrington would not hear of it; his firm had sent him to do a particular job, and by gum, he was going to do it or perish in the attempt. Then Anastasia Alexandrovna took him in hand. A singular friendship had arisen between the pair. Mr Harrington thought her a very remarkable and deeply wronged woman; he told her all about his wife and his two sons, he told her all about the Constitution of the United States; she on her side told him all about Vladimir Semenovich, and she told him about Tolstoi, Turgenieff and Dostoievsky. They had great times together. He said he couldn't manage to call her Anastasia Alexandrovna, it was too much of a mouthful; so he called her Delilah. And now she placed her inexhaustible energy at his service and they went together to the persons who might be useful to him. But things were coming to a head. Riots broke out and the streets were growing dangerous. Now and then armoured cars filled with discontented reservists careered widely along the Nevsky Prospekt and in order to show that they were not happy took pot-shots at the passers-by. On one occasion when Mr Harrington and Anastasia Alexandrovna were in a tram together shots peppered the windows and they had to lie down on the floor for safety. Mr Harrington was highly indignant.

'An old fat woman was lying right on top of me and when I wriggled to get out Delilah caught me a clip on the side of the head and said, stop still, you fool. I don't like your Russian ways, Delilah.'

'Anyhow you stopped still,' she giggled.

'What you want in this country is a little less art and a litte more civilization.'

'You are bourgeoisie, Mr Harrington, you are not a member of the intelligentsia.'

'You are the first person who's ever said that,

Delilah. If I'm not a member of the intelligentsia I
don't know who is,' retorted Mr Harrington with
dignity.

Then one day when Ashenden was working
in his room there was a knock at the door and
Anastasia Alexandrovna stalked in followed, somewhat sheepishly, by Mr Harrington. Ashenden
saw that she was excited.

'What's the matter?' he asked.

'Unless this man goes back to America he'll get
killed. You really must talk to him. If I hadn't been
there something very unpleasant might have happened to him.'

'Not at all, Delilah,' said Mr Harrington, with
asperity. 'I'm perfectly capable of taking care of
myself and I wasn't in the smallest danger.'

'What is it all about?' asked Ashenden.

'I'd taken Mr Harrington to the Lavra of Alexander Nevsky to see Dostoievsky's grave,' said
Anastasia Alexandrovna, 'and on our way back we
saw a soldier being rather rough with an old
woman.'

'Rather rough!' cried Mr Harrington. 'There was
an old woman walking along the side-walk with a
basket of provisions on her arm. Two soldiers came
up behind her and one of them snatched the basket
from her and walked off with it. She burst out
screaming and crying, I don't know what she was
saying, but I can guess, and the other soldier took
his gun and with the butt-end of it hit her over the
head. Isn't that right, Delilah?'

'Yes,' she answered, unable to help smiling. 'And
before I could prevent it Mr Harrington jumped
out of the cab and ran up to the soldier who had the
basket, wrenched it from him and began to abuse
the pair of them like pickpockets. At first they were

so taken aback they didn't know what to do and then they got in a rage. I ran after Mr Harrington and explained to them that he was a foreigner and drunk.'

'Drunk?' cried Mr Harrington.

'Yes, drunk. Of course a crowd collected. It looked as though it wasn't going to be very nice.'

Mr Harrington smiled with those large, pale-blue eyes of his.

'It sounded to me as though you were giving them a piece of your mind, Delilah. It was as good as a play to watch you.'

'Don't be stupid, Mr Harrington,' cried Anastasia, in a sudden fury, stamping her foot. 'Don't you know that those soldiers might very easily have killed you and me too, and not one of the bystanders would have raised a finger to help us?'

'Me? I'm an American citizen, Delilah. They wouldn't dare touch a hair of my head.'

'They'd have difficulty in finding one,' said Anastasia Alexandrovna, who when she was in a temper had no manners. 'But if you think Russian soldiers are going to hesitate to kill you because you're an American citizen you'll get a big surprise one of these days.'

'Well, what happened to the old woman?' asked Ashenden.

'The soldiers went off after a little and we went back to her.'

'Still with the basket?'

'Yes. Mr Harrington clung on to that like grim death. She was lying on the ground with the blood pouring from her head. We got her into the cab and when she could speak enough to tell us where she lived we drove her home. She was bleeding dreadfully and we had some difficulty in staunching the blood.'

Anastasia Alexandrovna gave Mr Harrington an odd look and to his surprise Ashenden saw him turn scarlet.

'What's the matter now?'

'You see, we had nothing to bind her up with. Mr Harrington's handkerchief was soaked. There was only one thing about me that I could get off quickly and so I took off my . . .'

But before she could finish Mr Harrington interrupted her.

'You need not tell Mr Ashenden what you took off. I'm a married man and I know ladies wear them, but I see no need to refer to them in general society.'

Anastasia Alexandrovna giggled.

'Then you must kiss me, Mr Harrington. If you don't I shall say.'

Mr Harrington hesitated a moment, considering evidently the pros and cons of the matter, but he saw that Anastasia Alexandrovna was determined.

'Go on then, you may kiss me, Delilah, though I'm bound to say I don't see what pleasure it can be to you.'

She put her arms round his neck and kissed him on both cheeks, then without a word of warning burst into a flood of tears.

'You're a brave little man, Mr Harrington. You're absurd but magnificent,' she sobbed.

Mr Harrington was less surprised than Ashenden would have expected him to be. He looked at Anastasia with a thin, quizzical smile and gently patted her.

'Come, come, Delilah, pull yourself together. It gave you a nasty turn, didn't it? You're quite upset. I shall have terrible rheumatism in my shoulder if you go on weeping all over it.'

The scene was ridiculous and touching. Ashenden laughed, but he had the beginnings of a lump in his throat.

When Anastasia Alexandrovna had left them Mr Harrington sat in a brown study.

'They're very queer, these Russians. Do you know what Delilah did?' he said, suddenly. 'She stood up in the cab, in the middle of the street, with people passing on both sides, and took her pants off. She tore them in two and gave me one to hold while she made a bandage of the other. I was never so embarrassed in my life.'

'Tell me what gave you the idea of calling her Delilah?' smiled Ashenden.

Mr Harrington reddened a little.

'She's a very fascinating woman, Mr Ashenden. She's been deeply wronged by her husband and I naturally felt a great deal of sympathy for her. These Russians are very emotional people and I did not want her to mistake my sympathy for anything else. I told her I was very much attached to Mrs Harrington.'

'You're not under the impression that Delilah was Potiphar's wife?' asked Ashenden.

'I don't know what you mean by that, Mr Ashenden,' replied Mr Harrington. 'Mrs Harrington has always given me to understand that I'm very fascinating to women, and I thought if I called our little friend Delilah it would make my position quite clear.'

'I don't think Russia's any place for you, Mr

Harrington,' said Ashenden smiling. 'If I were you I'd get out of it as quick as I could.'

'I can't go now. I've got them to agree to my terms at last and we're going to sign next week. Then I shall pack my grip and go.'

'I wonder if your signatures will be worth the paper they're written on,' said Ashenden.

He had at length devised a plan of campaign. It took him twenty-four hours' hard work to code a telegram in which he put his scheme before the persons who had sent him to Petrograd. It was accepted and he was promised all the money he needed. Ashenden knew he could do nothing unless the Provisional Government remained in power for another three months; but winter was at hand and food was getting scarcer every day. The army was mutinous. The people clamoured for peace. Every evening at the Europe Ashenden drank a cup of chocolate with Professor Z and discussed with him how best to make use of his devoted Czechs. Anastasia Alexandrovna had a flat in a retired spot and here he had meetings with all manner of persons. Plans were drawn up. Measures were taken. Ashenden argued, persuaded, promised. He had to overcome the vacillation of one and wrestle with the fatalism of another. He had to judge who was resolute and who was self-sufficient, who was honest and who was infirm of purpose. He had to curb his impatience with the Russian verbosity; he had to be good-tempered with people who were willing to talk of everything but the matter in hand; he had to listen sympathetically to ranting and rhodomontade. He had to beware of treachery. He had to humour the vanity of fools and elude the greed of the ambitious. Time was pressing. The rumours grew hot and many of the activities of the Bolsheviks. Kerensky ran hither and thither like a frightened hen.

Then the blow fell. On the night of November 7th, 1917, the Bolsheviks rose, Kerensky's ministers were arrested and the Winter Palace was sacked by the mob; the reins of power were seized by Lenin and Trotsky.

Anastasia Alexandrovna came to Ashenden's room at the hotel early in the morning. Ashenden was coding a telegram. He had been up all night, first at the Smolny, and then at the Winter Palace. He was tired out. Her face was white and her shining brown eyes were tragic.

'Have you heard?' she asked Ashenden.

He nodded.

'It's all over then. They say Kerensky has fled. They never even showed fight.' Rage seized her. 'The buffoon!' she screamed.

At that moment there was a knock at the door and Anastasia Alexandrovna looked at it with sudden apprehension.

'You know the Bolsheviks have got a list of people they've decided to execute. My name is on it, and it may be that yours is too.'

'If it's they and they want to come in they only have to turn the handle,' said Ashenden, smiling, but with ever so slightly odd a feeling at the pit of his stomach. 'Come in.'

The door was opened and Mr Harrington stepped into the room. He was as dapper as ever, in his short black coat and striped trousers, his shoes neatly polished and a derby on his bald head. He took it off when he saw Anastasia Alexandrovna.

'Oh, fancy finding you here so early. I looked in on my way out, I wanted to tell you my news. I tried to find you yesterday evening, but couldn't. You didn't come in to dinner.'

'No, I was at a meeting,' said Ashenden.

'You must both congratulate me, I got my signatures yesterday, and my business is done.'

Mr Harrington beamed on them, the picture of self-satisfaction, and he arched himself like a bantam-cock who has chased away all rivals. Anastasia Alexandrovna burst into a sudden shriek of hysterical laughter. He stared at her in perplexity.

'Why, Delilah, what is the matter?' he said.

Anastasia laughed till the tears ran from her eyes and then began to sob in earnest. Ashenden explained.

'The Bolsheviks have overthrown the Government. Kerensky's ministers are in prison. The Bolsheviks are out to kill. Delilah says her name is on the list. Your minister signed your documents yesterday because he knew it did not matter what he did then. Your contracts are worth nothing. The Bolsheviks are going to make peace with Germany as soon as they can.'

Anastasia Alexandrovna had recovered her self-control as quickly as she had lost it.

'You had better get out of Russia as soon as you can, Mr Harrington. It's no place for a foreigner now and it may be that in a few days you won't be able to.'

Mr Harrington looked from one to the other.

'O my,' he said. 'O my!' It seemed inadequate. 'Are you going to tell me that that Russian minister was just making a fool of me?'

Ashenden shrugged his shoulders.

'How can one tell what he was thinking of? He may have a keen sense of humour and perhaps he thought it funny to sign a fifty million dollar contract yesterday when there was every chance of his being stood against the wall and shot today. Anastasia Alexandrovna's right, Mr Harrington, you'd better take the first train that'll get you to Sweden.'

'And what about you?'

'There's nothing for me to do here any more. I'm cabling for instructions and I shall go as soon as I get leave. The Bolsheviks have got in ahead of us and the people I was working with will have their work cut out to save their lives.'

'Boris Petrovich was shot this morning,' said Anastasia Alexandrovna with a frown.

They both looked at Mr Harrington and he stared at the floor. His pride in this achievement of his was shattered and he sagged like a pricked balloon. But in a minute he looked up. He gave Anastasia Alexandrovna a little smile and for the first time Ashenden noticed how attractive and kindly his smile was. There was something peculiarly disarming about it.

'If the Bolsheviks are after you, Delilah, don't you think you'd better come with me? I'll take care of you and if you like to come to America I'm sure Mrs Harrington would be glad to do anything she could for you.'

'I can see Mrs Harrington's face if you arrived in Philadelphia with a Russian refugee,' laughed Anastasia Alexandrovna. 'I'm afraid it would need more explaining than you could ever manage. No, I shall stay here.'

'But if you're in danger?'

'I'm a Russian. My place is here. I will not leave my country when most my country needs me.'

'That is the bunk, Delilah,' said Mr Harrington very quietly.

Anastasia Alexandrovna had spoken with deep emotion, but now with a little start she shot a sudden quizzical look at him.

'I know it is, Samson,' she answered. 'To tell you the truth I think we're all going to have a hell of a time, God knows what's going to happen, but I want to see; I wouldn't miss a minute of it for the world.'

Mr Harrington shook his head.

'Curiosity is the bane of your sex, Delilah,' he said.

'Go along and do your packing, Mr Harrington,' said Ashenden, smiling, 'and then we'll take you to the station. The train will be besieged.'

'Very well, I'll go. And I shan't be sorry either. I haven't had a decent meal since I came here and I've done a thing I never thought I should have to do in my life, I've drunk my coffee without sugar and when I've been lucky enough to get a little piece of black bread I've had to eat it without butter. Mrs Harrington will never believe me when I tell her what I've gone through. What this country wants is organization.'

When he left them Ashenden and Anastasia Alexandrovna talked over the situation. Ashenden was depressed because all his careful schemes had come to nothing, but Anastasia Alexandrovna was excited and she hazarded every sort of guess about the outcome of this new revolution. She pretended to be very serious, but in her heart she looked upon it all very much as a thrilling play. She wanted more and more things to happen. Then there was another knock at the door and before Ashenden could answer Mr Harrington burst in.

'Really the service at this hotel is a scandal,' he cried heatedly, 'I've been ringing my bell for fifteen minutes and I can't get anyone to pay the smallest attention to me.'

'Service?' exclaimed Anastasia Alexandrovna. 'There is not a servant left in the hotel.'

'But I want my washing. They promised to let me have it back last night.'

'I'm afraid you haven't got much chance of getting it now,' said Ashenden.

'I'm not going to leave without my washing. Four shirts, two union suits, a pair of pyjamas, and four collars. I wash my handkerchiefs and socks in my room. I want my washing and I'm not going to leave this hotel without it.'

'Don't be a fool,' cried Ashenden. 'What you've got to do is to get out of here while the going's good. If there are no servants to get it you'll just have to leave your washing behind you.'

'Pardon me, sir, I shall do nothing of the kind. I'll go and fetch it myself. I've suffered enough at the hands of this country and I'm not going to leave four perfectly good shirts to be worn by a lot of dirty Bolsheviks. No, sir. I do not leave Russia till I have my washing.'

Anastasia Alexandrovna stared at the floor for a moment; then with a little smile looked up. It seemed to Ashenden that there was something in her that responded to Mr Harrington's futile obstinacy. In her Russian way she understood that Mr Harrington could not leave Petrograd without his washing. His insistence had given it the value of a symbol.

'I'll go downstairs and see if I can find anybody about who knows where the laundry is and if I can, I'll go with you and you can bring your washing away with you.'

Mr Harrington unbent. He answered with that sweet and disarming smile of his.

'That's terribly kind of you, Delilah. I don't mind if it's not ready or not, I'll take it just as it is.'

Anastasia Alexandrovna left them.

'Well, what do you think of Russia and the Russians now?' Mr Harrington asked Ashenden.

'I'm fed up with them. I'm fed up with Tolstoi, I'm fed up with Turgenieff and Dostoievsky, I'm fed up with Chekoff. I'm fed up with the Intelligentsia. I hanker after people who know their mind from one minute to another, who mean what they say an hour after they've said it, whose word you can rely on; I'm sick of fine phrases, and oratory and attitudinizing.'

Ashenden, bitten by the prevailing ill, was about to make a speech when he was interrupted by a rattle as of peas on a drum. In the city, so strangely silent, it sounded abrupt and odd.

'What's that?' asked Mr Harrington.

'Rifle firing. On the other side of the river I should think.'

Mr Harrington gave a funny little look. He laughed, but his face was a trifle pale; he did not like it, and Ashenden did not blame him.

'I think it's high time I got out. I shouldn't so much mind for myself, but I've got a wife and children to think of. I haven't had a letter from Mrs Harrington for so long I'm a bit worried.' He paused an instant. 'I'd like you to know Mrs Harrington, she's a very wonderful woman. She's the best wife a man ever had. Until I came here I'd not been separated from her for more than three days since we were married.'

Anastasia Alexandrovna came back and told them that she had found the address.

'It's about forty minutes' walk from here and if you'll come now I'll go with you,' she said.

'I'm ready.'

'You'd better look out,' said Ashenden. 'I don't believe the streets are very healthy today.'

Anastasia Alexandrovna looked at Mr Harrington.

'I must have my washing, Delilah,' he said. 'I should never rest in peace if I left it behind me and Mrs Harrington would never let me hear the last of it.'

'Come on then.'

They set out and Ashenden went on with the dreary business of translating into a very complicated code the shattering news he had to give. It was a long message, and then he had to ask for instructions upon his own movements. It was a mechanical job and yet it was one in which you could not allow your attention to wander. The mistake of a single figure might make a whole sentence incomprehensible.

Suddenly his door was burst open and Anastasia Alexandrovna flung into the room. She had lost her hat and was dishevelled. She was panting. Her eyes were starting out of her head and she was obviously in a state of great excitement.

'Where's Mr Harrington?' she cried. 'Isn't he here?'

'No.'

'Is he in his bedroom?'

'I don't know. Why, what's the matter? We'll go and look if you like. Why didn't you bring him along with you?'

They walked down the passage and knocked at Mr Harrington's door; there was no answer; they tried the handle; the door was locked.

'He's not there.'

They went back to Ashenden's room. Anastasia Alexandrovna sank into a chair.

'Give me a glass of water, will you. I'm out of breath. I've been running.'

She drank the water Ashenden poured out for her. She gave a sudden sob.

'I hope he's all right. I should never forgive myself if he was hurt. I was hoping he would have got here before me. He got his washing all right. We found the place. There was only an old woman there and they didn't want to let us take it, but we insisted. Mr Harrington was furious because it hadn't been touched. It was exactly as he had sent it. They'd promised it last night and it was still in the bundle that Mr Harrington had made himself. I said that was Russia and Mr Harrington said he preferred coloured people. I'd led him by side streets because I thought it was better, and we started to come back again. We passed at the top of a street and at the bottom of it I saw a little crowd. There was a man addressing them.

'"Let's go and hear what he's saying," I said.

'I could see they were arguing. It looked exciting. I wanted to know what was happening.

'"Come along, Delilah," he said. "Let us mind our own business."'

'"You go back to the hotel and do your packing. I'm going to see the fun," I said.

'I ran down the street and he followed me. There were about two or three hundred people there and a student was addressing them. There were some working men and they were shouting at him. I love a row and I edged my way into the crowd. Suddenly we heard the sound of shots and before you could realize what was happening two armoured cars came dashing down the street. There were soldiers in them and they were firing as they went. I don't know why. For fun, I suppose, or because they were drunk. We all scattered like a lot of rabbits. We just ran for our lives. I lost Mr Harrington. I can't make out why he isn't here. Do you think something has happened to him?'

Ashenden was silent for a while.

'We'd better go out and look for him,' he said. 'I don't know why the devil he couldn't leave his washing.'

'I understand, I understand so well.'

'That's a comfort,' said Ashenden irritably. 'Let's go.'

He put on his hat and coat, and they walked downstairs. The hotel seemed strangely empty. They went out into the street. There was hardly anyone to be seen. They walked along. The trams were not running and the silence in the great city was uncanny. The shops were closed. It was quite startling when a motor car dashed by at breakneck speed. The people they passed looked frightened and downcast. When they had to go through a main thoroughfare they hastened their steps. A lot of people were there and they stood about irresolutely as though they did not know what to do next.

Reservists in their shabby grey were walking down the middle of the roadway in little bunches. They did not speak. They looked like sheep looking for their shepherd. Then they came to the street down which Anastasia Alexandrovna had run, but they entered it from the opposite end. A number of windows had been broken by the wild shooting. It was quite empty. You could see where the people had scattered, for strewn about were articles they had dropped in their haste, books, a man's hat, a lady's bag and a basket. Anastasia Alexandrovna touched Ashenden's arm to draw his attention: sitting on the pavement, her head bent right down to her lap, was a woman and she was dead. A little way on two men had fallen together. They were dead too. The wounded, one supposed, had managed to drag themselves away or their friends had carried them. Then they found Mr Harrington. His derby had rolled in the gutter. He lay on his face, in a pool of blood, his bald head, with its prominent bones, very white; his neat black coat smeared and muddy. But his hand was clenched tight on the parcel that contained four shirts, two union suits, a pair of pyjamas and four collars. Mr Harrington had not let his washing go.

FROM

Creatures of
Circumstance

(1947)

Sanatorium

For the first six weeks that Ashenden was at the
sanatorium he stayed in bed. He saw nobody but
the doctor who visited him morning and evening,
the nurses who looked after him and the maid who
brought him his meals. He had contracted
tuberculosis of the lungs and since at the time there
were reasons that made it difficult for him to go to
Switzerland the specialist he saw in London had
sent him up to a sanatorium in the north of Scotland. At last the day came that he had been
patiently looking forward to when the doctor told
him he could get up; and in the afternoon his nurse,
having helped him to dress, took him down to the
veranda, placed cushions behind him, wrapped
him up in rugs and left him to enjoy the sun that
was streaming down from a cloudless sky. It was
mid-winter. The sanatorium stood on the top of a
hill and from it you had a spacious view of the
snow-clad country. There were people lying all
along the veranda in deck-chairs, some chatting
with their neighbours and some reading. Every
now and then one would have a fit of coughing and
you noticed that at the end of it he looked anxiously
at his handkerchief. Before the nurse left Ashenden
she turned with a kind of professional briskness to
the man who was lying in the next chair.

'I want to introduce Mr Ashenden to you,' she said. And then to Ashenden: 'This is Mr McLeod. He and Mr Campbell have been here longer than anyone else.'

On the other side of Ashenden was lying a pretty girl, with red hair and bright blue eyes; she had on no make-up, but her lips were very red and the colour on her cheeks was high. It emphasized the astonishing whiteness of her skin. It was lovely even when you realized that its delicate texture was due to illness. She wore a fur coat and was wrapped up in rugs, so that you could see nothing of her body, but her face was extremely thin, so thin that it made her nose, which wasn't really large, look a trifle prominent. She gave Ashenden a friendly look, but did not speak, and Ashenden, feeling rather shy among all those strange people, waited to be spoken to.

'First time they've let you get up, is it?' said McLeod.

'Yes.'

'Where's your room?'

Ashenden told him.

'Small. I know every room in the place. I've been here for seventeen years. I've got the best room here and so I damned well ought to have. Campbell's been trying to get me out of it, he wants it himself, but I'm not going to budge; I've got a right to it, I came here six months before he did.'

McLeod, lying there, gave you the impression that he was immensely tall; his skin was stretched tight over his bones, his cheeks and temples hollow, so that you could see the formation of his skull under it; and in that emaciated face, with its great bony nose, the eyes were preternaturally large.

'Seventeen years is a long time,' said Ashenden, because he could think of nothing else to say.

'Time passes very quickly. I like it here. At first, after a year or two, I went away in the summer, but I don't any more. It's my home now. I've got a brother and two sisters; but they're married and now they've got families; they don't want me. When you've been here a few years and you go back to ordinary life, you feel a bit out of it, you know. Your pals have gone their own ways and you've got nothing in common with them any more. It all seems an awful rush. Much ado about nothing, that's what it is. It's noisy and stuffy. No, one's better off here. I shan't stir again till they carry me out feet first in my coffin.'

The specialist had told Ashenden that if he took care of himself for a reasonable time he would get well, and he looked at McLeod with curiosity.

'What do you do with yourself all day long?' he asked.

'Do? Having TB is a whole time job, my boy. There's my temperature to take and then I weigh myself. I don't hurry over my dressing. I have breakfast, I read the papers and go for a walk. Then I have my rest. I lunch and play bridge. I have another rest and then I dine. I play a bit more bridge and I go to bed. They've got quite a decent library here, we get all the new books, but I don't really have much time for reading. I talk to people. You meet all sorts here, you know. They come and they go. Sometimes they go because they think they're cured, but a lot of them come back, and sometimes they go because they die. I've seen a lot of people out and before I go I expect to see a lot more.'

The girl sitting on Ashenden's other side suddenly spoke.

'I should tell you that few persons can get a heartier laugh out of a hearse than Mr McLeod,' she said.

McLeod chuckled.

'I don't know about that, but it wouldn't be human nature if I didn't say to myself: Well, I'm just as glad it's him and not me they're taking for a ride.'

It occurred to him that Ashenden didn't know the pretty girl, so he introduced him.

'By the way, I don't think you've met Mr Ashenden – Miss Bishop. She's English, but not a bad girl.'

'How long have *you* been here?' asked Ashenden.

'Only two years. This is my last winter. Dr Lennox says I shall be all right in a few months and there's no reason why I shouldn't go home.'

'Silly, I call it,' said McLeod. 'Stay where you're well off, that's what I say.'

At that moment a man, leaning on a stick, came walking slowly along the veranda.

'Oh, look, there's Major Templeton,' said Miss Bishop, a smile lighting up her blue eyes; and then, as he came up: 'I'm glad to see you up again.'

'Oh, it was nothing. Only a bit of a cold. I'm quite all right now.'

The words were hardly out of his mouth when he began to cough. He leaned heavily on his stick. But when the attack was over he smiled gaily.

'Can't get rid of this damned cough,' he said. 'Smoking too much. Dr Lennox says I ought to give it up, but it's no good – I can't.'

He was a tall fellow, good-looking in a slightly

theatrical way, with a dusky, sallow face, fine very dark eyes and a neat black moustache. He was wearing a fur coat with an Astrakhan collar. His appearance was smart and perhaps a trifle showy. Miss Bishop made Ashenden known to him. Major Templeton said a few civil words in an easy, cordial way, and then asked the girl to go for a stroll with him; he had been ordered to walk to a certain place in the wood behind the sanatorium and back again. McLeod watched them as they sauntered off.

'I wonder if there's anything between those two,' he said. 'They do say Templeton was a devil with the girls before he got ill.'

'He doesn't look up to much in that line just now,' said Ashenden.

'You never can tell. I've seen a lot of rum things here in my day. I could tell you no end of stories if I wanted to.'

'You evidently do, so why don't you?'

McLeod grinned.

'Well, I'll tell you one. Three or four years ago there was a woman here who was pretty hot stuff. Her husband used to come and see her every other week-end, he was crazy about her, used to fly up from London; but Dr Lennox was pretty sure she was carrying on with somebody here, but he couldn't find out who. So one night when we'd all gone to bed he had a thin coat of paint put down just outside her room and next day he had everyone's slippers examined. Neat, wasn't it? The fellow whose slippers had paint on them got the push. Dr Lennox has to be particular, you know. He doesn't want the place to get a bad name.'

'How long has Templeton been here?'

'Three or four months. He's been in bed most of

the time. He's for it all right. Ivy Bishop'll be a damned fool if she gets stuck on him. She's got a good chance of getting well. I've seen so many of them, you know, I can tell. When I look at a fellow I make up my mind at once whether he'll get well or whether he won't, and if he won't I can make a pretty shrewd guess how long he'll last. I'm very seldom mistaken. I give Templeton about two years myself.'

McLeod gave Ashenden a speculative look and Ashenden, knowing what he was thinking, though he tried to be amused, could not help feeling somewhat concerned. There was a twinkle in McLeod's eyes. He plainly knew what was passing through Ashenden's mind.

'You'll get all right. I wouldn't have mentioned it if I hadn't been pretty sure of that. I don't want Dr Lennox to hoof me out for putting the fear of God into his bloody patients.'

Then Ashenden's nurse came to take him back to bed. Even though he had only sat out for an hour, he was tired, and was glad to find himself once more between the sheets. Dr Lennox came in to see him in the course of the evening. He looked at his temperature chart.

'That's not so bad,' he said.

Dr Lennox was small, brisk and genial. He was a good enough doctor, an excellent business man, and an enthusiastic fisherman. When the fishing season began he was inclined to leave the care of his patients to his assistants; the patients grumbled a little, but were glad enough to eat the young salmon he brought back to vary their meals. He was fond of talking, and now, standing at the end of Ashenden's bed, he asked him, in his broad Scots, whether he had got into conversation with any of the patients that afternoon. Ashenden told him the nurse had introduced him to McLeod. Dr Lennox laughed.

'The oldest living inhabitant. He knows more about the sanatorium and its inmates than I do. How he gets his information I haven't an idea, but there's not a thing about the private lives of anyone under this roof that he doesn't know. There's not an old maid in the place with a keener nose for a bit of scandal. Did he tell you about Campbell?'

'He mentioned him.'

'He hates Campbell, and Campbell hates him. Funny, when you come to think of it, those two men, they've been here for seventeen years and they've got about one sound lung between them. They loathe the sight of one another. I've had to refuse to listen to the complaints about one another that they come to me with. Campbell's room is just below McLeod's and Campbell plays the fiddle. It drives McLeod wild. He says he's been listening to the same tunes for fifteen years, but Campbell says McLeod doesn't know one tune from another. McLeod wants me to stop Campbell playing, but I can't do that, he's got a perfect right to play so long as he doesn't play in the silence hours. I've offered to change McLeod's room, but he won't do that. He says Campbell only plays to drive him out of the room because it's the best in the house, and he's damned if he's going to have it. It's queer, isn't it, that two middle-aged men should think it worth while to make life hell for one another. Neither can leave the other alone. They have their meals at the same table, they play bridge together; and not a day passes without a row. Sometimes I've threatened to turn them both out if they don't behave like sensible fellows. That keeps them quiet for a bit. They don't want to go. They've been here so long, they've got no one any more who gives a damn for them, and they can't cope with the world outside. Campbell went away for a couple of months' holiday some years ago. He came back after a week; he said he couldn't stand the racket, and the sight of so many people in the streets scared him.'

It was a strange world into which Ashenden found himself thrown when, his health gradually improving, he was able to mix with his fellow patients. One morning Dr Lennox told him he could thenceforward lunch in the dining-room. This was a large, low room, with great window space; the windows were always wide open and on fine days the sun streamed in. There seemed to be a great many people and it took him some time to sort them out. They were of all kinds, young, middle-aged and old. There were some, like McLeod and Campbell, who had been at the sanatorium for years and expected to die there. Others had only been there for a few months. There was one middle-aged spinster called Miss Atkin who had been coming every winter for a long time and in the summer went to stay with friends and relations. She had nothing much the matter with her any more, and might just as well have stayed away altogether, but she liked the life. Her long residence had given her a sort of position, she was honorary librarian and hand in glove with the matron. She was always ready to gossip with you, but you were soon warned that everything you said was passed on. It was useful to Dr Lennox to know that his patients were getting on well together and were happy, that they did nothing imprudent and followed his instructions. Little escaped Miss Atkin's sharp eyes, and from her it went to the matron and so to Dr Lennox. Because she had been coming for so many years, she sat at the same table as McLeod and Campbell, together with an old general who had been put there on account of his rank. The table was in no way different from any other, and it was not more advantageously placed, but because the oldest residents sat there it was looked upon as the most desirable place to sit, and several elderly women were bitterly resentful because Miss Atkin, who went away for four or five months every summer, should be given a place there while they who spent the whole year in the sanatorium sat at other tables. There was an old Indian civilian who had been at the sanatorium longer than anyone but McLeod and Campbell; he was a man who in his day had ruled a province, and he was waiting irascibly for either McLeod or Campbell to die so that he might take his place at the first table. Ashenden made the acquaintance of Campbell. He was a long, big-boned fellow with a bald head, so thin that you wondered how his limbs held together; and when he sat crumpled in an arm-chair he gave you the uncanny impression of a mannikin in a puppet-show. He was brusque, touchy and bad-tempered. The first thing he asked Ashenden was:

'Are you fond of music?

'Yes.'

'No one here cares a damn for it. I play the violin. But if you like it, come to my room one day and I'll play to you.'

'Don't you go,' said McLeod, who heard him. 'It's torture.'

'How can you be so rude?' cried Miss Atkin. 'Mr Campbell plays very nicely.'

'There's no one in this beastly place that knows one note from another,' said Campbell.

With a derisive chuckle McLeod walked off. Miss Atkin tried to smooth things down.

'You mustn't mind what Mr McLeod said.'

'Oh, I don't. I'll get back on him all right.'

He played the same tune over and over again all that afternoon. McLeod banged on the floor, but Campbell went on. He sent a message by a maid to say that he had a headache and would Mr Campbell mind not playing; Campbell replied that he had a perfect right to play and if Mr McLeod didn't like it he could lump it. When next they met high words passed.

Ashenden was put on a table with the pretty Miss Bishop, with Templeton, and with a London man, an accountant, called Henry Chester. He was a stocky, broad-shouldered, wiry little fellow, and the last person you would ever have thought would be attacked by TB. It had come upon him as a sudden and unexpected blow. He was a perfectly ordinary man, somewhere between thirty and forty, married, with two children. He lived in a decent suburb. He went up to the city every morning and read the morning paper; he came down from the city every evening and read the evening paper. He had no interests except his business and his family. He liked his work; he made enough money to live in comfort, he put by a reasonable sum every year, he played golf on Saturday afternoon and on Sunday, he went every August for a three weeks' holiday to the same place on the east coast; his children would grow up and marry, then he would turn his business over to his son and retire with his wife to a little house in the country where he could potter about till death claimed him at a ripe old age. He asked nothing more from life than that, and it was a life that thousands upon thousands of his fellow-men lived with satisfaction. He was the average citizen. Then this thing happened. He had caught cold playing golf, it had gone to his chest, and he had had a cough that he couldn't shake off. He had always been strong and healthy, and had no opinion of doctors; but at last at his wife's persuasion he had consented to see one. It was a shock to him, a fearful shock, to learn that there was tubercle in both his lungs and that his only chance of life was to go immediately to a sanatorium. The specialist he saw then told him that he might be able to go back to work in a couple of years, but two years had passed and Dr Lennox advised him not to think of it for at least a year more. He showed him the bacilli in his sputum, and in an X-ray photograph the actively diseased patches in his lungs. He lost heart. It seemed to him a cruel and unjust trick that fate had played upon him. He could have understood it if he had led a wild life, if he had drunk too much, played around with women or kept late hours. He would have deserved it then. But he had done none of these things. It was monstrously unfair. Having no resources in himself, no interest in books, he had nothing to do but think of his health. It became an obsession. He watched his symptoms anxiously. They had to deprive him of a thermometer because he took his temperature a dozen times a day. He got it into his head that the doctors were taking his case too indifferently, and in order to force their attention used every method he could devise to make the thermometer register a temperature that would alarm;

and when his tricks were foiled he grew sulky and querulous. But he was by nature a jovial, friendly creature, and when he forgot himself he talked and laughed gaily; then on a sudden he remembered that he was a sick man and you would see in his eyes the fear of death.

At the end of every month his wife came up to spend a day or two in a lodging-house nearby. Dr Lennox did not much like the visits that relatives paid the patients, it excited and unsettled them. It was moving to see the eagerness with which Henry Chester looked forward to his wife's arrival; but it was strange to notice that once she had come he seemed less pleased than one would have expected. Mrs Chester was a pleasant, cheerful little woman, not pretty, but neat, as commonplace as her husband, and you only had to look at her to know that she was a good wife and mother, a careful housekeeper, a nice, quiet body who did her duty and interfered with nobody. She had been quite happy in the dull, domestic life they had led for so many years, her only dissipation a visit to the pictures, her great thrill the sales in the big London shops; and it had never occurred to her that it was monontonous. It completely satisfied her. Ashenden liked her. He listened with interest while she prattled about her children and her house in the suburbs, her neighbours and her trivial occupations. On one occasion he met her in the road. Chester for some reason connected with his treatment had stayed in and she was alone. Ashenden suggested that they should walk together. They talked for a little of indifferent things. Then she suddenly asked him how he thought her husband was.

'I think he seems to be getting on all right.'

'I'm so terribly worried.'

'You must remember it's a slow, long business. One has to have patience.'

They walked on a little and then he saw she was crying.

'You mustn't be unhappy about him,' said Ashenden gently.

'Oh, you don't know what I have to put up with when I come here. I know I ought not to speak about it, but I must. I can trust you, can't I?'

'Of course.'

'I love him. I'm devoted to him. I'd do anything in the world I could for him. We've never quarrelled, we've never even differed about a single thing. He's beginning to hate me and it breaks my heart.'

'Oh, I can't believe that. Why, when you're not here he talks of you all the time. He couldn't talk more nicely. He's devoted to you.'

'Yes, that's when I'm not here. It's when I'm here, when he sees me well and strong, that it comes over him. You see, he resents it so terribly that he's ill and I'm well. He's afraid he's going to die and he hates me because I'm going to live. I have to be on my guard all the time: almost everything I say, if I speak of the children, if I speak of the future, exasperates him, and he says bitter, wounding things. When I speak of something I've had to do to the house or a servant I've had to change it irritates him beyond endurance. He complains that I treat him as if he didn't count any more. We used to be so united, and now I feel there's a great wall of antagonism between us. I know I shouldn't blame him, I know it's only his

(351)

illness, he's a dear good man really, and kindness itself, normally he's the easiest man in the world to get on with; and now I simply dread coming here and I go with relief. He'd be terribly sorry if I had TB but I know that in his heart of hearts it would be a relief. He could forgive me, he could forgive fate, if he thought I was going to die too. Sometimes he tortures me by talking about what I shall do when he's dead, and when I get hysterical and cry out to him to stop, he says I needn't grudge him a little pleasure when he'll be dead so soon and I can go on living for years and years and have a good time. Oh, it's so frightful to think that this love we've had for one another all these years should die in this sordid, miserable way.'

Mrs Chester sat down on a stone by the roadside and gave way to passionate weeping. Ashenden looked at her with pity, but could find nothing to say that might comfort her. What she had told him did not come quite as a surprise.

'Give me a cigarette,' she said at last. 'I mustn't let my eyes get all red and swollen, or Henry'll know I've been crying and he'll think I've had bad news about him. Is death so horrible? Do we all fear death like that?'

'I don't know,' said Ashenden.

'When my mother was dying she didn't seem to mind a bit. She knew it was coming and she even made little jokes about it. But she was an old woman.'

Mrs Chester pulled herself together and they set off again. They walked for a while in silence.

'You won't think any the worse of Henry for what I've told you?' she said at last.

'Of course not.'

'He's been a good husband and a good father. I've never known a better man in my life. Until this illness I don't think an unkind or ungenerous thought ever passed through his head.'

The conversation left Ashenden pensive. People often said he had a low opinion of human nature. It was because he did not always judge his fellows by the usual standards. He accepted, with a smile, a tear or a shrug of the shoulders, much that filled others with dismay. It was true that you would never have expected that good-natured, commonplace little chap to harbour such bitter and unworthy thoughts; but who has ever been able to tell to what depths man may fall or to what heights rise? The fault lay in the poverty of his ideals. Henry Chester was born and bred to lead an average life, exposed to the normal vicissitudes of existence, and when an unforeseeable accident befell him he had no means of coping with it. He was like a brick made to take its place with a million others in a huge factory, but by chance with a flaw in it so that it is inadequate to its purpose. And the brick too, if it had a mind, might cry: What have I done that I cannot fulfil my modest end, but must be taken away from all these other bricks that support me and thrown on the dust-heap? It was no fault of Henry Chester's that he was incapable of the conceptions that might have enabled him to bear his calamity with resignation. It is not everyone who can find solace in art or thought. It is the tragedy of our day that these humble souls have lost their faith in God, in whom lay hope, and their belief in a resurrection that might bring them the happiness that has been denied them on earth; and have found nothing to put in their place.

There are people who say that suffering ennobles. It is not true. As a general rule it makes man petty, querulous and selfish; but here in this sanatorium there was not much suffering. In certain stages of tuberculosis the slight fever that accompanies it excites rather than depresses, so that the patient feels alert and, upborne by hope, faces the future blithely; but for all that the idea of death haunts the subconscious. It is a sardonic theme song that runs through a sprightly operetta. Now and again the gay, melodious arias, the dance measures, deviate strangely into tragic strains that throb menacingly down the nerves; the petty interests of every day, the small jealousies and trivial concerns are as nothing; pity and terror make the heart on a sudden stand still and the awfulness of death broods as the silence that precedes a tropical storm broods over the tropical jungle. After Ashenden had been for some time at the sanatorium there came a boy of twenty. He was in the navy, a sub-lieutenant in a submarine, and he had what they used to call in novels galloping consumption. He was a tall, good-looking youth, with curly brown hair, blue eyes and a very sweet smile. Ashenden saw him two or three times lying on the terrace in the sun and passed the time of day with him. He was a cheerful lad. He talked of musical shows and film stars; and he read the paper for the football results and the boxing news. Then he was put to bed and Ashenden saw him no more. His relations were sent for and in two months he was dead. He died uncomplaining. He understood what was happening to him as little as an animal. For a day or two there was the same malaise in the sanatorium as there is in a prison when a man has been hanged; and then, as though by universal consent, in obedience to an instinct of self-preservation, the boy was put out of mind: life, with its three meals a day, its golf on the miniature course, its regulated exercise, its prescribed rests, its quarrels and jealousies, its scandal-mongering and petty vexations, went on as before. Campbell, to the exasperation of McLeod, continued to play the prize-song and 'Annie Laurie' on his fiddle. McLeod continued to boast of his bridge and gossip about other people's health and morals. Miss Atkin continued to backbite. Henry Chester continued to complain that the doctors gave him insufficient attention and railed against fate because, after the model life he had led, it had played him such a dirty trick. Ashenden continued to read, and with amused tolerance to watch the vagaries of his fellow-creatures.

He became intimate with Major Templeton. Templeton was perhaps a little more than forty years of age. He had been in the Grenadier Guards, but had resigned his commission after the war. A man of ample means, he had since then devoted himself entirely to pleasure. He raced in the racing season, shot in the shooting season and hunted in the hunting season. When this was over he went to Monte Carlo. He told Ashenden of the large sums he had made and lost at baccarat. He was very fond of women and if his stories could be believed they were very fond of him. He loved good food and good drink. He knew by their first names the head waiters of every restaurant in London where you ate well. He belonged to half a dozen clubs. He had led for years a useless, selfish, worthless life, the sort of life which maybe it will be impossible for anyone to live in the future, but he had lived it without misgiving and had enjoyed it. Ashenden asked him once what he would do if he had his time over again and he answered that he would do exactly what he had done. He was an amusing talker, gay and pleasantly ironic, and he dealt with the surface of things, which was all he knew, with a light, easy and assured touch. He always had a pleasant word for the dowdy spinsters in the sanatorium and a joking one for the peppery old gentlemen, for he combined good manners with a natural kindliness. He knew his way about the superficial world of the people who have more money than they know what to do with as well as he knew his way about Mayfair. He was the kind of man who would always have been willing to take a bet, to help a friend and to give a tenner to a rogue. If he had never done much good in the world he had never done much harm. He amounted to nothing. But he was a more agreeable companion than many of more sterling character and of more admirable qualities. He was very ill now. He was dying and he knew it. He took it with the same easy, laughing nonchalance as he had taken all the rest. He'd had a thundering good time, he regretted nothing, it was rotten tough luck getting TB, but to hell with it, no one can live for ever, and when you came to think of it, he might have been killed in the war or broken his bloody neck in a point-to-point. His principle all through life had been, when you've made a bad bet, pay up and forget about it. He'd had a good run for his money and he was ready to call it a day. It had been a damned good party while it lasted, but every party's got to come to an end, and next day it doesn't matter much if you went home with the milk or if you left while the fun was in full swing.

Of all those people in the sanatorium he was probably from the moral standpoint the least worthy, but he was the only one who genuinely accepted the inevitable with unconcern. He snapped his fingers in the face of death, and you could choose whether to call his levity unbecoming or his insouciance gallant.

The last thing that ever occurred to him when he came to the sanatorium was that he might fall more deeply in love there than he had ever done before. His amours had been numerous, but they had been light; he had been content with the politely mercenary love of chorus girls and with ephemeral unions with women of easy virtue whom he met at house parties. He had always taken care to avoid any attachment that might endanger his freedom. His only aim in life had been to get as much fun out of it as possible, and where sex was concerned he found every advantage and no inconvenience in ceaseless variety. But he liked women. Even when they were quite old he could not talk to them without a caress in his eyes and a tenderness in his voice. He was prepared to do anything to please them. They were conscious of his interest in them and were agreeably flattered, and they felt, quite mistakenly, that they could trust him never to let them down. He once said a thing that Ashenden thought showed insight.

'You know, any man can get any woman he wants if he tries hard enough, there's nothing in that, but once he's got her, only a man who thinks the world of women can get rid of her without humiliating her.'

It was simply from habit that he began to make love to Ivy Bishop. She was the prettiest and the youngest girl in the sanatorium. She was in point of fact not so young as Ashenden had first thought her, she was twenty-nine, but for the last eight years she had been wandering from one sanatorium to another, in Switzerland, England and Scotland, and the sheltered invalid life had preserved her youthful appearance so that you might easily have taken her for twenty. All she knew of the world she had learnt in these establishments, so that she combined rather curiously extreme innocence with extreme sophistication. She had seen a number of love affairs run their course. A good many men, of various nationalities, had made love to her; she accepted their attentions with self-possession and humour, but she had at her disposal plenty of firmness when they showed an inclination to go too far. She had a force of character unexpected in anyone who looked so flower-like and when it came to a show-down knew how to express her meaning in plain, cool and decisive words. She was quite ready to have a flirtation with George Templeton. It was a game she understood, and though always charming to him, it was with a bantering lightness that showed quite clearly that she had summed him up and had no mind to take the affair more seriously than he did. Like Ashenden, Templeton went to bed every evening at six and dined in his room, so that he saw Ivy only by day. They went for little walks together, but otherwise were seldom alone. At lunch the conversation between the four of them, Ivy, Templeton, Henry Chester and

Ashenden, was general, but it was obvious that it was for neither of the two men that Templeton took so much trouble to be entertaining. It seemed to Ashenden that he was ceasing to flirt with Ivy to pass the time, and that his feeling for her were growing deeper and more sincere; but he could not tell whether she was conscious of it nor whether it meant anything to her. Whenever Templeton hazarded a remark that was more intimate than the occasion warranted she countered it with an ironic one that made them all laugh. But Templeton's laugh was rueful. He was no longer content to have her take him as a play-boy. The more Ashenden knew Ivy Bishop the more he liked her. There was something pathetic in her sick beauty, with that lovely transparent skin, the thin face in which the eyes were so large and so wonderfully blue; and there was something pathetic in her plight, for like so many others in the sanatorium she seemed to be alone in the world. Her mother led a busy social life, her sisters were married; they took but a perfunctory interest in the young woman from whom they had been separated now for eight years. They corresponded, they came to see her occasionally, but there was no longer very much between them. She accepted the situation without bitterness. She was friendly with everyone and prepared always to listen with sympathy to the complaints and the distress of all and sundry. She went out of her way to be nice to Henry Chester and did what she could to cheer him.

'Well, Mr Chester,' she said to him one day at lunch, 'it's the end of the month, your wife will be coming tomorrow. That's something to look forward to.'

'No, she's not coming this month,' he said quietly, looking down at his plate.

'Oh, I am sorry. Why not? The children are all right, aren't they?'

'Dr Lennox thinks it's better for me that she shouldn't come.'

There was a silence. Ivy looked at him with troubled eyes.

'That's tough luck, old man,' said Templeton in his hearty way. 'Why didn't you tell Lennox to go to hell?'

'He must know best,' said Chester.

Ivy gave him another look and began to talk of something else.

Looking back, Ashenden realized that she had at once suspected the truth. For next day he happened to walk with Chester.

'I'm awfully sorry your wife isn't coming,' he said. 'You'll miss her visit dreadfully.'

'Dreadfully.'

He gave Ashenden a sidelong glance. Ashenden felt that he had something he wanted to say, but could not bring himself to say it. He gave his shoulders an angry shrug.

'It's my fault if she's not coming. I asked Lennox to write and tell her not to. I couldn't stick it any more. I spend the whole month looking forward to her coming and then when she's here I hate her. You see, I resent so awfully having this filthy disease. She's strong and well and full of beans. It maddens me when I see the pain in her eyes. What does it matter to her really? Who cares if you're ill? They pretend to care, but they're jolly glad it's you and not them. I'm a swine aren't I?'

Ashenden remembered how Mrs Chester had sat on a stone by the side of the road and wept.

'Aren't you afraid you'll make her very unhappy, not letting her come?'

'She must put up with that. I've got enough with my own unhappiness without bothering with hers.'

Ashenden did not know what to say and they walked on in silence. Suddenly Chester broke out irritably.

'It's all very well for you to be disinterested and unselfish, you're going to live. I'm going to die, and God damn it, I don't want to die. Why should I? It's not fair.'

Time passed. In a place like the sanatorium where there was little to occupy the mind it was inevitable that soon everyone should know that George Templeton was in love with Ivy Bishop. But it was not so easy to tell what her feelings were. It was plain that she liked his company, but she did not seek it, and indeed it looked as though she took pains not to be alone with him. One or two of the middle-aged ladies tried to trap her into some compromising admission, but ingenuous as she was, she was easily a match for them. She ignored their hints and met their straight questions with incredulous laughter. She succeeded in exasperating them.

'She can't be so stupid as not to see that he's mad about her.'

'She has no right to play with him like that.'

'I believe she's just as much in love with him as he is with her.'

'Dr Lennox ought to tell her mother.'

No one was more incensed than McLeod.

'Too ridiculous. After all, nothing can come of it. He's riddled with TB and she's not much better.'

Campbell on the other hand was sardonic and gross.

'I'm all for their having a good time while they can. I bet there's a bit of hanky-panky going on if one only knew, and I don't blame 'em.'

'You cad,' said McLeod.

'Oh, come off it. Templeton isn't the sort of chap to play bumble-puppy bridge with a girl like that unless he's getting something out of it, and she knows a thing or two, I bet.'

Ashenden, who saw most of them, knew them better than any of the others. Templeton at last had taken him into his confidence. He was rather amused at himself.

'Rum thing at my time of life, falling in love with a decent girl. Last thing I'd ever expected of myself. And it's no good denying it, I'm in it up to the neck; if I were a well man I'd ask her to marry me tomorrow. I never knew a girl could be as nice as that. I've always thought girls, decent girls, I mean, damned bores. But she isn't a bore, she's as clever as she can stick. And pretty too. My God, what a skin! And that hair: but it isn't any of that that's bowled me over like a row of ninepins. D'you know what's got me? Damned ridiculous when you come to think of it. An old rip like me. Virtue. Makes me laugh like a hyena. Last thing I've ever wanted in a woman, but there it is, no getting away from it, she's good, and it makes me feel like a worm. Surprises you, I suppose?'

'Not a bit,' said Ashenden 'You're not the first rake who's fallen to innocence. It's merely the sentimentality of middle age.'

'Dirty dog,' laughed Templeton.

'What does she say to it?'

'Good God, you don't suppose I've told her. I've never said a word to her that I wouldn't have said before anyone else. I may be dead in six months, and besides, what have I got to offer a girl like that?'

Ashenden by now was pretty sure that she was just as much in love with Templeton as he was with her. He had seen the flush that coloured her cheeks when Templeton came into the dining-room and he had noticed the soft glance she gave him now and then when he was not looking at her. There was a peculiar sweetness in her smile when she listened to him telling some of his old experiences. Ashenden had the impression that she basked comfortably in his love as the patients on the terrace, facing the snow, basked in the hot sunshine; but it might very well be that she was content to leave it at that, and it was certainly no business of his to tell Templeton what perhaps she had no wish that he should know.

Then an incident occurred to disturb the monotony of life. Though McLeod and Campbell were always at odds they played bridge together because, till Templeton came, they were the best players in the sanatorium. They bickered incessantly, their post-mortems were endless, but after so many years each knew the other's game perfectly and they took a keen delight in scoring off one another. As a rule Templeton refused to play with them; though a fine player he preferred to play with Ivy Bishop, and McLeod and Campbell were agreed on this, that she ruined the game. She was the kind of player who, having made a mistake that lost the rubber, would laugh and say: Well, it only made the difference of a trick. But one afternoon, since Ivy was staying in her room with a headache, Templeton consented to play with Campbell and

McLeod. Ashenden was the fourth. Though it was the end of March there had been heavy snow for several days, and they played, in a veranda open on three sides to the wintry air, in fur coats and caps, with mittens on their hands. The stakes were too small for a gambler like Templeton to take the game seriously and his bidding was overbold, but he played so much better than the other three that he generally managed to make his contract or at least to come near it. But there was much doubling and redoubling. The cards ran high, so that an inordinate number of small slams were bid; it was a tempestuous game, and McLeod and Campbell lashed one another with their tongues. Half-past five arrived and the last rubber was started, for at six the bell rang to send everyone to rest. It was a hard-fought rubber, with sets on both sides, for McLeod and Campbell were opponents and each was determined that the other should not win. At ten minutes to six it was game all and the last hand was dealt. Templeton was McLeod's partner and Ashenden Campbell's. The bidding started with two clubs from McLeod; Ashenden said nothing; Templeton showed that he had substantial help, and finally McLeod called a grand slam. Campbell doubled and McLeod redoubled. Hearing this, the players at other tables who had broken off gathered round and the hands were played in deadly silence to a little crowd of onlookers. McLeod's face was white with excitement and there were beads of sweat on his brow. His hands trembled. Campbell was very grim. McLeod had to take two finesses and they both came off. He finished with a squeeze and got the last of the thirteen tricks. There was a burst of applause from the onlookers. McLeod, arrogant in victory, sprang to his feet. He shook his clenched fist at Campbell.

'Play that off on your blasted fiddle,' he shouted. 'Grand slam doubled and redoubled. I've wanted to get it all my life and now I've got it. By God. By God.'

He gasped. He staggered forward and fell across the table. A stream of blood poured from his mouth. The doctor was sent for. Attendants came. He was dead.

He was buried two days later, early in the morning so that the patients should not be disturbed by the sight of a funeral. A relation in black came from Glasgow to attend it. No one had liked him. No one regretted him. At the end of a week so far as one could tell, he was forgotten. The Indian civilian took his place at the principal table and Campbell moved into the room he had so long wanted.

'Now we shall have peace,' said Dr Lennox to Ashenden. 'When you think that I've had to put up with the quarrels and complaints of those two men for years and years. . . Believe me, one has to have patience to run a sanatorium. And to think that after all the trouble he's given me he had to end up like that and scare all those people out of their wits.'

'It was a bit of a shock, you know,' said Ashenden.

'He was a worthless fellow and yet some of the women have been quite upset about it. Poor little Miss Bishop cried her eyes out.'

'I suspect that she was the only one who cried for him and not for herself.'

But presently it appeared that there was one person who had not forgotten him. Campbell went about like a lost dog. He wouldn't play bridge. He wouldn't talk. There was no doubt about it, he was moping for McLeod. For several days he remained in his room, having his meals brought to him, and then went to Dr Lennox and said he didn't like it as well as his old one and wanted to be moved back. Dr Lennox lost his temper, which he rarely did, and told him he had been pestering him to give him that room for years and now he could stay there or get out of the sanatorium. He returned to it and sat gloomily brooding.

'Why don't you play your violin?' the matron asked him at length. 'I haven't heard you play for a fortnight.'

'I haven't.'

'Why not?'

'It's no fun any more. I used to get a kick out of playing because I knew it maddened McLeod. But now nobody cares if I play or not. I shall never play again.'

Nor did he for all the rest of the time that Ashenden was at the sanatorium. It was strange, now that McLeod was dead life had lost its savour for him. With no one to quarrel with, no one to infuriate, he had lost his incentive and it was plain that it would not be long before he followed his enemy to the grave.

But on Templeton McLeod's death had another effect, and one which was soon to have unexpected consequences. He talked to Ashenden about it in his cool, detached way.

'Grand, passing out like that in his moment of triumph. I can't make out why everyone got in such a state about it. He'd been here for years, hadn't he?'

'Eighteen, I believe.'

'I wonder if it's worth it. I wonder if it's not better to have one's fling and take the consequences.'

'I suppose it depends on how much you value life.'

'But is this life?'

Ashenden had no answer. In a few months he could count on being well, but you only had to look at Templeton to know that he was not going to recover. The death-look was on his face.

'D'you know what I've done?' asked Templeton. 'I've asked Ivy to marry me.'

Ashenden was startled.

'What did she say?'

'Bless her little heart, she said it was the most ridiculous idea she'd ever heard in her life and I was crazy to think of such a thing.'

'You must admit she was right.'

'Quite. But she's going to marry me.'

'It's madness.'

'I daresay it is; but anyhow, we're going to see Lennox and ask him what he thinks about it.'

The winter had broken at last; there was still snow on the hills, but in the valleys it was melted and on the lower slopes the birch-trees were in bud all ready to burst into delicate leaf. The enchantment of spring was in the air. The sun was hot. Everyone felt alert and some felt happy. The old stagers who came only for the winter were making their plans to go south. Templeton and Ivy went to see Dr Lennox together. They told him what they had in mind. He examined them; they were X-rayed and various tests were taken. Dr Lennox fixed a day when he would tell them the results and in light of this discuss their proposal. Ashenden saw them just before they went to keep the appointment. They were anxious, but did their best to make a joke of it. Dr Lennox showed them the results of his examination and explained to them in plain language what their condition was.

'All that's very fine and large,' said Templeton then, 'but what we want to know is whether we can get married.'

'It would be highly imprudent.'

'We know that, but does it matter?'

'And criminal if you had a child.'

'We weren't thinking of having one,' said Ivy.

'Well, then I'll tell you in very few words how the matter stands. Then you must decide for yourselves.'

Templeton gave Ivy a little smile and took her hand. The doctor went on.

'I don't think Miss Bishop will ever be strong enough to lead a normal life, but if she continues to live as she has been doing for the last eight years . . .'

'In sanatoriums?'

'Yes. There's no reason why she shouldn't live very comfortably, if not to a ripe old age, as long as any sensible person wants to live. The disease is quiescent. If she marries, if she attempts to live an ordinary life, the foci of infection may very well light up again, and what the results of that may be no one can foretell. So far as you are concerned, Templeton, I can put it even more shortly. You've seen the X-ray photos yourself. Your lungs are riddled with tubercle. If you marry you'll be dead in six months.'

'And if I don't how long can I live?'

The doctor hesitated.

'Don't be afraid. You can tell me the truth.'

'Two or three years.'

'Thank you, that's all we wanted to know.'

They went as they had come, hand in hand; Ivy was crying softy. No one knew what they said to one another; but when they came into luncheon they were radiant. They told Ashenden and Chester that they were going to be married as soon as they could get a licence. Then Ivy turned to Chester.

'I should so much like your wife to come up for my wedding. D'you think she would?'

'You're not going to be married here?'

'Yes. Our respective relations will only disapprove, so we're not going to tell them until it's all over. We shall ask Dr Lennox to give me away.'

She looked mildly at Chester, waiting for him to speak, for he had not answered her. The other two men watched him. His voice shook a little when he spoke.

'It's very kind of you to want her. I'll write and ask her.'

When the news spread among the patients, though everyone congratulated them, most of them privately told one another that it was very injudicious; but when they learnt, as sooner or later everything that happened in the sanatorium was learnt, that Dr Lennox had told Templeton that if he married he would be dead in six months, they were awed to silence. Even the dullest were moved at the thought of these two persons who loved one another so much that they were prepared to sacrifice their lives. A spirit of kindliness and good will descended on the sanatorium: people who hadn't been speaking spoke to one another again; others forgot for a brief space their own anxieties. Everyone seemed to share in the happiness of the happy pair. And it was not only the spring that filled those sick hearts with new hope, the great love that had taken possession of the man and the girl seemed to spread its effulgence on all that came near them. Ivy was quietly blissful; the excitement became her and she looked younger and prettier. Templeton seemed to walk on air. He laughed and joked as if he hadn't a care in the world. You would have said that he looked forward to long years of uninterrupted felicity. But one day he confided in Ashenden.

'This isn't a bad place, you know,' he said. 'Ivy's promised me that when I hand in my checks she'll come back here. She knows the people and she won't be so lonely.'

'Doctors are often mistaken,' said Ashenden. 'If you live reasonably I don't see why you shouldn't go on for a long time yet.'

'I'm only asking for three months. If I can only have that it'll be worth it.'

Mrs Chester came up two days before the wedding. She had not seen her husband for several months and they were shy with one another. It was easy to guess that when they were alone they felt awkward and constrained. Yet Chester did his best to shake off the depression that was now habitual and at all events at meal-times showed himself the jolly, hearty little fellow that he must have been before he fell ill. On the eve of the wedding day they all dined together, Templeton and Ashenden both sitting up for dinner; they drank champagne and stayed up till ten joking, laughing and enjoying themselves. The wedding took place next morning in the kirk. Ashenden was best man. Everyone in the sanatorium who could stand on his feet attended it. The newly married couple were setting out by car immediately after lunch. Patients, doctors and nurses assembled to see them off. Someone had tied an old shoe on the back of the car, and as Templeton and his wife came out of the door of the sanatorium rice was flung over them. A cheer was raised as they drove away, as they drove away to love and death. The crowd separated slowly. Chester and his wife went silently side by side. After they had gone a little way he shyly took her hand. Her heart seemed to miss a beat. With a sidelong glance she saw that his eyes were wet with tears.

'Forgive me, dear,' he said. 'I've been very unkind to you.'

'I knew you didn't mean it,' she faltered.

'Yes, I did. I wanted you to suffer because I was suffering. But not any more. All this about Templeton and Ivy Bishop – I don't know how to put it, it's made me see everything differently. I don't mind dying any more. I don't think death's very important, not so important as love. And I want you to live and be happy. I don't grudge you anything any more and I don't resent anything. I'm glad now it's me that must die and not you. I wish for you everything that's good in the world. I love you.'

FROM

The Gentleman in the Parlour

(1930)

The Princess and the Nightingale

First the King of Siam had two daughters and he called them Night and Day. Then he had two more, so he changed the names of the first ones and called the four of them after the seasons, Spring and Autumn, Winter and Summer. But in course of time he had three others and he changed their names again and called all seven by the days of the week. But when his eighth daughter was born he did not know what to do till he suddenly thought of the months of the year. The Queen said there were only twelve and it confused her to have to remember so many new names, but the King had a methodical mind and when he made it up he never could change it if he tried. He changed the names of all his daughters and called them January, February, March (though of course in Siamese) till he came to the youngest who was called August, and the next one was called September.

'That only leaves October, November, and December,' said the Queen. 'And after that we shall have to begin all over again.'

'No, we shan't,' said the King, 'because I think twelve daughters are enough for any man and after the birth of dear little December I shall be reluctantly compelled to cut off your head.'

He cried bitterly when he said this, for he was extremely fond of the Queen. Of course it made the

Queen very uneasy because she knew that it would distress the King very much if he had to cut off her head. And it would not be very nice for her. But it so happened that there was no need for either of them to worry because September was the last daughter they ever had. The Queen only had sons after that and they were called by the letters of the alphabet, so there was no cause for anxiety there for a long time, since she only reached the letter J.

Now the King of Siam's daughters had had their characters permanently embittered by having to change their names in this way, and the older ones whose names of course had been changed oftener than the others had their characters more permanently embittered. But September who had never known what it was to be called anything but September (except of course by her sisters who because their characters were embittered called her all sorts of names) had a very sweet and charming nature.

The King of Siam had a habit which I think might be usefully imitated in Europe. Instead of receiving presents on his birthday he gave them and it looks as though he liked it, for he used often to say he was sorry he had only been born on one day and so only had one birthday in the year. But in this way he managed in course of time to give away all his wedding presents and the loyal addresses which the mayors of the cities in Siam presented him with and all his old crowns which had gone out of fashion. One year on his birthday, not having anything else handy, he gave each of his daughters a beautiful green parrot in a beautiful golden cage. There were nine of them and on each cage was written the name of the month which was the name of the Princess it belonged to. The nine Princesses were very proud of their parrots and they spent an hour every day (for like their father they were of a methodical turn of mind) in teaching them to talk. Presently all the parrots could say God Save the King (in Siamese, which is very difficult) and some of them could say Pretty Polly in no less than seven oriental languages. But one day when the Princess September went to say good-morning to her parrot she found it lying dead at the bottom of its golden cage. She burst into a flood of tears, and nothing that her Maids of Honour could say comforted her. She cried so much that the Maids of Honour, not knowing what to do, told the Queen, and the Queen said it was stuff and nonsense and the child had better go to bed without any supper. The Maids of Honour wanted to go to a party, so they put the Princess September to bed as quickly as they could and left her by herself. And while she lay in her bed, crying still even though she felt rather hungry, she saw a little bird hop into her room. She took her thumb out of her mouth and sat up. Then the little bird began to sing and he sang a beautiful song all about the lake in the King's garden and the willow-trees that looked at themselves in the still water and the gold fish that glided in and out of the branches that were reflected in it. When he had finished the Princess was not crying any more and she quite forgot that she had had no supper.

'That was a very nice song,' she said.

The little bird gave her a bow, for artists have naturally good manners, and they like to be appreciated.

'Would you care to have me instead of your

parrot?' said the little bird. 'It's true that I'm not so pretty to look at, but on the other hand I have a much better voice.'

The Princess September clapped her hands with delight and then the little bird hopped on to the end of her bed and sang her to sleep.

When she awoke next day the little bird was still sitting there, and as she opened her eyes he said good-morning. The Maids of Honour brought in her breakfast, and he ate rice out of her hand and he had his bath in her saucer. He drank out of it too. The Maids of Honour said they didn't think it was very polite to drink one's bath water, but the Princess September said that was the artistic temperament. When he had finished his breakfast he began to sing again so beautifully that the Maids of Honour were quite surprised, for they had never heard anything like it, and the Princess September was very proud and happy.

'Now I want to show you to my eight sisters,' said the Princess.

She stretched out the first finger of her right hand so that it served as a perch and the little bird flew down and sat on it. Then, followed by her Maids of Honour, she went through the palace and called on each of the Princesses in turn, starting with January, for she was mindful of etiquette, and going all the way down to August. And for each of the Princesses the little bird sang a different song. But the parrots could only say God save the King and Pretty Polly. At last she showed the little bird to the King and Queen. They were surprised and delighted.

'I knew I was right to send you to bed without any supper,' said the Queen.

'This bird sings much better than the parrots,' said the King.

'I should have thought you got quite tired of hearing people say God save the King,' said the Queen. 'I can't think why those girls wanted to teach their parrots to say it too.'

'The sentiment is admirable,' said the King, 'and I never mind how often I hear it. But I do get tired of hearing those parrots say Pretty Polly.'

'They say it in seven different languages,' said the Princesses.

'I daresay they do,' said the King, 'but it reminds me too much of my Councillors. They say the same thing in seven different ways and it never means anything in any way they say it.'

The Princesses, their characters as I have already said being naturally embittered, were vexed at this, and the parrots looked very glum indeed. But the Princess September ran through all the rooms of the palace, singing like a lark, while the little bird flew round and round her, singing like a nightingale, which indeed it was.

Things went on like this for several days and then the eight Princesses put their heads together. They went to September and sat down in a circle round her, hiding their feet as is proper for Siamese princesses to do.

'My poor September,' they said. 'We are sorry for the death of your beautiful parrot. It must be dreadful for you not to have a pet bird as we have. So we have all put our pocket-money together and we are going to buy you a lovely green and yellow parrot.'

'Thank you for nothing,' said September. (This was not very civil of her, but Siamese princesses are sometimes a little short with one another.) 'I have a pet bird which sings the most charming songs to me and I don't know what on earth I should do with a green and yellow parrot.'

January sniffed, then February sniffed, then March sniffed: in fact all the Princesses sniffed, but in their proper order of precedence. When they had finished September asked them:

'Why do you sniff? Have you all got colds in the head?'

'Well, my dear,' they said, 'it's absurd to talk of *your* bird when the little fellow flies in and out just as he likes.' They looked round the room and raised their eyebrows so high that their foreheads entirely disappeared.

'You'll get dreadful wrinkles,' said September.

'Do you mind our asking where your bird is now?' they said.

'He's gone to pay a visit to his father-in-law,' said the Princess September.

'And what makes you think he'll come back?' asked the Princesses.

'He always does come back,' said September.

'Well, my dear,' said the eight Princesses, 'if you'll take our advice you won't run any risks like that. If he comes back, and mind you, if he does you'll be lucky, pop him into the cage and keep him there. That's the only way you can be sure of him.'

'But I like to have him fly about the room,' said the Princess September.

'Safety first,' said her sisters ominously.

They got up and walked out of the room, shaking their heads, and they left September very uneasy. It seemed to her that her little bird was away a long time and she could not think what he was doing. Something might have happened to him. What with hawks and men with snares you never knew what trouble he might get into. Besides, he might forget her, or he might take a fancy to somebody else; that would be dreadful; oh, she wished he were safely back again, and in the golden cage that stood there empty and ready. For when the Maids of Honour had buried the dead parrot they had left the cage in its old place.

Suddenly September heard a tweet-tweet just behind her ear and she saw the little bird sitting on her shoulder. He had come in so quietly and alighted so softly that she had not heard him.

'I wondered what on earth had become of you,' said the Princess.

'I thought you'd wonder that,' said the little bird. 'The fact is I very nearly didn't come back tonight at all. My father-in-law was giving a party and they all wanted me to stay, but I thought you'd be anxious.'

Under the circumstances this was a very unfortunate remark for the little bird to make.

September felt her heart go thump, thump against her chest, and she made up her mind to take no more risks. She put up her hand and took hold of the bird. This he was quite used to, she liked feeling his heart go pit-a-pat, so fast, in the hollow of her hand, and I think he liked the soft warmth of her little hand. So the bird suspected nothing and he was so surprised when she carried him over to the cage, popped him in, and shut the door on him that for a moment he could think of nothing to say. But in a moment or two he hopped up on the ivory perch and said:

'What is the joke?'

'There's no joke,' said September, 'but some of mamma's cats are prowling about tonight, and I think you're much safer in there.'

'I can't think why the Queen wants to have all those cats,' said the little bird, rather crossly.

'Well, you see, they're very special cats,' said the Princess, 'they have blue eyes and a kink in their tails, and they're a speciality of the royal family, if you understand what I mean.'

'Perfectly,' said the little bird, 'but why did you put me in this cage without saying anything about it? I don't think it's the sort of place I like.'

'I shouldn't have slept a wink all night if I hadn't known you were safe.'

'Well, just for this once I don't mind,' said the little bird, 'so long as you let me out in the morning.'

He ate a very good supper and then began to sing. But in the middle of his song he stopped.

'I don't know what is the matter with me,' he said, 'but I don't feel like singing tonight.'

'Very well,' said September, 'go to sleep instead.'

So he put his head under his wing and in a minute was fast asleep. September went to sleep too. But when the dawn broke she was awakened by the little bird calling her at the top of his voice.

'Wake up, wake up,' he said. 'Open the door of this cage and let me out. I want to have a good fly while the dew is still on the ground.'

'You're much better off where you are,' said September. 'You have a beautiful golden cage. It was made by the best workman in my papa's kingdom, and my papa was so pleased with it that he cut off his head so that he should never make another.'

'Let me out, let me out,' said the little bird.

'You'll have three meals a day served by my Maids of Honour; you'll have nothing to worry you from morning till night, and you can sing to your heart's content.'

'Let me out, let me out,' said the little bird. And he tried to slip through the bars of the cage, but of course he couldn't, and he beat against the door but of course he couldn't open it. Then the eight Princesses came in and looked at him. They told September she was very wise to take their advice. They said he would soon get used to the cage and in a few days would quite forget that he had ever been free. The little bird said nothing at all while they were there, but as soon as they were gone he began to cry again: 'Let me out, let me out.'

'Don't be such an old silly,' said September. 'I've only put you in the cage because I'm so fond of you. *I* know what's good for you much better than you do yourself. Sing me a little song and I'll give you a piece of brown sugar.'

But the little bird stood in the corner of his cage, looking out at the blue sky, and never sang a note. He never sang all day.

'What's the good of sulking?' said September. 'Why don't you sing and forget your troubles?'

'How can I sing?' answered the bird. 'I want to see the trees and the lake and the green rice growing in the fields.'

'If that's all you want I'll take you for a walk,' said September.

She picked up the cage and went out and she walked down to the lake round which grew the willow-trees, and she stood at the edge of the rice fields that stretched as far as the eye could see.

'I'll take you out every day,' she said. 'I love you and I only want to make you happy.'

'It's not the same thing,' said the little bird. 'The rice fields and the lake and the willow-trees look quite different when you see them through the bars of a cage.'

So she brought him home again and gave him his supper. But he wouldn't eat a thing. The Princess was a little anxious at this, and asked her sisters what they thought about it.

'You must be firm,' they said.

'But if he won't eat, he'll die,' she answered.

'That would be very ungrateful of him,' they said. 'He must know that you're only thinking of his own good. If he's obstinate and dies it'll serve him right and you'll be well rid of him.'

September didn't see how that was going to do *her* very much good, but they were eight to one and all older than she, so she said nothing.

'Perhaps he'll have got used to his cage by tomorrow,' she said.

And next day when she awoke she cried out good-morning in a cheerful voice. She got no answer. She jumped out of bed and ran to the cage. She gave a startled cry, for there the little bird lay, at the bottom, on his side, with his eyes closed, and he looked as if he were dead. She opened the door and putting her hand in lifted him out. She gave a sob of relief, for she felt that his little heart was beating still.

'Wake up, wake up, little bird,' she said.

She began to cry and her tears fell on the little bird. He opened his eyes and felt that the bars of the cage were no longer round him.

'I cannot sing unless I'm free and if I cannot sing, I die,' he said.

The Princess gave a great sob.

'Then take your freedom,' she said, 'I shut you in a golden cage because I loved you and wanted to have you all to myself. But I never knew it would kill you. Go. Fly away among the trees that are round the lake and fly over the green rice fields. I love you enough to let you be happy in your own way.'

She threw open the window and gently placed the little bird on the sill. He shook himself a little.

'Come and go as you will, little bird,' she said. 'I will never put you in a cage any more.'

'I will come because I love you, little Princess,' said the bird. 'And I will sing you the loveliest songs I know. I shall go far away, but I shall always come back, and I shall never forget you.' He gave himself another shake. 'Good gracious me, how still I am,' he said.

Then he opened his wings and flew right away into the blue. But the little Princess burst into tears, for it is very difficult to put the happiness of someone you love before your own, and with her little bird far out of sight she felt on a sudden very lonely. When her sisters knew what had happened they mocked her and said that the little bird would never return. But he did at last. And he sat on September's shoulder and ate out of her hand and sang her the beautiful songs he had learned while he was flying up and down the fair places of the world. September kept her window open day and night so that the little bird might come into her room whenever he felt inclined, and this was very good for her; so she grew extremely beautiful. And when she was old enough she married the King of

Cambodia and was carried all the way to the city in which he lived on a white elephant. But her sisters never slept with their windows open, so they grew extremely ugly as well as disagreeable, and when the time came to marry them off they were given away to the King's Councillors with a pound of tea and a Siamese cat.

FROM

*Six Stories Written in the
First Person Singular*

(1931)

The Round Dozen

I like Elsom. It is a seaside resort in the South of England, not very far from Brighton, and it has something of the late Georgian charm of that agreeable town. But it is neither bustling nor garish. Ten years ago, when I used to go there not infrequently, you might still see here and there an old house, solid and pretentious in no unpleasing fashion (like a decayed gentlewoman of good family whose discreet pride in her ancestry amuses rather than offends you) which was built in the reign of the First Gentleman in Europe and where a courtier of fallen fortunes may well have passed his declining years. The main street had a lackadaisical air and the doctor's motor seemed a trifle out of place. The housewives did their housekeeping in a leisurely manner. They gossiped with the butcher as they watched him cut from his great joint of South Down a piece of the best-end of the neck, and they asked amiably after the grocer's wife as he put half a pound of tea and a packet of salt into their string bag. I do not know whether Elsom was ever fashionable: it certainly was not so then; but it was respectable and cheap. Elderly ladies, maiden and widowed, lived there, Indian civilians and retired soldiers: they looked forward with little shudders of dismay to August and September which would bring holiday-makers; but did not disdain to let them their houses and on the proceeds spend a few worldly weeks in a Swiss pension. I never knew Elsom at that hectic time when the lodging-houses were full and young men in blazers sauntered along the front, when Pierrots performed on the beach and in the billiard-room at the Dolphin you heard the click of balls till eleven at night. I only knew it in winter. Then in every house on the sea-front, stucco houses with bow-windows built a hundred years ago, there was a sign to inform you that apartments were to let; and the guests of the Dolphin were waited on by a single waiter and the boots. At ten o'clock the porter came into the smoking-room and looked at you in so marked a manner that you got up and went to bed. Then Elsom was a restful place and the Dolphin a very comfortable inn. It was pleasing to think that the Prince Regent drove over with Mrs Fitzherbert more than once to drink a dish of tea in its coffee-room. In the hall was a framed letter from Mr Thackeray ordering a sitting-room and two bedrooms overlooking the sea and giving instructions that a fly should be sent to the station to meet him.

One November, two or three years after the war, having had a bad attack of influenza, I went down to Elsom to regain my strength. I arrived in the afternoon and when I had unpacked my things went for a stroll on the front. The sky was overcast and the calm sea grey and cold. A few seagulls flew close to the shore. Sailing boats, their masts taken down for the winter, were drawn up high on the shingly beach and the bathing huts stood side by side in a long, grey and tattered row. No one was sitting on the benches that the town council had put here and there, but a few people were trudging up and down for exercise. I passed an old colonel with a red nose who stamped along in plus fours followed by a terrier, two elderly women in short skirts and stout shoes and a plain girl in a Tam o' Shanter. I had never seen the front so deserted. The lodging-houses looked like bedraggled old maids waiting for lovers who would never return, and even the friendly Dolphin seemed wan and desolate. My heart sank. Life on a sudden seemed very drab. I returned to the hotel, drew the curtains of my sitting-room, poked the fire and with a book sought to dispel my melancholy. But I was glad enough when it was time to dress for dinner. I went into the coffee-room and found the guests of the hotel already seated. I gave them a casual glance. There was one lady of middle age by herself and there were two elderly gentlemen, golfers probably, with red faces and baldish heads, who ate their food in moody silence. The only other persons in the room were a group of three who sat in the bow-window, and they immediately attracted my surprised attention. The party consisted of an old gentleman and two ladies, one of whom was old and probably his wife, while the other was younger and possibly his daughter. It was the old lady who first excited my interest. She wore a voluminous dress of black silk and a black lace cap; on her wrists were heavy gold bangles and round her neck a substantial gold chain from which hung a large gold locket; at her neck was a large gold brooch. I did not know that anyone still wore jewellery of that sort. Often, passing second-hand jewellers and pawnbrokers, I had lingered for a moment to look at these strangely old-fashioned articles, so solid, costly and hideous, and thought, with a smile in which there was a tinge of sadness, of the women long since dead who had worn them. They suggested the period when the bustle and the flounce were taking the place of the crinoline and the pork-pie hat was ousting the poke-bonnet. The British people liked things solid and good in those days. They went to church on Sunday morning and after church walked in the Park. They gave dinner-parties of twelve courses where the master of the house carved the beef and the chickens, and after dinner the ladies who could play favoured the company with Mendelssohn's Songs Without Words and the gentleman with the fine baritone voice sang an old English ballad.

The younger woman had her back turned to me and at first I could see only that she had a slim and youthful figure. She had a great deal of brown hair which seemed to be elaborately arranged. She wore a grey dress. The three of them were chatting in low tones and presently she turned her head so that I saw her profile. It was astonishingly beautiful. The nose was straight and delicate, the line of the cheek exquisitely modelled; I saw then that she wore her hair after the manner of Queen Alexandra. The dinner proceeded to its close and the party got up. The old lady sailed out of the room, looking neither to the right nor to the left, and the young one followed her. Then I saw with a shock that she was old. Her frock was simple enough, the skirt was longer than was at that time worn, and there was something slightly old-fashioned in the cut, I daresay the waist was more clearly indicated than was then usual, but it was a girl's frock. She was tall, like a heroine of Tennyson's, slight, with long legs and a graceful carriage. I had seen the nose before, it was the nose of a Greek goddess, her mouth was beautiful, and her eyes were large and blue. Her skin was of course a little tight on the bones and there were wrinkles on her forehead and about her eyes, but in youth it must have been lovely. She reminded you of those Roman ladies with features of an exquisite regularity whom Alma Tadema used to paint, but who, notwithstanding their antique dress, were so stubbornly English. It was a type of cold perfection that one had not seen for five-and-twenty years. Now it is as dead as the epigram. I was like an archaeologist who finds some long-buried statue and I was thrilled in so unexpected a manner to hit upon this survival of a past era. For no day is so dead as the day before yesterday.

The gentleman rose to his feet when the two ladies left, and then resumed his chair. A waiter brought him a glass of heavy port. He smelt it, sipped it, and rolled it round his tongue. I observed him. He was a little man, much shorter than his imposing wife, well-covered without being stout, with a fine head of curling grey hair. His face was much wrinkled and it bore a faintly humorous expression. His lips were tight and his chin was square. He was, according to our present notions, somewhat extravagantly dressed. He wore a black velvet jacket, a frilled shirt with a low collar and a large black tie, and very wide evening trousers. It gave you vaguely the effect of costume. Having drunk his port with deliberation, he got up and sauntered out of the room.

When I passed through the hall, curious to know who these singular people were, I glanced at the visitors' book. I saw written in an angular feminine hand, the writing that was taught to young ladies in modish schools forty years or so ago, the names: Mr and Mrs Edwin St Clair and Miss Porchester. Their address was given as 68, Leinster Square, Bayswater, London. These must be the names and this the address of the persons who had so much interested me. I asked the manageress who Mr St Clair was and she told me that she believed he was something in the City. I went into the billiard-room and knocked the balls about for a little while and then on my way upstairs passed through the lounge. The two red-faced gentlemen were reading the evening paper and the elderly lady was dozing over a novel. The party of three sat in a corner. Mrs St Clair was knitting, Miss Porchester was busy with embroidery, and Mr St Clair was reading aloud in a discreet but resonant tone. As I passed I discovered that he was reading *Bleak House*.

I read and wrote most of the next day, but in the afternoon I went for a walk and on my way home I sat down for a little on one of those convenient benches on the sea-front. It was not quite so cold as the day before and the air was pleasant. For want of anything better to do I watched a figure advancing towards me from a distance. It was a man and as he came nearer I saw that it was rather a shabby little man. He wore a thin black greatcoat and a somewhat battered bowler. He walked with his hands in his pockets and looked cold. He gave me a glance as he passed by, went on a few steps, hesitated, stopped and turned back. When he came up once more to the bench on which I sat he took a hand out of his pocket and touched his hat. I noticed that he wore shabby black gloves, and surmised that he was a widower in straitened circumstances.

Or he might have been a mute recovering, like myself, from influenza.

'Excuse me, sir,' he said, 'but could you oblige me with a match?'

'Certainly.'

He sat down beside me and while I put my hand in my pocket for matches he hunted in his for cigarettes. He took out a small packet of Goldflakes and his face fell.

'Dear, dear, how very annoying! I haven't got a cigarette left.'

'Let me offer you one,' I replied, smiling.

I took out my case and he helped himself.

'Gold?' he asked, giving the case a tap as I closed it. 'Gold? That's a thing I never could keep. I've had three. All stolen.'

His eyes rested in a melancholy way on his boots which were sadly in need of repair. He was a wizened little man with a long thin nose and pale blue eyes. His skin was sallow and he was much lined. I could not tell what his age was; he might have been five-and-thirty or he might have been sixty. There was nothing remarkable about him except his insignificance. But though evidently poor he was neat and clean. He was respectable and he clung to respectability. No, I did not think he was a mute, I thought he was a solicitor's clerk who had lately buried his wife and been sent to Elsom by an indulgent employer to get over the first shock of his grief.

'Are you making a long stay, sir?' he asked me.

'Ten days or a fortnight.'

'Is this your first visit to Elsom, sir?'

'I have been here before.'

'I know it well, sir. I flatter myself there are very

few seaside resorts that I have not been to at one time or another. Elsom is hard to beat, sir. You get a very nice class of people here. There's nothing noisy or vulgar about Elsom if you understand what I mean. Elsom has very pleasant recollections for me, sir. I knew Elsom well in bygone days. I was married in St Martin's Church, sir.'

'Really,' I said feebly.

'It was a very happy marriage, sir.'

'I'm very glad to hear it,' I returned.

'Nine months that one lasted,' he said reflectively.

Surely the remark was a trifle singular. I had not looked forward with any enthusiasm to the probability which I so clearly foresaw that he would favour me with an account of his matrimonial experiences, but now I waited if not with eagerness at least with curiosity for a further observation. He made none. He sighed a little. At last I broke the silence.

'There don't seem to be very many people about,' I remarked.

'I like it so. I'm not one for crowds. As I was saying just now I reckon I've spent a good many years at one seaside resort after the other, but I never came in the season. It's the winter I like.'

'Don't you find it a little melancholy?'

He turned towards me and placed his black-gloved hand for an instant on my arm.

'It is melancholy. And because it's melancholy a little ray of sunshine is very welcome.'

The remark seemed to me perfectly idiotic and I did not answer. He withdrew his hand from my arm and got up.

'Well, I mustn't keep you, sir. Pleased to have made your acquaintance.'

He took off his dingy hat very politely and strolled away. It was beginning now to grow chilly and I thought I would return to the Dolphin. As I reached its broad steps a landau drove up, drawn by two scraggy horses, and from it stepped Mr St Clair. He wore a hat that looked like the unhappy result of a union between a bowler and a top-hat. He gave his hand to his wife and then to his niece. The porter carried in after them rugs and cushions. As Mr St Clair paid the driver I heard him tell him to come at the usual time next day and I understood that the St Clairs took a drive every afternoon in a landau. It would not have surprised me to learn that none of them had even been in a motor-car.

The manageress told me that they kept very much to themselves and sought no acquaintance among the other persons staying at the hotel. I rode my imagination on a loose rein. I watched them eat three meals a day. I watched Mr and Mrs St Clair sit at the top of the hotel steps in the morning. He read *The Times* and she knitted. I suppose Mrs St Clair had never read a paper in her life, for they never took anything but *The Times* and Mr St Clair of course took it with him every day to the City. At about twelve Miss Porchester joined them.

'Have you enjoyed your walk, Eleanor?' asked Mrs St Clair.

'It was very nice, Aunt Gertrude,' answered Miss Porchester.

And I understood that just as Mrs St Clair took 'her drive' every afternoon Miss Porchester took 'her walk' every morning.

'When you have come to the end of your row,

my dear,' said Mr St Clair, with a glance at his wife's knitting, 'we might go for a constitutional before luncheon.'

'That will be very nice,' answered Mrs St Clair. She folded up her work and gave it to Miss Porchester. 'If you're going upstairs, Eleanor, will you take my work?'

'Certainly, Aunt Gertrude.'

'I daresay you're a little tired after your walk, my dear.'

'I shall have a little rest before luncheon.'

Miss Porchester went into the hotel and Mr and Mrs St Clair walked slowly along the sea-front, side by side, to a certain point, and then walked slowly back.

When I met one of them on the stairs I bowed and received an unsmiling, polite bow in return, and in the morning I ventured upon a good-day, but there the matter ended. It looked as though I should never have a chance to speak to any of them. But presently I thought that Mr St Clair gave me now and then a glance, and thinking he had heard my name I imagined, perhaps vainly, that he looked at me with curiosity. And a day or two after that I was sitting in my room when the porter came in with a message.

'Mr St Clair presents his compliments and could you oblige him with the loan of Whitaker's Almanack.'

I was astonished.

'Why on earth should he think that I have a Whitaker's Almanack?'

'Well, sir, the manageress told him you wrote.'

I could not see the connection.

'Tell Mr St Clair that I'm very sorry that I

haven't got a Whitaker's Almanack, but if I had I would very gladly lend it to him.'

Here was my opportunity. I was by now filled with eagerness to know these fantastic persons more closely. Now and then in the heart of Asia I have come upon a lonely tribe living in a little village among an alien population. No one knows how they came there or why they settled in that spot. They live their own lives, speak their own language, and have no communication with their neighbours. No one knows whether they are the descendants of a band that was left behind when their nation swept in a vast horde across the continent or whether they are the dying remnant of some great people that in that country once held empire. They are a mystery. They have no future and no history. This odd little family seemed to me to have something of the same character. They were of an era that is dead and gone. They reminded me of persons in one of those leisurely, old-fashioned novels that one's father read. They belonged to the eighties and they had not moved since then. How extraordinary it was that they could have lived through the last forty years as though the world stood still! They took me back to my childhood and I recollected people who are long since dead. I wonder if it is only distance that gives me the impression that they were more peculiar than anyone is now. When a person was described then as 'quite a character', by heaven, it meant something.

So that evening after dinner I went into the lounge and boldly addressed Mr St Clair.

'I'm so sorry I haven't got a Whitaker's Almanack,' I said, 'but if I have any other book that can be of service to you I shall be delighted to lend it to you.'

Mr St Clair was obviously startled. The two ladies kept their eyes on their work. There was an embarrassed hush.

'It does not matter at all, but I was given to understand by the manageress that you were a novelist.'

I racked my brain. There was evidently some connection between my profession and Whitaker's Almanack that escaped me.

'In days gone by Mr Trollope used often to dine with us in Leinster Square and I remember him saying that the two most useful books to a novelist were the Bible and Whitaker's Almanack.'

'I see that Thackeray once stayed in this hotel,' I remarked, anxious not to let the conversation drop.

'I never very much cared for Mr Thackeray, though he dined more than once with my wife's father, the late Mr Sargeant Saunders. He was too cynical for me. My niece has not read *Vanity Fair* to this day.'

Miss Porchester blushed slightly at this reference to herself. A waiter brought in the coffee and Mrs St Clair turned to her husband.

'Perhaps, my dear, this gentleman would do us the pleasure to have his coffee with us.'

Although not directly addressed I answered promptly:

'Thank you very much.'

I sat down.

'Mr Trollope was always my favourite novelist,' said Mr St Clair. 'He was so essentially a gentleman. I admire Charles Dickens. But Charles Dickens could never draw a gentleman. I am given to understand that young people nowadays find Mr Trollope a little slow. My niece, Miss Porchester, prefers the novels of Mr William Black.'

'I'm afraid I've never read any,' I said.

'Ah, I see that you are like me; you are not up-to-date. My niece once persuaded me to read a novel by a Miss Rhoda Broughton, but I could not manage more than a hundred pages of it.'

'I did not say I liked it, Uncle Edwin,' said Miss Porchester, defending herself, with another blush, 'I told you it was rather fast, but everybody was talking about it.'

'I'm quite sure it is not the sort of book your Aunt Gertrude would have wished you to read, Eleanor.'

'I remember Miss Broughton telling me once that when she was young people said her books were fast and when she was old they said they were slow, and it was very hard since she had written exactly the same sort of book for forty years.'

'Oh, did you know Miss Broughton?' asked Miss Porchester, addressing me for the first time. 'How very interesting! And did you know Ouida?'

'My dear Eleanor, what will you say next! I'm quite sure you've never read anything by Ouida.'

'Indeed, I have, Uncle Edwin. I've read *Under Two Flags* and I liked it very much.'

'You amaze and shock me. I don't know what girls are coming to nowadays.'

'You always said that when I was thirty you gave me complete liberty to read anything I liked.'

'There is a difference, my dear Eleanor, between liberty and licence,' said Mr St Clair, smiling a little in order not to make his reproof offensive, but with a certain gravity.

I do not know if in recounting this conversation I have managed to convey the impression it gave me of a charming and old-fashioned air. I could have listened all night to them discussing the depravity of an age that was young in the eighteen-eighties. I would have given a good deal for a glimpse of their large and roomy house in Leinster Square. I should have recognized the suite covered in red brocade that stood stiffly about the drawing-room, each piece in its appointed place; and the cabinets filled with Dresden china would have brought me back my childhood. In the dining-room, where they habitually sat, for the drawing-room was used only for parties, was a Turkey carpet and a vast mahogany sideboard 'groaning' with silver. On the walls were the pictures that had excited the admiration of Mrs Humphrey Ward and her uncle Matthew in the Academy of eighteen-eighty.

Next morning, strolling through a pretty lane at the back of Elsom, I met Miss Porchester, who was taking 'her walk'. I should have liked to go a little way with her, but felt certain that it would embarrass this maiden of fifty to saunter alone with a man even of my respectable years. She bowed as I passed her and blushed. Oddly enough, a few yards behind her I came upon the funny shabby little man in black gloves with whom I had spoken for a few minutes on the front. He touched his old bowler hat.

'Excuse me, sir, but could you oblige me with a match?' he said.

'Certainly,' I retorted, 'but I'm afraid I have no cigarettes on me.'

'Allow me to offer you one of mine,' he said, taking out the paper case. It was empty. 'Dear,

dear, I haven't got one either. What a curious coincidence!'

He went on and I had a notion that he a little hastened his steps. I was beginning to have my doubts about him. I hoped he was not going to bother Miss Porchester. For a moment I thought of walking back, but I did not. He was a civil little man and I did not believe he would make a nuisance of himself to a single lady.

I saw him again that very afternoon. I was sitting on the front. He walked towards me with little, halting steps. There was something of a wind and he looked like a dried leaf being driven before it. This time he did not hesitate, but sat down beside me.

'We meet again, sir. The world is a small place. If it will not inconvenience you perhaps you will allow me to rest a few minutes. I am a wee bit tired.'

'This is a public bench, and you have just as much right to sit on it as I.'

I did not wait for him to ask me for a match, but at once offered him a cigarette.

'How very kind of you, sir! I have to limit myself to so many cigarettes a day, but I enjoy those I smoke. As one grows older the pleasures of life diminish, but my experience is that one enjoys more those that remain.'

'That is a very consoling thought.'

'Excuse me, sir, but am I right in thinking that you are the well-known author?'

'I am an author,' I replied. 'But what made you think it?'

'I have seen your portrait in the illustrated papers. I suppose you don't recognize me?'

I looked at him again, a weedy little man in neat, but shabby black clothes, with a long nose and watery blue eyes.

'I'm afraid I don't.'

'I daresay I've changed,' he sighed. 'There was a time when my photograph was in every paper in the United Kingdom. Of course, those press photographs never do you justice. I give you my word, sir, that if I hadn't seen my name underneath I should never have guessed that some of them were meant for me.'

He was silent for a while. The tide was out and beyond the shingle of the beach was a strip of yellow mud. The breakwaters were half buried in it like the backbones of prehistoric beasts.

'It must be a wonderfully interesting thing to be an author, sir. I've often thought I had quite a turn for writing myself. At one time and another I've done a rare lot of reading. I haven't kept up with it much lately. For one thing my eyes are not so good as they used to be. I believe I could write a book if I tried.'

'They say anybody can write one,' I answered.

'Not a novel, you know. I'm not much of a one for novels; I prefer histories and that like. But memoirs. If anybody was to make it worth my while I wouldn't mind writing my memoirs.'

'It's very fashionable just now.'

'There are not many people who've had the experiences I've had in one way and another. I did write to one of the Sunday papers about it some little while back, but they never answered my letter.'

He gave me a long, appraising look. He had too respectable an air to be about to ask me for half a crown.

'Of course you don't know who I am, sir, do you?'

'I honestly don't.'

He seemed to ponder for a moment, then he smoothed down his black gloves on his fingers, looked for a moment at a hole in one of them, and then turned to me not without self-consciousness.

'I am the celebrated Mortimer Ellis,' he said.

'Oh?'

I did not know what other ejaculation to make, for to the best of my belief I had never heard the name before. I saw a look of disappointment come over his face, and I was a trifle embarrassed.

'Mortimer Ellis,' he repeated. 'You're not going to tell me you don't know.'

'I'm afraid I must. I'm very often out of England.'

I wondered to what he owed his celebrity. I passed over in my mind various possibilities. He could never have been an athlete, which alone in England gives a man real fame, but he might have been a faith-healer or a champion billiard-player. There is of course no one so obscure as a cabinet minister out of office and he might have been the President of the Board of Trade in a defunct administration. But he had none of the look of a politician.

'That's fame for you,' he said bitterly. 'Why, for weeks I was the most talked-about man in England. Look at me. You must have seen my photograph in the papers. Mortimer Ellis.'

'I'm sorry,' I said, shaking my head.

He paused a moment to give his disclosure effectiveness.

'I am the well-known bigamist.'

Now what are you to reply when a person who is practically a stranger to you informs you that he is a well-known bigamist? I will confess that I have sometimes had the vanity to think that I am not as a rule at a loss for a retort, but here I found myself speechless.

'I've had eleven wives, sir,' he went on.

'Most people find one about as much as they can manage.'

'Ah, that's want of practice. When you've had eleven there's very little you don't know about women.'

'But why did you stop at eleven?'

'There now, I knew you'd say that. The moment I set eyes on you I said to myself he's got a clever face. You know, sir, that's the thing that always grizzles me. Eleven does seem a funny number, doesn't it? There's something unfinished about it. Now three anyone might have, and seven's all right, they say nine's lucky, and there's nothing wrong with ten. But eleven! That's the one thing I regret. I shouldn't have minded anything if I could have brought it up to the Round Dozen.'

He unbuttoned his coat and from an inside pocket produced a bulging and very greasy pocket-book. From this he took a large bundle of newspaper cuttings; they were worn and creased and dirty. But he spread out two or three.

'Now just you look at those photographs. I ask you, are they like me? It's an outrage. Why, you'd think I was a criminal to look at them.'

The cuttings were of imposing length. In the opinion of sub-editors Mortimer Ellis had obviously been a news item of value. One was headed, A Much Married Man; another, Heartless Ruffian Brought to Book; a third, Contemptible Scoundrel Meets his Waterloo.

'Not what you would call a good press,' I murmured.

'I never pay any attention to what the newspapers say,' he answered, with a shrug of his thin shoulders. 'I've known too many journalists myself for that. No, it's the judge I blame. He treated me shocking and it did him no good, mind you: he died within the year.'

I ran my eyes down the report I held.

'I see he gave you five years.'

'Disgraceful, I call it, and see what it says.' He pointed to a place with his forefinger. '"Three of his victims pleaded for mercy to be shown to him." That shows what they thought of me. And after that he gave me five years. And just look what he called me, a heartless scoundrel – me, the best-hearted man that ever lived – a pest of society and a danger to the public. Said he wished he had the power to give me the cat. I don't so much mind his giving me five years, though you'll never get me to say it wasn't excessive, but I ask you, had he the right to talk to me like that? No, he hadn't, and I'll never forgive him, not if I live to be a hundred.'

The bigamist's cheeks flushed and his watery eyes were filled for a moment with fire. It was a sore subject with him.

'May I read them?' I asked him.

'That's what I gave them you for. I want you to read them, sir. And if you can read them without saying that I'm a much wronged man, well, you're not the man I took you for.'

As I glanced through one cutting after another I saw why Mortimer Ellis had so wide an acquaintance with the seaside resorts of England. They were his hunting-ground. His method was to go to some place when the season was over and take apartments in one of the empty lodging-houses. Apparently it did not take him long to make acquaintance with some woman or other, widow or spinster, and I noticed that their ages at the time were between thirty-five and fifty. They stated in the witness-box that they had met him first on the sea-front. He generally proposed marriage to them within a fortnight of this and they were married shortly after. He induced them in one way or another to entrust him with their savings and in a few months, on the pretext that he had to go to London on business, he left them never to return. Only one had ever seen him again till, obliged to give evidence, they saw him in the dock. They were women of a certain respectability; one was the daughter of a doctor and another of a clergyman; there was a lodging-house keeper, there was the widow of a commercial traveller, and there was a retired dressmaker. For the most part, their fortunes ranged from five hundred to a thousand pounds, but whatever the sum the misguided women were stripped of every penny. Some of them told really pitiful stories of the destitution to which they had been reduced. But they all acknowledged that he had been a good husband to them. Not only had three actually pleaded for mercy to be shown him; but one said in the witness-box that, if he was willing to come, she was ready to take him back. He noticed that I was reading this.

'And she'd have worked for me,' he said, 'there's no doubt about that. But I said, better let bygones be bygones. No one likes a cut off the best end of the neck better than I do, but I'm not much of a one for cold roast mutton, I will confess.'

It was only by an accident that Mortimer Ellis did not marry his twelfth wife and so achieve the Round Dozen which I understand appealed to his love of symmetry. For he was engaged to be married to a Miss Hubbard – 'two thousand pounds she had, if she had a penny, in war-loan,' he confided to me – and the banns had been read, when one of his former wives saw him, made inquiries, and communicated with the police. He was arrested on the very day before his twelfth wedding.

'She was a bad one, she was,' he told me. 'She deceived me something cruel.'

'How did she do that?'

'Well, I met her at Eastbourne, one December it was, on the pier, and she told me in course of conversation that she'd been in the millinery business and had retired. She said she'd made a tidy bit of money. She wouldn't say exactly how much it was, but she gave me to understand it was something like fifteen hundred pounds. And when I married her, would you believe it, she hadn't got three hundred. And that's the one who gave me away. And mind you, I'd never blamed her. Many a man would have cut up rough when he found out he'd been made a fool of. I never showed her that I was disappointed even, I just went away without a word.'

'But not without the three hundred pounds, I take it.'

'Oh come, sir, you must be reasonable,' he returned in an injured tone. 'You can't expect three hundred pounds to last for ever and I'd been married to her four months before she confessed the truth.'

'Forgive my asking,' I said, 'and pray don't think my question suggests a disparaging view of your personal attractions, but – why did they marry you?'

'Because I asked them,' he answered, evidently very much surprised at my inquiry.

'But did you never have any refusals?'

'Very seldom. Not more than four or five in the whole course of my career. Of course I didn't propose till I was pretty sure of my ground and I don't say I didn't draw a blank sometimes. You can't expect to click every time, if you know what I mean, and I've often wasted several weeks making up to a woman before I saw there was nothing doing.'

I surrendered myself for a time to my reflections. But I noticed presently that a broad smile spread over the mobile features of my friend.

'I understand what you mean,' he said. 'It's my appearance that puzzles you. You don't know what it is they see in me. That's what comes of reading novels and going to the pictures. You think what women want is the cowboy type, or the romance of old Spain touch, flashing eyes, an olive skin, and a beautiful dancer. You make me laugh.'

'I'm glad,' I said.

'Are you a married man, sir?'

'I am. But I only have one wife.'

'You can't judge by that. You can't generalize from a single instance, if you know what I mean. Now, I ask you, what would you know about dogs if you'd never had anything but one bull-terrier?'

The question was rhetorical and I felt sure did not require an answer. He paused for an effective moment and went on.

'You're wrong, sir. You're quite wrong. They may take a fancy to a good-looking young fellow, but they don't want to marry him. They don't really care about looks.

'Douglas Jerrold, who was as ugly as he was witty, used to say that if he was given ten minutes' start with a woman he could cut out the handsomest man in the room.

'They don't want wit. They don't want a man to be funny; they think he's not serious. They don't want a man who's too handsome; they think he's not serious either. That's what they want, they want a man who's serious. Safety first. And then – attention. I may not be handsome and I may not be amusing, but believe me, I've got what every woman wants. Poise. And the proof is, I've made every one of my wives happy.'

'It certainly is much to your credit that three of them pleaded for mercy to be shown to you and that one was willing to take you back.'

'You don't know what an anxiety that was to me all the time I was in prison. I thought she'd be waiting for me at the gate when I was released and I said to the Governor, for God's sake, sir, smuggle me out so as no one can see me.'

He smoothed his gloves again over his hands and his eye once more fell upon the hole in the first finger.

'That's what comes of living in lodgings, sir. How's a man to keep himself neat and tidy without a woman to look after him? I've been married too often to be able to get along without a wife. There are men who don't like being married. I can't understand them. The fact is, you can't do a thing really well unless you've got your heart in it, and I like being a married man. It's no difficulty to me to do the little things that women like and that some men can't be bothered with. As I was saying just now, it's attention a woman wants. I never went out of the house without giving my wife a kiss and I never came in without giving her another. And it was very seldom I came in without bringing her some chocolates or a few flowers. I never grudged the expense.'

'After all, it was her money you were spending,' I interposed.

'And what if it was? It's not the money that you've paid for a present that signifies, it's the spirit you give it in. That's what counts with women. No, I'm not one to boast, but I will say this for myself, I am a good husband.'

I looked desultorily at the reports of the trial which I still held.

'I'll tell you what surprises me,' I said. 'All these women were very respectable, of a certain age, quiet, decent persons. And yet they married you without any inquiry after the shortest possible acquaintance.'

He put his hand impressively on my arm.

'Ah, that's what you don't understand, sir. Women have got a craving to be married. It doesn't matter how young they are or how old they are, if they're short or tall, dark or fair, they've all got one thing in common: they want to be married. And mind you, I married them in church. No woman feels really safe unless she's married in church. You say I'm no beauty, well, I never thought I was, but if I had one leg and a hump on my back I could find any number of women who'd jump at the chance of marrying me. It's not the man they care about, it's marriage. It's a mania with them. It's a disease. Why, there's hardly one of them who wouldn't have accepted me the second time I saw her only I like to make sure of my ground before I commit myself. When it all came out there was a rare to-do because I'd married eleven times. Eleven times? Why it's nothing, it's not even a Round Dozen. I could have married thirty times if I'd wanted to. I give you my word, sir, when I consider my opportunities, I'm astounded at my moderation.'

'You told me you were very fond of reading history.'

'Yes, Warren Hastings said that, didn't he? It struck me at the time I read it. It seemed to fit me like a glove.'

'And you never found these constant courtships a trifle monotonous?'

'Well, sir, I think I've got a logical mind, and it always gave me a rare lot of pleasure to see how the same effects followed on the same causes if you know what I mean. Now, for instance, with a woman who'd never been married before I always passed myself off as a widower. It worked like a charm. You see, a spinster likes a man who knows a thing or two. But with a widow I always said I was a bachelor: a widow's afraid a man who's been married before knows too much.'

I gave him back his cuttings; he folded them up neatly and replaced them in his greasy pocket-book.

'You know, sir, I always think I've been mis-judged. Just see what they say about me: a pest of society, unscrupulous villain, contemptible scoundrel. Now just look at me. I ask you, do I look that sort of man? You know me, you're a judge of character, I've told you all about myself; do you think me a bad man?'

'My acquaintance with you is very slight,' I answered with what I thought considerable tact.

'I wonder if the judge, I wonder if the jury, I wonder if the public ever thought about my side of the question. The public booed me when I was taken into court and the police had to protect me from their violence. Did any of them think what I'd done for these women?'

'You took their money.'

'Of course I took their money. I had to live the same as anybody has to live. But what did I give them in exchange for their money?'

This was another rhetorical question and though he looked at me as though he expected an answer I held my tongue. Indeed I did not know the answer. His voice was raised and he spoke with emphasis. I could see that he was serious.

'I'll tell you what I gave them in exchange for their money. Romance. Look at this place.' He made a wide, circular gesture that embraced the sea and the horizon. 'There are a hundred places in England like this. Look at that sea and that sky; look at these lodging-houses; look at that pier and the front. Doesn't it make your heart sink? It's dead as mutton. It's all very well for you who come down here for a week or two because you're run down. But think of all those women who live here from one year's end to another. They haven't a chance. They hardly know anyone. They've just got enough money to live on and that's all. I wonder if you know how terrible their lives are. Their lives are just like the front, a long, straight, cemented walk that goes on and on from one seaside resort to another. Even in the season there's nothing for them. They're out of it. They might as well be dead. And then I come along. Mind you, I never made advances to a woman who wouldn't have gladly acknowledged to thirty-five. And I give them love. Why, many of them had never known what it was to have a man do them up behind. Many of them had never known what it was to sit on a bench in the dark with a man's arm round their waist. I bring them change and excitement. I give them a new pride in themselves. They were on the shelf and I come along quite quietly and I deliberately take them down. A little ray of sunshine in those drab lives, that's what I was. No wonder they jumped at me, no wonder they wanted me to go back to them. The only one who gave me away was the milliner, she said she was a widow, my private opinion is that she'd never been married at all. You say I did the dirty on them; why, I brought happiness and glamour into eleven lives that never thought they had even a dog's chance of it again. You say I'm a villain and a scoundrel, you're wrong. I'm a philanthropist. Five years, they gave me; they should have given me the medal of the Royal Humane Society.'

He took out his empty packet of Goldflakes and looked at it with a melancholy shake of the head. When I handed him my cigarette case he helped himself without a word. I watched the spectacle of a good man struggling with his emotion.

'And what did I get out of it, I ask you?' he continued presently. 'Board and lodging and enough to buy cigarettes. But I never was able to save and the proof is that now, when I'm not so young as I was, I haven't got half a crown in my pocket.' He gave me a sidelong glance. 'It's a great come-down for me to find myself in this position. I've always paid my way and I've never asked a friend for a loan in all my life. I was wondering, sir, if you could oblige me with a trifle. It's humiliating to me to have to suggest it, but the fact is, if you could oblige me with a pound it would mean a great deal to me.'

Well, I had certainly had a pound's worth of entertainment out of the bigamist and I dived for my pocket-book.

'I shall be very glad,' I said.

He looked at the notes I took out.

'I suppose you couldn't make it two, sir?'

'I think I could.'

I handed him a couple of pound notes and he gave a little sigh as he took them.

'You don't know what it means to a man who's used to the comforts of home life not to know where to turn for a night's lodging.'

'But there is one thing I should like you to tell me,' I said. 'I shouldn't like you to think me cynical, but I had a notion that women on the whole take the maxim, it is more blessed to give than to receive, as applicable exclusively to our sex. How did you persuade these respectable, and no doubt thrifty, women to entrust you so confidently with all their savings?'

An amused smile spread over his undistinguished features.

'Well, sir, you know what Shakespeare said about ambition o'erleaping itself. That's the explanation. Tell a woman you'll double her capital in six months if she'll give it to you to handle and she won't be able to give you the money quick enough. Greed, that's what it is. Just greed.'

It was a sharp sensation, stimulating to the appetite (like hot sauce with ice cream) to go from this diverting ruffian to the respectability, all lavender bags and crinolines, of the St Clairs and Miss Porchester. I spent every evening with them now. No sooner had the ladies left him than Mr St Clair sent his compliments to my table and asked me to drink a glass of port with him. When we had finished it we went into the lounge and drank coffee. Mr St Clair enjoyed his glass of old brandy. The hour I thus spent with them was so exquisitely boring that it had for me a singular fascination. They were told by the manageress that I had written plays.

'We used often to go to the theatre when Sir Henry Irving was at the Lyceum,' said Mr St Clair. 'I once had the pleasure of meeting him. I was taken to supper at the Garrick Club by Sir Everard Millais and I was introduced to Mr Irving as he then was.'

'Tell him what he said to you, Edwin,' said Mrs St Clair.

Mr St Clair struck a dramatic attitude and gave not at all a bad imitation of Henry Irving.

'"You have the actor's face, Mr St Clair," he said to me. "If you ever think of going on the stage, come to me and I will give you a part."' Mr St Clair resumed his natural manner. 'It was enough to turn a young man's head.'

'But it didn't turn yours,' I said.

'I will not deny that if I had been otherwise

situated I might have allowed myself to be tempted. But I had my family to think of. It would have broken my father's heart if I had not gone into the business.'

'What is that?' I asked.

'I am a tea-merchant, sir. My firm is the oldest in the City of London. I have spent forty years of my life in combating to the best of my ability the desire of my fellow-countrymen to drink Ceylon tea instead of the China tea which was universally drunk in my youth.'

I thought it charmingly characteristic of him to spend a lifetime in persuading the public to buy something they didn't want rather than something they did.

'But in his younger days my husband did a lot of amateur acting and he was thought very clever,' said Mrs St Clair.

'Shakespeare, you know, and sometimes *The School for Scandal*. I would never consent to act trash. But that is a thing of the past. I had a gift, perhaps it was a pity to waste it, but it's too late now. When we have a dinner-party I sometimes let the ladies persuade me to recite the great soliloquies of Hamlet. But that is all I do.'

Oh! Oh! Oh! I thought with shuddering fascination of those dinner-parties and wondered whether I should ever be asked to one of them. Mrs St Clair gave me a little smile, half shocked, half prim.

'My husband was very bohemian as a young man,' she said.

'I sowed my wild oats. I knew quite a lot of painters and writers, Wilkie Collins, for instance, and even men who wrote for the papers. Watts painted a portrait of my wife, and I bought a picture of Millais. I knew a number of the pre-Raphaelites.'

'Have you a Rossetti?' I asked.

'No. I admired Rossetti's talent, but I could not approve of his private life. I would never buy a picture by an artist whom I should not care to ask to dinner at my house.'

My brain was reeling when Miss Porchester, looking at her watch, said: 'Are you not going to read to us tonight, Uncle Edwin?'

I withdrew.

It was while I was drinking a glass of port with Mr St Clair one evening that he told me the sad story of Miss Porchester. She was engaged to be married to a nephew of Mrs St Clair, a barrister, when it was discovered that he had had an intrigue with the daughter of his laundress.

'It was a terrible thing,' said Mr St Clair. 'A terrible thing. But of course my niece took the only possible course. She returned him his ring, his letters and his photograph, and said that she could never marry him. She implored him to marry the young person he had wronged and said she would be a sister to her. It broke her heart. She has never cared for any one since.'

'And did he marry the young person?'

Mr St Clair shook his head and sighed.

'No, we were greatly mistaken in him. It has been a sore grief to my dear wife to think that a nephew of hers should behave in such a dishonourable manner. Some time later we heard that he was engaged to a young lady in a very good position with ten thousand pounds of her own. I considered it my duty to write to her father and put the facts before him. He answered my letter in a most insolent fashion. He said he would much rather his son-in-law had a mistress before marriage than after.'

'What happened then?'

'They were married and now my wife's nephew is one of His Majesty's Judges of the High Court, and his wife is My Lady. But we've never consented to receive them. When my wife's nephew was knighted Eleanor suggested that we should ask them to dinner, but my wife said that he should never darken our doors and I upheld her.'

'And the laundress's daughter?'

'She married in her own class of life and has a public-house at Canterbury. My niece, who has a little money of her own, did everything for her and is godmother to her eldest child.'

Poor Miss Porchester. She had sacrificed herself on the altar of Victorian morality and I am afraid the consciousness that she had behaved beautifully was the only benefit she had got from it.

'Miss Porchester is a woman of striking appearance,' I said. 'When she was younger she must have been perfectly lovely. I wonder she never married somebody else.'

'Miss Porchester was considered a great beauty. Alma Tadema admired her so much that he asked her to sit as a model for one of his pictures, but of course we couldn't very well allow that.' Mr St Clair's tone conveyed that the suggestion had deeply outraged his sense of decency. 'No, Miss Porchester never cared for anyone but her cousin. She never speaks of him and it is now thirty years since they parted, but I am convinced that she loves him still. She is a true woman, my dear sir, one life, one love, and though perhaps I regret that she has

been deprived of the joys of marriage and mother-
hood I am bound to admire her fidelity.'

But the heart of woman is incalculable and rash is
the man who thinks she will remain in one stay.
Rash, Uncle Edwin. You have known Eleanor for
many years, for when, her mother having fallen
into a decline and died, you brought the orphan to
your comfortable and even luxurious house in
Leinster Square, she was but a child; but what,
when it comes down to brass tacks, Uncle Edwin,
do you really know of Eleanor?

It was but two days after Mr St Clair had confided to me the touching story which explained
why Miss Porchester had remained a spinster that,
coming back to the hotel in the afternoon after a
round of golf, the manageress came up to me in an
agitated manner.

'Mr St Clair's compliments and will you go up to
number twenty-seven the moment you come in.'

'Certainly. But why?'

'Oh, there's a rare upset. They'll tell you.'

I knocked at the door. I heard a 'come in, come
in', which reminded me that Mr St Clair had
played Shakespearean parts in probably the most
refined amateur dramatic company in London. I
entered and found Mrs St Clair lying on the sofa
with a handkerchief soaked in eau-de-Cologne on
her brow and a bottle of smelling salts in her hand.
Mr St Clair was standing in front of the fire in such
a manner as to prevent anyone else in the room
from obtaining any benefit from it.

'I must apologize for asking you to come up in
this unceremonious fashion, but we are in great

(421)

distress, and we thought you might be able to throw some light on what has happened.'

His perturbation was obvious.

'What *has* happened?'

'Our niece, Miss Porchester, has eloped. This morning she sent in a message to my wife that she had one of her sick headaches. When she has one of her sick headaches she likes to be left absolutely alone and it wasn't till this afternoon that my wife went to see if there was anything she could do for her. The room was empty. Her trunk was packed. Her dressing-case with silver fittings was gone. And on the pillow was a letter telling us of her rash act.'

'I'm very sorry,' I said. 'I don't know exactly what I can do.'

'We were under the impression that you were the only gentleman at Elsom with whom she had any acquaintance.'

His meaning flashed across me.

'I haven't eloped with her,' I said. 'I happen to be a married man.'

'I see you haven't eloped with her. At the first moment we thought perhaps . . . but if it isn't you, who is it?'

'I'm sure I don't know.'

'Show him the letter, Edwin,' said Mrs St Clair from the sofa.

'Don't move, Gertrude. It will bring on your lumbago.'

Miss Porchester had 'her' sick headaches and Mrs St Clair had 'her' lumbago. What had Mr St Clair? I was willing to bet a fiver that Mr St Clair had 'his' gout. He gave me the letter and I read it with an air of decent commiseration.

'Dear Uncle Edwin and Aunt Gertrude,

When you receive this I shall be far away. I am going to be married this morning to a gentleman who is very dear to me. I know I am doing wrong in running away like this, but I was afraid you would endeavour to set obstacles in the way of my marriage and since nothing would induce me to change my mind I thought it would save us all much unhappiness if I did it without telling you anything about it. My fiancé is a very retiring man, owing to his long residence in tropical countries not in the best of health, and he thought it much better that we should be married quite privately. When you know how radiantly happy I am I hope you will forgive me. Please send my box to the luggage office at Victoria Station.

Your loving niece,
Eleanor.'

'I will never forgive her,' said Mr St Clair as I returned him the letter. 'She shall never darken my doors again. Gertrude, I forbid you ever to mention Eleanor's name in my hearing.'

Mrs St Clair began to sob quietly.

'Aren't you rather hard?' I said. 'Is there any reason why Miss Porchester shouldn't marry?'

'At her age,' he answered angrily. 'It's ridiculous. We shall be the laughing-stock of everyone in Leinster Square. Do you know how old she is? She's fifty-one.'

'Fifty-four,' said Mrs St Clair through her sobs.

'She's been the apple of my eye. She's been like a daughter to us. She's been an old maid for years. I think it's positively improper for her to think of marriage.'

'She was always a girl to us, Edwin,' pleaded Mrs St Clair.

'And who is this man she's married? It's the deception that rankles. She must have been carrying on with him under our very noses. She does not even tell us his name. I fear the very worst.'

Suddenly I had an inspiration. That morning after breakfast I had gone out to buy myself some cigarettes and at the tobacconist's I ran across Mortimer Ellis. I had not seen him for some days.

'You're looking very spruce,' I said.

His boots had been repaired and were neatly blacked, his hat was brushed, he was wearing a clean collar and new gloves. I thought he had laid out my two pounds to advantage.

'I have to go to London this morning on business,' he said.

I nodded and left the shop.

I remembered that a fortnight before, walking in the country, I had met Miss Porchester and, a few yards behind, Mortimer Ellis. Was it possible that they had been walking together and he had fallen back as they caught sight of me? By heaven, I saw it all.

'I think you said that Miss Porchester had money of her own,' I said.

'A trifle. She has three thousand pounds.'

Now I was certain. I looked at them blankly. Suddenly Mrs St Clair, with a cry, sprang to her feet.

'Edwin, Edwin, supposing he doesn't marry her?'

Mr St Clair at this put his hand to his head and in a state of collapse sank into a chair.

'The disgrace would kill me,' he groaned.

'Don't be alarmed,' I said. 'He'll marry her all right. He always does. He'll marry her in church.'

They paid no attention to what I said. I suppose they thought I'd suddenly taken leave of my senses. I was quite sure now. Mortimer Ellis had achieved his ambition after all. Miss Porchester completed the Round Dozen.

Jane

I remember very well the occasion on which I first saw Jane Fowler. It is indeed only because the details of the glimpse I had of her then are so clear that I trust my recollection at all, for, looking back, I must confess that I find it hard to believe that it had not played me a fantastic trick. I had lately returned to London from China and was drinking a dish of tea with Mrs Tower. Mrs Tower had been seized with the prevailing passion for decoration; and with the ruthlessness of her sex had sacrificed chairs in which she had comfortably sat for years, tables, cabinets, ornaments on which her eyes had dwelt in peace since she was married, pictures that had been familiar to her for a generation; and delivered herself into the hands of an expert. Nothing remained in her drawing-room with which she had any association, or to which any sentiment was attached; and she had invited me that day to see the fashionable glory in which she now lived. Everything that could be pickled was pickled and what couldn't be pickled was painted. Nothing matched, but everything harmonized.

'Do you remember that ridiculous drawing-room suite that I used to have?' asked Mrs Tower.

The curtains were sumptuous yet severe; the sofa was covered with Italian brocade; the chair on which I sat was in *petit point*. The room was beautiful, opulent without garishness and original without affectation; yet to me it lacked something; and while I praised with my lips I asked myself why I so much preferred the rather shabby chintz of the despised suite, the Victorian water-colours that I had known so long, and the ridiculous Dresden china that had adorned the chimney-piece. I wondered what it was that I missed in all these rooms that the decorators were turning out with a profitable industry. Was it heart? But Mrs Tower looked about her happily.

'Don't you like my alabaster lamps?' she said. 'They give such a soft light.'

'Personally I have a weakness for a light that you can see by,' I smiled.

'It's so difficult to combine that with a light that you can't be too much seen by,' laughed Mrs Tower.

I had no notion what her age was. When I was quite a young man she was a married woman a good deal older than I, but now she treated me as her contemporary. She constantly said that she made no secret of her age, which was forty, and then added with a smile that all women took five years off. She never sought to conceal the fact that she dyed her hair (it was a very pretty brown with reddish tints), and she said she did this because hair was hideous while it was going grey; as soon as hers was white she would cease to dye it.

'Then they'll say what a young face I have.'

Meanwhile it was painted, though with discretion, and her eyes owed not a little of their vivacity to art. She was a handsome woman, exquisitely gowned, and in the sombre glow of the alabaster lamps did not look a day more than the forty she gave herself.

'It is only at my dressing-table that I can suffer the naked brightness of a thirty-two candle electric bulb,' she added with smiling cynicism. 'There I need it to tell me first the hideous truth and then to enable me to take the necessary steps to correct it.'

We gossiped pleasantly about our common friends and Mrs Tower brought me up to date in the scandal of the day. After roughing it here and there it was very agreeable to sit in a comfortable chair, the fire burning brightly on the hearth, charming tea-things set out on a charming table, and talk with this amusing, attractive woman. She treated me as a prodigal returning from his husks and was disposed to make much of me. She prided herself on her dinner-parties; she took no less trouble to have her guests suitably assorted than to give them excellent food; and there were few persons who did not look upon it as a treat to be bidden to one of them. Now she fixed a date and asked me whom I would like to meet.

'There's only one thing I must tell you. If Jane Fowler is still here I shall have to put it off.'

'Who is Jane Fowler?' I asked.

Mrs Tower gave a rueful smile.

'Jane Fowler is my cross.'

'Oh!'

'Do you remember a photograph that I used to have on the piano before I had my room done, of a woman in a tight dress with tight sleeves and a gold locket, with her hair drawn back from a broad forehead and her ears showing and spectacles on a rather blunt nose? Well, that was Jane Fowler.'

'You had so many photographs about the room in your unregenerate days,' I said, vaguely.

'It makes me shudder to think of them. I've made them into a huge brown-paper parcel and hidden them in an attic.'

'Well, who is Jane Fowler?' I asked again, smiling.

'She's my sister-in-law. She was my husband's sister and she married a manufacturer in the North. She's been a widow for many years, and she's very well to do.'

'And why is she your cross?'

'She's worthy, she's dowdy, she's provincial. She looks twenty years older than I do and she's quite capable of telling anyone she meets that we were at school together. She has an overwhelming sense of family affection and because I am her only living connection she's devoted to me. When she comes to London it never occurs to her that she should stay anywhere but here – she thinks it would hurt my feelings – and she'll pay me visits of three or four weeks. We sit here and she knits and reads. And sometimes she insists on taking me to dine at Claridge's and she looks like a funny old char-woman and everyone I particularly don't want to be seen by is sitting at the next table. When we are driving home she says she loves giving me a little treat. With her own hands she makes me tea-cosies that I am forced to use when she is here and doilies and centrepieces for the dining-room table.'

Mrs Tower paused to take breath.

'I should have thought a woman of your tact would find a way to deal with a situation like that.'

'Ah, but don't you see, I haven't a chance. She's so immeasurably kind. She has a heart of gold. She bores me to death, but I wouldn't for anything let her suspect it.'

'And when does she arrive?'

'Tomorrow.'

But the answer was hardly out of Mrs Tower's mouth when the bell rang. There were sounds in the hall of a slight commotion and in a minute or two the butler ushered in an elderly lady.

'Mrs Fowler,' he announced.

'Jane,' cried Mrs Tower, springing to her feet. 'I wasn't expecting you today.'

'So your butler has just told me. I certainly said today in my letter.'

Mrs Tower recovered her wits.

'Well, it doesn't matter. I'm very glad to see you whenever you come. Fortunately I'm doing nothing this evening.'

'You mustn't let me give you any trouble. If I can have a boiled egg for my dinner that's all I shall want.'

A faint grimace for a moment distorted Mrs Tower's handsome features. A boiled egg!

'Oh, I think we can do a little better than that.'

I chuckled inwardly when I recollected that the two ladies were contemporaries. Mrs Fowler looked a good fifty-five. She was a rather big woman; she wore a black straw hat with a wide brim and from it a black lace veil hung over her shoulders, a cloak that oddly combined severity with fussiness, a long black dress, voluminous as though she wore several petticoats under it, and stout boots. She was evidently short-sighted, for she looked at you through large gold-rimmed spectacles.

'Won't you have a cup of tea?' asked Mrs Tower.

'If it wouldn't be too much trouble. I'll take off my mantle.'

She began by stripping her hands of the black gloves she wore, and then took off her cloak. Round her neck was a solid gold chain from which hung a large gold locket in which I felt certain was a photograph of her deceased husband. Then she took off her hat and placed it neatly with her gloves and cloak on the sofa corner. Mrs Tower pursed her lips. Certainly those garments did not go very well with the austere but sumptuous beauty of Mrs Tower's redecorated drawing-room. I wondered where on earth Mrs Fowler had found the extraordinary clothes she wore. They were not old and the materials were expensive. It was astounding to think that dressmakers still made things that had not been worn for a quarter of a century. Mrs Fowler's grey hair was very plainly done, showing all her forehead and her ears, with a parting in the middle. It had evidently never known the tongs of Monsieur Marcel. Now her eyes fell on the tea-table with its teapot of Georgian silver and its cups in old Worcester.

'What have you done with the tea-cosy I gave you last time I came up, Marion? she asked. 'Don't you use it?'

'Yes, I used it every day, Jane,' answered Mrs Tower glibly. 'Unfortunately we had an accident with it a little while ago. It got burnt.'

'But the last one I gave you got burnt.'

'I'm afraid you'll think us very careless.'

'It doesn't really matter,' smiled Mrs Fowler. 'I shall enjoy making you another. I'll go to Liberty's tomorrow and buy some silks.'

Mrs Tower kept her face bravely.

'I don't deserve it, you know.' Doesn't your vicar's wife need one?'

'Oh, I've just made her one,' said Mrs Fowler brightly.

I noticed that when she smiled she showed white, small and regular teeth. They were a real beauty. Her smile was certainly very sweet.

But I felt it high time for me to leave the two ladies to themselves, so I took my leave.

Early next morning Mrs Tower rang me up and I heard at once from her voice that she was in high spirits.

'I've got the most wonderful news for you,' she said. 'Jane is going to be married.'

'Nonsense.'

'Her fiancé is coming to dine here tonight to be introduced to me and I want you to come too.'

'Oh, but I shall be in the way.'

'No, you won't. Jane suggested herself that I should ask you. Do come.'

She was bubbling over with laughter.

'Who is he?'

'I don't know. She tells me he's an architect. Can you imagine the sort of man Jane would marry?'

I had nothing to do and I could trust Mrs Tower to give me a good dinner.

When I arrived Mrs Tower, very splendid in a tea-gown a little too young for her, was alone.

'Jane is putting the finishing touches to her appearance. I'm longing for you to see her. She's all in a flutter. She says he adores her. His name is Gilbert and when she speaks of him her voice gets all funny and tremulous. It makes me want to laugh.'

'I wonder what he's like.'

'Oh, I'm sure I know. Very big and massive, with a bald head and an immense gold chain across an immense tummy. A large, fat, clean-shaven, red face and a booming voice.'

Mrs Fowler came in. She wore a very stiff black silk dress with a wide skirt and a train. At the neck it was cut into a timid V and the sleeves came down to the elbows. She wore a necklace of diamonds set in silver. She carried in her hands a long pair of black gloves and a fan of black ostrich feathers. She managed (as so few people do) to look exactly what she was. You could never have thought her anything in the world but the respectable relict of a North-country manufacturer of ample means.

'You've really got quite a pretty neck, Jane,' said Mrs Tower with a kindly smile.

It was indeed astonishingly young when you compared it with her weather-beaten face. It was smooth and unlined and the skin was white. And I noticed then that her head was very well placed on her shoulders.

'Has Marion told you my news?' she said, turning to me with that really charming smile of hers as if we were already old friends.

'I must congratulate you,' I said.

'Wait to do that till you've seen my young man.'

'I think it's too sweet to hear you talk of your young man,' smiled Mrs Tower.

Mrs Fowler's eyes certainly twinkled behind her preposterous spectacles.

'Don't expect anyone too old. You wouldn't like me to marry a decrepit old gentleman with one foot in the grave, would you?'

This was the only warning she gave us. Indeed there was no time for any further discussion, for the butler flung open the door and in a loud voice announced:

'Mr Gilbert Napier.'

There entered a youth in a very well-cut dinner jacket. He was slight, not very tall, with fair hair in which there was a hint of a natural wave, clean-shaven and blue-eyed. He was not particularly good-looking, but he had a pleasant, amiable face. In ten years he would probably be wizened and sallow; but now, in extreme youth, he was fresh and clean and blooming. For he was certainly not more than twenty-four. My first thought was that this was the son of Jane Fowler's fiancé (I had not known he was a widower) come to say that his father was prevented from dining by a sudden attack of gout. But his eyes fell immediately on Mrs Fowler, his face lit up, and he went towards her with both hands outstretched. Mrs Fowler gave him hers, a demure smile on her lips, and turned to her sister-in-law.

'This is my young man, Marion,' she said.

He held out his hand.

'I hope you'll like me, Mrs Tower,' he said. 'Jane tells me you're the only relation she has in the world.'

Mrs Tower's face was wonderful to behold. I saw then to admiration how bravely good breeding and social usage could combat the instincts of the natural woman. For the astonishment and then the dismay that for an instant she could not conceal were quickly driven away, and her face assumed an expression of affable welcome. But she was evidently at a loss for words. It was not unnatural if Gilbert felt a certain embarrassment and I was too busy preventing myself from laughing to think of anything to say. Mrs Fowler alone kept perfectly calm.

'I know you'll like him, Marion. There's no one enjoys good food more than he does.' She turned to the young man. 'Marion's dinners are famous.'

'I know,' he beamed.

Mrs Tower made some quick rejoinder and we went downstairs. I shall not soon forget the exquisite comedy of that meal. Mrs Tower could not make up her mind whether the pair of them were playing a practical joke on her or whether Jane by wilfully concealing her fiancé's age had hoped to make her look foolish. But then Jane never jested and she was incapable of doing a malicious thing. Mrs Tower was amazed, exasperated and per-plexed. But she had recovered her self-control, and for nothing would she have forgotten that she was a perfect hostess whose duty it was to make her party go. She talked vivaciously; but I wondered if Gilbert Napier saw how hard and vindictive was the expression of her eyes behind the mask of friendliness that she turned to him. She was measuring him. She was seeking to delve into the secret of his soul. I could see that she was in a passion, for under her rouge her cheeks glowed with an angry red.

'You've got a very high colour, Marion,' said Jane, looking at her amiably through her great round spectacles.

'I dressed in a hurry. I daresay I put on too much rouge.'

'Oh, is it rouge? I thought it was natural. Otherwise I shouldn't have mentioned it.' She gave Gilbert a shy little smile. 'You know Marion and I were at school together. You would never think it to look at us now, would you? But of course I've lived a very quiet life.'

I do not know what she meant by these remarks; it was almost incredible that she made them in complete simplicity; but anyhow they goaded Mrs Tower to such a fury that she flung her own vanity to the winds. She smiled brightly.

'We shall neither of us see fifty again, Jane,' she said.

If the observation was meant to discomfit the widow it failed.

'Gilbert says I mustn't acknowledge to more than forty-nine for his sake,' she answered blandly.

Mrs Tower's hands trembled slightly, but she found a retort.

'There is of course a certain disparity of age between you,' she smiled.

'Twenty-seven years,' said Jane. 'Do you think it's too much? Gilbert says I'm very young for my age. I told you I shouldn't like to marry a man with one foot in the grave.'

I was really obliged to laugh and Gilbert laughed too. His laughter was frank and boyish. It looked as though he were amused at everything Jane said. But Mrs Tower was almost at the end of her tether and I was afraid that unless relief came she would for once forget that she was a woman of the world. I came to the rescue as best I could.

'I suppose you're very busy buying your trousseau,' I said.

'No. I wanted to get my things from the dress-maker in Liverpool I've been to ever since I was first married. But Gilbert won't let me. He's very masterful, and of course he has wonderful taste.'

She looked at him with a little affectionate smile, demurely, as though she were a girl of seventeen.

Mrs Tower went quite pale under her make-up.

'We're going to Italy for our honeymoon. Gilbert has never had a chance of studying Renaissance architecture and of course it's important for an architect to see things for himself. And we shall stop in Paris on the way and get my clothes there.'

'Do you expect to be away long?'

'Gilbert has arranged with his office to stay away for six months. It will be such a treat for him, won't it? You see, he's never had more than a fortnight's holiday before.'

'Why not?' asked Mrs Tower in a tone that no effort of will could prevent from being icy.

'He's never been able to afford it, poor dear.'

'Ah!' said Mrs Tower, and into the exclamation put volumes.

Coffee was served and the ladies went upstairs. Gilbert and I began to talk in the desultory way in which men talk who have nothing whatever to say to one another; but in two minutes a note was brought in to me by the butler. It was from Mrs Tower and ran as follows:

'Come upstairs quickly and then go as soon as you can. Take him with you. Unless I have it out with Jane at once I shall have a fit.'

I told a facile lie.

'Mrs Tower has a headache and wants to go to bed. I think if you don't mind we'd better clear out.'

'Certainly,' he answered.

We went upstairs and five minutes later were on the doorstep. I called a taxi and offered the young man a lift.

'No thanks,' he answered. 'I'll just walk to the corner and jump on a bus.'

Mrs Tower sprang to the fray as soon as she heard the front-door close behind us.

'Are you crazy, Jane?' she cried.

'Not more than most people who don't habitually live in a lunatic asylum, I trust,' Jane answered blandly.

'May I ask why you're going to marry this young man?' asked Mrs Tower with formidable politeness.

'Partly because he won't take no for an answer. He's asked me five times. I grew positively tired of refusing him.'

'And why do you think he's so anxious to marry you?'

'I amuse him.'

Mrs Tower gave an exclamation of annoyance.

'He's an unscrupulous rascal. I very nearly told him so to his face.'

'You would have been wrong, and it wouldn't have been very polite.'

'He's penniless and you're rich. You can't be such a besotted fool as not to see that he's marrying you for your money.'

Jane remained perfectly composed. She observed her sister-in-law's agitation with detachment.

'I don't think he is, you know,' she replied. 'I think he's very fond of me.'

'You're an old woman, Jane.'

'I'm the same age as you are, Marion,' she smiled.

'I've never let myself go. I'm very young for my age. No one would think I was more than forty.

But even I wouldn't dream of marrying a boy twenty years younger than myself.'

'Twenty-seven,' corrected Jane.

'Do you mean to tell me that you can bring yourself to believe that it's possible for a young man to care for a woman old enough to be his mother?'

'I've lived very much in the country for many years. I daresay there's a great deal about human nature that I don't know. They tell me there's a man called Freud, an Austrian, I believe . . .'

But Mrs Tower interrupted her without any politeness at all.

'Don't be ridiculous, Jane. It's so undignified. It's so ungraceful. I always thought you were a sensible woman. Really you're the last person I should ever have thought likely to fall in love with a boy.'

'But I'm not in love with him. I've told him that. Of course I like him very much or I wouldn't think of marrying him. I thought it only fair to tell him quite plainly what my feelings were towards him.'

Mrs Tower gasped. The blood rushed to her head and her breathing oppressed her. She had no fan, but she seized the evening paper and vigorously fanned herself with it.

'If you're not in love with him why do you want to marry him?'

'I've been a widow a very long time and I've led a very quiet life. I thought I'd like a change.'

'If you want to marry just to be married why don't you marry a man of your own age?'

'No man of my own age has asked me five times. In fact no man of my own age has asked me at all.'

Jane chuckled as she answered. It drove Mrs Tower to the final pitch of frenzy.

'Don't laugh, Jane. I won't have it. I don't think you can be right in your mind. It's dreadful.'

It was altogether too much for her and she burst into tears. She knew that at her age it was fatal to cry, her eyes would be swollen for twenty-four hours and she would look a sight. But there was no help for it. She wept. Jane remained perfectly calm. She looked at Marion through her large spectacles and reflectively smoothed the lap of her black silk dress.

'You're going to be so dreadfully unhappy,' Mrs Tower sobbed, dabbing her eyes cautiously in the hope that the black on her lashes would not smudge.

'I don't think so, you know,' Jane answered in those equable, mild tones of hers, as if there were a little smile behind the words. 'We've talked it over very thoroughly. I always think I'm a very easy person to live with. I think I shall make Gilbert very happy and comfortable. He's never had anyone to look after him properly. We're only marrying after mature consideration. And we've decided that if either of us wants his liberty the other will place no obstacles in the way of his getting it.'

Mrs Tower had by now recovered herself sufficiently to make a cutting remark.

'How much has he persuaded you to settle on him?'

'I wanted to settle a thousand a year on him, but he wouldn't hear of it. He was quite upset when I made the suggestion. He says he can earn quite enough for his own needs.'

'He's more cunning than I thought,' said Mrs Tower acidly.

Jane paused a little and looked at her sister-in-law with kindly, but resolute eyes.

'You see, my dear, it's different for you,' she said. 'You've never been so very much a widow, have you?'

Mrs Tower looked at her. She blushed a little. She even felt slightly uncomfortable. But of course Jane was much too simple to intend an innuendo. Mrs Tower gathered herself together with dignity.

'I'm so upset that I really must go to bed,' she said. 'We'll resume the conversation tomorrow morning.'

'I'm afraid that won't be very convenient, dear. Gilbert and I are going to get the licence tomorrow morning.'

Mrs Tower threw up her hands in a gesture of dismay, but she found nothing more to say.

The marriage took place at a registrar's office. Mrs Tower and I were the witnesses. Gilbert in a smart blue suit looked absurdly young and he was obviously nervous. It is a trying moment for any man. But Jane kept her admirable composure. She might have been in the habit of marrying as frequently as a woman of fashion. Only a slight colour on her cheeks suggested that beneath her calm was some faint excitement. It is a thrilling moment for any woman. She wore a very full dress of silver grey velvet in the cut of which I recognized the hand of the dressmaker in Liverpool (evidently a widow of unimpeachable character), who had made her gowns for so many years; but she had so far succumbed to the frivolity of the occasion as to wear a large picture hat covered with blue ostrich feathers. Her gold-rimmed spectacles made it extraordinarily grotesque. When the ceremony was over the registrar (somewhat taken aback, I thought, by the difference of age between the pair he was marrying) shook hands with her, tendering his strictly official congratulations; and the bride-groom, blushing slightly, kissed her. Mrs Tower, resigned but implacable, kissed her; and then the bride looked at me expectantly. It was evidently fitting that I should kiss her too. I did. I confess that I felt a little shy as we walked out of the registrar's office past loungers who waited cynically to see the bridal pairs, and it was with relief that I stepped into Mrs Tower's car. We drove to Victoria Station, for the happy couple were to go over to Paris by the two o'clock train, and Jane had insisted that the wedding-breakfast should be eaten at the station restaurant. She said it always made her nervous not to be on the platform in good time. Mrs Tower, present only from a strong sense of family duty, was able to do little to make the party go off well; she ate nothing (for which I could not blame her, since the food was execrable, and any-way I hate champagne at luncheon) and talked in a strained voice. But Jane went through the menu conscientiously.

'I always think one should make a hearty meal before starting out on a journey,' she said.

We saw them off, and I drove Mrs Tower back to her house.

'How long do you give it?' she said. 'Six months?'

'Let's hope for the best,' I smiled.

'Don't be so absurd. There can be no best. You don't think he's marrying her for anything but her money, do you? Of course it can't last. My only hope is that she won't have to go through as much suffering as she deserves.'

I laughed. The charitable words were spoken in such a tone as to leave me in small doubt of Mrs Tower's meaning.

'Well, if it doesn't last you'll have the consolation of saying: I told you so,' I said.

'I promise you I'll never do that.'

'Then you'll have the satisfaction of congratulating yourself on your self-control in not saying: I told you so.'

'She's old and dowdy and dull.'

'Are you sure she's dull?' I said. 'It's true she doesn't say very much, but when she says anything it's very much to the point.'

'I've never heard her make a joke in my life.'

I was once more in the Far East when Gilbert and Jane returned from their honeymoon and this time I remained away for nearly two years. Mrs Tower was a bad correspondent and though I sent her an occasional picture-postcard I received no news from her. But I met her within a week of my return to London; I was dining out and found that I was seated next to her. It was an immense party, I think we were four-and-twenty like the blackbirds in the pie, arriving somewhat late, I was too confused by the crowd in which I found myself to notice who was there. But when we sat down, looking round the long table I saw that a good many of my fellow-guests were well known to the public from their photographs in the illustrated papers. Our hostess had a weakness for the persons technically known as celebrities and this was an unusually brilliant gathering. When Mrs Tower and I had exchanged the conventional remarks that two people make when they have not seen one another for a couple of years I asked about Jane.

'She's very well,' said Mrs Tower with a certain dryness.

'How has the marriage turned out?'

Mrs Tower paused a little and took a salted almond from the dish in front of her.

'It appears to be quite a success.'

'You were wrong then?'

'I said it wouldn't last and I still say it won't last. It's contrary to human nature.'

'Is she happy?'

'They're both happy.'

'I suppose you don't see very much of them.'

'At first I saw quite a lot of them. But now . . .' Mrs Tower pursed her lips a little. 'Jane is becoming very grand.'

'What *do* you mean?' I laughed.

'I think I should tell you that she's here tonight.'

'Here?'

I was startled. I looked round the table again. Our hostess was a delightful and an entertaining woman, but I could not imagine that she would be likely to invite to a dinner such as this the elderly and dowdy wife of an obscure architect. Mrs Tower saw my perplexity and was shrewd enough to see what was in my mind. She smiled thinly.

'Look on the left of our host.'

I looked. Oddly enough the woman who sat there had by her fantastic appearance attracted my attention the moment I was ushered into the crowded drawing-room. I thought I noticed a gleam of recognition in her eye, but to the best of my belief I had never seen her before. She was not a young woman, for her hair was iron-grey; it was cut very short and clustered thickly round her well-shaped head in tight curls. She made no attempt at youth, for she was conspicuous in that gathering by using neither lipstick, rouge nor powder. Her face, not a particularly handsome one, was red and weather-beaten; but because it owed nothing to artifice had a naturalness that was very pleasing. It contrasted oddly with the whiteness of her shoulders. They were really magnificent. A woman of thirty might have been proud of them. But her dress was extra-ordinary. I had not seen often anything more auda-cious. It was cut very low, with short skirts, which were then the fashion, in black and yellow; it had almost the effect of fancy-dress and yet so became her that though on anyone else it would have been outrageous, on her it had the inevitable simplicity of nature. And to complete the impression of an eccentricity in which there was no pose and of an extravagance in which there was no ostentation she wore, attached by a broad black ribbon, a single eyeglass.

'You're not going to tell me *that* is your sister-in-law,' I gasped.

'That is Jane Napier,' said Mrs Tower icily.

At that moment she was speaking. Her host was turned towards her with an anticipatory smile. A baldish white-haired man, with a sharp, intelligent face, who sat on her left, was leaning forward eagerly, and the couple who sat opposite, ceasing to talk with one another listened intently. She said her say and they all, with a sudden movement, threw themselves back in their chairs and burst into vociferous laughter. From the other side of the table a man addressed Mrs Tower: I recognized a famous statesman.

'Your sister-in-law has made another joke, Mrs Tower,' he said.

Mrs Tower smiled.

'She's priceless, isn't she?'

'Let me have a long drink of champagne and then for heaven's sake tell me about it all,' I said.

Well, this is how I gathered it had all happened. At the beginning of their honeymoon Gilbert took Jane to various dressmakers in Paris and he made no objection to her choosing a number of 'gowns' after her own heart; but he persuaded her to have a 'frock' or two made according to his own design. It appeared that he had a knack for that kind of work. He engaged a smart French maid. Jane had never had such a thing before. She did her own mending and when she wanted 'doing up' was in the habit of ringing for the housemaid. The dresses Gilbert had devised were very different from anything she had worn before; but he had been careful not to go too far too quickly, and because it pleased him she persuaded herself, though not without misgivings, to wear them in preference to those she had chosen herself. Of course she could not wear them with the voluminous petticoats she had been in the habit of using, and these, though it cost her an anxious moment, she discarded.

'Now if you please,' said Mrs Tower, with something very like a sniff of disapproval, 'she wears nothing but thin silk tights. It's a wonder to me she doesn't catch her death of cold at her age.'

Gilbert and the French maid taught her how to wear her clothes, and, unexpectedly enough, she was very quick at learning. The French maid was in raptures over Madame's arms and shoulders. It was a scandal not to show anything so fine.

'Wait a little, Alphonsine,' said Gilbert. 'The next lot of clothes I design for Madame we'll make the most of her.'

The spectacles of course were dreadful. No one could look really well in gold-rimmed spectacles. Gilbert tried some with tortoise-shell rims. He shook his head.

'They'd look all right on a girl,' he said. 'You're too old to wear spectacles, Jane.' Suddenly he had an inspiration. 'By George, I've got it. You must wear an eyeglass.'

'Oh, Gilbert, I couldn't.'

She looked at him and his excitement, the excitement of the artist, made her smile. He was so sweet to her she wanted to do what she could to please him.

'I'll try,' she said.

When they went to an optician and, suited with the right size, she placed an eyeglass jauntily in her eye Gilbert clapped his hands. There and then, before the astonished shopman, he kissed her on both cheeks.

'You look wonderful,' he cried.

So they went down to Italy and spent happy months studying Renaissance and Baroque architecture. Jane not only grew accustomed to her changed appearance, but found she liked it. At first she was a little shy when she went into the dining-room of a hotel and people turned round to stare at her, no one had ever raised an eyelid to look at her before, but presently she found that the sensation was not disagreeable. Ladies came up to her and asked her where she got her dress.

'Do you like it?' she answered demurely. 'My husband designed it for me.'

'I should like to copy it if you don't mind.'

Jane had certainly for many years lived a very quiet life, but she was by no means lacking in the normal instincts of her sex. She had her answer ready.

'I'm so sorry, but my husband's very particular and he won't hear of anyone copying my frocks. He wants me to be unique.'

She had an idea that people would laugh when she said this, but they didn't; they merely answered: 'Oh, of course I quite understand. You *are* unique.'

But she saw them making mental notes of what she wore, and for some reason this quite 'put her about'. For once in her life that she wasn't wearing what everybody else did, she reflected, she didn't see why everybody else should want to wear what she did.

'Gilbert,' she said, quite sharply for her, 'next time you're designing dresses for me I wish you'd design things that people *can't* copy.'

'The only way to do that is to design things that only you can wear.'

'Can't you do that?'

'Yes, if you'll do something for me.'

'What is it?'

'Cut off your hair.'

I think this was the first time that Jane jibbed. Her hair was long and thick and as a girl she had been quite vain of it; to cut it off was a very drastic proceeding. This really was burning her boats behind her. In her case it was not the first step that cost so much, it was the last; but she took it ('I

know Marion will think me a perfect fool, and I
shall *never* be able to go to Liverpool again,' she
said), and when they passed through Paris on their
way home Gilbert led her (she felt quite sick, her
heart was beating so fast) to the best hairdresser in
the world. She came out of his shop with a jaunty,
saucy, impudent head of crisp grey curls. Pyg-
malion had finished his fantastic masterpiece:
Galatea was come to life.

'Yes,' I said, 'but that isn't enough to explain
why Jane is here tonight amid this crowd of
duchesses, cabinet ministers and such like; nor why
she is sitting on one side of her host with an
Admiral of the Fleet on the other.'

'Jane is a humorist,' said Mrs Tower. 'Didn't you
see them all laughing at what she said?'

There was no doubt now of the bitterness in Mrs
Tower's heart.

'When Jane wrote and told me they were back
from their honeymoon I thought I must ask them
both to dinner. I didn't much like the idea, but I
felt it had to be done. I knew the party would be
deadly and I wasn't going to sacrifice any of the
people who really mattered. On the other hand I
didn't want Jane to think I hadn't any nice friends.
You know I never have more than eight, but on this
occasion I thought it would make things go better if
I had twelve. I'd been too busy to see Jane until the
evening of the party. She kept us all waiting a little
– that was Gilbert's cleverness – and at last she
sailed in. You could have knocked me down with a
feather. She made the rest of the women look
dowdy and provincial. She made me feel like a
painted old trollop.'

Mrs Tower drank a little champagne.

'I wish I could describe the frock to you. It would have been quite impossible on anyone else; on her it was perfect. And the eyeglass! I'd known her for thirty-five years and I'd never seen her without spectacles.'

'But you knew she had a good figure.'

'How should I? I'd never seen her except in the clothes you first saw her in. Did *you* think she had a good figure? She seemed not to be unconscious of the sensation she made but to take it as a matter of course. I thought of my dinner and I heaved a sigh of relief. Even if she was a little heavy in hand, with that appearance it didn't so very much matter. She was sitting at the other end of the table and I heard a good deal of laughter, I was glad to think that the other people were playing up well; but after dinner I was a good deal taken aback when no less than three men came up to me and told me that my sister-in-law was priceless, and did I think she would allow them to call on her. I didn't quite know whether I was standing on my head or my heels. Twenty-four hours later our hostess of tonight rang me up and said she had heard my sister-in-law was in London and she was priceless and would I ask her to luncheon to meet her. She has an infallible instinct, that woman: in a month everyone was talking about Jane. I am here tonight, not because I've known our hostess for twenty years and have asked her to dinner a hundred times, but because I'm Jane's sister-in-law.'

Poor Mrs Tower. The position was galling, and though I could not help being amused, for the tables were turned on her with a vengeance, I felt that she deserved my sympathy.

'People never can resist those who make them laugh,' I said, trying to console her.

'She never makes *me* laugh.'

Once more from the top of the table I heard a guffaw and guessed that Jane had said another amusing thing.

'Do you mean to say that you are the only person who doesn't think her funny?' I asked, smiling.

'Had it struck *you* that she was a humorist?'

'I'm bound to say it hadn't.'

'She says just the same things as she's said for the last thirty-five years. I laugh when I see everyone else does because I don't want to seem a perfect fool, but I am not amused.'

'Like Queen Victoria,' I said.

It was a foolish jest and Mrs Tower was quite right sharply to tell me so. I tried another tack.

'Is Gilbert here?' I asked, looking down the table.

'Gilbert was asked because she won't go out without him, but tonight he's at a dinner of the Architects' Institute or whatever it's called.'

'I'm dying to renew my acquaintance with her.'

'Go and talk to her after dinner. She'll ask you to her Tuesdays.'

'Her Tuesdays?'

'She's at home every Tuesday evening. You'll meet there everyone you ever heard of. They're the best parties in London. She's done in one year what I've failed to do in twenty.'

'But what you tell me is really miraculous. How has it been done?'

Mrs Tower shrugged her handsome, but adipose shoulders.

'I shall be glad if you'll tell me,' she replied.

After dinner I tried to make my way to the sofa

on which Jane was sitting, but I was intercepted and it was not till a little later that my hostess came up to me and said:

'I must introduce you to the star of my party. Do you know Jane Napier? She's priceless. She's much more amusing than your comedies.'

I was taken up to the sofa. The admiral who had been sitting beside her at dinner was with her still. He showed no sign of moving and Jane, shaking hands with me, introduced me to him.

'Do you know Sir Reginald Frobisher?'

We began to chat. It was the same Jane as I had known before, perfectly simple, homely and unaffected, but her fantastic appearance certainly gave a peculiar savour to what she said. Suddenly I found myself shaking with laughter. She had made a remark, sensible and to the point, but not in the least witty, which her manner of saying and the bland look she gave me through her eyeglass made perfectly irresistible. I felt light-hearted and buoyant. When I left her she said to me:

'If you've got nothing better to do, come and see us on Tuesday evening. Gilbert will be so glad to see you.'

'When he's been a month in London he'll know that he *can* have nothing better to do,' said the admiral.

So, on Tuesday but rather late, I went to Jane's. I confess I was a little surprised at the company. It was quite a remarkable collection of writers, painters and politicians, actors, great ladies and great beauties: Mrs Tower was right, it was a grand party; I had seen nothing like it in London since Stafford House was sold. No particular entertainment was provided. The refreshments were adequate without being luxurious. Jane in her quiet way seemed to be enjoying herself; I could not see that she took a great deal of trouble with her guests, but they seemed to like being there, and the gay, pleasant party did not break up till two in the morning. After that I saw much of her. I not only went often to her house, but seldom went out to luncheon or to dinner without meeting her. I am an amateur of humour and I sought to discover in what lay her peculiar gift. It was impossible to repeat anything she said, for the fun, like certain wines, would not travel. She had no gift for epigram. She never made a brilliant repartee. There was no malice in her remarks nor sting in her rejoinders. There are those who think that impropriety, rather than brevity, is the soul of wit; but she never said a thing that could have brought a blush to a Victorian cheek. I think her humour was unconscious and I am sure it was unpremeditated. It flew like a butterfly from flower to flower, obedient only to its own caprice and pursuivant of neither method nor intention. It depended on the way she spoke and on the way she looked. Its subtlety gained by the flaunting and extravagant appearance that Gilbert had achieved for her; but her appearance was only an element in it. Now of course she was the fashion and people laughed if she but opened her mouth. They no longer wondered that Gilbert had married a wife so much older than himself. They saw that Jane was a woman with whom age did not count. They thought him a devilish lucky young fellow. The admiral quoted Shakespeare to me: 'Age cannot wither her, nor custom stale her infinite variety.' Gilbert was delighted with her success. As I came to know him better I grew to like him. It was quite evident that he was neither a rascal nor a fortune-hunter. He was not only immensely proud of Jane but genuinely devoted to her. His kindness to her was touching. He was a very unselfish and sweet-tempered young man.

'Well, what do you think of Jane now?' he said to me once, with boyish triumph.

'I don't know which of you is more wonderful,' I said. 'You or she.'

'Oh, I'm nothing.'

'Nonsense. You don't think I'm such a fool as not to see that it's you, and you only, who've made Jane what she is.'

'My only merit is that I saw what was there when it wasn't obvious to the naked eye,' he answered.

'I can understand your seeing that she had in her the possibility of that remarkable appearance, but how in the world have you made her into a humorist?'

'But I always thought the things she said a perfect scream. She was always a humorist.'

'You're the only person who ever thought so.'

Mrs Tower, not without magnanimity, acknowledged that she had been mistaken in Gilbert. She grew quite attached to him. But notwithstanding appearances she never faltered in her opinion that the marriage could not last. I was obliged to laugh at her.

'Why, I've never seen such a devoted couple,' I said.

'Gilbert is twenty-seven now. It's just the time for a pretty girl to come along. Did you notice the other evening at Jane's that pretty little niece of Sir Reginald's? I thought Jane was looking at them both with a good deal of attention, and I wondered to myself.'

'I don't believe Jane fears the rivalry of any girl under the sun.'

'Wait and see,' said Mrs Tower.

'You gave it six months.'

'Well, now I give it three years.'

When anyone is very positive in an opinion it is only human nature to wish him proved wrong. Mrs Tower was really too cocksure. But such a satisfaction was not mine, for the end that she had always and confidently predicted to the ill-assorted match did in point of fact come. Still, the fates seldom give us what we want in the way we want it, and though Mrs Tower could flatter herself that she had been right, I think after all she would sooner have been wrong. For things did not happen at all in the way she expected.

One day I received an urgent message from her and fortunately went to see her at once. When I was shown into the room Mrs Tower rose from her chair and came towards me with the stealthy swiftness of a leopard stalking his prey. I saw that she was excited.

'Jane and Gilbert have separated,' she said.

'Not really? Well, you were right after all.'

Mrs Tower looked at me with an expression I could not understand.

'Poor Jane,' I muttered.

'Poor Jane!' she repeated, but in tones of such derision that I was dumbfounded.

She found some difficulty in telling me exactly what had occurred.

Gilbert had left her a moment before she leaped

to the telephone to summon me. When he entered the room, pale and distraught, she saw at once that something terrible had happened. She knew what he was going to say before he said it.

'Marion, Jane has left me.'

She gave him a little smile and took his hand.

'I knew you'd behave like a gentleman. It would have been dreadful for her for people to think that *you* had left her.'

'I've come to you because I knew I could count on your sympathy.'

'Oh, I don't blame you, Gilbert,' said Mrs Tower, very kindly. 'It was bound to happen.'

He sighed.

'I suppose so. I couldn't hope to keep her always. She was too wonderful and I'm a perfectly commonplace fellow.'

Mrs Tower patted his hand. He was really behaving beautifully.

'And what is going to happen now?'

'Well, she's going to divorce me.'

'Jane always said she'd put no obstacle in your way if ever you wanted to marry a girl.'

'You don't think it's likely I should ever be willing to marry anyone else after being Jane's husband,' he answered.

Mrs Tower was puzzled.

'Of course you mean that *you've* left Jane.'

'I? That's the last thing I should ever do.'

'Then why is she divorcing you?'

'She's going to marry Sir Reginald Frobisher as soon as the decree is made absolute.'

Mrs Tower positively screamed. Then she felt so faint that she had to get her smelling salts.

'After all you've done for her?'

'I've done nothing for her.'

'Do you mean to say you're going to allow yourself to be made use of like that?'

'We arranged before we married that if either of us wanted his liberty the other should put no hindrance in the way.'

'But that was done on your account. Because you were twenty-seven years younger than she was.'

'Well, it's come in very useful for her,' he answered bitterly.

Mrs Tower expostulated, argued and reasoned; but Gilbert insisted that no rules applied to Jane, and he must do exactly what she wanted. He left Mrs Tower prostrate. It relieved her a good deal to give me a full account of this interview. It pleased her to see that I was as surprised as herself and if I was not so indignant with Jane as she was she ascribed that to the criminal lack of morality incident to my sex. She was still in a state of extreme agitation when the door was opened and the butler showed in – Jane herself. She was dressed in black and white as no doubt befitted her slightly ambiguous position, but in a dress so original and fantastic, in a hat so striking, that I positively gasped at the sight of her. But she was as ever bland and collected. She came forward to kiss Mrs Tower, but Mrs Tower withdrew herself with icy dignity.

'Gilbert has been here,' she said.

'Yes, I know,' smiled Jane. 'I told him to come and see you. I'm going to Paris tonight and I want you to be very kind to him while I am away. I'm afraid just at first he'll be rather lonely and I shall feel more comfortable if I can count on your keeping an eye on him.'

Mrs Tower clasped her hands.

'Gilbert has just told me something that I can hardly bring myself to believe. He tells me that you're going to divorce him to marry Reginald Frobisher.'

'Don't you remember, before I married Gilbert you advised me to marry a man of my own age. The admiral is fifty-three.'

'But, Jane, you owe everything to Gilbert,' said Mrs Tower indignantly. 'You wouldn't exist without him. Without him to design your clothes, you'll be nothing.'

'Oh, he's promised to go on designing my clothes,' Jane answered blandly.

'No woman could want a better husband. He's always been kindness itself to you.'

'Oh, I know he's been sweet.'

'How *can* you be so heartless?'

'But I was never in love with Gilbert,' said Jane. 'I always told him that. I'm beginning to feel the need of the companionship of a man of my own age. I think I've probably been married to Gilbert long enough. The young have no conversation.' She paused a little and gave us both a charming smile. 'Of course I shan't lose sight of Gilbert. I've arranged that with Reginald. The admiral has a niece that would just suit him. As soon as we're married we'll ask them to stay with us at Malta – you know that the admiral is to have the Mediterranean Command – and I shouldn't be at all surprised if they fell in love with one another.'

Mrs Tower gave a little sniff.

'And have you arranged with the admiral that if you want your liberty neither should put any hindrance in the way of the other?'

'I suggested it,' Jane answered with composure. 'But the admiral says he knows a good thing when he sees it and he won't want to marry anyone else, and if anyone wants to marry me – he has eight twelve-inch guns on his flagship and he'll discuss the matter at short range.' She gave us a look through her eyeglass which even the fear of Mrs Tower's wrath could not prevent me from laughing at. 'I think the admiral's a very passionate man.'

Mrs Tower indeed gave me an angry frown.

'I never thought you funny, Jane,' she said. 'I never understood why people laughed at the things you said.'

'I never thought I was funny myself, Marion,' smiled Jane, showing her bright, regular teeth. 'I am glad to leave London before too many people come round to our opinion.'

'I wish you'd tell me the secret of your astonishing success,' I said.

She turned to me with that bland, homely look I knew so well.

'You know, when I married Gilbert and settled in London and people began to laugh at what I said no one was more surprised than I was. I'd said the same things for thirty years and no one ever saw anything to laugh at. I thought it must be my clothes or my bobbed hair or my eyeglass. Then I discovered it was because I spoke the truth. It was so unusual that people thought it humorous. One of these days someone else will discover the secret and when people habitually tell the truth of course there'll be nothing funny in it.'

'And why am I the only person not to think it funny?' asked Mrs Tower.

Jane hesitated a little as though she were honestly

searching for a satisfactory explanation.

'Perhaps you don't know the truth when you see it, Marion dear,' she answered in her mild good-natured way.

It certainly gave her the last word. I felt that Jane would always have the last word. She *was* priceless.

The Alien Corn

I had known the Blands a long time before I discovered that they had any connection with Ferdy
Rabenstein. Ferdy must have been nearly fifty
when I first knew him and at the time of which I
write he was well over seventy. He had altered
little. His hair, coarse but abundant and curly, was
white, but he had kept his figure and held himself
as gallantly as ever. It was not hard to believe that
in youth he had been as beautiful as people said. He
had still his fine Semitic profile and the lustrous
black eyes that had caused havoc in so many a
Gentile breast. He was very tall, lean, with an oval
face and a clear skin. He wore his clothes very well
and in evening dress, even now, he was one of the
handsomest men I had ever seen. He wore then
large black pearls in his shirt front and platinum
and sapphire rings on his fingers. Perhaps he was
rather flashy, but you felt it was so much in character that it would have ill become him to be anything
else.

'After all, I am an Oriental,' he said. 'I can carry
a certain barbaric magnificence.'

I have often thought that Ferdy Rabenstein
would make an admirable subject for a biography.
He was not a great man, but within the limits he set
himself he made of his life a work of art. It was a

masterpiece in little, like a Persian miniature, and derived its interest from its perfection. Unfortunately the materials are scanty. They would consist of letters that may very well have been destroyed and the recollections of people who are old now and will soon be dead. His memory is extraordinary, but he would never write his memoirs, for he looks upon his past as a source of purely private entertainment; and he is a man of the most perfect discretion. Nor do I know anyone who could do justice to the subject but Max Beerbohm. There is no one else in this hard world of today who can look upon the trivial with such tender sympathy and wring such a delicate pathos from futility. I wonder that Max who must have known Ferdy much better than I, and long before, was never tempted to exercise his exquisite fancy on such a theme. He was born for Max to write about. And who should have illustrated the elegant book that I see in my mind's eye but Aubrey Beardsley? Thus would have been erected a monument of triple brass and the ephemera imprisoned to succeeding ages in the amber's exquisite translucency.

Ferdy's conquests were social and his venue was the great world. He was born in South Africa and did not come to England till he was twenty. For some time he was on the Stock Exchange, but on the death of his father he inherited a considerable fortune, and retiring from business devoted himself to the life of a man about town. At that period English society was still a closed body and it was not easy for a Jew to force its barriers, but to Ferdy they fell like the walls of Jericho. He was handsome, he was rich, he was a sportsman and he was good company. He had a house in Curzon Street, furnished with the most beautiful French furniture, and a French chef, and a brougham. It would be interesting to know the first steps in his wonderful career: they are lost in the dark abysm of time. When I first met him he had been long established as one of the smartest men in London: this was at a very grand house in Norfolk to which I had been asked as a promising young novelist by the hostess who took an interest in letters, but the company was very distinguished and I was overawed. We were sixteen, and I felt shy and alone among these cabinet ministers, great ladies and peers of the realm who talked of people and things of which I knew nothing. They were civil to me, but indifferent, and I was conscious that I was somewhat of a burden to my hostess. Ferdy saved me. He sat with me, walked with me and talked with me. He discovered that I was a writer and we discussed the drama and the novel; he learnt that I had lived much on the continent and he talked to me pleasantly of France, Germany and Spain. He seemed really to seek my society. He gave me the flattering impression that he and I stood apart from the other members of the company and by our conversation upon affairs of the spirit made that of the rest of them, the political situation, the scandal of somebody's divorce and the growing disinclination of pheasants to be killed, seem a little ridiculous. But if Ferdy had at the bottom of his heart a feeling of ever so faint a contempt for the hearty British gentry that surrounded us I am sure that it was only to me that he allowed an inkling of it to appear, and looking back I cannot but wonder whether it was not after all a suave and very delicate compliment that he paid me. I think of course that he liked to exercise his charm and I daresay the obvious pleasure his conversation gave me gratified him, but he could have had no motive for taking so much trouble over an obscure novelist other than his real interest in art and letters. I felt that he and I at bottom were equally alien in that company, I because I was a writer and he because he was a Jew, but I envied the ease with which he bore himself. He was completely at home. Everyone called him Ferdy. He seemed to be always in good spirits. He was never at a loss for a quip, a jest or a repartee. They liked him in that house because he made them laugh, but never made them uncomfortable by talking above their heads. He brought a faint savour of Oriental romance into their lives, but so cleverly that they only felt more English. You could never be dull when he was by and with him present you were safe from the fear of the devastating silences that sometimes overwhelm a British company. A pause looked inevitable and Ferdy Rabenstein had broken into a topic that interested everyone. An invaluable asset to any party. He had an inexhaustible fund of Jewish stories. He was a very good mimic and he assumed the Yiddish accent and reproduced the Jewish gestures to perfection; his head sank into his body, his face grew cunning, his voice oily, and he was a rabbi or an old clothes merchant or a smart commercial traveller or a fat procuress in Frankfort. It was as good as a play. Because he was himself a Jew and insisted on it you laughed without reserve, but for my own part not without an undercurrent of discomfort. I was not quite sure of a sense of humour that made such cruel fun of his own race. I discovered afterwards that Jewish stories were his speciality and I seldom met him anywhere without hearing him tell sooner or later the last he had heard.

But the best story he told me on this occasion was not a Jewish one. It struck me so that I have never forgotten it, but for one reason or another I have never had occasion to tell it again. I give it here because it is a curious little incident concerning persons whose names at least will live in the social history of the Victorian Era and I think it would be a pity if it were lost. He told me then that once when quite a young man he was staying in the country in a house where Mrs Langtry, at that time at the height of her beauty and astounding reputation, was also a guest. It happened to be within driving distance of that in which lived the Duchess of Somerset, who had been Queen of Beauty at the Eglinton Tournament, and knowing her slightly, it occurred to him that it would be interesting to bring the two women together. He suggested it to Mrs Langtry, who was willing, and forthwith wrote to the Duchess asking if he might bring the celebrated beauty to call on her. It was fitting, he said, that the loveliest woman of this generation (this was in the eighties) should pay her respects to the loveliest woman of the last. 'Bring her by all means,' answered the Duchess, 'but I warn you that it will be a shock to her.' They drove over in a carriage and pair, Mrs Langtry in a close-fitting blue bonnet with long satin strings, which showed the exquisite shape of her head and made her blue eyes even bluer, and were received by a little ugly old hag who looked with irony out of her beady eyes at the radiant beauty who had come to see her. They had tea, they talked and they drove home again. Mrs Langtry was very silent and when

Ferdy looked at her he saw that she was quietly weeping. When they got back to the house she went to her room and would not come down to dinner that night. For the first time she had realized that beauty dies.

Ferdy asked me for my address and a few days after I got back to London invited me to dinner. There were only six of us, an American woman married to an English peer, a Swedish painter, an actress and a well-known critic. We ate very good food and drank excellent wine. The conversation was easy and intelligent. After dinner Ferdy was persuaded to play the piano. He only played Viennese waltzes, I discovered later that they were his speciality, and the light, tuneful and sensual music seemed to accord well with his discreet flamboyance. He played without affectation, with a lilt, and he had a graceful touch. This was the first of a good many dinners I had with him, he would ask me two or three times a year, and as time passed I met him more and more frequently at other people's houses. I rose in the world and perhaps he came down a little. Of late years I had sometimes found him at parties where other Jews were and I fancied that I read in his shining liquid eyes, resting for a moment on these members of his race, a certain good-natured amusement at the thought of what the world was coming to. There were people who said he was a snob, but I do not think he was; it just happened that in his early days he had never met any but the great. He had a real passion for art and in his commerce with those that produced it was at his best. With them he had never that faint air of persiflage which when he was with very grand persons made you suspect that he was never quite the dupe of their grandeur. His taste was exquisite and many of his friends were glad to avail themselves of his knowledge. He was one of the first to value old furniture and he rescued many an exquisite piece from the attics of ancestral mansions and gave it an honourable place in the drawing-room. It amused him to saunter round the auction rooms and he was always willing to give his advice to great ladies who desired at once to acquire a beautiful thing and make a profitable investment. He was rich and good-natured. He liked to patronize the arts and would take a great deal of trouble to get commissions for some young painter whose talent he admired or an engagement to play at a rich man's house for a violinist who could in no other way get a hearing. But he never let his rich man down. His taste was too good to deceive and civil though he might be to the mediocre he would not lift a finger to help them. His own musical parties, very small and carefully chosen, were a treat.

He never married.

'I am a man of the world,' he said, 'and I flatter myself that I have no prejudices, *tous les goûts sont dans la nature*, but I do not think I could bring myself to marry a Gentile. There's no harm in going to the opera in a dinner jacket, but it just would never occur to me to do so.'

'Then why didn't you marry a Jewess?'

(I did not hear this conversation, but the lively and audacious creature who thus tackled him told me of it.)

'Oh, my dear, our women are so prolific. I could

not bear the thought of peopling the world with a little Ikey and a little Jacob and a little Rebecca and a little Leah and a little Rachel.'

But he had had affairs of note and the glamour of past romance still clung to him. He was in his youth of an amorous complexion. I have met old ladies who told me that he was irresistible, and when in reminiscent mood they talked to me of this woman and that who had completely lost her head over him, I divined that, such was his beauty, they could not find it in their hearts to blame them. It was interesting to hear of great ladies that I had read of in the memoirs of the day or had met as respectable dowagers garrulous over their grandsons at Eton or making a mess of a hand at bridge and bethink myself that they had been consumed with sinful passion for the handsome Jew. Ferdy's most notorious amour was with the Duchess of Hereford, the loveliest, the most gallant and dashing of the beauties of the end of Queen Victoria's reign. It lasted for twenty years. He had doubtless flirtations meanwhile, but their relations were stable and recognized. It was proof of his marvellous tact that when at last they ended he exchanged an ageing mistress for a loyal friend. I remember meeting the pair not so very long ago at luncheon. She was an old woman, tall and of a commanding presence, but with a mask of paint on a ravaged face. We were lunching at the Carlton and Ferdy, our host, came a few minutes late. He offered us a cocktail and the Duchess told him we had already had one.

'Ah, I wondered why your eyes were so doubly bright,' he said.

The old raddled woman flushed with pleasure.

My youth passed, I grew middle-aged, I wondered how soon I must begin to describe myself as elderly; I wrote books and plays, I travelled, I underwent experiences, I fell in love and out of it; and still I kept meeting Ferdy at parties. War broke out and was waged, millions of men were killed and the face of the world was changed. Ferdy did not like the war. He was too old to take part in it and his German name was awkward, but he was discreet and took care not to expose himself to humiliation. His old friends were faithful to him and he lived in a dignified but not too strict seclusion. But then peace came and with courage he set himself to making the best of changed conditions. Society was mixed now, parties were rowdy, but Ferdy fitted himself to the new life. He still told his funny Jewish stories, he still played charmingly the waltzes of Strauss, he still went round auction rooms and told the new rich what they ought to buy. I went to live abroad, but whenever I was in London I saw Ferdy and now there was something a little uncanny in him. He did not give in. He had never known a day's illness. He seemed never to grow tired. He still dressed beautifully. He was interested in everybody. His mind was alert and people asked him to dinner, not for old times' sake, but because he was worth his salt. He still gave charming little concerts at his house in Curzon Street.

It was when he invited me to one of these that I made the discovery that started the recollections of him I have here set down. We were dining at a house in Hill Street, a large party, and the women having gone upstairs Ferdy and I found ourselves side by side. He told me that Lea Makart was coming to play for him on the following Friday evening and he would be glad if I would come.

'I'm awfully sorry,' I said, 'but I'm going down to the Blands.'

'What Blands?'

'They live in Sussex at a place called Tilby.'

'I didn't know you knew them.'

He looked at me rather strangely. He smiled. I didn't know what amused him.

'Oh, yes, I've known them for years. It's a very nice house to stay at.'

'Adolph is my nephew.'

'Sir Adolphus?'

'It suggests one of the bucks of the Regency, doesn't it? But I will not conceal from you that he was named Adolph.'

'Everyone I know calls him Freddy.'

'I know, and I understand that Miriam, his wife, only answers to the name of Muriel.'

'How does he happen to be your nephew?'

'Because Hannah Rabenstein, my sister, married Alphonse Bleikogel, who ended life as Sir Alfred Bland, first Baronet and Adolph, their only son, in due course became Sir Adolphus Bland, second Baronet.'

'Then Freddy Bland's mother, the Lady Bland who lives in Portland Place, is your sister?'

'Yes, my sister Hannah. She was the eldest of the family. She's eighty, but in full possession of her faculties and a remarkable woman.'

'I've never met her.'

'I think your friends the Blands would just as soon you didn't. She has never lost her German accent.'

'Do you never see them?' I asked.

'I haven't spoken to them for twenty years. I am such a Jew and they are so English.' He smiled. 'I could never remember that their names were Freddy and Muriel. I used to come out with an Adolph or a Miriam at awkward moments. And they didn't like my stories. It was better that we should not meet. When the war broke out and I would not change my name it was the last straw. It was too late, I could never have accustomed my friends to think of me as anything but Ferdy Rabenstein, I was quite content. I was not ambitious to be a Smith, a Brown or a Robinson.'

Though he spoke facetiously, there was in his tone the faintest possible derision and I felt, hardly felt even, the sensation was so shadowy, that, as it had often vaguely seemed to me before, there was in the depth of his impenetrable heart a cynical contempt for the Gentiles he had conquered.

'Then you don't know the two boys?' I said.

'No.'

'The eldest is called George, you know. I don't think he's so clever as Harry, the other one, but he's an engaging youth. I think you'd like him.'

'Where is he now?'

'Well, he's just been sent down from Oxford. I suppose he's at home. Harry's still at Eton.'

'Why don't you bring George to lunch with me?'

'I'll ask him. I should think he'd love to come.'

'It has reached my ears that he's been a little troublesome.'

'Oh, I don't know. He wouldn't go into the army, which is what they wanted. They rather fancied the Guards. And so he went to Oxford instead. He didn't work and he spent a great deal of money and he painted the town red. It was all quite normal.'

'What was he sent down for?'

'I don't know. Nothing of any consequence.'

At that moment our host rose and we went upstairs. When Ferdy bade me good-night he asked me not to forget about his great-nephew.

'Ring me up,' he said. 'Wednesday would suit me. Or Friday.'

Next day I went down to Tilby. It was an Elizabethan mansion standing in a spacious park, in which roamed fallow deer, and from its windows you had wide views of rolling downs. It seemed to me that as far as the eye could reach the land belonged to the Blands. His tenants must have found Sir Adolphus a wonderful landlord, for I never saw farms kept in such order, the barns and cow-sheds were spick and span and the pigsties were a picture; the public houses looked like old English water-colours and the cottages he had built on the estate combined admirably picturesqueness and convenience. It must have cost him a pot of money to run the place on these lines. Fortunately he had it. The park with its grand old trees (and its nine-hole golf course) was tended like a garden, and the wide-stretching gardens were the pride of the neighbourhood. The magnificent house, with its steep roofs and mullioned windows, had been restored by the most celebrated architect in England and furnished by Lady Bland with taste and knowledge, in a style that perfectly fitted it.

'Of course it's very simple,' she said. 'Just an English house in the country.'

The dining-room was adorned with old English sporting pictures and the Chippendale chairs were of incredible value. In the drawing-room were portraits by Reynolds and Gainsborough and landscapes by Old Crome and Richard Wilson. Even in my bedroom with its four-post bed were watercolours by Birket Foster. It was very beautiful and a treat to stay there, but though it would have distressed Muriel Bland beyond anything to know it, it missed oddly enough entirely the effect she had sought. It did not give you for a moment the impression of an English house. You had the feeling that every object had been bought with a careful eye to the general scheme. You missed the dull Academy portraits that hung in the dining-room beside a Carlo Dolci that an ancestor had brought back from the grand tour, and the water-colours painted by a great-aunt that cluttered up the drawing-room so engagingly. There was no ugly Victorian sofa that had always been there and that it never occurred to anybody to take away and no needlework chairs that an unmarried daughter had so painstakingly worked at about the time of the Great Exhibition. There was beauty but no sentiment.

And yet how comfortable it was and how well looked after you were! And what a cordial greeting the Blands gave you! They seemed really to like people. They were generous and kindly. They were never happier than when they were entertaining the county, and though they had not owned the property for more than twenty years they had established themselves firmly in the favour of their neighbours. Except perhaps in their splendour and the competent way in which the estate was run there was nothing to suggest that they had not been settled there for centuries.

Freddy had been at Eton and Oxford. He was now in the early fifties. He was quiet in manner, courtly, very clever, I imagine, but a trifle reserved. He had great elegance, but it was not an English elegance; he had grey hair and a short pointed grey beard, fine dark eyes and an aquiline nose. He was just above middle-height; I don't think you would have taken him for a Jew, but rather for a foreign diplomat of some distinction. He was a man of character, but gave you strangely enough, notwithstanding the success he had had in life, an impression of faint melancholy. His successes had been financial and political; in the world of sport, for all his perseverance, he had never shone. For many years he had followed hounds, but he was a bad rider and I think it must have been a relief to him when he could persuade himself that middle-age and pressure of business forced him to give up hunting. He had excellent shooting and gave grand parties for it, but he was a poor shot; and despite the course in his park he never succeeded in being more than an indifferent golfer. He knew only too well how much these things meant in England and his incapacity was a bitter disappointment to him. However George would make up for it.

George was scratch at golf, and though tennis was not his game he played much better than the average; the Blands had had him taught to shoot as soon as he was old enough to hold a gun and he was a fine shot; they had put him on a pony when he was two and Freddy, watching him mount his horse, knew that out hunting when the boy came to a fence he felt exhilaration and not that sickening feeling in the pit of his stomach which, though he had chased the fox with such grim determination, had always made the sport a torture to him. George was so tall and slim, his curly hair, of a palish brown, was so fine, his eyes were so blue, he was the perfect type of the young Englishman. He had the engaging candour of the breed. His nose was straight, though perhaps a trifle fleshy, and his lips were perhaps a little full and sensual, but he had beautiful teeth, and his smooth skin was like ivory. George was the apple of his father's eye. He did not like Harry, his second son, so well. He was rather stocky, broad-shouldered and strong for his age, but his black eyes, shining with cleverness, his coarse dark hair and his big nose revealed his race. Freddy was severe with him, and often impatient, but with George he was all indulgence. Harry would go into the business, he had brains and push, but George was the heir. George would be an English gentleman.

George had offered to motor me down in the roadster his father had given him as a birthday present. He drove very fast and we arrived before the rest of the guests. The Blands were sitting on the lawn and tea was laid out under a magnificent cedar.

'By the way,' I said presently, 'I saw Ferdy Rabenstein the other day and he wants me to bring George to lunch with him.'

I had not mentioned the invitation to George on the way because I thought that if there had been a family coldness I had better address his parents as well.

'Who in God's name is Ferdy Rabenstein?' said George.

How brief is human glory! A generation back such a question would have seemed grotesque.

'He's by way of being your great-uncle,' I replied.

A glance had passed from father to mother when I first spoke.

'He's a horrid old man,' said Muriel.

'I don't think it's in the least necessary for George to resume relationships that were definitely severed before he was born,' said Freddy with decision.

'Anyhow I've delivered the message,' said I, feeling somewhat snubbed.

'I don't want to see the old blighter,' said George.

The conversation was broken off by the arrival of other guests and in a little while George went off to play golf with one of his Oxford friends.

It was not till next day that the matter was referred to again. I had played an indifferent round with Freddy Bland in the morning and several sets of what is known as country house tennis in the afternoon and was sitting alone with Muriel on the terrace. In England we have so much bad weather that it is only fair that a beautiful day should be more beautiful than anywhere in the world and this June evening was perfect. The blue sky was cloudless and the air was balmy; before us stretched green rolling downs, and woods, and in the distance you saw the red roofs of a little village and the grey tower of the village church. It was a day when to be alive was sufficient happiness. Detached lines of poetry hovered vaguely in my memory. Muriel and I had been chatting desultorily.

'I hope you didn't think it rather horrid of us to

refuse to let George lunch with Ferdy,' she said suddenly. 'He's such a fearful snob, isn't he?'

'D'you think so? He's always been very nice to me.'

'We haven't been on speaking terms for twenty years. Freddy never forgave him for his behaviour during the war. So unpatriotic, I thought, and one really must draw the line somewhere. You know, he absolutely refused to drop his horrible German name. With Freddy in Parliament and running munitions and all that sort of thing it was quite impossible. I don't know why he should want to see George. He can't mean anything to him.'

'He's an old man. George and Harry are his great-nephews. He must leave his money to someone.'

'We'd rather not have his money,' said Muriel coldly.

Of course I didn't care a row of pins whether George went to lunch with Ferdy Rabenstein, and I was quite willing to let the matter drop, but evidently the Blands had talked it over and Muriel felt that some explanation was due to me.

'Of course you know that Freddy has Jewish blood in him,' she said.

She looked at me sharply. Muriel was rather a big blonde woman and she spent a great deal of time trying to keep down the corpulence to which she was predisposed. She had been very pretty when young and even now was a comely person; but her round blue eyes, slightly prominent, her fleshy nose, the shape of her face and the back of her neck, her exuberant manner, betrayed her race. No Englishwoman, however fair-haired, ever looked like that. And yet her observation was designed to make me take it for granted that she was a Gentile. I answered discreetly:

'So many people have nowadays.'

'I know. But there's no reason to dwell on it, is there? After all, we're absolutely English; no one could be more English than George, in appearance and manner and everything; I mean, he's such a fine sportsman and all that sort of thing, I can't see any object in his knowing Jews just because they happen to be distant connections of his.'

'It's very difficult in England now not to know Jews, isn't it?'

'Oh, I know, in London one does meet a good many, and I think some of them are very nice. They're so artistic. I don't go so far as to say that Freddy and I deliberately avoid them, of course I wouldn't do that, but it just happens that we don't really know any of them very well. And down here, there simply aren't any to know.'

I could not but admire the convincing manner in which she spoke. It would not have surprised me to be told that she really believed every word she said.

'You say that Ferdy might leave George his money. Well, I don't believe it's so very much anyway; it was quite a comfortable fortune before the war, but that's nothing nowadays. Besides, we're hoping that George will go in for politics when he's a little older, and I don't think it would do him any good in the constituency to inherit money from a Mr Rabenstein.'

'Is George interested in politics?' I asked, to change the conversation.

'Oh, I do hope so. After all, there's the family constituency waiting for him. It's a safe Conservative seat and one can't expect Freddy to go on with the grind of the House of Commons indefinitely.'

Muriel was grand. She talked already of the constituency as though twenty generations of Blands had sat for it. Her remark, however, was my first intimation that Freddy's ambition was not satisfied.

'I suppose Freddy would go to the House of Lords when George was old enough to stand.'

'We've done a good deal for the party,' said Muriel.

Muriel was a Catholic and she often told you that she had been educated in a convent – 'Such sweet women, those nuns, I always said that if I had a daughter I should have sent her to a convent too' – but she liked her servants to be Church of England, and on Sunday evenings we had what was called supper because the fish was cold and there was ice-cream, so that they could go to church, and we were waited on by two footmen instead of four. It was still light when we finished and Freddy and I, smoking our cigars, walked up and down the terrace in the gloaming. I suppose Muriel had told him of her conversation with me, and it may be that his refusal to let George see his great-uncle still troubled him, but being subtler than she he attacked the question more indirectly. He told me that he had been very much worried about George. It had been a great disappointment that he had refused to go into the army.

'I should have thought he'd have loved the life,' he said.

'And he would certainly have looked marvellous in his Guards uniform.'

'He would, wouldn't he?' returned Freddy, ingenuously. 'I wonder he could resist that.'

He had been completely idle at Oxford; although

his father had given him a very large allowance, he had got monstrously into debt; and now he had been sent down. But though he spoke so tartly I could see that he was not a little proud of his scapegrace son, he loved him with oh, such an unEnglish love, and in his heart it flattered him that George had cut such a dash.

'Why should you worry?' I said. 'You don't really care if George has a degree or not.'

Freddy chuckled.

'No, I don't suppose I do really. I always think the only important thing about Oxford is that people know you were there, and I daresay that George isn't any wilder than the other young men in his set. It's the future I'm thinking of. He's so damned idle. He doesn't seem to want to do anything but have a good time.'

'He's young, you know.'

'He's not interested in politics, and though he's so good at games he's not even very keen on sport. He seems to spend most of his time strumming the piano.'

'That's a harmless amusement.'

'Oh, yes, I don't mind that, but he can't go on loafing indefinitely. You see, all this will be his one day.' Freddy gave a sweeping gesture that seemed to embrace the whole county, but I knew that he did not own it all yet. 'I'm very anxious that he should be fit to assume his responsibilities. His mother is very ambitious for him, but I only want him to be an English gentleman.'

Freddy gave me a sidelong glance as though he wanted to say something but hesitated in case I thought it ridiculous; but there is one advantage in being a writer that, since people look upon you as of no account, they will often say things to you that they would not to their equals. He thought he would risk it.

'You know, I've got an idea that nowhere in the world now is the Greek ideal of life so perfectly cultivated as by the English country gentleman living on his estates. I think his life has the beauty of a work of art.'

I could not but smile when I reflected that it was impossible for the English country gentleman in these days to do anything of the sort without a packet of money safely invested in American Bonds, but I smiled with sympathy. I thought it rather touching that this Jewish financier should cherish so romantic a dream.

'I want him to be a good landlord. I want him to take his part in the affairs of the country. I want him to be a thorough sportsman.'

'Poor mutt,' I thought, but said: 'Well, what are your plans for George now?'

'I think he has a fancy for the diplomatic service. He's suggested going to Germany to learn the language.'

'A very good idea, I should have thought.'

'For some reason he's got it into his head that he wants to go to Munich.'

'A nice place.'

Next day I went back to London and shortly after my arrival rang up Ferdy.

'I'm sorry, but George isn't able to come to lunch on Wednesday?'

'What about Friday?'

'Friday's no good either.' I thought it useless to

beat about the bush. 'The fact is, his people aren't keen on his lunching with you.'

There was a moment's silence. Then:

'I see. Well, will you come on Wednesday anyway?'

'Yes, I'd like to,' I answered.

So on Wednesday at half-past one I strolled round to Curzon Street. Ferdy received me with the somewhat elaborate graciousness that he cultivated. He made no reference to the Blands. We sat in the drawing-room and I could not help reflecting what an eye for beautiful objects that family had. The room was more crowded than the fashion of today approves and the gold snuff-boxes in vitrines, the French china, appealed to a taste that was not mine; but they were no doubt choice pieces; and the Louis XV suite, with its beautiful *petit point*, must have been worth an enormous lot of money. The pictures on the walls by Lancret, Pater and Watteau did not greatly interest me, but I recognized their intrinsic excellence. It was a proper setting for this aged man of the world. It fitted his period. Suddenly the door opened and George was announced. Ferdy saw my surprise and gave me a little smile of triumph.

'I'm very glad you were able to come after all,' he said as he shook George's hand.

I saw him in a glance take in his great-nephew whom he saw today for the first time. George was very elegantly dressed. He wore a short black coat, striped trousers and the grey double-breasted waistcoat which at that time was the mode. You could only wear it with elegance if you were tall and thin and your belly was slightly concave. I felt sure that Ferdy knew exactly who George's tailor was and what haberdasher he went to and approved of them. George, so smart and trim, wearing his clothes so beautifully, certainly looked very handsome. We went down to luncheon. Ferdy had the social graces at his fingers' ends and he put the boy at his ease, but I saw that he was carefully appraising him; then, I do not know why, he began to tell some of his Jewish stories. He told them with gusto and with his wonderful mimicry. I saw George flush, and though he laughed at them, I could see that it was with embarrassment. I wondered what on earth had induced Ferdy to be so tactless. But he was watching George and he told story after story. It looked as though he would never stop. I wondered if for some reason I could not grasp he was taking a malicious pleasure in the boy's obvious discomfiture. At last we went upstairs and to make things easier I asked Ferdy to play the piano. He played us three or four little waltzes. He had lost none of his exquisite lightness nor his sense of their lilting rhythm. Then he turned to George.

'Do you play?' he asked him.

'A little.'

'Won't you play something?'

'I'm afraid I only play classical music. I don't think it would interest you.'

Ferdy smiled slightly, but did not insist. I said it was time for me to go and George accompanied me.

'What a filthy old Jew,' he said as soon as we were in the street. 'I hated those stories of his.'

'They're his great stunt. He always tells them.'

'Would you if you were a Jew?'

I shrugged my shoulders.

'How is it you came to lunch after all?' I asked George.

He chuckled. He was a light-hearted creature, with a sense of humour, and he shook off the slight irritation his great-uncle had caused him.

'He went to see Granny. You don't know Granny, do you?'

'No.'

'She treats daddy like a kid in Etons. Granny said I was to go to lunch with great-uncle Ferdy and what Granny says goes.'

'I see.'

A week or two later George went to Munich to learn German. I happened then to go on a journey and it was not till the following spring that I was again in London. Soon after my arrival I found myself sitting next to Muriel Bland at dinner. I asked after George.

'He's still in Germany,' she said.

'I see in the papers that you're going to have a great beano at Tilby for his coming of age.'

'We're going to entertain the tenants and they're making George a presentation.'

She was less exuberant than usual, but I did not pay much attention to the fact. She led a strenuous life and it might be that she was tired. I knew she liked to talk of her son, so I continued.

'I suppose George has been having a grand time in Germany,' I said.

She did not answer for a moment and I gave her a glance. I was surprised to see that her eyes were filled with tears.

'I'm afraid George has gone mad,' she said.

'What *do* you mean?'

'We've been so frightfully worried. Freddy's so angry, he won't even discuss it. I don't know what we're going to do.'

Of course it immediately occurred to me that George, who, I supposed, like most young Englishmen sent to learn the language, had been put with a German family, had fallen in love with the daughter of the house and wanted to marry her. I had a pretty strong suspicion that the Blands were intent on his making a very grand marriage.

'Why, what's happened?' I asked.

'He wants to become a pianist.'

'A what?'

'A professional pianist.'

'What on earth put that idea in his head?'

'Heaven knows. We didn't know anything about it. We thought he was working for his exam. I went out to see him. I thought I'd like to know that he was getting on all right. Oh, my dear. He looks like nothing on earth. And he used to be so smart; I could have cried. He told me he wasn't going in for the exam and had never had any intention of doing so; he'd only suggested the diplomatic service so that we'd let him go to Germany and he'd be able to study music.'

'But has he any talent?'

'Oh, that's neither here nor there. Even if he had the genius of Paderewski we couldn't have George traipsing around the country playing at concerts. No one can deny that I'm very artistic, and so is Freddy, we love music and we've always known a lot of artists, but George will have a very great position, it's out of the question. We've set our hearts on his going into Parliament. He'll be very rich one day. There's nothing he can't aspire to.'

'Did you point all that out to him?'

'Of course I did. He laughed at me. I told him he'd break his father's heart. He said his father could always fall back on Harry. Of course I'm devoted to Harry, and he's as clever as a monkey, but it was always understood that he was to go into the business; even though I am his mother I can see that he hasn't got the advantages that George has. Do you know what he said to me? He said that if his father would settle five pounds a week on him he would resign everything in Harry's favour and Harry could be his father's heir and succeed to the baronetcy and everything. It's too ridiculous. He said that if the Crown Prince of Roumania could abdicate a throne he didn't see why he couldn't abdicate a baronetcy. But you can't do that. Nothing can prevent him from being third baronet and if Freddy should be granted a peerage from succeeding to it at Freddy's death. Do you know, he even wants to drop the name of Bland and take some horrible German name.'

I could not help asking what.

'Bleikogel or something like that,' she answered.

That was a name I recognized. I remembered Ferdy telling me that Hannah Rabenstein had married Alphonse Bleikogel who became eventually Sir Alfred Bland, first Baronet. It was all very strange. I wondered what had happened to the charming and so typically English boy whom I had seen only a few months before.

'Of course when I came home and told Freddy he was furious. I've never seen him so angry. He foamed at the mouth. He wired to George to come back immediately and George wired back to say he couldn't on account of his work.'

'Is he working?'

'From morning till night. That's the maddening part of it. He never did a stroke of work in his life. Freddy used to say he was born idle.'

'H'm.'

'Then Freddy wired to say that if he didn't come he'd stop his allowance and George wired back: Stop it. That put the lid on. You don't know what Freddy can be when his back is up.'

I knew that Freddy had inherited a large fortune, but I knew also that he had immensely increased it, and I could well imagine that behind the courteous and amiable Squire of Tilby there was a ruthless man of affairs. He had been used to having his own way and I could believe that when crossed he would be hard and cruel.

'We'd been making George a very handsome allowance, but you know how frightfully extravagant he was. We didn't think he'd be able to hold out long and in point of fact within a month he wrote to Ferdy and asked him to lend him a hundred pounds. Ferdy went to my mother-in-law, she's his sister, you know, and asked her what it meant. Though they hadn't spoken for twenty years Freddy went to see him and begged him not to send George a penny, and he promised he wouldn't. I don't know how George has been making both ends meet. I'm sure Freddy's right, but I can't help being rather worried. If I hadn't given Freddy my word of honour that I wouldn't send him anything I think I'd have slipped a few notes in a letter in case of accident. I mean, it's awful to think that perhaps he hasn't got enough to eat.'

'It'll do him no harm to go short for a bit.'

'We were in an awful hole, you know. We'd made all sorts of preparations for his coming of age, and I'd issued hundreds of invitations. Suddenly George said he wouldn't come. I was simply frantic. I wrote and wired. I would have gone over to

Germany only Freddy wouldn't let me. I practically went down on my bended knees to George. I begged him not to put us in such a humiliating position. I mean, it's the sort of thing it's so difficult to explain. Then my mother-in-law stepped in. You don't know her, do you? She's an extraordinary old woman. You'd never think she was Freddy's mother. She was German originally, but of very good family.'

'Oh?'

'To tell you the truth I'm rather frightened of her. She tackled Freddy and then she wrote to George herself. She said that if he'd come home for his twenty-first birthday, she'd pay any debts he had in Munich and we'd all give a patient hearing to anything he had to say. He agreed to that and we're expecting him one day next week. But I'm not looking forward to it, I can tell you.'

She gave a deep sigh. When we were walking upstairs after dinner Freddy addressed me.

'I see Muriel has been telling you about George. The damned fool! I have no patience with him. Fancy wanting to be a pianist. It's so ungentlemanly.'

'He's very young, you know,' I said soothingly.

'He's had things too easy for him. I've been much too indulgent. There's never been a thing he wanted that I haven't given him. I'll learn him.'

The Blands had a discreet apprehension of the uses of advertisement and I gathered from the papers that the celebrations at Tilby of George's twenty-first birthday were conducted in accordance with the usage of English county families. There was a

dinner party and a ball for the gentry and a colla-
tion and a dance in marquees on the lawn for the
tenants. Expensive bands were brought down from
London. In the illustrated papers were pictures of
George surrounded by his family being presented
with a solid silver tea set by the tenantry. They had
subscribed to have his portrait painted, but since
his absence from the country had made it impossible for him to sit, the tea service had been sub-
stituted. I read in the columns of the gossip writers
that his father had given him a hunter, his mother a
gramophone that changed its own records, his
grandmother the dowager Lady Bland an
Encyclopaedia Britannica and his great-uncle
Ferdinand Rabenstein a Virgin and Child by Pel-
legrino da Modena. I could not help observing that
these gifts were bulky and not readily convertible
into cash. From Ferdy's presence at the festivities I
concluded that George's unaccountable vagary had
effected a reconciliation between uncle and
nephew. I was right. Ferdy did not at all like the
notion of his great-nephew becoming a professional
pianist. At the first hint of danger to its prestige the
family drew together and a united front was
presented to oppose George's designs. Since I was
not there I only know from hearsay what happened
when the birthday celebrations were over. Ferdy
told me something and so did Muriel, and later
George gave me his version. The Blands had very
much the impression that when George came home
and found himself occupying the centre of the
stage, when, surrounded by splendour, he saw for
himself once more how much it meant to be the
heir of a great estate, he would weaken. They surrounded him with love. They flattered him. They

hung on his words. They counted on the goodness of his heart and thought that if they were very kind to him he would not have the courage to cause them pain. They seemed to take it for granted that he had no intention of going back to Germany and in conversation included him in all their plans. George did not say very much. He seemed to be enjoying himself. He did not open a piano. Things looked as though they were going very well. Peace descended on the troubled house. Then one day at luncheon when they were discussing a garden party to which they had all been asked for one day of the following week, George said pleasantly:

'Don't count on me. I shan't be here.'

'Oh, George, why not?' asked his mother.

'I must get back to my work. I'm leaving for Munich on Monday.'

There was an awful pause. Everyone looked for something to say, but was afraid of saying the wrong thing, and at last it seemed impossible to break it. Luncheon was finished in silence. Then George went into the garden and the others, old Lady Bland and Ferdy, Muriel and Sir Adolphus, into the morning-room. There was a family council. Muriel wept. Freddy flew into a temper. Presently from the drawing-room they heard the sound of someone playing a nocturne of Chopin. It was George. It was as though now he had announced his decision he had gone for comfort, rest and strength to the instrument he loved. Freddy sprang to his feet.

'Stop that noise,' he cried. 'I won't have him play the piano in my house.'

Muriel rang for a servant and gave him a message.

'Will you tell Mr Bland that her ladyship has a bad headache and would he mind not playing the piano.'

Ferdy, the man of the world, was deputed to have a talk with George. He was authorized to make him certain promises if he would give up the idea of becoming a pianist. If he did not wish to go into the diplomatic service his father would not insist, but if he would stand for Parliament he was prepared to pay his election expenses, give him a flat in London and make him an allowance of five thousand a year. I must say it was a handsome offer. I do not know what Ferdy said to the boy. I suppose he painted to him the life that a young man could lead in London on such an income. I am sure he made it very alluring. It availed nothing. All George asked was five pounds a week to be able to continue his studies and to be left alone. He was indifferent to the position that he might some day enjoy. He didn't want to hunt. He didn't want to shoot. He didn't want to be a Member of Parliament. He didn't want to be a millionaire. He didn't want to be a baronet. He didn't want to be a peer. Ferdy left him defeated and in a state of considerable exasperation.

After dinner that evening there was a battle royal. Freddy was a quick-tempered man, unused to opposition, and he gave George the rough side of his tongue. I gather that it was very rough indeed. The women who sought to restrain his violence were sternly silenced. Perhaps for the first time in his life Freddy would not listen to his mother. George was obstinate and sullen. He had made up his mind and if his father didn't like it he could lump it. Freddy was peremptory. He forbade

George to go back to Germany. George answered that he was twenty-one and his own master. He would go where he chose. Freddy swore he would not give him a penny.

'All right, I'll earn money.'

'You! You've never done a stroke of work in your life. What do you expect to do to earn money?'

'Sell old clothes,' grinned George.

There was a gasp from all of them. Muriel was so taken aback that she said a stupid thing.

'Like a Jew?'

'Well, aren't I a Jew? And aren't you a Jewess and isn't daddy a Jew? We're all Jews, the whole gang of us, and everyone knows it and what the hell's the good of pretending we're not?'

Then a very dreadful thing happened. Freddy burst suddenly into tears. I'm afraid he didn't behave very much like Sir Adolphus Bland, Bart., MP, and the good old English gentleman he so much wanted to be, but like an emotional Adolph Bleikogel who loved his son and wept with mortification because the great hopes he had set on him were brought to nothing and the ambition of his life was frustrated. He cried noisily with great loud sobs and pulled his beard and beat his breast and rocked to and fro. Then they all began to cry, old Lady Bland and Muriel, and Ferdy, who sniffed and blew his nose and wiped the tears streaming down his face, and even George cried. Of course it was very painful, but to our rough Anglo-Saxon temperament I am afraid it must seem also a trifle ridiculous. No one tried to console anybody else. They just sobbed and sobbed. It broke up the party.

But it had no result on the situation. George

remained obdurate. His father would not speak to him. There were more scenes. Muriel sought to excite his pity; he was deaf to her piteous entreaties, he did not seem to mind if he broke her heart, he did not care two hoots if he killed his father. Ferdy appealed to him as a sportsman and a man of the world. George was flippant and indeed personally offensive. Old Lady Bland with her gutural German accent and strong common sense argued with him, but he would not listen to reason. It was she, however, who at last found a way out. She made George acknowledge that it was no use to throw away all the beautiful things the world laid at his feet unless he had talent. Of course he thought he had, but he might be mistaken. It was not worth while to be a second-rate pianist. His only excuse, his only justification, was genius. If he had genius his family had no right to stand in his way.

'You can't expect me to show genius already,' said George. 'I shall have to work for years.'

'Are you sure you are prepared for that?'

'It's my only wish in the world. I'll work like a dog. I only want to be given my chance.'

This was the proposition she made. His father was determined to give him nothing and obviously they could not let the boy starve. He had mentioned five pounds a week. Well, she was willing to give him that herself. He could go back to Germany and study for two years. At the end of that time he must come back and they would get some competent and disinterested person to hear him play, and if then that person said he showed promise of becoming a first-rate pianist no further obstacles would be placed in his way. He would be given every advantage, help and encouragement. If on the other hand that person decided that his natural gifts were not such as to ensure ultimate success he must promise faithfully to give up all thoughts of making music his profession and in every way accede to his father's wishes. George could hardly believe his ears.

'Do you mean that, Granny?'

'I do.'

'But will daddy agree?'

'I vil see dat he does,' she answered.

George seized her in his arms and impetuously kissed her on both cheeks.

'Darling,' he cried.

'Ah, but de promise?'

He gave her his solemn word of honour that he would faithfully abide by the terms of the arrangement. Two days later he went back to Germany. Though his father consented unwillingly to his going, and indeed could not help doing so, he would not be reconciled to him and when he left refused to say good-bye to him. I imagine that in no manner could he have caused himself such pain. I permit myself a trite remark. It is strange that men, inhabitants for so short a while of an alien and inhuman world, should go out of their way to cause themselves so much unhappiness.

George had stipulated that during his two years of study his family should not visit him, so that when Muriel heard some months before he was due to come home that I was passing through Munich on my way to Vienna, whither business called me, it was not unnatural that she should ask me to look

him up. She was anxious to have first-hand information about him. She gave me George's address
and I wrote ahead, telling him I was spending a day
in Munich, and asked him to lunch with me. His
answer awaited me at the hotel. He said he worked
all day and could not spare the time to lunch with
me, but if I would come to his studio about six he
would like to show me that and if I had nothing
better to do would love to spend the evening with
me. So soon after six I went to the address he gave
me. He lived on the second floor of a large block of
flats and when I came to his door I heard the sound
of piano-playing. It stopped when I rang and
George opened the door for me. I hardly
recognized him. He had grown very fat. His hair
was extremely long, it curled all over his head in
picturesque confusion; and he had certainly not
shaved for three days. He wore a grimy pair of
Oxford bags, a tennis shirt and slippers. He was
not very clean and his finger nails were rimmed
with black. It was a startling change from the
spruce, slim youth so elegantly dressed in such
beautiful clothes that I had last seen. I could not
but think it would be a shock to Ferdy to see him
now. The studio was large and bare; on the walls
were three or four unframed canvases of a highly
cubist nature, there were several arm-chairs much
the worse for wear, and a grand piano. Books were
littered about and old newspapers and art
magazines. It was dirty and untidy and there was a
frowzy smell of stale beer and stale smoke.

'Do you live here alone?' I asked.

'Yes, I have a woman who comes in twice a week
and cleans up. But I make my own breakfast and
lunch.'

'Can you cook?'

'Oh, I only have bread and cheese and a bottle of beer for lunch. I dine at a *Bierstube.*'

It was pleasant to discover that he was very glad to see me. He seemed in great spirits and extremely happy. He asked after his relations and we talked of one thing and another. He had a lesson twice a week and for the rest of the time practised. He told me that he worked ten hours a day.

'That's a change,' I said.

He laughed.

'Daddy said I was born tired. I wasn't really lazy. I didn't see the use of working at things that bored me.'

I asked him how he was getting on with the piano. He seemed to be satisfied with his progress and I begged him to play to me.

'Oh, not now, I'm all in, I've been at it all day. Let's go out and dine and come back here later and then I'll play. I generally go to the same place, there are several students I know there, and it's rather fun.'

Presently we set out. He put on socks and shoes and a very old golf-coat, and we walked together through the wide quiet streets. It was a brisk cold day. His step was buoyant. He looked round him with a sigh of delight.

'I love Munich,' he said. 'It's the only city in the world where there's art in the very air you breathe. After all art is the only thing that matters, isn't it? I loathe the idea of going home.'

'All the same I'm afraid you'll have to.'

'I know. I'll go all right, but I'm not going to think about it till the time comes.'

'When you do you might do worse than get a

hair-cut. If you don't mind my saying so you look almost too artistic to be convincing.'

'You English, you're such Philistines,' he said.

He took me to a rather large restaurant in a side street, crowded even at that early hour with people dining and furnished heavily in the German medieval style. A table covered with a red cloth, well away from the air, was reserved for George and his friends and when we went to it four or five youths were at it. There was a Pole studying Oriental languages, a student of philosophy, a painter (I suppose the author of George's cubist pictures), a Swede, and a young man who introduced himself to me, clicking his heels, as Hans Reiting, *Dichter*, namely Hans Reiting, poet. Not one of them was more than twenty-two and I felt a trifle out of it. They all addressed George as *du* and I noticed that his German was extremely fluent. I had not spoken it for some time and mine was rusty, so that I could not take much part in the lively conversation. But nevertheless I thoroughly enjoyed myself. They ate sparingly, but drank a good deal of beer. They talked of art and literature and life and ethics and motor-cars and women. They were very revolutionary and though gay very much in earnest. They were contemptuous of everyone you had ever heard of, and the only point on which they all agreed was that in this topsy-turvy world only the vulgar could hope for success. They argued points of technique with animation, and contradicted one another, and shouted and were obscene. They had a grand time.

At about eleven George and I walked back to his studio. Munich is a city that frolics demurely and except about the Marienplatz the streets were still and empty. When we got in he took off his coat and said:

'Now I'll play to you.'

I sat in one of the dilapidated arm-chairs and a broken spring stuck into my behind, but I made myself as comfortable as I could. George played Chopin. I know very little of music and that is one of the reasons for which I have found this story difficult to write. When I go to a concert at the Queen's Hall and in the intervals read the programme it is all Greek to me. I know nothing of harmony and counterpoint. I shall never forget how humiliated I felt once when having come to Munich for a Wagner Festival, I went to a wonderful performance of *Tristan and Isolde* and never heard a note of it. The first few bars sent me off and I began to think of what I was writing, my characters leapt into life and I heard their long conversations, I suffered their pains and was a party to their joy; the years swept by and all sorts of things happened to me, the spring brought me its rapture and in the winter I was cold and hungry; and I loved and I hated and I died. I suppose there were intervals in which I walked round and round the garden and probably ate *Schinken-Brödchen* and drank beer, but I have no recollection of them. The only thing I know is that when the curtain for the last time fell I woke with a start. I had had a wonderful time, but I could not help thinking it was very stupid of me to come such a long way and spend so much money if I couldn't pay attention to what I heard and saw.

I knew most of the things George played. They were the familiar pieces of concert programmes. He played with a great deal of dash. Then he played Beethoven's *Appassionata*. I used to play it myself when I played the piano (very badly) in my far distant youth and I still knew every note of it. Of course it is a classic and a great work, it would be foolish to deny it, but I confess that at this time of day it leaves me cold. It is like *Paradise Lost*, splendid, but a trifle stolid. This too George played with vigour. He sweated profusely. At first I could not make out what was the matter with his playing, something did not seem to me quite right, and then it struck me that the two hands did not exactly synchronize, so that there was ever so slight an interval between the bass and the treble; but I repeat, I am ignorant of these things; what disconcerted me might have been merely the effect of his having drunk a good deal of beer that evening or indeed only my fancy. I said all I could think of to praise him.

'Of course I know I need a lot more work. I'm only a beginner, but I know I can do it. I feel it in my bones. It'll take me ten years, but then I shall be a pianist.'

He was tired and came away from the piano. It was after midnight and I suggested going, but he would not hear of it. He opened a couple of bottles of beer and lit his pipe. He wanted to talk.

'Are you happy here?' I asked him.

'Very,' he answered gravely. 'I'd like to stay for ever. I've never had such fun in my life. This evening for instance. Wasn't it grand?'

'It was very jolly. But one can't go on leading the student's life. Your friends here will grow older and go away.'

'Others'll come. There are always students here and people like that.'

'Yes, but you'll grow older too. Is there anything more lamentable than the middle-aged man who tries to go on living the undergraduate's life? The old fellow who wants to be a boy among boys, and tries to persuade himself that they'll accept him as one of themselves – how ridiculous he is. It can't be done.'

'I feel so at home here. My poor father wants me to be an English gentleman. It gives me gooseflesh. I'm not a sportsman. I don't care a damn for hunting and shooting and playing cricket. I was only acting.'

'You gave a very natural performance.'

'It wasn't till I came here that I knew it wasn't real. I loved Eton, and Oxford was a riot, but all the same I knew I didn't belong. I played the part all right, because acting's in my blood, but there was always something in me that wasn't satisfied. The house in Grosvenor Square is a freehold and daddy paid a hundred and eighty thousand pounds for Tilby; I don't know if you understand what I mean, I felt they were just furnished houses we'd taken for the season and one of these days we'd pack up and the real owners would come back.'

I listened to him attentively, but I wondered how much he was describing what he had obscurely felt and how much he imagined now in his changed circumstances that he had felt.

'I used to hate hearing Great-Uncle Ferdy tell his Jewish stories. I thought it so damned mean. I understand now; it was a safety valve. My God, the strain of being a man about town. It's easier for daddy, he can play the old English squire at Tilby, but in the City he can be himself. He's all right. I've taken the make-up off and my stage clothes and at last I can be my real self too. What a relief! You know, I don't like English people. I never really know where I am with you. You're so dull and conventional. You never let yourselves go. There's no freedom in you, freedom of the soul, and you're such funks. There's nothing in the world you're so frightened of as doing the wrong thing.'

'Don't forget that you're English yourself, George,' I murmured.

He laughed.

'I? I'm not English. I haven't got a drop of English blood in me. I'm a Jew and you know it, and a German Jew into the bargain. I don't want to be English. I want to be a Jew. My friends are Jews. You don't know how much more easy I feel with them. I can be myself. We did everything we could to avoid Jews at home; mummy because she was blonde thought she could get away with it and pretended she was a Gentile. What rot! D'you know, I have a lot of fun wandering about the Jewish parts of Munich and looking at the people. I went to Frankfort once, there are a lot of them there, and I walked about and looked at the frowzy old men with their hooked noses and the fat women with their false hair. I felt such a sympathy for them, I felt I belonged to them, I could have kissed them. When they looked at me I wondered if they knew that I was one of them. I wish to God I knew Yiddish. I'd like to become friends with them, and go into their houses and eat Kosher food and all that sort of thing. I wanted to go to a synagogue, but I was afraid I'd do the wrong thing and be kicked out. I like the smell of the Ghetto and the sense of life, and the mystery and the dust and the squalor and the romance. I shall never get the longing for it out of my head now. That's the real thing. All the rest is only pretence.'

'You'll break your father's heart,' I said.

'It's his or mine. Why can't he let me go? There's Harry. Harry would love to be squire of Tilby. He'd be an English gentleman all right. You know, mummy's set her heart on my marrying a Christian. Harry would love to. He'll found the good old English family all right. After all, I ask so little. I only want five pounds a week, and they can keep the title and the park and the Gainsboroughs and the whole bag of tricks.'

'Well, the fact remains that you gave your solemn word of honour to go back after two years.'

'I'll go back all right,' he said sullenly. 'Lea Makart has promised to come and hear me play.'

'What'll you do if she says you're no good?'

'Shoot myself,' he said gaily.

'What nonsense,' I answered in the same tone.

'Do *you* feel at home in England?'

'No,' I said, 'but then I don't feel at home anywhere else.'

But he was quite naturally not interested in me.

'I loathe the idea of going back. Now that I know what life has to offer I wouldn't be an English country gentleman for anything in the world. My God, the boredom of it!'

'Money's a very nice thing and I've always understood it's very pleasant to be an English peer.'

'Money means nothing to me. I want none of the things it can buy, and I don't happen to be a snob.'

It was growing very late and I had to get up early next day. It seemed unnecessary for me to pay too much attention to what George said. It was the sort of nonsense a young man might very well indulge in when thrown suddenly among painters and poets. Art is strong wine and needs a strong head to carry it. The divine fire burns most efficiently in those who temper its fury with horse sense. After all, George was not twenty-three yet. Time teaches. And when all was said and done his future was no concern of mine. I bade him good-night and walked back to my hotel. The stars were shining in the indifferent sky. I left Munich in the morning.

I did not tell Muriel on my return to London what George had said to me, or what he looked like, but contented myself with assuring her that he was well and happy, working very hard, and seemed to be leading a virtuous and sober life. Six months later he came home. Muriel asked me to go down to Tilby for the week-end: Ferdy was bringing Lea Makart to hear George play and he particularly wished me to be there. I accepted. Muriel met me at the station.

'How did you find George?' I asked.

'He's very fat, but he seems in great spirits. I think he's pleased to be back again. He's been very sweet to his father.'

'I'm glad of that.'

'Oh, my dear, I do hope Lea Makart will say he's no good. It'll be such a relief to all of us.'

'I'm afraid it'll be a terrible disappointment to him.'

'Life is full of disappointments,' said Muriel crisply. 'But one learns to put up with them.'

I gave her a smile of amusement. We were sitting in a Rolls and there was a footman as well as a chauffeur on the box. She wore a string of pearls that had probably cost forty thousand pounds. I recollected that in the birthday honours Sir Adolphus Bland had not been one of the three gentlemen on whom the King had been pleased to confer a peerage.

Lea Makart was able to make only a flying visit. She was playing that evening at Brighton and would motor over to Tilby on the Sunday morning for luncheon. She was returning to London the same day because she had a concert in Manchester on the Monday. George was to play in the course of the afternoon.

'He's practising very hard,' his mother told me. 'That's why he didn't come with me to meet you.'

We turned in at the park gates and drove up the imposing avenue of elms that led to the house. I found that there was no party.

I met the dowager Lady Bland for the first time. I had always been curious to see her. I had had in my mind's eye a somewhat sensational picture of an old, old Jewish woman who lived alone in her grand house in Portland Place and, with a finger in every pie, ruled her family with a despotic hand. She did not disappoint me. She was of a commanding presence, rather tall, and stout without being corpulent. Her countenance was markedly Hebraic. She wore a rather heavy moustache and a wig of a peculiarly metallic brown. Her dress was very grand, of black brocade, and she had a row of large diamond stars on her breast and round her neck a chain of diamonds. Diamond rings gleamed on her wrinkled hands. She spoke in a rather loud harsh voice and with a strong German accent. When I was introduced to her she fixed me with shining eyes. She summed me up with dispatch and to my fancy at all events made no attempt to conceal from me that the judgement she formed was unfavourable.

'You have known my brother Ferdinand for many years, is it not so?' she said, rolling a guttural R. 'My brother Ferdinand has always moved in very good society. Where is Sir Adolphus, Muriel? Does he know your guest is arrived? And will you not send for George? If he does not know his pieces by now he will not know them by tomorrow.'

Muriel explained that Freddy was finishing a round of golf with his secretary and that she had had George told I was there. Lady Bland looked as though she thought Muriel's replies highly unsatisfactory and turned again to me.

'My daughter tells me you have been in Italy?'

'Yes, I've only just come back.'

'It is a beautiful country. How is the King?'

I said I did not know.

'I used to know him when he was a little boy. He was not very strong then. His mother, Queen Margherita, was a great friend of mine. They thought he would never marry. The Duchess of Aosta was very angry when he fell in love with that Princess of Montenegro.'

She seemed to belong to some long past period of history, but she was very alert and I imagine that little escaped her beady eyes. Freddy, very spruce in plus fours, presently came in. It was amusing and yet a little touching to see this grey-bearded man, as a rule somewhat domineering, so obviously on his best behaviour with the old lady. He called her Mamma. Then George came in. He was as fat as ever, but he had taken my advice and had his hair cut; he was losing his boyish looks, but he was a powerful and well set-up young man. It was good to see the pleasure he took in his tea. He ate quantities of sandwiches and great hunks of cake. He had still a boy's appetite. His father watched him with a tender smile and as I looked at him I could not be surprised at the attachment which they all so obviously felt for him. He had an ingenuousness, a charm and an enthusiasm which were certainly very pleasant. There was about him a generosity of demeanour, a frankness and a natural cordiality which could not but make people take to him. I do not know whether it was owing to a hint from his grandmother or merely of his own good nature, but it was plain that he was going out of his way to be nice to his father; and in his father's soft eyes, in the way he hung upon the boy's words, in his pleased, proud and happy look, you felt how bitterly the estrangement of the last two years had weighed on him. He adored George.

We played golf in the morning, a three-ball match, since Muriel, having to go to Mass, could not join us, and at one Ferdy arrived in Lea Makart's car. We sat down to luncheon. Of course Lea Makart's reputation was well known to me. She was acknowledged to be the greatest woman pianist in Europe. She was a very old friend of Ferdy's who with his interest and patronage had greatly helped her at the beginning of her career, and it was he who had arranged for her to come and give her opinion of George's chances. At one time I went as often as I could to hear her play. She had no affectations; she played as a bird sings, without any appearance of effort, very naturally, and the silvery notes dripped from her light fingers in a curiously spontaneous manner, so that it gave you the impression that she was improvising those complicated rhythms. They used to tell me that her technique was wonderful. I could never make up my mind how much the delight her playing gave me was due to her person. In those days she was the most ethereal thing you could imagine, and it was surprising that a creature so sylphlike should be capable of so much power. She was very slight, pale, with enormous eyes and magnificent black hair, and at the piano she had a child-like wistfulness that was most appealing. She was very beautiful in a hardly human way and when she played, a little smile on her closed lips, she seemed to be remembering things she had heard in another world. Now, however, a woman in the early forties, she was sylphlike no more; she was stout and her face had broadened; she had no longer that lovely remoteness, but the authority of her long succession of triumphs. She was brisk, business-like and somewhat overwhelming. Her vitality lit her with a natural spotlight as his sanctity surrounds the saint with a halo. She was not interested in anything very much but her own affairs, but since she had humour and knew the world she was able to invest them with gaiety. She held the conversation, but did not absorb it. George talked little. Every now and then she gave him a glance, but did not try to draw him in. I was the only Gentile at the table. All but old Lady Bland spoke perfect English, yet I could not help feeling that they did not speak like English people; I think they rounded their vowels more than we do, they certainly spoke louder, and the words seemed not to fall, but to gush from their lips. I think if I had been in another room where I could hear the tone but not the words of their speech I should have thought it was in a foreign language that they were conversing. The effect was slightly disconcerting.

Lea Makart wished to set out for London at about six, so it was arranged that George should play at four. Whatever the result of the audition, I felt that I, a stranger in the circle which her departure must render exclusively domestic, would be in the way and so, pretexting an early engagement in town next morning, I asked her if she would take me with her in her car.

At a little before four we all wandered into the drawing-room. Old Lady Bland sat on a sofa with Ferdy; Freddy, Muriel and I made ourselves comfortable in arm-chairs; and Lea Makart sat by herself. She chose instinctively a high-backed Jacobean chair that had somewhat the air of a throne, and in a yellow dress, with her olive skin, she looked very handsome. She had magnificent eyes. She was very much made up and her mouth was scarlet.

George gave no sign of nervousness. He was already seated at the piano when I went in with his father and mother, and he watched us quietly settling ourselves down. He gave me the shadow of a smile. When he saw that we were all at our ease he began to play. He played Chopin. He played two waltzes that were familiar to me, a polonaise and an *étude*. He played with a great deal of *brio*. I wish I knew music well enough to give an exact description of his playing. It had strength, and a youthful exuberance, but I felt that he missed what to me is the peculiar charm of Chopin, the tenderness, the nervous melancholy, the wistful gaiety and the slightly faded romance that reminds me always of an Early Victorian keepsake. And again I had the vague sensation, so slight that it almost escaped me, that the two hands did not quite synchronize. I looked at Ferdy and saw him give his sister a look of faint surprise, Muriel's eyes were fixed on the pianist, but presently she dropped them and for the rest of the time stared at the floor. His father looked at him too, and his eyes were steadfast, but unless I was much mistaken he went pale and his face betrayed something like dismay. Music was in the blood of all of them, all their lives they had heard the greatest pianists in the world, and they judged with instinctive precision. The only person whose face betrayed no emotion was Lea Makart. She listened very attentively. She was as still as an image in a niche.

At last he stopped and turning round on his seat faced her. He did not speak.

'What is it you want me to tell you?' she asked.

They looked into one another's eyes.

'I want you to tell me whether I have any chance of becoming in time a pianist in the first rank.'

'Not in a thousand years.'

For a moment there was a dead silence. Freddy's head sank and he looked down at the carpet at his feet. His wife put out her hand and took his. But George continued to look steadily at Lea Makart.

'Ferdy has told me the circumstances,' she said at last. 'Don't think I'm influenced by them. Nothing of this is very important.' She made a great sweeping gesture that took in the magnificent room with the beautiful things it contained and all of us. 'If I thought you had in you the makings of an artist I shouldn't hesitate to beseech you to give up everything for art's sake. Art is the only thing that matters. In comparison with art, wealth and rank and power are not worth a row of pins.' She gave us a look so sincere that it was void of insolence. 'We are the only people who count. We give the world significance. You are only our raw material.'

I was not too pleased to be included with the rest under that heading, but that is neither here nor there.

'Of course I can see that you've worked very hard. Don't think it's been wasted. It will always be a pleasure to you to be able to play the piano and it will enable you to appreciate great playing as no ordinary person can hope to do. Look at your hands. They're not a pianist's hands.'

Involuntarily I glanced at George's hands. I had never noticed them before. I was astounded to see how podgy they were and how short and stumpy the fingers.

'Your ear is not quite perfect. I don't think you can ever hope to be more than a very competent amateur. In art the difference between the amateur and the professional is immeasurable.'

George did not reply. Except for his pallor no one would have known that he was listening to the blasting of all his hopes. The silence that fell was quite awful. Lea Makart's eyes suddenly filled with tears.

'But don't take my opinion alone,' she said. 'After all, I'm not infallible. Ask somebody else. You know how good and generous Paderewski is. I'll write to him about you and you can go down and play to him. I'm sure he'll hear you.'

George now gave a little smile. He had very good manners and whatever he was feeling did not want to make the situation too difficult for others.

'I don't think that's necessary, I am content to accept your verdict. To tell you the truth it's not so very different from my master's in Munich.'

He got up from the piano and lit a cigarette. It eased the strain. The others moved a little in their chairs. Lea Makart smiled at George.

'Shall I play to you?' she said.

'Yes, do.'

She got up and went to the piano. She took off the rings with which her fingers were laden. She played Bach. I do not know the names of the pieces, but I recognized the stiff ceremonial of the frenchified little German courts and the sober, thrifty comfort of the burghers, and the dancing on the village green, the green trees that looked like Christmas trees, and the sunlight on the wide German country, and a tender cosiness; and in my nostrils there was a warm scent of the soil and I was conscious of a sturdy strength that seemed to have its roots deep in mother earth, and of an elemental power that was timeless and had no home in space. She played exquisitely, with a soft brilliance that made you think of the full moon shining at dusk in the summer sky. With another part of me I watched the others and I saw how intensely they were conscious of the experience. They were rapt. I wished with all my heart that I could get from music the wonderful exaltation that possessed them. She stopped, a smile hovered on her lips, and she put on her rings. George gave a little chuckle.

'That clinches it, I fancy,' he said.

The servants brought in tea and after tea Lea Makart and I bade the company farewell and got into the car. We drove up to London. She talked all the way, if not brilliantly at all events with immense gusto; she told me of her early years in Manchester and of the struggle of her beginnings. She was very interesting. She never even mentioned George; the episode was of no consequence; it was finished and she thought of it no more.

We little knew what was happening at Tilby. When we left George went out on the terrace and presently his father joined him. Freddy had won the day, but he was not happy. With his more than feminine sensitiveness he felt all that George was feeling, and George's anguish simply broke his heart. He had never loved his son more than then. When he appeared George greeted him with a little smile. Freddy's voice broke. In a sudden and overwhelming emotion he found it in him to surrender the fruits of his victory.

'Look here, old boy,' he said, 'I can't bear to think that you've had such a disappointment. Would you like to go back to Munich for another year and then see?'

George shook his head.

'No, it wouldn't be any good. I've had my chance. Let's call it a day.'

'Try not to take it too hard.'

'You see, the only thing in the world I want is to be a pianist. And there's nothing doing. It's a bit thick if you come to think of it.'

George, trying so hard to be brave, smiled wanly.

'Would you like to go round the world? You can get one of your Oxford pals to go with you and I'll pay all the expenses. You've been working very hard for a long time.'

'Thanks awfully, daddy, we'll talk about it. I'm just going for a stroll now.'

'Shall I come with you?'

'I'd rather go alone.'

Then George did a strange thing. He put his arm round his father's neck, and kissed him on the lips. He gave a funny little moved laugh and walked away. Freddy went back to the drawing-room. His mother, Ferdy and Muriel were sitting there.

'Freddy, why don't you marry the boy?' said the old lady. 'He is twenty-three. It would take his mind off his troubles and when he is married and has a baby he will soon settle down like everybody else.'

'Whom is he to marry, Mamma?' asked Sir Adolphus, smiling.

'That's not so difficult. Lady Frielinghausen came to see me the other day with her daughter Violet. She is a very nice maiden and she will have money of her own. Lady Frielinghausen gave me to understand that her Sir Jacob would come down very handsome if Violet made a good match.'

Muriel flushed.

'I hate Lady Frielinghausen. George is much too young to marry. He can afford to marry anyone he likes.'

Old Lady Bland gave her daughter a strange look.

'You are a very foolish girl, Miriam,' she said, using the name Muriel had long discarded. 'As long as I am here I shall not allow you to commit a foolishness.'

She knew as well as if Muriel had said it in so many words that she wanted George to marry a Gentile, but she knew also that so long as she was alive neither Freddy nor his wife would dare to suggest it.

But George did not go for a walk. Perhaps because the shooting season was about to open he took it into his head to go into the gun-room. He began to clean the gun that his mother had given him on his twentieth birthday. No one had used it since he went to Germany. Suddenly the servants were startled by a report. When they went into the gun-room they found George lying on the floor shot through the heart. Apparently the gun had been loaded and George while playing about with it had accidentally shot himself. One reads of such accidents in the paper often.

FROM

Ah King

(1933)

The Door of Opportunity

They got a first-class carriage to themselves. It was lucky, because they were taking a good deal in with them, Alban's suit-case and a hold-all, Anne's dressing-case and her hat-box. They had two trunks in the van, containing what they wanted immediately, but all the rest of their luggage Alban had put in the care of an agent who was to take it up to London and store it till they had made up their minds what to do. They had a lot, pictures and books, curios that Alban had collected in the East, his guns and saddles. They had left Sondurah for ever. Alban, as was his way, tipped the porter generously and then went to the bookstall and bought papers. He bought the *New Statesman* and the *Nation*, and the *Tatler* and the *Sketch*, and the last number of the *London Mercury*. He came back to the carriage and threw them on the seat.

'It's only an hour's journey,' said Anne.

'I know, but I wanted to buy them. I've been starved so long. Isn't it grand to think that tomorrow morning we shall have tomorrow's *Times*, and the *Express* and the *Mail*?'

She did not answer and he turned away, for he saw coming towards them two persons, a man and his wife, who had been fellow-passengers from Singapore.

'Get through the customs all right?' he cried to them cheerily.

The man seemed not to hear, for he walked straight on, but the woman answered.

'Yes, they never found the cigarettes.'

She saw Anne, gave her a friendly little smile, and passed on. Anne flushed.

'I was afraid they'd want to come in here,' said Alban. 'Let's have the carriage to ourselves if we can.'

She looked at him curiously.

'I don't think you need worry,' she answered. 'I don't think anyone will come in.'

He lit a cigarette and lingered at the carriage door. On his face was a happy smile. When they had passed through the Red Sea and found a sharp wind in the Canal, Anne had been surprised to see how much the men who had looked presentable enough in the white ducks in which she had been accustomed to see them, were changed when they left them off for warmer clothes. They looked like nothing on earth then. Their ties were awful and their shirts all wrong. They wore grubby flannel trousers and shabby old golf-coats that had too obviously been bought off the nail, or blue serge suits that betrayed the provincial tailor. Most of the passengers had got off at Marseilles, but a dozen or so, either because after a long period in the East they thought the trip through the Bay would do them good, or, like themselves, for economy's sake, had gone all the way to Tilbury, and now several of them walked along the platform. They wore solar topis or double-brimmed terais, and heavy great-coats, or else shapeless soft hats or bowlers, not too well brushed, that looked too small for them. It was a shock to see them. They looked suburban and a trifle second-rate. But Alban had already a London look. There was not a speck of dust on his smart greatcoat, and his black Homburg hat looked brand-new. You would never have guessed that he had not been home for three years. His collar fitted closely round his neck and his foulard tie was neatly tied. As Anne looked at him she could not but think how good-looking he was. He was just under six feet tall, and slim, and he wore his clothes well, and his clothes were well cut. He had fair hair, still thick, and blue eyes and the faintly yellow skin common to men of that complexion after they have lost the pink-and-white freshness of early youth. There was no colour in his cheeks. It was a fine head, well-set on rather a long neck, with a somewhat prominent Adam's apple; but you were more impressed with the distinction than with the beauty of his face. It was because his features were so regular, his nose so straight, his brow so broad that he photographed so well. Indeed, from his photographs you would have thought him extremely handsome. He was not that, perhaps because his eyebrows and his eyelashes were pale, and his lips thin, but he looked very intellectual. There was refinement in his face and a spirituality that was oddly moving. That was how you thought a poet should look; and when Anne became engaged to him she told her girl friends who asked her about him that he looked like Shelley. He turned to her now with a little smile in his blue eyes. His smile was very attractive.

'What a perfect day to land in England!'

It was October. They had steamed up the Channel on a grey sea under a grey sky. There was not a breath of wind. The fishing boats seemed to rest on the placid water as though the elements had for ever forgotten their old hostility. The coast was incredibly green, but with a bright cosy greenness quite unlike the luxuriant, vehement verdure of Eastern jungles. The red towns they passed here and there were comfortable and homelike. They seemed to welcome the exiles with a smiling friend-liness. And when they drew into the estuary of the Thames they saw the rich levels of Essex and in a little while Chalk Church on the Kentish shore, lonely in the midst of weather-beaten trees, and beyond it the woods of Cobham. The sun, red in a faint mist, set on the marshes, and night fell. In the station the arc-lamps shed a light that spotted the darkness with cold hard patches. It was good to see the porters lumbering about in their grubby uniforms and the station-master fat and important in his bowler hat. The station-master blew a whistle and waved his arm. Alban stepped into the carriage and seated himself in the corner opposite to Anne. The train started.

'We're due in London at six-ten,' said Alban. 'We ought to get to Jermyn Street by seven. That'll give us an hour to bath and change and we can get to the Savoy for dinner by eight-thirty. A bottle of pop tonight, my pet, and a slap-up dinner.' He gave a chuckle. 'I heard the Strouds and the Maundys arranging to meet at the Trocadero Grill-Room.'

He took up the papers and asked if she wanted any of them. Anne shook her head.

'Tired?' he smiled.

'No.'

'Excited?'

In order not to answer she gave a little laugh. He

began to look at the papers, starting with the publishers' advertisements, and she was conscious of the intense satisfaction it was to him to feel himself through them once more in the middle of things. They had taken in those same papers in Sondurah, but they arrived six weeks old, and though they kept them abreast of what was going on in the world that interested them both, they emphasized their exile. But these were fresh from the press. They smelt different. They had a crispness that was almost voluptuous. He wanted to read them all at once. Anne looked out of the window. The country was dark, and she could see little but the lights of their carriage reflected on the glass, but very soon the town encroached upon it, and then she saw little sordid houses, mile upon mile of them, with a light in a window here and there, and the chimneys made a dreary pattern against the sky. They passed through Barking and East Ham and Bromley – it was silly that the name on the platform as they went through the station should give her such a tremor – and then Stepney. Alban put down his papers.

'We shall be there in five minutes now.'

He put on his hat and took down from the racks the things the porter had put in them. He looked at her with shining eyes and his lips twitched. She saw that he was only just able to control his emotion. He looked out of the window, too, and they passed over brightly lighted thoroughfares, close packed with tram-cars, buses and motor-vans, and they saw the streets thick with people. What a mob! The shops were all lit up. They saw the hawkers with their barrows at the curb.

'London,' he said.

He took her hand and gently pressed it. His smile was so sweet that she had to say something. She tried to be facetious.

'Does it make you feel all funny inside?'

'I don't know if I want to cry or if I want to be sick.'

Fenchurch Street. He lowered the window and waved his arm for a porter. With a grinding of brakes the train came to a standstill. A porter opened the door and Alban handed him out one package after another. Then in his polite way, having jumped out, he gave his hand to Anne to help her down to the platform. The porter went to fetch a barrow and they stood by the pile of their luggage. Alban waved to two passengers from the ship who passed them. The man nodded stiffly.

'What a comfort it is that we shall never have to be civil to those awful people any more,' said Alban lightly.

Anne gave him a quick glance. He was really incomprehensible. The porter came back with his barrow, the luggage was put on and they followed him to collect their trunks. Alban took his wife's arm and pressed it.

'The smell of London. By God, it's grand.'

He rejoiced in the noise and the bustle, and the crowd of people who jostled them; the radiance of the arc-lamps and the black shadows they cast, sharp but full-toned, gave him a sense of elation. They got out into the street and the porter went off to get them a taxi. Alban's eyes glittered as he looked at the buses and the policemen trying to direct the confusion. His distinguished face bore a look of something like inspiration. The taxi came. Their luggage was stowed away and piled up

beside the driver, Alban gave the porter half-a-
crown, and they drove off. They turned down
Gracechurch Street and in Cannon Street were
held up by a block in the traffic. Alban laughed out
loud.

'What's the matter?' said Anne.

'I'm so excited.'

They went along the Embankment. It was
relatively quiet there. Taxis and cars passed them.
The bells of the trams were music in his ears. At
Westminster Bridge they cut across Parliament
Square and drove through the green silence of St
James's Park. They had engaged a room at a hotel
just off Jermyn Street. The reception clerk took
them upstairs and a porter brought up their
luggage. It was a room with twin beds and a
bathroom.

'This looks all right,' said Alban. 'It'll do us till
we can find a flat or something.'

He looked at his watch.

'Look here, darling, we shall only fall over one
another if we try to unpack together. We've got
oodles of time and it'll take you longer to get
straight and dress than me. I'll clear out. I want to
go to the club and see if there's any mail for me. I've
got my dinner-jacket in my suit-case and it'll only
take me twenty minutes to have a bath and dress.
Does that suit you?'

'Yes. That's all right.'

'I'll be back in an hour.'

'Very well.'

He took out of his pocket the little comb he
always carried and passed it through his long fair
hair. Then he put on his hat. He gave himself a
glance in the mirror.

'Shall I turn on the bath for you?'

'No, don't bother.'

'All right. So long.'

He went out.

When he was gone Anne took her dressing-case and her hat-box and put them on the top of her trunk. Then she rang the bell. She did not take off her hat. She sat down and lit a cigarette. When a servant answered the bell she asked for the porter. He came. She pointed to the luggage.

'Will you take those things and leave them in the hall for the present. I'll tell you what to do with them presently.'

'Very good, ma'am.'

She gave him a florin. He took the trunk out and the other packages and closed the door behind him. A few tears slid down Anne's cheeks, but she shook herself; she dried her eyes and powdered her face. She needed all her calm. She was glad that Alban had conceived the idea of going to his club. It made things easier and gave her a little time to think them out.

Now that the moment had come to do what she had for weeks determined, now that she must say the terrible things she had to say, she quailed. Her heart sank. She knew exactly what she meant to say to Alban, she had made up her mind about that long ago, and had said the very words to herself a hundred times, three or four times a day every day of the long journey from Singapore, but she was afraid that she would grow confused. She dreaded an argument. The thought of a scene made her feel slightly sick. It was something at all events to have an hour in which to collect herself. He would say she was heartless and ·cruel and unreasonable. She could not help it.

'No, no, no,' she cried aloud.

She shuddered with horror. And all at once she saw herself again in the bungalow, sitting as she had been sitting when the whole thing started. It was getting on towards tiffin time and in a few minutes Alban would be back from the office. It gave her pleasure to reflect that it was an attractive room for him to come back to, the large veranda which was their parlour, and she knew that though they had been there eighteen months he was still alive to the success she had made of it. The jalousies were drawn now against the midday sun and the mellowed light filtering through them gave an impression of cool silence. Anne was house-proud, and though they were moved from district to district according to the exigencies of the Service and seldom stayed anywhere very long, at each new post she started with new enthusiasm to make their house cosy and charming. She was very modern. Visitors were surprised because there were no knick-knacks. They were taken aback by the bold colour of her curtains and could not at all make out the tinted reproductions of pictures by Marie Laurencin and Gauguin in silvered frames which were placed on the walls with such cunning skill. She was conscious that few of them quite approved and the good ladies of Port Wallace and Pemberton thought such arrangements odd, affected and out of place; but this left her calm. They would learn. It did them good to get a bit of a jolt. And now she looked round the long, spacious veranda with the complacent sigh of the artist satisfied with his work. It was gay. It was bare. It was restful. It refreshed the spirit and gently excited the fancy. Three immense bowls of yellow cannas completed the colour scheme. Her eyes lingered for a moment on the book-shelves filled with books; that was another thing that disconcerted the colony, all the books they had, and strange books too, heavy they thought them for the most part; and she gave them a little affectionate look as though they were living things. Then she gave the piano a glance. A piece of music was still open on the rack, it was something of Debussy, and Alban had been playing it before he went to the office.

Her friends in the colony had condoled with her when Alban was appointed DO at Daktar, for it was the most isolated district in Sondurah. It was connected with the town which was the headquarters of the Government neither by telegraph nor telephone. But she liked it. They had been there for some time and she hoped they would remain till Alban went home on leave in another twelve months. It was as large as an English county, with a long coast-line, and the sea was dotted with little islands. A broad, winding river ran through it and on each side of this stretched hills densely covered with virgin forest. The station, a good way up the river, consisted of a row of Chinese shops and a native village nestling amid coconut trees, the District Office, the DO's bungalow, the Clerk's quarters and the barracks. Their only neighbours were the manager of a rubber estate a few miles up the river and the manager and his assistant, Dutchmen both, of a timber camp on one of the river's tributaries. The rubber estate's launch went up and down twice a month and was their only means of regular communication with the outside world. But though they were lonely they were not dull. Their days were full. Their ponies waited for them at dawn and they rode while the day was still fresh and in the bridle-paths through the jungle lingered the mystery of the tropical night. They came back, bathed, changed and had breakfast, and Alban went to the office. Anne spent the morning writing letters and working. She had fallen in love with the country from the first day she arrived in it and had taken pains to master the common language spoken. Her imagination was inflamed by the stories she heard of love and jealousy and death. She was told romantic tales of a time that was only just past. She sought to steep herself in the lore of those strange people. Both she and Alban read a great deal. They had for the country a considerable library and new books came from London by nearly every mail. Little that was noteworthy escaped them. Alban was fond of playing the piano. For an amateur he played very well. He had studied rather seriously, and he had an agreeable touch and a good ear; he could read music with ease, and it was always a pleasure to Anne to sit by him and follow the score when he tried something new. But their great delight was to tour the district. Sometimes they would be away for a fortnight at a time. They would go down the river in a prahu and then sail from one little island to another, bathe in the sea, and fish, or else row upstream till it grew shallow and the trees on either bank were so close to one another that you only saw a slim strip of sky between. Here the boatmen had to pole and they would spend the night in a native house. They bathed in a river pool so clear that you could see the sand shining silver at the bottom; and the spot was so lovely, so peaceful and remote, that you felt you could stay there for ever. Sometimes, on the other hand, they would tramp for days along the jungle paths, sleeping under canvas, and notwithstanding the mosquitoes that tormented them and the leeches that sucked their blood, enjoy every moment. Whoever slept so well as on a camp bed? And then there was the gladness of getting back, the delight in the comfort of the well-ordered establishment, the mail that had arrived with letters from home and all the papers, and the piano.

Alban would sit down to it then, his fingers itching to feel the keys, and in what he played, Stravinsky, Ravel, Darius, Miehaud, she seemed to feel that he put in something of his own, the sounds of the jungle at night, dawn over the estuary, the starry nights and the crystal clearness of the forest pools.

Sometimes the rain fell in sheets for days at a time. Then Alban worked at Chinese. He was learning it so that he could communicate with the Chinese of the country in their own language, and Anne did the thousand-and-one things for which she had not had time before. Those days brought them even more closely together; they always had plenty to talk about, and when they were occupied with their separate affairs they were pleased to feel in their bones that they were near to one another. They were wonderfully united. The rainy days that shut them up within the walls of the bungalow made them feel as if they were one body in face of the world.

On occasion they went to Port Wallace. It was a

change, but Anne was always glad to get home. She was never quite at her ease there. She was conscious that none of the people they met liked Alban. They were very ordinary people, middle-class and suburban and dull, without any of the intellectual interests that made life so full and varied to Alban and her, and many of them were narrow-minded and ill-natured; but since they had to pass the better part of their lives in contact with them, it was tiresome that they should feel so unkindly towards Alban. They said he was conceited. He was always very pleasant with them, but she was aware that they resented his cordiality. When he tried to be jovial they said he was putting on airs, and when he chaffed them they thought he was being funny at their expense.

Once they stayed at Government House, and Mrs Hannay, the Governor's wife, who liked her, talked to her about it. Perhaps the Governor had suggested that she should give Anne a hint.

'You know, my dear, it's a pity your husband doesn't try to be more come-hither with people. He's very intelligent; don't you think it would be better if he didn't let others see he knows it quite so clearly? My husband said to me only yesterday: of course I know Alban Torel is the cleverest young man in the Service, but he does manage to put my back up more than anyone I know. I am the Governor, but when he talks to me he always gives me the impression that he looks upon me as a damned fool.'

The worst of it was that Anne knew how low an opinion Alban had of the Governor's parts.

'He doesn't mean to be superior,' Anne answered, smiling. 'And he really isn't in the least conceited. I think it's only because he has a straight nose and high cheek-bones.'

'You know, they don't like him at the club. They call him Powder-Puff Percy.'

Anne flushed. She had heard that before and it made her very angry. Her eyes filled with tears.

'I think it's frightfully unfair.'

Mrs Hannay took her hand and gave it an affectionate little squeeze.

'My dear, you know I don't want to hurt your feelings. Your husband can't help rising very high in the Service. He'd make things so much easier for himself if he were a little more human. Why doesn't he play football?'

'It's not his game. He's always only too glad to play tennis.'

'He doesn't give that impression. He gives the impression that there's no one here who's worth his while to play with.'

'Well, there isn't,' said Anne, stung.

Alban happened to be an extremely good tennis-player. He had played a lot of tournaments in England and Anne knew that it gave him a grim satisfaction to knock those beefy, hearty men all over the court. He could make the best of them look foolish. He could be maddening on the tennis court and Anne was aware that sometimes he could not resist the temptation.

'He does play to the gallery, doesn't he?' said Mrs Hannay.

'I don't think so. Believe me, Alban has no idea he isn't popular. As far as I can see he's always pleasant and friendly with everybody.'

'It's then he's most offensive,' said Mrs Hannay dryly.

'I know people don't like us very much,' said Anne, smiling a little. 'I'm very sorry, but really I don't know what we can do about it.'

'Not you, my dear,' cried Mrs Hannay. 'Everybody adores you. That's why they put up with your husband. My dear, who could help liking you?'

'I don't know why they should adore me,' said Anne.

But she did not say it quite sincerely. She was deliberately playing the part of the dear little woman and within her she bubbled with amusement. They disliked Alban because he had such an air of distinction, and because he was interested in art and literature; they did not understand these things and so thought them unmanly; and they disliked him because his capacity was greater than theirs. They disliked him because he was better bred than they. They thought him superior; well, he was superior, but not in the sense they meant. They forgave her because she was an ugly little thing. That was what she called herself, but she wasn't that, or if she was it was with an ugliness that was most attractive. She was like a little monkey, but a very sweet little monkey and very human. She had a neat figure. That was her best point. That and her eyes. They were very large, of a deep brown, liquid and shining; they were full of fun, but they could be tender on occasion with a charming sympathy. She was dark, her frizzy hair was almost black, and her skin was swarthy; she had a small fleshy nose, with large nostrils, and much too big a mouth. But she was alert and vivacious. She could talk with a show of real interest to the ladies of the colony about their husbands and their servants and their children in England, and she could listen appreciatively to the men who told her stories that she had often heard before. They thought her a jolly good sort. They did not know what clever fun she made of them in private. It never occurred to them that she thought them narrow, gross and pretentious. They found no glamour in the East because they looked at it vulgarly with material eyes. Romance lingered at their threshold and they drove it away like an importunate beggar. She was aloof. She repeated to herself Landor's line:

'Nature I loved, and next to nature, art.'

She reflected on her conversation with Mrs Hannay, but on the whole it left her unconcerned. She wondered whether she should say anything about it to Alban; it had always seemed a little odd to her that he should be so little aware of his unpopularity; but she was afraid that if she told him of it he would become self-conscious. He never noticed the coldness of the men at the club. He made them feel shy and therefore uncomfortable. His appearance then caused a sort of awkwardness, but he, happily insensible, was breezily cordial to all and sundry. The fact was that he was strangely unconscious of other people. She was in a class by herself, she and a little group of friends they had in London, but he could never quite realize that the people of the colony, the government officials and the planters and their wives, were human beings. They were to him like pawns in a game. He laughed with them, chaffed them, and was amiably tolerant of them; with a chuckle Anne told herself that he was rather like the master of a preparatory school taking little boys out on a picnic and anxious to give them a good time.

She was afraid it wasn't much good telling Alban. He was incapable of the dissimulation which, she happily realized, came so easily to her. What was one to do with these people? The men had come out to the colony as lads from second-rate schools, and life had taught them nothing. At fifty they had the outlook of hobbledehoys. Most of them drank a great deal too much. They read nothing worth reading. Their ambition was to be like everybody else. Their highest praise was to say that a man was a damned good sort. If you were interested in the things of the spirit you were a prig. They were eaten up with envy of one another and devoured by petty jealousies. And the women, poor things, were obsessed by petty rivalries. They made a circle that was more provincial than any in the smallest town in England. They were prudish and spiteful. What did it matter if they did not like Alban? They would have to put up with him because his ability was so great. He was clever and energetic. They could not say that he did not do his work well. He had been successful in every post he had occupied. With his sensitiveness and his imagination he understood the native mind and he was able to get the natives to do things that no one in his position could. He had a gift for languages, and he spoke all the local dialects. He not only knew the common tongue that most of the government officials spoke, but was acquainted with the niceties of the language and on occasion could make use of a ceremonial speech that flattered and impressed the chiefs. He had a gift for organization. He was not afraid of responsibility. In due course he was bound to be made a Resident. Alban had some interest in England; his father was a brigadier-general killed in the war, and though he had no private means he had influential friends. He spoke of them with pleasant irony.

'The great advantage of democratic government,' he said, 'is that merit, with influence to back it, can be pretty sure of receiving its due reward.'

Alban was so obviously the ablest man in the Service that there seemed no reason why he should not eventually be made Governor. Then, thought Anne, his air of superiority, of which they complained, would be in place. They would accept him as their master and he would know how to make himself respected and obeyed. The position she foresaw did not dazzle her. She accepted it as a right. It would be fun for Alban to be Governor and for her to be the Governor's wife. And what an opportunity! They were sheep, the government servants and the planters; when Government House was the seat of culture they would soon fall into line. When the best way to the Governor's favour was to be intelligent, intelligence would become the fashion. She and Alban would cherish the native arts and collect carefully the memorials of a vanished past. The country would make an advance it had never dreamed of. They would develop it, but along lines of order and beauty. They would instil into their subordinates a passion for that beautiful land and a loving interest in these romantic races. They would make them realize what music meant. They would cultivate literature. They would create beauty. It would be the golden age.

Suddenly she heard Alban's footstep. Anne awoke from her day-dream. All that was far away in the future. Alban was only a District Officer yet and what was important was the life they were living now. She heard Alban go into the bath-house and splash water over himself. In a minute he came in. He had changed into a shirt and shorts. His fair hair was still wet.

'Tiffin ready?' he asked.

'Yes.'

He sat down at the piano and played the piece that he had played in the morning. The silvery notes cascaded coolly down the sultry air. You had an impression of a formal garden with great trees and elegant pieces of artificial water and of leisurely walks bordered with pseudo-classical statues. Alban played with an exquisite delicacy. Lunch was announced by the head boy. He rose from the piano. They walked into the dining-room hand in hand. A punkah lazily fanned the air. Anne gave the table a glance. With its bright-coloured tablecloth and the amusing plates it looked very gay.

'Anything exciting at the office this morning?' she asked.

'No, nothing much. A buffalo case. Oh, and Prynne has sent along to ask me to go up to the estate. Some coolies have been damaging the trees and he wants me to come along and look into it.'

Prynne was manager of the rubber estate up the river and now and then they spent a night with him. Sometimes when he wanted a change he came down to dinner and slept at the DO's bungalow. They both liked him. He was a man of five-and-thirty, with a red face, with deep furrows in it, and very black hair. He was quite uneducated, but cheerful and easy, and being the only Englishman within two days' journey they could not but be friendly with him. He had been a little shy of them at first. News spreads quickly in the East and long before they arrived in the district he heard that they were highbrows. He did not know what he would make of them. He probably did not know that he had charm, which makes up for many more commendable qualities, and Alban with his almost feminine sensibilities was peculiarly susceptible to this. He found Alban much more human than he expected, and of course Anne was stunning. Alban played ragtime for him, which he would not have done for the Governor, and played dominoes with him. When Alban was making his first tour of the district with Anne, and suggested that they would like to spend a couple of nights on the estate, he had thought it as well to warn him that he lived with a native woman and had two children by her. He would do his best to keep them out of Anne's sight, but he could not send them away, there was nowhere to send them. Alban laughed.

'Anne isn't that sort of woman at all. Don't dream of hiding them. She loves children.'

Anne quickly made friends with the shy, pretty little native woman and soon was playing happily with the children. She and the girl had long confidential chats. The children took a fancy to her. She brought them lovely toys from Port Wallace. Prynne, comparing her smiling tolerance with the disapproving acidity of the other white women of the colony, described himself as knocked all of a heap. He could not do enough to show his delight and gratitude.

'If all highbrows are like you,' he said, 'give me highbrows every time.'

He hated to think that in another year they would leave the district for good and the chances were that if the next DO was married, his wife would think it dreadful that, rather than live alone, he had a native woman to live with him and, what was more, was much attached to her.

But there had been a good deal of discontent on the estate of late. The coolies were Chinese and infected with communist ideas. They were disorderly. Alban had been obliged to sentence several of them for various crimes to terms of imprisonment.

'Prynne tells me that as soon as their term is up he's going to send them all back to China and get Javanese instead,' said Alban. 'I'm sure he's right. They're much more amenable.'

'You don't think there's going to be any serious trouble?'

'Oh, no. Prynne knows his job and he's a pretty determined fellow. He wouldn't put up with any nonsense and with me and our policemen to back him up I don't imagine they'll try any monkey tricks.' He smiled. 'The iron hand in the velvet glove.'

The words were barely out of his mouth when a sudden shouting arose. There was a commotion and the sounds of steps. Loud voices and cries.

'Tuan, Tuan.'

'What the devil's the matter?'

Alban sprang from his chair and went swiftly on to the veranda. Anne followed him. At the bottom of the steps was a group of natives. There was the sergeant, and three or four policeman, boatmen and several men from the kampong.

'What is it?' called Alban.

Two or three shouted back in answer. The sergeant pushed others aside and Alban saw lying on the ground a man in a shirt and khaki shorts. He ran down the steps. He recognized the man as the assistant manager of Prynne's estate. He was a half-caste. His shorts were covered with blood and there was clotted blood all over one side of his face and head. He was unconscious.

'Bring him up here,' called Anne.

Alban gave an order. The man was lifted up and carried on to the veranda. They laid him on the floor and Anne put a pillow under his head. She sent for water and for the medicine-chest in which they kept things for emergency.

'Is he dead?' asked Alban.

'No.'

'Better try to give him some brandy.'

The boatmen brought ghastly news. The Chinese coolies had risen suddenly and attacked the manager's office. Prynne was killed and the assistant manager, Oakley by name, had escaped only by the skin of his teeth. He had come upon the rioters when they were looting the office, he had seen Prynne's body thrown out of the window, and had taken to his heels. Some of the Chinese saw him and gave chase. He ran for the river and was wounded as he jumped into the launch. The launch managed to put off before the Chinese could get on board and they had come downstream for help as fast as they could go. As they went they saw flames rising from the office buildings. There was no doubt that the coolies had burned down everything that would burn.

Oakley gave a groan and opened his eyes. He was a little dark-skinned man, with flattened features and thick coarse hair. His great native eyes were filled with terror.

'You're all right,' said Anne. 'You're quite safe.'

He gave a sigh and smiled. Anne washed his face and swabbed it with antiseptics. The wound on his head was not serious.

'Can you speak yet?' said Alban.

'Wait a bit,' she said. 'We must look at his leg.'

Alban ordered the sergeant to get the crowd out of the veranda. Anne ripped up one leg of the shorts. The material was clinging to the coagulated wound.

'I've been bleeding like a pig,' said Oakley.

It was only a flesh wound. Alban was clever with his fingers, and though the blood began to flow again they stanched it. Alban put on a dressing and a bandage. The sergeant and a policeman lifted Oakley on to a long chair. Alban gave him a brandy and soda, and soon he felt strong enough to speak. He knew no more than the boatmen had already told. Prynne was dead and the estate was in flames.

'And the girl and the children?' asked Anne.

'I don't know.'

'Oh, Alban.'

'I must turn out the police. Are you sure Prynne is dead?'

'Yes, sir. I saw him.'

'Have the rioters got fire-arms?'

'I don't know, sir.'

'How d'you mean, you don't know?' Alban cried irritably. 'Prynne had a gun, hadn't he?'

'Yes, sir.'

'There must have been more on the estate. You had one, didn't you? The head overseer had one.'

The half-caste was silent. Alban looked at him sternly.

'How many of those damned Chinese are there?'

'A hundred and fifty.'

Anne wondered that he asked so many questions. It seemed waste of time. The important thing was to collect coolies for the transport up-river, prepare the boats and issue ammunition to the police.

'How many policemen have you got, sir?' asked Oakley.

'Eight and the sergeant.'

'Could I come too? That would make ten of us. I'm sure I shall be all right now I'm bandaged.'

'I'm not going,' said Alban.

'Alban, you must,' cried Anne. She could not believe her ears.

'Nonsense. It would be madness. Oakley's obviously useless. He's sure to have a temperature in a few hours. He'd only be in the way. That leaves nine guns. There are a hundred and fifty Chinese and they've got fire-arms and all the ammunition in the world.'

'How d'you know?'

'It stands to reason they wouldn't have started a show like this unless they had. It would be idiotic to go.'

Anne stared at him with open mouth. Oakley's eyes were puzzled.

'What are you going to do?'

'Well, fortunately we've got the launch. I'll send it to Port Wallace with a request for reinforcements.'

'But they won't be here for two days at least.'

'Well, what of it? Prynne's dead and the estate burned to the ground. We couldn't do any good by going up now. I shall send a native to reconnoitre so that we can find out exactly what the rioters are doing.' He gave Anne his charming smile. 'Believe me, my pet, the rascals won't lose anything by waiting a day or two for what's coming to them.'

Oakley opened his mouth to speak, but perhaps he hadn't the nerve. He was a half-caste assistant manager and Alban, the DO, represented the power of the Government. But the man's eyes sought Anne's and she thought she read in them an earnest and personal appeal.

'But in two days they're capable of committing the most frightful atrocities,' she cried. 'It's quite unspeakable what they may do.'

'Whatever damage they do they'll pay for. I promise you that.'

'Oh, Alban, you can't sit still and do nothing. I beseech you to go yourself at once.'

'Don't be silly. I can't quell a riot with eight policemen and a sergeant. I haven't got the right to take a risk of that sort. We'd have to go in boats. You don't think we could get up unobserved. The lalang along the banks is perfect cover and they could just take pot shots at us as we came along. We shouldn't have a chance.'

'I'm afraid they'll only think it weakness if nothing is done for two days, sir,' said Oakley.

'When I want your opinion I'll ask for it,' said Alban acidly. 'So far as I can see when there was danger the only thing you did was to cut and run. I can't persuade myself that your assistance in a crisis would be very valuable.'

The half-caste reddened. He said nothing more. He looked straight in front of him with troubled eyes.

'I'm going down to the office,' said Alban. 'I'll just write a short report and send it down the river by launch at once.'

He gave an order to the sergeant who had been standing all this time stiffly at the top of the steps. He saluted and ran off. Alban went into a little hall they had to get his topi. Anne swiftly followed him.

'Alban, for God's sake listen to me a minute,' she whispered.

'I don't want to be rude to you, darling, but I am pressed for time. I think you'd much better mind your own business.'

'You can't do nothing, Alban. You must go. Whatever the risk.'

'Don't be such a fool,' he said angrily.

He had never been angry with her before. She seized his hand to hold him back.

'I tell you I can do no good by going.'

'You don't know. There's the woman and Prynne's children. We must do something to save them. Let me come with you. They'll kill them.'

'They've probably killed them already.'

'Oh, how can you be so callous! If there's a chance of saving them it's your duty to try.'

'It's my duty to act like a reasonable human being. I'm not going to risk my life and my policemen's for the sake of a native woman and her half-caste brats. What sort of a damned fool do you take me for?'

'They'll say you were afraid.'

'Who?'

'Everyone in the colony.'

He smiled disdainfully.

'If you only knew what a complete contempt I have for the opinion of everyone in the colony.'

She gave him a long searching look. She had been married to him for eight years and she knew every expression of his face and every thought in his mind. She stared into his blue eyes as if they were open windows. She suddenly went quite pale. She dropped his hand and turned away. Without another word she went back on to the veranda. Her ugly little monkey face was a mask of horror.

Alban went to his office, wrote a brief account of the facts, and in a few minutes the motor launch was pounding down the river.

The next two days were endless. Escaped natives brought them news of happenings on the estate. But from their excited and terrified stories it was impossible to get an exact impression of the truth. There had been a good deal of bloodshed. The head overseer had been killed. They brought wild tales of cruelty and outrage. Anne could hear nothing of Prynne's woman and the two children. She shuddered when she thought of what might have been their fate. Alban collected as many natives as he could. They were armed with spears and swords. He commandeered boats. The situation was serious, but he kept his head. He felt that he had done all that was possible and nothing remained but for him to carry on normally. He did his official work. He played the piano a great deal. He rode with Anne in the early morning. He appeared to have forgotten that they had had the first serious difference of opinion in the whole of their married life. He took it that Anne had accepted the wisdom of his decision. He was as amusing, cordial and gay with her as he had always been. When he spoke of the rioters it was with grim irony: when the time came to settle matters a good many of them would wish they had never been born.

'What'll happen to them?' asked Anne.

'Oh, they'll hang.' He gave a shrug of distaste. 'I hate having to be present at executions. It always makes me feel rather sick.'

He was very sympathetic to Oakley, whom they had put to bed and whom Anne was nursing. Perhaps he was sorry that in the exasperation of the moment he had spoken to him offensively, and he went out of his way to be nice to him.

Then on the afternoon of the third day, when they were drinking their coffee after luncheon, Alban's quick ears caught the sound of a motor boat approaching. At the same moment a policeman ran up to say that the government launch was sighted.

'At last,' cried Alban.

He bolted out of the house. Anne raised one of the jalousies and looked out at the river. Now the sound was quite loud and in a moment she saw the boat come round the bend. She saw Alban on the landing-stage. He got into a prahu and as the launch dropped her anchor he went on board. She told Oakley that the reinforcements had come.

'Will the DO go up with them when they attack?' he asked her.

'Naturally,' said Anne coldly.

'I wondered.'

Anne felt a strange feeling in her heart. For the last two days she had had to exercise all her self-control not to cry. She did not answer. She went out of the room.

A quarter of an hour later Alban returned to the bungalow with the captain of constabulary who had been sent with twenty Sikhs to deal with the rioters. Captain Stratton was a little red-faced man with a red moustache and bow legs, very hearty and dashing, whom she had met often at Port Wallace.

'Well, Mrs Torel, this is a pretty kettle of fish,' he cried, as he shook hands with her, in a loud jolly voice. 'Here I am, with my army all full of pep and ready for a scrap. Up, boys, and at 'em. Have you got anything to drink in this benighted place?'

'Boy,' she cried, smiling.

'Something long and cool and faintly alcoholic, and then I'm ready to discuss the plan of campaign.'

His breeziness was very comforting. It blew away the sullen apprehension that had seemed ever since the disaster to brood over the lost peace of the bungalow. The boy came in with a tray and Stratton mixed himself a stengah. Alban put him in possession of the facts. He told them clearly, briefly and with precision.

'I must say I admire you,' said Stratton. 'In your place I should never have been able to resist the temptation to take my eight cops and have a whack at the blighters myself.'

'I thought it was a perfectly unjustifiable risk to take.'

'Safety first, old boy, eh, what?' said Stratton jovially. 'I'm jolly glad you didn't. It's not often we get the chance of a scrap. It would have been a dirty trick to keep the whole show to yourself.'

Captain Stratton was all for steaming straight up the river and attacking at once, but Alban pointed out to him the inadvisability of such a course. The sound of the approaching launch would warn the rioters. The long grass at the river's edge offered them cover and they had enough guns to make a landing difficult. It seemed useless to expose the attacking force to their fire. It was silly to forget that they had to face a hundred and fifty desperate men and it would be easy to fall into an ambush.

Alban expounded his own plan. Stratton listened to it. He nodded now and then. The plan was evidently a good one. It would enable them to take the rioters on the rear, surprise them, and in all probability finish the job without a single casualty. He would have been a fool not to accept it.

'But why didn't you do that yourself?' asked Stratton.

'With eight men and a sergeant?'

Stratton did not answer.

'Anyhow it's not a bad idea and we'll settle on it. It gives us plenty of time, so with your permission, Mrs Torel, I'll have a bath.'

They set out at sunset, Captain Stratton and his twenty Sikhs, Alban with his policemen and the natives he had collected. The night was dark and moonless. Trailing behind them were the dug-outs that Alban had gathered together and into which after a certain distance they proposed to transfer their force. It was important that no sound should give warning of their approach. After they had gone for about three hours by launch they took to the dug-outs and in them silently paddled upstream. They reached the border of the vast estate and landed. Guides led them along a path so narrow that they had to march in single file. It had been long unused and the going was heavy. They had twice to ford a stream. The path led them circuitously to the rear of the coolie lines, but they did not wish to reach them till nearly dawn and presently Stratton gave the order to halt. It was a long cold wait. At last the night seemed to be less dark; you did not see the trunks, but were vaguely sensible of them against its darkness. Stratton had been sitting with his back to a tree.

He gave a whispered order to a sergeant and in a few minutes the column was once more on the march. Suddenly they found themselves on a road. They formed fours. The dawn broke and in the ghostly light the surrounding objects were wanly visible. The column stopped on a whispered order. They had come in sight of the coolie lines. Silence reigned in them. The column crept on again and again halted. Stratton, his eyes shining, gave Alban a smile.

'We've caught the blighters asleep.'

He lined up his men. They inserted cartridges in their guns. He stepped forward and raised his hand. The carbines were pointed at the coolie lines.

'Fire.'

There was a rattle as the volley of shots rang out. Then suddenly there was a tremendous din and the Chinese poured out, shouting and waving their arms, but in front of them, to Alban's utter bewilderment, bellowing at the top of his voice and shaking his fist at them, was a white man.

'Who the hell's that?' cried Stratton.

A very big, very fat man, in khaki trousers and a singlet, was running towards them as fast as his fat legs would carry him and as he ran shaking both fists at them and yelling:

'*Smerige flikkers! Verlockte ploerten!*'

'My God, it's Van Hasseldt,' said Alban.

This was the Dutch manager of the timber camp which was situated on a considerable tributary of the river about twenty miles away.

'What the hell do you think you're doing?' he puffed as he came up to them.

'How the hell did you get here?' asked Stratton in turn.

He saw that the Chinese were scattering in all directions and gave his men instructions to round them up. Then he turned again to Van Hasseldt.

'What's it mean?'

'Mean? Mean?' shouted the Dutchman furiously. 'That's what I want to know. You and your damned policemen. What do you mean by coming here at this hour in the morning and firing a damned volley. Target practice? You might have killed me. Idiots!'

'Have a cigarette,' said Stratton.

'How did you get here, Van Hasseldt?' asked Alban again, very much at sea. 'This is the force they've sent from Port Wallace to quell the riot.'

'How did I get here? I walked. How did you think I got here? Riot be damned. I quelled the riot. If that's what you came for you can take your damned policemen home again. A bullet came within a foot of my head.'

'I don't understand,' said Alban.

'There's nothing to understand,' spluttered Van Hasseldt, still fuming. 'Some coolies came to my estate and said the chinks had killed Prynne and burned the bally place down, so I took my assistant and my head overseer and a Dutch friend I had staying with me and came over to see what the trouble was.'

Captain Stratton opened his eyes wide.

'Did you just stroll in as if it was a picnic?' he asked.

'Well, you don't think after all the years I've been in this country I'm going to let a couple of hundred chinks put the fear of God into me? I found them all scared out of their lives. One of them had the nerve to pull a gun on me and I blew his bloody brains out. And the rest surrendered. I've got the leaders tied up. I was going to send a boat down to you this morning to come up and get them.'

Stratton stared at him for a minute and then burst into a shout of laughter. He laughed till the tears ran down his face. The Dutchman looked at him angrily, then began to laugh too; he laughed with the big belly laugh of a very fat man and his coils of fat heaved and shook. Alban watched them sullenly. He was very angry.

'What about Prynne's girl and the kids?' he asked.

'Oh, they got away all right.'

It just showed how wise he had been not to let himself be influenced by Anne's hysteria. Of course the children had come to no harm. He never thought they would.

Van Hasseldt and his little party started back for the timber camp, and as soon after as possible Stratton embarked his twenty Sikhs and leaving Alban with his sergeant and his policemen to deal with the situation departed for Port Wallace. Alban gave him a brief report for the Governor. There was much for him to do. It looked as though he would have to stay for a considerable time; but since every house on the estate had been burned to the ground and he was obliged to install himself in the coolie lines he thought it better that Anne should not join him. He sent her a note to that effect. He was glad to be able to reassure her of the safety of poor Prynne's girl. He set to work at once to make his preliminary inquiry. He examined a host of witnesses. But a week later he received an order to go to Port Wallace at once. The launch that brought it was to take him and he was able to see

Anne on the way down for no more than an hour. Alban was a trifle vexed.

'I don't know why the Governor can't leave me to get things straight without dragging me off like this. It's extremely inconvenient.'

'Oh, well, the Government never bothers very much about the convenience of its subordinates, does it?' smiled Anne.

'It's just red-tape. I would offer to take you along, darling, only I shan't stay a minute longer than I need. I want to get my evidence together for the Sessions Court as soon as possible. I think in a country like this it's very important that justice should be prompt.'

When the launch came in to Port Wallace one of the harbour police told him that the harbour-master had a chit for him. It was from the Governor's secretary and informed him that His Excellency desired to see him as soon as convenient after his arrival. It was ten in the morning. Alban went to the club, had a bath and shaved, and then in clean ducks, his hair neatly brushed, he called a rickshaw and told the boy to take him to the Governor's office. He was at once shown in to the secretary's room. The secretary shook hands with him.

'I'll tell HE you're here,' he said. 'Won't you sit down?'

The secretary left the room and in a little while came back.

'HE will see you in a minute. Do you mind if I get on with my letters?'

Alban smiled. The secretary was not exactly come-hither. He waited, smoking a cigarette, and amused himself with his own thoughts. He was making a good job of the preliminary inquiry. It interested him. Then an orderly came in and told Alban that the Governor was ready for him. He rose from his seat and followed him into the Governor's room.

'Good-morning, Torel.'

'Good-morning, sir.'

The Governor was sitting at a large desk. He nodded to Alban and motioned to him to take a seat. The Governor was all grey. His hair was grey, his face, his eyes; he looked as though the tropical suns had washed the colour out of him; he had been in the country for thirty years and had risen one by one through all the ranks of the Service; he looked tired and depressed. Even his voice was grey. Alban liked him because he was quiet; he did not think him clever, but he had an unrivalled knowledge of the country, and his great experience was a very good substitute for intelligence. He looked at Alban for a full moment without speaking and the odd idea came to Alban that he was embarrassed. He very nearly gave him a lead.

'I saw Van Hasseldt yesterday,' said the Governor suddenly.

'Yes, sir?'

'Will you give me your account of the occurrences at the Alud Estate and of the steps you took to deal with them.'

Alban had an orderly mind. He was self-possessed. He marshalled his facts well and was able to state them with precision. He chose his words with care and spoke them fluently.

'You had a sergeant and eight policemen. Why did you not immediately go to the scene of the disturbance?'

'I thought the risk was unjustifiable.'

A thin smile was outlined on the Governor's grey face.

'If the officers of this Government had hesitated to take the unjustifiable risks it would never have become a province of the British Empire.'

Alban was silent. It was difficult to talk to a man who spoke obvious nonsense.

'I am anxious to hear your reasons for the decision you took.'

Alban gave them coolly. He was quite convinced of the rightness of his action. He repeated, but more fully, what he had said in the first place to Anne. The Governor listened attentively.

'Van Hasseldt, with his manager, a Dutch friend of his, and a native overseer, seems to have coped with the situation very efficiently,' said the Governor.

'He had a lucky break. That doesn't prevent him from being a damned fool. It was madness to do what he did.'

'Do you realize that by leaving a Dutch planter to do what you should have done yourself, you have covered the Government with ridicule?'

'No, sir.'

'You've made yourself a laughing-stock in the whole colony.'

Alban smiled.

'My back is broad enough to bear the ridicule of persons to whose opinion I am entirely indifferent.'

'The utility of a government official depends very largely on his prestige, and I'm afraid his prestige is likely to be inconsiderable when he lies under the stigma of cowardice.'

Alban flushed a little.

THE DOOR OF OPPORTUNITY

'I don't quite know what you mean by that, sir.'

'I've gone into the matter very carefully. I've seen Captain Stratton, and Oakley, poor Prynne's assistant, and I've seen Van Hasseldt. I've listened to your defence.'

'I didn't know that I was defending myself, sir.'

'Be so good as not to interrupt me. I think you committed a grave error of judgement. As it turns out the risk was very small, but whatever it was, I think you should have taken it. In such matters promptness and firmness are essential. It is not for me to conjecture what motive led you to send for a force of constabulary and do nothing till they came. I am afraid, however, that I consider that your usefulness in the Service is no longer very great.'

Alban looked at him with astonishment.

'But would you have gone under the circumstances?' he asked him.

'I should.'

Alban shrugged his shoulders.

'Don't you believe me?' rapped out the Governor.

'Of course I believe you, sir. But perhaps you will allow me to say that if you had been killed the colony would have suffered an irreparable loss.'

The Governor drummed on the table with his fingers. He looked out of the window and then looked again at Alban. When he spoke it was not unkindly.

'I think you are unfitted by temperament for this rather rough-and-tumble life, Torel. If you'll take my advice you'll go home. With your abilities I feel sure that you'll soon find an occupation much better suited to you.'

'I'm afraid I don't understand what you mean, sir.'

'Oh come, Torel, you're not stupid. I'm trying to make things easy for you. For your wife's sake as well as for your own I do not wish you to leave the colony with the stigma of being dismissed from the Service for cowardice. I'm giving you the opportunity of resigning.'

'Thank you very much, sir. I'm not prepared to avail myself of the opportunity. If I resign I admit that I committed an error and that the charge you make against me is justified. I don't admit it.'

'You can please yourself. I have considered the matter very carefully and I have no doubt about it in my mind. I am forced to discharge you from the Service. The necessary papers will reach you in due course. Meanwhile you will return to your post and hand over to the officer appointed to succeed you on his arrival.'

'Very good, sir,' replied Alban, a twinkle of amusement in his eyes. 'When do you desire me to return to my post?'

'At once.'

'Have you any objection to my going to the club and having tiffin before I go?'

The Governor looked at him with surprise. His exasperation was mingled with an unwilling admiration.

'Not at all. I'm sorry, Torel, that this unhappy incident should have deprived the Government of a servant whose zeal has always been so apparent and whose tact, intelligence and industry seemed to point him out in the future for very high office.'

'Your Excellency does not read Schiller, I suppose. You are probably not acquainted with his celebrated line: *mit der Dummheit kämpfen die Götter selbstvergebens.*'

'What does it mean?'

'Roughly: against stupidity the gods themselves battle in vain.'

'Good-morning.'

With his head in the air, a smile on his lips, Alban left the Governor's office. The Governor was human, and he had the curiosity to ask his secretary later in the day if Alban Torel had really gone to the club.

'Yes, sir. He had tiffin there.'

'It must have wanted some nerve.'

Alban entered the club jauntily and joined the group of men standing at the bar. He talked to them in the breezy, cordial tone he always used with them. It was designed to put them at their ease. They had been discussing him ever since Stratton had come back to Port Wallace with his story, sneering at him and laughing at him, and all that had resented his superciliousness, and they were the majority, were triumphant because his pride had had a fall. But they were so taken aback at seeing him now, so confused to find him as confident as ever, that it was they who were embarrassed.

One man, though he knew perfectly, asked him what he was doing in Port Wallace.

'Oh, I came about the riot on the Alud Estate. HE wanted to see me. He does not see eye to eye with me about it. The silly old ass has fired me. I'm going home as soon as he appoints a DO to take over.'

There was a moment of awkwardness. One, more kindly disposed than the others, said:

'I'm awfully sorry.'

Alban shrugged his shoulders.

'My dear fellow, what can you do with a perfect damned fool? The only thing is to let him stew in his own juice.'

When the Governor's secretary had told his chief as much of this as he thought discreet, the Governor smiled.

'Courage is a queer thing. I would rather have shot myself than go to the club just then and face all those fellows.'

A fortnight later, having sold to the incoming DO all the decorations that Anne had taken so much trouble about, with the rest of their things in packing-cases and trunks, they arrived at Port Wallace to await the local steamer that was to take them to Singapore. The padre's wife invited them to stay with her, but Anne refused; she insisted that they should go to the hotel. An hour after their arrival she received a very kind little letter from the Governor's wife asking her to go and have tea with her. She went. She found Mrs Hannay alone, but in a minute the Governor joined them. He expressed his regret that she was leaving and told her how sorry he was for the cause.

'It's very kind of you to say that,' said Anne, smiling gaily, 'but you mustn't think I take it to heart. I'm entirely on Alban's side. I think what he did was absolutely right and if you don't mind my saying so I think you've treated him most unjustly.'

'Believe me, I hated having to take the step I took.'

'Don't let's talk about it,' said Anne.

'What are your plans when you get home?' asked Mrs Hannay.

Anne began to chat brightly. You would have thought she had not a care in the world. She seemed in great spirits at going home. She was jolly and amusing and made little jokes. When she took leave of the Governor and his wife she thanked them for all their kindness. The Governor escorted her to the door.

The next day but one, after dinner, they went on board the clean and comfortable little ship. The padre and his wife saw them off. When they went into their cabin they found a large parcel on Anne's bunk. It was addressed to Alban. He opened it and saw that it was an immense powder-puff.

'Hullo, I wonder who sent us this,' he said, with a laugh. 'It must be for you, darling.'

Anne gave him a quick look. She went pale. The brutes! How could they be so cruel? She forced herself to smile.

'It's enormous, isn't it? I've never seen such a large powder-puff in my life.'

But when he had left the cabin and they were out at sea, she threw it passionately overboard.

And now, now that they were back in London and Sondurah was nine thousand miles away, she clenched her hands as she thought of it. Somehow, it seemed the worst thing of all. It was so wantonly unkind to send that absurd object to Alban, Powder-Puff Percy; it showed such a petty spite. Was that their idea of humour? Nothing had hurt her more and even now she felt that it was only by holding on to herself that she could prevent herself from crying. Suddenly she started, for the door opened and Alban came in. She was still sitting in the chair in which he had left her.

'Hullo, why haven't you dressed? He looked about the room. 'You haven't unpacked.'

'No.'

'Why on earth not?'

'I'm not going to unpack. I'm not going to stay here. I'm leaving you.'

'What are you talking about?'

'I've stuck it out till now. I made up my mind I would till we got home. I set my teeth, I've borne more than I thought it possible to bear, but now it's finished. I've done all that could be expected of me. We're back in London now and I can go.'

He looked at her in utter bewilderment.

'Are you mad, Anne?'

'Oh, my God, what I've endured! The journey to Singapore, with all the officers knowing, and even the Chinese stewards. And at Singapore, the way people looked at us at the hotel, and the sympathy I had to put up with, the bricks they dropped and their embarrassment when they realized what they'd done. My God, I could have killed them. That interminable journey home. There wasn't a single passenger on the ship who didn't know. The contempt they had for you and the kindness they went out of their way to show me. And you so self-complacent and so pleased with yourself, seeing nothing, feeling nothing. You must have the hide of a rhinoceros. The misery of seeing you so chatty and agreeable. Pariahs, that's what we were. You seemed to ask them to snub you. How can anyone be so shameless?'

She was flaming with passion. Now that at last she need not wear the mask of indifference and pride that she had forced herself to assume she cast aside all reserve and all self-control. The words poured from her trembling lips in a virulent stream.

'My dear, how can you be so absurd?' he said good-naturedly, smiling. 'You must be very nervous and high-strung to have got such ideas in your head. Why didn't you tell me? You're like a country bumpkin who comes to London and thinks everyone is staring at him. Nobody bothered about us and if they did what on earth did it matter? You ought to have more sense than to bother about what a lot of fools say. And what do you imagine they were saying?'

'They were saying you'd been fired.'

'Well, that was true,' he laughed.

'They said you were a coward.'

'What of it?'

'Well, you see, that was true too.'

He looked at her for a moment reflectively. His lips tightened a little.

'And what makes you think so?' he asked acidly.

'I saw it in your eyes, that day the news came, when you refused to go to the estate and I followed you into the hall when you went to fetch your topi. I begged you to go, I felt that whatever the danger you must take it, and suddenly I saw the fear in your eyes. I nearly fainted with the horror.'

'I should have been a fool to risk my life to no purpose. Why should I? Nothing that concerned me was at stake. Courage is the obvious virtue of the stupid. I don't attach any particular importance to it.'

'How do you mean that nothing that concerned you was at stake? If that's true then your whole life is a sham. You've given away everything you stood for, everything we both stand for. You've let all of us down. We did set ourselves up on a pinnacle, we

did think ourselves better than the rest of them
because we loved literature and art and music, we
weren't content to live a life of ignoble jealousies
and vulgar tittle-tattle, we did cherish the things of
the spirit, and we loved beauty. It was our food and
drink. They laughed at us and sneered at us. That
was inevitable. The ignorant and the common
naturally hate and fear those who are interested in
things they don't understand. We didn't care. We
called them Philistines. We despised them and we
had a right to despise them. Our justification was
that we were better and nobler and wiser and
braver than they were. And you weren't better,
you weren't nobler, you weren't braver. When the
crisis came you slunk away like a whipped cur with
his tail between his legs. You of all people hadn't
the right to be a coward. They despise *us* now and
they have the right to despise us. Us and all we
stood for. Now they can say that art and beauty are
all rot; when it comes to a pinch people like us
always let you down. They never stopped looking
for a chance to turn and rend us and you gave it to
them. They can say that they always expected it.
It's a triumph for them. I used to be furious because
they called you Powder-Puff Percy. Did you know
they did?'

'Of course. I thought it very vulgar, but it left me
entirely indifferent.'

'It's funny that their instinct should have been so
right.'

'Do you mean to say you've been harbouring this
against me all these weeks? I should never have
thought you capable of it.'

'I couldn't let you down when everyone was
against you. I was too proud for that. Whatever

happened I swore to myself that I'd stick to you till we got home. It's been torture.'

'Don't you love me any more?'

'Love you? I loathe the very sight of you.'

'Anne.'

'God knows I loved you. For eight years I worshipped the ground you trod on. You were everything to me. I believed in you as some people believe in God. When I saw the fear in your eyes that day, when you told me that you weren't going to risk your life for a kept woman and her half-caste brats, I was shattered. It was as though someone had wrenched my heart out of my body and trampled on it. You killed my love there and then, Alban. You killed it stone-dead. Since then when you've kissed me I've had to clench my hands so as not to turn my face away. The mere thought of anything else makes me feel physically sick. I loathe your complacence and your frightful insensitiveness. Perhaps I could have forgiven it if it had been just a moment's weakness and if afterwards you'd been ashamed. I should have been miserable, but I think my love was so great that I should only have felt pity for you. But you're incapable of shame. And now I believe in nothing. You're only a silly, pretentious vulgar poseur. I would rather be the wife of a second-rate planter so long as he had the common human virtues of a man than the wife of a fake like you.'

He did not answer. Gradually his face began to discompose. Those handsome, regular features of his horribly distorted and suddenly he broke out into loud sobs. She gave a little cry.

'Don't, Alban, don't.'

'Oh, darling, how can you be so cruel to me? I

adore you. I'd give my whole life to please you. I can't live without you.'

She put out her arms as though to ward off a blow.

'No, no, Alban, don't try to move me. I can't. I must go. I can't live with you any more. It would be frightful. I can never forget. I must tell you the truth, I have only contempt for you and repulsion.'

He sank down at her feet and tried to cling to her knees. With a gasp she sprang up and he buried his head in the empty chair. He cried painfully with sobs that tore his chest. The sound was horrible. The tears streamed from Anne's eyes and, putting her hands to her ears to shut out that dreadful, hysterical sobbing, blindly stumbling she rushed to the door and ran out.

The Vessel of Wrath

There are few books in the world that contain more meat than the *Sailing Directions* published by the Hydrographic Department by order of the Lords Commissioners of the Admiralty. They are handsome volumes, bound (very flimsily) in cloth of different colours, and the most expensive of them is cheap. For four shillings you can buy the *Yangste Kiang Pilot*, 'containing a description of, and sailing directions for, the Yangste Kiang from the Wusung river to the highest navigable point, including the Han Kiang, the Kialing Kiang, and the Min Kiang'; and for three shillings you can get Part III of the *Eastern Archipelago Pilot*, 'comprising the NE end of Celebes, Molucca and Gilolo passages, Banda and Arafura Seas, and North, West, and South-West coasts of New Guinea'. But it is not very safe to do so if you are a creature of settled habits that you have no wish to disturb or if you have an occupation that holds you fast to one place. These business-like books take you upon enchanted journeys of the spirit; and their matter-of-fact style, the admirable order, the concision with which the material is set before you, the stern sense of the practical that informs every line, cannot dim the poetry that, like the spice-laden breeze that assails your senses with a more than material languor when you approach some of those magic islands of the Eastern seas, blows you so sweet a fragrance through the printed pages. They tell you the anchorages and the landing-places, what supplies you can get at each spot, and where you can get water; they tell you the lights and buoys, tides, winds and weather that you will find there. They give you brief information about the population and the trade. And it is strange when you think how sedately it is all set down, with no words wasted, that so much else is given you besides. What? Well, mystery and beauty, romance and the glamour of the unknown. It is no common book that offers you casually turning its pages such a paragraph as this: 'Supplies. A few jungle fowl are preserved, the island is also the resort of vast numbers of sea birds. Turtle are found in the lagoon, as well as quantities of various fish, including grey mullet, shark, and dog-fish; the seine cannot be used with any effect; but there is a fish which may be taken on a rod. A small store of tinned provisions and spirits is kept in a hut for the relief of shipwrecked persons. Good water may be obtained from a well near the landing-place.' Can the imagination want more material than this to go on a journey through time and space?

In the volume from which I have copied this passage, the compilers with the same restraint have described the Alas Islands. They are composed of a group or chain of islands, 'for the most part low and wooded, extending about 75 miles east and west, and 40 miles north and south'. The information about them, you are told, is very slight; there are channels between the different groups, and several vessels have passed through them, but the passages have not been thoroughly explored, and the positions of many of the dangers not yet determined; it is therefore advisable to avoid them. The population of the group is estimated at about 8,000, of whom 200 are Chinese and 400 Mohammedans. The rest are heathen. The principal island is called Baru, it is surrounded by a reef and here lives a Dutch Contrôleur. His white house with its red roof on the top of a little hill is the most prominent object that the vessels of the Royal Netherlands Steam Packet Company see when every other month on their way up to Macassar and every four weeks on their way down to Merauke in Dutch New Guinea they touch at the island.

At a certain moment of the world's history the Contrôleur was Mynheer Evert Gruyter and he ruled the people who inhabited the Alas Islands with firmness tempered by a keen sense of the ridiculous. He had thought it a very good joke to be placed at the age of twenty-seven in a position of such consequence and at thirty he was still amused by it. There was no cable communication between his islands and Batavia, and the mail arrived after so long a delay that even if he asked advice, by the time he received it, it was useless, and so he equably did what he thought best and trusted to his good fortune to keep out of trouble with the authorities. He was very short, not more than five feet four in height, and extremely fat; he was of a florid complexion. For coolness' sake he kept his head shaved and his face was hairless. It was round and red. His eyebrows were so fair that you hardly saw them; and he had little twinkling blue eyes. He knew that he had no dignity, but for the sake of his position made up for it by dressing very dapperly. He never went to his office, nor sat in court, nor walked abroad but in spotless white. His stengah-shifter, with its bright brass buttons, fitted him very tightly and displayed the shocking fact that, young though he was, he had a round and protruding belly. His good-humoured face shone with sweat and he constantly fanned himself with a palm-leaf fan.

But in his house Mr Gruyter preferred to wear nothing but a sarong and then with his white podgy little body he looked like a fat funny boy of sixteen. He was an early riser and his breakfast was always ready for him at six. It never varied. It consisted of a slice of papaia, three cold fried eggs, Edam cheese, sliced thin, and a cup of black coffee. When he had eaten it, he smoked a large Dutch cigar, read the papers if he had not read them through and through already, and then dressed to go down to his office.

One morning while he was thus occupied his head boy came into his bedroom and told him that Tuan Jones wanted to know if he could see him. Mr Gruyter was standing in front of a looking-glass. He had his trousers on and was admiring his smooth chest. He arched his back in order to throw it out and throw in his belly and with a good deal of satisfaction gave his breast three or four resounding slaps. It was a manly chest. When the boy brought the message he looked at his own eyes in the mirror and exchanged a slightly ironic smile with them. He asked himself what the devil his visitor could want. Evert Gruyter spoke English, Dutch and Malay with equal facility, but he thought in Dutch. He liked to do this. It seemed to him a pleasantly ribald language.

'Ask the Tuan to wait and say I shall come

directly.' He put on his tunic, over his naked body, buttoned it up, and strutted into the sitting-room. The Rev. Owen Jones got up.

'Good-morning, Mr Jones,' said the Contrôleur. 'Have you come in to have a peg with me before I start my day's work?'

Mr Jones did not smile.

'I've come to see you upon a very distressing matter, Mr Gruyter,' he answered.

The Contrôleur was not disconcerted by his visitor's gravity nor depressed by his words. His little blue eyes beamed amiably.

'Sit down, my dear fellow, and have a cigar.'

Mr Gruyter knew quite well that the Rev. Owen Jones neither drank nor smoked, but it tickled something prankish in his nature to offer him a drink and a smoke whenever they met. Mr Jones shook his head.

Mr Jones was in charge of the Baptist Mission on the Alas Islands. His headquarters were at Baru, the largest of them, with the greatest population, but he had meeting-houses under the care of native helpers in several other islands of the group. He was a tall, thin melancholy man, with a long face, sallow and drawn, of about forty. His brown hair was already white on the temples and it receded from the forehead. This gave him a look of somewhat vacuous intellectuality. Mr Gruyter both disliked and respected him. He disliked him because he was narrow-minded and dogmatic. Himself a cheerful pagan who liked the good things of the flesh and was determined to get as many of them as his circumstances permitted, he had no patience with a man who disapproved of them all. He thought the customs of the country suited its

inhabitants and had no patience with the missionary's energetic efforts to destroy a way of life that
for centuries had worked very well. He respected
him because he was honest, zealous and good. Mr
Jones, an Australian of Welsh descent, was the only
qualified doctor in the group and it was a comfort to
know that if you fell ill you need not rely only on a
Chinese practitioner, and none knew better than
the Contrôleur how useful to all Mr Jones's skill
had been and with what charity he had given it. On
the occasion of an epidemic of influenza the missionary had done the work of ten men and no storm
short of a typhoon could prevent him from crossing
to one island or another if his help was needed.

He lived with his sister in a little white house
about half a mile from the village and when the
Contrôleur had arrived, came on board to meet him
and begged him to stay until he could get his own
house in order. The Contrôleur had accepted and
soon saw for himself with what simplicity the
couple lived. It was more than he could stand. Tea
at three sparse meals a day and when he lit his cigar
Mr Jones politely but firmly asked him to be good
enough not to smoke, since both his sister and he
strongly disapproved of it. In twenty-four hours
Mr Gruyter moved into his own house. He fled,
with panic in his heart, as though from a plague-
stricken city. The Contrôleur was fond of a joke
and he liked to laugh; to be with a man who took
your nonsense in deadly earnest and never even
smiled at your best story was more than flesh and
blood could stand. The Rev. Owen Jones was a
worthy man, but as a companion he was impossible. His sister was worse. Neither had a sense of
humour, but whereas the missionary was of a

melancholy turn, doing his duty so conscientiously, with the obvious conviction that everything in the world was hopeless, Miss Jones was
resolutely cheerful. She grimly looked on the
bright side of things. With the ferocity of an aven-
ging angel she sought out the good in her fellow-
men. Miss Jones taught in the mission school and
helped her brother in his medical work. When he
did operations she gave the anaesthetic and was
matron, dresser and nurse of the tiny hospital
which on his own initiative Mr Jones had added to
the mission. But the Contrôleur was an obstinate
little fellow and he never lost his capacity of extrac-
ting amusement from the Rev. Owen's dour struggle with the infirmities of human nature, and Miss
Jones's ruthless optimism. He had to get his fun
where he could. The Dutch boats came in three
times in two months for a few hours and then he
could have a good old crack with the captain and
chief engineer, and once in a blue moon a pearling
lugger came in from Thursday Island or Port
Darwin and for two or three days he had a grand
time. They were rough fellows, the pearlers, for
the most part, but they were full of guts, and they
had plenty of liquor on board, and good stories to
tell, and the Contrôleur had them up to his house
and gave them a fine dinner and the party was only
counted a success if they were all too drunk to get
back on the lugger again that night. But beside the
missionary the only white man who lived on Baru
was Ginger Ted, and he, of course, was a disgrace
to civilization. There was not a single thing to be
said in his favour. He cast discredit on the white
race. All the same, but for Ginger Ted the Contrôleur sometimes thought he would find life on the

island of Baru almost more than he could bear.

Oddly enough it was on account of this scamp that Mr Jones, when he should have been instructing the pagan young in the mysteries of the Baptist faith, was paying Mr Gruyter this early visit.

'Sit down, Mr Jones,' said the Contrôleur. 'What can I do for you?'

'Well, I've come to see you about the man they call Ginger Ted. What are you going to do now?'

'Why, what's happened?'

'Haven't you heard? I thought the sergeant would have told you.'

'I don't encourage the members of my staff to come to my private house unless the matter is urgent,' said the Contrôleur rather grandly. 'I am unlike you, Mr Jones, I only work in order to have leisure and I like to enjoy my leisure without disturbance.'

But Mr Jones did not care much for small talk and he was not interested in general reflections.

'There was a disgraceful row in one of the Chinese shops last night. Ginger Ted wrecked the place and half killed a Chinaman.'

'Drunk again, I suppose,' said the Contrôleur placidly.

'Naturally. When is he anything else? They sent for the police and he assaulted the sergeant. They had to have six men to get him to the gaol.'

'He's a hefty fellow,' said the Contrôleur.

'I suppose you'll send him to Macassar.'

Evert Gruyter returned the missionary's outraged look with a merry twinkle. He was no fool and he knew already what Mr Jones was up to. It gave him considerable amusement to tease him a little.

'Fortunately my powers are wide enough to

enable me to deal with the situation myself,' he answered.

'You have power to deport anyone you like, Mr Gruyter, and I'm sure it would save a lot of trouble if you got rid of the man altogether.'

'I have the power of course, but I am sure you would be the last person to wish me to use it arbitrarily.'

'Mr Gruyter, the man's presence here is a public scandal. He's never sober from morning till night; it's notorious that he has relations with one native woman after another.'

'That is an interesting point, Mr Jones. I had always heard that alcoholic excess, though it stimulated sexual desire, prevented its gratification. What you tell me about Ginger Ted does not seem to bear out this theory.'

The missionary flushed a dull red.

'These are physiological matters which at the moment I have no wish to go into,' he said, frigidly. 'The behaviour of this man does incalculable damage to the prestige of the white race, and his example seriously hampers the efforts that are made in other quarters to induce the people of these islands to lead a less vicious life. He's an out-and-out bad lot.'

'Pardon my asking, but have you made any attempts to reform him?'

'When he first drifted here I did my best to get in touch with him. He repelled all my advances. When there was that first trouble I went to him and talked to him straight from the shoulder. He swore at me.'

'No one has a greater appreciation than I of the excellent work that you and other missionaries do on these islands, but are you sure that you always exercise your calling with all the tact possible?'

The Contrôleur was rather pleased with this phrase. It was extremely courteous and yet contained a reproof that he thought worth administering. The missionary looked at him gravely. His sad brown eyes were full of sincerity.

'Did Jesus exercise tact when he took a whip and drove the money-changers from the Temple? No, Mr Gruyter. Tact is the subterfuge the lax avail themselves of to avoid doing their duty.'

Mr Jones's remark made the Contrôleur feel suddenly that he wanted a bottle of beer. The missionary leaned forward earnestly.

'Mr Gruyter, you know this man's transgressions just as well as I do. It's unnecessary for me to remind you of them. There are no excuses for him. Now he really has overstepped the limit. You'll never have a better chance than this. I beg you to use the power you have and turn him out once for all.'

The Contrôleur's eyes twinkled more brightly than ever. He was having a lot of fun. He reflected that human beings were much more amusing when you did not feel called upon in dealing with them to allot praise or blame.

'But, Mr Jones, do I understand you right? Are you asking me to give you an assurance to deport this man before I've heard the evidence against him and listened to his defence?'

'I don't know what his defence can be.'

The Contrôleur rose from his chair and really he managed to get quite a little dignity into his five feet four inches.

'I am here to administer justice according to the

laws of the Dutch Government. Permit me to tell you that I am exceedingly surprised that you should attempt to influence me in my judicial functions.'

The missionary was a trifle flustered. It had never occurred to him that this young whipper-snapper of a boy, ten years younger than himself, would dream of adopting such an attitude. He opened his mouth to explain and apologize, but the Contrôleur raised a podgy little hand.

'It is time for me to go to my office, Mr Jones. I wish you good-morning.'

The missionary, taken aback, bowed and without another word walked out of the room. He would have been surprised to see what the Contrôleur did when his back was turned. A broad grin broke on his lips and he put his thumb to his nose and cocked a snook at the Rev. Owen Jones.

A few minutes later he went down to his office. His head clerk, who was a Dutch half-caste, gave him his version of the previous night's row. It agreed pretty well with Mr Jones's. The court was sitting that day.

'Will you take Ginger Ted first, sir?' asked the clerk.

'I see no reason to do that. There are two or three cases held over from the last sitting. I will take him in his proper order.'

'I thought perhaps as he was a white man you would like to see him privately, sir.'

'The majesty of the law knows no difference between white and coloured, my friend,' said Mr Gruyter, somewhat pompously.

The court was a big square room with wooden benches on which, crowded together, sat natives of all kinds, Polynesians, Bugis, Chinese, Malays, and they all rose when a door was opened and a sergeant announced the arrival of the Contrôleur. He entered with his clerk and took his place on a little dais at a table of varnished pitch pine. Behind him was a large engraving of Queen Wilhelmina. He dispatched half a dozen cases and then Ginger Ted was brought in. He stood in the dock, hand-cuffed, with a warder on either side of him. The Contrôleur looked at him with a grave face, but he could not keep the amusement out of his eyes.

Ginger Ted was suffering from a hang-over. He swayed a little as he stood and his eyes were vacant. He was a man still young, thirty perhaps, of somewhat over the middle height, rather fat, with a bloated red face and a shock of curly red hair. He had not come out of the tussle unscathed. He had a black eye and his mouth was cut and swollen. He wore khaki shorts, very dirty and ragged, and his singlet had been almost torn off his back. A great rent showed the thick mat of red hair with which his chest was covered, but showed also the astonishing whiteness of his skin. The Contrôleur looked at the charge sheet. He called the evidence. When he had heard it, when he had seen the China-man whose head Ginger Ted had broken with a bottle, when he had heard the agitated story of the sergeant who had been knocked flat when he tried to arrest him, when he had listened to the tale of the havoc wrought by Ginger Ted who in his drunken fury had smashed everything he could lay hands on, he turned and addressed the accused in English.

'Well, Ginger, what have you got to say for yourself?'

'I was blind. I don't remember a thing about it. If they say I half killed 'im I suppose I did. I'll pay the damage if they'll give me time.'

'You will, Ginger,' said the Contrôleur, 'but it's me who'll give you time.'

He looked at Ginger Ted for a minute in silence. He was an unappetizing object. A man who had gone completely to pieces. He was horrible. It made you shudder to look at him and if Mr Jones had not been so officious, at that moment the Contrôleur would certainly have ordered him to be deported.

'You've been a trouble ever since you came to the islands, Ginger. You're a disgrace. You're incorrigibly idle. You've been picked up in the street dead drunk time and time again. You've kicked up row after row. You're hopeless. I told you the last time you were brought here that if you were arrested again I should deal with you severely. You've gone the limit this time and you're for it. I sentence you to six months' hard labour.'

'Me?'

'You.'

'By God, I'll kill you when I come out.'

He burst into a string of oaths both filthy and blasphemous. Mr Gruyter listened scornfully. You can swear much better in Dutch than in English and there was nothing that Ginger Ted said that he could not have effectively capped.

'Be quiet,' he ordered. 'You make me tired.'

The Contrôleur repeated his sentence in Malay and the prisoner was led struggling away.

Mr Gruyter sat down to tiffin in high good humour. It was astonishing how amusing life could be if you exercised a little ingenuity. There were people in Amsterdam, and even in Batavia and Surabaya, who looked upon his island home as a place of exile. They little knew how agreeable it was and what fun he could extract from unpromising material. They asked him whether he did not miss the club and the races and the cinema, the dances that were held once a week at the Casino and the society of Dutch ladies. Not at all. He liked comfort. The substantial furniture of the room in which he sat had a satisfying solidity. He liked reading French novels of a frivolous nature and he appreciated the sensation of reading one after the other without the uneasiness occasioned by the thought that he was wasting his time. It seemed to him a great luxury to waste time. When his young man's fancy turned to thoughts of love his head boy brought to the house a little dark-skinned bright-eyed creature in a sarong. He took care to form no connection of a permanent nature. He thought that change kept the heart young. He enjoyed freedom and was not weighed down by a sense of responsibility. He did not mind the heat. It made a sluice over with cold water half a dozen times a day a pleasure that had almost an aesthetic quality. He played the piano. He wrote letters to his friends in Holland. He felt no need for the conversation of intellectual persons. He liked a good laugh, but he could get that out of a fool just as well as out of a professor of philosophy. He had a notion that he was a very wise little man.

Like all good Dutchmen in the Far East he began his lunch with a small glass of Hollands gin. It has a musty acrid flavour, and the taste for it must be acquired, but Mr Gruyter preferred it to any cocktail. When he drank it he felt besides that he was upholding the traditions of his race. Then he had *rysttafel*. He had it every day. He heaped a soup-plate high with rice, and then, his three boys waiting on him, helped himself to the curry that one handed him, to the fried egg that another brought, and to the condiment presented by the third. Then each one brought another dish, of bacon, or bananas, or pickled fish, and presently his plate was piled high in a huge pyramid. He stirred it all together and began to eat. He ate slowly and with relish. He drank a bottle of beer.

He did not think while he was eating. His attention was applied to the mass in front of him and he consumed it with a happy concentration. It never palled on him and when he had emptied the great plate it was a compensation to think that next day he would have *rysttafel* again. He grew tired of it as little as the rest of us grow tired of bread. He finished his beer and lit his cigar. The boy brought him a cup of coffee. He leaned back in his chair then and allowed himself the luxury of reflection.

It tickled him to have sentenced Ginger Ted to the richly deserved punishment of six months' hard labour, and he smiled when he thought of him working on the roads with the other prisoners. It would have been silly to deport from the island the one man with whom he could occasionally have a heart-to-heart talk, and besides, the satisfaction it would have given the missionary would have been bad for that gentleman's character. Ginger Ted was a scamp and a scallywag, but the Contrôleur had a kindly feeling for him. They had drunk many a bottle of beer in one another's company and when the pearl fishers from Port Darwin came in and they all made a night of it, they had got gloriously tight together. The Contrôleur liked the reckless way in which Ginger Ted squandered the priceless treasure of life.

Ginger Ted had wandered in one day on the ship that was going up from Merauke to Macassar. The captain did not know how he had found his way there, but he had travelled steerage with the natives, and he stopped off at the Alas Islands because he liked the look of them. Mr Gruyter had a suspicion that their attraction consisted perhaps in their being under the Dutch flag and so out of British jurisdiction. But his papers were in order, so there was no reason why he should not stay. He said that he was buying pearl-shell for an Australian firm, but it soon appeared that his commercial undertakings were not serious. Drink, indeed, took up so much of his time that he had little left over for other pursuits. He was in receipt of two pounds a week, paid monthly, which came regularly to him from England. The Contrôleur guessed that this sum was paid only so long as he kept well away from the persons who sent it. It was anyway too small to permit him any liberty of movement. Ginger Ted was reticent. The Contrôleur discovered that he was an Englishman, this he learnt from his passport, which described him as Edward Wilson, and that he had been in Australia. But why he had left England and what he had done in Australia he had no notion. Nor could he ever quite tell to what class Ginger Ted belonged. When you saw him in a filthy singlet and a pair of ragged trousers, a battered topi on his head, with the pearl fishers and heard his conversation, coarse, obscene and illiterate, you thought he must be a sailor before the mast who had deserted his ship, or a labourer, but when you saw his handwriting you were surprised to find that it was that of a man not without at least some education, and on occasion when you got him alone, if he had had a few drinks but was not yet drunk, he would talk of matters that neither a sailor nor a labourer would have been likely to know anything about. The Contrôleur had a certain sensitiveness and he realized that Ginger Ted did not speak to him as an inferior to a superior but as an equal. Most of his remittance was mortgaged before he received it, and the Chinamen to whom he owed money were standing at his elbow when the monthly letter was delivered to him, but with what was left he proceeded to get drunk. It was then that he made trouble, for when drunk he grew violent and was then likely to commit acts that brought him into the hands of the police. Hitherto Mr Gruyter had contented himself with keeping him in gaol till he was sober and giving him a talking to. When he was out of money he cadged what drink he could from anyone who would give it him. Rum, brandy, arak, it was all the same to him. Two or three times Mr Gruyter had got him work on plantations run by Chinese in one or other of the islands, but he could not stick to it, and in a few weeks was back again at Baru on the beach. It was a miracle how he kept body and soul together. He had, of course, a way with him. He picked up the various dialects spoken on the islands, and knew how to make the natives laugh. They despised him, but they respected his physical strength, and they liked his company. He was as a result never at a loss for a meal or a mat to sleep on. The strange thing was, and it was this that chiefly outraged the Rev. Owen Jones, that he could do anything he liked with a woman. The Contrôleur could not imagine what it was they saw in him. He was casual with them and rather brutal. He took what they gave him, but seemed incapable of gratitude. He used them for his pleasure and then flung them indifferently away. Once or twice this had got him into trouble, and Mr Gruyter had had to sentence an angry father for sticking a knife in Ginger Ted's back one night, and a Chinese woman had sought to poison herself by swallowing opium because he had deserted her. Once Mr Jones came to the Contrôleur in a great state because the beachcomber had seduced one of his converts. The Contrôleur agreed that it was very deplorable, but could only advise Mr Jones to keep a sharp eye on these young persons. The Contrôleur liked it less when he discovered that a girl whom he fancied a good deal himself and had been seeing for several weeks had all the time been according her favours also to Ginger Ted. When he thought of this particular incident he smiled again at the thought of Ginger Ted doing six months' hard labour. It is seldom in this life that in the process of doing your bounden duty you can get back on a fellow who has played you a dirty trick.

A few days later Mr Gruyter was taking a walk partly for exercise and partly to see that some job he wanted done was being duly proceeded with, when he passed a gang of prisoners working under the charge of a warder. Among them he saw Ginger Ted. He wore the prison sarong, a dingy tunic called in Malay a baju, and his own battered topi. They were repairing the road, and Ginger Ted was wielding a heavy pick. The way was narrow and the Contrôleur saw that he must pass within a foot of him. He remembered his threats. He knew that Ginger Ted was a man of violent passion and the language he had used in the dock made it plain that he had not seen what a good joke it was of the Contrôleur's to sentence him to six months' hard labour. If Ginger Ted suddenly attacked him with the pick, nothing on God's earth could save him. It was true that the warder would immediately shoot him down, but meanwhile the Contrôleur's head would be bashed in. It was with a funny little feeling in the pit of his stomach that Mr Gruyter walked through the gang of prisoners. They were working in pairs a few feet from one another. He set his mind on neither hastening his pace nor slackening it. As he passed Ginger Ted, the man swung his pick into the ground and looked up at the Contrôleur and as he caught his eye winked. The Contrôleur checked the smile that rose to his lips and with official dignity strode on. But that wink, so lusciously full of sardonic humour, filled him with satisfaction. If he had been the Caliph of Bagdad instead of a junior official in the Dutch Civil Service, he would forthwith have released Ginger Ted, sent slaves to bath and perfume him, and having clothed him in a golden robe entertained him to a sumptuous repast.

Ginger Ted was an exemplary prisoner and in a month or two the Contrôleur, having occasion to send a gang to do some work on one of the outlying islands, included him in it. There was no gaol there, so the ten fellows he sent, under the charge of a warder, were billeted on the natives and after their day's work lived like free men. The job was sufficient to take up the rest of Ginger Ted's sentence. The Contrôleur saw him before he left.

'Look here, Ginger,' he said to him, 'here's ten guilder for you so that you can buy yourself tobacco when you're gone.'

'Couldn't you make it a bit more? There's eight pounds a month coming in regularly.'

'I think that's enough. I'll keep the letters that come for you, and when you get back you'll have a tidy sum. You'll have enough to take you anywhere you want to go.'

'I'm very comfortable here,' said Ginger Ted.

'Well, the day you come back, clean yourself up and come over to my house. We'll have a bottle of beer together.'

'That'll be fine. I guess I'll be ready for a good crack then.'

Now chance steps in. The island to which Ginger Ted had been sent was called Maputiti, and like all the rest of them it was rocky, heavily wooded and surrounded by a reef. There was a village among coconuts on the sea-shore opposite the opening of the reef and another village on a brackish lake in the middle of the island. Of this some of the inhabitants had been converted to Christianity. Communications with Baru was effected by a launch that touched at the various islands at irregular intervals. It carried passengers and produce. But the villagers were seafaring folk, and if they had to communicate urgently with Baru, manned a prahu and sailed the fifty miles or so that separated them from it. It happened that when Ginger Ted's sentence had but another fortnight to run the Christian headman of the village on the lake was taken suddenly ill. The native remedies availed him nothing and he writhed in agony. Messengers were sent to Baru imploring the missionary's help; but as ill luck would have it Mr Jones was suffering at the moment from an attack of malaria. He was in bed and unable to move. He talked the matter over with his sister.

'It sounds like acute appendicitis,' he told her.

'You can't go, Owen,' she said.

'I can't let the man die.'

Mr Jones had a temperature of a hundred and four. His head was aching like mad. He had been delirious all night. His eyes were shining strangely and his sister felt that he was holding on to his wits by a sheer effort of will.

'You couldn't operate in the state you're in.'

'No, I couldn't. Then Hassan must go.'

Hassan was the dispenser.

'You couldn't trust Hassan. He'd never dare to do an operation on his own responsibility. And they'd never let him. I'll go. Hassan can stay here and look after you.'

'You can't remove an appendix?'

'Why not? I've seen you do it. I've done lots of minor operations.'

Mr Jones felt he didn't quite understand what she was saying.

'Is the launch in?'

'No, it's gone to one of the islands. But I can go in the prahu the men came in.'

'You? I wasn't thinking of you. You can't go.'

'I'm going, Owen.'

'Going where?' he said.

She saw that his mind was wandering already. She put her hand soothingly on his dry forehead. She gave him a dose of medicine. He muttered something and she realized that he did not know where he was. Of course she was anxious about him, but she knew that his illness was not dangerous, and she could leave him safely to the mission boy who was helping her nurse him and to the native dispenser. She slipped out of the room. She put her toilet things, a night-dress, and a change of clothes into a bag. A little chest with surgical instruments, bandages and antiseptic dressings was kept always ready. She gave them to the two natives who had come over from Maputiti, and telling the dispenser what she was going to do gave him instructions to inform her brother when he was able to listen. Above all he was not to be anxious about her. She put on her topi and sallied forth. The mission was about half a mile from the village. She walked quickly. At the end of the jetty the prahu was waiting. Six men manned it. She took her place in the stern and they set off with a rapid stroke. Within the reef the sea was calm, but when they crossed the bar they came upon a long swell. But this was not the first journey of the sort Miss Jones had taken and she was confident in the seaworthiness of the boat she was in. It was noon and the sun beat down from a sultry sky. The only thing that harassed her was that they could not arrive before dark, and if she found it necessary to operate at once she could count only on the light of hurricane lamps.

Miss Jones was a woman of hard on forty. Nothing in her appearance would have prepared you for such determination as she had just shown. She had an odd drooping gracefulness, which suggested that she might be swayed by every breeze; it was almost an affectation; and it made the strength of character which you soon discovered in her seem positively monstrous. She was flat-chested, tall and extremely thin. She had a long sallow face and she was much afflicted with prickly heat. Her lank brown hair was drawn back straight from her forehead. She had rather small eyes, grey in colour, and because they were somewhat too close they gave her face a shrewish look. Her nose was long and thin and a trifle red. She suffered a good deal from indigestion. But this infirmity availed nothing against her ruthless determination to look upon the bright side of things. Firmly persuaded that the world was evil and men unspeakably vicious, she extracted any little piece of decency she could find in them with the modest pride with which a conjurer extracts a rabbit from a hat. She was quick, resourceful and competent. When she arrived on the island she saw that there was not a moment to lose if she was to save the headman's life. Under the greatest difficulties, showing a native how to give the anaesthetic, she operated, and for the next three days nursed the patient with anxious assiduity. Everything went very well and she realized that her brother could not have made a better job of it. She waited long enough to take out the stitches and then prepared to go home. She could flatter herself that she had not wasted her time. She had given medical attention to such as needed it, she had strengthened the small Christian community in its faith, admonished such as were lax and cast the good seed in places where it might be hoped under divine providence to take root.

The launch, coming from one of the other islands, put in somewhat late in the afternoon, but it was full moon and they expected to reach Baru before midnight. They brought her things down to the wharf and the people who were seeing her off stood about repeating their thanks. Quite a little crowd collected. The launch was loaded with sacks of copra, but Miss Jones was used to its strong smell and it did not incommode her. She made herself as comfortable a place to sit in as she could, and waiting for the launch to start, chatted with her grateful flock. She was the only passenger. Suddenly a group of natives emerged from the trees that embowered the little village on the lagoon and she saw that among them was a white man. He wore a prison sarong and a baju. He had long red hair. She at once recognized Ginger Ted. A policeman was with him. They shook hands and Ginger Ted shook hands with the villagers who accompanied him. They bore bundles of fruit and a jar which Miss Jones guessed contained native spirit, and these they put in the launch. She discovered to her surprise that Ginger Ted was coming with her. His term was up and instructions had arrived that he was to be returned to Baru in the launch. He gave her a glance, but did not nod – indeed Miss Jones turned away her head – and stepped in. The mechanic started his engine and in a moment they were jug-jugging through the channel in the lagoon. Ginger Ted clambered on to a pile of sacks and lit a cigarette.

Miss Jones ignored him. Of course she knew him very well. Her heart sank when she thought that he was going to be once more in Baru, creating a scandal and drinking, a peril to the women and a thorn in the flesh of all decent people. She knew the steps her brother had taken to have him deported and she had no patience with the Contrôleur, who would not see a duty that stared him so plainly in the face. When they had crossed the bar and were

in the open sea Ginger Ted took the stopper out of
the jar of arak and putting his mouth to it took a
long pull. Then he handed the jar to the two
mechanics who formed the crew. One was a middle-aged man and the other a youth.

'I do not wish you to drink anything while we are
on the journey,' said Miss Jones sternly to the elder
one.

He smiled at her and drank.

'A little arak can do no one any harm,' he
answered. He passed the jar to his companion, who
drank also.

'If you drink again I shall complain to the Contrôleur,' said Miss Jones.

The elder man said something she could not
understand, but which she suspected was very
rude, and passed the jar back to Ginger Ted. They
went along for an hour or more. The sea was like
glass and the sun set radiantly. It set behind one of
the islands and for a few minutes changed it into a
mystic city of the skies. Miss Jones turned round to
watch it and her heart was filled with gratitude for
the beauty of the world.

'And only man is vile,' she quoted to herself.

They went due east. In the distance was a little
island which she knew they passed close by. It was
uninhabited. A rocky islet thickly grown with
virgin forest. The boatman lit his lamps. The night
fell and immediately the sky was thick with stars.
The moon had not yet risen. Suddenly there was a
slight jar and the launch began to vibrate strangely.
The engine rattled. The head mechanic, calling to
his mate to take the helm, crept under the housing.
They seemed to be going more slowly. The engine
stopped. She asked the youth what was the matter,

but he did not know. Ginger Ted got down from the top of the copra sacks and slipped under the housing. When he reappeared she would have liked to ask him what had happened, but her dignity prevented her. She sat still and occupied herself with her thoughts. There was a long swell and the launch rolled slightly. The mechanic emerged once more into view and started the engine. Though it rattled like mad they began to move. The launch vibrated from stem to stern. They went very slowly. Evidently something was amiss, but Miss Jones was exasperated rather than alarmed. The launch was supposed to do six knots, but now it was just crawling along; at that rate they would not get into Baru till long, long after midnight. The mechanic, still busy under the housing, shouted out something to the man at the helm. They spoke in Bugi, of which Miss Jones knew very little. But after a while she noticed that they had changed their course and seemed to be heading for the little uninhabited island a good deal to the lee of which they should have passed.

'Where are we going?' she asked the helmsman with sudden misgiving.

He pointed to the islet. She got up and went to the housing and called to the man to come out.

'You're not going there? Why? What's the matter?'

'I can't get to Baru,' he said.

'But you must. I insist. I order you to go to Baru.'

The man shrugged his shoulders. He turned his back on her and slipped once more under the housing. Then Ginger Ted addressed her.

'One of the blades of the propeller has broken

off. He thinks he can get as far as that island. We shall have to stay the night there and he'll put on a new propeller in the morning when the tide's out.'

'I can't spend the night on an uninhabited island with three men,' she cried.

'A lot of women would jump at it.'

'I insist on going to Baru. Whatever happens we must get there tonight.'

'Don't get excited, old girl. We've got to beach the boat to put a new propeller on, and we shall be all right on the island.'

'How dare you speak to me like that. I think you're very insolent.'

'You'll be OK. We've got plenty of grub and we'll have a snack when we land. You have a drop of arak and you'll feel like a house on fire.'

'You're an impertinent man. If you don't go to Baru I'll have you all put in prison.'

'We're not going to Baru. We can't. We're going to that island and if you don't like it you can get out and swim.'

'Oh, you'll pay for this.'

'Shut up, you old cow,' said Ginger Ted.

Miss Jones gave a gasp of anger. But she controlled herself. Even out there, in the middle of the ocean, she had too much dignity to bandy words with that vile wretch. The launch, the engine rattling horribly, crawled on. It was pitch dark now, and she could no longer see the island they were making for. Miss Jones, deeply incensed, sat with lips tight shut and a frown on her brow; she was not used to being crossed. Then the moon rose and she could see the bulk of Ginger Ted sprawling on the top of the piled sacks of copra. The glimmer of his cigarette was strangely sinister. Now the island was vaguely outlined against the sky. They reached it and the boatman ran the launch on to the beach. Suddenly Miss Jones gave a gasp. The truth had dawned on her and her anger changed to fear. Her heart beat violently. She shook in every limb. She felt dreadfully faint. She saw it all. Was the broken propeller a put-up job or was it an accident? She could not be certain; anyhow, she knew that Ginger Ted would seize the opportunity. Ginger Ted would rape her. She knew his character. He was mad about women. That was what he had done, practically, to the girl at the mission, such a good little thing she was and an excellent sempstress; they would have prosecuted him for that and he would have been sentenced to years of imprisonment only very unfortunately the innocent child had gone back to him several times and indeed had only complained of his ill usage when he left her for somebody else. They had gone to the Contrôleur about it, but he had refused to take any steps, saying in that coarse way of his that even if what the girl said was true, it didn't look very much as though it had been an altogether unpleasant experience. Ginger Ted was a scoundrel. And she was a white woman. What chance was there that he would spare her? None. She knew men. But she must pull herself together. She must keep her wits about her. She must have courage. She was determined to sell her virtue dearly, and if he killed her – well, she would rather die than yield. And if she died she would rest in the arms of Jesus. For a moment a great light blinded her eyes and she saw the mansions of her Heavenly Father. They were a grand and sumptuous mixture of a picture palace and a railway station. The mechanics and Ginger

Ted jumped out of the launch and, waist-deep in water, gathered round the broken propeller. She took advantage of their preoccupation to get her case of surgical instruments out of the box. She took out the four scalpels it contained and secreted them in her clothing. If Ginger Ted touched her she would not hesitate to plunge a scalpel in his heart.

'Now then, miss, you'd better get out,' said Ginger Ted. 'You'll be better off on the beach than in the boat.'

She thought so too. At least there she would have freedom of action. Without a word she clambered over the copra sacks. He offered her his hand.

'I don't want your help,' she said coldly.

'You can go to hell,' he answered.

It was a little difficult to get out of the boat without showing her legs, but by the exercise of considerable ingenuity she managed it.

'Damned lucky we've got something to eat. We'll make a fire and then you'd better have a snack and a nip of arak.'

'I want nothing. I only want to be left alone.'

'It won't hurt me if you go hungry.'

She did not answer. She walked, with head erect, along the beach. She held the largest scalpel in her closed fist. The moon allowed her to see where she was going. She looked for a place to hide. The thick forest came down to the very edge of the beach; but, afraid of its darkness (after all, she was but a woman), she dared not plunge into its depth. She did not know what animals lurked there or what dangerous snakes. Besides, her instinct told her that it was better to keep those three bad men in sight; then if they came towards her she would be prepared. Presently she found a little hollow. She looked round. They seemed to be occupied with their own affairs and they could not see her. She slipped in. There was a rock between them and her so that she was hidden from them and yet could watch them. She saw them go to and from the boat carrying things. She saw them build a fire. It lit them luridly and she saw them sit around it and eat, and she saw the jar of arak passed from one to the other. They were all going to get drunk. What would happen to her then? It might be that she could cope with Ginger Ted, though his strength terrified her, but against three she would be powerless. A mad idea came to her to go to Ginger Ted and fall on her knees before him and beg him to spare her. He must have some spark of decent feeling in him and she had always been so convinced that there was good even in the worst of men. He must have had a mother. Perhaps he had a sister. Ah, but how could you appeal to a man blinded with lust and drunk with arak? She began to feel terribly weak. She was afraid she was going to cry. That would never do. She needed all her self-control. She bit her lip. She watched them, like a tiger watching his prey; no, not like that, like a lamb watching three hungry wolves. She saw them put more wood on the fire and Ginger Ted, in his sarong, silhouetted by the flames. Perhaps after he had had his will of her he would pass her on to the others. How could she go back to her brother when such a thing had happened to her? Of course he would be sympathetic, but would he ever feel quite the same to her again? It would break his heart. And perhaps he would think that she ought to have resisted more. For his sake perhaps it would be better if she said nothing about it. Naturally the men would say nothing. It would mean twenty years in prison for them. But then supposing she had a baby. Miss Jones instinctively clenched her hands with horror and nearly cut herself with the scalpel. Of course it would only infuriate them if she resisted.

'What shall I do?' she cried. 'What have I done to deserve this?'

She flung herself down on her knees and prayed to God to save her. She prayed long and earnestly. She reminded God that she was a virgin and just mentioned, in case it had slipped the divine memory, how much St Paul had valued that excellent state. And then she peeped round the rock again. The three men appeared to be smoking and the fire was dying down. Now was the time that Ginger Ted's lewd thoughts might be expected to turn to the woman who was at his mercy. She smothered a cry, for suddenly he got up and walked in her direction. She felt all her muscles grow taut, and though her heart was beating furiously she clenched the scalpel firmly in her hand. But it was for another purpose that Ginger Ted had got up. Miss Jones blushed and looked away. He strolled slowly back to the others and sitting down again raised the jar of arak to his lips. Miss Jones, crouching behind the rock, watched with straining eyes. The conversation round the fire grew less and presently she divined, rather than saw, that the two natives wrapped themselves in blankets and composed themselves to slumber. She understood. This was the moment Ginger Ted had been waiting for. When they were fast asleep he would get up cautiously and without a sound, in order not to wake the others, creep stealthily towards her. Was it that he was unwilling to share her with them or did he know that his deed was so dastardly that he did not wish them to know of it? After all, he was a white man and she was a white woman. He could not have sunk so low as to allow her to suffer the violence of natives. But his plan, which was so obvious to her, had given her an idea; when she saw him coming she would scream, she would scream so loudly that it would wake the two mechanics. She remembered now that the elder, though he had only one eye, had a kind face. But Ginger Ted did not move. She was feeling terribly tired. She began to fear that she would not have the strength now to resist him. She had gone through too much. She closed her eyes for a minute.

When she opened them it was broad daylight. She must have fallen asleep and, so shattered was she by emotion, have slept till long after dawn. It gave her quite a turn. She sought to rise, but something caught in her legs. She looked and found that she was covered with two empty copra sacks. Someone had come in the night and put them over her. Ginger Ted! She gave a little scream. The horrible thought flashed through her mind that he had outraged her in her sleep. No. It was impossible. And yet he had had her at his mercy. Defenceless. And he had spared her. She blushed furiously. She raised herself to her feet, feeling a little stiff, and arranged her disordered dress. The scalpel had fallen from her hand and she picked it up. She took the two copra sacks and emerged from her hiding-place. She walked towards the boat. It was floating in the shallow water of the lagoon.

'Come on, Miss Jones,' said Ginger Ted. 'We've

finished. I was just going to wake you up.'

She could not look at him, but she felt herself as red as a turkey cock.

'Have a banana?' he said.

Without a word she took it. She was very hungry, and ate it with relish.

'Step on this rock and you'll be able to get in without wetting your feet.'

Miss Jones felt as though she could sink into the ground with shame, but she did as he told her. He took hold of her arm – good heavens! his hand was like an iron vice, never, never could she have struggled with him – and helped her into the launch. The mechanic started the engine and they slid out of the lagoon. In three hours they were at Baru.

That evening, having been officially released, Ginger Ted went to the Contrôleur's house. He wore no longer the prison uniform, but the ragged singlet and the khaki shorts in which he had been arrested. He had had his hair cut and it fitted his head now like a little curly red cap. He was thinner. He had lost his bloated flabbiness and looked younger and better. Mr Gruyter, a friendly grin on his round face, shook hands with him and asked him to sit down. The boy brought two bottles of beer.

'I'm glad to see you hadn't forgotten my invitation, Ginger,' said the Contrôleur.

'Not likely. I've been looking forward to this for six months.'

'Here's luck, Ginger Ted.'

'Same to you, Contrôleur.'

They emptied their glasses and the Contrôleur clapped his hands. The boy brought two more bottles.

'Well, you don't bear me any malice for the sentence I gave you, I hope.'

'No bloody fear. I was mad for a minute, but I got over it. I didn't have half a bad time, you know. Nice lot of girls on that island, Contrôleur. You ought to give 'em a look over one of these days.'

'You're a bad lot, Ginger.'

'Terrible.'

'Good beer, isn't it?'

'Fine.'

'Let's have some more.'

Ginger Ted's remittance had been arriving every month and the Contrôleur now had fifty pounds for him. When the damage he had done to the Chinaman's shop was paid for there would still be over thirty.

'That's quite a lot of money, Ginger. You ought to do something useful with it.'

'I mean to,' answered Ginger. 'Spend it.'

The Contrôleur sighed.

'Well, that's what money's for, I guess.'

The Contrôleur gave his guest the news. Not much had happened during the last six months. Time on the Alas Islands did not matter very much and the rest of the world did not matter at all.

'Any wars anywhere?' asked Ginger Ted.

'No. Not that I've noticed. Harry Jervis found a pretty big pearl. He says he's going to ask a thousand quid for it.'

'I hope he gets it.'

'And Charlie McCormack's married.'

'He always was a bit soft.'

Suddenly the boy appeared and said Mr Jones wished to know if he might come in. Before the Contrôleur could give an answer Mr Jones walked in.

'I won't detain you long,' he said. 'I've been try-ing to get hold of this good man all day and when I heard he was here I thought you wouldn't mind my coming.'

'How is Miss Jones?' asked the Contrôleur politely. 'None the worse for her night in the open, I trust.'

'She's naturally a bit shaken. She had a temperature and I've insisted on her going to bed, but I don't think it's serious.'

The two men had got up on the missionary's entrance, and now the missionary went up to Ginger Ted and held out his hand.

'I want to thank you. You did a great and noble thing. My sister is right, one should always look for the good in their fellow-men; I am afraid I mis-judged you in the past: I beg your pardon.'

He spoke very solemnly. Ginger Ted looked at him with amazement. He had not been able to prevent the missionary taking his hand. He still held it.

'What the hell are you talking about?'

'You had my sister at your mercy and you spared her. I thought you were all evil and I am ashamed. She was defenceless. She was in your power. You had pity on her. I thank you from the bottom of my heart. Neither my sister nor I will ever forget. God bless and guard you always.'

Mr Jones's voice shook a little and he turned his head away. He released Ginger Ted's hand and strode quickly to the door. Ginger Ted watched him with a blank face.

'What the blazes does he mean?' he asked.

The Contrôleur laughed. He tried to control himself, but the more he did the more he laughed. He shook and you saw the folds of his fat belly ripple under the sarong. He leaned back in his long chair and rolled from side to side. He did not laugh only with his face, he laughed with his whole body, and even the muscles of his podgy legs shook with mirth. He held his aching ribs. Ginger Ted looked at him frowning, and because he did not understand what the joke was he grew angry. He seized one of the empty beer bottles by the neck.

'If you don't stop laughing, I'll break your bloody head open,' he said.

The Contrôleur mopped his face. He swallowed a mouthful of beer. He sighed and groaned because his sides were hurting him.

'He's thanking you for having respected the virtue of Miss Jones,' he spluttered at last.

'Me?' cried Ginger Ted.

The thought took quite a long time to travel through his head, but when at last he got it he flew into a violent rage. There flowed from his mouth such a stream of blasphemous obscenities as would have startled a marine.

'That old cow,' he finished. 'What does he take me for?'

'You have the reputation of being rather hot stuff with the girls, Ginger,' giggled the little Contrôleur.

'I wouldn't touch her with the fag-end of a barge-pole. It never entered my head. The nerve. I'll wring his blasted neck. Look here, give me my money, I'm going to get drunk.'

'I don't blame you,' said the Contrôleur.

'That old cow,' repeated Ginger Ted. 'That old cow.'

He was shocked and outraged. The suggestion really shattered his sense of decency.

The Contrôleur had the money at hand and having got Ginger Ted to sign the necessary papers gave it to him.

'Go and get drunk, Ginger Ted,' he said, 'but I warn you, if you get into mischief it'll be twelve months next time.'

'I shan't get into mischief,' said Ginger Ted sombrely. He was suffering from a sense of injury. 'It's an insult,' he shouted at the Contrôleur. 'That's what it is, it's a bloody insult.'

He lurched out of the house, and as he went he muttered to himself: 'dirty swine, dirty swine'. Ginger Ted remained drunk for a week. Mr Jones went to see the Contrôleur again.

'I'm very sorry to hear that poor fellow has taken up his evil course again,' he said. 'My sister and I are dreadfully disappointed. I'm afraid it wasn't very wise to give him so much money at once.'

'It was his own money. I had no right to keep it back.'

'Not a legal right, perhaps, but surely a moral right.'

He told the Contrôleur the story of that fearful night on the island. With her feminine instinct, Miss Jones had realized that the man, inflamed with lust, was determined to take advantage of her, and, resolved to defend herself to the last, had armed herself with a scalpel. He told the Contrôleur how she had prayed and wept and how she had hidden herself. Her agony was indescribable, and she knew that she could never have survived the shame. She rocked to and fro and every moment she thought he was coming. And there was no help anywhere and at last she had fallen asleep; she was tired out, poor thing, she had undergone more than any human being could stand, and then when she awoke she found that he had covered her with copra sacks. He had found her asleep, and surely it was her innocence, her very helplessness that had moved him, he hadn't the heart to touch her; he covered her gently with two copra sacks and crept silently away.

'It shows you that deep down in him there is something sterling. My sister feels it's our duty to save him. We must do something for him.'

'Well, in your place, I wouldn't try till he's got through all his money,' said the Contrôleur, 'and then if he's not in gaol you can do what you like.'

But Ginger Ted didn't want to be saved. About a fortnight after his release from prison he was sitting on a stool outside a Chinaman's shop looking vacantly down the street when he saw Miss Jones coming along. He stared at her for a minute and once more amazement seized him. He muttered to himself and there can be little doubt that his mutterings were disrespectful. But then he noticed that Miss Jones had seen him and he quickly turned his head away; he was conscious, notwithstanding, that she was looking at him. She was walking briskly, but she sensibly diminished her pace as she approached him. He thought she was going to stop and speak to him. He got up quickly and went into the shop. He did not venture to come out for at least five minutes. Half an hour later Mr Jones himself came along and he went straight up to Ginger Ted with outstretched hand.

'How do you do, Mr Edward? My sister told me I should find you here.'

Ginger Ted gave him a surly look and did not take the proffered hand. He made no answer.

'We'd be so very glad if you'd come to dinner with us next Sunday. My sister's a capital cook and she'll make you a real Australian dinner.'

'Go to hell,' said Ginger Ted.

'That's not very gracious,' said the missionary, but with a little laugh to show that he was not affronted. 'You go and see the Contrôleur from time to time, why shouldn't you come and see us? It's pleasant to talk to white people now and then. Won't you let bygones be bygones? I can assure you of a very cordial welcome.'

'I haven't got clothes fit to go out in,' said Ginger Ted sulkily.

'Oh, never mind about that. Come as you are.'

'I won't.'

'Why not? You must have a reason.'

Ginger Ted was a blunt man. He had no hesitation in saying what we should all like to when we receive unwelcome invitations.

'I don't want to.'

'I'm sorry. My sister will be very disappointed.'

Mr Jones, determined to show that he was not in the least offended, gave him a breezy nod and walked on. Forty-eight hours later there mysteriously arrived at the house in which Ginger Ted lodged a parcel containing a suit of ducks, a tennis shirt, a pair of socks and some shoes. He was unaccustomed to receiving presents and next time he saw the Contrôleur asked him if it was he who had sent the things.

'Not on your life,' replied the Contrôleur. 'I'm perfectly indifferent to the state of your wardrobe.'

'Well, then, who the hell can have?'

'Search me.'

It was necessary from time to time for Miss

Jones to see Mr Gruyter on business and shortly after this she came to see him one morning in his office. She was a capable woman and though she generally wanted him to do something he had no mind to, she did not waste his time. He was a little surprised then to discover that she had come on a very trivial errand. When he told her that he could not take cognizance of the matter in question, she did not as was her habit try to convince him, but accepted his refusal as definite. She got up to go and then as though it were an after-thought said:

'Oh, Mr Gruyter, my brother is very anxious that we should have the man they call Ginger Ted to supper with us and I've written him a little note inviting him for the day after tomorrow. I think he's rather shy, and I wonder if you'd come with him.'

'That's very kind of you.'

'My brother feels that we ought to do something for the poor fellow.'

'A woman's influence and all that sort of thing,' said the Contrôleur demurely.

'Will you persuade him to come? I'm sure he will if you make a point of it, and when he knows the way he'll come again. It seems such a pity to let a young man like that go to pieces altogether.'

The Contrôleur looked up at her. She was several inches taller than he. He thought her very unattractive. She reminded him strangely of wet linen hung on a clothes-line to dry. His eyes twinkled, but he kept a straight face.

'I'll do my best,' he said.

'How old is he?' she asked.

'According to his passport he's thirty-one.'

'And what is his real name?'

'Wilson.'

'Edward Wilson,' she said softly.

'It's astonishing that after the life he's led he should be so strong,' murmured the Contrôleur. 'He has the strength of an ox.'

'Those red-headed men sometimes are very powerful,' said Miss Jones, but spoke as though she were choking.

'Quite so,' said the Contrôleur.

Then for no obvious reason Miss Jones blushed. She hurriedly said good-bye to the Contrôleur and left his office.

'*Godverdomme!*' said the Contrôleur.

He knew now who had sent Ginger Ted the new clothes.

He met him during the course of the day and asked him whether he had heard from Miss Jones. Ginger Ted took a crumpled ball of paper out of his pocket and gave it to him. It was the invitation. It ran as follows:

'Dear Mr Wilson,

My brother and I would be so very glad if you would come and have supper with us next Thursday at 7.30. The Contrôleur has kindly promised to come. We have some new records from Australia which I am sure you will like. I am afraid I was not very nice to you last time we met, but I did not know you so well then, and I am big enough to admit it when I have committed an error. I hope you will forgive me and let me be your friend.

Yours sincerely,
Martha Jones.'

The Contrôleur noticed that she addressed him as Mr Wilson and referred to his own promise to go, so that when she told him she had already invited Ginger Ted she had a little anticipated the truth.

'What are you going to do?'

'I'm not going, if that's what you mean. Damned nerve.'

'You must answer the letter.'

'Well, I won't.'

'Now look here, Ginger, you put on those new clothes and you come as a favour to me. I've got to go, and damn it all, you can't leave me in the lurch. It won't hurt you just once.'

Ginger Ted looked at the Contrôleur suspiciously, but his face was serious and his manner sincere: he could not guess that within him the Dutchman bubbled with laughter.

'What the devil do they want me for?'

'I don't know. The pleasure of your society, I suppose.'

'Will there be any booze?'

'No, but come up to my house at seven, and we'll have a tiddly before we go.'

'Oh, all right,' said Ginger Ted sulkily.

The Contrôleur rubbed his little fat hands with joy. He was expecting a great deal of amusement from the party. But when Thursday came and seven o'clock, Ginger Ted was dead drunk and Mr Gruyter had to go alone. He told the missionary and his sister the plain truth. Mr Jones shook his head.

'I'm afraid it's no good, Martha, the man's hopeless.'

For a moment Miss Jones was silent and the Contrôleur saw two tears trickle down her long thin nose. She bit her lip.

'No one is hopeless. Everyone has some good in him. I shall pray for him every night. It would be wicked to doubt the power of God.'

Perhaps Miss Jones was right in this, but the divine providence took a very funny way of effecting its ends. Ginger Ted began to drink more heavily than ever. He was so troublesome that even Mr Gruyter lost patience with him. He made up his mind that he could not have the fellow on the islands any more and resolved to deport him on the next boat that touched at Baru. Then a man died under mysterious circumstances after having been for a trip to one of the islands and the Contrôleur learnt that there had been several deaths on the same island. He sent the Chinese who was the official doctor of the group to look into the matter, and very soon received intelligence that the deaths were due to cholera. Two more took place at Baru and the certainty was forced upon him that there was an epidemic.

The Contrôleur cursed freely. He cursed in Dutch, he cursed in English and he cursed in Malay. Then he drank a bottle of beer and smoked a cigar. After that he took thought. He knew the Chinese doctor would be useless. He was a nervous little man from Java and the natives would refuse to obey his orders. The Contrôleur was efficient and knew pretty well what must be done, but he could not do everything single-handed. He did not like Mr Jones, but just then he was thankful that he was at hand, and he sent for him at once. In ten minutes

Mr Jones was in the office. He was accompanied by his sister.

'You know what I want to see you about, Mr Jones,' he said abruptly.

'Yes. I've been expecting a message from you. That is why my sister has come with me. We are ready to put all our resources at your disposal. I need not tell you that my sister is as competent as a man.'

'I know. I shall be very glad of her assistance.'

They set to without further delay to discuss the steps that must be taken. Hospital huts would have to be erected and quarantine stations. The inhabitants of the various villages on the islands must be forced to take proper precautions. In a good many cases the infected villages drew their water from the same well as the uninfected, and in each case this difficulty would have to be dealt with according to circumstances. It was necessary to send round people to give orders and make sure that they were carried out. Negligence must be ruthlessly punished. The worst of it was that the natives would not obey other natives, and orders given by native policemen, themselves unconvinced of their efficacy, would certainly be disregarded. It was advisable for Mr Jones to stay at Baru where the population was largest and his medical attention most wanted; and what with the official duties that forced him to keep in touch with his headquarters, it was impossible for Mr Gruyter to visit all the other islands himself. Miss Jones must go; but the natives of some of the outlying islands were wild and treacherous; the Contrôleur had had a good deal of trouble with them. He did not like the idea of exposing her to danger.

'I'm not afraid,' she said.

'I daresay. But if you have your throat cut I shall get into trouble, and besides, we're so short-handed I don't want to risk losing your help.'

'Then let Mr Wilson come with me. He knows the natives better than anyone and can speak all their dialects.'

'Ginger Ted?' The Contrôleur stared at her. 'He's just getting over an attack of DTs.'

'I know,' she answered.

'You know a great deal, Miss Jones.'

Even though the moment was so serious Mr Gruyter could not but smile. He gave her a sharp look, but she met it coolly.

'There's nothing like responsibility for bringing out what there is in a man, and I think something like this may be the making of him.'

'Do you think it would be wise to trust yourself for days at a time to a man of such infamous character?' said the missionary.

'I put my trust in God,' she answered gravely.

'Do you think he'd be any use?' asked the Contrôleur. 'You know what he is.'

'I'm convinced of it.' Then she blushed. 'After all, no one knows better than I that he's capable of self-control.'

The Contrôleur bit his lip.

'Let's send for him.'

He gave a message to the sergeant and in a few minutes Ginger Ted stood before them. He looked ill. He had evidently been much shaken by his recent attack and his nerves were all to pieces. He was in rags and he had not shaved for a week. No one could have looked more disreputable.

'Look here, Ginger,' said the Contrôleur, 'it's

about this cholera business. We've got to force the natives to take precautions and we want you to help us.'

'Why the hell should I?'

'No reason at all. Except philanthropy.'

'Nothing doing, Contrôleur. I'm not a phil-anthropist.'

'That settles that. That was all. You can go.'

But as Ginger Ted turned to the door Miss Jones stopped him.

'It was my suggestion, Mr Wilson. You see, they want me to go to Labobo and Sakunchi, and the natives there are so funny I was afraid to go alone. I thought if you came I should be safer.'

He gave her a look of extreme distaste.

'What do you suppose I care if they cut your throat?'

Miss Jones looked at him and her eyes filled with tears. She began to cry. He stood and watched her stupidly.

'There's no reason why you should.' She pulled herself together and dried her eyes. 'I'm being silly. I shall be all right. I'll go alone.'

'It's damned foolishness for a woman to go to Labobo.'

She gave him a little smile.

'I daresay it is, but you see, it's my job and I can't help myself. I'm sorry if I offended you by asking you. You must forget about it. I daresay it wasn't quite fair to ask you to take such a risk.'

For quite a minute Ginger Ted stood and looked at her. He shifted from one foot to the other. His surly face seemed to grow black.

'Oh, hell, have it your own way,' he said at last. 'I'll come with you. When d'you want to start?'

They set out next day, with drugs and disinfectants, in the Government launch. Mr Gruyter as soon as he had put the necessary work in order was to start off in a prahu in the other direction. For four months the epidemic raged. Though everything possible was done to localize it one island after another was attacked. The Contrôleur was busy from morning to night. He had no sooner got back to Baru from one or other of the islands to do what was necessary there than he had to set off again. He distributed food and medicine. He cheered the terrified people. He supervised everything. He worked like a dog. He saw nothing of Ginger Ted, but he heard from Mr Jones that the experiment was working out beyond all hopes. The scamp was behaving himself. He had a way with the natives; and by cajolery, firmness and on occasion the use of his fist, managed to make them take the steps necessary for their own safety. Miss Jones could congratulate herself on the success of the scheme. But the Contrôleur was too tired to be amused. When the epidemic had run its course he rejoiced because out of a population of eight thousand only six hundred had died.

Finally he was able to give the district a clean bill of health.

One evening he was sitting in his sarong on the veranda of his house and he read a French novel with the happy consciousness that once more he could take things easy. His head boy came in and told him that Ginger Ted wished to see him. He got up from his chair and shouted to him to come in. Company was just what he wanted. It had crossed the Contrôleur's mind that it would be pleasant to get drunk that night, but it is dull to get drunk alone, and he had regretfully put the thought aside. And heaven had sent Ginger Ted in the nick of time. By God, they would make a night of it. After four months they deserved a bit of fun. Ginger Ted entered. He was wearing a clean suit of white ducks. He was shaved. He looked another man.

'Why, Ginger, you look as if you'd been spending a month at a health resort instead of nursing a pack of natives dying of cholera. And look at your clothes. Have you just stepped out of a band-box?'

Ginger Ted smiled rather sheepishly. The head boy brought two bottles of beer and poured them out.

'Help yourself, Ginger,' said the Contrôleur as he took his glass.

'I don't think I'll have any, thank you.'

The Contrôleur put down his glass and looked at Ginger Ted with amazement.

'Why, what's the matter? Aren't you thirsty?'

'I don't mind having a cup of tea.'

'A cup of what?'

'I'm on the wagon. Martha and I are going to be married.'

'Ginger!'

The Contrôleur's eyes popped out of his head. He scratched his shaven pate.

'You can't marry Miss Jones,' he said. 'No one could marry Miss Jones.'

'Well, I'm going to. That's what I've come to see you about. Owen's going to marry us in chapel but we want to be married by Dutch law as well.'

'A joke's a joke, Ginger. What's the idea?'

'She wanted it. She fell for me that night we spent on the island when the propeller broke. She's not a bad old girl when you get to know her. It's her last chance, if you understand what I mean, and I'd like to do something to oblige her. And she wants someone to take care of her, there's no doubt about that.'

'Ginger, Ginger, before you can say knife she'll make you into a damned missionary.'

'I don't know that I'd mind that so much if we had a little mission of our own. She says I'm a bloody marvel with the natives. She says I can do more with a native in five minutes than Owen can do in a year. She says she's never known anyone with the magnetism I have. It seems a pity to waste a gift like that.'

The Contrôleur looked at him without speaking and slowly nodded his head three or four times. She'd nobbled him all right.

'I've converted seventeen already,' said Ginger Ted.

'You? I didn't know you believed in Christianity.'

'Well, I don't know that I did exactly, but when I talked to 'em and they just came into the fold like a lot of blasted sheep, well, it gave me quite a turn. Blimey, I said, I daresay there's something in it after all.'

'You should have raped her, Ginger. I wouldn't have been hard on you. I wouldn't have given you more than three years and three years is soon over.'

'Look here, Contrôleur, don't you ever let on that the thought never entered my head. Women are touchy, you know, and she'd be as sore as hell if she knew that.'

'I guessed she'd got her eye on you, but I never thought it would come to this.' The Contrôleur in an agitated manner walked up and down the veranda. 'Listen to me, old boy,' he said after an interval of reflection, 'we've had some grand times together and a friend's a friend. I'll tell you what I'll do, I'll lend you the launch and you can go and hide on one of the islands till the next ship comes along and then I'll get 'em to slow down and take you on board. You've only got one chance now and that's to cut and run.'

Ginger Ted shook his head.

'It's no good, Contrôleur, I know you mean well, but I'm going to marry the blasted woman, and that's that. You don't know the joy of bringing all them bleeding sinners to repentance, and Christ! that girl can make a treacle pudding. I haven't eaten a better one since I was a kid.'

The Contrôleur was very much disturbed. The drunken scamp was his only companion on the islands and he did not want to lose him. He discovered that he had even a certain affection for him. Next day he went to see the missionary.

'What's this I hear about your sister marrying Ginger Ted?' he asked him. 'It's the most extraordinary thing I've ever heard in my life.'

'It's true nevertheless.'

'You must do something about it. It's madness.'

'My sister is of full age and entitled to do as she pleases.'

'But you don't mean to tell me you approve of it. You know Ginger Ted. He's a bum and there are no two ways about it. Have you told her the risk she's running? I mean, bringing sinners to repentance and all that sort of thing's all right, but there are limits. And does the leopard ever change his spots?'

Then for the first time in his life the Contrôleur saw a twinkle in the missionary's eye.

'My sister is a very determined woman, Mr Gruyter,' he replied. 'From that night they spent on the island he never had a chance.'

The Contrôleur gasped. He was as surprised as the prophet when the Lord opened the mouth of the ass, and she said unto Balaam, What have I done unto thee, that thou hast smitten me these three times? Perhaps Mr Jones was human after all.

'*Allejesus!*' muttered the Contrôleur.

Before anything more could be said Miss Jones swept into the room. She was radiant. She looked ten years younger. Her cheeks were flushed and her nose was hardly red at all.

'Have you come to congratulate me, Mr Gruyter?' she cried, and her manner was sprightly and girlish. 'You see, I was right after all. Everyone has some good in them. You don't know how splendid Edward has been all through this terrible time. He's a hero. He's a saint. Even I was surprised.'

'I hope you'll be very happy, Miss Jones.'

'I know I shall. Oh, it would be wicked of me to doubt it. For it is the Lord who has brought us together.'

'Do you think so?'

'I know it. Don't you see? Except for the cholera Edward would never have found himself. Except for the cholera we should never have learnt to know one another. I have never seen the hand of God more plainly manifest.'

The Contrôleur could not but think that it was rather a clumsy device to bring those two together that necessitated the death of six hundred innocent persons, but not being well versed in the ways of omnipotence he made no remark.

'You'll never guess where we're going for our honeymoon,' said Miss Jones, perhaps a trifle archly.

'Java?'

'No, if you'll lend us the launch, we're going to that island where we were marooned. It has very tender recollections for both of us. It was there that I first guessed how fine and good Edward was. It's there I want him to have his reward.'

The Contrôleur caught his breath. He left quickly, for he thought that unless he had a bottle of beer at once he would have a fit. He was never so shocked in his life.

The Book-Bag

Some people read for instruction, which is praiseworthy, and some for pleasure, which is innocent,
but not a few read from habit, and I suppose that
this is neither innocent nor praiseworthy. Of that
lamentable company am I. Conversation after a
time bores me, games tire me and my own
thoughts, which we are told are the unfailing
resource of a sensible man, have a tendency to run
dry. Then I fly to my book as the opium-smoker to
his pipe. I would sooner read the catalogue of the
Army and Navy Stores or Bradshaw's Guide than
nothing at all, and indeed I have spend many
delightful hours over both these works. At one time
I never went out without a second-hand bookseller's list in my pocket. I know no reading more
fruity. Of course to read in this way is as reprehen-
sible as doping, and I never cease to wonder at the
impertinence of great readers who, because they
are such, look down on the illiterate. From the
standpoint of what eternity is it better to have read
a thousand books than to have ploughed a million
furrows? Let us admit that reading with us is just a
drug that we cannot do without – who of this band
does not know the restlessness that attacks him
when he has been severed from reading too long,
the apprehension and irritability, and the sigh of

relief which the sight of a printed page extracts from him? – and so let us be no more vainglorious than the poor slaves of the hypodermic needle or the pint-pot.

And like the dope-fiend who cannot move from place to place without taking with him a plentiful supply of his deadly balm I never venture far without a sufficiency of reading matter. Books are so necessary to me that when in a railway train I have become aware that fellow-travellers have come away without a single one I have been seized with a veritable dismay. But when I am starting on a long journey the problem is formidable. I have learnt my lesson. Once, imprisoned by illness for three months in a hill-town in Java, I came to the end of all the books I had brought with me, and knowing no Dutch was obliged to buy the school-books from which intelligent Javanese, I suppose, acquired knowledge of French and German. So I read again after five-and-twenty years the frigid plays of Goethe, the fables of La Fontaine and the tragedies of the tender and exact Racine. I have the greatest admiration for Racine, but I admit that to read his plays one after the other requires a certain effort in a person who is suffering from colitis. Since then I have made a point of travelling with the largest sack made for carrying soiled linen and filling it to the brim with books to suit every possible occasion and every mood. It weighs a ton and strong porters reel under its weight. Custom-house officials look at it askance, but recoil from it with consternation when I give them my word that it contains nothing but books. Its inconvenience is that the particular work I suddenly hanker to read is always at the bottom and it is impossible for me to get it without emptying the book-bag's entire contents upon the floor. Except for this, however, I should perhaps never have heard the singular history of Olive Hardy.

I was wandering about Malaya, staying here and there, a week or two if there was a rest-house or a hotel, and a day or so if I was obliged to inflict myself on a planter or a District Officer whose hospitality I had no wish to abuse; and at the moment I happened to be at Penang. It is a pleasant little town, with a hotel that has always seemed to me very agreeable, but the stranger finds little to do there and time hung a trifle heavily on my hands. One morning I received a letter from a man I knew only by name. This was Mark Featherstone. He was Acting Resident, in the absence on leave of the Resident, at a place called Tenggarah. There was a sultan there and it appeared that a water festival of some sort was to take place which Featherstone thought would interest me. He said that he would be glad if I would come and stay with him for a few days. I wired to tell him that I should be delighted and next day took the train to Tenggarah. Featherstone met me at the station. He was a man of about thirty-five, I should think, tall and handsome, with fine eyes and a strong, stern face. He had a wiry black moustache and bushy eyebrows. He looked more like a soldier than a government official. He was very smart in white ducks, with a white topi, and he wore his clothes with elegance. He was a little shy, which seemed odd in a strapping fellow of resolute mien, but I surmised that this was only because he was unused to the society of that strange fish, a writer, and I hoped in a little to put him at his ease.

'My boys'll look after your barang,' he said.

'We'll go down to the club. Give them your keys and they'll unpack before we get back.'

I told him that I had a good deal of luggage and thought it better to leave everything at the station but what I particularly wanted. He would not hear of it.

'It doesn't matter a bit. It'll be safer at my house. It's always better to have one's barang with one.'

'All right.'

I gave my keys and the ticket for my trunk and my book-bag to a Chinese boy who stood at my host's elbow. Outside the station a car was waiting for us and we stepped in.

'Do you play bridge?' asked Featherstone.

'I do.'

'I thought most writers didn't.'

'They don't,' I said. 'It's generally considered among authors a sign of deficient intelligence to play cards.'

The club was a bungalow, pleasing but unpretentious; it had a large reading-room, a billiard-room with one table, and a small card-room. When we arrived it was empty but for one or two persons reading the English weeklies, and we walked through to the tennis courts where a couple of sets were being played. A number of people were sitting on the veranda, looking on, smoking and sipping long drinks. I was introduced to one or two of them. But the light was failing and soon the players could hardly see the ball. Featherstone asked one of the men I had been introduced to if he would like a rubber. He said he would. Featherstone looked about for a fourth. He caught sight of a man sitting a little by himself, paused for a second, and went up to him. The two exchanged a few words and then came towards us. We strolled in to the card-room. We had a very nice game. I did not pay much attention to the two men who made up the four. They stood me drinks and I, a temporary member of the club, returned the compliment. The drinks were very small, quarter whiskies, and in the two hours we played each of us able to show his open-handedness without an excessive consumption of alcohol. When the advancing hour suggested that the next rubber must be the last we changed from whisky to gin pahits. The rubber came to an end. Featherstone called for the book and the winnings and losings of each one of us were set down. One of the men got up.

'Well, I must be going,' he said.

'Going back to the Estate?' asked Featherstone.

'Yes,' he nodded. He turned to me. 'Shall you be here tomorrow?'

'I hope so.'

He went out of the room.

'I'll collect my mem and get along home to dinner,' said the other.

'We might be going too,' said Featherstone.

'I'm ready whenever you are,' I replied.

We got into the car and drove to his house. It was a longish drive. In the darkness I could see nothing much, but presently I realized that we were going up a rather steep hill. We reached the Residency.

It had been an evening like any other, pleasant, but not at all exciting, and I had spent I don't know how many just like it. I did not expect it to leave any sort of impression on me.

Featherstone led me into his sitting-room. It

looked comfortable, but it was a trifle ordinary. It had large basket arm-chairs covered with cretonne and on the walls were a great many framed photographs; the tables were littered with papers, magazines and official reports, with pipes, yellow tins of straight-cut cigarettes and pink tins of tobacco. In a row of shelves were untidily stacked a good many books, their bindings stained with damp and the ravages of white ants. Featherstone showed me my room and left me with the words:

'Shall you be ready for a gin pahit in ten minutes?'

'Easily,' I said.

I had a bath and changed and went downstairs. Featherstone, ready before me, mixed our drink as he heard me clatter down the wooden staircase. We dined. We talked. The festival which I had been invited to see was the next day but one, but Featherstone told me he had arranged for me before that to be received by the Sultan.

'He's a jolly old boy,' he said. 'And the palace is a sight for sore eyes.'

After dinner we talked a little more, Featherstone put on the gramophone, and we looked at the latest illustrated papers that had arrived from England. Then we went to bed. Featherstone came to my room to see that I had everything I wanted.

'I suppose you haven't any books with you,' he said. 'I haven't got a thing to read.'

'Books?' I cried.

I pointed to my book-bag. It stood upright, bulging oddly, so that it looked like a humpbacked gnome somewhat the worse for liquor.

'Have you got books in there? I thought that was your dirty linen or a camp-bed or something. Is there anything you can lend me?'

'Look for yourself.'

Featherstone's boys had unlocked the bag, but quailing before the sight that then discovered itself had done no more. I knew from long experience how to unpack it. I threw it over on its side, seized its leather bottom and, walking backwards, dragged the sack away from its contents. A river of books poured on to the floor. A look of stupefaction came upon Featherstone's face.

'You don't mean to say you travel with as many books as that? By George, what a snip!'

He bent down and turning them over rapidly looked at the titles. There were books of all kinds. Volumes of verse, novels, philosophical works, critical studies (they say books about books are profitless, but they certainly make very pleasant reading), biographies, history; there were books to read when you were ill and books to read when your brain, all alert, craved for something to grapple with; there were books that you had always wanted to read, but in the hurry of life at home had never found time to; there were books to read at sea when you were meandering through narrow waters on a tramp steamer, and there were books for bad weather when your whole cabin creaked and you had to wedge yourself in your bunk in order not to fall out; there were books chosen solely for their length, which you took with you when on some expedition you had to travel light, and there were the books you could read when you could read nothing else. Finally Featherstone picked out a life of Byron that had recently appeared.

'Hullo, what's this?' he said. 'I read a review of it some time ago.'

'I believe it's very good,' I replied. 'I haven't read it yet.'

'May I take it? It'll do me for tonight at all events.'

'Of course. Take anything you like.'

'No, that's enough. Well, good night. Breakfast at eight-thirty.'

When I came down next morning the head boy told me that Featherstone, who had been at work since six, would be in shortly. While I waited for him I glanced at his shelves.

'I see you've got a grand library of books on bridge,' I remarked as we sat down to breakfast.

'Yes, I get every one that comes out. I'm very keen on it.'

'That fellow we were playing with yesterday plays a good game.'

'Which? Hardy?'

'I don't know. Not the one who said he was going to collect his wife. The other.'

'Yes, that was Hardy. That was why I asked him to play. He doesn't come to the club very often.'

'I hope he will tonight.'

'I wouldn't bank on it. He has an estate about thirty miles away. It's a longish ride to come just for a rubber of bridge.'

'Is he married?'

'No. Well, yes. But his wife is in England.'

'It must be awfully lonely for those men who live by themselves on those estates,' I said.

'Oh, he's not so badly off as some. I don't think he much cares about seeing people. I think he'd be just as lonely in London.'

There was something in the way Featherstone spoke that struck me as a little strange. His voice had what I can only describe as a shuttered tone. He seemed suddenly to have moved away from me.

It was as though one were passing along a street at night and paused for a second to look in at a lighted window that showed a comfortable room and suddenly an invisible hand pulled down a blind. His eyes, which habitually met those of the person he was talking to with frankness, now avoided mine and I had a notion that it was not only my fancy that read in his face an expression of pain. It was drawn for a moment as it might be by a twinge of neuralgia. I could not think of anything to say and Featherstone did not speak. I was conscious that his thoughts, withdrawn from me and what we were about, were turned upon a subject unknown to me. Presently he gave a little sigh, very slight, but unmistakable, and seemed with a deliberate effort to pull himself together.

'I'm going down to the office immediately after breakfast,' he said. 'What are you going to do with yourself?'

'Oh, don't bother about me. I shall slack around. I'll stroll down and look at the town.'

'There's not much to see.'

'All the better. I'm fed up with sights.'

I found that Featherstone's veranda gave me sufficient entertainment for the morning. It had one of the most enchanting views I had seen in the FMS. The Residency was built on the top of a hill and the garden was large and well cared for. Great trees gave it almost the look of an English park. It had vast lawns and there Tamils, black and emaciated, were scything with deliberate and beautiful gestures. Beyond and below, the jungle grew thickly to the bank of a broad, winding and swiftly flowing river, and on the other side of this, as far as the eye could reach, stretched the wooded hills of

Tenggarah. The contrast between the trim lawns, so strangely English, and the savage growth of the jungle beyond pleasantly titillated the fancy. I sat and read and smoked. It is my business to be curious about people and I asked myself how the peace of this scene, charged nevertheless with a tremulous and dark significance, affected Featherstone who lived with it. He knew it under every aspect: at dawn when the mist rising from the river shrouded it with a ghostly pall; in the splendour of noon; and at last when the shadowy gloaming crept softly out of the jungle, like an army making its way with caution in unknown country, and presently enveloped the green lawns and the great flowering trees and the flaunting cassias in the silent night. I wondered whether, unbeknownst to him, the tender and yet strangely sinister aspect of the scene, acting on his nerves and his loneliness, imbued him with some mystical quality so that the life he led, the life of the capable administrator, the sportsman and the good fellow, on occasion seemed to him not quite real. I smiled at my own fancies, for certainly the conversation we had had the night before had not indicated in him any stirrings of the soul. I had thought him quite nice. He had been at Oxford and was a member of a good London club. He seemed to attach a good deal of importance to social things. He was a gentleman and slightly conscious of the fact that he belonged to a better class than most of the Englishmen his life brought him in contact with. I gathered from the various silver pots that adorned his dining-room that he excelled in games. He played tennis and billiards. When he went on leave he hunted and, anxious to keep his weight down, he dieted carefully. He talked a good deal of what he would do when he retired. He hankered after the life of a country gentleman. A little house in Leicestershire, a couple of hunters and neighbours to play bridge with. He would have his pension and he had a little money of his own. But meanwhile he worked hard and did his work, if not brilliantly, certainly with competence. I have no doubt that he was looked upon by his superiors as a reliable officer. He was cut upon a pattern that I knew too well to find very interesting. He was like a novel that is careful, honest and efficient, yet a little ordinary, so that you seem to have read it all before, and you turn the pages listlessly, knowing that it will never afford you a surprise or move you to excitement.

But human beings are incalculable and he is a fool who tells himself that he knows what a man is capable of.

In the afternoon Featherstone took me to see the Sultan. We were received by one of his sons, a shy, smiling youth who acted as his ADC. He was dressed in a neat blue suit, but round his waist he wore a sarong, white flowers on a yellow ground, on his head a red fez, and on his feet knobbly American shoes. The palace, built in the Moorish style, was like a very big doll's house and it was painted bright yellow, which is the royal colour. We were led into a spacious room, furnished with the sort of furniture you would find in an English lodging-house at the seaside, but the chairs were covered with yellow silk. On the floor was a Brussels carpet and on the walls photographs in very grand gilt frames of the Sultan at various state functions. In a cabinet was a large collection of all kinds of fruit done entirely in crochet work. The Sultan came in with several attendants. He was a man of fifty, perhaps, short and stout, dressed in trousers and tunic of a large white-and-yellow check; round his middle he wore a very beautiful yellow sarong and on his head a white fez. He had large handsome friendly eyes. He gave us coffee to drink, sweet cakes to eat and cheroots to smoke. Conversation was not difficult, for he was affable, and he told me that he had never been to a theatre or played cards, for he was very religious, and he had four wives and twenty-four children. The only bar to the happiness of his life seemed to be that common decency obliged him to divide his time equally between his four wives. He said that an hour with one was a month and with another five minutes. I remarked that Professor Einstein – or was it Bergson? – had made similar observations upon time and indeed on this question had given the world much to ponder over. Presently we took our leave and the Sultan presented me with some beautiful white Malaccas.

In the evening we went to the club. One of the men we had played with the day before got up from his chair as we entered.

'Ready for a rubber?' he said.

'Where's our fourth?' I asked.

'Oh, there are several fellows here who'll be glad to play.'

'What about that man we played with yesterday?' I had forgotten his name.

'Hardy? He's not here.'

'It's not worth while waiting for him,' said Featherstone.

'He very seldom comes to the club. I was surprised to see him last night.'

I did not know why I had the impression that behind the very ordinary words of these two men there was an odd sense of embarrassment. Hardy had made no impression on me and I did not even remember what he looked like. He was just a fourth at the bridge table. I had a feeling that they had something against him. It was no business of mine and I was quite content to play with a man who at that moment joined us. We certainly had a more cheerful game than before. A good deal of chaff passed from one side of the table to the other. We played less serious bridge. We laughed. I wondered if it was only that they were less shy of the stranger who had happened in upon them or if the presence of Hardy had caused in the other two a certain constraint. At half-past eight we broke up and Featherstone and I went back to dine at his house.

After dinner we lounged in arm-chairs and smoked cheroots. For some reason our conversation did not flow easily. I tried topic after topic, but could not get Featherstone to interest himself in any of them. I began to think that in the last twenty-four hours he had said all he had to say. I fell somewhat discouraged into silence. It prolonged itself and again, I did not know why, I had a faint sensation that it was charged with a significance that escaped me. I felt slightly uncomfortable. I had that queer feeling that one sometimes has when sitting in an empty room that one is not by oneself. Presently I was conscious that Featherstone was steadily looking at me. I was sitting by a lamp, but he was in shadow so that the play of his features was hidden from me. But he had very large brilliant eyes and in the half darkness they seemed to shine dimly. They were like new boot-buttons that caught a reflected light. I wondered why he looked at me like that. I gave him a glance and catching his eyes insistently fixed upon me faintly smiled.

'Interesting book that one you lent me last night,' he said suddenly, and I could not help thinking his voice did not sound quite natural. The words issued from his lips as though they were pushed from behind.

'Oh, the *Life of Byron*?' I said breezily. 'Have you read it already?'

'A good deal of it. I read till three.'

'I've heard it's very well done. I'm not sure that Byron interests me so much as all that. There was so much in him that was so frightfully second-rate. It makes one rather uncomfortable.'

'What do you think is the real truth of that story about him and his sister?'

'Augusta Leigh? I don't know very much about it. I've never read *Astarte*.'

'Do you think they were really in love with one another?'

'I suppose so. Isn't it generally believed that she was the only woman he ever genuinely loved?'

'Can you understand it?'

'I can't really. It doesn't particularly shock me. It just seems to me very unnatural. Perhaps "unnatural" isn't the right word. It's incomprehensible to me. I can't throw myself into the state of feeling in which such a thing seems possible. You know, that's how a writer gets to know the people he writes about, by standing himself in their shoes and feeling with their hearts.'

I knew I did not make myself very clear, but I

was trying to describe a sensation, an action of the subconscious, which from experience was perfectly familiar to me, but which no words I knew could precisely indicate. I went on.

'Of course she was only his half-sister, but just as habit kills love I should have thought habit would prevent its arising. When two persons have known one another all their lives and lived together in close contact I can't imagine how or why that sudden spark should flash that results in love. The probabilities are that they would be joined by mutual affection and I don't know anything that is more contrary to love than affection.'

I could just see in the dimness the outline of a smile flicker for a moment on my host's heavy, and it seemed to me then, somewhat saturnine face.

'You only believe in love at first sight?'

'Well, I suppose I do, but with the proviso that people may have met twenty times before seeing one another. "Seeing" has an active side and a passive one. Most people we run across mean so little to us that we never bestir ourselves to look at them. We just suffer the impression they make on us.'

'Oh, but one's often heard of couples who've known one another for years and it's never occurred to one they cared two straws for each other and suddenly they go and get married. How do you explain that?'

'Well, if you're going to bully me into being logical and consistent, I should suggest that their love is of a different kind. After all, passion isn't the only reason for marriage. It may not even be the best one. Two people may marry because they're lonely or because they're good friends or for convenience' sake. Though I said that affection was the greatest enemy of love, I would never deny that it's a very good substitute. I'm not sure that a marriage founded on it isn't the happiest.'

'What did you think of Tim Hardy?'

I was a little surprised at the sudden question, which seemed to have nothing to do with the subject of our conversation.

'I didn't think of him very much. He seemed quite nice. Why?'

'Did he seem to you just like everybody else?'

'Yes. Is there anything peculiar about him? If you'd told me that I'd have paid more attention to him.'

'He's very quiet, isn't he? I suppose no one who knew nothing about him would give him a second thought.'

I tried to remember what he looked like. The only thing that had struck me when we were playing cards was that he had fine hands. It passed idly through my mind that they were not the sort of hands I should have expected a planter to have. But why a planter should have different hands from anybody else I did not trouble to ask myself. His were somewhat large, but very well formed, with peculiarly long fingers, and the nails were of an admirable shape. They were virile and yet oddly sensitive hands. I noticed this and thought no more about it. But if you are a writer instinct and the habit of years enable you to store up impressions that you are not aware of. Sometimes of course they do not correspond with the facts and a woman for example may remain in your subconsciousness as a dark, massive and ox-eyed creature when she is indeed rather small and of a nondescript colouring. But that is of no consequence. The impression may very well be more exact than the sober truth. And now, seeking to call up from the depths of me a picture of this man I had a feeling of some ambiguity. He was clean-shaven and his face, oval but not thin, seemed strangely pale under the tan of long exposure to the tropical sun. His features were vague. I did not know whether I remembered it or only imagined now that his rounded chin gave one the impression of a certain weakness. He had thick brown hair, just turning grey, and a long wisp fell down constantly over his forehead. He pushed it back with a gesture that had become habitual. His brown eyes were rather large and gentle, but perhaps a little sad; they had a melting softness which, I could imagine, might be very appealing.

After a pause Featherstone continued:

'It's rather strange that I should run across Tim Hardy here after all these years. But that's the way of the FMS. People move about and you find yourself in the same place as a man you'd known years before in another part of the country. I first knew Tim when he had an estate near Sibuku. Have you ever been there?'

'No. Where is it?'

'Oh, it's up north. Towards Siam. It wouldn't be worth your while to go. It's just like every other place in the FMS. But it was rather nice. It had a very jolly little club and there were some quite decent people. There was the schoolmaster and the head of the police, the doctor, the padre and the government engineer. The usual lot, you know. A few planters. Three or four women. I was ADO. It was one of my first jobs. Tim Hardy had an estate about twenty-five miles away. He lived there with his sister. They had a bit of money of their own and he'd bought the place. Rubber was pretty good then and he wasn't doing at all badly. We rather cottoned on to one another. Of course it's a toss-up with planters. Some of them are very good fellows, but they're not exactly . . .' he sought for a word or a phrase that did not sound snobbish. 'Well, they're not the sort of people you'd be likely to meet at home. Tim and Olive were of one's own class, if you understand what I mean.'

'Olive was the sister?'

'Yes. They'd had a rather unfortunate past. Their parents had separated when they were quite small, seven or eight, and the mother had taken Olive and the father had kept Tim. Tim went to Clifton, they were West Country people, and only came home for the holidays. His father was a retired naval man who lived at Fowey. But Olive went with her mother to Italy. She was educated in Florence; she spoke Italian perfectly and French too. For all those years Tim and Olive never saw one another once, but they used to write to one another regularly. They'd been very much attached when they were children. As far as I could understand, life when their people were living together had been rather stormy with all sorts of scenes and upsets, you know the sort of thing that happens when two people who are married don't get on together, and that had thrown them on their own resources. They were left a good deal to themselves. Then Mrs Hardy died and Olive came home to England and went back to her father. She was eighteen then and Tim was seventeen. A year later the war broke out. Tim joined up and his father, who was over fifty, got some job at Portsmouth. I take it he had been a hard liver and a heavy drinker.

He broke down before the end of the war and died after a lingering illness. They don't seem to have had any relations. They were the last of a rather old family; they had a fine old house in Dorsetshire that had belonged to them for a good many generations, but they had never been able to afford to live in it and it was always let. I remember seeing photographs of it. It was very much a gentleman's house, of grey stone and rather stately, with a coat of arms carved over the front door and mullioned windows. Their great ambition was to make enough money to be able to live in it. They used to talk about it a lot. They never spoke as though either of them would marry, but always as though it were a settled thing that they would remain together. It was rather funny considering how young they were.'

'How old were they then?' I asked.

'Well, I suppose he was twenty-five or twenty-six and she was a year older. They were awfully kind to me when I first went up to Sibuku. They took a fancy to me at once. You see, we had more in common than most of the people there. I think they were glad of my company. They weren't particularly popular.'

'Why not?' I asked.

'They were rather reserved and you couldn't help seeing that they liked their own society better than other people's. I don't know if you've noticed it, but that always seems to put people's backs up. They resent it somehow if they have a feeling that you can get along very well without them.'

'It's tiresome, isn't it?' I said.

'It was rather a grievance to the other planters that Tim was his own master and had private means. They had to put up with an old Ford to get about in, but Tim had a real car. Tim and Olive were very nice when they came to the club and they played in the tennis tournaments and all that sort of thing, but you had an impression that they were always glad to get away again. They'd dine out with people and make themselves very pleasant, but it was pretty obvious that they'd just as soon have stayed at home. If you had any sense you couldn't blame them. I don't know if you've been much to planters' houses. They're a bit dreary. A lot of gimcrack furniture and silver ornaments and tiger skins. And the food's uneatable. But the Hardys had made their bungalow rather nice. There was nothing very grand in it; it was just easy and homelike and comfortable. Their living-room was like a drawing-room in an English country house. You felt that their things meant something to them and that they had had them a long time. It was a very jolly house to stay at. The bungalow was in the middle of the estate, but it was on the brow of a little hill and you looked right over the rubber trees to the sea in the distance. Olive took a lot of trouble with her garden and it was really topping. I never saw such a show of cannas. I used to go there for week-ends. It was only about half an hour's drive to the sea and we'd take our lunch with us and bathe and sail. Tim kept a small boat there. Those days were grand. I never knew one could enjoy oneself so much. It's a beautiful bit of coast and it was really extraordinarily romantic. Then in the evenings we'd play patience and chess or turn on the gramophone. The cooking was damned good too. It was a change from what one generally got. Olive had taught their cook to make all sorts of Italian dishes and we used to have great wallops of macaroni and risotto and gnocchi and things like that. I couldn't help envying them their life, it was so jolly and peaceful, and when they talked of what they'd do when they went back to England for good I used to tell them they'd always regret what they'd left.

'"We've been very happy here," said Olive.

'She had a way of looking at Tim, with a slow, sidelong glance from under her long eyelashes, that was rather engaging.

'In their own house they were quite different from what they were when they went out. They were so easy and cordial. Everybody admitted that and I'm bound to say that people enjoyed going there. They often asked people over. They had the gift of making you feel at home. It was a very happy house, if you know what I mean. Of course no one could help seeing how attached they were to one another. And whatever people said about their being standoffish and self-centred, they were bound to be rather touched by the affection they had for one another. People said they couldn't have been more united if they were married, and when you saw how some couples got on you couldn't help thinking they made most marriages look rather like a wash-out. They seemed to think the same things at the same time. They had little private jokes that made them laugh like children. They were so charming with one another, so gay and happy, that really to stay with them was, well, a spiritual refreshment. I don't know what else you could call it. When you left them, after a couple of days at the bungalow, you felt that you'd absorbed some of their peace and their sober gaiety. It was as though your soul had been sluiced with cool clear water. You felt strangely purified.'

It was singular to hear Featherstone talking in this exalted strain. He looked so spruce in his smart white coat, technically known as a bum-freezer, his moustache was so trim, his thick curly hair so carefully brushed, that his high-flown language made me a trifle uncomfortable. But I realized that he was trying to express in his clumsy way a very sincerely felt emotion.

'What was Olive Hardy like?' I asked.

'I'll show you. I've got quite a lot of snapshots.'

He got up from his chair and going to a shelf brought me a large album. It was the usual thing, indifferent photographs of people in groups and unflattering likenesses of single figures. They were in bathing dress or in shorts or tennis things, generally with their faces screwed up because the sun blinded them, or puckered by the distortion of laughter. I recognized Hardy, not much changed after ten years, with his wisp of hair hanging across his forehead. I remembered him better now that I saw the snapshots. In them he looked nice and fresh and young. He had an alertness of expression that was attractive and that I certainly had not noticed when I saw him. In his eyes was a sort of eagerness for life that danced and sparkled through the fading print. I glanced at the photographs of his sister. Her bathing dress showed that she had a good figure, well-developed, but slender; and her legs were long and slim.

'They look rather alike,' I said.

'Yes, although she was a year older they might have been twins, they were so much alike. They both had the same oval face and that pale skin without any colour in the cheeks, and they both had those soft brown eyes, very liquid and appealing, so that you felt whatever they did you could never be angry with them. And they both had a sort of careless elegance that made them look charming whatever they wore and however untidy they were. He's lost that now, I suppose, but he certainly had it when I first knew him. They always rather reminded me of the brother and sister in *Twelfth Night*. You know whom I mean.'

'Viola and Sebastian.'

'They never seemed to belong quite to the present. There was something Elizabethan about them. I don't think it was only because I was very young then that I couldn't help feeling they were strangely romantic somehow. I could see them living in Illyria.'

I gave one of the snapshots another glance.

'The girl looks as though she had a good deal more character than her brother,' I remarked.

'She had. I don't know if you'd have called Olive beautiful, but she was awfully attractive. There was something poetic in her, a sort of lyrical quality, as it were, that coloured her movements, her acts and everything about her. It seemed to exalt her above common cares. There was something so candid in her expression, so courageous and independent in her bearing, that – oh, I don't know, it made mere beauty just flat and dull.'

'You speak as if you'd been in love with her,' I interrupted.

'Of course I was. I should have thought you'd guessed that at once. I was frightfully in love with her.'

'Was it love at first sight?' I smiled.

'Yes, I think it was, but I didn't know it for a month or so. When it suddenly struck me that what I felt for her – I don't know how to explain it, it was a sort of shattering turmoil that affected every bit of me – that that was love, I knew I'd felt it all along. It was not only her looks, though they were awfully alluring, the smoothness of her pale skin and the way her hair fell over her forehead and the grave sweetness of her brown eyes, it was more than that; you had a sensation of well-being when you were with her, as though you could relax and be quite natural and needn't pretend to be anything you weren't. You felt she was incapable of meanness. It was impossible to think of her as envious of other people or catty. She seemed to have a natural generosity of soul. One could be silent with her for an hour at a time and yet feel that one had had a good time.'

'A rare gift,' I said.

'She was a wonderful companion. If you made a suggestion to do something she was always glad to fall in with it. She was the least exacting girl I ever knew. You could throw her over at the last minute and however disappointed she was it made no dif-ference. Next time you saw her she was just as cordial and serene as ever.'

'Why didn't you marry her?'

Featherstone's cheroot had gone out. He threw the stub away and deliberately lit another. He did not answer for a while. It may seem strange to persons who live in a highly civilized state that he should confide these intimate things to a stranger; it did not seem strange to me. I was used to it. People who live so desperately alone, in the remote places of the earth, find it a relief to tell someone whom in all probability they will never meet again the story that has burdened perhaps for years their waking thoughts and their dreams at night. And I have an inkling that the fact of your being a writer attracts their confidence. They feel that what they tell you will excite your interest in an impersonal way that makes it easier for them to discharge their souls. Besides, as we all know from our own experience, it is never unpleasant to talk about oneself.

'Why didn't you marry her?' I had asked him.

'I wanted to badly enough,' Featherstone answered at length. 'But I hesitated to ask her. Although she was always so nice to me and so easy to get on with, and we were such good friends, I always felt that there was something a little mysterious in her. Although she was so simple, so frank and natural, you never quite got over the feeling of an inner kernel of aloofness, as if deep in her heart she guarded, not a secret, but a sort of privacy of the soul that not a living person would ever be allowed to know. I don't know if I make myself clear.'

'I think so.'

'I put it down to her upbringing. They never talked of their mother, but somehow I got the impression that she was one of those neurotic, emotional women who wreck their own happiness and are a pest to everyone connected with them. I had a suspicion that she'd led rather a hectic life in Florence and it struck me that Olive owed her beautiful serenity to a disciplined effort of her own will and that her aloofness was a sort of citadel she'd built to protect herself from the knowledge of all sorts of shameful things. But of course that aloofness was awfully captivating. It was strangely exciting to think that if she loved you, and you were married to her, you would at last pierce right into the hidden heart of that mystery; and you felt that if you could share that with her it would be as it were a consummation of all you'd ever desired in your life. Heaven wouldn't be in it. You know, I felt about it just like Bluebeard's wife about the forbidden chamber in the castle. Every room was open to me, but I should never rest till I had gone into that last one that was locked against me.'

My eye was caught by a chik-chak, a little brown house lizard with a large head, high up on the wall. It is a friendly little beast and it is good to see it in a house. It watched a fly. It was quite still. On a sudden it made a dart and then as the fly flew away fell back with a sort of jerk into a strange immobility.

'And there was another thing that made me hesitate. I couldn't bear the thought that if I proposed to her and she refused me she wouldn't let me come to the bungalow in the same old way. I should have hated that, I enjoyed going there so awfully. It made me so happy to be with her. But you know, sometimes one can't help oneself. I did ask her at last, but it was almost by accident. One evening, after dinner, when we were sitting on the veranda by ourselves, I took her hand. She withdrew it at once.

'"Why did you do that?" I asked her.

'"I don't very much like being touched," she said. She turned her head a little and smiled. "Are you hurt? You mustn't mind, it's just a funny feeling I have. I can't help it."

'"I wonder if it's ever occurred to you that I'm frightfully fond of you," I said.

'I expect I was terribly awkward about it, but I'd

never proposed to anyone before.' Featherstone gave a little sound that was not quite a chuckle and not quite a sigh. 'For the matter of that, I've never proposed to anyone since. She didn't say anything for a minute. Then she said:

'"I'm very glad, but I don't think I want you to be anything more than that."

'"Why not?" I asked.

'"I could never leave Tim."

'"But supposing he marries?"

'"He never will."

'I'd gone so far then that I thought I'd better go on. But my throat was so dry that I could hardly speak. I was shaking with nervousness.

'"I'm frightfully in love with you, Olive. I want to marry you more than anything in the world."

'She put her hand very gently on my arm. It was like a flower falling to the ground.

'"No, dear, I can't," she said.

'I was silent. It was difficult for me to say what I wanted to. I'm naturally rather shy. She was a girl. I couldn't very well tell her that it wasn't quite the same thing living with a husband and living with a brother. She was normal and healthy; she must want to have babies; it wasn't reasonable to starve her natural instincts. It was such waste of her youth. But it was she who spoke first.

'"Don't let's talk about this any more," she said. "D'you mind? It did strike me once or twice that perhaps you cared for me. Tim noticed it. I was sorry because I was afraid it would break up our friendship. I don't want it to do that, Mark. We do get on so well together, the three of us, and we have such jolly times. I don't know what we should do without you now."

'"I thought of that too," I said.

'"D'you think it need?" she asked me.

'"My dear, I don't want it to," I said. "You must know how much I love coming here. I've never been so happy anywhere before!"

'"You're not angry with me?"

'"Why should I be? It's not your fault. It only means that you're not in love with me. If you were you wouldn't care a hang about Tim."

'"You are rather sweet," she said.

'She put her arm round my neck and kissed me lightly on the cheek. I had a notion that in her mind it settled our relation. She adopted me as a second brother.

'A few weeks later Tim went back to England. The tenant of their house in Dorset was leaving and though there was another in the offing, he thought he ought to be on the spot to conduct negotiations. And he wanted some new machinery for the estate. He thought he'd get it at the same time. He didn't expect to be gone more than three months and Olive made up her mind not to go. She knew hardly anyone in England, and it was practically a foreign country to her, she didn't mind being left alone, and she wanted to look after the estate. Of course they could have put a manager in charge, but that wasn't the same thing. Rubber was falling and in case of accidents it was just as well that one or other of them should be there. I promised Tim I'd look after her and if she wanted me she could always call me up. My proposal hadn't changed anything. We carried on as though nothing had happened. I don't know whether she'd told Tim. He made no sign that he knew. Of course I loved her as much as ever, but I kept it to myself. I have a good deal of self-control, you know. I had a sort of feeling I hadn't a chance. I hoped eventually my love would change into something else and we could just be wonderful friends. It's funny, it never has, you know. I suppose I was hit too badly ever to get quite over it.

'She went down to Penang to see Tim off and when she came back I met her at the station and drove her home. I couldn't very well stay at the bungalow while Tim was away, but I went over every Sunday and had tiffin and we'd go down to the sea and have a bathe. People tried to be kind to her and asked her to stay with them, but she wouldn't. She seldom left the estate. She had plenty to do. She read a lot. She was never bored. She seemed quite happy in her own company, and when she had visitors it was only from a sense of duty. She didn't want them to think her ungracious. But it was an effort and she told me she heaved a sigh of relief when she saw the last of them and could again enjoy without disturbance the peaceful loneliness of the bungalow. She was a very curious girl. It was strange that at her age she should be so indifferent to parties and the other small gaieties the station afforded. Spiritually, if you know what I mean, she was entirely self-supporting. I don't know how people found out that I was in love with her; I thought I'd never given myself away in anything, but I had hints here and there that they knew. I gathered they thought Olive hadn't gone home with her brother on my account. One woman, a Mrs Sergison, the policeman's wife, actually asked me when they were going to be able to congratulate me. Of course I pretended I didn't know what she was talking about, but it didn't go down very well. I couldn't help being amused. I meant so little to Olive in that way that I really believe she'd entirely forgotten that I'd asked her to marry me. I can't say she was unkind to me, I don't think she could have been unkind to anyone; but she treated me with just the casualness with which a sister might treat a younger brother. She was two or three years older than I. She was always terribly glad to see me, but it never occurred to her to put herself out for me, she was almost amazingly intimate with me; but unconsciously, you know, as you might be with a person you'd known so well all your life that you never thought of putting on frills with him. I might not have been a man at all, but an old coat that she wore all the time because it was easy and comfortable and she didn't mind what she did in it. I should have been crazy not to see that she was a thousand miles away from loving me.

'Then one day, three or four weeks before Tim was due back, when I went to the bungalow I saw she'd been crying. I was startled. She was always so composed. I'd never seen her upset over anything.

'"Hullo, what's the matter?" I said.

'"Nothing."

'"Come off it, darling," I said. "What have you been crying about?"

'She tried to smile.

'"I wish you hadn't got such sharp eyes," she said. "I think I'm being silly. I've just had a cable from Tim to say he's postponed his sailing."

'"Oh, my dear, I am sorry," I said. "You must be awfully disappointed."

'"I've been counting the days. I want him back so badly."

'"Does he say why he's postponing?" I asked.

'"No, he says he's writing. I'll show you the cable."

'I saw that she was very nervous. Her slow quiet eyes were filled with apprehension and there was a little frown of anxiety between her brows. She went into her bedroom and in a moment came back with the cable. I felt that she was watching me anxiously as I read. So far as I remember it ran: *Darling, I cannot sail on the seventh after all. Please forgive me. Am writing fully. Fondest love. Tim.*

'"Well, perhaps the machinery he wanted isn't ready and he can't bring himself to sail without it," I said.

'"What could it matter if it came by a later ship? Anyhow, it'll be hung up at Penang."

'"It may be something about the house."

'"If it is why doesn't he say so? He must know how frightfully anxious I am."

'"It wouldn't occur to him," I said. "After all, when you're away you don't realize that the people you've left behind don't know something that you take as a matter of course."

'She smiled again, but now more happily.

'"I daresay you're right. In point of fact Tim is a little like that. He's always been rather slack and casual. I daresay I've been making a mountain out of a molehill. I must just wait patiently for his letter."

'Olive was a girl with a lot of self-control and I saw her by an effort of will pull herself together. The little line between her eyebrows vanished and she was once more her serene, smiling and kindly self. She was always gentle: that day she had a mildness so heavenly that it was shattering. But for the rest of the time I could see that she kept her restlessness in check only by the deliberate exercise of her common sense. It was as though she had a foreboding of ill. I was with her the day before the mail was due. Her anxiety was all the more pitiful to see because she took such pains to hide it. I was always busy on mail day, but I promised to go up to the estate later on and hear the news. I was just thinking of starting when Hardy's seis came along in the car with a message from the amah asking me to go at once to her mistress. The amah was a decent, elderly woman to whom I had given a dollar or two and said that if anything went wrong on the estate she was to let me know at once. I jumped into my car. When I arrived I found the amah waiting for me on the steps.

'"A letter came this morning," she said.

'I interrupted her. I ran up the steps. The sitting-room was empty.

'"Olive," I called.

'I went into the passage and suddenly I heard a sound that froze my heart. The amah had followed me and now she opened the door of Olive's room. The sound I had heard was the sound of Olive crying. I went in. She was lying on her bed, on her face, and her sobs shook her from head to foot. I put my hand on her shoulder.

'"Olive, what is it?" I asked.

'"Who's that?" she cried. She sprang to her feet suddenly, as though she was scared out of her wits. And then: "Oh, it's you," she said. She stood in front of me, with her head thrown back and her eyes closed, and the tears streamed from them. It was dreadful. "Tim's married," she gasped, and her face screwed up in a sort of grimace of pain.

'I must admit that for one moment I had a thrill of exultation, it was like a little electric shock tingling through my heart; it struck me that now I had a chance, she might be willing to marry me; I know it was terribly selfish of me; you see, the news had taken me by surprise; but it was only for a moment, after that I was melted by her awful distress and the only thing I felt was deep sorrow because she was unhappy. I put my arm round her waist.

'"Oh, my dear, I'm so sorry," I said. "Don't stay here. Come into the sitting-room and sit down and we'll talk about it. Let me give you something to drink."

'She let me lead her into the next room and we sat down on the sofa. I told the amah to fetch the whisky and syphon and I mixed her a good strong stengah and made her drink a little. I took her in my arms and rested her head on my shoulder. She let me do what I liked with her. The great tears streamed down her poor face.

'"How could he?" she moaned. "How could he?"

'"My darling," I said, "it was bound to happen sooner or later. He's a young man. How could you expect him never to marry? It's only natural."

'"No, no, no," she gasped.

'Tight-clenched in her hand I saw that she had a letter and I guessed that it was Tim's.

'"What does he say?" I asked.

'She gave a frightened movement and clutched the letter to her heart as though she thought I would take it from her.

'"He says he couldn't help himself. He says he had to. What does it mean?"

'"Well, you know, in his way he's just as attractive as you are. He has so much charm. I suppose he just fell madly in love with some girl and she with him."

'"He's so weak," she moaned.

'"Are they coming out?" I asked.

'"They sailed yesterday. He says it won't make any difference. He's insane. How *can* I stay here?"'

'She began to cry hysterically. It was torture to see that girl, usually so calm, utterly shattered by her emotion. I had always felt that her lovely serenity masked a capacity for deep feeling. But the abandon of her distress simply broke me up. I held her in my arms and kissed her, her eyes and her wet cheek and her hair. I don't think she knew what I was doing. I was hardly conscious of it myself. I was so deeply moved.

'"What shall I do?" she wailed.

'"Why won't you marry me?" I said.

'She tried to withdraw herself from me, but I wouldn't let her go.

'"After all, it would be a way out," I said.

'"How can I marry you?" she moaned. "I'm years older than you are."

'"Oh, what nonsense, two or three. What do I care?"

'"No, no."

'"Why not?" I said.

'"I don't love you," she said.

'"What does that matter? I love you."

'I don't know what I said. I told her that I'd try to make her happy. I said I'd never ask anything from her but what she was prepared to give me. I talked and talked. I tried to make her see reason. I felt that she didn't want to stay there, in the same place as Tim, and I told her that I'd be moved soon to some other district. I thought that might tempt her. She couldn't deny that we'd always got on awfully well together. After a time she did seem to grow a little quieter. I had a feeling that she was listening to me. I had even a sort of feeling that she knew that she was lying in my arms and that it comforted her. I made her drink a drop more whisky. I gave her a cigarette. At last I thought I might be just mildly facetious.

'"You know, I'm not a bad sort really," I said. "You might do worse."

'"You don't know me," she said. "You know nothing whatever about me."

'"I'm capable of learning," I said.

'She smiled a little.

'"You're awfully kind, Mark," she said.

'"Say yes, Olive," I begged.

'She gave a deep sigh. For a long time she stared at the ground. But she did not move and I felt the softness of her body in my arms. I waited. I was frightfully nervous and the minutes seemed endless.

'"All right," she said at last, as though she were not conscious that any time had passed between my prayer and her answer.

'I was so moved that I had nothing to say. But when I wanted to kiss her lips, she turned her face away, and wouldn't let me. I wanted us to be married at once, but she was quite firm that she wouldn't. She insisted on waiting till Tim came back. You know how sometimes you see so clearly in people's thoughts that you're more certain of them than if they'd spoken them; I saw that she couldn't quite believe that what Tim had written was true and that she had a sort of miserable hope that it was all a mistake and he wasn't married after all. It gave me a pang, but I loved her so much, I just bore it. I was willing to bear anything. I adored her. She wouldn't even let me tell anyone that we were engaged. She made me promise not to say a word till Tim's return. She said she couldn't bear the thought of the congratulations and all that. She wouldn't even let me make any announcement of Tim's marriage. She was obstinate about it. I had a notion that she felt if the fact were spread about it gave it a certainty that she didn't want it to have.

'But the matter was taken out of her hands. News travels mysteriously in the East. I don't know what Olive had said in the amah's hearing when first she received the news of Tim's marriage; anyhow, the Hardys' seis told the Sergisons' and Mrs Sergison attacked me the next time I went into the club.

'"I hear Tim Hardy's married," she said.

'"Oh?" I answered, unwilling to commit myself.

'She smiled at my blank face, and told me that her amah having told her the rumour she had rung up Olive and asked her if it was true. Olive's answer had been rather odd. She had not exactly confirmed it, but said that she had received a letter from Tim telling her he was married.

'"She's a strange girl," said Mrs Sergison. "When I asked her for details she said she had none to give and when I said: 'Aren't you thrilled?' she didn't answer."

'"Olive's devoted to Tim, Mrs Sergison," I said. "His marriage has naturally been a shock to her. She knows nothing about Tim's wife. She's nervous about her."

'"And when are you two going to be married?" she asked me abruptly.

'"What an embarrassing question!" I said, trying to laugh it off.

'She looked at me shrewdly.

'"Will you give me your word of honour that you're not engaged to her?"

'I didn't like to tell her a deliberate lie, nor to ask her to mind her own business, and I'd promised Olive faithfully that I would say nothing till Tim got back. I hedged.

'"Mrs Sergison," I said, "when there's anything to tell I promise that you'll be the first person to hear it. All I can say to you now is that I do want to marry Olive more than anything in the world."

'"I'm very glad that Tim's married," she answered. "And I hope she'll marry you very soon. It was a morbid and unhealthy life that they led up there, those two, they kept far too much to themselves and they were far too much absorbed in one another."

'I saw Olive practically every day. I felt that she didn't want me to make love to her, and I contented myself with kissing her when I came and when I went. She was very nice to me, kindly and thoughtful; I knew she was glad to see me and sorry when it was time for me to go. Ordinarily, she was apt to fall into silence, but during this time she talked more than I had ever heard her talk before. But never of the future and never of Tim and his wife. She told me a lot about her life in Florence with her mother. She had led a strange lonely life, mostly with servants and governesses, while her mother, I suspected, engaged in one affair after another with vague Italian counts and Russian princes. I guessed that by the time she was fourteen there wasn't much she didn't know. It was natural for her to be quite unconventional: in the only world she knew till she was eighteen conventions weren't mentioned because they didn't exist. Gradually, Olive seemed to regain her serenity and I should have thought that she was beginning to accustom herself to the thought of Tim's marriage if it hadn't been that I couldn't but notice how pale and tired she looked. I made up my mind that the moment he arrived I'd press her to marry me at once. I could get short leave whenever I asked for it, and by the time that was up I thought I could manage a transfer to some other post. What she wanted was change of air and fresh scenes.

'We knew, of course, within a day when Tim's ship would reach Penang, but it was a question whether she'd get in soon enough for him to catch the train and I wrote to the P & O agent asking him to telegraph as soon as he had definite news. When I got the wire and took it up to Olive I found that she'd just received one from Tim. The ship had docked early and he was arriving next day. The train was supposed to get in at eight o'clock in the morning, but it was liable to be anything from one to six hours late, and I bore with me an invitation from Mrs Sergison asking Olive to come back with me to stay the night with her so that she would be on the spot and need not go to the station till the news came through that the train was coming.

'I was immensely relieved. I thought that when the blow at last fell Olive wouldn't feel it so much. She had worked herself up into such a state that I couldn't help thinking that she must have a reaction now. She might take a fancy to her sister-in-law. There was no reason why they shouldn't all three get on very well together. To my surprise Olive said she wasn't coming down to the station to meet them.

'"They'll be awfully disappointed," I said.

'"I'd rather wait here," she answered. She smiled a little. "Don't argue with me, Mark, I've quite made up my mind."

'"I've ordered breakfast in my house," I said.

'"That's all right. You meet them and take them to your house and give them breakfast, and then they can come along here afterwards. Of course I'll send the car down."

'"I don't suppose they'll want to breakfast if you're not there," I said.

'"Oh, I'm sure they will. If the train gets in on time they wouldn't have thought of breakfasting before it arrived and they'll be hungry. They won't want to take this long drive without anything to eat."

'I was puzzled. She had been looking forward so intensely to Tim's coming, it seemed strange that she should want to wait all by herself while the rest of us were having a jolly breakfast. I supposed she was nervous and wanted to delay as long as possible meeting the strange woman who had come to take her place. It seemed unreasonable, I couldn't see that an hour sooner or an hour later could make any difference, but I knew women were funny, and anyhow I felt Olive wasn't in the mood for me to press it.

'"Telephone when you're starting so that I shall know when to expect you," she said.

'"All right," I said, "but you know I shan't be able to come with them. It's my day for going to Lahad."

'This was a town that I had to go to once a week

to take cases. It was a good way off and one had to ferry across a river, which took some time, so that I never got back till late. There were a few Europeans there and a club. I generally had to go on there for a bit to be sociable and see that things were getting along all right.

'"Besides," I added, "with Tim bringing his wife home for the first time I don't suppose he'll want me about. But if you'd like to ask me to dinner I'll be glad to come to that."

'Olive smiled.

'"I don't think it'll be my place to issue any more invitations, will it?" she said. "You must ask the bride."

'She said this so lightly that my heart leaped. I had a feeling that at last she had made up her mind to accept the altered circumstances and, what was more, was accepting them with cheerfulness. She asked me to stay to dinner. Generally I left about eight and dined at home. She was very sweet, almost tender, and I was happier than I'd been for weeks. I had never been more desperately in love with her. I had a couple of gin pahits and I think I was in rather good form at dinner. I know I made her laugh. I felt that at last she was casting away the load of misery that had oppressed her. That was why I didn't let myself be very much disturbed by what happened at the end.

'"Don't you think it's about time you were leaving a presumably maiden lady?" she said.

'She spoke in a manner that was so quietly gay that I answered without hesitation:

'"Oh, my dear, if you think you've got a shred of reputation left you deceive yourself. You're surely not under the impression that the ladies of Sibuku don't know that I've been coming to see you every day for a month. The general feeling is that if we're not married it's high time we were. Don't you think it would be just as well if I broke it to them that we're engaged?"

'"Oh, Mark, you mustn't take our engagement very seriously," she said.

'I laughed.

'"How else do you expect me to take it? It is serious."

'She shook her head a little.

'"No. I was upset and hysterical that day. You were being very sweet to me. I said yes because I was too miserable to say no. But now I've had time to collect myself. Don't think me unkind. I made a mistake. I've been very much to blame. You must forgive me."

'"Oh, darling, you're talking nonsense. You've got nothing against me."

'She looked at me steadily. She was quite calm. She had even a little smile at the back of her eyes.

'"I can't marry you. I can't marry anyone. It was absurd of me ever to think I could."

'I didn't answer at once. She was in a queer state and I thought it better not to insist.

'"I suppose I can't drag you to the altar by main force," I said.

'I held out my hand and she gave me hers. I put my arm round her, and she made no attempt to withdraw. She suffered me to kiss her as usual on her cheek.

'Next morning I met the train. For once in a way it was punctual. Tim waved to me as his carriage passed the place where I was standing, and by the time I had walked up he had already jumped out and was handing down his wife. He grasped my hand warmly.

'"Where's Olive?" he said, with a glance along the platform. "This is Sally."

'I shook hands with her and at the same time explained why Olive was not there.

'"It was frightfully early, wasn't it?" said Mrs Hardy.

'I told them that the plan was for them to come and have a bit of breakfast at my house and then drive home.

'"I'd love a bath," said Mrs Hardy.

'"You shall have one," I said.

'She was really an extremely pretty little thing, very fair, with enormous blue eyes and a lovely little straight nose. Her skin, all milk and roses, was exquisite. A little of the chorus girl type, of course, and you may happen to think that rather namby-pamby, but in that style she was enchanting. We drove to my house, they both had a bath and Tim a shave; I just had two minutes alone with him. He asked me how Olive had taken his marriage. I told him she'd been upset.

'"I was afraid so," he said, frowning a little. He gave a short sigh. "I couldn't do anything else."

'I didn't understand what he meant. At that moment Mrs Hardy joined us and slipped her arm through her husband's. He took her hand in his and gently pressed it. He gave her a look that had in it something pleased and humorously affectionate, as though he didn't take her quite seriously, but enjoyed his sense of proprietorship and was proud of her beauty. She really was lovely. She was not at all shy, she asked me to call her Sally before we'd known one another ten minutes, and she was quick in the uptake. Of course, just then she was excited at arriving. She'd never been East and everything thrilled her. It was quite obvious that she was head over heels in love with Tim. Her eyes never left him and she hung on his words. We had a jolly breakfast and then we parted. They got into their car to go home and I into mine to go to Lahad. I promised to go straight to the estate from there and in point of fact it was out of my way to pass by my house. I took a change with me. I didn't see why Olive shouldn't like Sally very much, she was frank and gay, and ingenuous; she was extremely young, she couldn't have been more than nineteen, and her wonderful prettiness couldn't fail to appeal to Olive. I was just as glad to have had a reasonable excuse to leave the three of them by themselves for the day, but as I started out from Lahad I had a notion that by the time I arrived they would all be pleased to see me. I drove up to the bungalow and blew my horn two or three times, expecting someone to appear. Not a soul. The place was in total darkness. I was surprised. It was absolutely silent. I couldn't make it out. They must be in. Very odd, I thought. I waited a moment, then got out of the car and walked up the steps. At the top of them I stumbled over something. I swore and bent down to see what it was; it had felt like a body. There was a cry and I saw it was the amah. She shrank back cowering as I touched her and broke into loud wails.

'"What the hell's the matter?" I cried, and then I felt a hand on my arm and heard a voice: Tuan, Tuan. I turned and in the darkness recognized Tim's head boy. He began to speak in little frightened gasps. I listened to him with horror.

What he told me was unspeakable. I pushed him aside and rushed into the house. The sitting-room was dark. I turned on the light. The first thing I saw was Sally huddled up in an arm-chair. She was startled by my sudden appearance and cried out. I could hardly speak. I asked her if it was true. When she told me it was I felt the room suddenly going round and round me. I had to sit down. As the car that bore Tim and Sally drove up the road that led to the house and Tim sounded the claxon to announce their arrival and the boys and the amah ran out to greet them there was the sound of a shot. They ran to Olive's room and found her lying in front of the looking-glass in a pool of blood. She had shot herself with Tim's revolver.

'"Is she dead?" I said.

'"No, they sent for the doctor, and he took her to the hospital."

'I hardly knew what I was doing. I didn't even trouble to tell Sally where I was going. I got up and staggered to the door. I got into the car and told my seis to drive like hell to the hospital. I rushed in. I asked where she was. They tried to bar my way, but I pushed them aside. I knew where the private rooms were. Someone clung to my arm, but I shook him off. I vaguely understood that the doctor had given instructions that no one was to go into the room. I didn't care about that. There was an orderly at the door; he put his arm to prevent me from passing. I swore at him and told him to get out of my way. I suppose I made a row, I was beside myself; the door was opened and the doctor came out.

'"Who's making all this noise?" he said. "Oh, it's you. What do you want?"

'"Is she dead?" I asked.

'"No. But she's unconscious. She never regained consciousness. It's only a matter of an hour or two."

'"I want to see her."

'"You can't."

'"I'm engaged to her."

'"You?" he cried, and even at that moment I was aware that he looked at me strangely. "That's all the more reason."

'I didn't know what he meant. I was stupid with horror.

'"Surely you can do something to save her," I cried.

'He shook his head.

'"If you saw her you wouldn't wish it," he said.

'I stared at him aghast. In the silence I heard a man's convulsive sobbing.

'"Who's that?" I asked.

'"Her brother."

'Then I felt a hand on my arm. I look round and saw it was Mrs Sergison.

'"My poor boy," she said, "I'm so sorry for you."

'"What on earth made her do it?" I groaned.

'"Come away, my dear," said Mrs Sergison. "You can do no good here."

'"No, I must stay," I said.

'"Well, go and sit in my room," said the doctor.

'I was so broken that I let Mrs Sergison take me by the arm and lead me into the doctor's private room. She made me sit down. I couldn't bring myself to realize that it was true. I thought it was a horrible nightmare from which I must awake. I don't know how long we sat there. Three hours. Four hours. At last the doctor came in.

'"It's all over," he said.

'Then I couldn't help myself, I began to cry. I didn't care what they thought of me. I was so frightfully unhappy.

'We buried her next day.

'Mrs Sergison came back to my house and sat with me for a while. She wanted me to go to the club with her. I hadn't the heart. She was very kind, but I was glad when she left me by myself. I tried to read, but the words meant nothing to me. I felt dead inside. My boy came in and turned on the lights. My head was aching like mad. Then he came back and said that a lady wished to see me. I asked who it was. He wasn't quite sure, but he thought it must be the new wife of the tuan at Putatan. I couldn't imagine what she wanted. I got up and went to the door. He was right. It was Sally. I asked her to come in. I noticed that she was deathly white. I felt sorry for her. It was a frightful experience for a girl of that age and for a bride a miserable home-coming. She sat down. She was very nervous. I tried to put her at her ease by saying conventional things. She made me very uncomfortable because she stared at me with those enormous blue eyes of hers, and they were simply ghastly with horror. She interrupted me suddenly.

'"You're the only person here I know," she said. "I had to come to you. I want you to get me away from here."

'I was dumbfounded.

'"What *do* you mean?" I said.

'"I don't want you to ask me any questions. I just want you to get me away. At once. I want to go back to England!"

'"But you can't leave Tim like that just now," I said. "My dear, you must pull yourself together. I know it's been awful for you. But think of Tim. I mean, he'll be miserable. If you have any love for him the least you can do is to try and make him a little less unhappy."

'"Oh, you don't know," she cried. "I can't tell you. It's too horrible. I beseech you to help me. If there's a train tonight let me get on it. If I can only get to Penang I can get a ship. I can't stay in this place another night. I shall go mad."

'I was absolutely bewildered.

'"Does Tim know?" I asked her.

'"I haven't seen Tim since last night. I'll never see him again. I'd rather die."

'I wanted to gain a little time.

'"But how can you go without your things? Have you got any luggage?"

'"What does that matter?" she cried impatiently. "I've got what I want for the journey."

'"Have you any money?"

'"Enough. Is there a train tonight?"

'"Yes," I said. "It's due just after midnight."

'"Thank God. Will you arrange everything? Can I stay here till then?"

'"You're putting me in a frightful position," I said. "I don't know what to do for the best. You know, it's an awfully serious step you're taking."

'"If you knew everything you'd know it was the only possible thing to do."

'"It'll create an awful scandal here. I don't know what people'll say. Have you thought of the effect on Tim?" I was worried and unhappy. "God knows I don't want to interfere in what isn't my business. But if you want me to help you I ought to know enough to feel justified in doing so. You must tell me what's happened."

'"I can't. I can only tell you that I know everything."

'She hid her face with her hands and shuddered. Then she gave herself a shake as though she were recoiling from some frightful sight.

'"He had no right to marry me. It was monstrous."

'And as she spoke her voice rose shrill and piercing. I was afraid she was going to have an attack of hysterics. Her pretty doll-like face was terrified and her eyes stared as though she could never close them again.

'"Don't you love him any more?" I asked.

'"After that?"

'"What will you do if I refuse to help you?" I said.

'"I suppose there's a clergyman here or a doctor. You can't refuse to take me to one of them."

'"How did you get here?"

'"The head boy drove me. He got a car from somewhere."

'"Does Tim know you've gone?"

'"I left a letter for him."

'"He'll know you're here."

'"He won't try to stop me. I promise you that. He daren't. For God's sake don't you try either. I tell you I shall go mad if I stay here another night."

'I sighed. After all she was of an age to decide for herself.'

I, the writer of this, hadn't spoken for a long time.

'Did you know what she meant?' I asked Featherstone.

He gave me a long, haggard look.

'There was only one thing she could mean. It was unspeakable. Yes, I knew all right. It explained everything. Poor Olive. Poor sweet. I suppose it was unreasonable of me, at that moment I only felt a horror of that little pretty fair-haired thing with her terrified eyes. I hated her. I didn't say anything for a while. Then I told her I'd do as she wished. She didn't even say thank you. I think she knew what I felt about her. When it was dinner-time I made her eat something and then she asked me if there was a room she could go and lie down in till it was time to go to the station. I showed her into my spare room and left her. I sat in the sitting-room and waited. My God, I don't think the time has ever passed so slowly for me. I thought twelve would never strike. I rang up the station and was told the train wouldn't be in till nearly two. At midnight she came back to the sitting-room and we sat there for an hour and a half. We had nothing to say to one another and we didn't speak. Then I took her to the station and put her on the train.'

'Was there an awful scandal?'

Featherstone frowned.

'I don't know. I applied for short leave. After that I was moved to another post. I heard that Tim had sold the estate and bought another. But I didn't know where. It was a shock to me at first when I found him here.'

Featherstone, getting up, went over to a table and mixed himself a whisky and soda. In the silence that fell I heard the monotonous chorus of the croaking frogs. And suddenly the bird that is known as the fever-bird, perched in a tree close to the house, began to call. First, three notes in a descending, chromatic scale, then five, then four. The varying notes of the scale succeeded one another with maddening persistence. One was compelled to listen and to count them, and because one did not know how many there would be it tortured one's nerves.

'Blast that bird,' said Featherstone. 'That means no sleep for me tonight.'

FROM

Cosmopolitans

(1936)

Salvatore

I wonder if I can do it.

I knew Salvatore first when he was a boy of fifteen with a pleasant, ugly face, a laughing mouth and care-free eyes. He used to spend the morning lying about the beach with next to nothing on and his brown body was as thin as a rail. He was full of grace. He was in and out of the sea all the time, swimming with the clumsy, effortless stroke common to the fisher boys. Scrambling up the jagged rocks on his hard feet, for except on Sundays he never wore shoes, he would throw himself into the deep water with a cry of delight. His father was a fisherman who owned his own little vineyard and Salvatore acted as nursemaid to his two younger brothers. He shouted to them to come in shore when they ventured out too far and made them dress when it was time to climb the hot, vineclad hill for the frugal midday meal.

But boys in those Southern parts grow apace and in a little while he was madly in love with a pretty girl who lived on the Grande Marina. She had eyes like forest pools and held herself like a daughter of the Caesars. They were affianced, but they could not marry till Salvatore had done his military service, and when he left the island which he had never left in his life before, to become a sailor in the navy of King Victor Emmanuel, he wept like a child. It was hard for one who had never been less free than the birds to be at the beck and call of others; it was harder still to live in a battleship with strangers instead of in a little white cottage among the vines; and when he was ashore, to walk in noisy, friendless cities with streets so crowded that he was frightened to cross them, when he had been used to silent paths and the mountains and the sea. I suppose it had never struck him that Ischia, which he looked at every evening (it was like a fairy island in the sunset) to see what the weather would be like next day, or Vesuvius, pearly in the dawn, had anything to do with him at all; but when he ceased to have them before his eyes he realized in some dim fashion that they were as much part of him as his hands and his feet. He was dreadfully homesick. But it was hardest of all to be parted from the girl he loved with all his passionate young heart. He wrote to her (in his childlike hand-writing) long, ill-spelt letters in which he told her how constantly he thought of her and how much he longed to be back. He was sent here and there, to Spezzia, to Venice, to Bari and finally to China. Here he fell ill of some mysterious ailment that kept him in hospital for months. He bore it with the mute and uncomprehending patience of a dog. When he learnt that it was a form of rheumatism that made him unfit for further service his heart exulted, for he could go home; and he did not bother, in fact he scarcely listened, when the doctors told him that he would never again be quite well. What did he care when he was going back to the little island he loved so well and the girl who was waiting for him?

When he got into the rowing-boat that met the steamer from Naples and was rowed ashore he saw his father and mother standing on the jetty and his two brothers, big boys now, and he waved to them. His eyes searched among the crowd that waited there, for the girl. He could not see her. There was a great deal of kissing when he jumped up the steps and they all, emotional creatures, cried a little as they exchanged their greetings. He asked where the girl was. His mother told him that she did not know; they had not seen her for two or three weeks; so in the evening when the moon was shining over the placid sea and the lights of Naples twinkled in the distance he walked down to the Grande Marina to her house. She was sitting on the doorstep with her mother. He was a little shy because he had not seen her for so long. He asked her if she had not received the letter that he had written to her to say that he was coming home. Yes, they had received a letter, and they had been told by another of the island boys that he was ill. Yes, that was why he was back; was it not a piece of luck? Oh, but they had heard that he would never be quite well again. The doctors talked a lot of nonsense, but he knew very well that now he was home again he would recover. They were silent for a little, and then the mother nudged the girl. She did not try to soften the blow. She told him straight out, with the blunt directness of her race, that she could not marry a man who would never be strong enough to work like a man. They had made up their minds, her mother and father and she, and her father would never give his consent.

When Salvatore went home he found that they all knew. The girl's father had been to tell them what they had decided, but they had lacked the courage to tell him themselves. He wept on his mother's bosom. He was terribly unhappy, but he did not blame the girl. A fisherman's life is hard and it needs strength and endurance. He knew very well that a girl could not afford to marry a man who might not be able to support her. His smile was very sad and his eyes had the look of a dog that has been beaten, but he did not complain, and he never said a hard word of the girl he had loved so well. Then, a few months later, when he had settled down to the common round, working in his father's vineyard and fishing, his mother told him that there was a young woman in the village who was willing to marry him. Her name was Assunta.

'She's as ugly as the devil,' he said.

She was older than he, twenty-four or twenty-five, and she had been engaged to a man who, while doing his military service, had been killed in Africa. She had a little money of her own and if Salvatore married her she could buy him a boat of his own and they could take a vineyard that by a happy chance happened at that moment to be without a tenant. His mother told him that Assunta had seen him at the *festa* and had fallen in love with him. Salvatore smiled his sweet smile and said he would think about it. On the following Sunday, dressed in the stiff black clothes in which he looked so much less well than in the ragged shirt and trousers of every day, he went up to High Mass at the parish church and placed himself so that he could have a good look at the young woman. When he came down again he told his mother that he was willing.

Well, they were married and they settled down

in a tiny white-washed house in the middle of a handsome vineyard. Salvatore was now a great big husky fellow, tall and broad, but still with that ingenuous smile and those trusting, kindly eyes that he had had as a boy. He had the most beautiful manners I have ever seen in my life. Assunta was a grim-visaged female, with decided features, and she looked old for her years. But she had a good heart and she was no fool. I used to be amused by the little smile of devotion that she gave her husband when he was being very masculine and masterful; she never ceased to be touched by his gentle sweetness. But she could not bear the girl who had thrown him over, and notwithstanding Salvatore's smiling expostulations she had nothing but harsh words for her. Presently children were born to them.

It was a hard enough life. All through the fishing season towards evening he set out in his boat with one of his brothers for the fishing grounds. It was a long pull of six or seven miles, and he spent the night catching the profitable cuttlefish. Then there was the long row back again in order to sell the catch in time for it to go on the early boat to Naples. At other times he was working in his vineyard from dawn till the heat drove him to rest and then again, when it was a trifle cooler, till dusk. Often his rheumatism prevented him from doing anything at all and then he would lie about the beach, smoking cigarettes, with a pleasant word for everyone notwithstanding the pain that racked his limbs. The foreigners who came down to bathe and saw him there said that these Italian fishermen were lazy devils.

Sometimes he used to bring his children down to

give them a bath. They were both boys and at this time the elder was three and the younger less than two. They sprawled about at the water's edge stark naked and Salvatore, standing on a rock would dip them in the water. The elder one bore it with stoicism, but the baby screamed lustily. Salvatore had enormous hands, like legs of mutton, coarse and hard from constant toil, but when he bathed his children, holding them so tenderly, drying them with delicate care, upon my word they were like flowers. He would seat the naked baby on the palm of his hand and hold him up, laughing a little at his smallness, and his laugh was like the laughter of an angel. His eyes then were as candid as his child's.

I started by saying that I wondered if I could do it and now I must tell you what it is that I have tried to do. I wanted to see whether I could hold your attention for a few pages while I drew for you the portrait of a man, just an ordinary Italian fisherman who possessed nothing in the world except a quality which is the rarest, the most precious and the loveliest that anyone can have. Heaven only knows why he should so strangely and unexpectedly have possessed it. All I know is that it shone in him with a radiance that, if it had not been so unconscious and so humble, would have been to the common run of men hardly bearable. And in case you have not guessed what the quality was, I will tell you. Goodness, just goodness.

The Judgement Seat

They awaited their turn patiently, but patience was no new thing to them; they had practised it, all three of them, with grim determination, for thirty years. Their lives had been a long preparation for this moment and they looked forward to the issue now, if not with self-confidence, for that on so awful an occasion would have been misplaced, at all events with hope and courage. They had taken the strait and narrow path when the flowery meads of sin stretched all too invitingly before them; with heads held high, though with breaking hearts, they had resisted temptation; and now, their arduous journey done, they expected their reward. There was no need for them to speak, since each knew the others' thoughts, and they felt that in all three of them the same emotion of relief filled their bodiless souls with thanksgiving. With what anguish now would they have been wrung if they had yielded to the passion which then had seemed so nearly irresistible and what a madness it would have been if for a few short years of bliss they had sacrificed that Life Everlasting which with so bright a light at long last shone before them! They felt like men who with the skin of their teeth have escaped a sudden and violent death and touch their feet and hands and, scarce able to believe that they are still alive, look about them in amazement. They had done nothing with which they could reproach themselves and when presently their angels came and told them that the moment was come, they would advance, as they had passed through the world that was now so far behind, happily conscious that they had done their duty. They stood a little on one side, for the press was great. A terrible war was in progress and for years the soldiers of all nations, men in the full flush of their gallant youth, had marched in an interminable procession to the Judgement Seat; women and children too, their lives brought to a wretched end by violence or, more unhappily, by grief, disease and starvation; and there was in the courts of heaven not a little confusion.

It was on account of this war, too, that these three wan, shivering ghosts stood in expectation of their doom. For John and Mary had been passengers on a ship which was sunk by the torpedo of a submarine; and Ruth, broken in health by the arduous work to which she had so nobly devoted herself, hearing of the death of the man whom she had loved with all her heart, sank beneath the blow and died. John, indeed, might have saved himself if he had not tried to save his wife; he hated her; he had hated her to the depths of his soul for thirty years; but he had always done his duty by her and now, in the moment of dreadful peril, it never occurred to him that he could do otherwise.

At last their angels took them by the hand and led them to the Presence. For a little while the Eternal took not the slightest notice of them. If the truth must be told he was in a bad humour. A moment before there had come up for judgement a philosopher, deceased full of years and honours, who had told the Eternal to his face that he did not believe in him. It was not this that would have disturbed the serenity of the King of Kings, this could only have made him smile; but the philosopher, taking perhaps an unfair advantage of the regrettable happenings just then upon Earth, had asked him how, considering them dispassionately, it was possible to reconcile his All-Power with his All-Goodness.

'No one can deny the fact of Evil,' said the philosopher, sententiously. 'Now, if God cannot prevent Evil he is not all-powerful, and if he can prevent it and will not, he is not all-good.'

This argument was of course not new to the Omniscient, but he had always refused to consider the matter; for the fact is, though he knew everything, he did not know the answer to this. Even God cannot make two and two five. But the philosopher, pressing his advantage, and, as philosophers often will, drawing from a reasonable premise an unjustifiable inference, the philosopher had finished with a statement that in the circumstances was surely preposterous.

'I will not believe,' he said, 'in a God who is not All-Powerful and All-Good.'

It was not then perhaps without relief that the Eternal turned his attention to the three shades who stood humbly and yet hopefully before him. The quick, with so short a time to live, when they talk of themselves, talk too much; but the dead, with eternity before them, are so verbose that only angels could listen to them with civility. But this in brief is the story that these three recounted. John and Mary had been happily married for five years and till John met Ruth they loved each other, as married couples for the most part do, with sincere affection and mutual respect. Ruth was eighteen, ten years younger than he was, a charming, graceful animal, with a sudden and all-conquering loveliness; she was as healthy in mind as she was in body, and, eager for the natural happiness of life, was capable of achieving that greatness which is beauty of soul. John fell in love with her and she with him. But it was no ordinary passion that seized them; it was something so overwhelming that they felt as if the whole long history of the world signified only because it had led to the time and place that had brought them together. They loved as Daphnis and Chloe or as Paolo and Francesca. But after that first moment of ecstasy when each discovered the other's love they were seized with dismay. They were decent people and they respected themselves, the beliefs in which they had been bred, and the society in which they lived. How could he betray an innocent girl, and what had she to do with a married man? Then they grew conscious that Mary was aware of their love. The confident affection with which she had regarded her husband was shaken; and there arose in her feelings of which she would never have thought herself capable, jealousy and the fear that he would desert her, anger because her possession of his heart was threatened and a strange hunger of the soul which was more painful than love. She felt that she would die if he left her; and yet she knew that if he loved it was because love had come to him, not because he had sought it. She did not blame him. She prayed for strength; she wept silent, bitter tears. John and Ruth saw her pine

away before their eyes. The struggle was long and
bitter. Sometimes their hearts failed them and they
felt that they could not resist the passion that
burned the marrow of their bones. They resisted.
They wrestled with evil as Jacob wrestled with the
angel of God and at last they conquered. With
breaking hearts, but proud in their innocence, they
parted. They offered up to God, as it were a sacrifice, their hopes of happiness, the joy of life and the
beauty of the world.

Ruth had loved too passionately ever to love
again and with a stony heart she turned to God and
to good works. She was indefatigable. She tended
the sick and assisted the poor. She founded
orphanages and managed charitable institutions.
And little by little her beauty which she cared for
no longer left her and her face grew as hard as her
heart. Her religion was fierce and narrow; her very
kindness was cruel because it was founded not on
love but on reason; she became domineering,
intolerant and vindictive. And John resigned, but
sullen and angry, dragged himself along the weary
years waiting for the release of death. Life lost its
meaning to him; he had made his effort and in
conquering was conquered; the only emotion that
remained with him was the unceasing, secret
hatred with which he looked upon his wife. He
used her with kindness and consideration; he did
everything that could be expected of a man who
was a Christian and a gentleman. He did his duty.
Mary, a good, faithful and (it must be confessed)
exceptional wife, never thought to reproach her
husband for the madness that had seized him; but
all the same she could not forgive him for the sacrifice he had made for her sake. She grew acid and

querulous. Though she hated herself for it, she could not refrain from saying the things that she knew would wound him. She would willingly have sacrificed her life for him, but she could not bear that he should enjoy a moment's happiness when she was so wretched that a hundred times she had wished she was dead. Well, now she was and so were they; grey and drab had life been, but that was passed; they had not sinned and now their reward was at hand.

They finished and there was silence. There was silence in all the courts of heaven. Go to hell were the words that came to the Eternal's lips, but he did not utter them, for they had a colloquial association that he rightly thought unfitting to the solemnity of the occasion. Nor indeed would such a decree have met the merits of the case. But his brows darkened. He asked himself if it was for this that he had made the rising sun shine on the boundless sea and the snow glitter on the mountain tops; was it for this that the brooks sang blithely as they hastened down the hillsides and the golden corn waved in the evening breeze?

'I sometimes think,' said the Eternal, 'that the stars never shine more brightly than when reflected in the muddy waters of a wayside ditch.'

But the three shades stood before him and now that they had unfolded their unhappy story they could not but feel a certain satisfaction. It had been a bitter struggle, but they had done their duty. The Eternal blew lightly, he blew as a man might blow out a lighted match, and behold! where the three poor souls had stood – was nothing. The Eternal annihilated them.

'I have often wondered why men think I attach

so much importance to sexual irregularity,' he said. 'If they read my works more attentively they would see that I have always been sympathetic to that particular form of human frailty.'

Then he turned to the philosopher who was still waiting for a reply to his remarks.

'You cannot but allow,' said the Eternal, 'that on this occasion I have very happily combined my All-Power with my All-Goodness.'

FROM

The Mixture as Before

(1940)

Gigolo and Gigolette

The bar was crowded. Sandy Westcott had had a couple of cocktails and he was beginning to feel hungry. He looked at his watch. He had been asked to dinner at half-past nine and it was nearly ten. Eva Barrett was always late and he would be lucky if he got anything to eat by ten-thirty. He turned to the barman to order another cocktail and caught sight of a man who at that moment came up to the bar.

'Hullo, Cotman,' he said. 'Have a drink?'

'I don't mind if I do, sir.'

Cotman was a nice-looking fellow, of thirty perhaps, short, but with so good a figure that he did not look it, very smartly dressed in a double-breasted dinner jacket, a little too much waisted, and a butterfly tie a good deal too large. He had a thick mat of black, wavy hair, very sleek and shiny, brushed straight back from his forehead, and large flashing eyes. He spoke with great refinement, but with a cockney accent.

'How's Stella?' asked Sandy.

'Oh, she's all right. Likes to have a lay-down before the show, you know. Steadies the old nerves, she says.'

'I wouldn't do that stunt of hers for a thousand pounds.'

'I don't suppose you would. No one can do it but

her, not from that height, I mean, and only five foot of water.'

'It's the most sick-making thing I've ever seen.'

Cotman gave a little laugh. He took this as a compliment. Stella was his wife. Of course she did the trick and took the risk, but it was he who had thought of the flames, and it was the flames that had taken the public fancy and made the turn the huge success it was. Stella dived into a tank from the top of a ladder sixty feet high, and as he said, there were only five feet of water in the tank. Just before she dived they poured enough petrol on to cover the surface and he set it alight; the flames soared up and she dived straight into them.

'Paco Espinel tells me it's the biggest draw the Casino has ever had,' said Sandy.

'I know. He told me they'd served as many dinners in July as they generally do in August. And that's you, he says to me.'

'Well, I hope you're making a packet.'

'Well, I can't exactly say that. You see, we've got our contract and naturally we didn't know it was going to be a riot, but Mr Espinel's talking of booking us for next month, and I don't mind telling you he's not going to get us on the same terms or anything like it. Why, I had a letter from an agent only this morning saying they wanted us to go to Deauville.'

'Here are my people,' said Sandy.

He nodded to Cotman and left him. Eva Barrett sailed in with the rest of her guests. She had gathered them together downstairs. It was a party of eight.

'I knew we should find you here, Sandy,' she said. 'I'm not late, am I?'

'Only half an hour.'

'Ask them what cocktails they want and then we'll dine.'

While they were standing at the bar, emptying now, for nearly everyone had gone down to the terrace for dinner, Paco Espinel passed through and stopped to shake hands with Eva Barrett. Paco Espinel was a young man who had run through his money and now made his living by arranging the turns with which the Casino sought to attract visitors. It was his duty to be civil to the rich and great. Mrs Chaloner Barrett was an American widow of vast wealth; she not only entertained expensively, but also gambled. And after all, the dinners and suppers and the two cabaret shows that accompanied them were only provided to induce people to lose their money at the tables.

'Got a good table for me, Paco?' said Eva Barrett.

'The best.' His eyes, fine, dark Argentine eyes, expressed his admiration of Mrs Barrett's opulent, ageing charms. This also was business. 'You've seen Stella?'

'Of course. Three times. It's the most terrifying thing I've ever seen.'

'Sandy comes every night.'

'I want to be in at the death. She's bound to kill herself one of these nights and I don't want to miss that if I can help it.'

Paco laughed.

'She's been such a success, we're going to keep her on another month. All I ask is that she shouldn't kill herself till the end of August. After that she can do as she likes.'

'Oh, God, have I got to go on eating trout and roast chicken every night till the end of August?' cried Sandy.

'You brute, Sandy,' said Eva Barrett. 'Come on,

let's go in to dinner. I'm starving.'

Paco Espinel asked the barman if he'd seen Cotman. The barman said he'd had a drink with Mr Westcott.

'Oh, well, if he comes in here again, tell him I want a word with him.'

Mrs Barrett paused at the top of the steps that led down to the terrace long enough for the press representative, a little haggard woman with an untidy head, to come up with her note-book. Sandy whispered the names of the guests. It was a representative Riviera party. There was an English Lord and his Lady, long and lean both of them, who were prepared to dine with anyone who would give them a free meal. They were certain to be as tight as drums before midnight. There was a gaunt Scots woman, with a face like a Peruvian mask that has been battered by the storms of ten centuries, and her English husband. Though a broker by profession, he was bluff, military and hearty. He gave you an impression of such integrity that you were almost more sorry for him than for yourself when the good thing he had put you on to as a special favour turned out to be a dud. There was an Italian countess who was neither Italian nor a countess, but played a beautiful game of bridge, and there was a Russian prince who was ready to make Mrs Barrett a princess and in the meantime sold champagne, motor cars and Old Masters on commission. A dance was in progress and Mrs Barrett, waiting for it to end, surveyed with a look which her short upper lip made scornful the serried throng on the dance floor. It was a gala night and the dining tables were crowded together. Beyond the terrace the sea was calm and silent. The music stopped and the head waiter, affably smiling, came up to guide her to her table. She swept down the steps with majestic gait.

'We shall have quite a good view of the dive,' she said as she sat down.

'I like to be next door to the tank,' said Sandy, 'so that I can see her face.'

'Is she pretty?' asked the Countess.

'It's not that. It's the expression of her eyes. She's scared to death every time she does it.'

'Oh, I don't believe that,' said the City gentleman, Colonel Goodhart by name, though no one had ever discovered how he came by the title. 'I mean, the whole bally stunt's only a trick. There's no danger really, I mean.'

'You don't know what you're talking about. Diving from that height in as little water as that, she's got to turn like a flash the moment she touches the water. And if she doesn't do it right she's bound to bash her head against the bottom and break her back.'

'That's just what I'm telling you, old boy,' said the Colonel, 'it's a trick. I mean, there's no argument.'

'If there's no danger there's nothing to it, anyway,' said Eva Barrett. 'It's over in a minute. Unless she's risking her life it's the biggest fraud of modern times. Don't say we've come to see this over and over again and it's only a fake.'

'Pretty well everything is. You can take my word for that.'

'Well, you ought to know,' said Sandy.

If it occurred to the Colonel that this might be a nasty dig he admirably concealed it. He laughed.

'I don't mind saying I know a thing or two,' he

admitted. 'I mean, I've got my eyes peeled all right. You can't put much over on me.'

The tank was on the far left of the terrace, and behind it, supported by stays, was an immensely tall ladder at the top of which was a tiny platform. After two or three dances more, when Eva Barrett's party were eating asparagus, the music stopped and the lights were lowered. A spot was turned on the tank. Cotman was visible in the brilliance. He ascended half a dozen steps so that he was on a level with the top of the tank.

'Ladies and gentlemen,' he cried out, in a loud clear voice, 'you are now going to see the most marvellous feat of the century. Madam Stella, the greatest diver in the world, is about to dive from a height of sixty feet into a lake of flames five foot deep. This is a feat that has never been performed before, and Madam Stella is prepared to give one hundred pounds to anyone who will attempt it. Ladies and gentlemen, I have the honour to present Madam Stella.'

A little figure appeared at the top of the steps that led on to the terrace, ran quickly up to the tank, and bowed to the applauding audience. She wore a man's silk dressing-gown and on her head a bathing-cap. Her thin face was made up as if for the stage. The Italian countess looked at her through her *face-à-main*.

'Not pretty,' she said.

'Good figure,' said Eva Barrett. 'You'll see.'

Stella slipped out of her dressing-gown and gave it to Cotman. He went down the steps. She stood for a moment and looked at the crowd. They were in darkness and she could only see vague white faces and white shirt-fronts. She was small, beautifully made, with legs long for her body and slim hips. Her bathing costume was very scanty.

'You're quite right about the figure, Eva,' said the Colonel. 'Bit undeveloped, of course, but I know you girls think that's quite the thing.'

Stella began to climb the ladder and the spot-light followed her. It seemed an incredible height. An attendant poured petrol on the surface of the water. Cotman was handed a flaming torch. He watched Stella reach the top of the ladder and settle herself on the platform.

'Ready?' he cried.

'Yes.'

'Go,' he shouted.

And as he shouted he seemed to plunge the burn-ing torch into the water. The flames sprang up, leaping high, and really terrifying to look at. At the same moment Stella dived. She came down like a streak of lightning and plunged through the flames, which subsided a moment after she had reached the water. A second later she was at the surface and jumped out to a roar, a storm of applause. Cotman wrapped the dressing-gown round her. She bowed and bowed. The applause went on. Music struck up. With a final wave of the hand she ran down the steps and between the tables to the door. The lights went up and the waiters hurried along with their neglected service.

Sandy Westcott gave a sigh. He did not know whether he was disappointed or relieved.

'Top hole,' said the English peer.

'It's a bally fake,' said the Colonel, with his British pertinacity. 'I bet you anything you like.'

'It's over so quickly,' said her English ladyship. 'I mean, you don't get your money's worth really.'

Anyhow it wasn't her money. That it never was. The Italian countess leaned forward. She spoke fluent English, but with a strong accent.

'Eva, my darling, who are those extraordinary people at the table near the door under the balcony?'

'Packet of fun, aren't they?' said Sandy. 'I simply haven't been able to take my eyes off them.'

Eva Barrett glanced at the table the Countess indicated, and the Prince, who sat with his back to it, turned round to look.

'They can't be true,' cried Eva. 'I must ask Angelo who they are.'

Mrs Barrett was the sort of woman who knew the head waiters of all the principal restaurants in Europe by their first names. She told the waiter who was at that moment filling her glass to send Angelo to her.

It was certainly an odd pair. They were sitting by themselves at a small table. They were very old. The man was big and stout, with a mass of white hair, great bushy white eyebrows and an enormous white moustache. He looked like the late King Humbert of Italy, but much more like a king. He sat bolt upright. He wore full evening dress, with a white tie and a collar that has been out of fashion for hard on thirty years. His companion was a little old lady in a black satin ball dress, cut very low and tight at the waist. Round her neck were several chains of coloured beads. She wore what was obviously a wig, and a very ill-fitting one at that; it was very elaborate, all curls and sausages, and raven black. She was outrageously made-up, bright blue under the eyes and on the eyelids, the eyebrows heavily black, a great patch of very pink rouge on each cheek and the lips a livid scarlet. The skin hung loosely on her face in deep wrinkles. She had large bold eyes and they darted eagerly from table to table. She was taking everything in, and every other minute called the old man's attention to someone or other. The appearance of the couple was so fantastic in that fashionable crowd, the men in dinner jackets, the women in thin, pale-coloured frocks, that many eyes were turned on them. The staring did not seem to incommode the old lady. When she felt certain persons were looking at her she raised her eyebrows archly, smiled and rolled her eyes. She seemed on the point of acknowledging applause.

Angelo hurried up to the good customer that Eva Barrett was.

'You wished to see me, my lady?'

'Oh, Angelo, we're simply dying to know who those absolutely marvellous people are at the next table to the door.'

Angelo gave a look and then assumed a deprecating air. The expression of his face, the movement of his shoulders, the turn of his spine, the gesture of his hands, probably even the twiddle of his toes, all indicated a half-humorous apology.

'You must overlook them, my lady.' He knew of course that Mrs Barrett had no right to be thus addressed, just as he knew that the Italian countess was neither Italian nor a countess and that the English lord never paid for a drink if anyone else would pay for it, but he also knew that to be thus addressed did not displease her. 'They begged me to give them a table because they wanted to see Madame Stella do her dive. They were in the profession themselves once. I know they're not the sort of people one expects to see dining here, but they made such a point of it I simply hadn't the heart to refuse.'

'But I think they're a perfect scream. I adore them.'

'I've known them for many years. The man indeed is a compatriot of mine.' The head waiter gave a condescending little laugh. 'I told them I'd give them a table on the condition that they didn't dance. I wasn't taking any risks, my lady.'

'Oh, but I should have loved to see them dance.'

'One has to draw the line somewhere, my lady,' said Angelo gravely.

He smiled, bowed again and withdrew.

'Look,' cried Sandy, 'they're going.'

The funny old couple were paying their bill. The old man got up and put round his wife's neck a large white, but not too clean, feather boa. She rose. He gave her his arm, holding himself very erect, and she, small in comparison, tripped out beside him. Her black satin dress had a long train, and Eva Barrett (who was well over fifty) screamed with joy.

'Look, I remember my mother wearing a dress like that when I was in the school-room.'

The comic pair walked, still arm in arm, through the spacious rooms of the Casino till they came to the door. The old man addressed a commissionaire.

'Be so good as to direct me to the artistes' dressing-rooms. We wish to pay our respects to Madam Stella.'

The commissionaire gave them a look and summed them up. They were not people with whom it was necessary to be very polite.

'You won't find her there.'

'She has not gone? I thought she gave a second performance at two.'

'That's true. They might be in the bar.'

'It won't 'urt us just to go an' 'ave a look, Carlo,' said the old lady.

'Right-o, my love,' he answered with a great roll of the R.

They walked slowly up the great stairs and entered the bar. It was empty but for the deputy-barman and a couple sitting in two armchairs in the corner. The old lady released her husband's arm and tripped up with outstretched hands.

"Ow are you, dear? I felt I just 'ad to come and congratulate you, bein' English same as you are. And in the profession meself. It's a grand turn, my dear, it deserves to be a success.' She turned to Cotman. 'And is this your 'usband?'

Stella got out of her armchair and a shy smile broke on her lips as she listened with some confusion to the voluble old lady.

'Yes, that's Syd.'

'Pleased to meet you,' he said.

'And this is mine,' said the old lady, with a little dig of the elbow in the direction of the tall, white-haired man. 'Mr Penezzi. 'E's a count really, and I'm the Countess Penezzi by rights, but when we retired from the profession we dropped the title.'

'Will you have a drink?' said Cotman.

'No, you 'ave one with us,' said Mrs Penezzi, sinking into an armchair. 'Carlo, you order.'

The barman came, and after some discussion three bottles of beer were ordered. Stella would not have anything.

'She never has anything till after the second show,' explained Cotman.

Stella was slight and small, about twenty-six, with light brown hair, cut short and waved, and grey eyes. She had reddened her lips, but wore little rouge on her face. Her skin was pale. She was not very pretty, but she had a neat little face. She wore a very simple evening frock of white silk. The beer was brought and Mr Penezzi, evidently not very talkative, took a long swig.

'What was your line?' asked Syd Cotman, politely.

Mrs Penezzi gave him a rolling glance of her flashing, made-up eyes and turned to her husband.

'Tell 'em who I am, Carlo,' she said.

'The 'uman cannon-ball,' he announced.

Mrs Penezzi smiled brightly and with a quick, bird-like glance looked from one to the other. They stared at her in dismay.

'Flora,' she said. 'The 'uman cannon-ball.'

She so obviously expected them to be impressed that they did not quite know what to do. Stella gave her Syd a puzzled look. He came to the rescue.

'It must have been before our time.'

'Naturally it was before your time. Why, we retired from the profession definitely the year poor Queen Victoria died. It made quite a sensation when we did too. But you've 'eard of me, of course.' She saw the blank look on their faces; her tone changed a little. 'But I was the biggest draw in London. At the Old Aquarium, that was. All the swells came to see me. The Prince of Wales and I don't know who all. I was the talk of the town. Isn't that true, Carlo?'

'She crowded the Aquarium for a year.'

'It was the most spectacular turn they'd ever 'ad there. Why, only a few years ago I went up and introduced myself to Lady de Bathe. Lily Langtry, you know. She used to live down 'ere. She remembered me perfectly. She told me she'd seen me ten times.'

'What did you do?' asked Stella.

'I was fired out of a cannon. Believe me, it was a sensation. And after London I went all over the world with it. Yes, my dear, I'm an old woman now and I won't deny it. Seventy-eight Mr Penezzi is and I shall never see seventy again, but I've 'ad me portrait on every 'oardin' in London. Lady de Bathe said to me: my dear, you was as celebrated as I was. But you know what the public is, give 'em a good thing and they go mad over it, only they want change; 'owever good it is, they get sick of it and then they won't go and see it any more. It'll 'appen to you, my dear, same as it 'appened to me. It comes to all of us. But Mr Penezzi always 'ad 'is 'ead screwed on 'is shoulders the right way. Been in the business since 'e was so 'igh. Circus, you know. Ringmaster. That's 'ow I first knew 'im. I was in a troupe of acrobacks. Trapeze act, you know. 'E's a fine-lookin' man now, but you should 'ave seen 'im then, in 'is Russian boots, and ridin' breeches, and a tight-fittin' coat with frogs all down the front of it, crackin' 'is long whip as 'is 'orses galloped round the ring, the 'andsomest man I ever see in my life.'

Mr Penezzi did not make any remark, but thoughtfully twisted his immense white moustache.

'Well, as I was tellin' you, 'e was never one to throw money about and when the agents couldn't get us bookin's any more 'e said, let's retire. An 'e was quite right, after 'avin' been the biggest star in London, we couldn't go back to circus work any more, I mean, Mr Penezzi bein' a count really, 'e 'ad 'is dignity to think of, so we come down 'ere and we bought a 'ouse and started a pension. It always 'ad been Mr Penezzi's ambition to do something like that. Thirty-five years we been 'ere now. We 'aven't done so badly, not until the last two or three years, and the slump came, though visitors are very different from what they was when we first started, the things they want, electric-light and runnin' water in their bedrooms and I don't know what all. Give them a card, Carlo. Mr Penezzi does the cookin' 'imself, and if ever you want a real 'ome from 'ome, you'll know where to find it. I like professional people and we'd 'ave a rare lot to talk about, you and me, dearie. Once a professional always a professional, I say.'

At that moment the head-barman came back from his supper. He caught sight of Syd.

'Oh, Mr Cotman, Mr Espinel was looking for you, wants to see you particularly.'

'Oh, where is he?'

'You'll find him around somewhere.'

'We'll be going,' said Mrs Penezzi, getting up. 'Come and 'ave lunch with us one day, will you? I'd like to show you my old photographs and me press cuttin's. Fancy you not 'avin' 'eard of the 'uman cannon-ball. Why, I was as well known as the Tower of London.'

Mrs Penezzi was not vexed at finding that these young people had never even heard of her. She was simply amused.

They bade one another good-bye, and Stella sank back again into her chair.

'I'll just finish my beer,' said Syd, 'and then I'll go and see what Paco wants. Will you stay here,

ducky, or would you like to go to your
dressing-room?'

Stella's hands were tightly clenched. She did not
answer. Syd gave her a look and then quickly
glanced away.

'Perfect riot, that old girl,' he went on, in his
hearty way. 'Real figure of fun. I suppose it's true
what she said. It's difficult to believe, I must say.
Fancy 'er drawing all London, what, forty years
ago? And the funny thing is, her thinking anybody
remembered. Seemed as though she simply
couldn't understand us not having heard of her
even.'

He gave Stella another glance, from the corner of
his eye so that she should not see he was looking at
her, and he saw she was crying. He faltered. The
tears were rolling down her pale face. She made no
sound.

'What's the matter, darling?'

'Syd, I can't do it again tonight,' she sobbed.

'Why on earth not?'

'I'm afraid.'

He took her hand.

'I know you better than that,' he said. 'You're the
bravest little woman in the world. Have a brandy,
that'll pull you together.'

'No, that'd only make it worse.'

'You can't disappoint your public like that.'

'That filthy public. Swine who eat too much and
drink too much. A pack of chattering fools with
more money than they know what to do with. I
can't stick them. What do they care if I risk my
life?'

'Of course, it's the thrill they come for, there's no

denying that,' he replied uneasily. 'But you know and I know, there's no risk, not if you keep your nerve.'

'But I've lost my nerve, Syd. I shall kill myself.'

She had raised her voice a little, and he looked round quickly at the barman. But the barman was reading the *Eclaireur de Nice* and paying no attention.

'You don't know what it looks like from up there, the top of the ladder, when I look down at the tank. I give you my word, tonight I thought I was going to faint. I tell you I can't do it again tonight, you've got to get me out of it, Syd.'

'If you funk it tonight it'll be worse tomorrow.'

'No, it won't. It's having to do it twice kills me. The long wait and all that. You go and see Mr Espinel and tell I can't give two shows a night. It's more than my nerves'll stand.'

'He'll never stand for that. The whole supper trade depends on you. It's only to see you they come in then at all.'

'I can't help it, I tell you I can't go on.'

He was silent for a moment. The tears still streamed down her pale little face, and he saw that she was quickly losing control of herself. He had felt for some days that something was up and he had been anxious. He had tried not to give her an opportunity to talk. He knew obscurely that it was better for her not to put into words what she felt. But he had been worried. For he loved her.

'Anyhow Espinel wants to see me,' he said.

'What about?'

'I don't know. I'll tell him you can't give the show more than once a night and see what he says. Will you wait here?'

'No, I'll go along to the dressing-room.'

Ten minutes later he found her there. He was in great spirits and his step was jaunty. He burst open the door.

'I've got grand news for you, honey. They're keeping us on next month at twice the money.'

He sprang forward to take her in his arms and kiss her, but she pushed him away.

'Have I got to go on again tonight?'

'I'm afraid you must. I tried to make it only one show a night, but he wouldn't hear of it. He says it's quite essential you should do the supper turn. And after all, for double the money, it's worth it.'

She flung herself down on the floor and this time burst into a storm of tears.

'I can't, Syd, I can't. I shall kill myself.'

He sat down on the floor and raised her head and took her in his arms and petted her.

'Buck up, darling. You can't refuse a sum like that. Why, it'll keep us all the winter and we shan't have to do a thing. After all there are only four more days to the end of July and then it's only August.'

'No, no, no. I'm frightened. I don't want to die, Syd. I love you.'

'I know you do, darling, and I love you. Why, since we married I've never looked at another woman. We've never had money like this before and we shall never get it again. You know what these things are, we're a riot now, but we can't expect it to go on for ever. We've got to strike while the iron's hot.'

'D'you want me to die, Syd?'

'Don't talk so silly. Why, where should I be without you? You mustn't give way like this.

You've got your self-respect to think of. You're famous all over the world.'

'Like the human cannon-ball was,' she cried with a laugh of fury.

'That damned old woman,' he thought.

He knew that was the last straw. Bad luck, Stella taking it like that.

'That was an eye-opener to me,' she went on. 'What do they come and see me over and over again for? On the chance they'll see me kill myself. And a week after I'm dead they'll have forgotten even my name. That's what the public is. When I looked at the painted old hag I saw it all. Oh, Syd, I'm so miserable.' She threw her arms round his neck and pressed her face to his. 'Syd, it's no good, I can't do it again.'

'Tonight, d'you mean? If you really feel like that about it, I'll tell Espinel you've had a fainting fit. I daresay it'll be all right just for once.'

'I don't mean tonight, I mean never.'

She felt him stiffen a little.

'Syd, dear, don't think I'm being silly. It's not just today, it's been growing on me. I can't sleep at night thinking of it, and when I do drop off I see myself standing at the top of the ladder and looking down. Tonight I could hardly get up it, I was trembling so, and when you lit the flames and said go, something seemed to be holding me back. I didn't even know I'd jumped. My mind was a blank till I found myself on the platform and heard them clapping. Syd, if you loved me you wouldn't want me to go through such torture.'

He sighed. His own eyes were wet with tears. For he loved her devotedly.

'You know what it means,' he said. 'The old life. Marathons and all.'

'Anything's better than this.'

The old life. They both remembered it. Syd had been a dancing gigolo since he was eighteen, he was very good-looking in his dark Spanish way and full of life, old women and middle-aged women were glad to pay to dance with him, and he was never out of work. He had drifted from England to the Continent and there he had stayed, going from hotel to hotel, to the Riviera in the winter, to watering-places in France in the summer. It wasn't a bad life they led, there were generally two or three of them together, the men, and they shared a room in cheap lodgings. They didn't have to get up till late, and they only dressed in time to go to the hotel at twelve to dance with stout women who wanted to get their weight down. Then they were free till five, when they went to the hotel again and sat at a table, the three of them together, keeping a sharp eye open for anyone who looked a likely client. They had their regular customers. At night they went to the restaurant and the house provided them with quite a decent meal. Between the courses they danced. It was good money. They generally got fifty or a hundred francs from anyone they danced with. Sometimes a rich woman, after dancing a good deal with one of them for two or three nights, would give him as much as a thousand francs. Sometimes a middle-aged woman would ask one to spend a night with her, and he would get two hundred and fifty francs for that. There was always the chance of a silly old fool losing her head, and then there were platinum and sapphire rings, cigarette-cases, clothes and a wrist-watch to be got. One of Syd's friends had married one of them, who was old enough to be his mother, but she gave him a car and money to gamble with, and they lived in a beautiful villa at Biarritz. Those were the good days when everybody had money to burn. The slump came and hit the gigolos hard. The hotels were empty, and the clients didn't seem to want to pay for the pleasure of dancing with a nice-looking young fellow. Often and often Syd passed a whole day without earning the price of a drink, and more than once a fat old girl who weighed a ton had had the nerve to give him ten francs. His expenses didn't go down, for he had to be smartly dressed or the manager of the hotel made remarks, washing cost a packet, and you'd be surprised the amount of linen he needed; then shoes, those floors were terribly hard on shoes, and they had to look new. He had his room to pay for and his lunch.

It was then he met Stella. It was at Evian, and the season was disastrous. She was a swimming instructress. She was Australian, and a beautiful diver. She gave exhibitions every morning and afternoon. At night she was engaged to dance at the hotel. They dined together at a little table in the restaurant apart from the guests, and when the band began to play they danced together to induce the customers to come on to the floor. But often no one followed them and they danced by themselves. Neither of them got anything much in the way of paying partners. They fell in love with one another, and at the end of the season got married.

They had never regretted it. They had gone through hard times. Even though for business

reasons (elderly ladies didn't so much like the idea
of dancing with a married man when his wife was
there) they concealed their marriage, it was not so
easy to get an hotel job for the pair of them and Syd
was far from being able to earn enough to keep
Stella, even in the most modest pension, without
working. The gigolo business had gone to pot.
They went to Paris and learnt a dancing act, but the
competition was fearful and cabaret engagements
were very hard to get. Stella was a good ballroom
dancer, but the rage was for acrobatics, and
however much they practised she never managed to
do anything startling. The public was sick of the
apache turn. They were out of a job for weeks at a
time. Syd's wrist-watch, his gold cigarette-case, his
platinum ring, all went up the spout. At last they
found themselves in Nice reduced to such straits
that Syd had to pawn his evening clothes. It was a
catastrophe. They were forced to enter for the
Marathon that an enterprising manager was starting. Twenty-four hours a day they danced, resting
every hour for fifteen minutes. It was frightful.
Their legs ached, their feet were numb. For long
periods they were unconscious of what they were
doing. They just kept time to the music, exerting
themselves as little as possible. They made a little
money, people gave them sums of a hundred
francs, or two hundred, to encourage them, and
sometimes to attract attention they roused themselves to give an exhibition dance. If the public was
in a good humour this might bring in a decent sum.
They grew terribly tired. On the eleventh day
Stella fainted and had to give up. Syd went on
by himself, moving, moving without pause,
grotesquely, without a partner. That was the worst

time they had ever had. It was the final degrada-
tion. It had left with them a recollection of horror
and misery.

But it was then that Syd had his inspiration. It
had come to him while he was slowly going round
the hall by himself. Stella always said she could
dive in a saucer. It was just a trick.

'Funny how ideas come,' he said afterwards.
'Like a flash of lightning.'

He suddenly remembered having seen a boy set
fire to some petrol that had been spilt on the pavement, and the sudden blaze-up. For of course it was
the flames on the water and the spectacular dive
into them that had caught the public fancy. He
stopped dancing there and then; he was too excited
to go on. He talked it over with Stella, and she was
enthusiastic. He wrote to an agent who was a friend
of his; everyone liked Syd, he was a nice little man,
and the agent put up the money for the apparatus.
He got them an engagement at a circus in Paris, and
the turn was a success. They were made. Engagements followed here and there, Syd bought himself
an entire outfit of new clothes, and the climax came
when they got a booking for the summer casino on
the coast. It was no exaggeration of Syd's when he
said that Stella was a riot.

'All our troubles are over, old girl,' he said
fondly. 'We can put a bit by now for a rainy day,
and when the public's sick of this I'll just think of
something else.'

And now, without warning, at the top of their
boom, Stella wanted to chuck it. He didn't know
what to say to her. It broke his heart to see her so
unhappy. He loved her more now even than when
he had married her. He loved her because of all

they'd gone through together; after all for five days once they'd had nothing to eat but a hunk of bread each and a glass of milk, and he loved her because she'd taken him out of all that; he had good clothes to wear again and his three meals a day. He couldn't look at her; the anguish in her dear grey eyes was more than he could bear. Timidly she stretched out her hand and touched his. He gave a deep sigh.

'You know what it means, honey. Our connection in the hotels has gone west, and the business is finished, anyway. What there is'll go to people younger than us. You know what these old women are as well as I do; it's a boy they want, and besides, I'm not tall enough really. It didn't matter so much when I was a kid. It's no good saying I don't look my age because I do.'

'Perhaps we can get into pictures.'

He shrugged his shoulders. They'd tried that before when they were down and out.

'I wouldn't mind what I did. I'd serve in a shop.'

'D'you think jobs can be had for the asking?'

She began to cry again.

'Don't, honey. It breaks my heart.'

'We've got a bit put by.'

'I know we have. Enough to last us six months. And then it'll mean starvation. First popping the bits and pieces, and then the clothes'll have to go, same as they did before. And then dancing in low-down joints for our supper and fifty francs a night. Out of a job for weeks together. And Marathons whenever we hear of one. And how long will the public stand for them?'

'I know you think I'm unreasonable, Syd.'

He turned and looked at her now. There were

tears in her eyes. He smiled, and the smile he gave her was charming and tender.

'No, I don't, ducky. I want to make you happy. After all, you're all I've got. I love you.'

He took her in his arms and held her. He could feel the beating of her heart. If Stella felt like that about it, well, he must just make the best of it. After all, supposing she were killed? No, no, let her chuck it and be damned to the money. She made a little movement.

'What is it, honey?'

She released herself and stood up. She went over to the dressing-table.

'I expect it's about time for me to be getting ready,' she said.

He started to his feet.

'You're not going to do a show tonight?'

'Tonight, and every night till I kill myself. What else is there? I know you're right, Syd. I can't go back to all that other, stinking rooms in fifth-rate hotels and not enough to eat. Oh, that Marathon. Why did you bring that up? Being tired and dirty for days at a time and then having to give up because flesh and blood just couldn't stand it. Perhaps I can go on another month and then there'll be enough to give you a chance of looking round.'

'No, darling, I can't stand for that. Chuck it. We'll manage somehow. We starved before; we can starve again.'

She slipped out of her clothes, and for a moment stood naked but for her stockings, looking at herself in the glass. She gave her reflection a hard smile.

'I mustn't disappoint my public,' she sniggered.

FROM

*Creatures of
Circumstance*

(1947)

The Colonel's Lady

All this happened two or three years before the outbreak of the war.

The Peregrines were having breakfast. Though they were alone and the table was long they sat at opposite ends of it. From the walls George Peregrine's ancestors, painted by the fashionable painters of the day, looked down upon them. The butler brought in the morning post. There were several letters for the colonel, business letters, *The Times* and a small parcel for his wife Evie. He looked at his letters and then, opening *The Times*, began to read it. They finished breakfast and rose from the table. He noticed that his wife hadn't opened the parcel.

'What's that?' he asked.

'Only some books.'

'Shall I open it for you?'

'If you like.'

He hated to cut string and so with some difficulty untied the knots.

'But they're all the same,' he said when he had unwrapped the parcel. 'What on earth d'you want six copies of the same book for?' He opened one of them. 'Poetry.' Then he looked at the title page. *When Pyramids Decay*, he read, by E. K. Hamilton. Eva Katherine Hamilton: that was his wife's maiden name. He looked at her with smiling surprise. 'Have you written a book, Evie? You are a slyboots.'

'I didn't think it would interest you very much. Would you like a copy?'

'Well, you know poetry isn't much in my line, but – yes, I'd like a copy; I'll read it. I'll take it along to my study. I've got a lot to do this morning.'

He gathered up *The Times*, his letters and the book, and went out. His study was a large and comfortable room, with a big desk, leather armchairs and what he called 'trophies of the chase' on the walls. On the bookshelves were works of reference, books on farming, gardening, fishing and shooting, and books on the last war in which he had won an MC and a DSO. For before his marriage he had been in the Welsh Guards. At the end of the war he retired and settled down to the life of a country gentleman in the spacious house, some twenty miles from Sheffield, which one of his forebears had built in the reign of George III. George Peregrine had an estate of some fifteen hundred acres which he managed with ability; he was a Justice of the Peace and performed his duties conscientiously. During the season he rode to hounds two days a week. He was a good shot, a golfer and though now a little over fifty could still play a hard game of tennis. He could describe himself with propriety as an all-round sportsman.

He had been putting on weight lately, but was still a fine figure of a man; tall, with grey curly hair, only just beginning to grow thin on the crown, frank blue eyes, good features and a high colour. He was a public-spirited man, chairman of any number of local organizations and, as became his class and station, a loyal member of the Conservative party. He looked upon it as his duty to see to the welfare of the people on his estate and it was a satisfaction to him to know that Evie could be trusted to tend the sick and succour the poor. He had built a cottage hospital on the outskirts of the village and paid the wages of a nurse out of his own pocket. All he asked of the recipients of his bounty was that at elections, county or general, they should vote for his candidate. He was a friendly man, affable to his inferiors, considerate with his tenants and popular with the neighbouring gentry. He would have been pleased and at the same time slightly embarrassed if someone had told him he was a jolly good fellow. That was what he wanted to be. He desired no higher praise.

It was hard luck that he had no children. He would have been an excellent father, kindly but strict, and would have brought up his sons as gentlemen's sons should be brought up, sent them to Eton, you know, taught them to fish, shoot and ride. As it was, his heir was a nephew, son of his brother killed in a motor accident, not a bad boy, but not a chip off the old block, no, sir, far from it; and would you believe it, his fool of a mother was sending him to a co-educational school. Evie had been a sad disappointment to him. Of course she was a lady, and she had a bit of money of her own; she managed the house uncommonly well and she was a good hostess. The village people adored her. She had been a pretty little thing when he married her, with a creamy skin, light brown hair and a trim figure, healthy too and not a bad tennis player; he couldn't understand why she'd had no children;

of course she was faded now, she must be getting on for five-and-forty; her skin was drab, her hair had lost its sheen and she was as thin as a rail. She was always neat and suitably dressed, but she didn't seem to bother how she looked, she wore no make-up and didn't even use lipstick; sometimes at night when she dolled herself up for a party you could tell that once she'd been quite attractive, but ordinarily she was – well, the sort of woman you simply didn't notice. A nice woman, of course, a good wife, and it wasn't her fault if she was barren, but it was tough on a fellow who wanted an heir of his own loins; she hadn't any vitality, that's what was the matter with her. He supposed he'd been in love with her when he asked her to marry him, at least sufficiently in love for a man who wanted to marry and settle down, but with time he discovered that they had nothing much in common. She didn't care about hunting, and fishing bored her. Naturally they'd drifted apart. He had to do her the justice to admit that she'd never bothered him. There'd been no scenes. They had no quarrels. She seemed to take it for granted that he should go his own way. When he went up to London now and then she never wanted to come with him. He had a girl there, well, she wasn't exactly a girl, she was thirty-five if she was a day, but she was blonde and luscious and he only had to wire ahead of time and they'd dine, do a show and spend the night together. Well, a man, a healthy normal man had to have some fun in his life. The thought crossed his mind that if Evie hadn't been such a good woman she'd have been a better wife; but it was not the sort of thought that he welcomed and he put it away from him.

George Peregrine finished his *Times* and being a considerate fellow rang the bell and told the butler to take it to Evie. Then he looked at his watch. It was half-past ten and at eleven he had an appointment with one of his tenants. He had half an hour to spare.

'I'd better have a look at Evie's book,' he said to himself.

He took it up with a smile. Evie had a lot of highbrow books in her sitting-room, not the sort of books that interested him, but if they amused her he had no objection to her reading them. He noticed that the volume he now held in his hand contained no more than ninety pages. That was all to the good. He shared Edgar Allan Poe's opinion that poems should be short. But as he turned the pages he noticed that several of Evie's had long lines of irregular length and didn't rhyme. He didn't like that. At his first school, when he was a little boy, he remembered learning a poem that began: *The boy stood on the burning deck*, and later, at Eton, one that started: *Ruin seize thee, ruthless king*; and then there was Henry V; they'd had to take that one half. He stared at Evie's pages with consternation.

'That's not what I call poetry,' he said.

Fortunately it wasn't all like that. Interspersed with the pieces that looked so odd, lines of three or four words and then a line of ten or fifteen, there were little poems, quite short, that rhymed, thank God, with the lines all the same length. Several of the pages were just headed with the word *Sonnet*, and out of curiosity he counted the lines; there were fourteen of them. He read them. They seemed all right, but he didn't quite know what they were all about. He repeated to himself: *Ruin seize thee, ruthless king*.

'Poor Evie,' he sighed.

At that moment the farmer he was expecting was ushered into the study, and putting the book down he made him welcome. They embarked on their business.

'I read your book, Evie,' he said as they sat down to lunch. 'Jolly good. Did it cost you a packet to have it printed?'

'No, I was lucky. I sent it to a publisher and he took it.'

'Not much money in poetry, my dear,' he said in his good-natured, hearty way.

'No, I don't suppose there is. What did Bannock want to see you about this morning?'

Bannock was the tenant who had interrupted his reading of Evie's poems.

'He's asked me to advance the money for a pedigree bull he wants to buy. He's a good man and I've half a mind to do it.'

George Peregrine saw that Evie didn't want to talk about her book and he was not sorry to change the subject. He was glad she had used her maiden name on the title page; he didn't suppose anyone would ever hear about the book, but he was proud of his own unusual name and he wouldn't have liked it if some damned penny-a-liner had made fun of Evie's effort in one of the papers.

During the few weeks that followed he thought it tactful not to ask Evie any questions about her venture into verse, and she never referred to it. It might have been a discreditable incident that they had silently agreed not to mention. But then a strange thing happened. He had to go to London on business and he took Daphne out to dinner. That was the name of the girl with whom he was in the habit of passing a few agreeable hours whenever he went to town.

'Oh, George,' she said, 'is that your wife who's written a book they're all talking about?'

'What on earth d'you mean?'

'Well, there's a fellow I know who's a critic. He took me out to dinner the other night and he had a book with him. "Got anything for me to read?" I said. "What's that?" "Oh, I don't think that's your cup of tea," he said. "It's poetry. I've just been reviewing it." "No poetry for me," I said. "It's about the hottest stuff I ever read," he said. "Selling like hot cakes. And it's damned good."'

'Who's the book by?' asked George.

'A woman called Hamilton. My friend told me that wasn't her real name. He said her real name was Peregrine. "Funny," I said, "I know a fellow called Peregrine." "Colonel in the army," he said. "Lives near Sheffield."'

'I'd just as soon you didn't talk about me to your friends,' said George with a frown of vexation.

'Keep your shirt on, dearie. Who d'you take me for? I just said: "It's not the same one."' Daphne giggled. 'My friend said: "They say he's a regular Colonel Blimp."'

George had a keen sense of humour.

'You could tell them better than that,' he laughed. 'If my wife had written a book I'd be the first to know about it, wouldn't I?'

'I suppose you would.'

Anyhow the matter didn't interest her and when the colonel began to talk of other things she forgot about it. He put it out of his mind too. There was nothing to it, he decided, and that silly fool of a critic had just been pulling Daphne's leg. He was amused at the thought of her tackling that book because she had been told it was hot stuff and then finding it just a lot of bosh cut up into unequal lines.

He was a member of several clubs and next day he thought he'd lunch at one in St James's Street. He was catching a train back to Sheffield early in the afternoon. He was sitting in a comfortable arm-chair having a glass of sherry before going into the dining-room when an old friend came up to him.

'Well, old boy, how's life?' he said. 'How d'you like being the husband of a celebrity?'

George Peregrine looked at his friend. He thought he saw an amused twinkle in his eyes.

'I don't know what you're talking about,' he answered.

'Come off it, George. Everyone knows E. K. Hamilton is your wife. Not often a book of verse has a success like that. Look here, Henry Dashwood is lunching with me. He'd like to meet you.'

'Who the devil is Henry Dashwood and why should he want to meet me?'

'Oh, my dear fellow, what do you do with yourself all the time in the country? Henry's about the best critic we've got. He wrote a wonderful review of Evie's book. D'you mean to say she didn't show it you?'

Before George could answer his friend had called a man over. A tall, thin man, with a high forehead, a beard, a long nose and a stoop, just the sort of man whom George was prepared to dislike at first sight. Introductions were effected. Henry Dashwood sat down.

'Is Mrs Peregrine in London by any chance? I

should very much like to meet her,' he said.

'No, my wife doesn't like London. She prefers the country,' said George stiffly.

'She wrote me a very nice letter about my review. I was pleased. You know, we critics get more kicks than halfpence. I was simply bowled over by her book. It's so fresh and original, very modern without being obscure. She seems to be as much at her ease in free verse as in the classical metres.' Then because he was a critic he thought he should criticize. 'Sometimes her ear is a trifle at fault, but you can say the same of Emily Dickinson. There are several of those short lyrics of hers that might have been written by Landor.'

All this was gibberish to George Peregrine. The man was nothing but a disgusting highbrow. But the colonel had good manners and he answered with proper civility: Henry Dashwood went on as though he hadn't spoken.

'But what makes the book so outstanding is the passion that throbs in every line. So many of these young poets are so anaemic, cold, bloodless, dully intellectual, but here you have real naked, earthy passion; of course deep, sincere emotion like that is tragic – ah, my dear Colonel, how right Heine was when he said that the poet makes little songs out of his great sorrows. You know, now and then, as I read and re-read those heart-rending pages I thought of Sappho.'

This was too much for George Peregrine and he got up.

'Well, it's jolly nice of you to say such nice things about my wife's little book. I'm sure she'll be delighted. But I must bolt, I've got to catch a train and I want to get a bite of lunch.'

'Damned fool,' he said irritably to himself as he walked upstairs to the dining-room.

He got home in time for dinner and after Evie had gone to bed he went into his study and looked for her book. He thought he'd just glance through it again to see for himself what they were making such a fuss about, but he couldn't find it. Evie must have taken it away.

'Silly,' he muttered.

He'd told her he thought it jolly good. What more could a fellow be expected to say? Well, it didn't matter. He lit his pipe and read the *Field* till he felt sleepy. But a week or so later it happened that he had to go into Sheffield for the day. He lunched there at his club. He had nearly finished when the Duke of Haverel came in. This was the great local magnate and of course the colonel knew him, but only to say how d'you do to; and he was surprised when the Duke stopped at his table.

'We're so sorry your wife couldn't come to us for the week-end,' he said, with a sort of shy cordiality. 'We're expecting rather a nice lot of people.'

George was taken aback. He guessed that the Haverels had asked him and Evie over for the week-end and Evie, without saying a word to him about it, had refused. He had the presence of mind to say he was sorry too.

'Better luck next time,' said the Duke pleasantly and moved on.

Colonel Peregrine was very angry and when he got home he said to his wife:

'Look here, what's this about our being asked over to Haverel? Why on earth did you say we couldn't go? We've never been asked before and it's the best shooting in the county.'

'I didn't think of that, I thought it would only bore you.'

'Damn it all, you might at least have asked me if I wanted to go.'

'I'm sorry.'

He looked at her closely. There was something in her expression that he didn't quite understand. He frowned.

'I suppose *I* was asked?' he barked.

Evie flushed a little.

'Well, in point of fact you weren't.'

'I call it damned rude of them to ask you without asking me.'

'I suppose they thought it wasn't your sort of party. The Duchess is rather fond of writers and people like that, you know. She's having Henry Dashwood, the critic, and for some reason he wants to meet me.'

'It was damned nice of you to refuse, Evie.'

'It's the least I could do,' she smiled. She hesitated a moment. 'George, my publishers want to give a little dinner party for me one day towards the end of the month and of course they want you to come too.'

'Oh, I don't think that's quite my mark. I'll come up to London with you if you like. I'll find someone to dine with.'

Daphne.

'I expect it'll be very dull, but they're making rather a point of it. And the day after, the American publisher who's taken my book is giving a cocktail party at Claridge's. I'd like you to come to that if you wouldn't mind.'

'Sounds like a crashing bore, but if you really want me to come I'll come.'

'It would be sweet of you.'

George Peregrine was dazed by the cocktail party. There were a lot of people. Some of them didn't look so bad, a few of the women were decently turned out, but the men seemed to him pretty awful. He was introduced to everyone as Colonel Peregrine, E. K. Hamilton's husband, you know. The men didn't seem to have anything to say to him, but the women gushed.

'You *must* be proud of your wife. Isn't it *wonderful*? You know, I read it right through at a sitting, I simply couldn't put it down, and when I'd finished I started again at the beginning and read it right through a second time. I was simply *thrilled*.'

The English publisher said to him:

'We've not had a success like this with a book of verse for twenty years. I've never seen such reviews.'

The American publisher said to him:

'It's swell. It'll be a smash hit in America. You wait and see.'

The American publisher had sent Evie a great spray of orchids. Damned ridiculous, thought George. As they came in, people were taken up to Evie, and it was evident that they said flattering things to her, which she took with a pleasant smile and a word or two of thanks. She was a trifle flushed with the excitement, but seemed quite at her ease. Though he thought the whole thing a lot of stuff and nonsense George noted with approval that his wife was carrying it off in just the right way.

'Well, there's one thing,' he said to himself, 'you can see she's a lady and that's a damned sight more than you can say of anyone else here.'

He drank a good many cocktails. But there was one thing that bothered him. He had a notion that some of the people he was introduced to looked at him in rather a funny sort of way, he couldn't quite make out what it meant, and once when he strolled by two women who were sitting together on a sofa he had the impression that they were talking about him and after he passed he was almost certain they tittered. He was very glad when the party came to an end.

In the taxi on their way back to their hotel Evie said to him:

'You were wonderful, dear. You made quite a hit. The girls simply raved about you; they thought you so handsome.'

'Girls,' he said bitterly. 'Old hags.'

'Were you bored, dear?'

'Stiff.'

She pressed his hand in a gesture of sympathy.

'I hope you won't mind if we wait and go down by the afternoon train. I've got some things to do in the morning.'

'No, that's all right. Shopping?'

'I do want to buy one or two things, but I've got to go and be photographed. I hate the idea, but they think I ought to be. For America, you know.'

He said nothing. But he thought. He thought it would be a shock to the American public when they saw the portrait of the homely, desiccated little woman who was his wife. He'd always been under the impression that they liked glamour in America.

He went on thinking, and next morning when Evie had gone out he went to his club and up to the library. There he looked up recent numbers of *The*

Times Literary Supplement, the *New Statesman* and the *Spectator*. Presently he found reviews of Evie's book. He didn't read them very carefully, but enough to see that they were extremely favourable. Then he went to the bookseller's in Piccadilly where he occasionally bought books. He'd made up his mind that he had to read this damned thing of Evie's properly, but he didn't want to ask her what she'd done with the copy she'd given him. He'd buy one for himself. Before going in he looked in the window and the first thing he saw was a display of *When Pyramids Decay*. Damned silly title! He went in. A young man came forward and asked if he could help him.

'No, I'm just having a look round.' It embarrassed him to ask for Evie's book and he thought he'd find it for himself and then take it to the salesman. But he couldn't see it anywhere and at last, finding the young man near him, he said in a carefully casual tone: 'By the way, have you got a book called *When Pyramids Decay*?'

'The new edition came in this morning. I'll get a copy.'

In a moment the young man returned with it. He was a short, rather stout young man, with a shock of untidy carroty hair and spectacles. George Peregrine, tall, upstanding, very military, towered over him.

'Is this a new edition then?' he asked.

'Yes, sir. The fifth. It might be a novel the way it's selling.'

George Peregrine hesitated a moment.

'Why d'you suppose it's such a success? I've always been told no one reads poetry.'

'Well, it's good, you know. I've read it meself.'

The young man, though obviously cultured had a slight cockney accent, and George quite instinctively adopted a patronizing attitude. 'It's the story they like. Sexy, you know, but tragic.'

George frowned a little. He was coming to the conclusion that the young man was rather impertinent. No one had told him anything about there being a story in the damned book and he had not gathered that from reading the reviews. The young man went on.

'Of course it's only a flash in the pan, if you know what I mean. The way I look at it, she was sort of inspired like by a personal experience, like Housman was with *The Shropshire Lad*. She'll never write anything else.'

'How much is the book?' said George coldly to stop his chatter. 'You needn't wrap it up, I'll just slip it into my pocket.'

The November morning was raw and he was wearing a greatcoat.

At the station he bought the evening papers and magazines and he and Evie settled themselves comfortably in opposite corners of a first-class carriage and read. At five o'clock they went along to the restaurant car to have tea and chatted a little. They arrived. They drove home in the car which was waiting for them. They bathed, dressed for dinner, and after dinner Evie, saying she was tired out, went to bed. She kissed him, as was her habit, on the forehead. Then he went into the hall, took Evie's book out of his greatcoat pocket and going into the study began to read it. He didn't read verse very easily and though he read with attention, every word of it, the impression he received was far from clear. Then he began at the beginning again and read it a second time. He read with increasing malaise, but he was not a stupid man and when he had finished he had a distinct understanding of what it was all about. Part of the book was in free verse, part in conventional metres, but the story it related was coherent and plain to the meanest intelligence. It was the story of a passionate love affair between an older woman, married, and a young man. George Peregrine made out the steps of it as easily as if he had been doing a sum in simple addition.

Written in the first person, it began with the tremulous surprise of the woman, past her youth, when it dawned upon her that the young man was in love with her. She hesitated to believe it. She thought she must be deceiving herself. And she was terrified when on a sudden she discovered that she was passionately in love with him. She told herself it was absurd; with the disparity of age between them nothing but unhappiness could come to her if she yielded to her emotion. She tried to prevent him from speaking, but the day came when he told her that he loved her and forced her to tell him that she loved him too. He begged her to run away with him. She couldn't leave her husband, her home; and what life could they look forward to, she an ageing woman, he so young? How could she expect his love to last? She begged him to have mercy on her. But his love was impetuous. He wanted her, he wanted her with all his heart, and at last trembling, afraid, desirous, she yielded to him. Then there was a period of ecstatic happiness. The world, the dull humdrum world of every day, blazed with glory. Love songs flowed from her pen. The woman worshipped the young, virile body of her lover. George flushed darkly when she praised his broad chest and slim flanks, the beauty of his legs and the flatness of his belly.

Hot stuff, Daphne's friend had said. It was that all right. Disgusting.

There were sad little pieces in which she lamented the emptiness of her life when as must happen he left her, but they ended with a cry that all she had to suffer would be worth it for the bliss that for a while had been hers. She wrote of the long, tremulous nights they passed together and the languor that lulled them to sleep in one another's arms. She wrote of the rapture of brief stolen moments when, braving all danger, their passion overwhelmed them and they surrendered to its call.

She thought it would be an affair of a few weeks, but miraculously it lasted. One of the poems referred to three years having gone by without lessening the love that filled their hearts. It looked as though he continued to press her to go away with him, far away, to a hill town in Italy, a Greek island, a walled city in Tunisia, so that they could be together always, for in another of the poems she besought him to let things be as they were. Their happiness was precarious. Perhaps it was owing to the difficulties they had to encounter and the rarity of their meetings that their love had retained for so long its first enchanting ardour. Then on a sudden the young man died. How, when or where George could not discover. There followed a long, heart-broken cry of bitter grief, grief she could not indulge in, grief that had to be hidden. She had to be cheerful, give dinner parties and go out to dinner, behave as she had always behaved, though the light had gone out of her life and she was bowed down with anguish. The last poem of all was a set of four short stanzas in which the writer, sadly resigned to her loss, thanked the dark powers that rule man's destiny that she had been privileged at least for a while to enjoy the greatest happiness that we poor human beings can ever hope to know.

It was three o'clock in the morning when George Peregrine finally put the book down. It had seemed to him that he heard Evie's voice in every line, over and over again he came upon turns of phrase he had heard her use, there were details that were as familiar to him as to her: there was no doubt about it; it was her own story she had told, and it was as plain as anything could be that she had had a lover and her lover had died. It was not anger so much that he felt, nor horror or dismay, though he was dismayed and he was horrified, but amazement. It was as inconceivable that Evie should have had a love affair, and a wildly passionate one at that, as that the trout in a glass case over the chimney piece in his study, the finest he had ever caught, should suddenly wag its tail. He understood now the meaning of the amused look he had seen in the eyes of that man he had spoken to at the club, he understood why Daphne when she was talking about the book had seemed to be enjoying a private joke, and why those two women at the cocktail party had tittered when he strolled past them.

He broke out into a sweat. Then on a sudden he was seized with fury and he jumped up to go and awake Evie and ask her sternly for an explanation. But he stopped at the door. After all what proof had he? A book. He remembered that he'd told Evie he thought it jolly good. True, he hadn't read it, but he'd pretended he had. He would look a perfect fool if he had to admit that.

'I must watch my step,' he muttered.

He made up his mind to wait for two or three days and think it all over. Then he'd decide what to do. He went to bed, but he couldn't sleep for a long time.

'Evie,' he kept on saying to himself. 'Evie, of all people.'

They met at breakfast next morning as usual. Evie was as she always was, quiet, demure and self-possessed, a middle-aged woman who made no effort to look younger than she was, a woman who had nothing of what he still called It. He looked at her as he hadn't looked at her for years. She had her usual placid serenity. Her pale blue eyes were untroubled. There was no sign of guilt on her candid brow. She made the same little casual remarks she always made.

'It's nice to get back to the country again after those two hectic days in London. What are you going to do this morning?'

It was incomprehensible.

Three days later he went to see his solicitor. Henry Blane was an old friend of George's as well as his lawyer. He had a place not far from Peregrine's and for years they had shot over one another's preserves. For two days a week he was a country gentleman and for the other five a busy lawyer in Sheffield. He was a tall, robust fellow, with a boisterous manner and a jovial laugh, which suggested that he liked to be looked upon essentially as a sportsman and a good fellow and only incidentally as a lawyer. But he was shrewd and worldly-wise.

'Well, George, what's brought you here today?' he boomed as the colonel was shown into his office. 'Have a good time in London? I'm taking my missus up for a few days next week. How's Evie?'

'It's about Evie I've come to see you,' said Peregrine, giving him a suspicious look. 'Have you read her book?'

His sensitivity had been sharpened during those last days of troubled thought and he was conscious of a faint change in the lawyer's expression. It was as though he were suddenly on his guard.

'Yes, I've read it. Great success, isn't it? Fancy Evie breaking out into poetry. Wonders will never cease.'

George Peregrine was inclined to lose his temper.

'It's made me look a perfect damned fool.'

'Oh, what nonsense, George! There's no harm in Evie's writing a book. You ought to be jolly proud of her.'

'Don't talk such rot. It's her own story. You know it and everyone else knows it. I suppose I'm the only one who doesn't know who her lover was.'

'There is such a thing as imagination, old boy. There's no reason to suppose the whole thing isn't just made up.'

'Look here, Henry, we've known one another all our lives. We've had all sorts of good times together. Be honest with me. Can you look me in the face and tell me you believe it's a made-up story?'

Harry Blane moved uneasily in his chair. He was disturbed by the distress in old George's voice.

'You've got no right to ask me a question like that. Ask Evie.'

'I daren't,' George answered after an anguished pause. 'I'm afraid she'd tell me the truth.'

There was an uncomfortable silence.

'Who was the chap?'

Harry Blane looked at him straight in the eye.

'I don't know, and if I did I wouldn't tell you.'

'You swine. Don't you see what a position I'm in? Do you think it's very pleasant to be made absolutely ridiculous?'

The lawyer lit a cigarette and for some moments silently puffed it.

'I don't see what I can do for you,' he said at last.

'You've got private detectives you employ, I suppose. I want you to put them on the job and let them find everything out.'

'It's not very pretty to put detectives on one's wife, old boy; and besides, taking for granted for a moment that Evie had an affair, it was a good many years ago and I don't suppose it would be possible to find out a thing. They seem to have covered their tracks pretty carefully.'

'I don't care. You put the detectives on. I want to know the truth.'

'I won't, George. If you're determined to do that you'd better consult someone else. And look here, even if you got evidence that Evie had been unfaithful to you what would you do with it? You'd look rather silly divorcing your wife because she'd committed adultery ten years ago.'

'At all events I could have it out with her.'

'You can do that now, but you know just as well as I do, that if you do she'll leave you. D'you want her to do that?'

George gave him an unhappy look.

'I don't know. I always thought she'd been a

damned good wife to me. She runs the house perfectly, we never have any servant trouble; she's done wonders with the garden and she's splendid with all the village people. But damn it, I have my self-respect to think of. How can I go on living with her when I know that she was grossly unfaithful to me?'

'Have you always been faithful to her?'

'More or less, you know. After all we've been married for nearly twenty-four years and Evie was never much for bed.'

The solicitor slightly raised his eyebrows, but George was too intent on what he was saying to notice.

'I don't deny that I've had a bit of fun now and then. A man wants it. Women are different.'

'We only have men's word for that,' said Harry Blane, with a faint smile.

'Evie's absolutely the last woman I'd have suspected of kicking over the traces. I mean, she's a very fastidious, reticent woman. What on earth made her write the damned book?'

'I suppose it was a very poignant experience and perhaps it was a relief to her to get it off her chest like that.'

'Well, if she had to write it why the devil didn't she write it under an assumed name?'

'She used her maiden name. I suppose she thought that was enough, and it would have been if the book hadn't had this amazing boom.'

George Peregrine and the lawyer were sitting opposite one another with a desk between them. George, his elbow on the desk, his cheek resting on his hand, frowned at his thought.

'It's so rotten not to know what sort of a chap he

was. One can't even tell if he was by way of being a gentleman. I mean, for all I know he may have been a farm-hand or a clerk in a lawyer's office.'

Harry Blane did not permit himself to smile and when he answered there was in his eyes a kindly, tolerant look.

'Knowing Evie so well I think the probabilities are that he was all right. Anyhow I'm sure he wasn't a clerk in my office.'

'It's been such a shock to me,' the colonel sighed. 'I thought she was fond of me. She couldn't have written that book unless she hated me.'

'Oh, I don't believe that. I don't think she's capable of hatred.'

'You're not going to pretend that she loves me.'

'No.'

'Well, what does she feel for me?'

Harry Blane leaned back in his swivel chair and looked at George reflectively.

'Indifference, I should say.'

The colonel gave a little shudder and reddened.

'After all, you're not in love with her, are you?'

George Peregrine did not answer directly.

'It's been a great blow to me not to have any children, but I've never let her see that I think she's let me down. I've always been kind to her. Within reasonable limits I've tried to do my duty by her.'

The lawyer passed a large hand over his mouth to conceal the smile that trembled on his lips.

'It's been such an awful shock to me,' Peregrine went on. 'Damn it all, even ten years ago Evie was no chicken and God knows, she wasn't much to look at. It's so ugly.' He sighed deeply. 'What would *you* do in my place?'

'Nothing.'

George Peregrine drew himself bolt upright in his chair and he looked at Harry with the stern set face that he must have worn when he inspected his regiment.

'I can't overlook a thing like this. I've been made a laughing-stock. I can never hold up my head again.'

'Nonsense,' said the lawyer sharply, and then in a pleasant, kindly manner. 'Listen, old boy: the man's dead; it all happened a long while back. Forget it. Talk to people about Evie's book, rave about it, tell 'em how proud you are of her. Behave as though you had so much confidence in her, you *knew* she could never have been unfaithful to you. The world moves so quickly and people's memories are so short. They'll forget.'

'I shan't forget.'

'You're both middle-aged people. She probably does a great deal more for you than you think and you'd be awfully lonely without her. I don't think it matters if you don't forget. It'll be all to the good if you can get it into that thick head of yours that there's a lot more in Evie than you ever had the gumption to see.'

'Damn it all, you talk as if *I* was to blame.'

'No, I don't think you were to blame, but I'm not so sure that Evie was either. I don't suppose she wanted to fall in love with this boy. D'you remember those verses right at the end? The impression they gave me was that though she was shattered by his death, in a strange sort of way she welcomed it. All through she'd been aware of the fragility of the tie that bound them. He died in the full flush of his first love and had never known that love so seldom endures; he'd only known its bliss and beauty. In her own bitter grief she found solace in the thought that he'd been spared all sorrow.'

'All that's a bit above my head, old boy. I see more or less what you mean.'

George Peregrine stared unhappily at the inkstand on the desk. He was silent and the lawyer looked at him with curious, yet sympathetic eyes.

'Do you realize what courage she must have had never by a sign to show how dreadfully unhappy she was?' he said gently.

Colonel Peregrine sighed.

'I'm broken. I suppose you're right; it's no good crying over spilt milk and it would only make things worse if I made a fuss.'

'Well?'

George Peregrine gave a pitiful little smile.

'I'll take your advice. I'll do nothing. Let them think me a damned fool and to hell with them. The truth is, I don't know what I'd do without Evie. But I'll tell you what, there's one thing I shall never understand till my dying day: What in the name of heaven did the fellow ever see in her?'

The Kite

I know this is an odd story. I don't understand it myself and if I set it down in black and white it is only with a faint hope that when I have written it I may get a clearer view of it, or rather with the hope that some reader, better acquainted with the complications of human nature than I am, may offer me an explanation that will make it comprehensible to me. Of course the first thing that occurs to me is that there is something Freudian about it. Now, I have read a good deal of Freud, and some books by his followers, and intending to write this story I have recently flipped through again the volume published by the Modern Library which contains his basic writings. It was something of a task, for he is a dull and verbose writer, and the acrimony with which he claims to have originated such and such a theory shows a vanity and a jealousy of others working in the same field which somewhat ill become the man of science. I believe, however, that he was a kindly and benign old party. As we know, there is often a great difference between the man and the writer. The writer may be bitter, harsh and brutal, while the man may be so meek and mild that he wouldn't say boo to a goose. But that is neither here nor there. I found nothing in my re-reading of Freud's works that cast any light on the subject I had in mind. I can only relate the facts and leave it at that.

First of all I must make it plain that it is not my story and that I knew none of the persons with whom it is concerned. It was told me one evening by my friend Ned Preston, and he told it me because he didn't know how to deal with the circumstances and he thought, quite wrongly as it happened, that I might be able to give him some advice which would help him. In a previous story* I have related what I thought the reader should know about Ned Preston, and so now I need only remind him that my friend was a prison visitor at Wormwood Scrubs. He took his duties very seriously and made the prisoners' troubles his own. We had been dining together at the Café Royal in that long, low room with its absurd and charming decoration which is all that remains of the old Café Royal that painters have loved to paint; and we were sitting over our coffee and liqueurs and, so far as Ned was concerned against his doctor's orders, smoking very long and very good Havanas.

'I've got a funny chap to deal with at the Scrubs just now,' he said after a pause, 'and I'm blowed if I know how to deal with him.'

'What's he in for?' I asked.

'He left his wife and the court ordered him to pay so much a week in alimony and he's absolutely refused to pay it. I've argued with him till I was blue in the face. I've told him he's only cutting off his nose to spite his face. He says he'll stay in gaol all his life rather than pay her a penny. I tell him he

---

*'Episode', W. Somerset Maugham, Collected Short Stories Vol. 4. Penguin Books, 1963.

can't let her starve, and all he says is: "Why not?"
He's perfectly well behaved, he's no trouble, he
works well, he seems quite happy, he's just getting
a lot of fun out of thinking what a devil of a time his
wife is having.'

'What's he got against her?'

'She smashed his kite.'

'She did what?' I cried.

'Exactly that. She smashed his kite. He says he'll
never forgive her for that till his dying day.'

'He must be crazy.'

'No, he isn't, he's a perfectly reasonable, quite
intelligent, decent fellow.'

Herbert Sunbury was his name, and his mother,
who was very refined, never allowed him to be
called Herb or Bertie, but always Herbert, just as
she never called her husband Sam but only Samuel.
Mrs Sunbury's first name was Beatrice, and when
she got engaged to Mr Sunbury and he ventured to
call her Bea she put her foot down firmly.

'Beatrice I was christened,' she said, 'and
Beatrice I always have been and always shall be, to
you and to my nearest and dearest.'

She was a little woman, but strong, active and
wiry, with a sallow skin, sharp, regular features
and small, beady eyes. Her hair, suspiciously black
for her age, was always very neat, and she wore it
in the style of Queen Victoria's daughters, which
she had adopted as soon as she was old enough to
put it up and had never thought fit to change. The
possibility that she did something to keep her hair
its original colour was, if such was the case, her
only concession to frivolity, for, far from using
rouge or lipstick, she had never in her life so much
as passed a powder-puff over her nose. She never

wore anything but black dresses of good material,
but made (by a little woman round the corner)
regardless of fashion after a pattern that was both
serviceable and decorous. Her only ornament was a
thin gold chain from which hung a small gold cross.

Samuel Sunbury was a little man too. He was as
thin and spare as his wife, but he had sandy hair,
gone very thin now so that he had to wear it very
long on one side and brush it carefully over the
large bald patch. He had pale blue eyes and his
complexion was pasty. He was a clerk in a lawyer's
office and had worked his way up from office boy to
a respectable position. His employer called him
Mr Sunbury and sometimes asked him to see an
unimportant client. Every morning for twenty-four
years Samuel Sunbury had taken the same train to
the City, except of course on Sundays and during
his fortnight's holiday at the seaside, and every
evening he had taken the same train back to the
suburb in which he lived. He was neat in his dress;
he went to work in quiet grey trousers, a black coat
and a bowler hat, and when he came home he put
on his slippers and a black coat which was too old
and shiny to wear at the office; but on Sundays
when he went to the chapel he and Mrs Sunbury
attended he wore a morning coat with his bowler.
Thus he showed his respect for the day of rest and
at the same time registered a protest against
the ungodly who went bicycling or lounged about
the streets until the pubs opened. On principle the
Sunburys were total abstainers, but on Sundays,
when to make up for the frugal lunch, consisting of
a scone and butter with a glass of milk, which
Samuel had during the week, Beatrice gave him a
good dinner of roast beef and Yorkshire pudding,

for his health's sake she liked him to have a glass of beer. Since she wouldn't for the world have kept liquor in the house, he sneaked out with a jug after morning service and got a quart from the pub round the corner; but nothing would induce him to drink alone, so, just to be sociable like, she had a glass too.

Herbert was the only child the Lord had vouchsafed to them, and this certainly through no precaution on their part. It just happened that way. They doted on him. He was a pretty baby and then a good-looking child. Mrs Sunbury brought him up carefully. She taught him to sit up at table and not put his elbows on it, and she taught him how to use his knife and fork like a little gentleman. She taught him to stretch out his little finger when he took his tea-cup to drink out of it and when he asked why, she said: 'Never you mind. That's how it's done. It shows you know what's what.'

In due course Herbert grew old enough to go to school. Mrs Sunbury was anxious because she had never let him play with the children in the street.

'Evil communications corrupt good manners,' she said. 'I always have kept myself to myself and I always shall keep myself to myself.'

Although they had lived in the same house ever since they were married she had taken care to keep her neighbours at a distance.

'You never know who people are in London,' she said. 'One thing leads to another, and before you know where you are you're mixed up with a lot of riff-raff and you can't get rid of them.'

She didn't like the idea of Herbert being thrown into contact with a lot of rough boys at the County Council school and she said to him:

'Now, Herbert, do what I do; keep yourself to yourself and don't have anything more to do with them than you can help.'

But Herbert got on very well at school. He was a good worker and far from stupid. His reports were excellent. It turned out that he had a good head for figures.

'If that's a fact,' said Samuel Sunbury, 'he'd better be an accountant. There's always a good job waiting for a good accountant.'

So it was settled there and then that this was what Herbert was to be. He grew tall.

'Why, Herbert,' said his mother, 'soon you'll be as tall as your dad.'

By the time he left school he was two inches taller, and by the time he stopped growing he was five feet ten.

'Just the right height,' said his mother. 'Not too tall and not too short.'

He was a nice-looking boy, with his mother's regular features and dark hair, but he had inherited his father's blue eyes, and though he was rather pale his skin was smooth and clear. Samuel Sunbury had got him into the office of the accountants who came twice a year to do the accounts of his own firm and by the time he was twenty-one he was able to bring back to his mother every week quite a nice little sum. She gave him back three half-crowns for his lunches and ten shillings for pocket money, and the rest she put in the Savings Bank for him against a rainy day.

When Mr and Mrs Sunbury went to bed on the night of Herbert's twenty-first birthday, and in passing I may say that Mrs Sunbury never went to bed, she retired, but Mr Sunbury who was not

quite so refined as his wife always said: 'Me for
Bedford' – when then Mr and Mrs Sunbury went
to bed, Mrs Sunbury said:

'Some people don't know how lucky they are;
thank the Lord, I do. No one's ever had a better son
than our Herbert. Hardly a day's illness in his life
and he's never given me a moment's worry. It just
shows if you bring up somebody right they'll be a
credit to you. Fancy him being twenty-one, I can
hardly believe it.'

'Yes, I suppose before we know where we are
he'll be marrying and leaving us.'

'What should he want to do that for?' asked Mrs
Sunbury with asperity. 'He's got a good home
here, hasn't he? Don't you go putting silly ideas
into his head, Samuel, or you and me'll have words
and you know that's the last thing I want. Marry
indeed! He's got more sense than that. He knows
when he's well off. He's got sense, Herbert has.'

Mr Sunbury was silent. He had long ago learnt
that it didn't get him anywhere with Beatrice to
answer back.

'I don't hold with a man marrying till he knows
his own mind,' she went on. 'And a man doesn't
know his own mind till he's thirty or thirty-five.'

'He was pleased with his presents,' said Mr
Sunbury to change the conversation.

'And so he ought to be,' said Mrs Sunbury still
upset.

They had in fact been handsome. Mr Sunbury
had given him a silver wrist-watch, with hands that
you could see in the dark, and Mrs Sunbury had
given him a kite. It wasn't by any means the first
one she had given him. That was when he was
seven years old, and it happened this way. There

was a large common near where they lived and on
Saturday afternoons when it was fine Mrs Sunbury
took her husband and son for a walk there. She said
it was good for Samuel to get a breath of fresh air
after being cooped up in a stuffy office all the week.
There were always a lot of people on the common,
but Mrs Sunbury who liked to keep herself to herself kept out of their way as much as possible.

'Look at them kites, Mum,' said Herbert suddenly one day.

There was a fresh breeze blowing and a number
of kites, small and large, were sailing through the
air.

'*Those*, Herbert, not them,' said Mrs Sunbury.

'Would you like to go and see where they start,
Herbert?' asked his father.

'Oh, yes, Dad.'

There was a slight elevation in the middle of the
common and as they approached it they saw boys
and girls and some men racing down it to give their
kites a start and catch the wind. Sometimes they
didn't and fell to the ground, but when they did
they would rise, and as the owner unravelled his
string go higher and higher. Herbert looked with
ravishment.

'Mum, can I have a kite?' he cried.

He had already learnt that when he wanted anything it was better to ask his mother first.

'Whatever for?' she said.

'To fly it, Mum.'

'If you're so sharp you'll cut yourself,' she said.

Mr and Mrs Sunbury exchanged a smile over the
little boy's head. Fancy him wanting a kite. Growing quite a little man he was.

'If you're a good boy and wash your teeth regular

every morning without me telling you I shouldn't be surprised if Santa Claus didn't bring you a kite on Christmas Day.'

Christmas wasn't far off and Santa Claus brought Herbert his first kite. At the beginning he wasn't very clever at managing it, and Mr Sunbury had to run down the hill himself and start it for him. It was a very small kite, but when Herbert saw it swim through the air and felt the little tug it gave his hand he was thrilled; and then every Saturday afternoon, when his father got back from the City, he would pester his parents to hurry over to the common. He quickly learnt how to fly it, and Mr and Mrs Sunbury, their hearts swelling with pride, would watch him from the top of the knoll while he ran down and as the kite caught the breeze lengthened the cord in his hand.

It became a passion with Herbert, and as he grew older and bigger his mother bought him larger and larger kites. He grew very clever at gauging the winds and could do things with his kite you wouldn't have thought possible. There were other kite-flyers on the common, not only children, but men, and since nothing brings people together so naturally as a hobby they share it was not long before Mrs Sunbury, notwithstanding her exclusiveness, found that she, her Samuel and her son were on speaking terms with all and sundry. They would compare their respective kites and boast of their accomplishments. Sometimes Herbert, a big boy of sixteen now, would challenge another kite-flyer. Then he would manoeuvre his kite to windward of the other fellow's, allow his cord to drift against his, and by a sudden jerk bring the enemy kite down. But long before this Mr Sunbury had succumbed to his son's enthusiasm and he would

often ask to have a go himself. It must have been a
funny sight to see him running down the hill in his
striped trousers, black coat and bowler hat. Mrs
Sunbury would trot sedately behind him and when
the kite was sailing free would take the cord from
him and watch it as it soared. Saturday afternoon
became the great day of the week for them, and
when Mr Sunbury and Herbert left the house in
the morning to catch their train to the City the first
thing they did was to look up at the sky to see if it
was flying weather. They liked best of all a gusty
day, with uncertain winds, for that gave them the
best chance to exercise their skill. All through the
week in the evenings, they talked about it. They
were contemptuous of smaller kites than theirs and
envious of bigger ones. They discussed the performances of other flyers as hotly, and as scornfully, as boxers or football players discuss their
rivals. Their ambition was to have a bigger kite
than anyone else and a kite that would go higher.
They had long given up a cord, for the kite they
gave Herbert on his twenty-first birthday was
seven feet high, and they used piano wire wound
round a drum. But that did not satisfy Herbert.
Somehow or other he had heard of a box-kite which
had been invented by somebody, and the idea
appealed to him at once. He thought he could
devise something of the sort himself and since he
could draw a little he set out making designs of it.
He got a small model made and tried it out one
afternoon, but it wasn't a success. He was a stub-
born boy and he wasn't going to be beaten. Something was wrong, and it was up to him to put it
right.

Then an unfortunate thing happened. Herbert
began to go out after supper. Mrs Sunbury didn't

like it much, but Mr Sunbury reasoned with her. After all, the boy was twenty-two, and it must be dull for him to stay at home all the time. If he wanted to go for a walk or see a movie there was no great harm. Herbert had fallen in love. One Saturday evening, after they'd had a wonderful time on the common, while they were at supper, out of a clear sky he said suddenly:

'Mum, I've asked a young lady to come in to tea tomorrow. Is that all right?'

'You done what?' said Mrs Sunbury, for a moment forgetting her grammar.

'You heard, Mum.'

'And may I ask who she is and how you got to know her?'

'Her name's Bevan, Betty Bevan, and I met her first at the pictures one Saturday afternoon when it was raining. It was an accident like. She was sitting next me and she dropped her bag and I picked it up and she said thank you and so naturally we got talking.'

'And d'you mean to tell me you fell for an old trick like that? Dropped her bag indeed!'

'You're making a mistake, Mum, she's a nice girl, she is really, and well educated too.'

'And when did all this happen?'

'About three months ago.'

'Oh, you met her three months ago and you've asked her to come to tea tomorrow?'

'Well, I've seen her since of course. That first day, after the show, I asked her if she'd come to the pictures with me on the Tuesday evening, and she said she didn't know, perhaps she would and perhaps she wouldn't. But she came all right.'

'She would. I could have told you that.'

(744)

'And we've been going to the pictures about twice a week ever since.'

'So that's why you've taken to going out so often?'

'That's right. But, look, I don't want to force her on you, if you don't want her to come to tea I'll say you've got a headache and take her out.'

'Your mum will have her to tea all right,' said Mr Sunbury. 'Won't you, dear? It's only that your mum can't abide strangers. She never has liked them.'

'I keep myself to myself,' said Mrs Sunbury gloomily. 'What does she do?'

'She works in a typewriting office in the City and she lives at home, if you call it home; you see, her mum died and her dad married again, and they've got three kids and she doesn't get on with her step-ma. Nag, nag, nag all the time, she says.'

Mrs Sunbury arranged the tea very stylishly. She took the knick-knacks off a little table in the sitting-room, which they never used, and put a tea-cloth on it. She got out the tea service and the plated tea-kettle which they never used either, and she made scones, baked a cake, and cut thin bread-and-butter.

'I want her to see that we're not just nobody,' she told her Samuel.

Herbert went to fetch Miss Bevan, and Mr Sunbury intercepted them at the door in case Herbert should take her into the dining-room where normally they ate and sat. Herbert gave the tea-table a glance of surprise as he ushered the young woman into the sitting-room.

'This is Betty, Mum,' he said.

'Miss Bevan, I presume,' said Mrs Sunbury.

'That's right, but call me Betty, won't you?'

'Perhaps the acquaintance is a bit short for that,' said Mrs Sunbury with a gracious smile. 'Won't you sit down, Miss Bevan?'

Strangely enough, or perhaps not strangely at all, Betty Bevan looked very much as Mrs Sunbury must have looked at her age. She had the same sharp features and the same rather small beady eyes, but her lips were scarlet with paint, her cheeks lightly rouged and her short black hair permanently waved. Mrs Sunbury took in all this at a glance, and she reckoned to a penny how much her smart rayon dress had cost, her extravagantly high-heeled shoes and the saucy hat on her head. Her frock was very short and she showed a good deal of flesh-coloured stocking. Mrs Sunbury, disapproving of her make-up and of her apparel, took an instant dislike to her, but she had made up her mind to behave like a lady, and if she didn't know how to behave like a lady nobody did, so that at first things went well. She poured out tea and asked Herbert to give a cup to his lady friend.

'Ask Miss Bevan if she'll have some bread-and-butter or a scone, Samuel, my dear.'

'Have both,' said Samuel, handing round the two plates, in his coarse way. 'I like to see people eat hearty.'

Betty insecurely perched a piece of bread-and-butter and a scone on her saucer and Mrs Sunbury talked affably about the weather. She had the satisfaction of seeing that Betty was getting more and more ill at ease. Then she cut the cake and pressed a large piece on her guest. Betty took a bite at it and when she put it in her saucer it fell to the ground.

'Oh, I am sorry,' said the girl, as she picked it up.

'It doesn't matter at all, I'll cut you another piece,' said Mrs Sunbury.

'Oh, don't bother. I'm not particular. The floor's clean.'

'I hope so,' said Mrs Sunbury with an acid smile, 'but I wouldn't dream of letting you eat a piece of cake that's been on the floor. Bring it here, Herbert, and I'll give Miss Bevan some more.'

'I don't want any more, Mrs Sunbury, I don't really.'

'I'm sorry you don't like my cake. I made it specially for you.' She took a bit. 'It tastes all right to me.'

'It's not that, Mrs Sunbury, it's a beautiful cake, it's only that I'm not hungry.'

She refused to have more tea and Mrs Sunbury saw she was glad to get rid of the cup. 'I expect they have their meals in the kitchen,' she said to herself. Then Herbert lit a cigarette.

'Give us a fag, Herb,' said Betty. 'I'm simply dying for a smoke.'

Mrs Sunbury didn't approve of women smoking, but she only raised her eyebrows slightly.

'We prefer to call him Herbert, Miss Bevan,' she said.

Betty wasn't such a fool as not to see that Mrs Sunbury had been doing all she could to make her uncomfortable, and now she saw a chance to get back on her.

'I know,' she said. 'When he told me his name was Herbert I nearly burst out laughing. Fancy calling anyone Herbert. A scream, I call it.'

'I'm sorry you don't like the name my son was given at his baptism. I think it's a very nice name.

But I suppose it all depends on what sort of class of people one is.'

Herbert stepped in to the rescue.

'At the office they call me Bertie, Mum.'

'Then all I can say is, they're a lot of very common men.'

Mrs Sunbury lapsed into a dignified silence and the conversation, such as it was, was maintained by Mr Sunbury and Herbert. It was not without satisfaction that Mrs Sunbury perceived that Betty was offended. She also perceived that the girl wanted to go, but didn't quite know how to manage it. She was determined not to help her. Finally Herbert took the matter into his own hands.

'Well, Betty, I think it's about time we were getting along,' he said. 'I'll walk back with you.'

'Must you go already?' said Mrs Sunbury, rising to her feet. 'It's been a pleasure, I'm sure.'

'Pretty little thing,' said Mr Sunbury tentatively after the young things had left.

'Pretty my foot. All that paint and powder. You take my word for it, she'd look very different with her face washed and without a perm. Common, that's what she is, common as dirt.'

An hour later Herbert came back. He was angry.

'Look here, Mum, what d'you mean by treating the poor girl like that? I was simply ashamed of you.'

'Don't you talk to your mother like that, Herbert,' she flared up. 'You didn't ought to have brought a woman like that into my house. Common, she is, common as dirt.'

When Mrs Sunbury got angry not only did her grammar grow shaky, but she wasn't quite safe on her aitches. Herbert took no notice of what she said.

'She said she'd never been so insulted in her life. I had a rare job pacifying her.'

'Well, she's never coming here again, I tell you that straight.'

'That's what you think. I'm engaged to her, so put that in your pipe and smoke it.'

Mrs Sunbury gasped.

'You're not?'

'Yes, I am. I've been thinking about it for a long time, and then she was so upset tonight I felt sorry for her, so I popped the question and I had a rare job persuading her, I can tell you.'

'You fool,' screamed Mrs Sunbury. 'You fool.'

There was quite a scene then. Mrs Sunbury and her son went at it hammer and tongs, and when poor Samuel tried to intervene they both told him roughly to shut up. At last Herbert flung out of the room and out of the house and Mrs Sunbury burst into angry tears.

No reference was made next day to what had passed. Mrs Sunbury was frigidly polite to Herbert and he was sullen and silent. After supper he went out. On Saturday he told his father and mother that he was engaged that afternoon and wouldn't be able to come to the common with them.

'I daresay we shall be able to do without you,' said Mrs Sunbury grimly.

It was getting on to the time for their usual fortnight at the seaside. They always went to Herne Bay, because Mrs Sunbury said you had a nice class of people there, and for years they had taken the same lodgings. One evening, in as casual a way as he could, Herbert said:

'By the way, Mum, you'd better write and tell them I shan't be wanting my room this year. Betty and me are getting married and we're going to Southend for the honeymoon.'

For a moment there was dead silence in the room.

'Bit sudden like, isn't it, Herbert?' said Mr Sunbury uneasily.

'Well, they're cutting down at Betty's office and she's out of a job, so we thought we'd better get married at once. We've taken two rooms in Dabney Street and we're furnishing out of my Savings Bank money.'

Mrs Sunbury didn't say a word. She went deathly pale and tears rolled down her thin cheeks.

'Oh, come on, Mum, don't take it so hard,' said Herbert. 'A fellow has to marry sometime. If Dad hadn't married you, I shouldn't be here now, should I?'

Mrs Sunbury brushed her tears away with an impatient hand.

'Your dad didn't marry me; I married 'im. I knew he was steady and respectable. I knew he'd make a good 'usband and father. I've never 'ad cause to regret it and no more 'as your dad. That's right, Samuel, isn't it?'

'Right as rain, Beatrice,' he said quickly.

'You know, you'll like Betty when you get to know her. She's a nice girl, she is really. I believe you'd find you had a lot in common. You must give her a chance, Mum.'

'She's never going to set foot in this house only over my dead body.'

'That's absurd, Mum. Why, everything'll be just the same if you'll only be reasonable. I mean, we can go flying on Saturday afternoons same as we always did. Just this time I've been engaged it's been difficult. You see, she can't see what there is in kite-flying, but she'll come round to it, and after I'm married it'll be different, I mean I can come and fly with you and Dad; that stands to reason.'

'That's what you think. Well, let me tell you that if you marry that woman you're not going to fly my kite. I never gave it you, I bought it out of the housekeeping money, and it's mine, see.'

'All right then, have it your own way. Betty says it's a kid's game anyway and I ought to be ashamed of myself, flying a kite at my age.'

He got up and once more stalked angrily out of the house. A fortnight later he was married. Mrs Sunbury refused to go to the wedding and wouldn't let Samuel go either. They went for their holiday and came back. They resumed their usual round. On Saturday afternoons they went to the common by themselves and flew their enormous kite. Mrs Sunbury never mentioned her son. She was determined not to forgive him. But Mr Sunbury used to meet him on the morning train they both took and they chatted a little when they managed to get into the same carriage. One morning Mr Sunbury looked up at the sky.

'Good flying weather today,' he said.

'D'you and Mum still fly?'

'What do you think? She's getting as clever as I am. You should see her with her skirts pinned up running down the hill. I give you my word I never knew she had it in her. Run? Why, she can run better than what I can.'

'Don't make me laugh, Dad?'

'I wonder you don't buy a kite of your own, Herbert. You've been always so keen on it.'

'I know I was. I did suggest it once, but you

know what women are, Betty said: "Be your age",
and oh, I don't know what all. I don't want a kid's
kite, of course, and them big kites cost money.
When we started to furnish Betty said it was
cheaper in the long run to buy the best and so we
went to one of them hire purchase places and what
with paying them every month and the rent, well, I
haven't got any more money than just what we can
manage on. They say it doesn't cost any more to
keep two than one, well, that's not my experience
so far.'

'Isn't she working?'

'Well, no, she says after working for donkeys'
years as you might say, now she's married she's
going to take it easy, and of course someone's got to
keep the place clean and do the cooking.'

So it went on for six months, and then one
Saturday afternoon when the Sunburys were as
usual on the common Mrs Sunbury said to her
husband:

'Did you see what I saw, Samuel?'

'I saw Herbert, if that's what you mean. I didn't
mention it because I thought it would only upset
you.'

'Don't speak to him. Pretend you haven't seen
him.'

Herbert was standing among the idle lookers-on.
He made no attempt to speak to his parents, but it
did not escape Mrs Sunbury that he followed with
all his eyes the flight of the big kite he had flown so
often. It began to grow chilly and the Sunburys
went home. Mrs Sunbury's face was brisk with
malice.

'I wonder if he'll come next Saturday,' said
Samuel.

'If I didn't think betting wrong I'd bet you six-pence he will, Samuel. I've been waiting for this all along.'

'You have?'

'I knew from the beginning he wouldn't be able to keep away from it.'

She was right. On the following Saturday and on every Saturday after that when the weather was fine Herbert turned up on the common. No inter-course passed. He just stood there for a while look-ing on and then strolled away. But after things had been going on like this for several weeks, the Sunburys had a surprise for him. They weren't flying the big kite which he was used to but a new one, a box-kite, a small one, on the model for which he had made the designs himself. He saw it was creating a lot of interest among the other kite-flyers; they were standing round it and Mrs Sunbury was talking volubly. The first time Samuel ran down the hill with it the thing didn't rise, but flopped miserably on the ground, and Herbert clenched his hands and ground his teeth. He couldn't bear to see it fail. Mr Sunbury climbed up the little hill again, and the second time the box-kite took the air. There was a cheer among the bystanders. After a while Mr Sunbury pulled it down and walked back with it to the hill. Mrs Sunbury went up to her son.

'Like to have a try, Herbert?'

He caught his breath.

'Yes, Mum, I should.'

'It's just a small one because they say you have to get the knack of it. It's not like the old-fashioned sort. But we've got specifications for a big one, and they say when you get to know about it and the wind's right you can go up to two miles with it.'

Mr Sunbury joined them.

'Samuel, Herbert wants to try the kite.'

Mr Sunbury handed it to him, a pleased smile on his face, and Herbert gave his mother his hat to hold. Then he raced down the hill, the kite took the air beautifully, and as he watched it rise his heart was filled with exultation. It was grand to see that little black thing soaring so sweetly, but even as he watched it he thought of the great big one they were having made. They'd never be able to manage that. Two miles in the air, Mum had said. Whew!

'Why don't you come back and have a cup of tea, Herbert,' said Mrs Sunbury, 'and we'll show you the designs for the new one they want to build for us. Perhaps you could make some suggestions.'

He hesitated. He'd told Betty he was just going for a walk to stretch his legs, she didn't know he'd been coming to the common every week, and she'd be waiting for him. But the temptation was irresistible.

'I don't mind if I do,' he said.

After tea they looked at the specifications. The kite was huge, with gadgets he had never seen before, and it would cost a lot of money.

'You'll never be able to fly it by yourselves,' he said.

'We can try.'

'I suppose you wouldn't like me to help you just at first?' he asked uncertainly.

'Mightn't be a bad idea,' said Mrs Sunbury.

It was late when he got home, much later than he thought, and Betty was vexed.

'Wherever have you been, Herb? I thought you were dead. Supper's waiting and everything.'

'I met some fellows and got talking.'

She gave him a sharp look, but didn't answer. She sulked.

After supper he suggested they should go to a movie, but she refused.

'You go if you want to,' she said. 'I don't care to.'

On the following Saturday he went again to the common and again his mother let him fly the kite. They had ordered the new one and expected to get it in three weeks. Presently his mother said to him:

'Elizabeth is here.'

'Betty?'

'Spying on you.'

It gave him a nasty turn, but he put on a bold front.

'Let her spy. I don't care.'

But he was nervous and wouldn't go back to tea with his parents. He went straight home. Betty was waiting for him.

'So that's the fellows you got talking to. I've been suspicious for some time, you going for a walk on Saturday afternoons, and all of a sudden I tumbled to it. Flying a kite, you, a grown man. Contemptible I call it.'

'I don't care what you call it. I like it, and if you don't like it you can lump it.'

'I won't have it and I tell you that straight. I'm not going to have you make a fool of yourself.'

'I've flown a kite every Saturday afternoon ever since I was a kid, and I'm going to fly a kite as long as ever I want to.'

'It's that old bitch, she's just trying to get you away from me. I know her. If you were a man you'd never speak to her again, not after the way she's treated me.'

'I won't have you call her that. She's my mother

and I've got the right to see her as often as ever I want to.'

The quarrel went on hour after hour. Betty screamed at him and Herbert shouted at her. They had had trifling disagreements before, because they were both obstinate, but this was the first serious row they had had. They didn't speak to one another on the Sunday, and during the rest of the week, though outwardly there was peace between them, their ill feeling rankled. It happened that the next two Saturdays it poured with rain. Betty smiled to herself when she saw the downpour, but if Herbert was disappointed he gave no sign of it. The recollection of their quarrel grew dim. Living in two rooms as they did, sleeping in the same bed, it was inevitable that they should agree to forget their differences. Betty went out of her way to be nice to her Herb, and she thought that now she had given him a taste of her tongue and he knew she wasn't going to be put upon by anyone, he'd be reasonable. He was a good husband in his way, generous with his money and steady. Give her time and she'd manage him all right.

But after a fortnight of bad weather it cleared.

'Looks as if were going to have good flying weather tomorrow,' said Mr Sunbury as they met on the platform to await their morning train. 'The new kite's come.'

'It has?'

'Your mum says of course we'd like you to come and help us with it, but no one's got the right to come between a man and his wife, and if you're afraid of Betty, her kicking up a rumpus, I mean, you'd better not come. There's a young fellow we've got to know on the common who's just mad about it, and he says he'll get it to fly if anybody can.'

Herbert was seized with a pang of jealousy.

'Don't you let any strangers touch our kite. I'll be there all right.'

'Well, you think it over, Herbert, and if you don't come we shall quite understand.'

'I'll come,' said Herbert.

So next day when he got back from the City he changed from his business clothes into slacks and an old coat. Betty came into the bedroom.

'What are you doing?'

'Changing,' he answered gaily. He was so excited, he couldn't keep the secret to himself. 'Their new kite's come and I'm going to fly it.'

'Oh, no, you're not,' she said. 'I won't have it.'

'Don't be a fool, Betty. I'm going, I tell you, and if you don't like it you can do the other thing.'

'I'm not going to let you, so that's that.'

She shut the door and stood in front of it. Her eyes flashed and her jaw was set. She was a little thing and he was a tall strong man. He took hold of her two arms to push her out of the way, but she kicked him violently on the shin.

'D'you want me to give you a sock on the jaw?'

'If you go you don't come back,' she shouted.

He caught her up, though she struggled and kicked, threw her on the bed and went out.

If the small box-kite had caused an excitement on the common it was nothing to what the new one caused. But it was difficult to manage, and though they ran and panted and other enthusiastic flyers helped them Herbert couldn't get it up.

'Never mind,' he said, 'we'll get the knack of it presently. The wind's not right today, that's all.'

He went back to tea with his father and mother and they talked it over just as they had talked in the old days. He delayed going because he didn't fancy the scene Betty would make him, but when Mrs Sunbury went into the kitchen to get supper ready he had to go home. Betty was reading the paper. She looked up.

'Your bag's packed,' she said.

'My what?'

'You heard what I said. I said if you went you needn't come back. I forgot about your things. Everything's packed. It's in the bedroom.'

He looked at her for a moment with surprise. She pretended to be reading again. He would have liked to give her a good hiding.

'All right, have it your own way,' he said.

He went into the bedroom. His clothes were packed in a suit-case, and there was a brown-paper parcel in which Betty had put whatever was left over. He took the bag in one hand, the parcel in the other, walked through the sitting-room without a word and out of the house. He walked to his mother's and rang the bell. She opened the door.

'I've come home, Mum,' he said.

'Have you, Herbert? Your room's ready for you. Put your things down and come in. We were just sitting down to supper.' They went into the dining-room. 'Samuel, Herbert's come home. Run out and get a quart of beer.'

Over supper and during the rest of the evening he told them the trouble he had had with Betty.

'Well, you're well out of it, Herbert,' said Mrs Sunbury when he had finished. 'I told you she was no wife for you. Common she is, common as dirt, and you who's always been brought up so nice.'

He found it good to sleep in his own bed, the bed he'd been used to all his life, and to come down to breakfast on the Sunday morning, unshaved and unwashed, and read the *News of the World*.

'We won't go to chapel this morning,' said Mrs Sunbury. It's been an upset to you, Herbert; we'll all take it easy today.'

During the week they talked a lot about the kite, but they also talked a lot about Betty. They discussed what she would do next.

'She'll try and get you back,' said Mrs Sunbury.

'A fat chance she's got of doing that,' said Herbert.

'You'll have to provide for her,' said his father.

'Why should he do that?' cried Mrs Sunbury. 'She trapped him into marrying her and now she's turned him out of the home he made for her.'

'I'll give her what's right as long as she leaves me alone.'

He was feeling more comfortable every day, in fact he was beginning to feel as if he'd never been away, he settled in like a dog in its own particular basket; it was nice having his mother to brush his clothes and mend his socks; she gave him the sort of things he'd always eaten and liked best; Betty was a scrappy sort of cook, it had been fun just at first, like picnicking, but it wasn't the sort of eating a man could get his teeth into, and he could never get over his mother's idea that fresh food was better than the stuff you bought in tins. He got sick of the sight of tinned salmon. Then it was nice to have space to move about in rather than be cooped up in two small rooms, one of which had to serve as a kitchen as well.

'I never made a bigger mistake in my life than

when I left home, Mum,' he said to her once.

'I know that, Herbert, but you're back now and you've got no cause ever to leave it again.'

His salary was paid on Friday and in the evening when they had just finished supper the bell rang.

'That's her,' they said with one voice.

Herbert went pale. His mother gave him a glance.

'You leave it to me,' she said. 'I'll see her.'

She opened to door. Betty was standing on the threshold. She tried to push her way in, but Mrs Sunbury prevented her.

'I want to see Herb.'

'You can't. He's out.'

'No, he isn't. I watched him go in with his dad and he hasn't come out again.'

'Well, he doesn't want to see you, and if you start making a disturbance I'll call the police.'

'I want my week's money.'

'That's all you've ever wanted of him.' She took out her purse. 'There's thirty-five shillings for you.'

'Thirty-five shillings? The rent's twelve shillings a week.'

'That's all you're going to get. He's got to pay his board here, hasn't he?'

'And then there's the instalments on the furniture.'

'We'll see about that when the time comes. D'you want the money or don't you?'

Confused, unhappy, browbeaten, Betty stood irresolutely. Mrs Sunbury thrust the money in her hand and slammed the door in her face. She went back to the dining-room.

'I've settled her hash all right,' she said.

The bell rang again, it rang repeatedly, but they

did not answer it, and presently it stopped. They guessed that Betty had gone away.

It was fine next day, with just the right velocity in the wind, and Herbert, after failing two or three times, found he had got the knack of flying the big box-kite. It soared into the air and up and up as he unreeled the wire.

'Why, it's a mile up if it's a yard,' he told his mother excitedly.

He had never had such a thrill in his life.

Several weeks passed by. They concocted a letter for Herbert to write in which he told Betty that so long as she didn't molest him or members of his family she would receive a postal order for thirty-five shillings every Saturday morning and he would pay the instalments on the furniture as they came due. Mrs Sunbury had been much against this, but Mr Sunbury, for once at variance with her, and Herbert agreed that it was the right thing to do. Herbert by then had learnt the ways of the new kite and was able to do great things with it. He no longer bothered to have contests with the other kite-flyers. He was out of their class. Saturday afternoons were his moments of glory. He revelled in the admiration he aroused in the bystanders and enjoyed the envy he knew he excited in the less fortunate flyers. Then one evening when he was walking back from the station with his father Betty waylaid him.

'Hulloa, Herb,' she said.

'Hulloa.'

'I want to talk to my husband alone, Mr Sunbury.'

'There's nothing you've got to say to me that my dad can't hear,' said Herbert sullenly.

She hesitated. Mr Sunbury fidgeted. He didn't know whether to stay or go.

'All right, then,' she said. 'I want you to come back home, Herb. I didn't mean it that night when I packed your bag. I only did it to frighten you. I was in a temper. I'm sorry for what I did. It's all so silly, quarrelling about a kite.'

'Well, I'm not coming back, see. When you turned me out you did me the best turn you ever did me.'

Tears began to trickle down Betty's cheeks.

'But I love you, Herb. If you want to fly your silly old kite, you fly it, I don't care so long as you come back.'

'Thank you very much, but it's not good enough. I know when I'm well off and I've had enough of married life to last me a lifetime. Come on, Dad.'

They walked on quickly and Betty made no attempt to follow them. On the following Sunday they went to chapel and after dinner Herbert went to the coal-shed where they kept the kite to have a look at it. He just couldn't keep away from it. He doted on it. In a minute he rushed back, his face white, with a hatchet in his hand.

'She's smashed it up. She did it with this.'

The Sunburys gave a cry of consternation and hurried to the coal-shed. What Herbert had said was true. The kite, the new, expensive kite, was in fragments. It had been savagely attacked with the hatchet, the woodwork was all in pieces, the reel was hacked to bits.

'She must have done it while we were at chapel. Watched us go out, that's what she did.'

'But how did she get in?' asked Mr Sunbury.

'I had two keys. When I came home I noticed one was missing, but I didn't think anything about it.'

'You can't be sure she did it, some of them fellows on the common have been very snooty, I wouldn't put it past them to have done this.'

'Well, we'll soon find out,' said Herbert. 'I'll go and ask her, and if she did it I'll kill her.'

His rage was so terrible that Mrs Sunbury was frightened.

'And get yourself hung for murder? No, Herbert, I won't let you go. Let your dad go, and when he comes back we'll decide what to do.'

'That's right, Herbert, let me go.'

They had a job to persuade him, but in the end Mr Sunbury went. In half an hour he came back.

'She did it all right. She told me straight out. She's proud of it. I won't repeat her language, it fair startled me, but the long and short of it was she was jealous of the kite. She said Herbert loved the kite more than he loved her and so she smashed it up and if she had to do it again she'd do it again.'

'Lucky she didn't tell me that. I'd have wrung her neck even if I'd had to swing for it. Well, she never gets another penny out of me, that's all.'

'She'll sue you,' said his father.

'Let her.'

'The instalment on the furniture is due next week, Herbert,' said Mrs Sunbury quietly. 'In your place I wouldn't pay it.'

'Then they'll just take it away,' said Samuel, 'and all the money he's paid on it so far will be wasted.'

'Well, what of it?' she answered. 'He can afford it. He's rid of her for good and all and we've got him back and that's the chief thing.'

'I don't care twopence about the money,' said Herbert. 'I can see her face when they come and take the furniture away. It meant a lot to her, it did, and the piano, she set a rare store on that piano.'

So on the following Friday he did not send Betty her weekly money, and when she sent him on a letter from the furniture people to say that if he didn't pay the instalment due by such and such a date they would remove it, he wrote back and said he wasn't in a position to continue the payments and they could remove the furniture at their convenience. Betty took to waiting for him at the station, and when he wouldn't speak to her followed him down the street screaming curses at him. In the evenings she would come to the house and ring the bell till they thought they would go mad, and Mr and Mrs Sunbury had the greatest difficulty in preventing Herbert from going out and giving her a sound thrashing. Once she threw a stone and broke the sitting-room window. She wrote obscene and abusive postcards to him at his office. At last she went to the magistrates' court and complained that her husband had left her and wasn't providing for her support. Herbert received a summons. They both told their story and if the magistrate thought it a strange one he didn't say so. He tried to effect a reconciliation between them, but Herbert resolutely refused to go back to his wife. The magistrate ordered him to pay Betty twenty-five shillings a week. He said he wouldn't pay it.

'Then you'll go to prison,' said the magistrate. 'Next case.'

But Herbert meant what he said. On Betty's complaint he was brought once more before the magistrate who asked him what reason he had for not obeying the order.

'I said I wouldn't pay her and I won't, not after she smashed my kite. And if you send me to prison I'll go to prison.'

The magistrate was stern with him this time.

'You're a very foolish young man,' he said. 'I'll give you a week to pay the arrears, and if I have any more nonsense from you you'll go to prison till you come to your senses.'

Herbert didn't pay, and that is how my friend Ned Preston came to know him and I heard the story.

'What d'you make of it?' asked Ned as he finished. 'You know, Betty isn't a bad girl. I've seen her several times, there's nothing wrong with her except her insane jealousy of Herbert's kite; and he isn't a fool by any means. In fact he's smarter than the average. What d'you suppose there is in kite-flying that makes the damned fool so mad about it?'

'I don't know,' I answered. I took my time to think. 'You see, I don't know a thing about flying a kite. Perhaps it gives him a sense of power as he watches it soaring towards the clouds and of mastery over the elements as he seems to bend the winds of heaven to his will. It may be that in some queer way he identifies himself with the kite flying so free and so high above him, and it's as it were an escape from the monotony of life. It may be that in some dim, confused way it represents an ideal of freedom and adventure. And you know, when a man once gets bitten with the virus of the ideal not all the King's doctors and not all the King's surgeons can rid him of it. But all this is very fanciful and I dare say it's just stuff and nonsense. I

think you'd better put your problem before
someone who knows a lot more about the
psychology of the human animal than I do.'

FROM

Orientations

(1899)

Daisy

I

It was Sunday morning – a damp, warm November morning, with the sky overhead grey and low. Miss Reed stopped a little to take breath before climbing the hill, at the top of which, in the middle of the churchyard, was Blackstable Church. Miss Reed panted, and the sultriness made her loosen her jacket. She stood at the junction of the two roads which led to the church, one from the harbour end of the town and the other from the station. Behind her lay the houses of Blackstable, the wind-beaten houses with slate roofs of the old fishing village and the red brick villas of the seaside resort which Blackstable was fast becoming; in the harbour were the masts of the ships, colliers that brought coal from the north; and beyond, the grey sea, very motionless, mingling in the distance with the sky ... The peal of the church bells ceased, and was replaced by a single bell, ringing a little hurriedly, querulously, which denoted that there were only ten minutes before the beginning of the service. Miss Reed walked on; she looked curiously at the people who passed her, wondering ...

'Good-morning, Mr Golding!' she said to a fisherman who pounded by her, ungainly in his Sunday clothes.

'Good-morning, Miss Reed!' he replied. 'Warm this morning.'

She wondered whether he knew anything of the subject which made her heart beat with excitement whenever she thought of it, and for thinking of it she hadn't slept a wink all night.

'Have you seen Mr Griffith this morning?' she asked, watching his face.

'No; I saw Mrs Griffith and George as I was walking up.'

'Oh! they are coming to church, then!' Miss Reed cried with the utmost surprise.

Mr Golding looked at her stupidly, not understanding her agitation. But they had reached the church. Miss Reed stopped in the porch to wipe her boots and pass an arranging hand over her hair. Then, gathering herself together, she walked down the aisle to her pew.

She arranged the hassock and knelt down, clasping her hands and closing her eyes; she said the Lord's Prayer; and being a religious woman, she did not immediately rise, but remained a certain time in the same position of worship to cultivate a proper frame of mind, her long, sallow face upraised, her mouth firmly closed, and her eyelids quivering a little from the devotional force with which she kept her eyes shut; her thin bust, very erect, was encased in a black jacket as in a coat of steel. But when Miss Reed considered that a due period had elapsed, she opened her eyes, and, as she rose from her knees, bent over to a lady sitting just in front of her.

'Have you heard about the Griffiths, Mrs Howlett?'

'No . . .! What is it?' answered Mrs Howlett, half turning round, intensely curious.

Miss Reed waited a moment to heighten the effect of her statement.

'Daisy Griffith has eloped – with an officer from the depot at Tercanbury.'

Mrs Howlett gave a little gasp.

'You don't say so!'

'It's all they could expect,' whispered Miss Reed. They ought to have known something was the matter when she went into Tercanbury three or four times a week.'

Blackstable is six miles from Tercanbury, which is a cathedral city and has a cavalry depot.

'I've seen her hanging about the barracks with my own eyes,' said Mrs Howlett, 'but I never suspected anything.'

'Shocking, isn't it?' said Miss Reed, with suppressed delight.

'But how did you find out?' asked Mrs Howlett.

'Ssh!' whispered Miss Reed – the widow, in her excitement, had raised her voice a little and Miss Reed could never suffer the least irreverence in church . . . 'She never came back last night and George Browning saw them get into the London train at Tercanbury.'

'Well, I never!' exclaimed Mrs Howlett.

'D'you think the Griffiths'll have the face to come to church?'

'I shouldn't if I was them,' said Miss Reed.

But at that moment the vestry door was opened and the organ began to play the hymn.

'I'll see you afterwards,' Miss Reed whispered hurriedly; and, rising from their seats, both ladies began to sing:

O Jesus, thou art standing
  Outside the fast closed door,
In lowly patience waiting
  To pass the threshold o'er;
We bear the name of Christians ...

Miss Reed held the book rather close to her face, being short-sighted; but, without even lifting her eyes, she had become aware of the entrance of Mrs Griffith and George. She glanced significantly at Mrs Howlett. Mr Griffith hadn't come, although he was churchwarden, and Mrs Howlett gave an answering look which meant that it was then evidently quite true. But they both gathered themselves together for the last verse, taking breath.

O Jesus, thou are pleading
  In accents meek and low ...

A—A—men! The congregation fell to its knees, and the curate, rolling his eyes to see who was in church, began gabbling the morning prayers – '*Dearly beloved brethren* ...'

2

At the Sunday dinner, the vacant place of Daisy Griffith stared at them. Her father sat at the head of the table, looking down at his plate, in silence; every now and then, without raising his head, he glanced up at the empty space, filled with a madness of grief ... He had gone into Tercanbury in the morning inquiring at the houses of all Daisy's friends, imagining that she had spent the night with one of them. He could not believe that George Browning's story was true; he could so easily have been mistaken in the semi-darkness of the station. And even he had gone to the barracks – his cheeks still burned with the humiliation – asking if they knew a Daisy Griffith.

He pushed his plate away with a groan. He wished passionately that it were Monday, so that he could work. And the post would surely bring a letter, explaining.

'The vicar asked where you were,' said Mrs Griffith.

Robert, the father, looked at her with his pained eyes, but her eyes were hard and shining, her lips almost disappeared in the tight closing of the mouth. She was willing to believe the worst. He looked at his son; he was frowning; he looked as coldly angry as the mother. He, too, was willing to believe everything, and they neither seemed very sorry . . . Perhaps they were even glad.

'I was the only one who loved her,' he muttered to himself, and pushing back his chair, he got up and left the room. He almost tottered; he had aged twenty years in the night.

'Aren't you going to have any pudding?' asked his wife.

He made no answer.

He walked out into the courtyard quite aimlessly, but the force of habit took him to the workshop, where, every Sunday afternoon, he was used to going after dinner to see that everything was in order, and today also he opened the window, put away a tool which the men had left about, examined the Saturday's work . . .

Mrs Griffith and George, stiff and ill at ease in

his clumsy Sunday clothes, went on with their dinner.

'D'you think the vicar knew?' he asked as soon as the father had closed the door.

'I don't think he'd have asked if he had. Mrs Gray might, but he's too simple – unless she put him up to it.'

'I thought I should never get round with the plate,' said George. Mr Griffith, being a carpenter, which is respectable and well-to-do, which is honourable, had been made churchwarden, and part of his duty was to take round the offertory plate. This duty George performed in his father's occasional absences, as when a coffin was very urgently required.

'I wasn't going to let them get anything out of me,' said Mrs Griffith, defiantly.

All through the service a number of eyes had been fixed on them, eager to catch some sign of emotion, full of horrible curiosity to know what the Griffiths felt and thought; but Mrs Griffith had been inscrutable.

3

Next day the Griffiths lay in wait for the postman; George sat by the parlour window, peeping through the muslin curtains.

'Fanning's just coming up the street,' he said at last. Until the post had come old Griffith could not work; in the courtyard at the back was heard the sound of hammering.

There was a rat-tat at the door, the sound of a letter falling on the mat, and Fanning the postman passed on. George leaned back quickly so that he might not see him. Mr Griffith fetched the letter, opened it with trembling hands . . . He gave a little gasp of relief.

'She's got a situation in London.'

'Is that all she says?' asked Mrs Griffith. 'Give me the letter,' and she almost tore it from her husband's hand.

She read it through and uttered a little ejaculation of contempt – almost of triumph. 'You don't mean to say you believe that?' she cried.

'Let's look, Mother,' said George. He read the letter and he too gave a snort of contempt.

'She says she's got a situation,' repeated Mrs Griffith, with a sneer at her husband, 'and we're not to be angry or anxious and she's quite happy – and we can write to Charing Cross Post Office. I know what sort of a situation she's got.'

Mr Griffith looked from his wife to his son.

'Don't you think it's true?' he asked helplessly. At the first moment he had put the fullest faith in Daisy's letter, he had been so anxious to believe it; but the scorn of the others . . .

'There's Miss Reed coming down the street,' said George. 'She's looking this way, and she's crossing over. I believe she's coming in.'

'What does she want?' asked Mrs Griffith, angrily.

There was another knock at the door, and through the curtains they saw Miss Reed's eyes looking towards them, trying to pierce the muslin. Mrs Griffith motioned the two men out of the room, and hurriedly put antimacassars on the chairs. The knock was repeated, and Mrs Griffith, catching hold of a duster, went to the door.

'Oh, Miss Reed! Who'd have thought of seeing you?' she cried with surprise.

'I hope I'm not disturbing,' answered Miss Reed, with an acid smile.

'Oh, dear no!' said Mrs Griffith. 'I was just doing the dusting in the parlour. Come in, won't you? The place is all upside down, but you won't mind that, will you?'

Miss Reed sat on the edge of a chair.

'I thought I'd just pop in to ask about dear Daisy. I met Fanning as I was coming along and he told me you'd had a letter.'

'Oh! Daisy?' Mrs Griffith had understood at once why Miss Reed came, but she was rather at a loss for an answer ... 'Yes, we have had a letter from her. She's up in London.'

'Yes, I knew that,' said Miss Reed. 'George Browning saw them getting into the London train, you know.'

Mrs Griffith saw it was no good fencing, but an idea occurred to her.

'Yes, of course her father and I are very distressed about – her eloping like that.'

'I can quite understand that,' said Miss Reed.

'But it was on account of his family. He didn't want anyone to know about it till he was married.'

'Oh!' said Miss Reed, raising her eyebrows very high.

'Yes,' said Mrs Griffith, 'that's what she said in her letter; they were married on Saturday at a registry office.'

'But, Mrs Griffith, I'm afraid she's been deceiving you. It's Captain Hogan ... and he's a married man.'

She could have laughed outright at the look of

dismay on Mrs Griffith's face. The blow was sudden, and, notwithstanding all her power of self-control, Mrs Griffith could not help herself. But at once she recovered, an angry flush appeared on her cheek-bones.

'You don't mean it?' she cried.

'I'm afraid it's quite true,' said Miss Reed, humbly. 'In fact I know it is.'

'Then she's a lying, deceitful hussy, and she's made a fool of all of us. I give you my word of honour that she told us she was married; I'll fetch you the letter.' Mrs Griffith rose from her chair, but Miss Reed put a hand to stop her.

'Oh, don't trouble, Mrs Griffith; of course I believe you,' she said, and Mrs Griffith immediately sat down again.

But she burst into a storm of abuse of Daisy, for her deceitfulness and wickedness. She vowed she would never forgive her. She assured Miss Reed again and again that she had known nothing about it. Finally she burst into a perfect torrent of tears. Miss Reed was mildly sympathetic; but now she was anxious to get away to impart her news to the rest of Blackstable. Mrs Griffith sobbed her visitor out of the front door, but when she had closed it, dried her tears. She went into the parlour and flung open the door that led to the back room. Griffith was sitting with his face hidden in his hands, and every now and then a sob shook his great frame. George was very pale, biting his nails.

'You heard what she said,' cried Mrs Griffith. 'He's married . . .!' She looked at her husband contemptuously. 'It's all very well for you to carry on like that now. It was you who did it; it was all your fault. If she'd been brought up as I wanted her to be, this wouldn't ever have happened.'

Again there was a knock, and George, going out, ushered in Mrs Gray, the vicar's wife. She rushed in when she heard the sound of voices.

'Oh, Mrs Griffith, it's dreadful! simply dreadful! Miss Reed has just told me all about it. What is to be done? And what'll the dissenters make of it? Oh, dear, it's simply dreadful!'

'You've just come in time, Mrs Gray,' said Mrs Griffith, angrily. 'It's not my fault. I can tell you that. It's her father who's brought it about. He would have her go into Tercanbury to be educated, and he would have her take singing lessons and dancing lessons. The Church school was good enough for George. It's been Daisy this and Daisy that all through. Me and George have been always put by for Daisy. I didn't want her brought up above her station, I can assure you. It's him who would have her brought up as a lady; and see what's come of it! And he let her spend any money she liked on her dress ... It wasn't me that let her go into Tercanbury every day in the week if she wanted to. I knew she was up to no good. There you see what you've brought her to; it's you who's disgraced us all!'

She hissed out the words with intense malignity, nearly screaming in the bitterness she felt towards the beautiful daughter of better education than herself, almost of different station. It was all but a triumph for her that this had happened. It brought her daughter down; she turned the tables, and now, from the superiority of her virtue, she looked down upon her with utter contempt.

4

On the following Sunday the people of Blackstable enjoyed an emotion; as Miss Reed said:

'It was worth going to church this morning, even for a dissenter.'

The vicar was preaching, and the congregation paid a very languid attention, but suddenly a curious little sound went through the church – one of those scarcely perceptible noises which no comparison can explain; it was a quick attraction of all eyes, an arousing of somnolent intelligences, a slight, quick drawing-in of the breath. The listeners had heeded very indifferently Mr Gray's admonitions to brotherly love and charity as matters which did not concern them other than abstractedly; but quite suddenly they had realized that he was bringing his discourse round to the subject of Daisy Griffith, and they pricked up both ears. They saw it coming directly along the highways of Vanity and Luxuriousness; and everyone became intensely wide awake.

'And we have in all our minds,' he said at last, 'the terrible fall which has almost broken the hearts of sorrowing parents and brought bitter grief – bitter grief and shame to all of us ...'

He went on hinting at the scandal in the matter of the personal columns in newspapers, and drawing a number of obvious morals. The Griffith family were sitting in their pew well in view of the congregation; and, losing even the shadow of decency, the people turned round and stared at them, ghoul-like ... Robert Griffith sat in the corner with his head bent down, huddled up, his rough face speaking in all its lines the terrible humiliation; his hair was all dishevelled. He was not more than fifty, and he looked an old man. But Mrs Griffith sat next him, very erect, not leaning against the back, with her head well up, her mouth firmly closed, and she looked straight in front of her, her little eyes sparkling, as if she had not an idea that a hundred people were staring at her. In the other corner was George, very white, looking up at the roof in simulation of indifference. Suddenly a sob came from the Griffiths' pew, and people saw that the father had broken down; he seemed to forget where he was, and he cried as if indeed his heart were broken. The great tears ran down his cheeks in the sight of all – the painful tears of men; he had not even the courage to hide his face in his hands. Still Mrs Griffith made no motion, she never gave a sign that she heard her husband's agony; but two little red spots appeared angrily on her cheek-bones, and perhaps she compressed her lips a little more tightly . . .

5

Six months passed. One evening, when Mr Griffith was standing at the door after work, smoking his pipe, the postman handed him a letter. He changed colour and his hand shook when he recognized the handwriting. He turned quickly into the house.

'A letter from Daisy,' he said. They had not replied to her first letter, and since then had heard nothing.

'Give it to me,' said his wife.

He drew it quickly towards him, with an instinctive gesture of retention.

'It's addressed to me.'

'Well, then, you'd better open it.'

He looked up at his wife; he wanted to take the letter away and read it alone, but her eyes were upon him, compelling him there and then to open it.

'She wants to come back,' he said in a broken voice.

Mrs Griffith snatched the letter from him.

'That means he's left her,' she said.

The letter was all incoherent, nearly incomprehensible, covered with blots, every other word scratched out. One could see that the girl was quite distraught, and Mrs Griffith's keen eyes saw the trace of tears on the paper . . . It was a long, bitter cry of repentance. She begged them to take her back, repeating again and again the cry of penitence, piteously beseeching them to forgive her.

'I'll go and write to her,' said Mr Griffith.

'Write what?'

'Why – that it's all right and she isn't to worry; and we want her back, and that I'll go up and fetch her.'

Mrs Griffith placed herself between him and the door.

'What d'you mean?' she cried. 'She's not coming back into my house.'

Mr Griffith started back.

'You don't want to leave her where she is! She says she'll kill herself.'

'Yes, I believe that,' she replied scornfully; and then, gathering up her anger, 'D'you mean to say

(781)

you expect me to have her in the house after what she's done? I tell you I won't. She's never coming in this house again as long as I live; I'm an honest woman and she isn't. She's a—' Mrs Griffith called her daughter the foulest name that can be applied to her sex.

Mr Griffith stood indecisively before his wife.

'But think what a state's she's in, Mother. She was crying when she wrote the letter.'

'Let her cry; she'll have to cry a lot more before she's done. And it serves her right; and it serves you right. She'll have to go through a good deal more than that before God forgives her, I can tell you.'

'Perhaps she's starving.'

'Let her starve, for all I care. She's dead to us; I've told everyone in Blackstable that I haven't got a daughter now, and if she came on her bended knees before me I'd spit on her.'

George had come in and listened to the conversation.

'Think what people would say, Father,' he said now; 'as it is, it's jolly awkward, I can tell you. No one would speak to us if she was back again. It's not as if people didn't know; everyone in Blackstable knows what she's been up to.'

'And what about George?' put in Mrs Griffith. 'D'you think the Polletts would stand it?' George was engaged to Edith Pollett.

'She'd be quite capable of breaking it off if Daisy came back,' said George. 'She's said as much.'

'Quite right too!' cried his mother. 'And I'm not going to be like Mrs Jay with Lottie. Everyone knows about Lottie's goings-on, and you can see how people treat them – her and her mother. When

Mrs Gray passes them in the street she always goes the other side. No, I've always held my head high, and I'm always going to. I've never done anything to be ashamed of as far as I know, and I'm not going to begin now. Everyone knows it was no fault of mine what Daisy did, and all through I've behaved so that no one should think the worse of me.'

Mr Griffith sank helplessly into a chair, the old habit of submission asserted itself, and his weakness gave way as usual before his wife's strong will. He had not the courage to oppose her.

'What shall I answer, then?' he asked.

'Answer? Nothing.'

'I must write something. She'll be waiting for the letter, and waiting and waiting.'

'Let her wait.'

6

A few days later another letter came from Daisy, asking pitifully why they didn't write, begging them again to forgive her and take her back. The letter was addressed to Mr Griffith; the girl knew that it was only from him she might expect mercy; but he was out when it arrived. Mrs Griffith opened it, and passed it on to her son. They looked at one another guiltily; the same thought had occurred to both, and each knew it was in the other's mind.

'I don't think we'd better let Father see it,' Mrs Griffith said, a little uncertainly; 'it'll do no good and it'll only distress him.'

'And it's no good making a fuss, because we can't have her back.'

'She'll never enter this door as long as I'm in the world . . . I think I'll lock it up.'

'I'd burn it, if I was you, Mother. It's safer.'

Then every day Mrs Griffith made a point of going to the door herself for the letters. Two more came from Daisy.

'I know it's not you; it's Mother and George. They've always hated me. Oh, don't be so cruel, Father! You don't know what I've gone through. I've cried and cried till I thought I should die. For God's sake write to me! They might let you write just once. I'm alone all day, day after day, and I think I shall go mad. You might take me back; I'm sure I've suffered enough, and you wouldn't know me now, I'm so changed. Tell Mother that if she'll only forgive me I'll be quite different. I'll do the housework and anything she tells me. I'll be a servant to you, and you can send the girl away. If you knew how I repent! Do forgive me and have me back. Oh, I know that no one would speak to me; but I don't care about that, if I can only be with you!'

'She doesn't think about us,' said George, 'what we should do if she was back. No one would speak to us, either.'

But the next letter said that she couldn't bear the terrible silence; if her father didn't write she'd come down to Blackstable. Mrs Griffith was furious.

'I'd shut the door in her face; I wonder how she can dare to come.'

'It's jolly awkward,' said George. 'Supposing Father found out we'd kept back the letters?'

'It was for his own good,' said Mrs Griffith,

angrily. 'I'm not ashamed of what I've done, and I'll tell him so to his face if he says anything to me.'

'Well, it is awkward. You know what Father is; if he saw her . . .'

Mrs Griffith paused a moment.

'You must go up and see her, George!'

'Me!' he cried in astonishment, a little in terror.

'You must go as if you came from her father to say we won't have anything more to do with her and she's not to write.'

7

Next day George Griffith, on getting out of the station at Victoria, jumped on a Fulham bus, taking his seat with the self-assertiveness of the countryman who intends to show the Londoners that he's as good as they are. He was in some trepidation and his best clothes. He didn't know what to say to Daisy, and his hands sweated uncomfortably. When he knocked at the door he wished she might be out – but that would only be postponing the ordeal.

'Does Mrs Hogan live here?'

'Yes. Who shall I say?'

'Say a gentleman wants to see her.'

He followed quickly on the landlady's heels and passed through the door the woman opened while she was giving the message. Daisy sprang to her feet with a cry.

'George!'

She was very pale, her blue eyes dim and lifeless, with the lids heavy and red; she was in a dressing gown, her beautiful hair dishevelled, wound loosely into a knot at the back of her head. She had not half the beauty of her old self ... George, to affirm the superiority of virtue over vice, kept his hat on.

She looked at him with frightened eyes, then her lips quivered, and, turning away her head, she fell on a chair and burst into tears. George looked at her sternly. His indignation was greater than ever now that he saw her. His old jealousy made him exult at the change in her.

'She's got nothing much to boast about now,' he said to himself, noting how ill she looked.

'Oh, George ...!' she began, sobbing; but he interrupted her.

'I've come from Father,' he said, 'and we don't want to have anything more to do with you, and you're not to write.'

'Oh!' She looked at him now with her eyes suddenly quite dry. They seemed to burn her in their sockets. 'Did he send you here to tell me that?'

'Yes; and you're not to come down.'

She put her hand to her forehead, looking vacantly before her.

'But what am I to do? I haven't got any money; I've pawned everything.'

George looked at her silently; but he was horribly curious.

'Why did he leave you?' he said.

She made no answer; she looked before her as if she were going out of her mind.

'Has he left you any money?' asked George.

Then she started up, her cheeks flaming red.

'I would not touch a halfpenny of his. I'd rather starve!' she screamed.

George shrugged his shoulders.

'Well, you understand?' he said.

'Oh, how can you! It's all you and Mother. You've always hated me. But I'll pay you out, by God! I'll pay you out. I know what you are, all of you – you and Mother, and all the Blackstable people. You're a set of damned hypocrites.'

'Look here, Daisy! I'm not going to stand here and hear you talk like that of me and Mother,' he replied with dignity; 'and as for the Blackstable people, you're not fit to – to associate with them. And I can see where you learnt your language.'

Daisy burst into hysterical laughter. George became more angry – virtuously indignant.

'Oh, you can laugh as much as you like! I know your repentance is a lot of damned humbug. You've always been a conceited little beast. And you've been stuck up and cocky because you thought yourself nice-looking, and because you were educated in Tercanbury. And no one was good enough for you in Blackstable. And I'm jolly glad that all this has happened to you; it serves you jolly well right. And if you dare to show yourself at Blackstable we'll send for the police.'

Daisy stepped up to him.

'I'm a damned bad lot,' she said, 'but I swear I'm not half as bad as you are … You know what you're driving me to.'

'You don't think I care what you do,' he answered, as he flung himself out of the door. He slammed it behind him, and he also slammed the front door to show that he was a man of high principles. And even George Washington, when he said, 'I cannot tell a lie; I did it with my little hatchet,' did not feel so righteous as George Griffith at that moment.

Daisy went to the window to see him go, and then, throwing up her arms, she fell on her knees, weeping, weeping, and she cried:

'My God, have pity on me!'

8

'I wouldn't go through it again for a hundred pounds,' said George, when he recounted his experience to his mother. 'And she wasn't a bit humble, as you'd expect.'

'Oh! that's Daisy all over. Whatever happens to her, she'll be as bold as brass.'

'And she didn't choose her language,' he said, with mingled grief and horror.

They heard nothing more of Daisy for over a year, when George went up to London for the choir treat. He did not come back till three o'clock in the morning, but he went at once to his mother's room.

He woke her very carefully, so as not to disturb his father. She started up, about to speak, but he prevented her with his hand.

'Come outside; I've got something to tell you.'

Mrs Griffith was about to tell him rather crossly to wait till the morrow, but he interrupted her:

'I've seen Daisy.'

She quickly got out of bed, and they went together into the parlour.

'I couldn't keep it till the morning,' he said ... 'What d'you think she's doing now? Well, after we came out of the Empire I went down Piccadilly, and – well, I saw Daisy standing there ... It did give me a turn, I can tell you; I thought some of the chaps would see her. I simply went cold all over. But they were on ahead and hadn't noticed her.'

'Thank God for that!' said Mrs Griffith, piously.

'Well, what d'you think I did? I went straight up to her and looked her full in the face. But d'you think she moved a muscle? She simply looked at me as if she'd never set eyes on me before. Well, I was taken aback, I can tell you. I thought she'd faint. Not a bit of it.'

'No, I know Daisy,' said Mrs Griffith; 'you think she's this and that, because she looks at you with those blue eyes of hers, as if she couldn't say boo to a goose, but she's got the very devil inside her . . . Well, I shall tell her father that, just so as to let him see what she has come to . . .'

The existence of the Griffith household went on calmly. Husband and wife and son led their life in the dull little fishing town, the seasons passed insensibly into one another, one year slid gradually into the next; and the five years that went by seemed like one long, long day. Mrs Griffith did not alter an atom; she performed her housework, went to church regularly, and behaved like a Christian woman in that state of life in which a merciful Providence had been pleased to put her. George got married, and on Sunday afternoons could be seen wheeling an infant in a perambulator along the street. He was a good husband and an excellent father. He never drank too much, he worked well, he was careful of his earnings, and he also went to church regularly; his ambition was to become churchwarden after his father. And even in Mr Griffith there was not so very much change. He was more bowed, his hair and beard were greyer.

His face was set in an expression of passive misery, and he was extremely silent. But as Mrs Griffith said:

'Of course, he's getting old. One can't expect to remain young for ever' – she was a woman who frequently said profound things – 'and I've known all along he wasn't the sort of man to make old bones. He's never had the go in him that I have. Why, I'd make two of him.'

The Griffiths were not so well-to-do as before. As Blackstable became a more important health resort, a regular undertaker opened a shop there; and his window, with two little model coffins and an arrangement of black Prince of Wales's feathers surrounded by a white wreath, took the fancy of the natives, so that Mr Griffith almost completely lost the most remunerative part of his business. Other carpenters sprang into existence and took away much of the trade.

'I've no patience with him,' said Mrs Griffith of her husband. 'He's let these newcomers come along and just take the bread out of his hands. Oh, if I was a man, I'd make things different, I can tell you! He doesn't seem to care . . .'

At last, one day George came to his mother in a state of tremendous excitement.

'I say, Mother, you know the pantomime they've got at Tercanbury this week?'

'Yes.'

'Well, the principal boy's Daisy.'

Mrs Griffith sank into a chair, gasping.

'Harry Ferne's been, and he recognized her at once. It's all over the town.'

Mrs Griffith, for the first time in her life, was completely at a loss for words.

'Tomorrow's the last night,' added her son, after a little while, 'and all the Blackstable people are going.'

'To think that this should happen to me!' said Mrs Griffith, distractedly. 'What have I done to deserve it? Why couldn't it happen to Mrs Garman or Mrs Jay? If the Lord had seen fit to bring it upon them – well, I shouldn't have wondered.'

'Edith wants us to go,' said George – Edith was his wife.

'You don't mean to say you're going, with all the Blackstable people there?'

'Well, Edith says we ought to go, just to show them we don't care.'

'Well, I shall come too!' cried Mrs Griffith.

9

Next evening half Blackstable took the special train to Tercanbury, which had been put on for the pantomime, and there was such a crowd at the doors that the impresario half thought of extending his stay. The Rev. Charles Gray and Mrs Gray were there, also James, their nephew. Mr Gray had some scruples about going to a theatre, but his wife said a pantomime was quite different; besides, curiosity may gently enter even a clerical bosom. Miss Reed was there in black satin, with her friend Mrs Howlett; Mrs Griffith sat in the middle of the stalls, flanked by her dutiful son and her daughter-in-law; and George searched for female beauty with his opera-glass, which is quite the proper thing to do on such occasions . . .

The curtain went up, and the villagers of Dick

Whittington's native place sang a chorus.

'Now she's coming,' whispered George.

All those Blackstable hearts stood still. And Daisy, as Dick Whittington, bounded on the stage – in flesh-coloured tights, with particularly scanty trunks, and her bodice – rather low. The vicar's nephew sniggered, and Mrs Gray gave him a reproachful glance; all the other Blackstable people looked pained; Miss Reed blushed. But as Daisy waved her hand and gave a kick, the audience broke out into prolonged applause; Tercanbury people have no moral sense, although Tercanbury is a cathedral city.

Daisy began to sing:

> *I'm a jolly sort of boy, tol, lol,*
> *And I don't care a damn who knows it.*
> *I'm fond of every joy, tol, lol,*
> *As you may very well suppose it.*
> *Tol, lol, lol,*
> *Tol, lol, lol.*

Then the audience, the audience of a cathedral city, as Mr Gray said, took up the refrain:

> *Tol, lol, lol,*
> *Tol, lol, lol.*

However, the piece went on to the bitter end, and Dick Whittington appeared in many different costumes and sang many songs, and kicked many kicks, till he was finally made Lord Mayor – in tights.

Ah, it was an evening of bitter humiliation for Blackstable people. Some of them, as Miss Reed said, behaved scandalously; they really appeared to enjoy it. And even George laughed at some of the jokes the cat made, though his wife and his mother sternly reproved him.

'I'm ashamed of you, George, laughing at such a time!' they said.

Afterwards the Grays and Miss Reed got into the same railway carriage with the Griffiths.

'Well, Mrs Griffith,' said the vicar's wife, 'what do you think of your daughter now?'

'Mrs Gray,' replied Mrs Griffith, solemnly, 'I haven't got a daughter.'

'That's a very proper spirit in which to look at it,' answered the lady ... 'She was simply covered with diamonds.'

'They must be worth a fortune,' said Miss Reed.

'Oh, I dare say they're not real,' said Mrs Gray; 'at that distance and with the limelight, you know, it's very difficult to tell.'

'I'm sorry to say,' said Mrs Griffith, with some asperity, feeling the doubt almost an affront to her, 'I'm sorry to say that I *know* they're real.'

The ladies coughed discreetly, scenting a little scandalous mystery which they must get out of Mrs Griffith at another opportunity.

'My nephew James says she earns at least thirty to forty pounds a week.'

Miss Reed sighed at the thought of such depravity.

'It's very sad,' she remarked, 'to think of such things happening to a fellow creature ...'

'But what I can't understand,' said Mrs Gray, next morning, at the breakfast-table, 'is how she got into such a position. We all know that at one time she was to be seen in – well, in a very questionable place, at an hour which left no doubt about her –

her means of livelihood. I must say I thought she was quite lost . . .'

'Oh well, I can tell you that easily enough,' replied her nephew. 'She's being kept by Sir Somebody Something, and he's running the show for her.'

'James, I wish you would be more careful about your language. It's not necessary to call a spade a spade, and you can surely find a less objectionable expression to explain the relationship between the persons . . . Don't you remember his name?'

'No; I heard it, but I've really forgotten.'

'I see in this week's *Tercanbury Times* that there's a Sir Herbert Ously-Farrowham staying at the George just now.'

'That's it. Sir Herbert Ously-Farrowham.'

'How sad! I'll look him out in Burke.'

She took down the reference book, which was kept beside the clergy list.

'Dear me, he's only twenty-nine . . . And he's got a house in Cavendish Square and a house in the country. He must be very well-to-do; and he belongs to the Junior Carlton and two other clubs . . . And he's got a sister who's married to Lord Edward Lake.' Mrs Gray closed the book and held it with a finger to mark the place, like a Bible. 'It's very sad to think of the dissipation of so many members of the aristocracy. It sets such a bad example to the lower classes.'

10

They showed old Griffith a portrait of Daisy in her theatrical costume.

'Has she come to that?' he said.

He looked at it a moment, then savagely tore it in pieces and flung it in the fire.

'Oh, my God!' he groaned; he could not get out of his head the picture, the shamelessness of the costume, the smile, the evident prosperity and content. He felt now that he had lost his daughter indeed. All these years he had kept his heart open to her, and his heart had bled when he thought of her starving, ragged, perhaps dead. He had thought of her begging her bread and working her beautiful hands to the bone in some factory. He had always hoped that some day she could return to him, purified by the fire of suffering ... But she was prosperous and happy and rich. She was applauded, worshipped; the papers were full of her praise. Old Griffith was filled with a feeling of horror, of immense repulsion. She was flourishing in her sin, and he loathed her. He had been so ready to forgive her when he thought her despairing and unhappy; but now he was implacable.

Three months later Mrs Griffith came to her husband, trembling with excitement, and handed him a cutting from a paper:

We hear that Miss Daisy Griffith, who earned golden opinions in the provinces last winter with her Dick Whittington, is about to be married to Sir Herbert Ously-Farrowham. Her friends, and their name is legion, will join with us in the heartiest congratulations.

He returned the paper without answering.

'Well?' asked his wife.

'It is nothing to me. I don't know either of the parties mentioned.'

At that moment there was a knock at the door, and Mrs Gray and Miss Reed entered, having met on the doorstep. Mrs Griffith at once regained her self-possession.

'Have you heard the news, Mrs Griffith?' said Miss Reed.

'D'you mean about the marriage of Sir Herbert Ously-Farrowham?' She mouthed the long name.

'Yes,' replied the two ladies together.

'It is nothing to me . . . I have no daughter, Mrs Gray.'

'I'm sorry to hear you say that, Mrs Griffith,' said Mrs Gray very stiffly. 'I think you show a most unforgiving spirit.'

'Yes,' said Miss Reed; 'I can't help thinking that if you'd treated poor Daisy in a – well, in a more *Christian* way, you might have saved her from a great deal.'

'Yes,' added Mrs Gray. 'I must say that all through I don't think you've shown a nice spirit at all. I remember poor, dear Daisy quite well, and she had a very sweet character. And I'm sure that if she'd been treated a little more gently, nothing of all this would have happened.'

Mrs Gray and Miss Reed looked at Mrs Griffith sternly and reproachfully; they felt themselves like God Almighty judging a miserable sinner. Mrs Griffith was extremely angry; she felt that she was being blamed most unjustly, and, moreover, she was not used to being blamed.

'I'm sure you're very kind, Mrs Gray and Miss Reed, but I must take the liberty of saying that I know best what my daughter was.'

'Mrs Griffith, all I say is this – you are not a good mother.'

'Excuse me, madam . . .' said Mrs Griffith, having

grown red with anger; but Mrs Gray interrupted.

'I am truly sorry to have to say it to one of my
parishioners, but you are not a good Christian. And
we all know that your husband's business isn't
going at all well, and I think it's a judgement of
Providence.'

'Very well, ma'am,' said Mrs Griffith getting up.
'You're at liberty to think what you please, but I
shall not come to church again. Mr Friend, the
Baptist minister, has asked me to go to his chapel,
and I'm sure he won't treat me like that.'

'I'm sure we don't want you to come to church in
that spirit, Mrs Griffith. That's not the spirit with
which you can please God, Mrs Griffith. I can
quite imagine now why dear Daisy ran away.
You're no Christian.'

'I'm sure I don't care what you think, Mrs Gray,
but I'm as good as you are.'

'Will you open the door for me, Mrs Griffith?'
said Mrs Gray, with outraged dignity.

'Oh, you can open it yourself, Mrs Gray!' replied
Mrs Griffith.

11

Mrs Griffith went to see her daughter-in-law.

'I've never been spoken to in that way before,'
she said. 'Fancy me not being a Christian! I'm a
better Christian than Mrs Gray, any day. I like Mrs
Gray, with the airs she gives herself – as if she'd got
anything to boast about . . .! No, Edith, I've said it,
and I'm not the woman to go back on what I've said
– I'll not go to church again. From this day I go to
chapel.'

But George came to see his mother a few days later.

'Look here, Mother, Edith says you'd better forgive Daisy now.'

'George,' cried his mother, 'I've only done my duty all through, and if you think it's my duty to forgive my daughter now she's going to enter the bonds of holy matrimony, I will do so. No one can say that I'm not a Christian, and I haven't said the Lord's Prayer night and morning ever since I remember for nothing.'

Mrs Griffith sat down to write, looking up to her son for inspiration.

'Dearest Daisy!' he said.

'No, George,' she replied, 'I'm not going to cringe to my daughter, although she is going to be a lady; I shall simply say, "Daisy."'

The letter was very dignified, gently reproachful, for Daisy had undoubtedly committed certain peccadilloes, although she was going to be a baronet's wife; but still it was completely forgiving, and Mrs Griffith signed herself, 'Your loving and forgiving mother, whose heart you nearly broke.'

But the letter was not answered, and a couple of weeks later the same Sunday paper contained an announcement of the date of the marriage and the name of the church. Mrs Griffith wrote a second time.

'My Darling Daughter, I am much surprised at receiving no answer to my long letter. All is forgiven. I should so much like to see you again before I die, and to have you married from your father's house. All is forgiven. Your loving mother.
Mary Ann Griffith.'

This time the letter was returned unopened.

'George,' cried Mrs Griffith, 'she's got her back up.'

'And the wedding's tomorrow,' he replied.

'It's most awkward, George. I've told all the Blackstable people that I've forgiven her and that Sir Herbert has written to say he wants to make my acquaintance. And I've got a new dress on purpose to go to the wedding. Oh! she's a cruel and exasperating thing, George; I never liked her. You were always my favourite.'

'Well, I do think she's not acting as she should,' replied George. 'And I'm sure I don't know what's to be done.'

But Mrs Griffith was a woman who made up her mind quickly.

'I shall go up to town and see her myself, George; and you must come too.'

'I'll come up with you, Mother, but you'd better go to her alone, because I expect she's not forgotten the last time I saw her.'

They caught a train immediately, and, having arrived at Daisy's house, Mrs Griffith went up the steps while George waited in a neighbouring public-house. The door was opened by a smart maid – much smarter than the Vicarage maid at Blackstable, as Mrs Griffith remarked with satisfaction. On finding that Daisy was at home, she sent up a message to ask if a lady could see her.

The maid returned.

'Would you give your name, madam? Miss Griffith cannot see you without.'

Mrs Griffith had foreseen the eventuality, and, unwilling to give her card, had written another little letter, using Edith as amanuensis, so that Daisy should at least open it. She sent it up. In a few minutes the maid came down again.

'There's no answer,' and she opened the door for Mrs Griffith to go out.

That lady turned very red. Her first impulse was to make a scene and call the housemaid to witness how Daisy treated her own mother; but immediately she thought how undignified she would appear in the maid's eyes. So she went out like a lamb ...

She told George all about it as they sat in the private bar of the public-house, drinking a little scotch whisky.

'All I can say,' she remarked, 'is that I hope she'll never live to repent it. Fancy treating her own mother like that! But I shall go to the wedding; I don't care. I will see my own daughter married.'

That had been her great ambition, and she would have crawled before Daisy to be asked to the ceremony ... But George dissuaded her from going uninvited. There were sure to be one or two Blackstable people present, and they would see that she was there as a stranger; the humiliation would be too great.

'I think she's an ungrateful girl,' said Mrs Griffith, as she gave way and allowed George to take her back to Blackstable.

12

But the prestige of the Griffiths diminished. Everyone in Blackstable came to the conclusion that the new Lady Ously-Farrowham had been very badly treated by her relatives, and many young ladies said they would have done just the same in her place. Also Mrs Gray induced her husband to ask Griffith to resign his churchwardenship.

'You know, Mr Griffith,' said the vicar deprecatingly, 'now that your wife goes to chapel I don't think we can have you as churchwarden any longer; and besides, I don't think you've behaved to your daughter in a Christian way.'

It was in the carpenter's shop; the business had dwindled till Griffith only kept one man and a boy; he put aside the saw he was using.

'What I've done to my daughter, I'm willing to take the responsibility for; I ask no one's advice and I want no one's opinion; and if you think I'm not fit to be churchwarden you can find someone else better.'

'Why don't you make it up with your daughter, Griffith?'

'Mind your own business!'

The carpenter had brooded and brooded over his sorrow till now his daughter's name roused him to fury. He had even asserted a little authority over his wife, and she dared not mention her daughter before him. Daisy's marriage had seemed like the consummation of her shame; it was vice riding triumphant in a golden chariot . . .

But the name of Lady Ously-Farrowham was hardly ever out of her mother's lips; and she spent a good deal more money in her dress to keep up her dignity.

'Why, that's another new dress you've got on!' said a neighbour.

'Yes,' said Mrs Griffith, complacently, 'you see we're in quite a different position now. I have to think of my daughter, Lady Ously-Farrowham, I don't want her to be ashamed of her mother. I had such a nice long letter from her the other day. She's so happy with Sir Herbert. And Sir Herbert's so good to her . . .'

'Oh, I didn't know you were . . .'

'Oh yes! Of course she was a little – well, a little wild when she was a girl, but *I've* forgiven that. It's her father won't forgive her. He always was a hard man, and he never loved her as I did. She wants to come and stay with me, but he won't let her. Isn't it cruel of him? I should so like to have Lady Ously-Farrowham down here . . .'

13

But at last the crash came. To pay for the new things which Mrs Griffith felt needful to preserve her dignity, she had drawn on her husband's savings in the bank; and he had been drawing on them himself for the last four years without his wife's knowledge. For, as his business declined, he had been afraid to give her less money than usual, and every week had made up the sum by taking something out of the bank. George only earned a pound a week – he had been made clerk to a coal merchant by his mother, who thought that more genteel than carpentering – and after his marriage he had constantly borrowed from his parents. At last Mrs Griffith learnt to her dismay that their savings had come to an end completely. She had a talk with her husband, and found out that he was earning almost nothing. He talked of sending his only remaining workman away and moving into a smaller place. If he kept his one or two old customers, they might just manage to make both ends meet.

Mrs Griffith was burning with anger. She looked at her husband, sitting in front of her with his helpless look.

'You fool!' she said.

She thought of herself coming down in the world, living in a poky little house away from the High Street, unable to buy new dresses, unnoticed by the chief people of Blackstable – she who had always held up her head with the best of them!

George and Edith came in, and she told them, hurling contemptuous sarcasms at her husband. He sat looking at them with his pained, unhappy eyes, while they stared back at him as if he were some despicable, noxious beast.

'But why didn't you say how things were going before, Father?' George asked him.

He shrugged his shoulders.

'I didn't like to,' he said hoarsely; those cold, angry eyes crushed him; he felt the stupid, useless fool he saw they thought him.

'I don't know what's to be done,' said George.

His wife looked at old Griffith with her hard grey eyes; the sharpness of her features, the firm, clear complexion, with all softness blown out of it by the east winds, expressed the coldest resolution.

'Father must get Daisy to help; she's got lots of money. She may do it for him.'

Old Griffith broke suddenly out of his apathy.

'I'd sooner go to the workhouse; I'll never touch a penny of hers!'

'Now then, Father,' said Mrs Griffith, quickly understanding, 'you drop that, you'll have to.'

George at the same time got pen and paper and

put them before the old man. They stood round him angrily. He stared at the paper; a look of horror came over his face.

'Go on! don't be a fool!' said his wife. She dipped the pen in the ink and handed it to him.

Edith's steel-grey eyes were fixed on him, coldly compelling.

'Dear Daisy,' she began.

'Father always used to 'call her Daisy darling,' said George; 'he'd better put that so as to bring back old times.'

They talked of him strangely, as if he were absent or had not ears to hear.

'Very well,' replied Edith, and she began again; the old man wrote bewilderedly, as if he were asleep. 'DAISY DARLING: ... Forgive me! ... I have been hard and cruel towards you ... On my knees I beg your forgiveness ... The business has gone wrong ... and I am ruined ... If you don't help me ... we shall have the brokers in ... and have to go to the workhouse ... For God's sake ... have mercy on me! You can't let me starve ... I know I have sinned towards you. Your broken-hearted ... FATHER.'

She read through the letter. 'I think that'll do; now the envelope', and she dictated the address.

When it was finished, Griffith looked at them with loathing, absolute loathing – but they paid no more attention to him. They arranged to send a telegram first, in case she should not open the letter:

Letter coming; for God's sake open! In great distress. FATHER.

George went out immediately to send the wire and post the letter.

14

The letter was sent on a Tuesday, and on Thursday morning a telegram came from Daisy to say she was coming down. Mrs Griffith was highly agitated.

'I'll go and put on my silk dress,' she said.

'No, Mother, that is a silly thing; be as shabby as you can.'

'How'll Father be?' asked George. 'You'd better speak to him, Edith.'

He was called, the stranger in his own house.

'Look here, Father, Daisy's coming this morning. Now, you'll be civil, won't you?'

'I'm afraid he'll go and spoil everything,' said Mrs Griffith, anxiously.

At that moment there was a knock at the door. 'It's her!'

Griffith was pushed into the back room; Mrs Griffith hurriedly put on a ragged apron and went to the door.

'Daisy!' she cried, opening her arms. She embraced her daughter and pressed her to her voluminous bosom. 'Oh, Daisy!'

Daisy accepted passively the tokens of affection, with a little sad smile. She tried not to be unsympathetic. Mrs Griffith led her daughter into the sitting-room, where George and Edith were sitting. George was very white.

'You don't mean to say you walked here!' said

Mrs Griffith, as she shut the front door. 'Fancy that, when you could have all the carriages in Blackstable to drive you about!'

'Welcome to your home again,' said George, with somewhat the air of a dissenting minister.

'Oh, George!' she said with the same sad, half-ironical smile, allowing herself to be kissed.

'Don't you remember me?' said Edith, coming forward. 'I'm George's wife; I used to be Edith Pollett.'

'Oh yes!' Daisy put out her hand.

They all three looked at her, and the women noticed the elegance of her simple dress. She was no longer the merry girl they had known, but a tall, dignified woman, and her great blue eyes were very grave. They were rather afraid of her; but Mrs Griffith made an effort to be cordial and at the same time familiar.

'Fancy you being a real lady!' she said.

Daisy smiled again.

'Where's Father?' she asked.

'In the next room.' They moved towards the door and entered. Old Griffith rose as he saw his daughter, but he did not come towards her. She looked at him a moment, then turned to the others.

'Please leave me alone with Father for a few minutes.'

They did not want to, knowing that their presence would restrain him; but Daisy looked at them so firmly that they were obliged to obey. She closed the door behind them.

'Father!' she said, turning towards him.

'They made me write the letter,' he said hoarsely.

'I thought so,' she said. 'Won't you kiss me?'

He stepped back as if in repulsion. She looked at him with her beautiful eyes full of tears.

'I'm so sorry I've made you unhappy. But I've been unhappy too – oh, you don't know what I've gone through . . .! Won't you forgive me?'

'I didn't write the letter,' he repeated hoarsely; 'they stood over me and made me.'

Her lips trembled, but with an effort she commanded herself. They looked at one another steadily, it seemed for a very long time; in his eyes was the look of a hunted beast . . . At last she turned away without saying anything more, and left him.

In the next room the three were anxiously waiting. She contemplated them a moment, and then, sitting down, asked about the affairs. They explained how things were.

'I talked to my husband about it,' she said; 'he's proposed to make you an allowance so that you can retire from business.'

'Oh, that's Sir Herbert all over,' said Mrs Griffith, greasily – she knew nothing about him but his name!

'How much do you think you could live on?' asked Daisy.

Mrs Griffith looked at George and then at Edith. What should they ask? Edith and George exchanged a glance; they were in agonies lest Mrs Griffith should demand too little.

'Well,' said that lady, at last, with a little cough of uncertainty, 'in our best years we used to make four pounds a week out of the business – didn't we, George?'

'Quite that!' answered he and his wife, in a breath.

'Then, shall I tell my husband that if he allows you five pounds a week you will be able to live comfortably?'

'Oh, that's very handsome!' said Mrs Griffith.

'Very well,' said Daisy, getting up.

'You're not going?' cried her mother.

'Yes.'

'Well, that is hard. After not seeing you all these years. But you know best, of course!'

'There's no train up to London for two hours yet,' said George.

'No; I want to take a walk through Blackstable.'

'Oh, you'd better drive, in your position.'

'I prefer to walk.'

'Shall George come with you?'

'I prefer to walk alone.'

Then Mrs Griffith again enveloped her daughter in her arms, and told her she had always loved her and that she was her only daughter; after which, Daisy allowed herself to be embraced by her brother and his wife. Finally they shut the door on her and watched her from the window walk slowly down the High Street.

'If you'd asked it, I believe she'd have gone up to six quid a week,' said George.

15

Daisy walked down the High Street slowly, looking at the houses she remembered, and her lips quivered a little; at every step smells blew across to her full of memories – the smell of a tannery, the blood smell of a butcher's shop, the sea-odour from a shop of fishermen's clothes ... At last she came on to the beach, and in the darkening November day she looked at the booths she knew so well, the boats drawn up for the winter, whose names she knew, whose owners she had known from her childhood; she noticed the new villas built in her absence. And she looked at the grey sea; a sob burst from her; but she was very strong, and at once she recovered herself. She turned back and slowly walked up the High Street again to the station. The lamps were lighted now, and the street looked as it had looked in her memory through the years; between the Green Dragon and the Duke of Kent were the same groups of men – farmers, townsfolk, fishermen – talking in the glare of the rival inns, and they stared at her curiously as she passed, a tall figure, closely veiled. She looked at the well-remembered shops, the stationery shop with its old-fashioned, fly-blown knick-knacks, the milliner's with cheap, gaudy hats, the little tailor's with his antiquated fashion plates. At last she came to the station, and sat in the waiting-room, her heart full of infinite sadness – the terrible sadness of the past . . .

And she could not shake it off in the train; she could only just keep back the tears.

At Victoria she took a cab and finally reached home. The servants said her husband was in his study.

'Hulloa!' he said. 'I didn't expect you tonight.'

'I couldn't stay; it was awful.' Then she went up to him and looked into his eyes. 'You do love me, Herbert, don't you?' she said, her voice suddenly breaking. 'I want your love so badly.'

'I love you with all my heart!' he said, putting his arms around her.

But she could restrain herself no longer; the strong arms seemed to take away the rest of her strength, and she burst into tears.

'I will try and be a good wife to you, Herbert,' she said, as he kissed them away.